ISBN 0-8123-7089-9 (softcover)
ISBN 0-8123-7098-8 (hardbound)

Copyright © 1993 by McDougal, Littell & Company
Box 1667, Evanston, Illinois 60204

Acknowledgments

Isaac Asimov "The Feeling of Power" from *The Best Science Fiction of Isaac Asimov* by Isaac Asimov. Copyright © 1986 by Nightfall, Inc. Reprinted by permission of the author.

Aunt Lute Books "The Youngest Doll" by Rosario Ferré from *Reclaiming Medusa: Short Stories by Contemporary Puerto Rican Women*, edited and translated by Diana Vélez. Copyright © 1988 by Diana Vélez. Reprinted by permission of Aunt Lute Books.

Bibliotheca Islamica, Inc. "The Happy Man" from *God's World* by Naguib Mahfouz, translated by Akef Abadir and Roger Allen. Copyright © 1973, 1988 by Akef Abadir and Roger Allen. Reprinted by permission of the publisher, Bibliotheca Islamica, Box 14474, Minneapolis, MN 55414.

Brandt & Brandt Literary Agents, Inc. "Searching for Summer" from *The Green Flash and Other Tales of Horror* by Joan Aiken. Copyright © 1958 by Joan Aiken. Reprinted by permission of Brandt & Brandt Literary Agents, Inc.

Confluence Press "The Secret Lion" from *The Iguana Killer: Twelve Stories of the Heart* by Alberto Alvaro Ríos. Copyright © 1984 by Alberto Alvaro Ríos. Reprinted by permission of Confluence Press at Lewis-Clark State College, Lewiston, Idaho.

Don Congdon Associates, Inc. "I Sing the Body Electric!" by Ray Bradbury. First published in *McCall's*. Copyright © 1969 by Ray Bradbury. Reprinted by permission of Don Congdon Associates, Inc.

Joan Daves "Action Will Be Taken" from *18 Stories* by Heinrich Böll, translated by Leila Vennewitz. Copyright © 1966 by Heinrich Böll. Reprinted by permission of Joan Daves.

Delacorte Press "The Lie" from *Welcome to the Monkey House* by Kurt Vonnegut, Jr. Copyright © 1962 by Kurt Vonnegut, Jr. Used by permission of Delacorte Press/Seymour Lawrence, a division of Bantam, Doubleday, Dell Publishing Group, Inc.

Doubleday "A Visit to Grandmother" from *Dancers on the Shore* by William Melvin Kelley. Copyright © 1962 by Fawcett Publications. Used by permission of Doubleday, a division of Bantam, Doubleday, Dell Publishing Group, Inc.

E. P. Dutton "All Cats Are Gray" by Andre Norton from *The Many Worlds of Science Fiction* edited by Ben Bova. Copyright © 1971 by Ben Bova. Reprinted by permission of the publisher, Dutton Children's Books, a division of Penguin USA, Inc.

Farrar, Straus and Giroux, Inc. "A Summer's Reading" from *The Magic Barrel* by Bernard Malamud. Copyright © 1956 by Bernard Malamud. Originally appeared in *The New Yorker*. Reprinted by permission of Farrar, Straus and Giroux, Inc. "What I Have Been Doing Lately" from *At the Bottom of the River* by Jamaica Kincaid. Copyright © 1978, 1979, 1981, 1982, 1983 by Jamaica Kincaid.

Blanche C. Gregory, Inc. "Out of Place" by Joyce Carol Oates. Originally published in *The Virginia Quarterly*, Summer 1968. Copyright © 1968 by Joyce Carol Oates. Reprinted by permission of the author.

Grove Press, Inc. "The Form of the Sword" from *Ficciones* by Jorge Luis Borges, translated by Anthony Kerrigan. Copyright © 1962 by Grove Press, Inc. Spanish translation copyright © 1956 by Emece Editores, Buenos Aires. "Rhinoceros" from *The*

CONTEMPORARY SHORT STORIES

Senior Consultants

ARTHUR N. APPLEBEE
State University of New York at Albany

JUDITH A. LANGER
State University of New York at Albany

Authors

DAVID W. FOOTE

MARGARET GRAUFF FORST

MARY HYNES-BERRY

JULIE WEST JOHNSON

BASIA C. MILLER

BRENDA PIERCE PERKINS

McDougal, Littell & Company
Evanston, Illinois
New York • Dallas • Sacramento • Columbia, SC

(Continued on page 436)

Authors & Consultants

SENIOR CONSULTANTS

The senior consultants guided all conceptual development for the *Responding to Literature* series. They participated actively in shaping tables of contents and prototype materials for all major components and features, and they reviewed completed units to assure consistency with current research and the philosophy of the series.

Arthur N. Applebee, Professor of Education, State University of New York at Albany; Director, Center for the Learning and Teaching of Literature

Judith A. Langer, Professor of Education, State University of New York at Albany; Co-Director, Center for the Learning and Teaching of Literature

AUTHORS

The authors of this text wrote lessons for the literary selections.

David W. Foote, Evanston Township High School, Evanston, Illinois

Margaret Grauff Forst, Lake Forest High School, Lake Forest, Illinois

Mary Hynes-Berry, Writer and Educator, Chicago, Illinois

Julie West Johnson, New Trier Township High School, Winnetka, Illinois

Basia C. Miller, Tutor on the Faculty at St. John's College, Santa Fe, New Mexico

Brenda Pierce Perkins, Lake Forest High School, Lake Forest, Illinois

ACADEMIC CONSULTANTS

The academic consultants worked with the senior consultants to establish the theoretical framework for the *Responding to Literature* series and the pedagogical design of the lessons. The consultants reviewed prototype lessons for the student book and Teacher's Guide, read selected units to assure philosophical consistency, and suggested writing assignments.

Susan Hynds, Director of English Education, Syracuse University, Syracuse, New York

James Marshall, Professor of English and Education, University of Iowa, Iowa City

Robert E. Probst, Professor of English Education, Georgia State University, Atlanta

William Sweigart, Assistant Professor of English, Indiana University Southeast, New Albany; formerly, Research Associate, Center for the Study of Writing, University of California at Berkeley

LITERARY CONSULTANTS

The literary consultants commented on selections and made suggestions for additional material.

Carlos J. Cumpián, Editor and Researcher, Hispanic Literature, Chicago, Illinois

Edris Makward, Professor, African Studies Program, University of Wisconsin, Madison

Peter Jaffe-Notier, Instructor of World Literature, Lyons Township High School, La Grange, Illinois

Carrie E. Reed, Pre-doctoral Teaching Associate I in Chinese, Department of Asian Language and Literature, University of Washington, Seattle

Michael W. Smith, Department of Curriculum and Instruction, University of Wisconsin, Madison

CONSULTANT-REVIEWERS

The consultant-reviewers evaluated the lesson design and reviewed selections for the purpose of assessing effectiveness and appropriateness for students and teachers.

Elizabeth Anderson, English Department Chairman, Olathe South High School, Olathe, Kansas

Joanne Bergman, English Department Chairman, Countryside High School, Clearwater, Florida

Michael F. Bernauer, Language Arts Instructor, Forest Lake Senior High School, Forest Lake, Minnesota

Nancy J. Boersma, Coordinator of English, White Plains Public Schools, White Plains, New York

Jennifer C. Boyd, Instructor of English, Nampa High School, Nampa, Idaho

Joanne Schenck Brower, Curriculum Specialist, Guilford County School System, Greensboro, North Carolina

Helen Brown, Educational Consultant, Baton Rouge, Louisiana

Clifton Browning, Department Head, English, Jefferson Davis High School, Montgomery, Alabama

Marilyn K. Buehler, Arizona State Teacher of the Year, 1989, English Instructor, North High School, Phoenix, Arizona

Patrick Cates, Chairman, English Department, Lubbock High School, Lubbock, Texas

Charles R. Chew, Director, Division of Communications Arts and Social Science Instruction, New York State Department of Education, Albany, New York

Willie Mae Crews, English Program Specialist, Birmingham Board of Education, Birmingham, Alabama

Bonnie M. Davis, Staff Development Teacher, Mehlville School District, St. Louis, Missouri

Harriet C. Fether, Language Arts Chairperson, Miami Senior High School, Miami, Florida

Contents

Connections:

Stories About the Family

Connections: Stories About the Family

Family ties . . . kinship bonds . . . the chain of generations. These phrases describe connections between members of a family. They are positive phrases, arousing feelings of warmth, love, strength, and continuity. But as most members of families know, family life can be painful as well as rewarding. Those bonds and chains can chafe sometimes.

Contemporary writers frequently concern themselves with family relationships. The stories in this first unit focus on connections between parents and children, between grandparents and grandchildren, between brothers, sisters, cousins. Often the connections are faulty—too tight, as in the case of a child chess prodigy who feels suffocated by her proud mother—or too loose, as in the case of a mother who watches helplessly as her teenage son drifts farther and farther from home. Some stories explore connections between generations of a family. For example, in one story two sisters clash over who will get the quilts made by their ancestors. In another, a young Israeli couple must decide whether or not to give their new baby a name that memorializes a dead relative and a destroyed culture.

As you read the stories in this unit, notice how the characters get along and what they seem to want from each other. Pay attention to the causes of strife between different generations. If you look at these fictional families closely, you may see your own family mirrored or magnified in them.

Literary Vocabulary

Irony. Irony is a contrast between appearance and actuality.

> **Situational irony** is the contrast between what a reader or character expects and what actually exists or happens.

> **Dramatic irony** is the contrast between what a character in a story knows about events and what the reader knows.

Theme. Theme is the central idea, or message, in a work of literature. It is the writer's perception about life or humanity that is shared with the reader.

Mood. Mood is the feeling, or atmosphere, that a writer creates for the reader. The mood of a work could be described as sinister, cheerful, exciting, dreamlike, or sentimental.

Setting. Setting is the time and place of the action of a story.

Symbol. A symbol is a person, place, activity, or object that represents something beyond itself.

Characterization. Characterization refers to the techniques a writer uses to develop characters. There are four basic methods of characterization: (1) through physical description; (2) through a character's speech, thoughts, feelings, or actions; (3) through the speech, thoughts, feelings, or actions of other characters; and (4) through the narrator's direct comments about a character.

Point of View. Point of view refers to the narrative method, or the kind of narrator, used in a literary work. Many stories use **third-person point of view:** the story is told by a narrative voice outside the action. Other stories, howeve, use **first-person point of view:** the narrator is a character in the story who tells everything in his or her own words.

Plot Structure. Plot refers to the actions and events in a literary work. In a traditional narrative, plot structure consists of the exposition, the rising action, the climax, and the falling action.

Dialogue. Dialogue is written conversation between two or more characters.

The Lie

KURT VONNEGUT, JR.

A biography of Vonnegut appears on page 428.

*A*pproaching the Story

Being the child of well-to-do parents can mean many things. For Eli Remenzel in this story, it means that his family expects him to attend an exclusive preparatory school, a private residential high school that prepares students for college. Prep schools are often partially funded by wealthy graduates who still feel ties to the school. In some families, several successive generations have attended the same school, so that the prep school becomes part of family tradition.

*B*uilding Vocabulary

These essential words are footnoted within the story.

reserve (ri zurv′): Sylvia enjoyed arguing with her husband about her lack of **reserve** and his excess of it. (page 6)

inconceivable (in′ kən sēv′ ə bəl): It was **inconceivable** to them that Eli could not go there. (page 8)

wretchedly (rech′ id lē): "I know," said Eli **wretchedly**. (page 9)

expansively (ek span′ siv lē): "Certainly, of course," said Doctor Remenzel **expansively**. (page 10)

incredulity (in′ krə do͞o′ lə tē): "A letter from me," said Doctor Warren, with growing **incredulity**. (page 10)

*C*onnecting Writing and Reading

In what areas of your life do you feel the most pressure to succeed? Make a pie graph in your journal showing how much pressure you feel in the following areas: academics, athletics, social relations, finances, other. For example, if you feel the most pressure to succeed as an athlete, you might label a large part of the pie graph "athletic pressure." As you read, note in your journal the pressures that you see affecting the characters in this story.

*I*T WAS EARLY springtime. Weak sunshine lay cold on old gray frost. Willow twigs against the sky showed the golden haze of fat catkins about to bloom. A black Rolls-Royce streaked up the Connecticut Turnpike from New York City. At the wheel was Ben Barkley, a black chauffeur.

"Keep it under the speed limit, Ben," said Doctor Remenzel. "I don't care how ridiculous any speed limit seems; stay under it. No reason to rush—we have plenty of time."

Ben eased off on the throttle. "Seems like in the springtime she wants to get up and go," he said.

"Do what you can to keep her down—OK?" said the doctor.

"Yes, sir!" said Ben. He spoke in a lower voice to the thirteen-year-old boy who was riding beside him, to Eli Remenzel, the doctor's son. "Ain't just people and animals feel good in the springtime," he said to Eli. "Motors feel good too."

"Um," said Eli.

"Everything feel good," said Ben. "Don't you feel good?"

"Sure, sure I feel good," said Eli emptily.

"Should feel good—going to that wonderful school," said Ben.

The wonderful school was the Whitehill School for Boys, a private preparatory school in North Marston, Massachusetts. That was where the Rolls-Royce was bound. The plan was that Eli would enroll for the fall semester, while his father, a member of the class of 1939, attended a meeting of the Board of Overseers of the school.

"Don't believe this boy's feeling so good, doctor," said Ben. He wasn't particularly serious about it. It was more a genial springtime blather.

"What's the matter, Eli?" said the doctor absently. He was studying blueprints, plans for a thirty-room addition to the Eli Remenzel Memorial Dormitory—a building named in honor of his great-great-grandfather. Doctor Remenzel had the plans draped over a walnut table that folded out of the back of the front seat. He was a massive, dignified man, a physician, a healer for healing's sake, since he had been born as rich as the Shah of Iran. "Worried about something?" he asked Eli without looking up from the plans.

"Nope," said Eli.

Eli's lovely mother, Sylvia, sat next to the doctor, reading the catalog of the Whitehill School. "If I were you," she said to Eli, "I'd be so excited I could hardly stand it. The best four years of your whole life are just about to begin."

"Sure," said Eli. He didn't show her his face. He gave her only the back of his head, a pinwheel of coarse brown hair above a stiff white collar, to talk to.

"I wonder how many Remenzels have gone to Whitehill," said Sylvia.

"That's like asking how many people are dead in a cemetery," said the doctor. He gave the answer to the old joke, and to Sylvia's question too. "All of 'em."

"If all the Remenzels who went to Whitehill were numbered, what number would Eli be?" said Sylvia. "That's what I'm getting at."

The question annoyed Doctor Remenzel a little. It didn't seem in very good taste. "It isn't the sort of thing you keep score on," he said.

"Guess," said his wife.

"Oh," he said, "you'd have to go back through all the records, all the way back to the end of the eighteenth century, even, to make any kind of a guess. And you'd have to decide whether to count the Schofields and the Haleys and the MacLellans as Remenzels."

"Please make a guess—" said Sylvia, "just people whose last names were Remenzel."

"Oh—" The doctor shrugged, rattled the plans. "Thirty maybe."

"So Eli is number thirty-one!" said Sylvia, delighted with the number. "You're number thirty-one, dear," she said to the back of Eli's head.

Doctor Remenzel rattled the plans again. "I don't want him going around saying something asinine, like he's number thirty-one," he said.

"Eli knows better than that," said Sylvia. She was a game, ambitious woman, with no money of her own at all. She had been married for sixteen years but was still openly curious and enthusiastic about the ways of families that had been rich for many generations.

"Just for my own curiosity—not so Eli can go around saying what number he is," said Sylvia, "I'm going to go wherever they keep the records and find out what number he is. That's what I'll do while you're at the meeting and Eli's doing whatever he has to do at the Admissions Office."

"All right," said Doctor Remenzel, "you go ahead and do that."

"I will," said Sylvia. "I think things like that are interesting, even if you don't." She waited for a rise[1] on that but didn't get one. Sylvia enjoyed arguing with her husband about her lack of reserve[2] and his excess of it, enjoyed saying, toward the end of arguments like that, "Well, I guess I'm just a simple-minded country girl at heart, and that's all I'll ever be; and I'm afraid you're going to have to get used to it."

But Doctor Remenzel didn't want to play that game. He found the dormitory plans more interesting.

"Will the new rooms have fireplaces?" said Sylvia. In the oldest part of the dormitory, several of the rooms had handsome fireplaces.

"That would practically double the cost of construction," said the doctor.

"I want Eli to have a room with a fireplace, if that's possible," said Sylvia.

"Those rooms are for seniors."

"I thought maybe through some fluke—" said Sylvia.

"What kind of fluke do you have in mind?" said the doctor. "You mean I should demand that Eli be given a room with a fireplace?"

"Not *demand*—" said Sylvia.

"Request firmly?" said the doctor.

"Maybe I'm just a simple-minded country girl at heart," said Sylvia, "but I look through this catalog, and I see all the buildings named after Remenzels, look through the back and see all the hundreds of thousands of dollars given by Remenzels for scholarships, and I just can't help thinking people named Remenzel are entitled to ask for a little something extra."

"Let me tell you in no uncertain terms," said Doctor Remenzel, "that you are not to ask for anything special for Eli—not anything."

"Of course I won't", said Sylvia. "Why do you always think I'm going to embarrass you?"

"I don't," he said.

"But I can still think what I think, can't I?" she said.

"If you have to," he said.

"I have to," she said cheerfully, utterly unrepentant. She leaned over the plans. "You think those people will like those rooms?"

"What people?" he said.

"The Africans," she said. She was talking about thirty Africans who, at the request of the State Department, were being admitted to Whitehill in the coming semester. It was because of them that the dormitory was being expanded.

"The rooms aren't for them," he said. "They aren't going to be segregated."

"Oh," said Sylvia. She thought about this awhile, and then she said, "Is there a chance Eli will have to have one of them for a roommate?"

---

1. rise (rīz): response to teasing or provoking; from the expression "a fish rising to the bait."

2. reserve (ri zʉrv'): strict control over the expression of thoughts and feelings.

"Freshmen draw lots for roommates," said the doctor. "That piece of information's in the catalog too."

"Eli?" said Sylvia.

"H'm?" said Eli.

"How would you feel about it if you had to room with one of those Africans?"

Eli shrugged listlessly.

"That's all right?" said Sylvia.

Eli shrugged again.

"I guess it's all right," said Sylvia.

"It had better be," said the doctor.

The Rolls-Royce pulled abreast of an old Chevrolet, a car in such bad repair that its back door was lashed shut with clothesline. Doctor Remenzel glanced casually at the driver, and then, with sudden excitement and pleasure, he told Ben Barkley to stay abreast of the car.

The doctor leaned across Sylvia, rolled down his window, yelled to the driver of the old Chevrolet, "Tom! Tom!"

The man was a Whitehill classmate of the doctor. He wore a Whitehill necktie, which he waved at Doctor Remenzel in gay recognition. And then he pointed to the fine young son who sat beside him, conveyed with proud smiles and nods that the boy was bound for Whitehill.

Doctor Remenzel pointed to the chaos of the back of Eli's head; beamed that his news was the same. In the wind blustering between the two cars they made a lunch date at the Holly House in North Marston, at the inn whose principal business was serving visitors to Whitehill.

"All right," said Doctor Remenzel to Ben Barkley, "drive on."

"You know," said Sylvia, "somebody really ought to write an article—" And she turned to look through the back window at the old car now shuddering far behind. "Somebody really ought to."

"What about?" said the doctor. He noticed that Eli had slumped way down in the front seat. "Eli!" he said sharply. "Sit up straight!" He turned his attention to Sylvia.

"Most people think prep schools are such snobbish things, just for people with money," said Sylvia, "but that isn't true." She leafed through the catalog and found the quotation she was after.

"The Whitehill School operates on the assumption," she read, *"that no boy should be deterred from applying for admission because his family is unable to pay the full cost of a Whitehill education. With this in mind, the Admissions Committee selects each year from approximately 3,000 candidates the 150 most promising and deserving boys, regardless of their parents' ability to pay the full $2,200 tuition. And those in need of financial aid are given it to the full extent of their need. In certain instances, the school will even pay for the clothing and transportation of a boy."*

Sylvia shook her head. "I think that's perfectly amazing. It's something most people don't realize at all. A truck driver's son can come to Whitehill."

"If he's smart enough," he said.

"Thanks to the Remenzels," said Sylvia with pride.

"And a lot of other people too," said the doctor.

Sylvia read out loud again: *"In 1799, Eli Remenzel laid the foundation for the present Scholarship Fund by donating to the school forty acres in Boston. The school still owns twelve of those acres, their current evaluation being $3,000,000."*

"Eli!" said the doctor. "Sit up! What's the matter with you?"

Eli sat up again, but began to slump almost immediately, like a snowman in the sun. Eli had good reason for slumping, for actually hoping to die or disappear. He could not bring himself to say what the reason was. He slumped because he knew he had been denied admission to Whitehill. He had failed the entrance examinations. Eli's parents did not know this, because Eli had found the awful notice in the mail and had torn it up.

Doctor Remenzel and his wife had no doubts whatsoever about their son's getting into Whitehill. It was inconceivable[3] to them that Eli could not go there, so they had no curiosity as to how Eli had done on the examinations, were not puzzled when no report ever came.

"What all will Eli have to do to enroll?" said Sylvia, as the black Rolls-Royce crossed the Rhode Island border.

"I don't know," said the doctor. "I suppose they've got it all complicated now with forms to be filled out in quadruplicate, and punch-card machines and bureaucrats. This business of entrance examinations is all new, too. In my day a boy simply had an interview with the headmaster. The headmaster would look him over, ask him a few questions, and then say, 'There's a Whitehill boy.'"

"Did he ever say, 'There isn't a Whitehill boy'?" said Sylvia.

"Oh sure," said Doctor Remenzel, "if a boy was impossibly stupid or something. There have to be standards. There have always been standards. The African boys have to meet the standards, just like anybody else. They aren't getting in just because the State Department wants to make friends. We made that clear. Those boys had to meet the standards."

"And they did?" said Sylvia.

"I suppose," said Doctor Remenzel. "I heard they're all in, and they all took the same examination Eli did."

"Was it a hard examination, dear?" Sylvia asked Eli. It was the first time she'd thought to ask.

"Um," said Eli.

"What?" she said.

"Yes," said Eli.

"I'm glad they've got high standards," she said, and then she realized that this was a fairly silly statement. "Of course they've got high standards," she said. "That's why it's such a famous school. That's why people who go there do so well in later life."

Sylvia resumed her reading of the catalog again, opened out a folding map of "The Sward," as the campus of Whitehill was traditionally called. She read off the names of features that memorialized Remenzels—the Sanford Remenzel Bird Sanctuary, the George MacLellan Remenzel Skating Rink, the Eli Remenzel Memorial Dormitory, and then she read out loud a quatrain printed on one corner of the map:

"When night falleth gently
Upon the green Sward,
It's Whitehill, dear Whitehill,
Our thoughts all turn toward."

"You know," said Sylvia, "school songs are so corny when you just read them. But when I hear the Glee Club sing those words, they sound like the most beautiful words ever written, and I want to cry."

"Um," said Doctor Remenzel.

"Did a Remenzel write them?"

"I don't think so," said Doctor Remenzel. And then he said, "No—Wait. That's the new song. A Remenzel didn't write it. Tom Hilyer wrote it."

"The man in that old car we passed?"

"Sure," said Doctor Remenzel. "Tom wrote it. I remember when he wrote it."

"A scholarship boy wrote it?" said Sylvia. "I think that's awfully nice. He was a scholarship boy, wasn't he?"

"His father was an ordinary automobile mechanic in North Marston."

---

3. **inconceivable** (in′ kən sēv′ ə bəl): that cannot be imagined or believed; unthinkable.

"You hear what a democratic school you're going to, Eli?" said Sylvia.

Half an hour later Ben Barkley brought the limousine to a stop before the Holly House, a rambling country inn twenty years older than the Republic. The inn was on the edge of the Whitehill Sward, glimpsing the school's rooftops and spires over the innocent wilderness of the Sanford Remenzel Bird Sanctuary.

Ben Barkley was sent away with the car for an hour and a half. Doctor Remenzel shepherded Sylvia and Eli into a familiar, low-ceilinged world of pewter, clocks, lovely old woods, agreeable servants, elegant food and drink.

Eli, clumsy with horror of what was surely to come, banged a grandmother clock with his elbow as he passed, made the clock cry.

Sylvia excused herself. Doctor Remenzel and Eli went to the threshold of the dining room, where a hostess welcomed them both by name. They were given a table beneath an oil portrait of one of the three Whitehill boys who had gone on to become President of the United States.

The dining room was filling quickly with families. What every family had was at least one boy about Eli's age. Most of the boys wore Whitehill blazers—black, with pale-blue piping, with Whitehill seals on the breast pockets. A few, like Eli, were not yet entitled to wear blazers, were simply hoping to get in.

The doctor ordered a drink, then turned to his son and said, "Your mother has the idea that you're entitled to special privileges around here. I hope you don't have that idea too."

"No, sir," said Eli.

"It would be a source of greatest embarrassment to me," said Doctor Remenzel with considerable grandeur, "if I were ever to hear that you had used the name Remenzel as though you thought Remenzels were something special."

"I know," said Eli wretchedly.[4]

"That settles it," said the doctor. He had nothing more to say about it. He gave abbreviated salutes to several people he knew in the dining room, speculated as to what sort of party had reserved a long banquet table that was set up along one wall. He decided that it was for a visiting athletic team. Sylvia arrived, and Eli had to be told in a sharp whisper to stand when a woman came to a table.

Sylvia was full of news. The long table, she related, was for the thirty boys from Africa. "I'll bet that's more black people than have eaten here since this place was founded," she said softly. "How fast things change these days!"

"You're right about how fast things change," said Doctor Remenzel. "You're wrong about the black people who've eaten here. This used to be a busy part of the Underground Railroad."[5]

"Really?" said Sylvia. "How exciting." She looked all about herself in a birdlike way. "I think everything's exciting here. I only wish Eli had a blazer on."

Doctor Remenzel reddened. "He isn't entitled to one," he said.

"I know that," said Sylvia.

"I thought you were going to ask somebody for permission to put a blazer on Eli right away," said the doctor.

"I wouldn't do that," said Sylvia, a little offended now. "Why are you always afraid I'll embarrass you?"

"Never mind. Excuse me. Forget it," said Doctor Remenzel.

Sylvia brightened again, put her hand on Eli's arm, and looked radiantly at a man in the dining-room doorway. "There's my favorite

---

4. wretchedly (rech′ id lē): very unhappily; miserably.
5. Underground Railroad: a system set up by opponents of slavery before the Civil War to help fugitive slaves escape to free states and Canada.

person in all the world, next to my son and husband," she said. She meant Dr. Donald Warren, headmaster of the Whitehill school. A thin gentleman in his early sixties, Doctor Warren was in the doorway with the manager of the inn, looking over the arrangements for the Africans.

It was then that Eli got up abruptly, fled the dining room, fled as much of the nightmare as he could possibly leave behind. He brushed past Doctor Warren rudely, though he knew him well, though Doctor Warren spoke his name. Doctor Warren looked after him sadly.

"I'll be darned," said Doctor Remenzel. "What brought that on?"

"Maybe he really *is* sick," said Sylvia.

The Remenzels had no time to react more elaborately, because Doctor Warren spotted them and crossed quickly to their table. He greeted them, some of his perplexity about Eli showing in his greeting. He asked if he might sit down.

"Certainly, of course," said Doctor Remenzel <u>expansively</u>.[6] "We'd be honored if you did. Heavens."

"Not to eat," said Doctor Warren. "I'll be eating at the long table with the new boys. I would like to talk, though." He saw that there were five places set at the table. "You're expecting someone?"

"We passed Tom Hilyer and his boy on the way," said Doctor Remenzel. "They'll be along in a minute."

"Good, good," said Doctor Warren absently. He fidgeted, looked again in the direction in which Eli had disappeared.

"Tom's boy will be going to Whitehill in the fall?" said Doctor Remenzel.

"H'm?" said Doctor Warren. "Oh—yes, yes. Yes, he will."

"Is he a scholarship boy, like his father?" said Sylvia.

"That's not a polite question," said Doctor Remenzel severely.

"I beg your pardon," said Sylvia.

"No, no—that's a perfectly proper question these days," said Doctor Warren. "We don't keep that sort of information very secret any more. We're proud of our scholarship boys, and they have every reason to be proud of themselves. Tom's boy got the highest score anyone's ever got on the entrance examinations. We feel privileged to have him."

"We never *did* find out Eli's score," said Doctor Remenzel. He said it with good-humored resignation, without expectation that Eli had done especially well.

"A good strong medium, I imagine," said Sylvia. She said this on the basis of Eli's grades in primary school, which had ranged from medium to terrible.

The headmaster looked surprised. "I didn't tell you his scores?" he said.

"We haven't seen you since he took the examinations," said Doctor Remenzel.

"The letter I wrote you—" said Doctor Warren.

"What letter?" said Doctor Remenzel. "Did we get a letter?"

"A letter from me," said Doctor Warren, with growing <u>incredulity</u>.[7] "The hardest letter I ever had to write."

Sylvia shook her head. "We never got any letter from you."

Doctor Warren sat back, looking very ill. "I mailed it myself," he said. "It was definitely mailed—two weeks ago."

Doctor Remenzel shrugged. "The U.S. mails don't lose much," he said, "but I guess that now and then something gets misplaced."

Doctor Warren cradled his head in his hands. "Oh, dear—oh, my, oh, Lord," he said. "I was surprised to see Eli here. I wondered

---

6. expansively (ek span′ siv lē): in an open, generous way.

7. incredulity (in′ krə doo′ lə tē): complete inability to believe.

that he would want to come along with you."

"He didn't come along just to see the scenery," said Doctor Remenzel. "He came to enroll."

"I want to know what was in the letter," said Sylvia.

Doctor Warren raised his head, folded his hands. "What the letter said was this, and no other words could be more difficult for me to say: '*On the basis of his work in primary school and his scores on the entrance examinations, I must tell you that your son and my good friend Eli cannot possibly do the work required of boys at Whitehill.*'" Doctor Warren's voice steadied, and so did his gaze. "'*To admit Eli to Whitehill, to expect him to do Whitehill work,*'" he said, "'*would be both unrealistic and cruel.*'"

Thirty African boys, escorted by several faculty members, State Department men, and diplomats from their own countries, filed into the dining room.

And Tom Hilyer and his boy, having no idea that something had just gone awfully wrong for the Remenzels, came in, too, and said hello to the Remenzels and Doctor Warren gaily, as though life couldn't possibly be better.

"I'll talk to you more about this later, if you like," Doctor Warren said to the Remenzels, rising. "I have to go now, but later on—" He left quickly.

"My mind's a blank," said Sylvia. "My mind's a perfect blank."

Tom Hilyer and his boy sat down. Hilyer looked at the menu before him, clapped his hands and said, "What's good? I'm hungry." And then he said, "Say—where's your boy?"

"He stepped out for a moment," said Doctor Remenzel evenly.

"We've got to find him," said Sylvia to her husband.

"In time, in due time," said Doctor Remenzel.

"That letter," said Sylvia; "Eli knew about it. He found it and tore it up. Of course he did!" She started to cry, thinking of the hideous trap Eli had caught himself in.

"I'm not interested right now in what Eli's done," said Doctor Remenzel. "Right now I'm a lot more interested in what some other people are going to do."

"What do you mean?" said Sylvia.

Doctor Remenzel stood impressively, angry and determined. "I mean," he said, "I'm going to see how quickly people can change their minds around here."

"Please," said Sylvia, trying to hold him, trying to calm him, "we've got to find Eli. That's the first thing."

"The first thing," said Doctor Remenzel quite loudly, "is to get Eli admitted to Whitehill. After that we'll find him, and we'll bring him back."

"But darling—" said Sylvia.

"No 'but' about it," said Doctor Remenzel. "There's a majority of the Board of Overseers in this room at this very moment. Every one of them is a close friend of mine, or a close friend of my father. If they tell Doctor Warren Eli's in, that's it—Eli's in. If there's room for all these other people," he said, "there's darn well room for Eli too."

He strode quickly to a table nearby, sat down heavily, and began to talk to a fierce-looking and splendid old gentleman who was eating there. The old gentleman was chairman of the board.

Sylvia apologized to the baffled Hilyers and then went in search of Eli.

Asking this person and that person, Sylvia found him. He was outside—all alone on a bench in a bower of lilacs that had just begun to bud.

Eli heard his mother's coming on the gravel path, stayed where he was, resigned. "Did you find out," he said, "or do I still have to tell you?"

"About you?" she said gently. "About not getting in? Doctor Warren told us."

"I tore his letter up," said Eli.

"I can understand that," she said. "Your father and I have always made you feel that you had to go to Whitehill, that nothing else would do."

"I feel better," said Eli. He tried to smile, found he could do it easily. "I feel so much better now that it's over. I tried to tell you a couple of times—but I just couldn't. I didn't know how."

"That's my fault, not yours," she said.

"What's father doing?" said Eli.

Sylvia was so intent on comforting Eli that she'd put out of her mind what her husband was up to. Now she realized that Doctor Remenzel was making a ghastly mistake. She didn't want Eli admitted to Whitehill, could see what a cruel thing that would be.

She couldn't bring herself to tell the boy what his father was doing, so she said, "He'll be along in a minute, dear. He understands." And then she said, "You wait here, and I'll go get him and come right back."

But she didn't have to go to Doctor Remenzel. At that moment, the big man came out of the inn and caught sight of his wife and son. He came to her and to Eli. He looked dazed.

"Well?" she said.

"They—they all said no," said Doctor Remenzel, very subdued.

"That's for the best," said Sylvia. "I'm relieved. I really am."

"Who said no?" said Eli. "Who said no to what?"

"The members of the board," said Doctor Remenzel, not looking anyone in the eye. "I asked them to make an exception in your case—to reverse their decision and let you in."

Eli stood, his face filled with incredulity and shame that were instant. "You what?" he said, and there was no childishness in the way he said it. Next came anger. "You shouldn't have done that!" he said to his father.

Doctor Remenzel nodded. "So I've already been told."

"That isn't done!" said Eli. "How awful! You shouldn't have!"

"You're right," said Doctor Remenzel, accepting the scolding lamely.

"Now I *am* ashamed," said Eli, and he showed that he was.

Doctor Remenzel, in his wretchedness, could find no strong words to say. "I apologize to you both," he said at last. "It was a very bad thing to try."

"Now a Remenzel *has* asked for something," said Eli.

"I don't suppose Ben's back yet with the car?" said Doctor Remenzel. It was obvious that Ben wasn't. "We'll wait out here for him," he said. "I don't want to go back in there now."

"A Remenzel asked for something—as though a Remenzel were something special," said Eli.

"I don't suppose—" said Doctor Remenzel, and he left the sentence unfinished, dangling in the air.

"You don't suppose what?" said his wife, her face puzzled.

"I don't suppose," said Doctor Remenzel, "that we'll ever be coming here any more."

A PERSONAL RESPONSE

sharing impressions

1. What do you think about the family relationships in this story? Briefly note your thoughts in your journal.

constructing interpretations

2. Who do you think feels the most pressure in this story, and why?

3. Compare the ways in which Doctor and Mrs. Remenzel react to the news that Eli has not been admitted to Whitehill.
   Think about
   • their behavior when they hear the news
   • the pressures that motivate their behavior
   • the losses they each face

4. At the beginning of the story, Doctor Remenzel appears to dominate both his wife and his son. How does this family relationship change during the story?

5. What situations in the story do you think the title refers to?
   Think about
   • who hides the truth in the story
   • the different ways the truth is hidden
   • why a character might choose to hide the truth

A CREATIVE RESPONSE

6. How might the story be different if Eli had been accepted to Whitehill but still did not want to go?

A CRITICAL RESPONSE

7. What events of the story would you describe as ironic?
   Think about
   • dramatic irony as the contrast between what a character in a story knows about events and what the reader knows
   • situational irony as the contrast between what the reader expects and what actually happens

8. In your view, how common are the pressures faced by the Remenzel family?

Analyzing the Writer's Craft

THEME

What do you think of the relationships within the Remenzel family?

Building a Literary Vocabulary. Theme is the central idea or message in a work of literature. It is the writer's perception about life or humanity that is shared with the reader. Often a clue to theme occurs in the title of a story. Interestingly for "The Lie," the letters in *lie* also spell *Eli*. However, Kurt Vonnegut shows that behind Eli's lie about Whitehill is a family relationship that fosters dishonesty. At the beginning of the story, Doctor and Mrs. Remenzel are so ambitious for their son's future at Whitehill that they fail to notice his silence and withdrawal on the way to the school. This insensitivity to Eli's feelings in the car reflects their larger ignorance of his academic abilities, for it seems clear from his low score on the extrance examination that Eli is not "a Whitehill boy." Because Doctor and Mrs. Remenzel have lost touch with their son, Eli does not feel free to express himself honestly. Thus the theme, or what Vonnegut may be saying through Eli's lie, is that a child's dishonesty often results from the parents' failure to recognize the child's individual needs, desires, and abilities. At the end of the story, Mrs. Remenzel reinforces this theme by acknowledging her mistake.

Application: Stating Themes. Most stories include several themes, one of which usually predominates. Look at what Vonnegut says about hypocrisy by having Doctor Remenzel ask the board at Whitehill to make an exception for Eli. Then think about the point Vonnegut makes about social snobbery through Mrs. Remenzel. Get together with a group of three classmates and come up with a statement that expresses each of these themes. Then share your thematic statements with other members of your class.

Connecting Reading and Writing

1. Analyze the character of Mrs. Remenzel in an **article** for the society page of the local newspaper.

Option: Analyze Mrs. Remenzel's character in a **character sketch**.

2. Choose one of the themes of "The Lie" and explain how that theme is expressed by the characters and events of the story. **Outline** your ideas for a friend who has not read the story and who has asked, "What is the story about?"

Option: Analyze the theme in an **expository essay** for a classmate who missed the discussion of this story.

3. In a **note** of warning to a good friend, describe a situation in which you told a lie, large or small, that was later discovered.

Option: Compose a **letter** that Eli might have written to Dr. Warren in response to the rejection notice.

No Dogs Bark

JUAN RULFO   1918–1986   MEXICO

A biography of Rulfo appears on page 427.

Approaching the Story

This story by Juan Rulfo (hwän r$\overline{oo}$l' fô) is told almost completely through dialogue. From the characters' speech you must make inferences about their relationship and the events they have experienced. The beginning of the story finds a father in the unusual situation of carrying his son on his back.

Connecting Writing and Reading

If you found yourself in serious trouble—for example, if you hurt someone in a fight or caused a fatal automobile accident—what would you expect your parents or guardians to do?

disown you   turn you in to the police
comfort you   pay damages to the victim
shame you   blame themselves
take no action   get legal or medical help for you

In your journal, jot down as many of these answers as apply; add others if you wish. As you read, compare your expectations with the reactions of the parent in this story.

No Dogs Bark

YOU UP THERE, Ignacio![1] Don't you hear something or see a light somewhere?"

"I can't see a thing."

"We ought to be near now."

"Yes, but I can't hear a thing."

"Look hard. Poor Ignacio."

The long black shadow of the men kept moving up and down, climbing over rocks, diminishing and increasing as it advanced along the edge of the arroyo.[2] It was a single, reeling shadow.

The moon came out of the earth like a round flare.

"We should be getting to that town, Ignacio. Your ears are uncovered, so try to see if you can't hear dogs barking. Remember they told us Tonaya[3] was right behind the mountain. And we left the mountain hours ago. Remember, Ignacio?"

"Yes, but I don't see a sign of anything."

"I'm getting tired."

"Put me down."

The old man backed up to a thick wall and shifted his load but didn't let it down from his shoulders. Though his legs were buckling on him, he didn't want to sit down, because then he would be unable to lift his son's body, which they had helped to sling on his back hours ago. He had carried him all this way.

"How do you feel?"

"Bad."

Ignacio didn't talk much. Less and less all the time. Now and then he seemed to sleep. At times he seemed to be cold. He trembled. When the trembling seized him, his feet dug into his father's flanks like spurs. Then his hands, clasped around his father's neck, clutched at the head and shook it as if it were a rattle.

The father gritted his teeth so he wouldn't bite his tongue, and when the shaking was over, he asked, "Does it hurt a lot?"

"Some," Ignacio answered.

First Ignacio had said, "Put me down here—leave me here—you go on alone. I'll catch up with you tomorrow or as soon as I get a little better." He'd said this some fifty times. Now he didn't say it.

There was the moon. Facing them. A large red moon that filled their eyes with light and stretched and darkened its shadow over the earth.

"I can't see where I'm going anymore," the father said.

No answer.

The son up there was illumined by the moon. His face, discolored, bloodless, reflected the opaque light. And he here below.

"Did you hear me, Ignacio? I tell you, I can't see very well."

No answer.

Falteringly, the father continued. He hunched his body over, then straightened up to stumble on again.

"This is no road. They told us Tonaya was behind the hill. We've passed the hill. And you can't see Tonaya or hear any sound that would tell us it is close. Why won't you tell me what you see up there, Ignacio?"

"Put me down, Father."

"Do you feel bad?"

---

1. Ignacio (ēg nä′ sē ô̂).

2. arroyo (ä rô̂′ yô̂): a narrow ravine where water once flowed.

3. Tonaya (tô̂ nä′ yä).

"Yes."

"I'll get you to Tonaya. There I'll find somebody to take care of you. They say there's a doctor in the town. I'll take you to him. I've already carried you for hours, and I'm not going to leave you lying here now for somebody to finish off."

He staggered a little. He took two or three steps to the side, then straightened up again.

"I'll get you to Tonaya."

"Let me down."

His voice was faint, scarcely a murmur. "I want to sleep a little."

"Sleep up there. After all, I've got a good hold on you."

The moon was rising, almost blue, in a clear sky. Now the old man's face, drenched with sweat, was flooded with light. He lowered his eyes so he wouldn't have to look straight ahead, since he couldn't bend his head, tightly gripped in his son's hands.

"I'm not doing all this for you. I'm doing it for your dead mother. Because you were her son. That's why I'm doing it. She would've haunted me if I'd left you lying where I found you and hadn't picked you up and carried you to be cured as I'm doing. She's the one who gives me courage, not you. From the first you've caused me nothing but trouble, humiliation, and shame."

He sweated as he talked. But the night wind dried his sweat. And over the dry sweat, he sweated again.

"I'll break my back, but I'll get to Tonaya with you so they can ease those wounds you got. I'm sure as soon as you feel well, you'll go back to your bad ways. But that doesn't matter to me anymore. As long as you go far away, where I won't hear anything more of you. As long as you do that—because as far as I'm concerned, you aren't my son anymore. I've cursed the blood you got from me. My part of it I've cursed. I said, 'Let the blood I gave him rot in his kidneys.' I said it when I heard you'd taken to the roads, robbing and killing people—good people. My old friend Tranquilino,[4] for instance. The one who baptized you. The one who gave you your name. Even he had the bad luck to run into you. From that time on I said, 'That one cannot be my son.'"

"See if you can't see something now. Or hear something. You'll have to do it from up there, because I feel deaf."

"I don't see anything."

"Too bad for you, Ignacio."

"I'm thirsty."

"You'll have to stand it. We must be near now. Because it's now very late at night, they must've turned out the lights in the town. But at least you should hear dogs barking. Try to hear."

"Give me some water."

"There's no water here. Just stones. You'll have to stand it. Even if there was water, I wouldn't let you down to drink. There's nobody to help me lift you up again, and I can't do it alone."

"I'm awfully thirsty and sleepy."

"I remember when you were born. You were that way then. You woke up hungry and ate and went back to sleep. Your mother had to give you water because you'd finished all her milk. You couldn't be filled up. And you were always mad and yelling. I never thought that in time this madness would go to your head. But it did. Your mother, may she rest in peace, wanted you to grow up strong. She thought when you grew up, you'd look after her. She only had you. The other child she tried to give birth to killed her. And you would've killed her again if she'd lived till now."

The man on his back stopped gouging with his knees. His feet began to swing loosely from side to side. And it seemed to the father that Ignacio's head, up there, was shaking as if he were sobbing.

---

4. **Tranquilino** (trän kē lē′ nô).

On his hair he felt thick drops fall.

"Are you crying, Ignacio? The memory of your mother makes you cry, doesn't it? But you never did anything for her. You always repaid us badly. Somehow your body got filled with evil instead of affection. And now you see? They've wounded it. What happened to your friends? They were all killed. Only they didn't have anybody. They might well have said, 'We have nobody to be concerned about.' But you, Ignacio?"

At last, the town. He saw roofs shining in the moonlight. He felt his son's weight crushing him as the back of his knees buckled in a final effort. When he reached the first dwelling, he leaned against the wall by the sidewalk. He slipped the body off, dangling, as if it had been wrenched from him.

With difficulty he unpried his son's fingers from around his neck. When he was free, he heard the dogs barking everywhere.

"And you didn't hear them, Ignacio?" he said. "You didn't even help me listen."

Thinking About the Story

A PERSONAL RESPONSE

sharing impressions

1. How did you feel after reading this story? Jot down your impressions in your journal.

constructing interpretations

2. Why do you think Ignacio does not tell his father that he hears dogs barking?

3. How would you judge Ignacio's father as a parent?

Think about
- the ordeal of carrying Ignacio to Tonaya
- what he feels toward Ignacio
- how the father's reactions to serious trouble compare with those you would expect from your parents or guardians

4. If Ignacio were to recover, do you think he would change? Explain your answer.

5. How would you describe the relationship between mood and setting in this story?

Think about
- mood as the feeling, or atmosphere, that the writer creates for the reader
- details of the setting, such as the rising moon, the arroyo, and the rocks that must be climbed

6. Most of what you learn about the characters is implied rather than stated. How successful did you find this method of storytelling?

7. George D. Schade, the translator of this story, describes a dominant theme of Rulfo's work in the following way: "Man is abject and lonely. He seeks communication but usually is thwarted." Discuss how this theme is brought out in "No Dogs Bark" and whether this view of the human condition is accurate in your opinion.

Connecting Reading and Writing

1. Write an **internal monologue** that reveals what Ignacio is thinking as his father carries him to Tonaya.

Option: Imagine that Ignacio recovers from his wounds. Compose a **letter** that he might write to his father shortly after his recovery.

2. Rewrite your own version of this **short story**, providing explanations of events and descriptions of characters that Rulfo does not. With your classmates create a collection of story variations to share with other English classes.

Option: Write your version of the story as a **screenplay**. Use flashbacks to depict the events that you have added to Rulfo's story.

3. Create an **editorial** that Rulfo might write about theories that attribute juvenile crime to parental neglect or about laws that would punish parents for their children's offenses.

Option: Write a **speech** that Rulfo might give to a group of youths at a juvenile detention center.

4. Compare this story with "Luvina" or another story from Rulfo's collection *The Burning Plain*. Design a **chart** for display in your school library that shows similarities and differences in plot, characters, setting, mood, and theme.

Option: Compare the two stories in a **report** for students interested in reading Rulfo's works.

The Heir

SŎ KIWŎN

A biography of Sŏ Kiwŏn appears on page 427.

Approaching the Story

This story by Sŏ Kiwŏn (sô kē′ wôn) is set in Korea. For many centuries Korea was governed by one royal family and an elite group of civil servants chosen by examination. Most people lived in rural areas and upheld family-centered values, particularly ancestor worship. In 1910 the Japanese took control of the government, seizing farmlands and so forcing many young people to leave the countryside and find work in cities. Japanese rule ended after World War II, but political and social turmoil remained.

"The Heir" was first published in 1963. In the story, an adolescent boy from Seoul, the capital of South Korea, goes to live with country relatives after his father dies.

Building Vocabulary

These essential words are footnoted within the story.

dissolute (dis′ ə l o͞ot′): Later he found out that his grandfather as a youth had led a **dissolute** life. (page 22)

keening (ken′ iŋ): He started **keening,** followed by everybody else. The grandfather's . . . was the loudest and the saddest. (page 25)

surreptitiously (sʉr′ əp tish′ əs lē): He half opened his eyes and looked up **surreptitiously.** (page 25)

punctilious (puŋk til′ ē əs): He heard the voice of his **punctilious** grandfather. (page 30)

Connecting Writing and Reading

If you had to go live with another family member, such as a stepparent, grandparent, aunt, or uncle, what adjustments would you find difficult? Describe these potential problems in your journal. As you read, see if the boy in this story has some of the same difficulties adjusting to a new family situation.

*I*T WAS THE monsoon season; rain was pouring down heavily, but he did not hear it. As he read to Sŏkhŭi,[1] he was conscious of the smell of straw emanating from his cousin's hair.

"Why did the man leave his home? Sŏgun,[2] brother Sŏgun?" asked Sŏkhŭi. They had come to the part of the story—the end of the first chapter—where the hero leaves home.

"Won't you let me break off here for today?" he asked her, closing the book. But she pestered him to go on, twisting at her waist.

He opened the book again and trained his eyes on the printed letters. On his cheeks he felt a blush appearing. He wished she would leave his room now. To be alone in a room with her made him uncomfortable.

Through the driving rain, he heard his grandfather's voice calling from across the courtyard.

"I think Grandfather's calling me." He raised his eyes from the book and strained his ears. Sŏkhŭi seemed not to care, whatever the old man might be wanting. She stared at his half-turned face intently. The call came louder.

"Coming!" he answered with a formal, grown-up voice and, leaving the room, put on the polite manner of a boy called to the presence of his elders. His name, Sŏgun, sounded much the same in the inarticulate pronunciation of the paralytic old man as those of his two other cousins, Sŏkpae[3] and Sŏkkŭn.[4] Often they answered to the old man's call together. His cousins, however, had not been seen around the house since morning.

"Greet the gentleman here," ordered the old man in the smoke-filled room, even before Sŏgun finished closing the double door. He bowed to the stranger who, like his grandfather, was wearing the old-style horsehair headgear. Sŏgun blushed as he did so, for he could never perform a kowtow without feeling embarrassment. He could not help feeling a momentary sense of disgrace whenever he had to kneel down on the floor with hands folded on his forehead.

"A fine-looking boy he is! Sit down." The stranger spoke in a low voice, caressing his long beard, which looked like the silk of an ear of corn.

"He takes after his father. Do you remember my son?"

"Yes," answered the stranger, and then, to express his sympathy, he clucked his tongue.

Seated respectfully with bowed head, Sŏgun listened to them while they talked about his dead father. He stole a glance at his grandfather. The old man seemed to be reluctant to satisfy the other man's curiosity. The old man seemed to have mixed feelings of pity and resentment about his son, who had died in a strange place.

"You may retire now," said Grandfather.

The rainwater had gathered into a mud pool in the courtyard. The rain was not likely to let up soon. Standing in the gloom of the entrance, he looked across toward his room, where Sŏkhŭi was waiting for his return. He had a pale forehead and long black eyebrows. Bashfulness lingered between his brows, which he narrowly knit, as if from biting a sour fruit.

To shelter himself from the rain, he stepped gingerly along the narrow strip of dry ground under the eaves. He entered the storeroom next to the room that stood beyond the garden, filled with the tepid warmth of straw decaying in the damp. The rafters stood out darkly from the mud-coated ceiling. He could smell the acrid odor of mud as the rats raced about the room. He looked up at the window set high in the wall. The paper was torn here and there, and a gray

---

1. **Sŏkhŭi** (sôk′ hwē).
2. **Sŏgun** (sô′ gσon).
3. **Sŏkpae** (sôk′ pa).
4. **Sŏkkŭn** (sôk′ kσon).

shaft of soft light entered, as at the dawn of a rainy day. The storehouse was divided into two sections. One of them served as a barn, where farming tools lay scattered all around. Winnows and baskets hung on the wall where the cornstalk wattles showed amidst the mud plaster. It was damp and stuffy in the poorly ventilated storehouse.

Sŏgun picked up a weeding hoe and made a hoeing motion in the air a few times. A weeding hoe with its long, curved neck always amused him. He thought there was something attractive in its curious curve. Looking around the room, he saw the connecting door to the other section of the storehouse. There used to be an iron lock on the door ring. To his surprise, however, the rusty lock had come loose. His heart throbbed.

This room had been an object of curiosity ever since he came to the country house—a vague fear and mysterious expectation mixed in his curiosity. Perhaps it was not right for him to enter the room without his grandfather's or uncle's permission. He hesitated a moment in front of the half-locked door, then finally took the lock off and stepped into the room. He assured himself that he was the heir of the family and was entitled to have a look at what was lawfully his. In fact, the word *heir* as it was said by Grandfather did not sound quite real to him. But now the boy once again uttered the word to himself.

Inside this part of the storehouse, it was darker than in the barn. There was a window the size of a portable table, but it opened on the dark entrance, providing no more illumination than a pale square of light like the night sky. There were soot-colored paper chests stacked one upon another on a corner of the shelf. He tiptoed to the shelf. At every stealthy step, the floor squeaked. Old books, tied up in small bundles with string and stacked high, were keeping a precarious balance. But the books interested him little. His

attention was on the soot-colored paper chests. He did not hear the rain outside. The day after his arrival here, Grandfather had taken him to this room. From among the paper chests, the old man opened the one that best kept its shape. Taking out a scroll, he said:

"This is a *hongp'ae*,[5] which the king issued to those who passed the civil service examination."

"What is a civil service examination?" asked Sŏgun.

"You had to pass it if you were to get an official position."

"Did you take it, Grandfather?"

"No, I did not."

"Why not?"

"By the time I was old enough for the examination, the Japanese were here, and the examination was banned."

There was embarrassment in the old man's tone. Later he found out that his grandfather as a youth had led a <u>dissolute</u>[6] life and did not apply himself to study. It was not because of the Japanese but because of his own laziness that the old man failed to take the examination. All this he learned from his aunt, who, having heard it from her mother-in-law, passed it on to him like a family secret. The boy had a good laugh out of it.

"You are the ninth heir of a family with as many as five *hongp'aes*," the old man would say. But hearing his grandfather, the boy would picture a young man with a rambunctious crew of his schoolmates who abhorred books, juxtaposed with the present figure of his grandfather. Thinking about this amusing incongruity when he was alone, he would laugh to himself.

He carefully took down the paper chest his grandfather had shown him. It was full of scrolls. He ransacked them to see if there was anything else in the chest. But there was noth-

---

5. *hongp'ae* (hôŋ' pa).

6. **dissolute** (dis' ə lo͞ot'): wasted and immoral.

ing except the grimy scrolls. He unrolled the one his grandfather had called *hongp'ae*, which looked like a sheet of flooring paper dyed red. A precocious boy who read difficult books beyond his age, he deciphered the faded characters. He found the three characters which made up his ancestor's name. They looked familiar to him.

He rolled up the paper and put it where it had been and shut the lid of the chest. Then he took down a leather case from a peg on the wall. It was a roughly made thing, heavy as an iron trunk. The old man told him it was a quiver. There was a broken brass lock on it like the one on the rice chest, though smaller. The key was hanging on the corner of the case, but he did not need to use it.

Among various trinkets and knickknacks, he caught sight of a small wooden box. Out of the box he took a pair of jade rings strung together. The jade was a soft, milky color.

He had no idea what these rings were for. The holes in the center would be too small even for the little finger of Sŏkhŭi. Maybe a kind of ornament for ladies, he thought.

He clicked the pieces of jade one against the other. They gave off a clear, sharp sound. Repeating the clicking several times, he listened to the sound intently. Then he strung the pieces together and put them into his pocket. His legs trembled. But hadn't he been told that everything there in the room was lawfully his? As he closed the leather case, his pale hands shook. He did not look into the other relics. He stole out of the room. The rain was beginning to turn to a drizzle.

At every mealtime, Sŏgun sat alone with Sŏkpae at the same table with his grandfather. The country cooking, which was so different from what he had been used to in the city, tasted bitter. What was more, the boy hated to sit close to Sŏkpae, their shoulders nearly touching. He felt repelled by the occasional contact with the other boy's skin. Sŏkpae, two

years his junior, was an epileptic. That his cousin looked like him disgusted him. As he looked at Sŏkpae, a secret shame seemed to stir in him.

It was not until a week after his arrival that he had found out about Sŏkpae's condition; the fit occurred at dinner time. The shredded squash seasoned with marinated shrimp gave off a foul smell. The soy sauce in the dark earthenware dish was no better. To swallow the squash, he had to hold his breath. A sense of loneliness choked him when he thought that he would be spending countless days from now on in this house, eating this food. Suddenly Sŏkpae fell over on his back, his spoon flung to the floor with a jangling sound. His eyes showing white, his foaming mouth thrust sideways, he struggled for air. Frightened, Sŏgun sat back from the table. The old man put his spoon down and sighed, turning away. The veins stood out in his eyes, either for grief or anger. Perhaps he was trying to keep the tears back.

Sŏkhŭi came in to serve the rice tea. Sŏgun felt pity for her. Perhaps the pity in his eyes touched her. He could see her eyes become moist. She hurriedly turned away and went out of the room.

Suddenly his uncle shouted angrily: "Take away the table!" He was moaning.

"What's the matter with you? Is he not your son, sick as he is?" Grandfather checked the outburst of the uncle. The uncle sat silently; a blue vein showed in the middle of his forehead.

"Don't be frightened, Sŏgun. He worries me so." His aunt tried to placate him in a tearful voice. Sŏgun wanted to run out of the room. But he felt that he had to see it through with the other members of the family until the fit was over.

Stiffness began to go out of Sŏkpae's twisted limbs, and he was breathing with more ease, but was still unconscious. He became soft like an uncoiled snake or a lump of sticky substance liquefying.

The boy gulped down some of the rice tea and left the room. The midsummer sun was going down, the clouds glowing in the twilit sky. Clear water, bubbling up from the well in the courtyard, prattled along in a little stream. They said a huge carp lived in the well among the moss-covered rocks.

His great-grandfather, returning from a long exile, had settled down here by the water, as his grandfather told the boy the story. Five gingko trees stood in line, dividing the path leading to the village and outer yard.

"I wish he were dead!" Sŏkhŭi's sharp-edged voice came from behind his back. He wondered a moment whom she meant, but he did not care whom she wanted to be dead. He was feeling desolate enough to take it calmly, even if it was himself she was referring to. He watched Sŏkhŭi as she came near. He tried hard to be casual, but he felt as if he were choking; she looked grown-up, more grown-up than himself. She was smiling.

"Cousin Sŏgun, tell me about Seoul."

He did not answer. He merely smiled. Sŏkhŭi sat on one of the rocks by the well and stretched her skinny red legs.

"I am the second tallest girl in class." She giggled, ducking her head. He wanted to find out more about her brother's illness, but he felt she feared to be questioned about it.

"You will be going to middle school next year. Perhaps the one in the county seat, right?" he asked.

"Grandpa won't let me go," Sŏkhŭi said in a thin, angry voice.

"I suppose not," mumbled the boy.

"You don't know anything." Sŏkhŭi rolled her eyes and was going to add something, then seemed to give up. The air did not stir. Evening was coming on. A dry coughing broke the spell which had hovered over the scene. He recognized the dry coughs of his grandfather, which he heard early mornings, while still in bed. His eyes searched around in the gathering dusk.

The smell of wild sesame-seed oil came drifting by; they must be frying something in the kitchen. He saw the white steam rising inside the dimly lighted kitchen. Grandpa had told him to get some sleep until called. Both his male cousins, Sŏkpae and Sŏkkŭn, seemed to like memorial services very much. They would poke their heads into the kitchen and get shouted at by their mother.

This was his first experience with sacrificial rites for the dead ancestors. He remembered his mother reminding his father about the rites and worrying. She would ask him if they shouldn't send some money to the country house to cover part of the expenses. Then his father would snap out sharply between his teeth: "How could we when they're having these rites every month of the year!" Sŏgun now seemed to understand why his father was so bitter about these rites. His uncle also looked angry and gloomy while getting the table and plates ready for the ritual. He could see his uncle considered these ancestral rites a burden.

Calming his restless spirit, he gazed at the tilted flame on top of the wooden lamp post. He made his bed and lay down, but sleep eluded him.

Sooty flames rose from the two candles burning in the discolored brass candlesticks set on either side of the sacrificial table. Through the thick wax paper covering the foods on the table came the pungent smell of fish. The grandfather, unwrapping a bundle of ancient hemp clothes, took out a long ceremonial robe and put it on.

The dusty robe wrapped around his thin, old body, the old man knelt down before the sacrificial table and respectfully kindled the incense in the burner. Thin wreaths of bluish smoke began to writhe up from the age-stained burner. The stink from the fish on the round, flat plate filled the room.

"The meat dishes should be set to the left. When will you learn the proper manner of setting the sacrificial table?" The man reprimanded his son and, holding up the sleeve of the robe with one hand, rearranged the dishes on the table with his free hand.

"This is for an ancestor of five generations ago," he told the boy for the third time this evening. The two elder men in the ceremonial robes made low bows; the children in the back rows did the same. Sŏgun nearly burst into laughter at the comic sight of the big flourish with which they brought their hands up to their foreheads before each kowtow. Yet his cousin Sŏkpae had a certain grace when he performed sacrificial bows. His soft and elastic body, unlike Sŏkkŭn's, fitted into the role with natural ease.

Sŏgun brought his hands up to his breast but dropped them; Sŏkpae was bowing away ecstatically, flourishing his two limbs, which looked longer than his torso, as if performing a dance.

Grandfather cleared his throat, coughing a few times, before he started reading the prayer to the dead in a low, tremulous voice. Finished, he started keening,[7] followed by everybody else. The grandfather's keening was the loudest and the saddest. The uncle was mumbling something in a low, indistinct voice.

Sŏgun remained still, his eyes and mouth shut tight. Yet he was not indifferent; he was tense and felt an unexplainable chill running down his spine. He half opened his eyes and looked up surreptitiously.[8] Insects had gathered around the candle flames, which cast their shadows over the sacrificial table. He had an illusion of a strange figure squatting in the gloom behind the tablet bearing the ancestral name.

When he died, his father became like a stranger, the way he heaved a last chilly breath toward him. Sŏgun had had to draw his hand by force out of his father's tightened grip. He feared that the hand would come and grip him again. He could not bring himself to touch his father. He could not cry. But when he came out of the death chamber, an inconsolable sorrow seized him, and he cried with abandon.

The boy closed his eyes again. The keening went on. His body shook from suppressed crying.

When the rite was over, Sŏgun went out to the well. Stars glittered in the night sky between the clouds. The pale starlight played on the ripples in the well. He dipped his hands in the cool water. He washed and rubbed his hands until he thought he had scrubbed the last odor of the rite from his hands.

"Sŏgun!" His grandfather called him.

In the hall were placed three tables, around which sat all the family. "We are going to partake of the ancestral food and receive the blessing of the ancestors," said the grandfather, pointing with his chin to the seat opposite him for Sŏgun. The bronze rice bowl that had been placed on the sacrificial table was now set in front of the old man, almost touching his beard. Sŏgun could still see, in the center of the heaped rice in the bowl, the hole which had been dug by the brass spoon in the course of the rite.

Sŏgun tried a sip from the brass wine cup his grandfather handed to him. He grimaced. Making much noise, everybody ate a bowl of soup with rice in it. The grandfather seemed displeased that Sŏgun did not eat like the others. He excused himself from the table, saying he had a stomachache, and returned to his room.

---

7. **keening** (kēn' iŋ): wailing or crying for the dead.
8. **surreptitiously** (sur' əp tish' əs lē): secretly.

"How like his father!" he heard the old man say in a cracked voice.

The grandfather, donning the new ramie cloth coat the aunt had finished for him overnight, left for town early in the morning. The boy waited until he was sure his cousins were all safely out playing and then took his suitcase down from the attic storeroom. He took stock of its contents. The first time he was engaged with his things in the suitcase after he came here, his cousins stuck their noses in and pestered him. He wanted to keep his things to himself. In the suitcase were several novels, his school texts, a glass weight with a goldfish swimming in it, a telescope made of millboard, and a wallet which his father had given him the day before he died. They were all very dear to him. He placed on his palm the jade rings he had taken from the storeroom on that rainy day. He listened to the music the milky jade made when clicked together. The sound was as clear and sharp as before. The sound, in fact, had improved with the weather, which had cleared in the meantime.

Somebody came into the room, unannounced.

"What are you doing?" It was Sŏkpae.

"Just checking on my things," the boy answered, very much confused and concealing his hand with the jade rings behind his back.

"Are you going somewhere?" asked Sŏkpae, drawing near.

"No."

Sŏkpae sneaked an eager look into the suitcase and then, grabbing at something, said:

"Won't you draw a picture of me, please?" The object Sŏkpae took hold of was a half-empty case of pastels. Sŏkpae's slit eyes winked at him.

"Oh, well." Sŏgun was pleased; he wanted to boast of his artistic talent. He felt much relieved that his cousin did not suspect anything. He spread out a sheet of paper on top of his suitcase and made Sŏkpae sit facing the doorway. He picked up a yellow crayon, taking a close look at his cousin. Sŏkpae sat, putting on an air of importance with his lower lip solemnly protruding. Sŏgun looked into the other boy's eyes and sat unmoving for a while, absorbed.

He felt dismay at a face that was so like his own. If Sŏkpae's features were taken separately, they would not noticeably resemble those of anyone in the family, let alone Sŏgun's. However, when Sŏgun looked at the whole face, it wasn't as though he were looking at a face other than his own.

"Aren't you going to draw?" Sŏkpae asked, only lowering his eyes.

Sŏgun began to draw. Sŏkpae's skin was darker, his features duller and fatter. From time to time, he slipped out a red, pointed tongue and licked his lips. Suddenly Sŏgun found himself wishing that Sŏkpae would have his fit there and then. A mixture of fear and curiosity came over him. He deliberately took time with his drawing.

"Here you are." The boy handed the finished picture over to his cousin, blushing.

"Why, it's you, not me, you drew!" Sŏkpae muttered.

"It's not true. It looks exactly like you!" he retorted angrily.

"Will you write down my name on this?"

He picked up a black crayon and wrote down the name.

Finally the grandfather found out about the missing jade. Sŏgun was sitting with his legs dangling on the low porch in back. The air was filled with the fragrant scent of balsam flowers, and beyond the mud wall towered the jagged ridges of the Mountain of the Moon against the cloudy, gray sky. In the direction of the courtyard, he heard the grandfather's querulous voice. Now being used to the old man's intonation, he could follow the old man as he bawled out in fury:

"Why, you ignorant ones! You think it's a toy or something, eh?"

"Oh, please, Father. I will take it back from the boy as soon as he comes home." His uncle tried to pacify the old man.

"It is all because you are so ignorant. You should have raised your boys to act like a gentleman's offspring. Instead, what do you have now?"

The old man did not attempt to choose his words in chiding his son, even when children were present. Sŏgun's heart sank. It was clear that Sŏkpae was being suspected of stealing the jade rings from the storeroom.

"That he could get so upset over such trash, after he has sold off every bit of property of any worth!" his uncle muttered after the old man disappeared into his quarters. Sŏgun trembled all over. He could not walk out of his hiding place and face the family. When he thought of what would take place after Sŏkpae came home, he felt an impulse to rush out to his grandfather and tell him everything. But still he could not move.

"I say, do you know what that is?" Grandfather, coming back, said now in a mocking voice.

"You told us it was jade beads, didn't you?" his uncle said.

"So you think it is just like any other jade, eh? It is no less than *tori* jade,[9] you hear?" The old man did not spare his son in taking him to task, as if they were not father and son but strangers to each other. Sŏgun did not know what jade beads were. They would not bring much money on the market, but they must still mean a great deal to his grandfather, the boy guessed.

He went out to the yard, dragging the rubber shoes which were too big for him. He was counting in his mind the money his father had left him along with that wallet. He thought he had enough to pay for board and room for four or five months. After his father died, his house, where he had a sunny study room, was sold by his uncle. He kept only the scuffed leather wallet and the bills in it.

"Let's go fishing together later on," said Sŏkhŭi, coming out to the yard with an armful of vegetables from the farm.

"It looks like rain again," he said.

Sŏkhŭi squatted down by the well and started washing the radishes.

"Pretty, isn't it?" Sŏkhŭi held out her wet hand, wiggling her pinkie to draw his attention to it. He noticed that it was dyed with balsam flowers. As he looked at the finger, she bobbed her head, puffing her cheeks, as she often did when she felt bashful. She was smiling. Sŏgun threw his head back and laughed like a grown-up. Looking at her from the back, in her white blouse and blue skirt, he could not think she was a cousin younger than himself.

"Do you know, Sŏkhŭi, what jade beads are?" asked Sŏgun, lowering his voice.

"Did you see the buttonlike things on Grandfather's headgear? They call them *kwanja*,"[10] Sŏkhŭi whispered back.

"They are not jade, are they?" He expressed his doubt.

"You hate my brother, don't you?" Sŏkhŭi, too, must be suspecting Sŏkpae of stealing the jade rings.

"Why should I?" Sŏgun feigned ignorance.

"I heard Grandpa once say there has been no one else like him in the family." Sŏkhŭi looked up from her work, stopping her washing for a moment.

Sŏgun did not say anything. What he had just heard hurt him somehow.

---

9. *tori* (tō′ dē) **jade:** jade rings or beads worn by those in the senior and junior first ranks of traditional Korean civil service.

10. *kwanja* (kwän′ jä): jade rings or beads worn on the hat of officials.

"Do you know he had his head cauterized with moxa?"[11] said Sŏkhŭi wearily.

Sŏgun stood up and, leaving Sŏkhŭi to her work, walked toward the stream. He kicked at the small rocks on the roadside.

Rain started again toward evening; thunder clapped and rain began to pour down in streaming showers. It was only then that the house became topsy-turvy. The old man kept pacing back and forth between the inner and the outer wings of the house, oblivious to the downpouring rain soaking his clothes.

"Where's your father? Of all the misfortunes of man!" The old man kept saying the same thing, wiping away the raindrops running down his beard. Sŏgun guessed the cause of all the commotion in the house. He saw in his imagination Sŏkpae's helpless body whirled in muddy torrents and then dashed against the rocks. His upturned eyes and foaming mouth were covered with the muddy water. "Grandfather, oh Grandfather! I didn't steal them!" But mud water filled his mouth, and not a moan came out of him. Sŏgun hugged his shaking knees. The uncle, who had just come back from the search, was going out again, this time taking Sŏkkŭn along with him.

"Let me go with you," asked Sŏgun.

"We don't need you." His uncle looked at him out of the corner of his eyes.

"I want to go," insisted Sŏgun.

"I said we didn't need you." His uncle flung back an answer with anger in his voice.

The old man groaned with agony and said, "You had better take several men along with you."

"All right, all right," answered the uncle, exasperated.

The moldy smell pervaded the room. A millipede crawled up the door frame and then down into the room. The sound of rain did not reach him. He thought he ought to walk over to the male quarters and keep the old man

company. He did not have the courage, however. He lit the lamp. He felt his forehead with his hand. Probably his hand was feverish, too. His forehead felt almost cold against his palm. He felt a chill running down his back. He was too sick to sit up and wait. He made the bed and lay down.

He could hear the light, pleasant music of the jade rings in the rain. For a moment, he wished Sŏkpae's wriggling body would stiffen into a chunk of wood. He wished that Sŏkpae would never show up again. Even after he was gone from this house, Sŏkpae must not show up before the grandfather.

When he awoke from sleep, Sŏkhŭi was sitting by him. Her body, outlined against the lamplight, was almost that of a woman. He felt a cool hand on his forehead. He did not shake it off. The palm grew warm and sticky.

"Anything new about Sŏkpae?" asked Sŏgun, turning toward her.

"Sŏkkŭn came back alone," answered Sŏkhŭi. "Father went to the Mountain of the Moon with the village people."

Sŏgun remained silent.

"This happened before," said Sŏkhŭi. "Everybody was terribly scared. Sŏkpae came back the next morning. Even he himself didn't know where he had been."

The uncle came back toward midnight, exhausted.

"Oh, that I might be struck dead!" The aunt wailed, beating the floor with her fists.

Sŏgun spent a sleepless night. Early in the morning, the villagers arrived with the news that Sŏmun[12] Bridge had been washed away overnight. It was a wooden bridge on the way from the village to the county seat.

It was hard to tell whether his uncle was laughing or crying. He was scowling darkly. He

---

11. moxa (mäks′ ə): a leafy herb whose leaves are burned on the skin for medicinal purposes.

12. Sŏmun (sô′ mo͞on).

sat on the damp floor and ordered the kitchen staff to prepare drinks for the guests and called in the people who stood around in the yard.

"Did you look into Snake Valley?" demanded the uncle.

"He can't have gone that far," said a man from the searching party, "and it rained so hard last night."

"The last time the bridge was washed out was five years ago," said another man and suggested: "Hadn't we better notify the police?"

The uncle stood up abruptly and, rolling up his trousers, started out. The rest of the men stood up, too, and, drying their wet lips with their hands, followed him out. The uncle disappeared out the front gate. But he seemed to have given up all hope.

"Oh, that I might be struck dead!" The aunt wailed in the main room. Her usual heartburn had gotten worse, and she had been fasting the previous day. When the heartburn got too painful, she nearly fainted but never forgot to exclaim: "Oh, that I might be struck dead!" as though it were some charm she had to repeat. She was not likely to recover from her mania unless Sŏkpae came back alive. She would rather cling to her sobbing, cling to her suffering, than seek a release from it, Sŏgun thought.

Sŏgun could not help feeling that Sŏkpae had gone out in the rain because of him. If only he had not come here, everything would have gone on in this moldy house as it had before his arrival. He was responsible for the untoward change in it.

Dark shadow covered the courtyard. No one stirred in the house. The whole place looked deserted. There was only the sound of heavy raindrops falling in the garden. The boy took up the jade rings in his hand and stole across the courtyard into the storehouse, shaking with excitement and fear. The rotten planks creaked and groaned under his light body.

He stifled an exclamation of surprise; a new lock was hanging from the quiver in place of the rusty old lock. The silver gleam of the new lock mocked him. A white, mean mocking was spreading all over the place: we have been waiting for you; we knew all along that you would come here to open the quiver again.

Sŏgun felt dizzy and had to lean against the muddy wall.

Sŏkpae's body was found lying among the rocks after the flood receded. It had once been as light and supple as a snake crossing the highway, but it was now as stiff and heavy as a water-soaked wooden tub, his once sleek skin turned dirty yellow by the working of the muddy water. His uncle loaded the body on his A-frame and carried it down the slope with unsteady steps.

Sŏgun thought he must go away from this house before Sŏkpae's body should come home. He must get away quickly because he could not face the dead body of someone virtually killed by him.

Sŏgun ran to his room and took down his trunk. He fished out the wallet his father gave him and put it deep into his pocket.

"Are you going someplace?" Sŏkhŭi's voice called from behind. He was startled but did not turn his head.

"Don't go, please. Don't go." Sŏkhŭi implored with tears in her voice. Sŏgun turned his head around and looked into her eyes. He shook his head sadly. His lips were trembling, and his throat choked so hard that he could hardly breathe. Sŏkhŭi was crying with her head lowered.

The smell of dry straw drifted from Sŏkhŭi's hair. Sŏgun walked out, leaving her alone in the room. The rain suddenly poured down in torrents. All he carried with him was an umbrella, the wallet with the scuffed edges, and the pair of jade rings. He started slowly toward the highway, all the time feeling with one hand the cool jade rings in his pocket. Rain soaked him. He heard the voice of his punctilious[13] grandfather saying: "Everything in here is yours."

Once he reached the highway, Sŏgun started running.

---

13. punctilious (puŋk til′ ē əs): very careful about every detail of behavior, ceremony, and so on.

Thinking About the Story

A PERSONAL RESPONSE

sharing impressions

1. How did you feel at the end of the story? Describe your feelings in your journal.

constructing interpretations

2. Why do you think Sŏgun leaves his relatives' home?

3. How would you describe Sŏgun's feelings toward his relatives?

Think about
- his relationships with his grandfather and his cousins Sŏkhŭi and Sŏkpae
- his thoughts as he kowtows to his grandfather's visitor
- his behavior during and after the sacrificial rites
- his decision to take the jade rings with him when he leaves

4. How would you characterize the grandfather?

> ***Think about***
> - what you learn about the relationship he had with Sŏgun's father
> - his views of the sacrificial rites
> - the exchange between the grandfather and uncle after the jade is discovered missing
> - the grandfather's comments about Sŏkpae
> - the reason that Sŏkhŭi will not attend school

5. Why do you think Sŏgun has difficulties adjusting to a new family situation?

6. Should Sŏgun feel responsible for Sŏkpae's death? Give reasons for your answer.

A CREATIVE RESPONSE

7. If Sŏkpae had returned home safely, would Sŏgun still have left?

A CRITICAL RESPONSE

8. What connections do you see between the setting and the emotional state of the characters? Cite examples from the story.

9. If Sŏgun were meant to represent an entire generation of youth, what might the writer be saying about Korea? Explain.

Analyzing the Writer's Craft

SYMBOL

Think about why the scuffed leather wallet is so important to Sŏgun.

Building a Literary Vocabulary. A symbol is a person, place, activity, or object that stands for something beyond itself. Cultural symbols are those that have meanings for people in the same culture. To many people in the United States, for example, an eagle symbolizes freedom and strength. Literary symbols take on meaning within the context of a literary work. To Sŏgun, the scuffed leather wallet symbolizes both the memory of his father and the means of surviving on his own.

Application: Interpreting Symbols. Form small groups and discuss the meaning of three other symbols in this story: the storehouse, the jade rings, and the rain. In a chart with three columns, write down ideas that each of these things might represent. Compare your group's ideas with those of other groups.

Connecting Reading and Writing

1. In a **character analysis** for a classmate who has also read the story, examine the character of Sŏgun, his grandfather, Sŏkpae, or Sŏkhŭi.

Option: Write a **dramatic monologue** for one of these characters, to be performed in front of the class.

2. Write a **short story** for an anthology of contemporary literature, adapting "The Heir" to a present-day American setting in which the main character has difficulties adjusting to a family situation.

Option: Write your adaptation as a **script** for television.

3. Draw a detailed **map** of the setting of this story to be displayed in your classroom. Label the features of the house and grounds and note what action occurs in each place.

Option: Create a set of **instructions** for a set designer who must reproduce the setting for a film.

4. Research one of the traditional Korean customs described in this story, such as the kowtow. Then create **notes** for a short lecture based on your findings.

Option: Write an **encyclopedia entry**, intended for an encyclopedia of Korean culture, explaining this custom.

Teenage Wasteland

ANNE TYLER

A biography of Tyler appears on page 428.

*A*pproaching the Story

During the last two decades, Anne Tyler has gained fame for writing stories and novels about families—usually, families in which one or more of the members are trying to escape the strains of family life. As a writer, Tyler is adept at using detail to create finely drawn characters. Such characters inhabit the story "Teenage Wasteland," in which Tyler portrays a family dealing with the school problems of a fifteen-year-old son. The story is told from the perspective of the mother, Daisy.

*B*uilding Vocabulary

The following essential words are footnoted within the story.

talisman (tal′ is mən): "'That's okay, Miss Evans,' he says. 'I have a tutor now.' Like a **talisman**!" (page 37)

temporized (tem′ pə rīzd′): She **temporized** and said, "The only thing I'm sure of is that they've kicked you out of school." (page 39)

*C*onnecting Writing and Reading

What advice would you give to a parent whose teenager is in trouble at school? Copy the following chart in your journal and check off the advice you would be most likely to give.

	Restrict television.		Supervise homework.
	See a psychologist.		Hire a tutor.
	Enforce a curfew.		Speak with teachers.
	Revoke driving privileges.		Limit the time spent with friends.
	Be patient and hope he or she matures.		Change schools.

As you read, compare the advice you have checked above with the advice Daisy and Matt receive about their son, and consider what seems to be the best thing to do.

Teenage Wasteland

*H*E USED TO have very blond hair—almost white—cut shorter than other children's so that on his crown a little cowlick always stood up to catch the light. But this was when he was small. As he grew older, his hair grew darker, and he wore it longer—past his collar even. It hung in lank, taffy-colored ropes around his face, which was still an endearing face, fine-featured, the eyes an unusual aqua blue. But his cheeks, of course, were no longer round, and a sharp new Adam's apple jogged in his throat when he talked.

In October, they called from the private school he attended to request a conference with his parents. Daisy went alone; her husband was at work. Clutching her purse, she sat on the principal's couch and learned that Donny was noisy, lazy, and disruptive; always fooling around with his friends, and he wouldn't respond in class.

In the past, before her children were born, Daisy had been a fourth-grade teacher. It shamed her now to sit before this principal as a parent, a delinquent parent, a parent who struck Mr. Lanham, no doubt, as unseeing or uncaring. "It isn't that we're not concerned," she said. "Both of us are. And we've done what we could, whatever we could think of. We don't let him watch TV on school nights. We don't let him talk on the phone till he's finished his homework. But he tells us he doesn't *have* any homework or he did it all in study hall. How are we to know what to believe?"

From early October through November, at Mr. Lanham's suggestion, Daisy checked Donny's assignments every day. She sat next to him as he worked, trying to be encouraging, sagging inwardly as she saw the poor quality of everything he did—the sloppy mistakes in math, the illogical leaps in his English themes, the history questions left blank if they required any research.

Daisy was often late starting supper, and she couldn't give as much attention to Donny's younger sister. "You'll never guess what happened at . . ." Amanda would begin, and Daisy would have to tell her, "Not now, honey."

By the time her husband, Matt, came home, she'd be snappish. She would recite the day's hardships—the fuzzy instructions in English, the botched history map, the morass of unsolvable algebra equations. Matt would look surprised and confused, and Daisy would gradually wind down. There was no way, really, to convey how exhausting all this was.

In December, the school called again. This time, they wanted Matt to come as well. She and Matt had to sit on Mr. Lanham's couch like two bad children and listen to the news: Donny had improved only slightly, raising a D in history to a C, and a C in algebra to a B-minus. What was worse, he had developed new problems. He had cut classes on at least three occasions. Smoked in the furnace room. Helped Sonny Barnett break into a freshman's locker. And last week, during athletics, he and three friends had been seen off the school grounds; when they returned, the coach had smelled beer on their breath.

Daisy and Matt sat silent, shocked. Matt rubbed his forehead with his fingertips. Imagine, Daisy thought, how they must look to Mr. Lanham: an overweight housewife in a cotton dress and a too-tall, too-thin insurance agent in a baggy, frayed suit. Failures, both of them—the kind of people who are always hurrying to catch up, missing the point of things that everyone else grasps at once. She wished she'd worn nylons instead of knee socks.

It was arranged that Donny would visit a psychologist for testing. Mr. Lanham knew just the person. He would set this boy straight, he said.

When they stood to leave, Daisy held her stomach in and gave Mr. Lanham a firm, responsible handshake.

Donny said the psychologist was a jackass and the tests were really dumb; but he kept all three of his appointments, and when it was time for the follow-up conference with the psychologist and both parents, Donny combed his hair and seemed unusually sober and subdued. The psychologist said Donny had no serious emotional problems. He was merely going through a difficult period in his life. He required some academic help and a better sense of self-worth. For this reason, he was suggesting a man named Calvin Beadle, a tutor with considerable psychological training.

In the car going home, Donny said he'd be damned if he'd let them drag him to some stupid tutor. His father told him to watch his language in front of his mother.

That night, Daisy lay awake pondering the term "self-worth." She had always been free with her praise. She had always told Donny he had talent, was smart, was good with his hands. She had made a big to-do over every little gift he gave her. In fact, maybe she had gone too far, although, Lord knows, she had meant every word. Was that his trouble?

She remembered when Amanda was born. Donny had acted lost and bewildered. Daisy had been alert to that, of course, but still, a new baby keeps you so busy. Had she really done all she could have? She longed—she ached—for a time machine. Given one more chance, she'd do it perfectly—hug him more, praise him more, or perhaps praise him less. Oh, who can say . . .

The tutor told Donny to call him Cal. All his kids did, he said. Daisy thought for a second that he meant his own children, then realized her mistake. He seemed too young, anyhow, to be a family man. He wore a heavy brown handlebar mustache. His hair was as long and stringy as Donny's, and his jeans as faded. Wire-rimmed spectacles slid down his nose. He lounged in a canvas director's chair with his fingers laced across his chest, and he casually, amiably questioned Donny, who sat upright and glaring in an armchair.

"So they're getting on your back at school," said Cal. "Making a big deal about anything you do wrong."

"Right," said Donny.

"Any idea why that would be?"

"Oh, well, you know, stuff like homework and all," Donny said.

"You don't do your homework?"

"Oh, well, I might do it sometimes but not just exactly like they want it." Donny sat forward and said, "It's like a prison there, you know? You've got to go to every class, you can never step off the school grounds."

"You cut classes sometimes?"

"Sometimes," Donny said, with a glance at his parents.

Cal didn't seem perturbed. "Well," he said, "I'll tell you what. Let's you and me try working together three nights a week. Think you could handle that? We'll see if we can show that school of yours a thing or two. Give it a month; then if you don't like it, we'll stop. If *I* don't like it, we'll stop. I mean, sometimes people just don't get along, right? What do you say to that?"

"Okay," Donny said. He seemed pleased.

"Make it seven o'clock till eight, Monday, Wednesday, and Friday," Cal told Matt and Daisy. They nodded. Cal shambled to his feet, gave them a little salute, and showed them to the door.

This was where he lived as well as worked,

evidently. The interview had taken place in the dining room, which had been transformed into a kind of office. Passing the living room, Daisy winced at the rock music she had been hearing, without registering it, ever since she had entered the house. She looked in and saw a boy about Donny's age lying on a sofa with a book. Another boy and a girl were playing Ping-Pong in front of the fireplace. "You have several here together?" Daisy asked Cal.

"Oh, sometimes they stay on after their sessions, just to rap. They're a pretty sociable group, all in all. Plenty of goof-offs like young Donny here."

He cuffed Donny's shoulder playfully. Donny flushed and grinned.

Climbing into the car, Daisy asked Donny, "Well? What did you think?"

But Donny had returned to his old evasive self. He jerked his chin toward the garage. "Look," he said. "He's got a basketball net."

Now on Mondays, Wednesdays, and Fridays, they had supper early—the instant Matt came home. Sometimes, they had to leave before they were really finished. Amanda would still be eating her dessert. "Bye, honey. Sorry," Daisy would tell her.

Cal's first bill sent a flutter of panic through Daisy's chest, but it was worth it, of course. Just look at Donny's face when they picked him up: alight and full of interest. The principal telephoned Daisy to tell her how Donny had improved. "Of course, it hasn't shown up in his grades yet, but several of the teachers have noticed how his attitude's changed. Yes, sir, I think we're onto something here."

At home, Donny didn't act much different. He still seemed to have a low opinion of his parents. But Daisy supposed that was unavoidable—part of being fifteen. He said his parents were too "controlling"—a word that made Daisy give him a sudden look. He said they acted like wardens. On weekends, they enforced a curfew. And any time he went to a party, they always telephoned first to see if adults would be supervising. "For God's sake!" he said. "Don't you trust me?"

"It isn't a matter of trust, honey . . ." But there was no explaining to him.

His tutor called one afternoon. "I get the sense," he said, "that this kid's feeling . . . underestimated, you know? Like you folks expect the worst of him. I'm thinking we ought to give him more rope."

"But see, he's still so suggestible," Daisy said. "When his friends suggest some mischief—smoking or drinking or such—why, he just finds it hard not to go along with them."

"Mrs. Coble," the tutor said, "I think this kid is hurting. You know? Here's a serious, sensitive kid, telling you he'd like to take on some grown-up challenges, and you're giving him the message that he can't be trusted. Don't you understand how that hurts?"

"Oh," said Daisy.

"It undermines his self-esteem—don't you realize that?"

"Well, I guess you're right," said Daisy. She saw Donny suddenly from a whole new angle: his pathetically poor posture, that slouch so forlorn that his shoulders seemed about to meet his chin . . . oh, wasn't it awful being young? She'd had a miserable adolescence herself and had always sworn no child of hers would ever be that unhappy.

They let Donny stay out later, they didn't call ahead to see if the parties were supervised, and they were careful not to grill him about his evening. The tutor had set down so many rules! They were not allowed any questions at all about any aspect of school, nor were they to speak with his teachers. If a teacher had some complaint, she should phone Cal. Only one teacher disobeyed—the history teacher, Miss Evans. She called one morning in February. "I'm a little concerned about Donny, Mrs. Coble."

"Oh, I'm sorry, Miss Evans, but Donny's tutor handles these things now . . ."

"I always deal directly with the parents. You are the parent," Miss Evans said, speaking very slowly and distinctly. "Now, here is the problem. Back when you were helping Donny with his homework, his grades rose from a D to a C, but now they've slipped back, and they're closer to an F."

"They are?"

"I think you should start overseeing his homework again."

"But Donny's tutor says . . ."

"It's nice that Donny has a tutor, but you should still be in charge of his homework. With you, he learned it. Then he passed his tests. With the tutor, well, it seems the tutor is more of a crutch. 'Donny,' I say, 'a quiz is coming up on Friday. Hadn't you better be listening instead of talking?' 'That's okay, Miss Evans,' he says. 'I have a tutor now.' Like a talisman![1] I really think you ought to take over, Mrs. Coble."

"I see," said Daisy. "Well, I'll think about that. Thank you for calling."

Hanging up, she felt a rush of anger at Donny. A talisman! For a talisman, she'd given up all luxuries, all that time with her daughter, her evenings at home!

She dialed Cal's number. He sounded muzzy. "I'm sorry if I woke you," she told him, "but Donny's history teacher just called. She says he isn't doing well."

"She should have dealt with me."

"She wants me to start supervising his homework again. His grades are slipping."

"Yes," said the tutor, "but you and I both know there's more to it than mere grades, don't we? I care about the *whole* child—his happiness, his self-esteem. The grades will come. Just give them time."

When she hung up, it was Miss Evans she was angry at. What a narrow woman!

It was Cal this, Cal that, Cal says this, Cal and I did that. Cal lent Donny an album by the Who. He took Donny and two other pupils to a rock concert. In March, when Donny began to talk endlessly on the phone with a girl named Miriam, Cal even let Miriam come to one of the tutoring sessions. Daisy was touched that Cal would grow so involved in Donny's life, but she was also a little hurt, because she had offered to have Miriam to dinner and Donny had refused. Now he asked them to drive her to Cal's house without a qualm.

This Miriam was an unappealing girl with blurry lipstick and masses of rough red hair. She wore a short, bulky jacket that would not have been out of place on a motorcycle. During the trip to Cal's she was silent, but coming back, she was more talkative. "What a neat guy, and what a house! All those kids hanging out, like a club. And the stereo playing rock . . . gosh, he's not like grown-up at all! Married and divorced and everything, but you'd think he was our own age."

"Mr. Beadle was married?" Daisy asked.

"Yeah, to this really controlling lady. She didn't understand him a bit."

"No, I guess not," Daisy said.

Spring came, and the students who hung around at Cal's drifted out to the basketball net above the garage. Sometimes, when Daisy and Matt arrived to pick up Donny, they'd find him there with the others—spiky and excited, jittering on his toes beneath the backboard. It was staying light much longer now, and the neighboring fence cast narrow bars across the bright grass. Loud music would be spilling from Cal's windows. Once it was the Who, which Daisy recognized from the time that Donny had borrowed the album. "Teenage Wasteland," she said aloud, identifying the song, and Matt gave a short, dry laugh. "It certainly is," he said. He'd misunderstood; he thought she was commenting on the scene spread before them. In fact, she might have been. The players looked like hoodlums, even her son. Why, one

---

1. talisman (tal′ is mən): a thing that is thought to produce magical effects.

of Cal's students had recently been knifed in a tavern. One had been shipped off to boarding school in midterm; two had been withdrawn by their parents. On the other hand, Donny had mentioned someone who'd been studying with Cal for five years. "Five years!" said Daisy. "Doesn't anyone ever stop needing him?"

Donny looked at her. Lately, whatever she said about Cal was read as criticism. "You're just feeling competitive," he said. "And controlling."

She bit her lip and said no more.

In April, the principal called to tell her that Donny had been expelled. There had been a locker check, and in Donny's locker they found five cans of beer and half a pack of cigarettes. With Donny's previous record, this offense meant expulsion.

Daisy gripped the receiver tightly and said, "Well, where is he now?"

"We've sent him home," said Mr. Lanham. "He's packed up all his belongings, and he's coming home on foot."

Daisy wondered what she would say to him. She felt him looming closer and closer, bringing this brand-new situation that no one had prepared her to handle. What other place would take him? Could they enter him in public school? What were the rules? She stood at the living room window, waiting for him to show up. Gradually, she realized that he was taking too long. She checked the clock. She stared up the street again.

When an hour had passed, she phoned the school. Mr. Lanham's secretary answered and told her in a grave, sympathetic voice that yes, Donny Coble had most definitely gone home. Daisy called her husband. He was out of the office. She went back to the window and thought awhile, and then she called Donny's tutor.

"Donny's been expelled from school," she said, "and now I don't know where he's gone. I wonder if you've heard from him?"

There was a long silence. "Donny's with me,

Mrs. Coble," he finally said.

"With you? How'd he get there?"

"He hailed a cab, and I paid the driver."

"Could I speak to him, please?"

There was another silence. "Maybe it'd be better if we had a conference," Cal said.

"I don't *want* a conference. I've been standing at the window picturing him dead or kidnapped or something, and now you tell me you want a—"

"Donny is very, very upset. Understandably so," said Cal. "Believe me, Mrs. Coble, this is not what it seems. Have you asked Donny's side of the story?"

"Well, of course not, how could I? He went running off to you instead."

"Because he didn't feel he'd be listened to."

"But I haven't even—"

"Why don't you come out and talk? The three of us," said Cal, "will try to get this thing in perspective."

"Well, all right," Daisy said. But she wasn't as reluctant as she sounded. Already, she felt soothed by the calm way Cal was taking this.

Cal answered the doorbell at once. He said, "Hi, there," and led her into the dining room. Donny sat slumped in a chair, chewing the knuckle of one thumb. "Hello, Donny," Daisy said. He flicked his eyes in her direction.

"Sit here, Mrs. Coble," said Cal, placing her opposite Donny. He himself remained standing, restlessly pacing. "So," he said.

Daisy stole a look at Donny. His lips were swollen, as if he'd been crying.

"You know," Cal told Daisy, "I kind of expected something like this. That's a very punitive school you've got him in—you realize that. And any half-decent lawyer will tell you they've violated his civil rights. Locker checks! Where's their search warrant?"

"But if the rule is—" Daisy said.

"Well, anyhow, let him tell you his side."

She looked at Donny. He said, "It wasn't my fault. I promise."

"They said your locker was full of beer."

"It was a put-up job! See, there's this guy that doesn't like me. He put all these beers in my locker and started a rumor going, so Mr. Lanham ordered a locker check."

"What was the boy's name?" Daisy asked.

"Huh?"

"Mrs. Coble, take my word, the situation is not so unusual," Cal said. "You can't imagine how vindictive kids can be sometimes."

"What was the boy's *name*," said Daisy, "so that I can ask Mr. Lanham if that's who suggested he run a locker check."

"You don't believe me," Donny said.

"And how'd this boy get your combination in the first place?"

"Frankly," said Cal, "I wouldn't be surprised to learn the school was in on it. Any kid that marches to a different drummer, why, they'd just love an excuse to get rid of him. The school is where I lay the blame."

"Doesn't *Donny* ever get blamed?"

"Now, Mrs. Coble, you heard what he—"

"Forget it," Donny told Cal. "You can see she doesn't trust me."

Daisy drew in a breath to say that of course she trusted him—a reflex. But she knew that bold-faced, wide-eyed look of Donny's. He had worn that look when he was small, denying some petty misdeed with the evidence plain as day all around him. Still, it was hard for her to accuse him outright. She temporized[2] and said, "The only thing I'm sure of is that they've kicked you out of school, and now I don't know what we're going to do."

"We'll fight it," said Cal.

"We can't. Even you must see we can't."

"I could apply to Brantly," Donny said.

Cal stopped his pacing to beam down at him. "Brantly! Yes. They're really onto where a kid is coming from, at Brantly. Why, I could get you into Brantly. I work with a lot of their students."

Daisy had never heard of Brantly, but already she didn't like it. And she didn't like Cal's smile, which struck her now as feverish and avid—a smile of hunger.

On the fifteenth of April, they entered Donny in a public school, and they stopped his tutoring sessions. Donny fought both decisions bitterly. Cal, surprisingly enough, did not object. He admitted he'd made no headway with Donny and said it was because Donny was emotionally disturbed.

Donny went to his new school every morning, plodding off alone with his head down. He did his assignments, and he earned average grades, but he gathered no friends, joined no clubs. There was something exhausted and defeated about him.

The first week in June, during final exams, Donny vanished. He simply didn't come home one afternoon, and no one at school remembered seeing him. The police were reassuring, and for the first few days, they worked hard. They combed Donny's sad, messy room for clues; they visited Miriam and Cal. But then they started talking about the number of kids who ran away every year. Hundreds, just in this city. "He'll show up, if he wants to," they said. "If he doesn't, he won't."

Evidently, Donny didn't want to.

It's been three months now and still no word. Matt and Daisy still look for him in every crowd of awkward, heartbreaking teenage boys. Every time the phone rings, they imagine it might be Donny. Both parents have aged. Donny's sister seems to be staying away from home as much as possible.

At night, Daisy lies awake and goes over Donny's life. She is trying to figure out what went wrong, where they made their first mistake. Often, she finds herself blaming Cal, although she knows he didn't begin it. Then at other times she excuses him, for without him, Donny might have left earlier. Who really

---

2. **temporized** (tem′ pə rīzd′): spoke only in order to gain time.

knows? In the end, she can only sigh and search for a cooler spot on the pillow. As she falls asleep, she occasionally glimpses something in the corner of her vision. It's something fleet and round, a ball—a basketball. It flies up, it sinks through the hoop, descends, lands in a yard littered with last year's leaves and striped with bars of sunlight as white as bones, bleached and parched and cleanly picked.

Thinking About the Story

A PERSONAL RESPONSE

sharing impressions

1. What are your impressions of Cal, Donny, and the other characters? Briefly note your thoughts in your journal.

constructing interpretations

2. Whom do you blame most for Donny's running away? Explain your answer.

3. How would you evaluate Daisy as a parent?
Think about
- the praise she gave Donny as a child
- the rules she and her husband have for Donny
- how she responds to the advice of Mr. Lanham, Cal, and Miss Evans
- how she treats her daughter
- what she does when Donny is expelled from school

4. What positives and negatives do you see in Cal?
Think about
- the way he relates to Donny
- the environment he provides for "his kids"
- the advice he gives Donny's parents
- what he says about his ex-wife

A CREATIVE RESPONSE

5. Do you think Donny will come home? Give specific reasons for your answer.

6. What could the character who you think is most to blame have done differently to make the situation turn out better?

A CRITICAL RESPONSE

7. Identify what you think is the most powerful example of irony in this story. Explain your choice.

8. Anne Tyler has said that she uses the family unit to describe "how people manage to endure each other—how they grate against each other, adjust, intrude, and protect themselves from intrusions, give up, and start all over again in the morning." How effectively has she described human beings in "Teenage Wasteland"? Use specific details from the story to support your answer.

*A*nalyzing the Writer's Craft

CHARACTERIZATION AND POINT OF VIEW

How would you describe Daisy's attitude toward herself? How do you learn about her?

Building a Literary Vocabulary. Characterization refers to the techniques that a writer uses to develop characters. There are four basic methods of characterization in fiction. Characters can be developed (1) through description of a character's physical appearance; (2) through a character's speech, thoughts, feelings, or actions; (3) through the speech, feelings, thoughts, or actions of other characters; and (4) through direct comments about a character's nature. In "Teenage Wasteland" Anne Tyler provides both details of Daisy's physical appearance and insight into Daisy's view of herself. For example, the second time Daisy visits Donny's principal, she imagines that to Mr. Lanham, she and her husband must look like "an overweight housewife in a cotton dress and a too-tall, too-thin insurance agent in a baggy, frayed suit. Failures, both of them—the kind of people who are always hurrying to catch up, missing the point of things that everyone else grasps at once. She wished she'd worn nylons instead of knee socks." Daisy is insecure—unhappy with her appearance and afraid that she isn't as smart as other people. Her wish

that she had dressed up reveals that she is anxious to please people she perceives to be in authority. These details demonstrate that she is the kind of character who will later accept whatever advice the "experts" give her about her son.

One reason the reader gains such insight into Daisy's character is that the story is told from her perspective. The reader sees who Daisy is from the inside because the story is written from the third-person limited point of view; that is, the narrator presents the inner thoughts and feelings of only one character.

Application: Analyzing Characterization and Point of View. Working in a small group, go back through the story and identify details that reveal something about the characters Daisy, Donny, and Cal. Choose at least three details for each character. Then, for each detail identify the method of characterization used by Tyler. Create a chart for each character similar to the one on the next page.

Decide how point of view determines the methods of characterization Tyler uses for each character. Compare your observations and conclusions with those of another group.

Detail that reveals character of _____	Method of Characterization

Connecting Reading and Writing

1. Write another **scene** to the story in which Daisy and Matt hire a private detective to try to find Donny.

Option: Write a **police report** that the officers who investigated Donny's case might file.

2. Write a **letter** telling a friend about this story. Describe the qualities of each character, and then tell which one you sympathize with most and why.

Option: Create brief **report cards** and grade Daisy, Donny, and Cal on qualities such as honesty, decisiveness, independence, judgment, fairness, industriousness, and devotion. Compare your report cards with those of classmates.

3. Read articles on what parents should do when they have runaway children. Then create a **list** of suggestions for Daisy and Matt to follow.

Option: Write an **advertisement** that Daisy might put in the newspaper to encourage Donny to come home.

4. Write a **persuasive speech** that could be delivered to the P.T.A., explaining how much control you think parents should exert over their teenage children. Use examples from the story and from your experience to support your opinions.

Option: Survey at least twenty teenagers, asking them who exerts the most influence in their lives: parents, teachers, friends, religious institutions, other sources. Convert your findings into percentages and illustrate them on a **bar graph** accompanied by an explanatory paragraph.

The Name

AHARON MEGGED

A biography of Megged appears on page 425.

Approaching the Story

"The Name" is about an elderly Jew who left his Ukrainian village in Eastern Europe before World War II to join his daughter and her family in what later became Israel. Here, settlers from many places came together to make a new life. In the background of the story is the Holocaust, the historic tragedy that occurred in Europe before and during World War II. More than six million Jews, along with millions of others, were systematically exterminated by the Nazis under Adolf Hitler. The story explores how this tragedy of the past affects the present lives of the characters and their decisions about the future.

Building Vocabulary

These essential words are footnoted within the story.

placatingly (plā′ kāt′ iŋ lē): She would smile at him **placatingly.** (page 45)

commiseration (kə miz′ ər ā′ shən): A strained silence of **commiseration** would descend. (page 46)

wont (wänt): Grandfather sat down on the chair and placed the palm of his hand on the edge of the table, as was his **wont.** (page 50)

chasm (kaz′ əm): It was as if a **chasm** gaped between a world that was passing and a world that was born. (page 53)

Connecting Writing and Reading

Think of any customs or traditions, such as using certain family names, that have been kept alive in your family or in the family of someone you know. Then imagine that you are about to start a family of your own. Describe in your journal one tradition you would like to continue and one that you cannot easily identify with, explaining how you feel about these traditions. As you read the following story, compare your feelings about family traditions with those expressed by the characters.

GRANDFATHER ZISSKIND lived in a little house in a southern suburb of the town. About once a month, on a Saturday afternoon, his granddaughter Raya and her young husband, Yehuda,[1] would go and pay him a visit.

Raya would give three cautious knocks on the door (an agreed signal between her and her grandfather ever since her childhood, when he had lived in their house together with the whole family), and they would wait for the door to be opened. "Now he's getting up," Raya would whisper to Yehuda, her face glowing, when the sound of her grandfather's slippers was heard from within, shuffling across the room. Another moment, and the key would be turned and the door opened.

"Come in," he would say somewhat absently, still buttoning up his pants, with the rheum of sleep in his eyes. Although it was very hot, he wore a yellow winter vest with long sleeves, from which his wrists stuck out—white, thin, delicate as a girl's, as was his bare neck with its taut skin.

After Raya and Yehuda had sat down at the table, which was covered with a white cloth showing signs of the meal he had eaten alone—crumbs from the Sabbath loaf, a plate with meat leavings, a glass containing some grape pips, a number of jars, and so on—he would smooth the crumpled pillows, spread a cover over the narrow bed, and tidy up. It was a small room, and its obvious disorder aroused pity for the old man's helplessness in running his home. In the corner was a shelf with two sooty kerosene burners, a kettle, and two or three saucepans, and next to it a basin containing plates, knives, and forks. In another corner was a stand holding books with thick leather bindings, leaning and lying on each other. Some of his clothes hung over the backs of the chairs. An ancient walnut cupboard with an empty buffet stood exactly opposite the door. On the wall hung a clock that had long since stopped.

"We ought to make Grandfather a present of a clock," Raya would say to Yehuda as she surveyed the room and her glance lighted on the clock; but every time the matter slipped her memory. She loved her grandfather, with his pointed white silky beard, his tranquil face from which a kind of holy radiance emanated, his quiet, soft voice that seemed to have been made only for uttering words of sublime wisdom. She also respected him for his pride, which had led him to move out of her mother's house and live by himself, accepting the hardship and trouble and the affliction of loneliness in his old age. There had been a bitter quarrel between him and his daughter. After Raya's father had died, the house had lost its grandeur and shed the trappings of wealth. Some of the antique furniture that they had retained—along with some crystalware and jewels, the dim luster of memories from the days of plenty in their native city—had been sold, and Rachel, Raya's mother, had been compelled to support the home by working as a dentist's nurse. Grandfather Zisskind, who had been supported by the family ever since he came to the country, wished to hand over to his daughter his small capital, which was deposited in a bank. She was not willing to accept it. She was stubborn and proud like

1. **Raya . . . Yehuda** (rä′ yə, ye hoo′ də).

him. Then, after a prolonged quarrel and several weeks of not speaking to each other, he took some of the things in his room and the broken clock and went to live alone. That had been about four years ago. Now Rachel would come to him once or twice a week, bringing with her a bag full of provisions, to clean the room and cook some meals for him. He was no longer interested in expenses and did not even ask about them, as though they were of no more concern to him.

"And now . . . what can I offer you?" Grandfather Zisskind would ask when he considered the room ready to receive guests. "There's no need to offer us anything, Grandfather; we didn't come for that," Raya would answer crossly.

But protests were of no avail. Her grandfather would take out a jar of fermenting preserves and put it on the table, then grapes and plums, biscuits and two glasses of strong tea, forcing them to eat. Raya would taste a little of this and that just to please the old man, while Yehuda, for whom all these visits were unavoidable torment, the very sight of the dishes arousing his disgust, would secretly indicate to her by making a sour face that he just couldn't touch the preserves. She would smile at him <u>placatingly</u>,[2] stroking his knee. But Grandfather insisted, so he would have to taste at least a teaspoonful of the sweet and nauseating stuff.

Afterwards Grandfather would ask about all kinds of things. Raya did her best to make the conversation pleasant in order to relieve Yehuda's boredom. Finally would come what Yehuda dreaded most of all and on account of which he had resolved more than once to refrain from these visits. Grandfather Zisskind would rise, take his chair and place it next to the wall, get up on it carefully, holding on to the back so as not to fall, open the clock, and take out a cloth bag with a black cord tied around it. Then he would shut the clock, get

off the chair, put it back in its place, sit down on it, undo the cord, take out of the cloth wrapping a bundle of sheets of paper, lay them in front of Yehuda, and say:

"I would like you to read this."

"Grandfather," Raya would rush to Yehuda's rescue, "but he's already read it at least ten times. . . ."

But Grandfather Zisskind would pretend not to hear and would not reply, so Yehuda was compelled each time to read there and then that same essay, spread over eight, long sheets in a large, somewhat shaky handwriting, which he almost knew by heart. It was a lament for Grandfather's native town in the Ukraine, which had been destroyed by the Germans, and all its Jews slaughtered. When he had finished, Grandfather would take the sheets out of his hand, fold them, sigh, and say:

"And nothing of all this is left. Dust and ashes. Not even a tombstone to bear witness. Imagine, of a community of twenty thousand Jews not even one survived to tell how it happened . . . Not a trace."

Then out of the same cloth bag, which contained various letters and envelopes, he would draw a photograph of his grandson Mendele,[3] who had been twelve years old when he was killed; the only son of his son Ossip, chief engineer in a large chemical factory. He would show it to Yehuda and say:

"He was a genius. Just imagine, when he was only eleven, he had already finished his studies at the Conservatory, won a scholarship from the government, and was considered an outstanding violinist. A genius! Look at that forehead. . . ." And after he had put the photograph back he would sigh and repeat, "Not a trace."

---

2. **placatingly** (plā' kat' iŋ lē): in a manner intended to calm or soothe.
3. **Mendele** (men' də le).

A strained silence of commiseration[4] would descend on Raya and Yehuda, who had already heard these same things many times over and no longer felt anything when they were repeated. And as he wound the cord around the bag the old man would muse: "And Ossip was also a prodigy. As a boy he knew Hebrew well and could recite Bialik's poems by heart. He studied by himself. He read endlessly, Gnessin, Frug, Bershadsky[5]... You didn't know Bershadsky; he was a good writer... He had a warm heart, Ossip had. He didn't mix in politics, he wasn't even a Zionist,[6] but even when they promoted him there, he didn't forget that he was a Jew... He called his son Mendele, of all names, after his dead brother,[7] even though it was surely not easy to have a name like that among the Russians... Yes, he had a warm, Jewish heart..."

He would turn to Yehuda as he spoke, since in Raya he always saw the child who used to sit on his knee listening to his stories, and for him she had never grown up, while he regarded Yehuda as an educated man who could understand someone else, especially inasmuch as Yehuda held a government job.

Raya remembered how the change had come about in her grandfather. When the war was over he was still sustained by uncertainty and hoped for some news of his son, for it was known that very many had succeeded in escaping eastward. Wearily he would visit all those who had once lived in his town, but none of them had received any sign of life from relatives. Nevertheless he continued to hope, for Ossip's important position might have helped to save him. Then Raya came home one evening and saw him sitting on the floor with a rent in his jacket.[8] In the house they spoke in whispers, and her mother's eyes were red with weeping. She, too, had wept at Grandfather's sorrow, at the sight of his stricken face, at the oppressive quiet in the rooms. For many weeks afterward it was as if he had

imposed silence on himself. He would sit at his table from morning to night, reading and rereading old letters, studying family photographs by the hour as he brought them close to his shortsighted eyes, or leaning backward on his chair, motionless, his hand touching the edge of the table and his eyes staring through the window in front of him, into the distance, as if he had turned to stone. He was no longer the same talkative, wise, and humorous grandfather who interested himself in the house, asked what his granddaughter was doing, instructed her, tested her knowledge, proving boastfully like a child that he knew more than her teachers. Now he seemed to cut himself off from the world and entrench himself in his thoughts and his memories, which none of the household could penetrate. Later, a strange perversity had taken hold of him that was hard to tolerate. He would insist that his meals be served at his table, apart, that no one should enter his room without knocking at the door, or close the shutters of his window against the sun. When anyone disobeyed these prohibitions, he would flare up and quarrel violently

---

4. **commiseration** (kə miz′ ər ā′ shən): the act of feeling or showing sorrow or pity for another's troubles; the act of showing sympathy.

5. **Bialik . . . Gnessin, Frug, Bershadsky** (bē ä′ lik, gne′ sin, frōōg, bər shäd′ skē): The Russian-born Hayyim Nahman Bialik (1873–1934) was a leading and influential poet in modern Hebrew literature. The other writers mentioned are less well-known.

6. **Zionist:** a follower of the movement to establish and maintain the Jewish national state of Israel.

7. **He called . . . brother:** It is a Jewish tradition to name a child after a loved one who is deceased. The name *Mendele* is Yiddish, the language spoken by East European Jews during the grandfather's time.

8. **rent in his jacket:** A rent is a tear in a cloth. It is a practice among some Jews to tear their clothing as an act of mourning for the loss of a loved one.

with his daughter. At times it seemed that he hated her.

When Raya's father died, Grandfather Zisskind did not show any signs of grief and did not even console his daughter. But when the days of mourning were past, it was as if he had been restored to new life, and he emerged from his silence. Yet he did not speak of his son-in-law, nor of his son Ossip, but only of his grandson Mendele. Often during the day he would mention the boy by name as if he were alive and would speak of him familiarly, although he had seen him only in photographs—as though deliberating aloud and turning the matter over, he would talk of how Mendele ought to be brought up. It was hardest of all when he started criticizing his son and his son's wife for not having foreseen the impending disaster, for not having rushed the boy away to a safe place, not having hidden him with non-Jews, not having tried to get him to the Land of Israel in good time. There was no logic in what he said; this would so infuriate Rachel that she would burst out with, "Oh, do stop! Stop it! I'll go out of my mind with your foolish nonsense!" She would rise from her seat in anger, withdraw to her room, and afterward, when she had calmed down, would say to Raya, "Sclerosis,[9] apparently. Loss of memory. He no longer knows what he's talking about."

One day—Raya would never forget this— she and her mother saw that Grandfather was wearing his best suit, the black one, and under it a gleaming white shirt; his shoes were polished, and he had a hat on. He had not worn these clothes for many months, and the family was dismayed to see him. They thought that he had lost his mind. "What holiday is it today?" her mother asked. "Really, don't you know?" asked her grandfather. "Today is Mendele's birthday!" Her mother burst out crying. She too began to cry and ran out of the house.

After that, Grandfather Zisskind went to live alone. His mind, apparently, had become settled, except that he would frequently forget things that had occurred a day or two before, though he clearly remembered, down to the smallest detail, things that had happened in his town and to his family more than thirty years ago. Raya would go and visit him, at first with her mother and, after her marriage, with Yehuda. What bothered them was that they were compelled to listen to his talk about Mendele his grandson and to read that same lament for his native town that had been destroyed.

Whenever Rachel happened to come there during their visit, she would scold Grandfather rudely. "Stop bothering them with your masterpiece," she would say, and would herself remove the papers from the table and put them back in their bag. "If you want them to keep on visiting you, don't talk to them about the dead. Talk about the living. They're young people, and they have no mind for such things." And as they left his room together she would say, turning to Yehuda in order to placate him, "Don't be surprised at him. Grandfather's already old. Over seventy. Loss of memory."

When Raya was seven months pregnant, Grandfather Zisskind had in his absent-mindedness not yet noticed it. But Rachel could no longer refrain from letting him share her joy and hope, and told him that a great-grandchild would soon be born to him. One evening the door of Raya and Yehuda's apartment opened, and Grandfather himself stood on the threshold in his holiday clothes, just as on the day of Mendele's birthday. This was the first time he had visited them at home, and Raya was so surprised that she hugged and kissed

---

9. sclerosis (skli rō′ sis): an abnormal hardening of body tissues, especially of the nervous system or the walls of major arteries.

him as she had not done since she was a child. His face shone, his eyes sparkled with the same intelligent and mischievous light they had in those far-off days before the calamity. When he entered, he walked briskly through the rooms, giving his opinion on the furniture and its arrangement and joking about everything around him. He was so pleasant that Raya and Yehuda could not stop laughing all the time he was speaking. He gave no indication that he knew what was about to take place, and for the first time in many months he did not mention Mendele.

"Ah, you naughty children," he said, "is this how you treat Grandfather? Why didn't you tell me you had such a nice place?"

"How many times have I invited you here, Grandfather?" asked Raya.

"Invited me? You ought to have *brought* me here, dragged me by force!"

"I wanted to do that too, but you refused."

"Well, I thought that you lived in some dark den, and I have a den of my own. Never mind, I forgive you."

And when he took leave of them he said:

"Don't bother to come to me. Now that I know where you're to be found and what a palace you have, I'll come to you . . . if you don't throw me out, that is."

Some days later, when Rachel came to their home and they told her about Grandfather's amazing visit, she was not surprised:

"Ah, you don't know what he's been contemplating during all these days, ever since I told him that you're about to have a child . . . He has one wish—that if it's a son, it should be named . . . after his grandson."

"Mendele?" exclaimed Raya, and involuntarily burst into laughter. Yehuda smiled as one smiles at the fond fancies of the old.

"Of course, I told him to put that out of his head," said Rachel, "but you know how obstinate he is. It's some obsession and he won't think of giving it up. Not only that, but he's

sure that you'll willingly agree to it, and especially you, Yehuda."

Yehuda shrugged his shoulders. "Crazy. The child would be unhappy all his life."

"But he's not capable of understanding that," said Rachel, and a note of apprehension crept into her voice.

Raya's face grew solemn. "We have already decided on the name," she said. "If it's a girl, she'll be called Osnath, and if it's a boy—Ehud."[10]

Rachel did not like either.

The matter of the name became almost the sole topic of conversation between Rachel and the young couple when she visited them, and it infused gloom into the air of expectancy that filled the house.

Rachel, midway between the generations, was of two minds about the matter. When she spoke to her father, she would scold and contradict him, flinging at him all the arguments she had heard from Raya and Yehuda as though they were her own; but when she spoke to the children, she sought to induce them to meet his wishes and would bring down their anger on herself. As time went on, the question of a name, to which in the beginning she had attached little importance, became a kind of mystery, concealing something preordained, fearful, and pregnant with life and death. The fate of the child itself seemed in doubt. In her innermost heart she prayed that Raya would give birth to a daughter.

"Actually, what's so bad about the name Mendele?" she asked her daughter. "It's a Jewish name like any other."

"What are you talking about, Mother"—

---

10. Osnath . . . Ehud (ŏs′ nät, e′ hōͦod): Hebrew names. In Israel, Hebrew—not Yiddish—is the official language. Raya and Yehuda associate Yiddish names with a troubled past and think this association will affect the child's happiness.

Raya rebelled against the thought—"a ghetto name, ugly, horrible! I wouldn't even be capable of letting it cross my lips. Do you want me to hate my child?"

"Oh, you won't hate your child. At any rate, not because of the name . . ."

"I should hate him. It's as if you'd told me that my child would be born with a hump! And anyway—why should I? What for?"

"You have to do it for Grandfather's sake," Rachel said quietly, although she knew that she was not speaking the whole truth.

"You know, Mother, that I am ready to do anything for Grandfather," said Raya. "I love him, but I am not ready to sacrifice my child's happiness on account of some superstition of his. What sense is there in it?"

Rachel could not explain the "sense in it" rationally, but in her heart she rebelled against her daughter's logic, which had always been hers too and now seemed very superficial, a symptom of the frivolity afflicting the younger generation. Her old father now appeared to her like an ancient tree whose deep roots suck up the mysterious essence of existence, of which neither her daughter nor she herself knew anything. Had it not been for this argument about the name, she would certainly never have got to meditating on the transmigration of souls[11] and the eternity of life. At night she would wake up covered in cold sweat. Hazily, she recalled frightful scenes of bodies of naked children, beaten and trampled under the jackboots of soldiers, and an awful sense of guilt oppressed her spirit.

Then Rachel came with a proposal for a compromise: that the child should be named Menahem. A Hebrew name, she said; an Israeli one, by all standards.[12] Many children bore it, and it occurred to nobody to make fun of them. Even Grandfather had agreed to it after much urging.

Raya refused to listen.

"We have chosen a name, Mother," she said, "which we both like, and we won't change it for another. Menahem is a name that reeks of old age, a name that for me is connected with sad memories and people I don't like. Menahem you could call only a boy who is short, weak, and not good-looking. Let's not talk about it any more, Mother."

Rachel was silent. She almost despaired of convincing them. At last she said:

"And are you ready to take the responsibility of going against Grandfather's wishes?"

Raya's eyes opened wide, and fear was reflected in them:

"Why do you make such a fateful thing of it? You frighten me!" she said, and burst into tears. She began to fear for her offspring as one fears the evil eye.[13]

"And perhaps there *is* something fateful in it . . ." whispered Rachel without raising her eyes. She flinched at her own words.

"What is it?" insisted Raya, with a frightened look at her mother.

"I don't know . . . ," she said. "Perhaps all the same we are bound to retain the names of the dead . . . in order to leave a remembrance of them . . ." She was not sure herself whether there was any truth in what she said or whether it was merely a stupid belief, but her

---

11. transmigration of souls: Some Jews believe that a soul transmigrates, or moves from a dead person to a living person. The tradition of naming a child after a deceased person is sometimes seen as a way to guarantee this transmigration.

12. Menahem . . . standards (me nä′ khem): *Mendel* and *Menahem* are Yiddish and Hebrew versions of the same name; both mean "comforter." Jews often adapt the tradition of naming a child after a loved one who is deceased by giving the child a different name that begins with the same letter. This allows for the use of more modern names.

13. the evil eye: a look which, in superstitious belief, is able to harm or bewitch the one stared at.

father's faith was before her, stronger than her own doubts and her daughter's simple and understandable opposition.

"But I don't always want to remember all those dreadful things, Mother. It's impossible that this memory should always hang about this house and that the poor child should bear it!"

Rachel understood. She, too, heard such a cry within her as she listened to her father talking, sunk in memories of the past. As if to herself, she said in a whisper:

"I don't know . . . at times it seems to me that it's not Grandfather who's suffering from loss of memory, but ourselves. All of us."

About two weeks before the birth was due, Grandfather Zisskind appeared in Raya and Yehuda's home for the second time. His face was yellow, angry, and the light had faded from his eyes. He greeted them, but did not favor Raya with so much as a glance, as if he had pronounced a ban upon the sinner. Turning to Yehuda he said, "I wish to speak to you."

They went into the inner room. Grandfather sat down on the chair and placed the palm of his hand on the edge of the table, as was his <u>wont</u>,[14] and Yehuda sat, lower than he, on the bed.

"Rachel has told me that you don't want to call the child by my grandchild's name," he said.

"Yes . . . ," said Yehuda diffidently.

"Perhaps you'll explain to me why?" he asked.

"We . . . ," stammered Yehuda, who found it difficult to face the piercing gaze of the old man. "The name simply doesn't appeal to us."

Grandfather was silent. Then he said, "I understand that Mendele doesn't appeal to you. Not a Hebrew name. Granted! But Menahem—what's wrong with Menahem?" It was obvious that he was controlling his feelings with difficulty.

"It's not . . . ," Yehuda knew that there was no use explaining; they were two generations

apart in their ideas. "It's not an Israeli name . . . it's from the *Golah*."[15]

"*Golah*," repeated Grandfather. He shook with rage, but somehow he maintained his self-control. Quietly he added, "We all come from the *Golah*. I, and Raya's father and mother. Your father and mother. All of us."

"Yes . . . ," said Yehuda. He resented the fact that he was being dragged into an argument that was distasteful to him, particularly with this old man whose mind was already not quite clear. Only out of respect did he restrain himself from shouting: That's that, and it's done with! . . . "Yes, but we were born in this country," he said aloud; "that's different."

Grandfather Zisskind looked at him contemptuously. Before him he saw a wretched boor, an empty vessel.

"You, that is to say, think that there's something new here," he said, "that everything that was there is past and gone. Dead, without sequel. That you are starting everything anew."

"I didn't say that. I only said that we were born in this country . . ."

"You were born here. Very nice . . . ," said Grandfather Zisskind with rising emotion. "So what of it? What's so remarkable about that? In what way are you superior to those who were born *there*? Are you cleverer than they? More cultured? Are you greater than they in Torah[16] or good deeds? Is your blood redder than theirs?" Grandfather Zisskind looked as if he could wring Yehuda's neck.

"I didn't say that either. I said that *here* it's different . . ."

Grandfather Zisskind's patience with idle words was exhausted.

---

14. wont (wänt): usual practice; habit.

15. *Golah* (gō lä′): the Diaspora, a term referring to the whole body of Jews living dispersed in various countries among non-Jews.

16. in Torah (tō′ rə): in the study of Jewish religious teachings.

"You good-for-nothing!" he burst out in his rage. "What do you know about what was there? What do you know of the *people* that were there? The communities? The cities? What do you know of the *life* they had there?"

"Yes," said Yehuda, his spirit crushed, "but we no longer have any ties with it."

"You have no ties with it?" Grandfather Zisskind bent toward him. His lips quivered in fury. "With what . . . with what *do* you have ties?"

"We have . . . with this country," said Yehuda and gave an involuntary smile.

"Fool!" Grandfather Zisskind shot at him. "Do you think that people come to a desert and make themselves a nation, eh? That you are the first of some new race? That you're not the son of your father? Not the grandson of your grandfather? Do you want to forget them? Are you ashamed of them for having had a hundred times more culture and education than you have? Why . . . why, everything here"—he included everything around him in the sweep of his arm—"is no more than a puddle of tap water against the big sea that was there! What have you here? A mixed multitude! Seventy languages! Seventy distinct groups! Customs? A way of life? Why, every home here is a nation in itself, with its own customs and its own names! And with this you have ties, you say . . ."

Yehuda lowered his eyes and was silent.

"I'll tell you what ties are," said Grandfather Zisskind calmly. "Ties are remembrance! Do you understand? The Russian is linked to his people because he remembers his ancestors. He is called Ivan, his father was called Ivan, and his grandfather was called Ivan, back to the first generation. And no Russian has said: 'From today onward I shall not be called Ivan because my fathers and my fathers' fathers were called that; I am the first of a new Russian nation which has nothing at all to do with the Ivans.' Do you understand?"

"But what has that got to do with it?" Yehuda protested impatiently. Grandfather Zisskind shook his head at him.

"And you—you're ashamed to give your son the name Mendele lest it remind you that there were Jews who were called by that name. You believe that his name should be wiped off the face of the earth. That not a trace of it should remain . . ."

He paused, heaved a deep sigh, and said:

"O children, children, you don't know what you're doing . . . You're finishing off the work which the enemies of Israel began. They took the bodies away from the world, and you—the name and the memory . . . No continuation, no evidence, no memorial, and no name. Not a trace . . ."

And with that he rose, took his stick, and with long strides went toward the door and left.

The newborn child was a boy, and he was named Ehud, and when he was about a month old, Raya and Yehuda took him in the carriage to Grandfather's house.

Raya gave three cautious knocks on the door, and when she heard a rustle inside she could also hear the beating of her anxious heart. Since the birth of the child, Grandfather had not visited them even once. "I'm terribly excited," she whispered to Yehuda with tears in her eyes. Yehuda rocked the carriage and did not reply. He was now indifferent to what the old man might say or do.

The door opened, and on the threshold stood Grandfather Zisskind, his face weary and wrinkled. He seemed to have aged. His eyes were sticky with sleep, and for a moment it seemed as if he did not see the callers.

"Good Sabbath, Grandfather," said Raya with great feeling. It seemed to her now that she loved him more than ever.

Grandfather looked at them as if surprised and then said absently, "Come in, come in."

"We've brought the baby with us!" said

Raya, her face shining, and her glance traveled from Grandfather to the infant sleeping in the carriage.

"Come in, come in," repeated Grandfather Zisskind in a tired voice. "Sit down," he said as he removed his clothes from the chairs and turned to tidy the disordered bedclothes.

Yehuda stood the carriage by the wall and whispered to Raya, "It's stifling for him here." Raya opened the window wide.

"You haven't seen our baby yet, Grandfather!" she said with a sad smile.

"Sit down, sit down," said Grandfather, shuffling over to the shelf, from which he took the jar of preserves and the biscuit tin, putting them on the table.

"There's no need, Grandfather, really there's no need for it. We didn't come for that," said Raya.

"Only a little something. I have nothing to offer you today . . . ," said Grandfather in a dull, broken voice. He took the kettle off the kerosene burner and poured out two glasses of tea, which he placed before them. Then he too sat down, said, "Drink, drink," and softly tapped his fingers on the table.

"I haven't seen Mother for several days now," he said at last.

"She's busy . . . ," said Raya in a low voice, without raising her eyes to him. "She helps me a lot with the baby . . ."

Grandfather Zisskind looked at his pale, knotted, and veined hands lying helplessly on the table; then he stretched out one of them and said to Raya, "Why don't you drink? The tea will get cold."

Raya drew up to the table and sipped the tea.

"And you—what are you doing now?" he asked Yehuda.

"Working as usual," said Yehuda, and added with a laugh, "I play with the baby when there's time."

Grandfather again looked down at his hands, the long thin fingers of which shook with the palsy of old age.

"Take some of the preserves," he said to Yehuda, indicating the jar with a shaking finger. "It's very good." Yehuda dipped the spoon in the jar and put it to his mouth.

There was a deep silence. It seemed to last a very long time. Grandfather Zisskind's fingers gave little quivers on the white tablecloth. It was hot in the room, and the buzzing of a fly could be heard.

Suddenly the baby burst out crying, and Raya started from her seat and hastened to quiet him. She rocked the carriage and crooned, "Quiet, child, quiet, quiet . . ." Even after he had quieted down, she went on rocking the carriage back and forth.

Grandfather Zisskind raised his head and said to Yehuda in a whisper:

"You think it was impossible to save him . . . it was possible. They had many friends. Ossip himself wrote to me about it. The manager of the factory had a high opinion of him. The whole town knew them and loved them . . . How is it they didn't think of it . . . ?" he said, touching his forehead with the palm of his hand. "After all, they knew that the Germans were approaching . . . It was still possible to do something . . ." He stopped a moment and then added, "Imagine that a boy of eleven had already finished his studies at the Conservatory—wild beasts!" He suddenly opened eyes filled with terror. "Wild beasts! To take little children and put them into wagons and deport them . . ."

When Raya returned and sat down at the table, he stopped and became silent, and only a heavy sigh escaped from deep within him.

Again there was a prolonged silence, and as it grew heavier Raya felt the oppressive weight on her bosom increasing till it could no longer be contained. Grandfather sat at the table tapping his thin fingers, and alongside the wall the infant lay in his carriage; it was as if a chasm[17] gaped between a world that was passing and a world that was born. It was no longer a single line to the fourth generation. The aged father did not recognize the great-grandchild whose life would be no memorial.

Grandfather Zisskind got up, took his chair, and pulled it up to the clock. He climbed on to it to take out his documents.

Raya could no longer stand the oppressive atmosphere.

"Let's go," she said to Yehuda in a choked voice.

"Yes, we must go," said Yehuda, and rose from his seat. "We have to go," he said loudly as he turned to the old man.

Grandfather Zisskind held the key of the clock for a moment more, then he let his hand fall, grasped the back of the chair, and got down.

"You have to go . . . ," he said with a tortured grimace. He spread his arms out helplessly and accompanied them to the doorway.

When the door had closed behind them, the tears flowed from Raya's eyes. She bent over the carriage and pressed her lips to the baby's chest. At that moment it seemed to her that he was in need of pity and of great love, as though he were alone, an orphan in the world.

---

17. **chasm** (kaz′ əm): a deep crack in the earth's surface.

Thinking About the Story

A PERSONAL RESPONSE

sharing impressions

1. What are your thoughts and feelings at the end of the story? Describe them briefly in your journal.

constructing interpretations

2. Do you think Raya and Yehuda do the right thing in choosing the name that they do?

Think about
- Raya's seeing her baby, at the end of the story, as "an orphan in the world"
- Raya's unwillingness to "sacrifice my child's happiness on account of some superstition" of her grandfather's
- the desire of the couple to dissociate from the past and identify with Israel

3. Why do you think that Grandfather Zisskind and the young couple are so divided in their feelings about the family tradition? Explain.

Think about
- Rachel's comparison of her father to "an ancient tree whose deep roots suck up the mysterious essence of existence"
- what you would have done in a similar situation

A CREATIVE RESPONSE

4. If Raya and Yehuda had named their son Mendele according to the family tradition, how do you think they would have felt about it in later life?

A CRITICAL RESPONSE

5. In what way do you think the clock belonging to the grandfather works as a symbol in this story?

Think about
- the definition of symbol as a person, place, object, or activity that stands for something beyond itself
- what the clock means to the characters in the story

6. Which of the themes, or messages, that can be drawn from "The Name" seems most relevant to your life?

Think about
- the effect of the past on the present
- the issue of cultural identity
- differences between youth and age
- questions of independence
- the possibility of compromise

7. How would you compare Raya and Yehuda's situation to that of Sŏgun in "The Heir" or that of Eli in "The Lie"?

Think about
- how the characters feel about family traditions
- the characters' relationships with their elders
- the seriousness of each character's situation

Analyzing the Writer's Craft

PLOT STRUCTURE

What are the key events in this story?

Building a Literary Vocabulary. Plot refers to the actions and events in a literary work. The plot moves forward because of a conflict, or struggle between opposing forces. In a traditional narrative, plot structure consists of the exposition, the rising action, the climax, and the falling action. The **exposition** is the explanation that lays the groundwork for the narrative and provides necessary background information. In "The Name," for example, exposition occurs in the first several pages so that the reader understands who the characters are, where they live, and what happened in the past to lead up to the present action. During the **rising action** of the plot, complications of the conflict build to a **climax,** or turning point. Interest and intensity reach their peak at this point. The events that follow the climax, called the **falling action,** show the results of the major events and resolve loose ends in the plot.

Application: Analyzing Plot Structure. Work in a small group to diagram the plot structure of "The Name." The main task will be to decide where the climax of the story occurs and where the falling action begins. Compare your findings with the findings of other groups in the class.

Connecting Reading and Writing

1. In this story Rachel sympathizes with the viewpoints of both her father and her daughter. Write a series of **diary entries** that Rachel might have written during the time this crisis was taking place.

Option: Create a **transcript** of a telephone conversation that Rachel might have with a friend shortly after the birth of her grandson.

2. Imagine that Grandfather writes a letter to his great-grandson Ehud. He puts this letter inside the old clock and tells Raya that the boy should read it when he grows into his teens. Write this **letter** as you imagine it would be.

Option: Create an **oral history** recorded by Grandfather that Ehud can listen to when he is twelve years old and curious about his ancestors.

3. To learn more about the culture of Russian and Ukrainian Jews in the late nineteenth and early twentieth centuries, read a few stories from one of Sholom Aleichem's collections, such as *Some Laughter, Some Tears.* Prepare a **report** for your class, explaining what these stories teach about the life that Grandfather Zisskind left behind in his native town.

Option: Using information from Sholom Aleichem's stories, create a **passage** to be added to "The Name" in which Grandfather describes life in his native town.

A Visit to Grandmother

WILLIAM MELVIN KELLEY

A biography of Kelley appears on page 423.

Approaching the Story

Parts of the story you are about to read recall the South before the era of civil rights, at a time when African Americans were forced to attend separate schools, made to use separate public facilities, and prevented from voting. In addition, they were sometimes lynched—hanged by lawless mobs. In this story an African-American doctor, living in the North in the early 1960's, returns to the South to visit his mother, whom he has not seen in many years. The visit is described from the viewpoint of the doctor's teenage son Chig, who has accompanied him.

Building Vocabulary

These essential words are footnoted within the story.

indulgence (in dul′ jəns): He had spoken of GL with the kind of **indulgence** he would have shown a cute, but ill-behaved and potentially dangerous, five-year-old. (page 57)

engaging (en gāj′ iŋ): He stood in the doorway, smiling broadly, an **engaging,** open, friendly smile, the innocent smile of a five-year-old. (page 61)

Connecting Writing and Reading

In which of the situations described below would it be fair to give a person special consideration? In which situations would it be unfair? Copy the box below and, for each statement, mark an **X** in the appropriate column. Give reasons for your responses.

	Fair	Unfair
The person is more attractive than others.	____	____
The person is less attractive than others.	____	____
The person is less responsible than others.	____	____

As you read this story about a mother and two sons, consider your thoughts about when someone should be indulged.

CHIG KNEW SOMETHING was wrong the instant his father kissed her. He had always known his father to be the warmest of men, a man so kind that when people ventured timidly into his office, it took only a few words from him to make them relax, and even laugh. Doctor Charles Dunford cared about people.

But when he had bent to kiss the old lady's black face, something new and almost ugly had come into his eyes: fear, uncertainty, sadness, and perhaps even hatred.

Ten days before in New York, Chig's father had decided suddenly he wanted to go to Nashville to attend his college class reunion, twenty years out. Both Chig's brother and sister, Peter and Connie, were packing for camp and besides were too young for such an affair. But Chig was seventeen, had nothing to do that summer, and his father asked if he would like to go along. His father had given him additional reasons: "All my running buddies got their diplomas and were snapped up by them crafty young gals, and had kids within a year—now all those kids, some of them gals, are your age."

The reunion had lasted a week. As they packed for home, his father, in a far too off-hand way, had suggested they visit Chig's grandmother. "We this close. We might as well drop in on her and my brothers."

So, instead of going north, they had gone farther south, had just entered her house. And Chig had a suspicion now that the reunion had been only an excuse to drive south, that his father had been heading to this house all the time.

His father had never talked much about his family, with the exception of his brother GL, who seemed part con man, part practical joker, and part Don Juan; he had spoken of GL with the kind of indulgence[1] he would have shown a cute, but ill-behaved and potentially dangerous, five-year-old.

Chig's father had left home when he was fifteen. When asked why, he would answer, "I wanted to go to school. They didn't have a black high school at home, so I went up to Knoxville and lived with a cousin and went to school."

They had been met at the door by Aunt Rose, GL's wife, and ushered into the living room. The old lady had looked up from her seat by the window. Aunt Rose stood between the visitors.

The old lady eyed his father. "Rose, who that? Rose?" She squinted. She looked like a doll, made of black straw, the wrinkles in her face running in one direction like the head of a broom. Her hair was white and coarse and grew out straight from her head. Her eyes were brown—the whites, too, seemed light brown—and were hidden behind thick glasses, which remained somehow on a tiny nose. "That Hiram?" That was another of his father's brothers. "No, it ain't Hiram; too big for Hiram." She turned then to Chig. "Now that man, he look like Eleanor, Charles's wife, but Charles wouldn't never send my grandson to see me. I never even hear from Charles." She stopped again.

"It Charles, Mama. That who it is." Aunt Rose, between them, led them closer. "It Charles come all the way from New York to see you, and brung little Charles with him."

The old lady stared up at them. "Charles? Rose, that really Charles?" She turned away, and reached for a handkerchief in the pocket of her clean, ironed, flowered housecoat, and wiped her eyes. "God have mercy. Charles." She spread her arms up to him, and he bent down and kissed her cheek. That was when Chig saw his face, grimacing. She hugged him; Chig watched the muscles in her arms as they tightened around his father's neck. She half rose out of her chair. "How are you, son?"

---

1. **indulgence** (in dul′ jəns): a yielding; lack of strictness.

Chig could not hear his father's answer.

She let him go, and fell back into her chair, grabbing the arms. Her hands were as dark as the wood, and seemed to become part of it. "Now, who that standing there? Who that man?"

"That's one of your grandsons, Mama." His father's voice cracked. "Charles Dunford, junior. You saw him once, when he was a baby, in Chicago. He's grown now."

"I can see that, boy!" She looked at Chig squarely. "Come here, son, and kiss me once." He did. "What they call you? Charles too?"

"No, ma'am, they call me Chig."

She smiled. She had all her teeth, but they were too perfect to be her own. "That's good. Can't have two boys answering to Charles in the same house. Won't nobody at all come. So you that little boy. You don't remember me, do you. I used to take you to church in Chicago, and you'd get up and hop in time to the music. You studying to be a preacher?"

"No, ma'am. I don't think so. I might be a lawyer."

"You'll be an honest one, won't you?"

"I'll try."

"Trying ain't enough! You be honest, you hear? Promise me. You be honest like your daddy."

"All right. I promise."

"Good. Rose, where's GL at? Where's that thief? He gone again?"

"I don't know, Mama." Aunt Rose looked embarrassed. "He say he was going by the store. He'll be back."

"Well, then where's Hiram? You call up those boys, and get them over here—now! You got enough to eat? Let me go see." She started to get up. Chig reached out his hand. She shook him off. "What they tell you about me, Chig? They tell you I'm all laid up? Don't believe it. They don't know nothing about old ladies. When I want help, I'll let you know. Only time I'll need help getting anywheres is when I dies and they lift me into the ground."

She was standing now, her back and shoulders straight. She came only to Chig's chest. She squinted up at him. "You eat much? Your daddy ate like two men."

"Yes, ma'am."

"That's good. That means you ain't nervous. Your mama, she ain't nervous. I remember that. In Chicago, she'd sit down by a window all afternoon and never say nothing, just knit." She smiled. "Let me see what we got to eat."

"I'll do that, Mama." Aunt Rose spoke softly. "You haven't seen Charles in a long time. You sit and talk."

The old lady squinted at her. "You can do the cooking if you promise it ain't because you think I can't."

Aunt Rose chuckled. "I know you can do it, Mama."

"All right. I'll just sit and talk a spell." She sat again and arranged her skirt around her short legs.

Chig did most of the talking, told all about himself before she asked. His father only spoke when he was spoken to, and then, only one word at a time, as if by coming back home, he had become a small boy again, sitting in the parlor while his mother spoke with her guests.

When Uncle Hiram and Mae, his wife, came, they sat down to eat. Chig did not have to ask about Uncle GL's absence; Aunt Rose volunteered an explanation: "Can't never tell where the man is at. One Thursday morning he left here and next thing we knew, he was calling from Chicago, saying he went up to see Joe Louis fight. He'll be here though; he ain't as young and footloose as he used to be." Chig's father had mentioned driving down that GL was about five years older than he was, nearly fifty.

Uncle Hiram was somewhat smaller than Chig's father; his short-cropped kinky hair was half gray, half black. One spot, just off his forehead, was totally white. Later, Chig found out it had been that way since he was twenty. Mae (Chig could not bring himself to call her Aunt) was a good deal younger than Hiram, pretty enough so that Chig would have looked at her twice on the street. She was a honey-colored woman, with long eyelashes. She was wearing a white sheath.

At dinner, Chig and his father sat on one side, opposite Uncle Hiram and Mae; his grandmother and Aunt Rose sat at the ends. The food was good; there was a lot and Chig ate a lot. All through the meal, they talked about the family as it had been thirty years before, and particularly about the young GL. Mae and Chig asked questions; the old lady answered; Aunt Rose directed the discussion, steering the old lady onto the best stories; Chig's father laughed from time to time; Uncle Hiram ate.

"Why don't you tell them about the horse, Mama?" Aunt Rose, over Chig's weak protest, was spooning mashed potatoes onto his plate. "There now, Chig."

"I'm trying to think." The old lady was holding her fork halfway to her mouth, looking at them over her glasses. "Oh, you talking about that crazy horse GL brung home that time."

"That's right, Mama." Aunt Rose nodded and slid another slice of white meat on Chig's plate.

Mae started to giggle. "Oh, I've heard this. This is funny, Chig."

The old lady put down her fork and began. "Well, GL went out of the house one day with an old, no-good chair I wanted him to take over to the church for a bazaar, and he met up with this man who'd just brung in some horses from out West. Now, I reckon you can expect one swindler to be in every town, but you don't rightly think there'll be two; and God forbid they should ever meet—but they did, GL and his chair, this man and his horses.

Well, I wished I'd-a been there; there must-a been some mighty high-powered talking going on. That man with his horses, he told GL them horses was half-Arab, half-Indian, and GL told that man the chair was an antique he'd stole from some rich white folks. So they swapped. Well, I was a-looking out the window and seen GL dragging this animal to the house. It looked pretty gentle and its eyes was most closed and its feet was shuffling.

"'GL, where'd you get that thing?' I says.

"'I swapped him for that old chair, Mama,' he says. 'And made myself a bargain. This is even better than Papa's horse.'

"Well, I'm a-looking at this horse and noticing how he be looking more and more wide awake every minute, sort of warming up like a teakettle until, I swears to you, that horse is blowing steam out its nose.

"'Come on, Mama,' GL says, 'come on and I'll take you for a ride.' Now George, my husband, God rest his tired soul, he'd brung home this white folks' buggy which had a busted wheel and fixed it and was to take it back that day and GL says: 'Come on, Mama, we'll use this fine buggy and take us a ride.'

"'GL,' I says, 'no, we ain't. Them white folks'll burn us alive if we use their buggy. You just take that horse right on back.' You see, I was sure that boy'd come by that animal ungainly.[2]

"'Mama, I can't take him back,' GL says.

"'Why not?' I says.

"'Because I don't rightly know where that man is at,' GL says.

"'Oh,' I says. 'Well, then I reckon we stuck with it.' And I turned around to go back into the house because it was getting late, near dinner time, and I was cooking for ten.

"'Mama,' GL says to my back. 'Mama, ain't you coming for a ride with me?'

---

2. **ungainly** (un gān′ lē): a colloquial term meaning "improperly, in an immoral or illegal manner."

"'Go on, boy. You ain't getting me inside kicking range of that animal.' I was eying that beast and it was boiling hotter all the time. I reckon maybe that man had drugged it. 'That horse is wild, GL,' I says.

"'No, he ain't. He ain't. That man say he is buggy and saddle broke and as sweet as the inside of a apple.'

"My oldest girl, Essie, had-a come out on the porch and she says, 'Go on, Mama. I'll cook. You ain't been out the house in weeks.'

"'Sure, come on, Mama,' GL says. 'There ain't nothing to be fidgety about. This horse is gentle as a rose petal.' And just then that animal snorts so hard it sets up a little dust storm around its feet.

"'Yes, Mama,' Essie says, 'you can see he gentle.' Well, I looked at Essie and then at that horse because I didn't think we could be looking at the same animal. I should-a figured how Essie's eyes ain't never been so good.

"'Come on, Mama,' GL says.

"'All right,' I says. So I stood on the porch and watched GL hitching that horse up to the white folks' buggy. For a while there, the animal was pretty quiet, pawing a little, but not much. And I was feeling a little better about riding with GL behind that crazy-looking horse. I could see how GL was happy I was going with him. He was scurrying around that animal buckling buckles and strapping straps, all the time smiling, and that made me feel good.

"Then he was finished, and I must say, that horse looked mighty fine hitched to that buggy and I knew anybody what climbed up there would look pretty good too. GL came around and stood at the bottom of the steps, and took off his hat and bowed and said, 'Madam,' and reached out his hand to me and I was feeling real elegant like a fine lady. He helped me up to the seat and then got up beside me and we moved out down our alley. And I remember how black folks come out on their porches and

shook their heads, saying, 'Lord now, will you look at Eva Dunford, the fine lady! Don't she look good sitting up there!' And I pretended not to hear and sat up straight and proud.

"We rode on through the center of town, up Market Street, and all the way out where Hiram is living now, which in them days was all woods, there not being even a farm in sight and that's when that horse must-a first realized he weren't at all broke or tame or maybe thought he was back out West again, and started to gallop.

"'GL,' I says, 'now you ain't joking with your mama, is you? Because if you is, I'll strap you purple if I live through this.'

"Well, GL was pulling on the reins with all his meager strength, and yelling, 'Whoa, you. Say now, whoa!' He turned to me just long enough to say, 'I ain't fooling with you, Mama. Honest!'

"I reckon that animal weren't too satisfied with the road, because it made a sharp right turn just then, down into a gulley, and struck out across a hilly meadow. 'Mama,' GL yells. 'Mama, do something!'

"I didn't know what to do, but I figured I had to do something so I stood up, hopped down onto the horse's back and pulled it to a stop. Don't ask me how I did that; I reckon it was that I was a mother and my baby asked me to do something, is all.

"Well, we walked that animal all the way home; sometimes I had to club it over the nose with my fist to make it come, but we made it, GL and me. You remember how tired we was, Charles?"

"I wasn't here at the time." Chig turned to his father and found his face completely blank, without even a trace of a smile or a laugh.

"Well, of course you was, son. That happened in . . . in . . . it was a hot summer that year and—"

"I left here in June of that year. You wrote me about it."

The old lady stared past Chig at him. They

all turned to him; Uncle Hiram looked up from his plate.

"Then you don't remember how we all laughed?"

"No, I don't, Mama. And I probably wouldn't have laughed. I don't think it was funny." They were staring into each other's eyes.

"Why not, Charles?"

"Because in the first place, the horse was gained by fraud. And in the second place, both of you might have been seriously injured or even killed." He broke off their stare and spoke to himself more than to any of them. "And if I'd done it, you would've beaten me good for it."

"Pardon?" The old lady had not heard him; only Chig had heard.

Chig's father sat up straight as if preparing to debate. "I said that if I had done it, if I had done just exactly what GL did, you would have beaten me good for it, Mama." He was looking at her again.

"Why you say that, son?" She was leaning toward him.

"Don't you know? Tell the truth. It can't hurt me now." His voice cracked, but only once. "If GL and I did something wrong, you'd beat me first and then be too tired to beat him. At dinner, he'd always get seconds and I wouldn't. You'd do things with him, like ride in that buggy; but if I wanted you to do something with me, you were always too busy." He paused and considered whether to say what he finally did say. "I cried when I left here. Nobody loved me, Mama. I cried all the way up to Knoxville. That was the last time I ever cried in my life."

"Oh, Charles." She started to get up, to come around the table to him.

He stopped her. "It's too late."

"But you don't understand."

"What don't I understand? I understood then; I understand now."

Tears now traveled down the lines in her face, but when she spoke, her voice was clear. "I thought you knew. I had ten children. I had to give all of them what they needed most." She nodded. "I paid more mind to GL. I had to. GL could-a ended up swinging if I hadn't. But you was smarter. You was more growed up than GL when you was five and he was ten, and I tried to show you that by letting you do what you wanted to do."

"That's not true, Mama. You know it. GL was light-skinned and had good hair and looked almost white and you loved him for that."

"Charles, no. No, son. I didn't love any one of you more than any other."

"That can't be true." His father was standing now, his fists clenched tight. "Admit it, Mama . . . please!" Chig looked at him, shocked; the man was actually crying.

"It may not-a been right what I done, but I ain't no liar." Chig knew she did not really understand what had happened, what he wanted of her. "I'm not lying to you, Charles."

Chig's father had gone pale. He spoke very softly. "You're about thirty years too late, Mama." He bolted from the table. Silverware and dishes rang and jumped. Chig heard him hurrying up to their room.

They sat in silence for awhile and then heard a key in the front door. A man with a new, lacquered straw hat came in. He was wearing brown-and-white two-tone shoes with very pointed toes and a white summer suit. "Say now! Man! I heard my brother was in town. Where he at? Where that rascal?"

He stood in the doorway, smiling broadly, an engaging,[3] open, friendly smile, the innocent smile of a five-year-old.

---

3. engaging (en gāj′ iŋ): tending to draw favorable attention; attractive.

Thinking About the Story

sharing impressions

1. What is your impression of Charles, GL, and their mother? Jot down some thoughts about these characters in your journal.

constructing interpretations

2. In your opinion, should GL have been indulged by his mother? Explain your answer.

> **Think about**
> - what his family's descriptions of him, particularly in the story about the horse, reveal about his character
> - what his mother means by saying that GL "could-a ended up swinging" if she had not paid more attention to him
> - the effect that the mother's indulgence of GL has had on her son Charles
> - your views about what entitles someone to be indulged

3. Is Charles right to feel that his mother does not love him? Tell why or why not.

A CREATIVE RESPONSE

4. What could the mother have done in the past, and what can she do now, to keep Charles from feeling such resentment?

5. How might GL view Charles?

A CRITICAL RESPONSE

6. What do you think are the advantages of telling this story from Chig's viewpoint instead of Charles's?

7. To what degree does the setting shape the events of this story?

> **Think about**
> - how the mother's actions are influenced by the time and place in which she lives
> - whether the same family tensions could have developed had she raised her children in the North or in today's South

8. In 1964 the critic Louis Rubin, Jr., wrote that this story "leaves one unsatisfied because the author has failed to bring out the rich potentialities of the situation. . . . This story isn't concerned enough with the race problem, and it also isn't sufficiently concerned with exploring the full human relationships." Tell whether you agree or disagree with these criticisms, and why.

Analyzing the Writer's Craft

DIALOGUE

What do you learn about the characters in "A Visit to Grandmother" from what they say to each other?

Building a Literary Vocabulary. Dialogue is written conversation between two or more characters. Realistic, well-placed dialogue enlivens narrative prose and provides the reader with insights into characters and their personalities. William Melvin Kelley relies heavily on dialogue to tell this story. The dialogue is consistent with his African-American characters, reproducing their rural Southern and urban Northern dialects. (A dialect is the particular variety of language spoken in one place by a distinct group of people.) The dialogue is also emotionally expressive, revealing the feelings and relationships of the characters. Reread the dialogue between the mother and Aunt Rose when Charles and Chig first enter the room (page 57). Here the reader learns that the mother cannot see well and that she has been hurt by never receiving visits from her son. She is profoundly moved that they have finally come to see her. The reader also learns that Aunt Rose is a peacemaker, happy to soothe the mother's feelings.

Application: Interpreting Dialogue. Look at three other passages of dialogue in the story: the exchanges between the mother, Aunt Rose, and Chig from when the mother asks where GL is until she sits down to talk to Chig (page 58); during the horse story, the exchanges between the mother, GL, and Essie from when the mother asks GL where he got the horse until she agrees to ride (pages 59–60); the exchange between the mother and Charles from when she finishes her story until Charles leaves the room (page 61). Several students, taking the parts of the characters, should read these exchanges aloud. The class should discuss what the dialogue reveals about the characters and the relationships between them.

Connecting Reading and Writing

1. Continue this story as a **dialogue** between Charles and his son Chig as they drive back to New York.

Option: Present Charles's view of the situation and the suggestions you would offer him in a **newspaper advice column** similar to "Dear Abby."

2. Write up **personality profiles** of GL and Charles that might appear in their high school yearbooks.

Option: Have the mother describe GL and Charles in an annual church **pamphlet** in which members and their families are profiled.

3. Interview a parent of two or more children, asking whether he or she treats all the children the same or treats them differently according to their special needs. Present this parent's experiences, and note any parallels in the story, in a **newspaper column** devoted to child rearing.

Option: As a class, combine your interview results in a **research report** for your teacher.

Everyday Use

ALICE WALKER

A biography of Walker appears on page 429.

*A*pproaching the Story ⸻

Alice Walker belongs to a generation of writers who benefited from the civil rights movement of the 1960's and the black pride movement of the 1970's. At the time that "Everyday Use" is set, many African Americans were not only discovering their African roots but also gaining a new appreciation for the heritage of the black experience in this country. As this story begins, the narrator waits with her daughter Maggie for her elder daughter, Dee, to return to the family farm in Georgia after a long absence.

I WILL WAIT for her in the yard that Maggie and I made so clean and wavy yesterday afternoon. A yard like this is more comfortable than most people know. It is not just a yard. It is like an extended living room. When the hard clay is swept clean as a floor and the fine sand around the edges lined with tiny, irregular grooves, anyone can come and sit and look up into the elm tree and wait for the breezes that never come inside the house.

Maggie will be nervous until after her sister goes. She will stand hopelessly in corners, homely and ashamed of the burn scars down her arms and legs, eyeing her sister with a mixture of envy and awe. She thinks her sister has held life always in the palm of one hand, that "no" is a word the world never learned to say to her.

You've no doubt seen those TV shows where the child who has "made it" is con-fronted, as a surprise, by her own mother and father, tottering in weakly from backstage. (A pleasant surprise, of course. What would they do if parent and child came on the show only to curse out and insult each other?) On TV, mother and child embrace and smile into each other's faces. Sometimes the mother and father weep, the child wraps them in her arms and leans across the table to tell how she would not have made it without their help. I have seen these programs.

Sometimes I dream a dream in which Dee and I are suddenly brought together on a TV program of this sort. Out of a dark and soft-seated limousine I am ushered into a bright room filled with many people. There I meet a smiling, gray, sporty man like Johnny Carson, who shakes my hand and tells me what a fine girl I have. Then we are on the stage and Dee is embracing me with tears in her eyes. She pins on my dress a large orchid, even though she had told me once that she thinks orchids are tacky flowers.

In real life I am a large, big-boned woman with rough, man-working hands. In the winter I wear flannel nightgowns to bed and overalls during the day. I can kill and clean a hog as mercilessly as a man. My fat keeps me hot in zero weather. I can work outside all day, breaking ice to get water for washing; I can eat pork liver cooked over the open fire minutes after it comes steaming from the hog. One winter I knocked a bull calf straight in the brain between the eyes with a sledge hammer and had the meat hung up to chill before nightfall. But of course all this does not show on television. I am the way my daughter would want me to be: a hundred pounds lighter, my skin like an uncooked barley pancake. My hair glistens in the hot bright lights. Johnny Carson has much to do to keep up with my quick and witty tongue.

But that is a mistake. I know even before I wake up. Who ever knew a Johnson with a quick tongue? Who can even imagine me looking a strange white man in the eye? It seems to me I have talked to them always with one foot raised in flight, with my head turned in whichever way is farthest from them. Dee, though. She would always look anyone in the eye. Hesitation was no part of her nature.

"How do I look, Mama?" Maggie says, showing just enough of her thin body enveloped in pink skirt and red blouse for me to know she's there, almost hidden by the door.

"Come out into the yard," I say.

Have you ever seen a lame animal, perhaps a dog run over by some careless person rich enough to own a car, sidle[1] up to someone who is ignorant enough to be kind to him? That is the way my Maggie walks. She has been like this, chin on chest, eyes on ground, feet in shuffle, ever since the fire that burned the other house to the ground.

Dee is lighter than Maggie, with nicer hair and a fuller figure. She's a woman now, though sometimes I forget. How long ago was it that the other house burned? Ten, twelve years? Sometimes I can still hear the flames and feel Maggie's arms sticking to me, her hair smoking and her dress falling off her in little black papery flakes. Her eyes seemed stretched open, blazed open by the flames reflected in them. And Dee. I see her standing off under the sweet gum tree she used to dig gum out of; a look of concentration on her face as she watched the last dingy gray board of the house fall in toward the red-hot brick chimney. Why don't you do a dance around the ashes? I'd wanted to ask her. She had hated the house that much.

I used to think she hated Maggie, too. But that was before we raised the money, the church and me, to send her to Augusta[2] to school. She used to read to us without pity; forcing words, lies, other folks' habits, whole lives upon us two, sitting trapped and ignorant underneath her voice. She washed us in a river of make-believe, burned us with a lot of knowledge we didn't necessarily need to know. Pressed us to her with the serious way she read, to shove us away at just the moment, like dimwits, we seemed about to understand.

Dee wanted nice things. A yellow organdy dress to wear to her graduation from high school; black pumps to match a green suit she'd made from an old suit somebody gave me. She was determined to stare down any disaster in her efforts. Her eyelids would not flicker for minutes at a time. Often I fought off the temptation to shake her. At sixteen she had a style of her own, and knew what style was.

I never had an education myself. After second grade the school was closed down. Don't ask me why; in 1927 blacks asked fewer ques-

---

1. **sidle** (sīd′ ′l): move sideways, especially in a way that does not draw attention.
2. **Augusta:** a city in Georgia.

tions than they do now. Sometimes Maggie reads to me. She stumbles along good-naturedly but can't see well. She knows she is not bright. Like good looks and money, quickness passed her by. She will marry John Thomas (who has mossy teeth in an earnest face), and then I'll be free to sit here and I guess just sing church songs to myself. Although I never was a good singer. Never could carry a tune. I was always better at a man's job. I used to love to milk till I was hooked in the side in '49. Cows are soothing and slow and don't bother you, unless you try to milk them the wrong way.

I have deliberately turned my back on the house. It is three rooms, just like the one that burned, except the roof is tin; they don't make shingle roofs any more. There are no real windows, just some holes cut in the sides, like the portholes in a ship, but not round and not square, with rawhide holding the shutters up on the outside. This house is in a pasture, too, like the other one. No doubt when Dee sees it, she will want to tear it down. She wrote me once that no matter where we "choose" to live, she will manage to come see us. But she will never bring her friends. Maggie and I thought about this and Maggie asked me, "Mama, when did Dee ever *have* any friends?"

She had a few. <u>Furtive</u>[3] boys in pink shirts hanging about on washday after school. Nervous girls who never laughed. Impressed with her, they worshiped the well-turned phrase, the cute shape, the scalding humor that erupted like bubbles in lye. She read to them.

When she was courting Jimmy T, she didn't have much time to pay to us, but turned all her faultfinding power on him. He *flew* to marry a cheap city girl from a family of ignorant, flashy people. She hardly had time to recompose herself.

When she comes I will meet—but there they are!

Maggie attempts to make a dash for the house, in her shuffling way, but I stay her with my hand. "Come back here," I say. And she stops and tries to dig a well in the sand with her toe.

It is hard to see them clearly through the strong sun. But even the first glimpse of leg out of the car tells me it is Dee. Her feet were always neat-looking, as if God himself had shaped them with a certain style. From the other side of the car comes a short, stocky man. Hair is all over his head a foot long and hanging from his chin like a kinky mule tail. I hear Maggie suck in her breath. "Uhnnnh," is what it sounds like. Like when you see the wriggling end of a snake just in front of your foot on the road. "Uhnnnh."

Dee next. A dress down to the ground, in this hot weather. A dress so loud it hurts my eyes. There are yellows and oranges enough to throw back the light of the sun. I feel my whole face warming from the heat waves it throws out. Earrings gold, too, and hanging down to her shoulders. Bracelets dangling and making noises when she moves her arm up to shake the folds of the dress out of her armpits. The dress is loose and flows, and as she walks closer, I like it. I hear Maggie go "Uhnnnh" again. It is her sister's hair. It stands straight up like the wool on a sheep. It is black as night and around the edges are two long pigtails that rope about like small lizards disappearing behind her ears.

"Wa-su-zo-Tean-o!" she says, coming on in that gliding way the dress makes her move. The short, stocky fellow with the hair to his navel is all grinning and he follows up with "Asalamalakim,[4] my mother and sister!" He moves to hug Maggie but she falls back, right

---

3. furtive (fɥr′ tiv): stealthy, sneaky.
4. Wa-su-zo-Tean-o . . . Asalamalakim (wä so͞o zō tēn′ ō, ä sə läm′ ä lī′ ko͝om′): African greetings. The second, an Arabic greeting used among Muslims, means "Peace to you."

up against the back of my chair. I feel her trembling there, and when I look up, I see the perspiration falling off her chin.

"Don't get up," says Dee. Since I am stout, it takes something of a push. You can see me trying to move a second or two before I make it. She turns, showing white heels through her sandals, and goes back to the car. Out she peeks next with a Polaroid. She stoops down quickly and lines up picture after picture of me sitting there in front of the house with Maggie cowering behind me. She never takes a shot without making sure the house is included. When a cow comes nibbling around the edge of the yard, she snaps it and me and Maggie *and* the house. Then she puts the Polaroid in the back seat of the car and comes up and kisses me on the forehead.

Meanwhile Asalamalakim is going through motions with Maggie's hand. Maggie's hand is as limp as a fish, and probably as cold, despite the sweat, and she keeps trying to pull it back. It looks like Asalamalakim wants to shake hands but wants to do it fancy. Or maybe he don't know how people shake hands. Anyhow, he soon gives up on Maggie.

"Well," I say. "Dee."

"No, Mama," she says. "Not 'Dee,'" Wangero Leewanika Kemanjo!"[5]

"What happened to 'Dee'?" I wanted to know.

"She's dead," Wangero said. "I couldn't bear it any longer, being named after the people who oppress me."

"You know as well as me you was named after your aunt Dicie," I said. Dicie is my sister. She named Dee. We called her "Big Dee" after Dee was born.

"But who was *she* named after?" asked Wangero.

"I guess after Grandma Dee," I said.

"And who was she named for?" asked Wangero.

"Her mother," I said, and saw Wangero was getting tired. "That's about as far back as I can trace it," I said. Though, in fact, I probably could have carried it back beyond the Civil War through the branches.

"Well," said Asalamalakim, "there you are."

"Uhnnnh," I heard Maggie say.

"There I was not," I said, "before 'Dicie' cropped up in our family, so why should I try to trace it that far back?"

He just stood there grinning, looking down on me like somebody inspecting a Model A car. Every once in a while he and Wangero sent eye signals over my head.

"How do you pronounce this name?" I asked.

"You don't have to call me by it if you don't want to," said Wangero.

"Why shouldn't I?" I asked. "If that's what you want us to call you, we'll call you."

"I know it might sound awkward at first," said Wangero.

"I'll get used to it," I said. "Ream it out again."

Well, soon we got the name out of the way. Asalamalakim had a name twice as long and three times as hard. After I tripped over it two or three times, he told me to just call him Hakim-a-barber.[6] I wanted to ask him was he a barber, but I really didn't think he was, so I didn't ask.

"You must belong to those beef-cattle peoples down the road," I said. They said "Asalamalakim" when they met you, too, but they didn't shake hands. Always too busy: feeding the cattle, fixing the fences, putting up salt lick shelters, throwing down hay. When the white folks poisoned some of the herd, the men stayed up all night with rifles in their hands. I walked a mile and a half just to see the sight.

---

5. **Wangero Leewanika Kemanjo** (wän gᵤr′ ō lē wä′ nē kə ke män′ jō).

6. **Hakim-a-barber** (hä kēm ä bär′ bər).

Hakim-a-barber said, "I accept some of their doctrines, but farming and raising cattle is not my style." (They didn't tell me, and I didn't ask, whether Wangero (Dee) had really gone and married him.)

We sat down to eat, and right away he said he didn't eat collards and pork was unclean. Wangero, though, went on through the chitlins and corn bread, the greens, and everything else. She talked a blue streak over the sweet potatoes. Everything delighted her. Even the fact that we still used the benches her daddy made for the table when we couldn't afford to buy chairs.

"Oh, Mama!" she cried. Then turned to Hakim-a-barber. "I never knew how lovely these benches are. You can feel the rump prints," she said, running her hands underneath her and along the bench. Then she gave a sigh, and her hand closed over Grandma Dee's butter dish. "That's it!" she said. "I knew there was something I wanted to ask you if I could have." She jumped up from the table and went over in the corner where the churn stood, the milk in it clabber by now. She looked at the churn and looked at it.

"This churn top is what I need," she said. "Didn't Uncle Buddy whittle it out of a tree you all used to have?"

"Yes," I said.

"Uh huh," she said happily. "And I want the dasher, too."

"Uncle Buddy whittle that, too?" asked the barber.

Dee (Wangero) looked up at me.

"Aunt Dee's first husband whittled the dash," said Maggie so low you almost couldn't hear her. "His name was Henry, but they called him Stash."

"Maggie's brain is like an elephant's," Wangero said, laughing. "I can use the churn top as a centerpiece for the alcove table," she said, sliding a plate over the churn, "and I'll think of something artistic to do with the dasher."

When she finished wrapping the dasher, the handle stuck out. I took it for a moment in my hands. You didn't even have to look close to see where hands pushing the dasher up and down to make butter had left a kind of sink in the wood. In fact, there were a lot of small sinks; you could see where thumbs and fingers had sunk into the wood. It was beautiful light yellow wood, from a tree that grew in the yard where Big Dee and Stash lived.

After dinner Dee (Wangero) went to the trunk at the foot of my bed and started rifling through it. Maggie hung back in the kitchen over the dishpan. Out came Wangero with two quilts. They had been pieced by Grandma Dee, and then Big Dee and me had hung them on the quilt frames on the front porch and quilted them. One was in the Lone Star pattern. The other was Walk Around the Mountain. In both of them were scraps of dresses Grandma Dee had worn fifty and more years ago. Bits and pieces of Grandpa Jarrell's paisley shirts. And one teeny faded blue piece, about the size of a penny matchbox, that was from Great Grandpa Ezra's uniform that he wore in the Civil War.

"Mama," Wangero said, sweet as a bird. "Can I have these old quilts?"

I heard something fall in the kitchen, and a minute later the kitchen door slammed.

"Why don't you take one or two of the others?" I asked. "These old things was just done by me and Big Dee from some tops your grandma pieced before she died."

"No," said Wangero, "I don't want those. They are stitched around the borders by machine."

"That'll make them last better," I said.

"That's not the point," said Wangero. "These are all pieces of dresses Grandma used to wear. She did all this stitching by hand. Imagine!" She held the quilts securely in her arms, stroking them.

"Some of the pieces, like those lavender

ones, come from old clothes her mother handed down to her," I said, moving up to touch the quilts. Dee (Wangero) moved back just enough so that I couldn't reach the quilts. They already belonged to her.

"Imagine!" she breathed again, clutching them closely to her bosom.

"The truth is," I said, "I promised to give them quilts to Maggie, for when she marries John Thomas."

She gasped like a bee had stung her.

"Maggie can't appreciate these quilts!" she said. "She'd probably be backward enough to put them to everyday use."

"I reckon she would," I said. "God knows I been saving 'em long enough with nobody using 'em. I hope she will!" I didn't want to bring up how I had offered Dee (Wangero) a quilt when she went away to college. Then she had told me they were old-fashioned, out of style.

"But they're *priceless!*" she was saying now, furiously; for she has a temper. "Maggie would put them on the bed and in five years they'd be in rags. Less than that!"

"She can always make some more," I said. "Maggie knows how to quilt."

Dee (Wangero) looked at me with hatred. "You just will not understand. The point is these quilts, *these* quilts!"

"Well," I said, stumped. "What would you do with them?"

"Hang them," she said. As if that was the only thing you *could* do with quilts.

Maggie by now was standing in the door. I could almost hear the sound her feet made as they scraped over each other.

"She can have them, Mama," she said, like somebody used to never winning anything, or having anything reserved for her. "I can 'member Grandma Dee without the quilts."

I looked at her hard. She had filled her bottom lip with checkerberry snuff, and it gave her face a kind of dopey, hangdog look. It was Grandma Dee and Big Dee who taught her how to quilt herself. She stood there with her scarred hands in the folds of her skirt. She looked at her sister with something like fear, but she wasn't mad at her. This was Maggie's portion. This was the way she knew God to work.

When I looked at her like that, something hit me in the top of my head and ran down to the soles of my feet. Just like when I'm in church and the spirit of God touches me and I get happy and shout. I did something I never had done before: hugged Maggie to me, then dragged her on into the room, snatched the quilts out of Miss Wangero's hands and dumped them into Maggie's lap. Maggie just sat there on my bed with her mouth open.

"Take one or two of the others," I said to Dee.

But she turned without a word and went out to Hakim-a-barber.

"You just don't understand," she said, as Maggie and I came out to the car.

"What don't I understand?" I wanted to know.

"Your heritage," she said. And then she turned to Maggie, kissed her, and said, "You ought to try to make something of yourself, too, Maggie. It's really a new day for us. But from the way you and Mama still live, you'd never know it."

She put on some sunglasses that hid everything above the tip of her nose and her chin.

Maggie smiled; maybe at the sunglasses. But a real smile, not scared. After we watched the car dust settle, I asked Maggie to bring me a dip of snuff. And then the two of us sat there just enjoying, until it was time to go in the house and go to bed.

Rules of the Game

AMY TAN

A biography of Tan appears on page 427.

Approaching the Story

Imagine that you are a child growing up in a culture that is foreign to your parents, or that you are a young player just learning the game of chess. Or perhaps you are the daughter of a loving, strong-willed mother. Telling this story is a young woman who is all of these. In each situation she must make adjustments—learn the "rules of the game."

This story was first published separately but was eventually incorporated into Amy Tan's novel *The Joy Luck Club,* which intertwines the stories of Chinese-American mothers and daughters.

I WAS SIX when my mother taught me the art of invisible strength. It was a strategy for winning arguments, respect from others, and eventually, though neither of us knew it at the time, chess games.

"Bite back your tongue," scolded my mother when I cried loudly, yanking her hand toward the store that sold bags of salted plums. At home, she said, "Wise guy, he not go against wind. In Chinese we say, Come from South, blow with wind—poom!—North will follow. Strongest wind cannot be seen."

The next week I bit back my tongue as we entered the store with the forbidden candies. When my mother finished her shopping, she quietly plucked a small bag of plums from the rack and put it on the counter with the rest of the items.

My mother imparted her daily truths so she could help my older brothers and me rise above our circumstances. We lived in San Francisco's Chinatown. Like most of the other Chinese children who played in the back alleys of restaurants and curio shops, I didn't think we were poor. My bowl was always full, three five-course meals every day, beginning with a soup full of mysterious things I didn't want to know the names of.

We lived on Waverly Place, in a warm, clean, two-bedroom flat that sat above a small Chinese bakery specializing in steamed pastries and dim sum.[1] In the early morning, when the alley was still quiet, I could smell fragrant red beans as they were cooked down to a pasty sweetness. By daybreak, our flat was heavy with the odor of fried sesame balls and sweet curried chicken crescents. From my bed, I would listen as my father got ready for work, then locked the door behind him, one-two-three clicks.

At the end of our two-block alley was a small sandlot playground with swings and

---

1. **dim sum:** Chinese dumplings.

slides well shined down the middle with use. The play area was bordered by wood-slat benches where old-country people sat cracking roasted watermelon seeds with their golden teeth and scattering the husks to an impatient gathering of gurgling pigeons. The best playground, however, was the dark alley itself. It was crammed with daily mysteries and adventures. My brothers and I would peer into the medicinal herb shop, watching old Li[2] dole out onto a stiff sheet of white paper the right amount of insect shells, saffron-colored seeds, and pungent leaves for his ailing customers. It was said that he once cured a woman dying of an ancestral curse that had eluded the best of American doctors. Next to the pharmacy was a printer who specialized in gold-embossed wedding invitations and festive red banners.

Farther down the street was Ping Yuen[3] Fish Market. The front window displayed a tank crowded with doomed fish and turtles struggling to gain footing on the slimy green-tiled sides. A handwritten sign informed tourists, "Within this store, is all for food, not for pet." Inside, the butchers with their bloodstained white smocks deftly gutted the fish while customers cried out their orders and shouted, "Give me your freshest," to which the butchers always protested, "All are freshest." On less crowded market days, we would inspect the crates of live frogs and crabs which we were warned not to poke, boxes of dried cuttlefish, and row upon row of iced prawns, squid, and slippery fish. The sanddabs made me shiver each time; their eyes lay on one flattened side and reminded me of my mother's story of a careless girl who ran into a crowded street and was crushed by a cab. "Was smash flat," reported my mother.

At the corner of the alley was Hong Sing's, a four-table cafe with a recessed stairwell in front that led to a door marked "Tradesmen." My brothers and I believed the bad people emerged from this door at night. Tourists never went to Hong Sing's, since the menu was printed only in Chinese. A Caucasian man with a big camera once posed me and my playmates in front of the restaurant. He had us move to the side of the picture window so the photo would capture the roasted duck with its head dangling from a juice-covered rope. After he took the picture, I told him he should go into Hong Sing's and eat dinner. When he smiled and asked me what they served, I shouted, "Guts and duck's feet and octopus gizzards!" Then I ran off with my friends, shrieking with laughter as we scampered across the alley and hid in the entryway grotto of the China Gem Company, my heart pounding with hope that he would chase us.

My mother named me after the street that we lived on: Waverly Place Jong, my official name for important American documents. But my family called me Meimei,[4] "Little Sister." I was the youngest, the only daughter. Each morning before school, my mother would twist and yank on my thick black hair until she had formed two tightly wound pigtails. One day, as she struggled to weave a hard-toothed comb through my disobedient hair, I had a sly thought.

I asked her, "Ma, what is Chinese torture?" My mother shook her head. A bobby pin was wedged between her lips. She wetted her palm and smoothed the hair above my ear, then pushed the pin in so that it nicked sharply against my scalp.

"Who say this word?" she asked without a trace of knowing how wicked I was being. I shrugged my shoulders and said, "Some boy in my class said Chinese people do Chinese torture."

"Chinese people do many things," she said simply. "Chinese people do business, do

2. **Li** (lē).

3. **Ping Yuen** (biŋ yüen).

4. **Meimei** (mā′ mā).

medicine, do painting. Not lazy like American people. We do torture. Best torture."

My older brother Vincent was the one who actually got the chess set. We had gone to the annual Christmas party held at the First Chinese Baptist Church at the end of the alley. The missionary ladies had put together a Santa bag of gifts donated by members of another church. None of the gifts had names on them. There were separate sacks for boys and girls of different ages.

One of the Chinese parishioners had donned a Santa Claus costume and a stiff paper beard with cotton balls glued to it. I think the only children who thought he was the real thing were too young to know that Santa Claus was not Chinese. When my turn came up, the Santa man asked me how old I was. I thought it was a trick question; I was seven according to the American formula and eight by the Chinese calendar. I said I was born on March 17, 1951. That seemed to satisfy him. He then solemnly asked if I had been a very, very good girl this year and did I believe in Jesus Christ and obey my parents. I knew the only answer to that. I nodded back with equal solemnity.

Having watched the other children opening their gifts, I already knew that the big gifts were not necessarily the nicest ones. One girl my age got a large coloring book of biblical characters, while a less greedy girl who selected a smaller box received a glass vial of lavender toilet water. The sound of the box was also important. A ten-year-old boy had chosen a box that jangled when he shook it. It was a tin globe of the world with a slit for inserting money. He must have thought it was full of dimes and nickels, because when he saw that it had just ten pennies, his face fell with such undisguised disappointment that his mother slapped the side of his head and led him out of the church hall, apologizing to the crowd for her son who had such bad manners he couldn't appreciate such a fine gift.

As I peered into the sack, I quickly fingered the remaining presents, testing their weight, imagining what they contained. I chose a heavy, compact one that was wrapped in shiny silver foil and a red satin ribbon. It was a twelve-pack of Life Savers and I spent the rest of the party arranging and rearranging the candy tubes in the order of my favorites. My brother Winston chose wisely as well. His present turned out to be a box of intricate plastic parts; the instructions on the box proclaimed that when they were properly assembled he would have an authentic miniature replica of a World War II submarine.

Vincent got the chess set, which would have been a very decent present to get at a church Christmas party, except it was obviously used, and as we discovered later, it was missing a black pawn and a white knight. My mother graciously thanked the unknown benefactor, saying, "Too good. Cost too much." At which point, an old lady with fine white, wispy hair nodded toward our family and said with a whistling whisper, "Merry, merry Christmas."

When we got home, my mother told Vincent to throw the chess set away. "She not want it. We not want it," she said, tossing her head stiffly to the side with a tight, proud smile. My brothers had deaf ears. They were already lining up the chess pieces and reading from the dog-eared instruction book.

I watched Vincent and Winston play during Christmas week. The chessboard seemed to hold elaborate secrets waiting to be untangled. The chessmen were more powerful than Old Li's magic herbs that cured ancestral curses. And my brothers wore such serious faces that I was sure something was at stake that was greater than avoiding the tradesmen's door to Hong Sing's.

"Let me! Let me!" I begged between games when one brother or the other would sit back with a deep sigh of relief and victory, the other annoyed, unable to let go of the outcome. Vincent at first refused to let me play, but when I offered my Life Savers as replacements for the buttons that filled in for the missing pieces, he relented. He chose the flavors: wild cherry for the black pawn and peppermint for the white knight. Winner could eat both.

As our mother sprinkled flour and rolled out small doughy circles for the steamed dumplings that would be our dinner that night, Vincent explained the rules, pointing to each piece. "You have sixteen pieces and so do I. One king and queen, two bishops, two knights, two castles, and eight pawns. The pawns can only move forward one step, except on the first move. Then they can move two. But they can only take men by moving crossways like this, except in the beginning, when you can move ahead and take another pawn."

"Why?" I asked as I moved my pawn. "Why can't they move more steps?"

"Because they're pawns," he said.

"But why do they go crossways to take other men? Why aren't there any women and children?"

"Why is the sky blue? Why must you always ask stupid questions?" asked Vincent. "This is a game. These are the rules. I didn't make them up. See. Here. In the book." He jabbed a page with a pawn in his hand. "Pawn. P-A-W-N. Pawn. Read it yourself."

My mother patted the flour off her hands. "Let me see book," she said quietly. She scanned the pages quickly, not reading the foreign English symbols, seeming to search deliberately for nothing in particular.

"This American rules," she concluded at last. "Every time people come out from foreign country, must know rules. You not know, judge say, Too bad, go back. They not telling you why so you can use their way go forward. They

say, Don't know why, you find out yourself. But they knowing all the time. Better you take it, find out why yourself." She tossed her head back with a satisfied smile.

I found out about all the whys later. I read the rules and looked up all the big words in a dictionary. I borrowed books from the Chinatown library. I studied each chess piece, trying to absorb the power each contained.

I learned about opening moves and why it's important to control the center early on; the shortest distance between two points is straight down the middle. I learned about the middle game and why tactics between two adversaries are like clashing ideas; the one who plays better has the clearest plans for both attacking and getting out of traps. I learned why it is essential in the endgame to have foresight, a mathematical understanding of all possible moves, and patience; all weaknesses and advantages become evident to a strong adversary and are obscured to a tiring opponent. I discovered that for the whole game one must gather invisible strengths and see the endgame before the game begins.

I also found out why I should never reveal "why" to others. A little knowledge withheld is a great advantage one should store for future use. That is the power of chess. It is a game of secrets in which one must show and never tell.

I loved the secrets I found within the sixty-four black and white squares. I carefully drew a handmade chessboard and pinned it to the wall next to my bed, where at night I would stare for hours at imaginary battles. Soon I no longer lost any games or Life Savers, but I lost my adversaries. Winston and Vincent decided they were more interested in roaming the streets after school in their Hopalong Cassidy cowboy hats.

On a cold spring afternoon, while walking home from school, I detoured through the playground at the end of our alley. I saw a group of old men, two seated across a folding table playing a game of chess, others smoking pipes, eating peanuts, and watching. I ran home and grabbed Vincent's chess set, which was bound in a cardboard box with rubber bands. I also carefully selected two prized rolls of Life Savers. I came back to the park and approached a man who was observing the game.

"Want to play?" I asked him. His face widened with surprise, and he grinned as he looked at the box under my arm.

"Little sister, been a long time since I play with dolls," he said, smiling benevolently. I quickly put the box down next to him on the bench and displayed my retort.[5]

Lau Po,[6] as he allowed me to call him, turned out to be a much better player than my brothers. I lost many games and many Life Savers. But over the weeks, with each diminishing roll of candies, I added new secrets. Lau Po gave me the names. The Double Attack from the East and West Shores. Throwing Stones on the Drowning Man. The Sudden Meeting of the Clan. The Surprise from the Sleeping Guard. The Humble Servant Who Kills the King. Sand in the Eyes of Advancing Forces. A Double Killing Without Blood.

There were also the fine points of chess etiquette. Keep captured men in neat rows, as well-tended prisoners. Never announce "Check" with vanity, lest someone with an unseen sword slit your throat. Never hurl pieces into the sandbox after you have lost a game, because then you must find them again, by yourself, after apologizing to all around you. By the end of the summer, Lau Po had taught me all he knew, and I had become a better chess player.

A small weekend crowd of Chinese people and tourists would gather as I played and defeated my opponents one by one. My mother would join the crowds during these outdoor exhibition games. She sat proudly on the bench, telling my admirers with proper Chinese humility, "Is luck."

A man who watched me play in the park suggested that my mother allow me to play in local chess tournaments. My mother smiled graciously, an answer that meant nothing. I desperately wanted to go, but I bit back my tongue. I knew she would not let me play among strangers. So as we walked home I said in a small voice that I didn't want to play in the local tournament. They would have American rules. If I lost, I would bring shame on my family.

"Is shame you fall down nobody push you," said my mother.

During my first tournament, my mother sat with me in the front row as I waited for my turn. I frequently bounced my legs to unstick them from the cold metal seat of the folding chair. When my name was called, I leapt up. My mother upwrapped something in her lap. It was her *chang*, a small tablet of red jade which held the sun's fire. "Is luck," she whispered, and tucked it into my dress pocket. I turned to my opponent, a fifteen-year-old boy from Oakland. He looked at me, wrinkling his nose.

As I began to play, the boy disappeared, the color ran out of the room, and I saw only my white pieces and his black ones waiting on the other side. A light wind began blowing past my ears. It whispered secrets only I could hear.

"Blow from the South," it murmured. "The wind leaves no trail." I saw a clear path, the traps to avoid. The crowd rustled. "Shhh! Shhh!" said the corners of the room. The wind blew stronger. "Throw sand from the East to distract him." The knight came forward ready for the sacrifice. The wind hissed, louder and louder. "Blow, blow, blow. He cannot see. He is blind now. Make him lean away from the wind so he is easier to knock down."

---

5. **retort:** a quick, sharp, or witty reply.
6. **Lau Po** (lou bô).

"Check," I said, as the wind roared with laughter. The wind died down to little puffs, my own breath.

My mother placed my first trophy next to a new plastic chess set that the neighborhood Tao society had given to me. As she wiped each piece with a soft cloth, she said, "Next time win more, lose less."

"Ma, it's not how many pieces you lose," I said. "Sometimes you need to lose pieces to get ahead."

"Better to lose less, see if you really need."

At the next tournament, I won again, but it was my mother who wore the triumphant grin.

"Lost eight piece this time. Last time was eleven. What I tell you? Better off lose less!" I was annoyed, but I couldn't say anything.

I attended more tournaments, each one farther away from home. I won all games, in all divisions. The Chinese bakery downstairs from our flat displayed my growing collection of trophies in its window, amidst the dust-covered cakes that were never picked up. The day after I won an important regional tournament, the window encased a fresh sheet cake with whipped-cream frosting and red script saying, "Congratulations, Waverly Jong, Chinatown Chess Champion." Soon after that, a flower shop, headstone engraver, and funeral parlor offered to sponsor me in national tournaments. That's when my mother decided I no longer had to do the dishes. Winston and Vincent had to do my chores.

"Why does she get to play and we do all the work?" complained Vincent.

"Is new American rules," said my mother. "Meimei play, squeeze all her brains out for win chess. You play, worth squeeze towel."

By my ninth birthday, I was a national chess champion. I was still some 429 points away from grand-master status, but I was touted as the Great American Hope, a child prodigy and a girl to boot. They ran a photo of me in *Life* magazine next to a quote in which Bobby Fischer[7] said, "There will never be a woman grand master." "Your move, Bobby," said the caption.

The day they took the magazine picture I wore neatly plaited braids clipped with plastic barrettes trimmed with rhinestones. I was playing in a large high school auditorium that echoed with phlegmy coughs and the squeaky rubber knobs of chair legs sliding across freshly waxed wooden floors. Seated across from me was an American man, about the same age as Lau Po, maybe fifty. I remember that his sweaty brow seemed to weep at my every move. He wore a dark, malodorous suit. One of his pockets was stuffed with a great white kerchief on which he wiped his palm before sweeping his hand over the chosen chess piece with great flourish.

In my crisp pink-and-white dress with scratchy lace at the neck, one of two my mother had sewn for these special occasions, I would clasp my hands under my chin, the delicate points of my elbows poised lightly on the table in the manner my mother had shown me for posing for the press. I would swing my patent leather shoes back and forth like an impatient child riding on a school bus. Then I would pause, suck in my lips, twirl my chosen piece in midair as if undecided, and then firmly plant it in its new threatening place, with a triumphant smile thrown back at my opponent for good measure.

I no longer played in the alley of Waverly Place. I never visited the playground where the pigeons and old men gathered. I went to school, then directly home to learn new chess secrets, cleverly concealed advantages, more escape routes.

But I found it difficult to concentrate at

---

7. **Bobby Fischer:** a well-known chess player who, at fifteen, was the world's youngest grand master.

home. My mother had a habit of standing over me while I plotted out my games. I think she thought of herself as my protective ally. Her lips would be sealed tight, and after each move I made, a soft "Hmmmmph" would escape from her nose.

"Ma, I can't practice when you stand there like that," I said one day. She retreated to the kitchen and made loud noises with the pots and pans. When the crashing stopped, I could see out of the corner of my eye that she was standing in the doorway. "Hmmmmph!" Only this one came out of her tight throat.

My parents made many concessions to allow me to practice. One time I complained that the bedroom I shared was so noisy that I couldn't think. Thereafter, my brothers slept in a bed in the living room, facing the street. I said I couldn't finish my rice; my head didn't work right when my stomach was too full. I left the table with half-finished bowls and nobody complained. But there was one duty I couldn't avoid. I had to accompany my mother on Saturday market days when I had no tournament to play. My mother would proudly walk with me, visiting many shops, buying very little. "This my daughter Wave-ly Jong," she said to whoever looked her way.

One day, after we left a shop I said under my breath, "I wish you wouldn't do that, telling everybody I'm your daughter." My mother stopped walking. Crowds of people with heavy bags pushed past us on the sidewalk, bumping into first one shoulder, then another.

"Aiii-ya. So shame be with mother?" She grasped my hand even tighter as she glared at me.

I looked down. "It's not that, it's just so obvious. It's just so embarrassing."

"Embarrass you be my daughter?" Her voice was cracking with anger.

"That's not what I meant. That's not what I said."

"What you say?"

I knew it was a mistake to say anything more, but I heard my voice speaking. "Why do you have to use me to show off? If you want to show off, then why don't you learn to play chess."

My mother's eyes turned into dangerous black slits. She had no words for me, just sharp silence.

I felt the wind rushing around my hot ears. I jerked my hand out of my mother's tight grasp and spun around, knocking into an old woman. Her bag of groceries spilled to the ground.

"Aii-ya! Stupid girl!" my mother and the woman cried. Oranges and tin cans careened down the sidewalk. As my mother stooped to help the old woman pick up the escaping food, I took off.

I raced down the street, dashing between people, not looking back as my mother screamed shrilly, "Meimei! Meimei!" I fled down an alley, past dark curtained shops and merchants washing the grime off their windows. I sped into the sunlight, into a large street crowded with tourists examining trinkets and souvenirs. I ducked into another dark alley, down another street, up another alley. I ran until it hurt and I realized I had nowhere to go, that I was not running from anything. The alleys contained no escape routes.

My breath came out like angry smoke. It was cold. I sat down on an upturned plastic pail next to a stack of empty boxes, cupping my chin with my hands, thinking hard. I imagined my mother, first walking briskly down one street or another looking for me, then giving up and returning home to await my arrival. After two hours, I stood up on creaking legs and slowly walked home.

The alley was quiet and I could see the yellow lights shining from our flat like two tiger's eyes in the night. I climbed the sixteen steps to the door, advancing quietly up each so as not to make any warning sounds. I turned the

Chess Players, 1931, EMORY LADANYI.
Courtesy of Kovesdy Gallery, New York.

knob; the door was locked. I heard a chair moving, quick steps, the locks turning—click! click! click!—and then the door opened.

"About time you got home," said Vincent. "Boy, are you in trouble."

He slid back to the dinner table. On a platter were the remains of a large fish, its fleshy head still connected to bones swimming upstream in vain escape. Standing there waiting for my punishment, I heard my mother speak in a dry voice.

"We not concerning this girl. This girl not have concerning for us."

Nobody looked at me. Bone chopsticks clinked against the insides of bowls being emptied into hungry mouths.

I walked into my room, closed the door, and lay down on my bed. The room was dark, the ceiling filled with shadows from the dinner-time lights of neighboring flats.

In my head, I saw a chessboard with sixty-four black and white squares. Opposite me was my opponent, two angry black slits. She wore a triumphant smile. "Strongest wind cannot be seen," she said.

Her black men advanced across the plane, slowly marching to each successive level as a single unit. My white pieces screamed as they scurried and fell off the board one by one. As her men drew closer to my edge, I felt myself growing light. I rose up into the air and flew out the window. Higher and higher, above the alley, over the tops of tiled roofs, where I was gathered up by the wind and pushed up toward the night sky until everything below me disappeared and I was alone.

I closed my eyes and pondered my next move.

Reviewing Concepts

SHORT STORY AND THEME: READING THE WRITER'S MESSAGE

*making
connections*

As you may recall, the central idea, or message, that a writer shares through his or her work is called the theme. The theme is not usually a statement mouthed by a character in a story but instead is a perception the reader gains from considering the story as a whole. The stories in this unit are rich in theme; they leave the reader with many ideas to ponder about family life. In "The Lie," for example, a theme that emerges is that parents can harm their children by focusing too much on their own wishes and ignoring the children's desires and abilities. Another theme related to parenthood is developed in "A Visit to Grandmother"—the insight that parents who treat each of their children differently, hoping to meet the children's differing needs, can unknowingly cause resentments lasting into adulthood. Other themes found in this unit center around a variety of family-related issues in addition to parenthood—issues such as heritage, tradition, love, and identity.

Choose a family-related issue—either one of those named above or any other you can think of. Think about how different stories in this unit express themes related to this issue. Then create a chart like the one below. After completing your chart, make similar charts for at least two other family-related issues.

Issue: PARENTHOOD

Title	Theme
"The Lie" by Kurt Vonnegut, Jr.	Parents can harm their children by focusing too much on their own wishes and ignoring the children's desires and abilities.
"A Visit to Grandmother" by William Melvin Kelley	Parents who treat their children differently, hoping to meet the children's differing needs, can unknowingly cause resentments lasting into adulthood.

*describing
connections*

Review your charts and decide which one contains the most interesting themes. On the basis of the stories, themes, and family-related issue identified in this chart, write an imaginary **dialogue** between the writers of the stories in which they express their views about the issue. For example, you might imagine a conversation between Kurt Vonnegut, Jr., William Melvin Kelley, Juan Rulfo, and Anne Tyler on parenthood. Have the writers illustrate their views by referring to characters and situations in their own stories.

© 1990, Phillip Cantor, Chicago.

Transitions:

Coming-of-Age
Stories

*"You are only young once. At the time
it seems endless, and is gone in a flash; and
then for a very long time you are old."*

SYLVIA TOWNSEND WARNER, 1893-1978
English novelist, short story writer, and poet

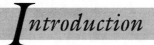

Transitions: Coming-of-Age Stories

Do you remember the first time you thought to yourself, "Well, I'm not a kid anymore," or the first time someone else made you aware of that fact? Perhaps this moment was one of disappointment, as when you found out that there is no Santa Claus or discovered that one of your heroes was not perfect after all. Perhaps it was a moment of triumph, as when you conquered a longtime fear or succeeded in a contest of skill.

Each of the main characters in these stories has a coming-of-age experience, undergoing a transition from one level of awareness to another. All of them make a discovery that changes how they view themselves and the world. In the words of one of the characters, "We grew up a little bit, and we couldn't go backward."

Some of the characters are very young children; others are teenagers. They find themselves at odds with their families, their teachers, their peers, and their own values. Small boys resist their mothers' protection. High school students weigh being independent against belonging to a group. Young women unwillingly glimpse the forces that have shaped the lives of older women. Notice what the characters learn and whether their coming of age is a source of power or pain. Their insights may be the same ones you have gained on your own path to maturity.

Literary Vocabulary

Style. Style is the way in which a piece of literature is written. Style refers not to what is said but to how it is said. Elements such as word choice, length of sentences, comparisons, tone, mood, and use of dialogue contribute to a writer's personal style. Juan Rulfo's style in "No Dogs Bark" might be described as restrained in its use of short sentences and minimal description.

Figurative Language. Figurative language is language that communicates ideas beyond the literal meanings of the words. Two common forms of figurative language are **simile** and **metaphor.** Similes and metaphors make comparisons between two things that are actually unlike yet have something in common. A simile usually contains the word *like* or *as.* In "Everyday Use" the simile "like portholes in a ship" describes the windowlike holes cut in the sides of a house.

Conflict. The plot of a story almost always involves some sort of conflict, or struggle between opposing forces. A conflict may be external, involving a character pitted against an outside force—another character, a physical obstacle, nature, or society. A conflict may also be internal, occurring within a character. In "The Lie" the conflict between Eli and his parents is external. At the same time, Eli's secret that he has not been accepted at the school creates an internal conflict.

Flashback. A flashback is a conversation, an episode, or an event that happened before the beginning of a story. Often a flashback interrupts the chronological flow of a story to give the reader information helpful in understanding a character's present situation. In "Teenage Wasteland" flashbacks occur throughout the story.

Description. Description helps a reader understand exactly what something is like. For example, the narrator of "Rules of the Game" describes the sights, sounds, and smells of San Francisco's Chinatown to convey the experience of living in this area.

Psychological Realism. The literary technique in which a writer explores the thoughts of a character confronted by a difficult moral choice is called psychological realism. Psychological means "having to do with the workings of the mind." Realism is a literary technique that aims for a truthful representation of life. "The Heir" is an example of psychological realism.

REVIEWED IN THIS UNIT

Setting   Mood   Plot   Theme   Symbol

The Secret Lion

ALBERTO ALVARO RÍOS

A biography of Ríos appears on page 427.

Approaching the Story

"The Secret Lion" centers on two important episodes in the life of a boy growing up in southern Arizona. In his own words, the boy recalls things he did and how he felt as a twelve-year-old entering junior high school and earlier, at the age of five. The style of the story is informal and conversational, as though the reader were right at the boy's side listening to his recollections.

Connecting Writing and Reading

What do you remember about starting junior high school or middle school? Think about how junior high or middle school was different from elementary school and about any changes you experienced during the transition. Jot down at least five things that you remember from that time in your life. Then, while you read, compare changes you remember with the changes described in "The Secret Lion."

Two Children Singing, 1957, ADOLFO MEXIAC.
Courtesy of the artist and the Mexican Fine Arts Center Museum, Chicago.

I WAS TWELVE and in junior high school and something happened that we didn't have a name for, but it was there nonetheless like a lion, and roaring, roaring that way the biggest things do. Everything changed. Just like that. Like the rug, the one that gets pulled—or better, like the tablecloth those magicians pull where the stuff on the table stays the same but the gasp! from the audience makes the staying-the-same part not matter. Like that.

What happened was there were teachers now, not just one teacher, teach-erz, and we felt personally abandoned somehow. When a person had all these teachers now, he didn't get taken care of the same way, even though six was more than one. Arithmetic went out the door when we walked in. And we saw girls now, but they weren't the same girls we used to know because we couldn't talk to them anymore, not the same way we used to, certainly not to Sandy, even though she was my neighbor, too. Not even to her. She just played the piano all the time. And there were words, oh there were words in junior high school, and we wanted to know what they were, and how a person did them—that's what school was supposed to be for. Only, in junior high school, school wasn't school, everything was backwardlike. If you went up to a teacher and said the word to try and find out what it meant you got in trouble for saying it. So we didn't. And we figured it must have been that way about other stuff, too, so we never said anything about anything—we weren't stupid.

But my friend Sergio and I, we solved junior high school. We would come home from school on the bus, put our books away, change shoes, and go across the highway to the arroyo.[1] It was the one place we were not supposed to go. So we did. This was, after all, what junior high had at least shown us. It was our river, though, our personal Mississippi, our friend from long back, and it was full of stories

and all the branch forts we had built in it when we were still the Vikings of America, with our own symbol, which we had carved everywhere, even in the sand, which let the water take it. That was good, we had decided; whoever was at the end of this river would know about us.

At the very very top of our growing lungs, what we would do down there was shout every dirty word we could think of, in every combination we could come up with, and we would yell about girls, and all the things we wanted to do with them, as loud as we could—we didn't know what we wanted to do with them, just things—and we would yell about teachers, and how we loved some of them, like Miss Crevelone, and how we wanted to dissect some of them, making signs of the cross, like priests, and we would yell this stuff over and over because it felt good, we couldn't explain why, it just felt good and for the first time in our lives there was nobody to tell us we couldn't. So we did.

One Thursday we were walking along shouting this way, and the railroad, the Southern Pacific, which ran above and along the far side of the arroyo, had dropped a grinding ball down there, which was, we found out later, a cannonball thing used in mining. A bunch of them were put in a big vat which turned around and crushed the ore. One had been dropped, or thrown—what do caboose men do when they get bored—but it got down there regardless and as we were walking along yelling about one girl or another, a particular Claudia, we found it, one of these things, looked at it, picked it up, and got very very excited, and held it and passed it back and forth, and we were saying, "Guythisis, this is, geeGuythis . . .": we had this perception about nature then, that nature is imperfect and that round things are perfect: we said, "GuyGodthis

---

1. **arroyo** (ə rȯi′ ō): a dry creek bed.

is perfect, thisisthis is perfect, it's round, round and heavy, it'sit's the best thing we'veverseen. Whatisit?" We didn't know. We just knew it was great. We just, whatever, we played with it, held it some more.

And then we had to decide what to do with it. We knew, because of a lot of things, that if we were going to take this and show it to anybody, this discovery, this best thing, was going to be taken away from us. That's the way it works with little kids, like all the polished quartz, the tons of it we had collected piece by piece over the years. Junior high kids too. If we took it home, my mother, we knew, was going to look at it and say, "Throw that dirty thing in the, get rid of it." Simple like, like that. "But ma it's the best thing I" "Getridofit." Simple.

So we didn't. Take it home. Instead, we came up with the answer. We dug a hole and we buried it. And we marked it secretly. Lots of secret signs. And came back the next week to dig it up and, we didn't know, pass it around some more or something, but we didn't find it. We dug up that whole bank, and we never found it again. We tried.

Sergio and I talked about that ball or whatever it was when we couldn't find it. All we used were small words, neat, good. Kid words. What we were really saying, but didn't know the words, was how much that ball was like that place, that whole arroyo: couldn't tell anybody about it, didn't understand what it was, didn't have a name for it. It just felt good. It was just perfect in the way it was that place, that whole going to that place, that whole junior high school lion. It was just iron-heavy, it had no name, it felt good or not, we couldn't take it home to show our mothers, and once we buried it, it was gone forever.

The ball was gone, like the first reasons we had come to that arroyo years earlier, like the first time we had seen the arroyo, it was gone like everything else that had been taken away. This was not our first lesson. We stopped going to the arroyo after not finding the thing, the same way we had stopped going there years earlier and headed for the mountains. Nature seemed to keep pushing us around one way or another, teaching us the same thing every place we ended up. Nature's gang was tough that way, teaching us stuff.

When we were young we moved away from town, me and my family. Sergio's was already out there. Out in the wilds. Or at least the new place seemed like the wilds since everything looks bigger the smaller a man is. I was five, I guess, and we had moved three miles north of Nogales,[2] where we had lived, three miles north of the Mexican border. We looked across the highway in one direction and there was the arroyo; hills stood up in the other direction. Mountains, for a small man.

When the first summer came the very first place we went to was of course the one place we weren't supposed to go, the arroyo. We went down in there and found water running, summer rainwater mostly, and we went swimming. But every third or fourth or fifth day, the sewage treatment plant that was, we found out, upstream, would release whatever it was that it released, and we would never know exactly what day that was, and a person really couldn't tell right off by looking at the water, not every time, not so a person could get out in time. So, we went swimming that summer and some days we had a lot of fun. Some days we didn't. We found a thousand ways to explain what happened on those other days, constructing elaborate stories about neighborhood dogs, and hadn't she, my mother, miscalculated her step before, too? But she knew something was up because we'd come running into the house those days, wanting to take a shower, even—if this can be imagined—in the middle of the day.

---

2. **Nogales** (nō gal′ əs).

That was the first time we stopped going to the arroyo. It taught us to look the other way. We decided, as the second side of summer came, we wanted to go into the mountains. They were still mountains then. We went running in one summer Thursday morning, my friend Sergio and I, into my mother's kitchen, and said, well, what'zin, what'zin those hills over there—we used her word so she'd understand us—and she said nothingdon'tworryaboutit. So we went out, and we weren't dumb, we thought with our eyes to each other, ohhoshe'stryingtokeep somethingfromus. We knew adults.

We had read the books, after all; we knew about bridges and castles and wildtreacherousraging alligatormouth rivers. We wanted them. So we were going to go out and get them. We went back that morning into that kitchen and we said, "We're going out there, we're going into the hills, we're going away for three days, don't worry." She said, "All right."

"You know," I said to Sergio, "if we're going to go away for three days, well, we ought to at least pack a lunch."

But we were two young boys with no patience for what we thought at the time was mom-stuff: making sa-and-wiches. My mother didn't offer. So we got our little kid knapsacks that my mother had sewn for us, and into them we put the jar of mustard. A loaf of bread. Knivesforksplates, bottles of Coke, a can opener. This was lunch for the two of us. And we were weighed down, humped over to be strong enough to carry this stuff. But we started walking, anyway, into the hills. We were going to eat berries and stuff otherwise. "Goodbye." My mom said that.

After the first hill we were dead. But we walked. My mother could still see us. And we kept walking. We walked until we got to where the sun is straight overhead, noon. That place. Where that is doesn't matter; it's time to eat. The truth is we weren't anywhere close to

that place. We just agreed that the sun was overhead and that it was time to eat, and by tilting our heads a little we could make that the truth.

"We really ought to start looking for a place to eat."

"Yeah. Let's look for a good place to eat." We went back and forth saying that for fifteen minutes, making it lunch time because that's what we always said back and forth before lunch times at home. "Yeah, I'm hungry all right." I nodded my head. "Yeah, I'm hungry all right too. I'm hungry." He nodded his head. I nodded my head back. After a good deal more nodding, we were ready, just as we came over a little hill. We hadn't found the mountains yet. This was a little hill.

And on the other side of this hill we found heaven.

It was just what we thought it would be.

Perfect. Heaven was green, like nothing else in Arizona. And it wasn't a cemetery or like that because we had seen cemeteries and they had gravestones and stuff and this didn't. This was perfect, had trees, lots of trees, had birds, like we had never seen before. It was like *The Wizard of Oz,* like when they got to Oz and everything was so green, so emerald, they had to wear those glasses, and we ran just like them, laughing, laughing that way we did that moment, and we went running down to this clearing in it all, hitting each other that good way we did.

We got down there, we kept laughing, we kept hitting each other, we unpacked our stuff, and we stared acting "rich." We knew all about how to do that, like blowing on our nails, then rubbing them on our chests for the shine. We made our sandwiches, opened our Cokes, got out the rest of the stuff, the salt and pepper shakers. I found this particular hole and I put my Coke right into it, a perfect fit, and I called it my Coke-holder. I got down next to it on my back, because everyone knows that rich people eat lying down, and I got my sandwich in one hand and put my other arm around the Coke in its holder. When I wanted a drink, I lifted my neck a little, put out my lips, and tipped my Coke a little with the crook of my elbow. Ah.

We were there, lying down, eating our sandwiches, laughing, throwing bread at each other and out for the birds. This was heaven. We were laughing and we couldn't believe it. My mother *was* keeping something from us, ah ha, but we had found her out. We even found water over at the side of the clearing to wash our plates with—we had brought plates. Sergio started washing his plates when he was done, and I was being rich with my Coke, and this day in summer was right.

When suddenly these two men came, from around a corner of trees and the tallest grass we had ever seen. They had bags on their backs, leather bags, bags and sticks.

We didn't know what clubs were, but I learned later, like I learned about the grinding balls. The two men yelled at us. Most specifically, one wanted me to take my Coke out of my Coke-holder so he could sink his golf ball into it.

Something got taken away from us that moment. Heaven. We grew up a little bit, and couldn't go backward. We learned. No one had ever told us about golf. They had told us about heaven. And it went away. We got golf in exchange.

We went back to the arroyo for the rest of that summer, and tried to have fun the best we could. We learned to be ready for finding the grinding ball. We loved it, and when we buried it we knew what would happen. The truth is, we didn't look so hard for it. We were two boys and twelve summers then, and not stupid. Things get taken away.

We buried it because it was perfect. We didn't tell my mother, but together it was all we talked about, till we forgot. It was the lion.

*T*hinking About the Story

A PERSONAL RESPONSE

sharing impressions

1. What is your overall impression of the experiences the boys have in this story? Jot down some of your thoughts and feelings in your journal.

constructing interpretations

2. How does the boys' experience at the golf course relate to their later experience with the grinding ball?

Think about
- what they think the golf course is at first, and why
- what the grinding ball means to them
- what they learn from each experience and how they change

3. What do you think the "lion" represents?

> **Think about**
> - what the boy telling the story says in the first and last paragraphs
> - why the lion is "secret"
> - how the title applies to the story as a whole

4. The boy telling the story says at the beginning, "We solved junior high school." Explain how you think he and Sergio did it.

> **Think about**
> - how he describes the differences between grade school and junior high
> - how his interactions with others change during junior high
> - why the boys go back to the arroyo during this time
> - what they do at the arroyo

5. How do your memories of junior high school or middle school compare with the boys' experience in this story?

A CREATIVE RESPONSE

6. If the boys lived in an urban environment, how would you expect this story to be different?

A CRITICAL RESPONSE

7. Go back through the story and find elements of style that you think add to the story.

> **Think about**
> - the definition of style as the way in which a piece of literature is written
> - some of the comparisons in the story
> - word choice, including the use of informal language to reflect the boy's speech
> - sentence lengths and patterns

8. Would you say that the desires and conflicts felt by the boys are unique to males or typical of both males and females as they grow up? Support your answer.

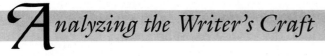

SETTING

How important do you think time and place are to this story?

Building a Literary Vocabulary. Setting refers to the time and place of the action of a story. Time in "The Secret Lion" is important in terms of the boys' ages. Place is essential to the events in the story because the arroyo and the hills determine the nature of the boys' experiences.

Application: Imagining Setting. Working with a group of classmates, carefully look through the story and write down all the locations that make up the setting, such as the narrator's home and the highway. Then use a large sheet of paper to draw a map showing these locations. Keep in mind that some locations in the story are described in relation to others. For example, the Southern Pacific railroad is located near the arroyo. For other locations, such as the school, you may have to guess where to put them on the map. After you have completed the map, trace the pattern of events in the story by drawing a line from location to location. You might use different-colored lines for the boys' experiences at different ages. Compare your map with the maps created by other groups.

Connecting Reading and Writing

1. "Things get taken away" is a realization that the narrator and Sergio come to as they grow out of childhood. Compile other words of wisdom they might share in a **handbook** for incoming junior high or middle school students.

Option: Write a **speech** that the boys might make to younger students about what they must learn in life.

2. What does the grinding ball symbolize for the boys? Give your views in a **letter** from the narrator as an adult writing to his own son.

Option: Imagine that this question appears on an essay exam and write an **interpretive essay** on the symbolism.

3. The style of this story is vivid and distinctive. Imitate this style in writing about an experience you remember having with a friend. Write a humorous **autobiographical sketch** that might appear in a magazine.

Option: Write a **dramatic monologue** retelling your experience, and deliver it to the class.

Games at Twilight

ANITA DESAI

A biography of Desai appears on page 421.

Approaching the Story

"Games at Twilight" by Indian-born Anita Desai (dā sī′) is about Ravi (ru′ vē), a young boy who is part of a large, wealthy family. Many families among the Indian upper classes still retain a preference for the Western values and social behaviors that they learned during Britain's long colonial rule in India, which ended in 1947. In this story, the children play games similar to those of English and American children. The rhyme that begins "Dip, Dip, Dip . . ." determines who will be "It," like the American rhyme "Eeny, Meeny, Miny, Mo."

Building Vocabulary

These essential words are footnoted within the story.

temerity (tə mer′ ə tē): He chuckled aloud with astonishment at his own **temerity**. (page 94)

lugubrious (lə goo′ brē əs): The children trooped under it . . . in a **lugubrious** circle. (page 96)

ignominy (ig′ nə min′ ē): The **ignominy** of being forgotten—how could he face it? (page 96)

Connecting Writing and Reading

Think back to a time when, as a child, you played games such as hide-and-seek or tag. In your journal write down words and phrases that come to mind about events that occurred and feelings that you had. As you read, compare your experiences and feelings with those of Ravi.

Games at Twilight

IT WAS STILL too hot to play outdoors. They had had their tea, they had been washed and had their hair brushed, and after the long day of confinement in the house that was not cool but at least a protection from the sun, the children strained to get out. Their faces were red and bloated with the effort, but their mother would not open the door; everything was still curtained and shuttered in a way that stifled the children, made them feel that their lungs were stuffed with cotton wool and their noses with dust and if they didn't burst out into the light and see the sun and feel the air, they would choke.

"Please, Ma, please," they begged. "We'll play in the veranda and porch—we won't go a step out of the porch."

"You will, I know you will, and then—"

"No—we won't, we won't," they wailed so horrendously that she actually let down the bolt of the front door, so that they burst out like seeds from a crackling, overripe pod into the veranda with such wild, maniacal yells that she retreated to her bath and the shower of talcum powder and the fresh sari that were to help her face the summer evening.

They faced the afternoon. It was too hot. Too bright. The white walls of the veranda glared stridently in the sun. The bougainvillea[1] hung about it, purple and magenta, in livid balloons. The garden outside was like a tray made of beaten brass, flattened out on the red gravel and the stony soil in all shades of metal—aluminum, tin, copper and brass. No life stirred at this arid time of day—the birds still drooped, like dead fruit, in the papery tents of the trees; some squirrels lay limp on the wet earth under the garden tap. The outdoor dog lay stretched as if dead on the veranda mat, his paws and ears and tail all reaching out like dying travellers in search of water. He rolled his eyes at the children—two white marbles rolling in the purple sockets, begging for sympathy—and attempted to lift his tail in a wag but could not. It only twitched and lay still.

Then, perhaps roused by the shrieks of the children, a band of parrots suddenly fell out of the eucalyptus tree, tumbled frantically in the still, sizzling air, then sorted themselves out into battle formation and streaked away across the white sky.

The children, too, felt released. They too began tumbling, shoving, pushing against each other, frantic to start. Start what? Start their business. The business of the children's day which is—play.

"Let's play hide-and-seek."

"Who'll be It?"

"You be It."

"Why should I? You be—"

"You're the eldest—"

"That doesn't mean—"

The shoves became harder. Some kicked out. The motherly Mira[2] intervened. She pulled the boys roughly apart. There was a tearing sound of cloth, but it was lost in the heavy panting and angry grumbling, and no one paid attention to the small sleeve hanging loosely off a shoulder.

"Make a circle, make a circle!" she shouted, firmly pulling and pushing till a kind of vague

---

1. **bougainvillea** ($b\overline{oo}'$ gən vil' ē ə): a woody tropical vine of the four o'clock family.
2. **Mira** (mē' rə).

circle was formed. "Now clap!" she roared, and clapping, they all chanted in melancholy unison: "Dip, dip, dip—my blue ship—" and every now and then one or the other saw he was safe by the way his hands fell at the crucial moment—palm on palm, or back of hand on palm—and dropped out of the circle with a yell and a jump of relief and jubilation.

Raghu[3] was It. He started to protest, to cry, "You cheated—Mira cheated—Anu[4] cheated—" but it was too late; the others had all already streaked away. There was no one to hear when he called out, "Only in the veranda—the porch—Ma said—Ma *said* to stay in the porch!" No one had stopped to listen; all he saw was their brown legs flashing through the dusty shrubs, scrambling up brick walls, leaping over compost heaps and hedges; and then the porch stood empty in the purple shade of the bougainvillea and the garden was as empty as before; even the limp squirrels had whisked away, leaving everything gleaming, brassy and bare.

Only small Manu[5] suddenly reappeared, as if he had dropped out of an invisible cloud or from a bird's claws, and stood for a moment in the center of the yellow lawn, chewing his finger and near to tears as he heard Raghu shouting, with his head pressed against the veranda wall, "Eighty-three, eighty-five, eighty-nine, ninety . . ." and then made off in a panic, half of him wanting to fly north, the other half counselling south. Raghu turned just in time to see the flash of his white shorts and the uncertain skittering of his red sandals and charged after him with such a blood-curdling yell that Manu stumbled over the hose pipe, fell into its rubber coils and lay there weeping, "I won't be It—you have to find them all—all—All!"

"I know I have to, idiot," Raghu said, superciliously kicking him with his toe. "You're dead," he said with satisfaction, licking the beads of perspiration off his upper lip, and then

stalked off in search of worthier prey, whistling spiritedly so that the hiders should hear and tremble.

Ravi heard the whistling and picked his nose in a panic, trying to find comfort by burrowing the finger deep—deep into that soft tunnel. He felt himself too exposed, sitting on an upturned flower pot behind the garage. Where could he burrow? He could run around the garage if he heard Raghu come—around and around and around—but he hadn't much faith in his short legs when matched against Raghu's long, hefty, hairy footballer legs. Ravi had a frightening glimpse of them as Raghu combed the hedge of crotons and hibiscus, trampling delicate ferns underfoot as he did so. Ravi looked about him desperately, swallowing a small ball of snot in his fear.

The garage was locked with a great, heavy lock to which the driver had the key in his room, hanging from a nail on the wall under his work shirt. Ravi had peeped in and seen him still sprawling on his string cot in his vest and striped underpants, the hair on his chest and the hair in his nose shaking with the vibrations of his phlegm-obstructed snores. Ravi had wished he were tall enough, big enough to reach the key on the nail, but it was impossible, beyond his reach for years to come. He had sidled away and sat dejectedly on the flower pot. That at least was cut to his own size.

But next to the garage was another shed with a big green door. Also locked. No one even knew who had the key to the lock. That shed wasn't opened more than once a year, when Ma turned out all the old broken bits of furniture and rolls of matting and leaking buckets, and the white ant hills were broken

---

3. **Raghu** (ru' gǒo).
4. **Anu** (u' nǒo).
5. **Manu** (mu' nǒo).

and swept away and Flit sprayed into the spider webs and rat holes so that the whole operation was like the looting of a poor, ruined and conquered city. The green leaves of the door sagged. They were nearly off their rusty hinges. The hinges were large and made a small gap between the door and the walls—only just large enough for rats, dogs and, possibly, Ravi to slip through.

Ravi had never cared to enter such a dark and depressing mortuary of defunct household goods seething with such unspeakable and alarming animal life, but, as Raghu's whistling grew angrier and sharper and his crashing and storming in the hedge wilder, Ravi suddenly slipped off the flower pot and through the crack and was gone. He chuckled aloud with astonishment at his own temerity[6] so that Raghu came out of the hedge, stood silent with his hands on his hips, listening, and finally shouted, "I heard you! I'm coming! *Got you—*" and came charging round the garage only to find the upturned flower pot, the yellow dust, the crawling of white ants in a mud hill against the closed shed door—nothing. Snarling, he bent to pick up a stick and went off, whacking it against the garage and shed walls as if to beat out his prey.

Ravi shook, then shivered with delight, with self-congratulation. Also with fear. It was dark, spooky in the shed. It had a muffled smell, as of graves. Ravi had once got locked into the linen cupboard and sat there weeping for half an hour before he was rescued. But at least that had been a familiar place and even smelt pleasantly of starch, laundry and, reassuringly, his mother. But the shed smelt of rats, ant hills, dust and spider webs. Also of less definable, less recognizable horrors. And it was dark. Except for the white-hot cracks along the door, there was no light. The roof was very low. Although Ravi was small, he felt as if he could reach up and touch it with his fingertips.

But he didn't stretch. He hunched himself into a ball so as not to bump into anything, touch or feel anything. What might there not be to touch him and feel him as he stood there, trying to see in the dark? Something cold or slimy—like a snake. Snakes! He leapt up as Raghu whacked the wall with his stick—then, quickly realizing what it was, felt almost relieved to hear Raghu, hear his stick. It made him feel protected.

But Raghu soon moved away. There wasn't a sound once his footsteps had gone around the garage and disappeared. Ravi stood frozen inside the shed. Then he shivered all over. Something had tickled the back of his neck. It took him a while to pick up the courage to lift his hand and explore. It was an insect—perhaps a spider—exploring *him*. He squashed it and wondered how many more creatures were watching him, waiting to reach out and touch him, the stranger.

There was nothing now. After standing in that position—his hand still on his neck, feeling the wet splodge of the squashed spider gradually dry—for minutes, hours, his legs began to tremble with the effort, the inaction. By now he could see enough in the dark to make out the large, solid shapes of old wardrobes, broken buckets and bedsteads piled on top of each other around him. He recognized an old bathtub—patches of enamel glimmered at him, and at last he lowered himself onto its edge.

He contemplated slipping out of the shed and into the fray. He wondered if it would not be better to be captured by Raghu and returned to the milling crowd as long as he could be in the sun, the light, the free spaces of the garden and the familiarity of his brothers, sisters and cousins. It would be evening soon. Their games would become legitimate. The

6. **temerity** (tə mer′ ə tē): foolish or rash boldness; recklessness.

parents would sit out on the lawn on cane basket chairs and watch them as they tore around
the garden or gathered in knots to share a loot
of mulberries or black, teeth-splitting *jamun*[7]
from the garden trees. The gardener would fix
the hose pipe to the water tap, and water
would fall lavishly through the air to the
ground, soaking the dry, yellow grass and the
red gravel and arousing the sweet, the intoxi-
cating, scent of water on dry earth—that
loveliest scent in the world. Ravi sniffed for a
whiff of it. He half rose from the bathtub, then
heard the despairing scream of one of the girls
as Raghu bore down upon her. There was the
sound of a crash and of rolling about in the
bushes, the shrubs, then screams and accusing
sobs of "I touched the den—" "You did not—"
"I did—" "You liar, you did *not*," and then a
fading away and silence again.

Ravi sat back on the harsh edge of the tub,
deciding to hold out a bit longer. What fun if
they were all found and caught—he alone left
unconquered! He had never known that sensation. Nothing more wonderful had ever happened to him than being taken out by an
uncle and bought a whole slab of chocolate all
to himself, or being flung into the soda man's
pony cart and driven up to the gate by the
friendly driver with the red beard and pointed
ears. To defeat Raghu—that hirsute, hoarse-
voiced football champion—and to be the winner in a circle of older, bigger, luckier children—that would be thrilling beyond imagination. He hugged his knees together and
smiled to himself almost shyly at the thought
of so much victory, such laurels.

There he sat smiling, knocking his heels
against the bathtub, now and then getting up
and going to the door to put his ear to the broad
crack and listening for sounds of the game, the
pursuer and the pursued, and then returning to
his seat with the dogged determination of the
true winner, a breaker of records, a champion.

It grew darker in the shed as the light at the
door grew softer, fuzzier, turned to a kind of
crumbling yellow pollen that turned to yellow
fur, blue fur, gray fur. Evening. Twilight. The
sound of water gushing, falling. The scent of
earth receiving water, slaking its thirst in great
gulps and releasing that green scent of freshness, coolness. Through the crack Ravi saw
the long purple shadows of the shed and the
garage lying still across the yard. Beyond that,
the white walls of the house. The bougainvillea had lost its lividity, hung in dark bundles
that quaked and twittered and seethed with
masses of homing sparrows. The lawn was shut
off from his view. Could he hear the children's
voices? It seemed to him that he could. It
seemed to him that he could hear them chanting, singing, laughing. But what about the
game? What had happened? Could it be over?
How could it when he was still not found?

It then occurred to him that he could have
slipped out long ago, dashed across the yard to
the veranda and touched the "den." It was
necessary to do that to win. He had forgotten.
He had only remembered the part of hiding
and trying to elude the seeker. He had done
that so successfully, his success had occupied
him so wholly, that he had quite forgotten that
success had to be clinched by that final dash to
victory and the ringing cry of "Den!"

With a whimper he burst through the crack,
fell on his knees, got up and stumbled on stiff,
benumbed legs across the shadowy yard, crying
heartily by the time he reached the veranda so
that when he flung himself at the white pillar
and bawled, "Den! Den! Den!" his voice broke
with rage and pity at the disgrace of it all, and
he felt himself flooded with tears and misery.

Out on the lawn, the children stopped
chanting. They all turned to stare at him in
amazement. Their faces were pale and triangu-
lar in the dusk. The trees and bushes around

---

7. *jamun* (jä' mmoon): a kind of plum.

them stood inky and sepulchral, spilling long shadows across them. They stared, wondering at his reappearance, his passion, his wild animal howling. Their mother rose from her basket chair and came toward him, worried, annoyed, saying, "Stop it, stop it, Ravi. Don't be a baby. Have you hurt yourself?" Seeing him attended to, the children went back to clasping their hands and chanting, "The grass is green, the rose is red. . . ."

But Ravi would not let them. He tore himself out of his mother's grasp and pounded across the lawn into their midst, charging at them with his head lowered so that they scattered in surprise. "I won, I won, I won," he bawled, shaking his head so that the big tears flew. "Raghu didn't find me. I won, I won—"

It took them a minute to grasp what he was saying, even who he was. They had quite forgotten him. Raghu had found all the others long ago. There had been a fight about who was to be It next. It had been so fierce that their mother had emerged from her bath and made them change to another game. Then they had played another and another. Broken mulberries from the tree and eaten them. Helped the driver wash the car when their father returned from work. Helped the gardener water the beds till he roared at them and swore he would complain to their parents. The parents had come out, taken up their positions on the cane chairs. They had begun to play again, sing and chant. All this time no one had remembered Ravi. Having disappeared from the scene, he had disappeared from their minds. Clean.

"Don't be a fool," Raghu said roughly, pushing him aside, and even Mira said, "Stop howling, Ravi. If you want to play, you can stand at the end of the line," and she put him there very firmly.

The game proceeded. Two pairs of arms reached up and met in an arc. The children trooped under it again and again in a lugubrious[8] circle, ducking their heads and intoning

"The grass is green,
The rose is red;
Remember me
When I am dead, dead, dead, dead . . ."

And the arc of thin arms trembled in the twilight, and the heads were bowed so sadly, and their feet tramped to that melancholy refrain so mournfully, so helplessly, that Ravi could not bear it. He would not follow them; he would not be included in this funereal game. He had wanted victory and triumph —not a funeral. But he had been forgotten, left out and he would not join them now. The ignominy[9] of being forgotten—how could he face it? He felt his heart go heavy and ache inside him unbearably. He lay down full length on the damp grass, crushing his face into it, no longer crying, silenced by a terrible sense of his insignificance.

---

8. lugubrious (lə g$\overline{oo}$′ brē əs): mournful, especially exaggeratedly or artificially mournful.
9. ignominy (ig′ nə min′ ē): shame and dishonor.

Thinking About the Story

A PERSONAL RESPONSE

sharing impressions

1. How do you feel about what happens to Ravi? Describe your feelings in your journal.

constructing interpretations

2. Why do you think Ravi's experience during the hide-and-seek game affects him so deeply?

Think about
- how this experience compares with the time he was locked in the linen cupboard
- his expectations about what winning will be like
- how the family reacts to his crying and to his declaration that he won
- why he refuses to join in the funeral game

3. How would you evaluate the way that Ravi's family behaves toward him?

Think about
- why the family forgets about him
- why they fail to respond according to his expectations

A CREATIVE RESPONSE

4. If Ravi came from a smaller family, how might his experience be different?

A CRITICAL RESPONSE

5. Describe the mood, or atmosphere, of this story and identify passages that you think are important in creating that mood.

Think about
- the children's feelings of being stifled inside the house at the beginning of the story
- what it is like inside the shed
- the references to death in the description of the dog and in both games the children play

6. One critic has written that the story conveys "Ravi's first experience of his own mortality, his sense of his own small, brief place in a vast and difficult universe." Using details from the story, explain whether you agree or disagree with this interpretation.

7. How would you compare Ravi's experience to the experience the boys have on the golf course in "The Secret Lion"?

Analyzing the Writer's Craft

FIGURATIVE LANGUAGE: SIMILE AND METAPHOR

The children bursting out of the house to play are described as being "like seeds from a crackling, overripe pod." Jot down some words or phrases that this comparison brings to mind.

Building a Literary Vocabulary. Figurative language is language that communicates ideas beyond the literal meanings of the words. A simile compares two things in a phrase that contains *like* or *as.* Desai's comparison of the children to seeds bursting from a dry, brittle pod is a simile that conveys the exuberant sense of release with which the children escape the protective "pod" of the house. The children are like seeds in their youthful energy and potential for growth.

A metaphor is another figure of speech that makes a comparison between two things that have something in common. While a simile contains the word *like* or *as,* a metaphor either makes the comparison directly or implies it. The same idea in

Desai's simile could be expressed as a metaphor by saying, "The children were seeds bursting out from a crackling, overripe pod."

Application: Identifying Figures of Speech. Working in a group, find at least five similes and metaphors in the story. For each example, create a diagram similar to the one that follows.

Example from story:

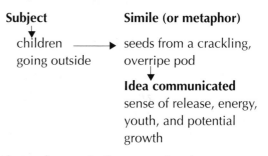

Choose the one simile or metaphor that your group likes best and diagram it for your class.

Connecting Reading and Writing

1. Write a **first-person narrative** recounting a situation like Ravi's in which your expectations were disappointed by the actual event. Share your narrative with a friend.

Option: Write about the event as a **diary entry.**

2. To what extent do you think children's games teach them to live in the adult world? Referring to both your own experience and the story, express your opinion in an **article** to be published in a magazine or newsletter for parents.

Option: Write on the topic of life lessons taught by children's games in a **memo** to be given to the teachers at a preschool.

3. Write an **episode** from a short story showing Ravi and his playmates playing games a week after the incident.

Option: Compose a **letter** that Ravi might write to either Raghu or Mira when they are adults, telling them how the experience of that afternoon affected him.

were dressed in the school uniform of white shirt and khaki shorts. Their official age was around sixteen, although, in fact, it ranged from Kojo's fifteen years to one or two boys of twenty-one.

Mr. Abu, the laboratory attendant, came in from the adjoining store and briskly cleaned the blackboard. He was a retired African sergeant from the Army Medical Corps and was feared by the boys. If he caught any of them in any petty thieving, he offered them the choice of a hard smack on the bottom or of being reported to the science masters. Most boys chose the former, as they knew the matter would end there, with no protracted[6] interviews, moral recrimination,[7] and an entry in the conduct book.

The science master stepped in and stood on his small platform. A tall, thin, dignified Negro, with graying hair and silver-rimmed spectacles badly fitting on his broad nose and always slipping down, making him look avuncular.[8] "Vernier"[9] was his nickname, as he insisted on exact measurement and exact speech "as fine as a vernier scale," he would say, which measured, of course, things in thousandths of a millimeter. Vernier set the experiments for the day and demonstrated them, then retired behind the *Church Times*, which he read seriously in between walking quickly down the aisles of lab benches, advising boys. It was a simple heat experiment to show that a dark surface gave out more heat by radiation than a bright surface.

During the class, Vernier was called away to the telephone and Abu was not about, having retired to the lavatory for a smoke. As soon as a posted sentinel announced that he was out of sight, minor pandemonium broke out. Some of the boys raided the store. The wealthier ones swiped rubber tubing to make catapults and to repair bicycles and helped themselves to chemicals for developing photographic films. The poorer boys were in deadlier earnest

and took only things of strict commercial interest which could be sold easily in the market. They emptied stuff into bottles in their pockets. Soda for making soap, magnesium sulphate for opening medicine, salt for cooking, liquid paraffin for women's hairdressing, and fine yellow iodoform powder much in demand for sprinkling on sores. Kojo protested mildly against all this. "Oh, shut up!" a few boys said. Sorie,[10] a huge boy who always wore a fez[11] indoors and who, rumor said, had already fathered a child, commanded respect and some leadership in the class. He was sipping his favorite mixture of diluted alcohol and bicarbonate—which he called "gin and fizz"—from a beaker. "Look here, Kojo, you are getting out of hand. What do you think our parents pay taxes and school fees for? For us to enjoy—or to buy a new car every year for Simpson?" The other boys laughed. Simpson was the European headmaster, feared by the small boys, adored by the boys in the middle school, and liked, in a critical fashion, with reservations, by some of the senior boys and African masters. He had a passion for new motorcars, buying one yearly.

"Come to think of it," Sorie continued to Kojo, "you must take something yourself; then we'll know we are safe." "Yes, you must," the other boys insisted. Kojo gave in and, unwillingly, took a little nitrate for some gunpowder experiments which he was carrying out at home.

"Someone!" the lookout called.

---

6. **protracted** (prō trak′ təd): drawn out; prolonged.

7. **recrimination** (ri krim′ ə nā′ shən): the act of answering an accuser by accusing him or her in return.

8. **avuncular** (ə vuŋ′ kyōō lər): of or like an uncle.

9. **Vernier** (vʉr′ nē ər).

10. **Sorie:** (sô′ rē).

11. **fez:** a man's brimless hat, shaped like a cone, with a flat top and a black tassel.

The boys dispersed in a moment. Sorie swilled out his mouth at the sink with some water. Mr. Abu, the lab attendant, entered and observed the innocent collective expression of the class. He glared round suspiciously and sniffed the air. It was a physics experiment, but the place smelled chemical. However, Vernier came in then. After asking if anyone was in difficulty, and finding that no one could momentarily think up anything, he retired to his chair and settled down to an article on Christian reunion, adjusting his spectacles and thoughtfully sucking an empty tooth socket.

Toward the end of the period, the class collected around Vernier and gave in their results, which were then discussed. One of the more political boys asked Vernier: if dark surfaces gave out more heat, was that why they all had black faces in West Africa? A few boys giggled. Basu looked down and tapped his clubfoot embarrassedly on the floor. Vernier was used to questions of this sort from the senior boys. He never committed himself, as he was getting near retirement and his pension, and became more guarded each year. He sometimes even feared that Simpson had spies among the boys.

"That may be so, although the opposite might be more convenient."

Everything in science had a loophole, the boys thought, and said so to Vernier.

"Ah! That is what is called research," he replied, enigmatically.[12]

Sorie asked a question. Last time, they had been shown that an electric spark with hydrogen and oxygen atoms formed water. Why was not that method used to provide water in town at the height of the dry season when there was an acute water shortage?

"It would be too expensive," Vernier replied, shortly. He disliked Sorie, not because of his different religion, but because he thought that Sorie was a bad influence and also asked ridiculous questions.

Sorie persisted. There was plenty of water during the rainy season. It could be split by lightning to hydrogen and oxygen in October and the gases compressed and stored, then changed back to water in March during the shortage. There was a faint ripple of applause from Sorie's admirers.

"It is an impracticable idea," Vernier snapped.

The class dispersed and started walking back across the hot grass. Kojo and Bandele heaved sighs of relief and joined Sorie's crowd, which was always the largest.

"Science is a bit of a swindle," Sorie was saying. "I do not for a moment think that Vernier believes any of it himself," he continued, "because, if he does, why is he always reading religious books?"

"Come back, all of you, come back!" Mr. Abu's stentorian[13] voice rang out, across to them.

They wavered and stopped. Kojo kept walking on in a blind panic.

"Stop," Bandele hissed across. "You fool." He stopped, turned, and joined the returning crowd, closely followed by Bandele. Abu joined Vernier on the platform. The loose semicircle of boys faced them.

"Mr. Abu just found this in the waste bin," Vernier announced, gray with anger. He held up the two broken halves of the thermometer. "It must be due to someone from this class, as the number of thermometers was checked before being put out."

A little wind gusted in through the window and blew the silence heavily this way and that.

"Who?"

No one answered. Vernier looked round and waited.

"Since no one has owned up, I am afraid I shall have to detain you for an hour after school as punishment," said Vernier.

---

12. **enigmatically** (e′ nig mat′ ə kal ē): mysteriously.
13. **stentorian** (sten tôr′ ē ən): very loud.

There was a murmur of dismay and anger. An important soccer house-match was scheduled for that afternoon. Some boys put their hands up and said that they had to play in the match.

"I don't care," Vernier shouted. He felt, in any case, that too much time was devoted to games and not enough to work.

He left Mr. Abu in charge and went off to fetch his things from the main building.

"We shall play 'Bible and Key,'" Abu announced as soon as Vernier had left. Kojo had been afraid of this, and new beads of perspiration sprang from his troubled brow. All the boys knew the details. It was a method of finding out a culprit by divination. A large door key was placed between the leaves of a Bible at the New Testament passage where Ananias and Sapphira[14] were struck dead before the Apostles for lying and the Bible suspended by two bits of string tied to both ends of the key. The combination was held up by someone, and the names of all present were called out in turn. When that of the sinner was called, the Bible was expected to turn round and round violently and fall.

Now Abu asked for a Bible. Someone produced a copy. He opened the first page and then shook his head and handed it back. "This won't do," he said. "It's a Revised Version; only the genuine Word of God will give us the answer."

An Authorized King James Version was then produced, and he was satisfied. Soon he had the contraption fixed up. He looked round the semicircle, from Sorie at one end, through the others, to Bandele, Basu, and Kojo at the other, near the door.

"You seem to have an honest face," he said to Kojo. "Come and hold it." Kojo took the ends of the string gingerly with both hands, trembling slightly.

Abu moved over to the low window and stood at attention, his sharp profile outlined against the red hibiscus flowers, the green trees, and the molten sky. The boys watched anxiously. A black-bodied lizard scurried up a wall and started nodding its pink head with grave impartiality.

Abu fixed his ageing, bloodshot eyes on the suspended Bible. He spoke hoarsely and slowly:

"Oh, Bible, Bible, on a key,
Kindly tell it unto me,
By swinging slowly round and true,
To whom this sinful act is due. . . ."

He turned to the boys and barked out their names in a parade-ground voice, beginning with Sorie and working his way round, looking at the Bible after each name.

To Kojo, trembling and shivering as if ice-cold water had been thrown over him, it seemed as if he had lost all power and that some gigantic being stood behind him holding up his tired, aching elbows. It seemed to him as if the key and Bible had taken on a life of their own, and he watched with fascination the whole combination moving slowly, jerkily, and rhythmically in short arcs as if it had acquired a heartbeat.

"Ayo Sogbenri, Sonnir Kargbo, Oji Ndebu." Abu was coming to the end now. "Tommy Longe, Ajayi Cole, Bandele Fagb . . ."[15]

Kojo dropped the Bible. "I am tired," he said, in a small scream. "I am tired."

"Yes, he is," Abu agreed, "but we are almost finished; only Bandele and Basu are left."

"Pick up that book, Kojo, and hold it up again." Bandele's voice whipped through the

---

14. Ananias and Sapphira (an' ə nī' əs; sə fī' rə): husband and wife who fell dead when Peter rebuked them for withholding from the apostles a part of the proceeds from a sale of their land.

15. Ayo Sogbenri . . . Fagb (ä' yō sŏg ben' rē; sŏn' nēr kärg' bŏ; ō' jē nde' boo; lŏn ge; ä jä' yē kōl; fägb).

air with cold fury. It sobered Kojo, and he picked it up.

"Will you continue, please, with my name, Mr. Abu?" Bandele asked, turning to the window.

"Go back to your place quickly, Kojo," Abu said. "Vernier is coming. He might be vexed. He is a strongly religious man and so does not believe in the Bible-and-Key ceremony."

Kojo slipped back with sick relief, just before Vernier entered.

In the distance the rest of the school was assembling for closing prayers. The class sat and stood around the blackboard and demonstration bench in attitudes of exasperation, resignation, and self-righteous indignation. Kojo's heart was beating so loudly that he was surprised no one else heard it.

"Once to every man and nation
Comes the moment to decide . . ."[16]

The closing hymn floated across to them, interrupting the still afternoon.

Kojo got up. He felt now that he must speak the truth, or life would be intolerable ever afterward. Bandele got up swiftly before him. In fact, several things seemed to happen all at the same time. The rest of the class stirred. Vernier looked up from a book review which he had started reading. A butterfly, with black and gold wings, flew in and sat on the edge of the blackboard, flapping its wings quietly and waiting too.

"Basu was here first before any of the class," Bandele said firmly.

Everyone turned to Basu, who cleared his throat.

"I was just going to say so myself, sir," Basu replied to Vernier's inquiring glance.

"Pity you had no thought of it before," Vernier said, dryly. "What were you doing here?"

"I missed the previous class, so I came straight to the lab and waited. I was over there

by the window, trying to look at the blue sky. I did not break the thermometer, sir."

A few boys tittered. Some looked away. The others muttered. Basu's breath always smelt of onions, but although he could play no games, some boys liked him and were kind to him in a tolerant way.

"Well, if you did not, someone did. We shall continue with the detention."

Vernier noticed Abu standing by. "You need not stay, Mr. Abu," he said to him. "I shall close up. In fact, come with me now and I shall let you out through the back gate."

He went out with Abu.

When he had left, Sorie turned to Basu and asked mildly:

"You are sure you did not break it?"

"No, I didn't."

"He did it," someone shouted.

"But what about the Bible-and-Key?" Basu protested. "It did not finish. Look at him." He pointed to Bandele.

"I was quite willing for it to go on," said Bandele. "You were the only one left."

Someone threw a book at Basu and said, "Confess!"

Basu backed on to a wall. "To God, I shall call the police if anyone strikes me," he cried fiercely.

"He thinks he can buy the police," a voice called.

"That proves it," someone shouted from the back.

"Yes, he must have done it," the others said, and they started throwing books at Basu. Sorie waved his arm for them to stop, but they did not. Books, corks, boxes of matches rained on Basu. He bent his head

---

16. Once to . . . decide: The words of the hymn are from "Present Crisis," a poem by the American poet James Russell Lowell (1819–1891). The theme of the poem is that a person must stand up for self or country when the need arises.

and shielded his face with his bent arm.

"I did not do it, I swear I did not do it. Stop it, you fellows," he moaned over and over again. A small cut had appeared on his temple, and he was bleeding. Kojo sat quietly for a while. Then a curious hum started to pass through him, and his hands began to tremble, his armpits to feel curiously wetter. He turned round and picked up a book and flung it with desperate force at Basu, and then another. He felt somehow that there was an awful swelling of guilt which he could only shed by punishing himself through hurting someone. Anger and rage against everything different seized him, because if everything and everyone had been the same, somehow he felt nothing would have been wrong and they would all have been happy. He was carried away now by a torrent which swirled and pounded. He felt that somehow Basu was in the wrong, must be in the wrong, and if he hurt him hard enough, he would convince the others and therefore himself that he had not broken the thermometer and that he had never done anything wrong. He groped for something bulky enough to throw, and picked up the Bible.

"Stop it," Vernier shouted through the open doorway. "Stop it, you hooligans, you beasts."

They all became quiet and shamefacedly put down what they were going to throw. Basu was crying quietly and hopelessly, his thin body shaking.

"Go home, all of you, go home. I am ashamed of you." His black face shone with anger. "You are an utter disgrace to your nation and to your race."

They crept away, quietly, uneasily, avoiding each other's eyes, like people caught in a secret passion.

Vernier went to the first-aid cupboard and started dressing Basu's wounds.

Kojo and Bandele came back and hid behind the door, listening. Bandele insisted that they should.

Vernier put Basu's bandaged head against his waistcoat and dried the boy's tears with his handkerchief, gently patting his shaking shoulders.

"It wouldn't have been so bad if I had done it, sir," he mumbled, snuggling his head against Vernier, "but I did not do it. I swear to God I did not."

"Hush, hush," said Vernier comfortingly.

"Now they will hate me even more," he moaned.

"Hush, hush."

"I don't mind the wounds so much; they will heal."

"Hush, hush."

"They've missed the football match and now they will never talk to me again; oh-ee, oh-ee, why have I been so punished?"

"As you grow older," Vernier advised, "you must learn that men are punished not always for what they do, but often for what people think they will do or for what they are. Remember that and you will find it easier to forgive them. 'To thine own self be true!'" Vernier ended with a flourish, holding up his clenched fist in a mock dramatic gesture, quoting from the Shakespeare examination set-book for the year and declaiming to the dripping taps and empty benches and still afternoon, to make Basu laugh.

Basu dried his eyes and smiled wanly and replied: "'And it shall follow as the night the day.' *Hamlet*, Act One, Scene Three, Polonius to Laertes."[17]

"There's a good chap. First Class Grade One. I shall give you a lift home."

---

17. And it shall . . . the day: The complete passage in Shakespeare's *Hamlet*, in which Polonius (pə lō' nē əs) advises his son Laertes, (lā ʉr' tēz) is "This above all—to thine own self be true,/And it must follow, as the night the day,/Thou can'st not then be false to any man." In other words, be honest with yourself and you will be honest with others.

Kojo and Bandele walked down the red laterite road together, Kojo dispiritedly kicking stones into the gutter.

"The fuss they made over a silly old thermometer," Bandele began.

"I don't know, old man, I don't know," Kojo said impatiently.

They had both been shaken by the scene in the empty lab. A thin, invisible wall of hostility and mistrust was slowly rising between them.

"Basu did not do it, of course," Bandele said.

Kojo stopped dead in his tracks. "Of course he did not do it," he shouted; "we did it."

"No need to shout, old man. After all, it was your idea."

"It wasn't," Kojo said furiously. "You suggested we try it."

"Well, you started the argument. Don't be childish." They tramped on silently, raising small clouds of dust with their bare feet.

"I should not take it too much to heart," Bandele continued. "That chap Basu's father hoards foodstuff like rice and palm oil until there is a shortage and then sells them at high prices. The police are watching him."

"What has that got to do with it?" Kojo asked.

"Don't you see, Basu might quite easily have broken that thermometer. I bet he has done things before that we have all been punished for." Bandele was emphatic.

They walked on steadily down the main road of the town, past the Syrian and Lebanese shops crammed with knickknacks and rolls of cloth, past a large Indian shop with dull red carpets and brass trays displayed in its windows, carefully stepping aside in the narrow road as the British officials sped by in cars to their hill-station bungalows for lunch and siesta.

Kojo reached home at last. He washed his feet and ate his main meal for the day. He sat about heavily and restlessly for some hours.

Night soon fell with its usual swiftness, at six, and he finished his homework early and went to bed. Lying in bed he rehearsed again what he was determined to do the next day. He would go up to Vernier:

"Sir," he would begin, "I wish to speak with you privately."

"Can it wait?" Vernier would ask.

"No, sir," he would say firmly, "as a matter of fact, it is rather urgent."

Vernier would take him to an empty classroom and say, "What is troubling you, Kojo Ananse?"[18]

"I wish to make a confession, sir. I broke the thermometer yesterday." He had decided he would not name Bandele; it was up to the latter to decide whether he would lead a pure life.

Vernier would adjust his slipping glasses up his nose and think. Then he would say:

"This is a serious matter, Kojo. You realize you should have confessed yesterday?"

"Yes, sir, I am very sorry."

"You have done great harm, but better late than never. You will, of course, apologize in front of the class and particularly to Basu, who has shown himself a finer chap than all of you."

"I shall do so, sir."

"Why have you come to me now to apologize? Were you hoping that I would simply forgive you?"

"I was hoping you would, sir. I was hoping you would show your forgiveness by beating me."

Vernier would pull his glasses up his nose again. He would move his tongue inside his mouth reflectively. "I think you are right. Do you feel you deserve six strokes or nine?"

"Nine, sir."

"Bend over!"

Kojo had decided he would not cry because he was almost a man.

_____

18. **Ananse** (ä nän' sē).

Whack! Whack!

Lying in bed in the dark thinking about it all as it would happen tomorrow, he clenched his teeth and tensed his buttocks in imaginary pain.

Whack! Whack! Whack!

Suddenly, in his little room, under his thin cotton sheet, he began to cry. Because he felt the sharp, lancing pain already cutting into him. Because of Basu and Simpson and the thermometer. For all the things he wanted to do and be which would never happen. For all the good men they had told them about—Jesus Christ, Mohammed, and George Washington, who never told a lie. For Florence Nightingale[19] and David Livingstone.[20] For Kagawa,[21] the Japanese man, for Gandhi,[22] and for Kwegyir Aggrey,[23] the African. Oh-ee, oh-ee. Because he knew he would never be as straight and strong and true as the school song said they should be. He saw, for the first time, what this thing would be like, becoming a man. He touched the edge of an inconsolable eternal grief. Oh-ee, oh-ee; always, he felt, always I shall be a disgrace to the nation and the race.

His mother passed by his bedroom door, slowly dragging her slippered feet as she always did. He pushed his face into his wet pillow to stifle his sobs, but she had heard him. She came in and switched on the light.

"What is the matter with you, my son?"

He pushed his face farther into his pillow.

"Nothing," he said, muffled and choking.

"You have been looking like a sick fowl all afternoon," she continued.

She advanced and put the back of her moist, cool fingers against the side of his neck.

"You have got fever," she exclaimed. "I'll get something from the kitchen."

When she had gone out, Kojo dried his tears and turned the dry side of the pillow up. His mother reappeared with a thermometer in one hand and some quinine mixture in the other.

"Oh, take it away, take it away," he shouted, pointing to her right hand and shutting his eyes tightly.

"All right, all right," she said, slipping the thermometer into her bosom.

He is a queer boy, she thought, with pride and a little fear as she watched him drink the clear, bitter fluid.

She then stood by him and held his head against her broad thigh as he sat up on the low bed, and she stroked his face. She knew he had been crying but did not ask him why, because she was sure he would not tell her. She knew he was learning, first slowly and now quickly, and she would soon cease to be his mother and be only one of the womenfolk in the family. Such a short time, she thought, when they are really yours and tell you everything. She sighed and slowly eased his sleeping head down gently.

The next day Kojo got to school early and set to things briskly. He told Bandele that he was going to confess but would not name him. He half hoped he would join him. But Bandele had said, threateningly, that he had better not mention his name, let him go and be a Boy Scout on his own. The sneer strengthened him, and he went off to the lab. He met Mr. Abu and asked for Vernier. Abu said Vernier was busy and what was the matter, anyhow.

---

19. **Florence Nightingale** (1820–1910): English nurse regarded as the founder of modern nursing.
20. **David Livingstone** (1813–1873): Scottish missionary and explorer in Africa.
21. **Kagawa** (kä′ gä wä′) (1888–1960): Japanese pacifist, social reformer, and Christian evangelist.
22. **Gandhi** (gän′ dē) (1869–1948): Hindu nationalist leader who preached nonviolence.
23. **Kwegyir Aggrey** (kweg′ yēr äg′ grā) (1875–1927): West African educator and orator.

"I broke the thermometer yesterday," Kojo said in a businesslike manner.

Abu put down the glassware he was carrying.

"Well, I never!" he said. "What do you think you will gain by this?"

"I broke it," Kojo repeated.

"Basu broke it," Abu said impatiently. "Sorie got him to confess, and Basu himself came here this morning and told the science master and myself that he knew now that he had knocked the thermometer by mistake when he came in early yesterday afternoon.

He had not turned round to look, but he had definitely heard a tinkle as he walked by. Someone must have picked it up and put it in the waste bin. The whole matter is settled, the palaver finished."

He tapped a barometer on the wall and, squinting, read the pressure. He turned again to Kojo.

"I should normally have expected him to say so yesterday and save you boys missing the game. But there you are," he added, shrugging and trying to look reasonable, "you cannot hope for too much from a Syrian boy."

Thinking About the Story

A PERSONAL RESPONSE

sharing impressions

1. How does the ending of this story make you feel? Jot down your impressions in your journal.

constructing interpretations

2. What do you think is the main reason that Basu confesses to breaking the thermometer?

Think about
- the kind of person he is
- his relationships with the other students

3. Who do you think suffers more from this experience, Basu or Kojo? Support your answer with references to the story.

4. Describe the lessons that you think Kojo learns about human relationships in this story.

A CREATIVE RESPONSE

5. How might this story have ended if Kojo had spoken to Mr. Vernier instead of to Mr. Abu?

A CRITICAL RESPONSE

6. Speculate about why the writer might have chosen a school laboratory as the setting of this story.

Think about
- a laboratory as a place where experiments and tests are conducted
- your own experiences in a school laboratory

7. While comforting Basu, Vernier quotes a line from Shakespeare's play *Hamlet*: "To thine own self be true." Which character in this story do you think comes closest to living up to this standard of conduct? Support your view with details from the story.

Analyzing the Writer's Craft

CONFLICT

Think about Kojo's moments of decision in this story.

Building a Literary Vocabulary. Conflict is a struggle between opposing forces. An external conflict involves a character pitted against an outside force—nature, a physical obstacle, or another character. An internal conflict is one that occurs between opposing tendencies within a character. In "Games at Twilight," for example, the external conflict is between Ravi and Raghu, whom Ravi is trying to elude. An internal conflict is between Ravi's determination to win the game and his fear of staying in the shed.

Application: Analyzing Internal Conflict. Get together with a partner and go back through this story, looking for passages that suggest Kojo's internal conflicts. Identify the tendencies within Kojo that are in opposition. Then evaluate how Kojo's character develops as a result of his internal conflicts.

1. Write an **autobiographical essay** in which Kojo explains why he lets Mr. Abu have the final say at the end of the story.

Option: Have Kojo explain his conduct in a **journal entry** written after his confrontation with Mr. Abu.

2. Imagine that you are on a committee appointed to select the Teacher of the Year in Sierra Leone and that Mr. Vernier is a candidate for that honor. Write a **memo** to your committee chairperson expressing your views of the candidate.

Option: Write a **letter** to Mr. Vernier explaining why you chose or rejected him for this honor.

3. Write the **dialogue** that may have taken place between Sorie and Basu when Basu agrees to confess to breaking the thermometer.

Option: Write a **monologue** in which Sorie tells his followers about his talk with Basu.

4. Write a draft of a **speech** to be delivered to your class about peer pressure at school. Include examples from this story.

Option: Write an **article** for your high school newspaper in which you support your ideas about peer pressure with examples from this story.

Seventeen Syllables

HISAYE YAMAMOTO

A biography of Yamamoto appears on page 429.

Approaching the Story

Like the character Rosie in this story, Hisaye Yamamoto (hē sä′ ye yä mä mô̄′ tô̄) was born in the United States to parents who emigrated from Japan. Much of her fiction, including "Seventeen Syllables," portrays the contrast between the thoughts and feelings of the two generations.

Building Vocabulary

These essential words are footnoted within the story.

vernaculars (vər nak′ yə lərz): Several Japanese **vernaculars** were printed there. (page 112)

anaesthetic (an′ əs thet′ ik): Rosie found the greater part of the evening practically **anaesthetic.** (page 113)

garrulous (gar′ ə ləs): Haru, the **garrulous** one, said . . .,"Oh, you must see my new coat!" (page 113)

infinitesimal (in′ fin i tes′ i məl), **repartee** (rep′ ər tē′): They laughed a great deal together over **infinitesimal repartee.** (page 115)

rapt: Mr. Kuroda was in his shirtsleeves expounding some *haiku* theory . . . , and her mother was **rapt.** (page 118)

vacillating (vas′ ə lāt′ iŋ): Frightened and **vacillating,** Rosie saw her father enter the house. (page 119)

indiscretion (in′ di skresh′ ən): She could no longer project herself . . . without refreshing in them the memory of her **indiscretion.** (page 119)

glib (glib): For an instant she turned away, and her mother, hearing the familiar **glib** agreement, released her. (page 120)

Connecting Writing and Reading

Think of a time when you witnessed a major conflict between two people who are close to you—friends, for example, or family members. In your journal, describe the conflict and how it made you feel. As you read, compare your feelings about the conflict you witnessed with Rosie's feelings about the conflict between her parents.

Seventeen Syllables

THE FIRST ROSIE knew that her mother had taken to writing poems was one evening when she finished one and read it aloud for her daughter's approval. It was about cats, and Rosie pretended to understand it thoroughly and appreciate it to no end, partly because she hesitated to disillusion her mother about the quantity and quality of Japanese she had learned in all the years now that she had been going to Japanese school every Saturday (and Wednesday, too, in the summer). Even so, her mother must have been skeptical about the depth of Rosie's understanding, because she explained afterwards about the kind of poem she was trying to write.

See, Rosie, she said, it was a haiku, a poem in which she must pack all her meaning into seventeen syllables only, which were divided into three lines of five, seven, and five syllables. In the one she had just read, she had tried to capture the charm of a kitten, as well as comment on the superstition that owning a cat of three colors meant good luck.

"Yes, yes, I understand. How utterly lovely," Rosie said, and her mother, either satisfied or seeing through the deception and resigned, went back to composing.

The truth was that Rosie was lazy; English lay ready on the tongue but Japanese had to be searched for and examined, and even then put forth tentatively (probably to meet with laughter). It was so much easier to say yes, yes, even when one meant no, no. Besides, this was what was in her mind to say: I was looking through one of your magazines from Japan last night, Mother, and toward the back I found some haiku in English that delighted me.

There was one that made me giggle off and on until I fell asleep—

It is morning, and lo!
I lie awake, *comme il faut*,[1]
sighing for some dough.

Now, how to reach her mother, how to communicate the melancholy song? Rosie knew formal Japanese by fits and starts, her mother had even less English, no French. It was much more possible to say yes, yes.

It developed that her mother was writing the haiku for a daily newspaper, the *Mainichi Shimbun*,[2] that was published in San Francisco. Los Angeles, to be sure, was closer to the farming community in which the Hayashi[3] family lived and several Japanese vernaculars[4] were printed there, but Rosie's parents said they preferred the tone of the northern paper. Once a week, the *Mainichi* would have a section devoted to haiku, and her mother became an extravagant contributor, taking for herself the blossoming pen name, Ume Hanazono.[5]

So Rosie and her father lived for a while with two women, her mother and Ume Hanazono. Her mother (Tome Hayashi by name) kept house, cooked, washed, and, along with her husband and the Carrascos, the Mexican family hired for the harvest, did her ample share of picking tomatoes out in the sweltering

---

1. *comme il faut* (kôm ēl fō) *French:* as one does.
2. *Mainichi Shimbun* (mä ē nē′ chē shēm′ bun).
3. **Hayashi** (hä yä′ shē).
4. **vernaculars** (vər nak′ ye lərz): newspapers printed in a native language.
5. **Ume Hanazono** (o͞o′ me hä nä zô′ nô).

fields and boxing them in tidy strata in the cool packing shed. Ume Hanazono, who came to life after the dinner dishes were done, was an earnest, muttering stranger who often neglected speaking when spoken to and stayed busy at the parlor table as late as midnight scribbling with pencil on scratch paper or carefully copying characters on good paper with her fat, pale green Parker.

The new interest had some repercussions on the household routine. Before, Rosie had been accustomed to her parents and herself taking their hot baths early and going to bed almost immediately afterward unless her parents challenged each other to a game of flower cards or unless company dropped in. Now if her father wanted to play cards, he had to resort to solitaire (at which he always cheated fearlessly), and if a group of friends came over, it was bound to contain someone who was also writing haiku, and the small assemblage would be split in two, her father entertaining the nonliterary members and her mother comparing ecstatic notes with the visiting poet.

If they went out, it was more of the same thing. But Ume Hanazono's life span, even for a poet's, was very brief—perhaps three months at most.

One night they went over to see the Hayano family in the neighboring town to the west, an adventure both painful and attractive to Rosie. It was attractive because there were four Hayano girls, all lovely and each one named after a season of the year (Haru, Natsu, Aki, Fuyu),[6] painful because something had been wrong with Mrs. Hayano ever since the birth of her first child. Rosie would sometimes watch Mrs. Hayano, reputed to have been the belle of her native village, making her way about a room, stooped, slowly shuffling, violently trembling (*always* trembling), and she would be reminded that this woman, in this same condition, had carried and given issue to three babies.

She would look wonderingly at Mr. Hayano, handsome, tall, and strong, and she would look at her four pretty friends. But it was not a matter she could come to any decision about.

On this visit, however, Mrs. Hayano sat all evening in the rocker, as motionless and unobtrusive as it was possible for her to be, and Rosie found the greater part of the evening practically anaesthetic.[7] Too, Rosie spent most of it in the girls' room, because Haru, the garrulous[8] one, said almost as soon as the bows and other greetings were over, "Oh, you must see my new coat!"

It was a pale plaid of gray, sand, and blue, with an enormous collar, and Rosie, seeing nothing special in it, said, "Gee, how nice."

"Nice?" said Haru, indignantly. "Is that all you can say about it? It's gorgeous! And so cheap, too. Only seventeen-ninety-eight, because it was a sale. The saleslady said it was twenty-five dollars regular."

"Gee," said Rosie. Natsu, who never said much and when she said anything said it shyly, fingered the coat covetously and Haru pulled it away.

"Mine," she said, putting it on. She minced in the aisle between the two large beds and smiled happily. "Let's see how your mother likes it."

She broke into the front room and the adult conversation and went to stand in front of Rosie's mother, while the rest watched from the door. Rosie's mother was properly envious. "May I inherit it when you're through with it?"

Haru, pleased, giggled and said yes, she could, but Natsu reminded gravely from the door, "You promised me, Haru."

Everyone laughed but Natsu, who shame-

---

6. **Haru, Natsu, Aki, Fuyu** (hä′ $r\overline{oo}$, nä′ ts$\overline{oo}$, ä′ kē, f$\overline{oo}$′ y$\overline{oo}$).

7. **anaesthetic** (an′ əs thet′ ik): numbing; making one fall asleep; dull.

8. **garrulous** (gar′ ə ləs): talkative.

facedly retreated into the bedroom. Haru came in laughing, taking off the coat. "We were only kidding, Natsu," she said. "Here, you try it on now."

After Natsu buttoned herself into the coat, inspected herself solemnly in the bureau mirror, and reluctantly shed it, Rosie, Aki, and Fuyu got their turns, and Fuyu, who was eight, drowned in it while her sisters and Rosie doubled up in amusement. They all went into the front room later, because Haru's mother quaveringly called to her to fix the tea and rice cakes and open a can of sliced peaches for everybody. Rosie noticed that her mother and Mr. Hayano were talking together at the little table—they were discussing a haiku that Mr. Hayano was planning to send to the *Mainichi*, while her father was sitting at one end of the sofa looking through a copy of *Life,* the new picture magazine. Occasionally, her father would comment on a photograph, holding it toward Mrs. Hayano and speaking to her as he always did—loudly, as though he thought someone such as she must surely be at least a trifle deaf also.

The five girls had their refreshments at the kitchen table, and it was while Rosie was showing the sisters her trick of swallowing peach slices without chewing (she chased each slippery crescent down with a swig of tea) that her father brought his empty teacup and untouched saucer to the sink and said, "Come on, Rosie, we're going home now."

"Already?" asked Rosie.

"Work tomorrow," he said.

He sounded irritated, and Rosie, puzzled, gulped one last yellow slice and stood up to go, while the sisters began protesting, as was their wont.

"We have to get up at five-thirty," he told them, going into the front room quickly, so that they did not have their usual chance to hang onto his hands and plead for an extension of time.

Rosie, following, saw that her mother and Mr. Hayano were sipping tea and still talking together, while Mrs. Hayano concentrated, quivering, on raising the handleless Japanese cup to her lips with both her hands and lowering it back to her lap. Her father, saying nothing, went out the door, onto the bright porch, and down the steps. Her mother looked up and asked, "Where is he going?"

"Where is he going?" Rosie said. "He said we were going home now."

"Going home?" Her mother looked with embarrassment at Mr. Hayano and his absorbed wife and then forced a smile. "He must be tired," she said.

Haru was not giving up yet. "May Rosie stay overnight?" she asked, and Natsu, Aki, and Fuyu came to reinforce their sister's plea by helping her make a circle around Rosie's mother. Rosie, for once having no desire to stay, was relieved when her mother, apologizing to the perturbed Mr. and Mrs. Hayano for her father's abruptness at the same time, managed to shake her head no at the quartet, kindly but adamant, so that they broke their circle and let her go.

Rosie's father looked ahead into the windshield as the two joined him. "I'm sorry," her mother said. "You must be tired." Her father, stepping on the starter, said nothing. "You know how I get when it's haiku," she continued, "I forget what time it is." He only grunted.

As they rode homeward silently, Rosie, sitting between, felt a rush of hate for both—for her mother for begging, for her father for denying her mother. I wish this old Ford would crash, right now, she thought, then immediately, no, no, I wish my father would laugh, but it was too late: already the vision had passed through her mind of the green pick-up crumpled in the dark against one of the mighty eucalyptus trees they were just riding past, of the three contorted, bleeding bodies, one of them hers.

Rosie ran between two patches of tomatoes, her heart working more rambunctiously than she had ever known it to. How lucky it was that Aunt Taka and Uncle Gimpachi[9] had come tonight, though, how very lucky. Otherwise she might not have really kept her half-promise to meet Jesus Carrasco. Jesus was going to be a senior in September at the same school she went to, and his parents were the ones helping with the tomatoes this year. She and Jesus, who hardly remembered seeing each other at Cleveland High where there were so many other people and two whole grades between them, had become great friends this summer—he always had a joke for her when he periodically drove the loaded pick-up up from the fields to the shed where she was usually sorting while her mother and father did the packing, and they laughed a great deal together over infinitesimal[10] repartee[11] during the afternoon break for chilled watermelon or ice cream in the shade of the shed.

What she enjoyed most was racing him to see which could finish picking a double row first. He, who could work faster, would tease her by slowing down until she thought she would surely pass him this time, then speeding up furiously to leave her several sprawling vines behind. Once he had made her screech hideously by crossing over, while her back was turned, to place atop the tomatoes in her green-stained bucket a truly monstrous, pale green worm (it had looked more like an infant snake). And it was when they had finished a contest this morning, after she had pantingly pointed a green finger at the immature tomatoes evident in the lugs[12] at the end of his row and he had returned the accusation (with justice), that he had startlingly brought up the matter of their possibly meeting outside the range of both their parents' dubious eyes.

"What for?" she had asked.

"I've got a secret I want to tell you," he said.

"Tell me now," she demanded.

"It won't be ready till tonight," he said.

She laughed. "Tell me tomorrow then."

"It'll be gone tomorrow," he threatened.

"Well, for seven hakes,[13] what is it?" she had asked, more than twice, and when he had suggested that the packing shed would be an appropriate place to find out, she had cautiously answered maybe. She had not been certain she was going to keep the appointment until the arrival of mother's sister and her husband. Their coming seemed a sort of signal of permission, of grace, and she had definitely made up her mind to lie and leave as she was bowing them welcome.

So as soon as everyone appeared settled back for the evening, she announced loudly that she was going to the privy outside, "I'm going to the *benjo*!" and slipped out the door. And now that she was actually on her way, her heart pumped in such an undisciplined way that she could hear it with her ears. It's because I'm running, she told herself, slowing to a walk. The shed was up ahead, one more patch away, in the middle of the fields. Its bulk, looming in the dimness, took on a sinisterness that was funny when Rosie reminded herself that it was only a wooden frame with a canvas roof and three canvas walls that made a slapping noise on breezy days.

Jesus was sitting on the narrow plank that was the sorting platform and she went around to the other side and jumped backwards to seat herself on the rim of a packing stand. "Well,

---

9. Aunt Taka (tä′ kä) **. . . Uncle Gimpachi** (gēm pä′ chē).

10. infinitesimal (in′ fin i tes′ i məl): too small to be measured; infinitely small.

11. repartee (rep′ ər tē′): quick, witty conversation.

12. lugs: shallow boxes in which fruit is shipped.

13. seven hakes: a play on the phrase "heaven's sake."

tell me," she said without greeting, thinking her voice sounded reassuringly familiar.

"I saw you coming out the door," Jesus said. "I heard you running part of the way, too."

"Uh-huh," Rosie said. "Now tell me the secret."

"I was afraid you wouldn't come," he said.

Rosie delved around on the chicken-wire bottom of the stall for number two tomatoes, ripe, which she was sitting beside, and came up with a left-over that felt edible. She bit into it and began sucking out the pulp and seeds. "I'm here," she pointed out.

"Rosie, are you sorry you came?"

"Sorry? What for?" she said. "You said you were going to tell me something."

"I will, I will," Jesus said, but his voice contained disappointment, and Rosie fleetingly felt the older of the two, realizing a brand-new power which vanished without category under her recognition.

"I have to go back in a minute," she said. "My aunt and uncle are here from Wintersburg. I told them I was going to the privy."

Jesus laughed. "You funny thing," he said. "You slay me!"

"Just because you have a bathroom *inside*," Rosie said. "Come on, tell me."

Chuckling, Jesus came around to lean on the stand facing her. They still could not see each other very clearly, but Rosie noticed that Jesus became very sober again as he took the hollow tomato from her hand and dropped it back into the stall. When he took hold of her empty hand, she could find no words to protest; her vocabulary had become distressingly constricted and she thought desperately that all that remained intact now was yes and no and oh, and even these few sounds would not easily out. Thus, kissed by Jesus, Rosie fell for the first time entirely victim to a helplessness delectable beyond speech. But the terrible, beautiful sensation lasted no more than a second, and the reality of Jesus' lips and tongue

and teeth and hands made her pull away with such strength that she nearly tumbled.

Rosie stopped running as she approached the lights from the windows of home. How long since she had left? She could not guess, but gasping yet, she went to the privy in back and locked herself in. Her own breathing deafened her in the dark, close space, and she sat and waited until she could hear at last the nightly calling of the frogs and crickets. Even then, all she could think to say was oh, my, and the pressure of Jesus' face against her face would not leave.

No one had missed her in the parlor, however, and Rosie walked in and through quickly, announcing that she was next going to take a bath. "Your father's in the bathhouse," her mother said, and Rosie, in her room, recalled that she had not seen him when she entered. There had been only Aunt Taka and Uncle Gimpachi with her mother at the table, drinking tea. She got her robe and straw sandals and crossed the parlor again to go outside. Her mother was telling them about the haiku competition in the *Mainichi* and the poem she had entered.

Rosie met her father coming out of the bathhouse. "Are you through, Father?" she asked. "I was going to ask you to scrub my back."

"Scrub your own back," he said shortly, going toward the main house.

"What have I done now?" she yelled after him. She suddenly felt like doing a lot of yelling. But he did not answer, and she went into the bathhouse. Turning on the dangling light, she removed her denims and T-shirt and threw them in the big carton for dirty clothes standing next to the washing machine. Her other things she took with her into the bath compartment to wash after her bath. After she had scooped a basin of hot water from the square wooden tub, she sat on the gray cement of the floor and soaped herself at exaggerated leisure, singing "Red Sails in the Sunset" at the top of her voice and using da-da-da where she suspected her words. Then, standing up, still singing, for she was possessed by the notion that any attempt now to analyze would result in spoilage and she believed that the larger her volume the less she would be able to hear herself think, she obtained more hot water and poured it on until she was free of lather. Only then did she allow herself to step into the steaming vat, one leg first, then the remainder of her body inch by inch until the water no longer stung and she could move around at will.

She took a long time soaking, afterwards remembering to go around outside to stoke the embers of the tin-lined fireplace beneath the tub and to throw on a few more sticks so that the water might keep its heat for her mother, and when she finally returned to the parlor, she found her mother still talking haiku with her aunt and uncle, the three of them on another round of tea. Her father was nowhere in sight.

At Japanese school the next day (Wednesday, it was), Rosie was grave and giddy by turns. Preoccupied at her desk in the row for students on Book Eight, she made up for it at recess by performing wild mimicry for the benefit of her friend Chizuko.[14] She held her nose and whined a witticism or two in what she considered was the manner of Fred Allen; she assumed intoxication and a British accent to go over the climax of the Rudy Vallee recording of the pub conversation about William Ewart Gladstone; she was the child Shirley Temple piping, "On the Good Ship Lollipop"; she was the gentleman soprano of the Four Inkspots[15] trilling, "If I Didn't Care." And she felt reasonably satisfied when Chizuko wept and gasped, "Oh, Rosie, you ought to be in the movies!"

Her father came after her at noon, bringing her sandwiches of minced ham and two nec-tarines to eat while she rode, so that she could pitch right into the sorting when they got home. The lugs were piling up, he said, and the ripe tomatoes in them would probably have to be taken to the cannery tomorrow if they were not ready for the produce haulers tonight. "This heat's not doing them any good. And we've got no time for a break today."

It *was* hot, probably the hottest day of the year, and Rosie's blouse stuck damply to her back even under the protection of the canvas. But she worked as efficiently as a flawless machine and kept the stalls heaped, with one part of her mind listening in to the parental murmuring about the heat and the tomatoes and with another part planning the exact words she would say to Jesus when he drove up with the first load of the afternoon. But when at last she saw that the pick-up was coming, her hands went berserk and the tomatoes started falling in the wrong stalls, and her father said, "Hey, hey! Rosie, watch what you're doing!"

"Well, I have to go to the *benjo*," she said, hiding panic.

"Go in the weeds over there," he said, only half-joking.

"Oh, Father!" she protested.

"Oh, go on home," her mother said. "We'll make out for a while."

In the privy Rosie peered through a knothole toward the fields, watching as much as she could of Jesus. Happily, she thought she saw him look in the direction of the house from

---

14. **Chizuko** (chē zōō′ kô).
15. **Fred Allen . . . Four Inkspots:** Fred Allen had a radio show during the 1930's and 1940's. Rudy Vallee was a singer during the 1920's and 1930's who had a radio comedy routine about Gladstone, a prime minister of England during the 1800's. Shirley Temple was the most popular child motion picture star of the 1930's. The Four Inkspots was an African-American singing group popular during the 1940's and 1950's.

time to time before he finished unloading and went back toward the patch where his mother and father worked. As she was heading for the shed, a very presentable black car purred up the dirt driveway to the house and its driver motioned to her. Was this the Hayashi home, he wanted to know. She nodded. Was she a Hayashi? Yes, she said, thinking that he was a good-looking man. He got out of the car with a huge, flat package and she saw that he warmly wore a business suit. "I have something here for your mother then," he said, in a more elegant Japanese than she was used to.

She told him where her mother was and he came along with her, patting his face with an immaculate white handkerchief and saying something about the coolness of San Francisco. To her surprised mother and father, he bowed and introduced himself as, among other things, the haiku editor of the *Mainichi Shimbun*, saying that since he had been coming as far as Los Angeles anyway, he had decided to bring her the first prize she had won in the recent contest.

"First prize?" her mother echoed, believing and not believing, pleased and overwhelmed. Handed the package with a bow, she bobbed her head up and down numerous times to express her utter gratitude.

"It is nothing much," he added, "but I hope it will serve as a token of our great appreciation for your contributions and our great admiration of your considerable talent."

"I am not worthy," she said, falling easily into his style. "It is I who should make some sign of my humble thanks for being permitted to contribute."

"No, no, to the contrary," he said, bowing again.

But Rosie's mother insisted, and then saying that she knew she was being unorthodox, she asked if she might open the package because her curiosity was so great. Certainly she might. In fact, he would like her reaction to it, for per-

sonally, it was one of his favorite *Hiroshiges*.[16]

Rosie thought it was a pleasant picture, which looked to have been sketched with delicate quickness. There were pink clouds, some graceful calligraphy, and a sea that was a pale blue except at the edges, containing four sampans[17] with indications of people in them. Pines edged the water and on the far-off beach there was a cluster of thatched huts towered over by pine-dotted mountains of gray and blue. The frame was scalloped and gilt.

After Rosie's mother pronounced it without peer and somewhat prodded her father into nodding agreement, she said Mr. Kuroda[18] must at least have a cup of tea after coming all this way, and although Mr. Kuroda did not want to impose, he soon agreed that a cup of tea would be refreshing and went along with her to the house, carrying the picture for her.

"Ha, your mother's crazy!" Rosie's father said, and Rosie laughed uneasily as she resumed judgment on the tomatoes. She had emptied six lugs when he broke into an imaginary conversation with Jesus to tell her to go and remind her mother of the tomatoes, and she went slowly.

Mr. Kuroda was in his shirtsleeves expounding some haiku theory as he munched a rice cake, and her mother was rapt.[19] Abashed in the great man's presence, Rosie stood next to her mother's chair until her mother looked up inquiringly, and then she started to whisper the message, but her mother pushed her gently away and reproached, "You are not being very polite to our guest."

---

16. *Hiroshiges* (hē *rô̄* shē′ ges): works by Hiroshige, master painter and designer of Japanese prints, considered one of Japan's most important artists.
17. sampans: small boats used in Japan, rowed with an oar at the front.
18. Mr. Kuroda (ko͞o *rô̄*′ dä).
19. rapt: completely absorbed; paying close attention.

"Father says the tomatoes . . ." Rosie said aloud, smiling foolishly.

"Tell him I shall only be a minute," her mother said, speaking the language of Mr. Kuroda.

When Rosie carried the reply to her father, he did not seem to hear and she said again, "Mother says she'll be back in a minute."

"All right, all right," he nodded, and they worked again in silence. But suddenly, her father uttered an incredible noise, exactly like the cork of a bottle popping, and the next Rosie knew, he was stalking angrily toward the house, almost running in fact, and she chased after him crying, "Father! Father! What are you going to do?"

He stopped long enough to order her back to the shed. "Never mind!" he shouted. "Get on with the sorting!"

And from the place in the fields where she stood, frightened and vacillating,[20] Rosie saw her father enter the house. Soon Mr. Kuroda came out alone, putting on his coat. Mr. Kuroda got into his car and backed out down the driveway onto the highway. Next her father emerged, also alone, something in his arms (it was the picture, she realized), and, going over to the bathhouse woodpile, he threw the picture on the ground and picked up the axe. Smashing the picture, glass and all (she heard the explosion faintly), he reached over for the kerosene that was used to encourage the bath fire and poured it over the wreckage. I am dreaming, Rosie said to herself, I am dreaming, but her father, having made sure that his act of cremation was irrevocable, was even then returning to the fields.

Rosie ran past him and toward the house. What had become of her mother? She burst into the parlor and found her mother at the back window watching the dying fire. They watched together until there remained only a feeble smoke under the blazing sun. Her mother was very calm.

"Do you know why I married your father?" she said without turning.

"No," said Rosie. It was the most frightening question she had ever been called upon to answer. Don't tell me now, she wanted to say, tell me tomorrow, tell me next week, don't tell me today. But she knew she would be told now, that the telling would combine with the other violence of the hot afternoon to level her life, her world to the very ground.

It was like a story out of the magazines illustrated in sepia,[21] which she had consumed so greedily for a period until the information had somehow reached her that those wretchedly unhappy autobiographies, offered to her as the testimonials of living men and women, were largely inventions: Her mother, at nineteen, had come to America and married her father as an alternative to suicide.

At eighteen she had been in love with the first son of one of the well-to-do families in her village. The two had met whenever and wherever they could, secretly, because it would not have done for his family to see him favor her —her father had no money; he was a drunkard and a gambler besides. She had learned she was with child; an excellent match had already been arranged for her lover. Despised by her family, she had given premature birth to a stillborn son, who would be seventeen now. Her family did not turn her out, but she could no longer project herself in any direction without refreshing in them the memory of her indiscretion.[22] She wrote to Aunt Taka, her favorite sister in America, threatening to kill herself if Aunt Taka would not send for her. Aunt Taka hastily arranged a marriage with a young man of whom she knew, but lately arrived from Japan, a young man of simple mind, it was

---

20. vacillating (vas′ ə lāt′ iŋ): wavering in opinion.

21. sepia: a dark reddish-brown color.

22. indiscretion (in′ di skresh′ ən): an act showing lack of good judgment.

said, but of kindly heart. The young man was never told why his unseen betrothed was so eager to hasten the day of meeting.

The story was told perfectly, with neither groping for words nor untoward passion. It was as though her mother had memorized it by heart, reciting it to herself so many times over that its nagging vileness had long since gone.

"I had a brother then?" Rosie asked, for this was what seemed to matter now; she would think about the other later, she assured herself, pushing back the illumination which threatened all that darkness that had hitherto been merely mysterious or even glamorous. "A half-brother?"

"Yes."

"I would have liked a brother," she said.

Suddenly, her mother knelt on the floor and took her by the wrists. "Rosie," she said urgently, "promise me you will never marry!" Shocked more by the request than the revela-

tion, Rosie stared at her mother's face. Jesus, Jesus, she called silently, not certain whether she was invoking the help of the son of the Carrascos or of God, until there returned sweetly the memory of Jesus' hand, how it had touched her and where. Still her mother waited for an answer, holding her wrists so tightly that her hands were going numb. She tried to pull free. Promise, her mother whispered fiercely, promise. Yes, yes, I promise, Rosie said. But for an instant she turned away, and her mother, hearing the familiar glib[23] agreement, released her. Oh, you, you, you, her eyes and twisted mouth said, you fool. Rosie, covering her face, began at last to cry, and the embrace and consoling hand came much later than she expected.

---

23. **glib** (glib): spoken in a smooth, careless manner, often in a way that is not convincing.

Thinking About the Story

A PERSONAL RESPONSE

sharing impressions

1. Which character were you most thinking of as you finished reading? Briefly record your thoughts about this character in your journal.

constructing interpretations

2. Do you think Mrs. Hayashi is justified in pressuring Rosie to promise not to marry? Give reasons for your answer.

Think about
- the nature of her marriage to Rosie's father
- what she wants for Rosie
- Rosie's immediate reaction to the demand

3. In your opinion, why does Rosie's father react as he does to Mrs. Hayashi's writing?

Think about
- the difference between the way Mrs. Hayashi and Mrs. Hayano act as wives
- what kind of wife Mr. Hayashi might prefer to have

- the pleasure Mrs. Hayashi takes in writing and discussing *haiku*
- the intensity of the farm work and the need for her labor
- the elegance of the prize Mrs. Hayashi wins and of the man who brings it
- the description of Mr. Hayashi as a man "of simple mind . . . but of kindly heart"

4. Is there anything Mrs. Hayashi can do to resolve the conflict between her husband's needs and her own desires? Explain your answer.

5. What incidents most clearly reveal to you how Rosie is affected by the conflict between her parents? Cite details from the story.

A CREATIVE RESPONSE

6. Do you think Rosie is more likely to follow her mother's advice not to marry, to model her behavior on her mother's, or to follow her own way?

Think about
- connections between Mrs. Hayashi's illicit romance in Japan and Rosie's budding romance with Jesus Carrasco
- the conflict between the way Rosie and her mother view Japanese culture and American culture
- similarities and differences between Rosie's personality and her mother's
- whether life in the United States will offer Rosie different opportunities from those her mother had

A CRITICAL RESPONSE

7. Between 1885 and 1924 many young Japanese men came to America seeking a new life. Some later returned to Japan to marry, while others, like Mr. Hayashi, found wives by exchanging photographs with Japanese women looking for husbands in America. What aspects of the Hayashi marriage do you think are directly related to these cultural circumstances, and what aspects could be present in any marriage? Cite examples from the story to support your answer.

8. According to one critic, Mrs. Hayashi's impassioned kneeling and clasping of Rosie at the end of the story is ironically similar to that of an ardent lover proposing marriage. Explain whether you agree or disagree with this critical interpretation, citing details from the story for support.

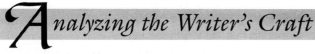
PLOT AND THEME ———————————————————

What do you think Yamamoto wants to communicate about Rosie and her adolescent awakening?

Building a Literary Vocabulary. Plot refers to the actions and events in a literary work. A short story sometimes has two or more plots that operate simultaneously. Each plot may suggest a theme, or central idea; all the plots and themes are somehow related. In "Seventeen Syllables" the development of Rosie's relationship with Jesus forms one plot line. In this part of the story, Yamamoto explores the conflicting emotions that often surround such a relationship. The second plot line involves Mrs. Hayashi's *haiku* writing and the conflicts she and her family experience because of it.

Application: Examining Plot and Theme. Working with a partner, create two time lines, one above the other. Indicate events related to Rosie's romance with Jesus on the top line and events connected with Mrs. Hayashi's *haiku* writing on the bottom one. Circle points on the time lines where the two plots overlap at crucial times. Then write a thematic statement that presents the central idea communicated by the two plots considered together. Share your time line and thematic statement with the class.

Connecting Reading and Writing

1. Write a *haiku* to share with a poetry reading group. Use the details about *haiku* presented in the story as a guide to writing your poem.

Option: Find examples of *haiku* to share with your poetry group and write **annotations** to accompany the poems.

2. Imagine that you are Rosie. In a **diary entry**, describe your feelings about your mother's forcing you to promise not to marry.

Option: Write a **note** that you might pass to your closest friend explaining what has happened in your family and asking for advice on what to do next.

3. Write the next **scene** for this story, in which Mr. and Mrs. Hayashi visit a close friend and advisor in an attempt to resolve their conflict.

Option: Write **journal notes** that the friend and advisor might write after the Hayashis' visit.

4. Read more about the picture brides who came to America to marry men they had never met. Share your findings with the class in the form of an **oral presentation**.

Option: Write a brief **dramatic scene** to communicate the thoughts and emotions of several picture brides when they meet their future husbands for the first time.

Marigolds

EUGENIA COLLIER

A biography of Collier appears on page 420.

Approaching the Story

The narrator of "Marigolds" is an adult who recalls a memory from her childhood, a memory that is as much about the feelings she had as a girl of fourteen as it is about her actions. The event she remembers takes place during the Great Depression, a time of economic hardship for the entire country but especially for those who lived in the shantytowns of the rural South.

Building Vocabulary

These essential words are footnoted within the story.

futile (fyo͞ot′ 'l), **impoverished** (im päv′ ər ishd): **Futile** waiting was the sorrowful background music of our **impoverished** little community. (page 124)

poignantly (poin′ yənt lē): As I think of those days I feel most **poignantly** the tag end of summer. (page 125)

stoicism (stō′ i siz′ əm): Her face had Indian-like features and the stern **stoicism** that one associates with Indian faces. (page 126)

perverse (pər vʉrs′): For some **perverse** reason, we children hated those marigolds. (page 126)

degradation (deg′ rə dā′ shən): The smoldering emotions of that summer swelled in me and burst—the great need for my mother . . ., the hopelessness of our poverty and **degradation**. (page 129)

contrition (kən trish′ ən): Despite my wild **contrition** she never planted marigolds again. (page 129)

Connecting Writing and Reading

Think about the kinds of things people do when they are unhappy. In your journal, briefly explain what unhappy people might do to themselves, to other people, and to things around them. Then as you read, notice how characters act when they suffer unhappiness or loss.

Marigolds

WHEN I THINK of the hometown of my youth, all that I seem to remember is dust—the brown, crumbly dust of late summer—arid, sterile dust that gets into the eyes and makes them water, gets into the throat and between the toes of bare brown feet. I don't know why I should remember only the dust. Surely there must have been lush green lawns and paved streets under leafy shade trees somewhere in town; but memory is an abstract painting—it does not present things as they are, but rather as they *feel*. And so, when I think of that time and that place, I remember only the dry September of the dirt roads and grassless yards of the shantytown where I lived. And one other thing I remember, another incongruency of memory—a brilliant splash of sunny yellow against the dust—Miss Lottie's marigolds.

Whenever the memory of those marigolds flashes across my mind, a strange nostalgia comes with it and remains long after the picture has faded. I feel again the chaotic emotions of adolescence, illusive as smoke, yet as real as the potted geranium before me now. Joy and rage and wild animal gladness and shame become tangled together in the multicolored skein of fourteen-going-on-fifteen as I recall that devastating moment when I was suddenly more woman than child, years ago in Miss Lottie's yard. I think of those marigolds at the strangest times. I remember them vividly now as I desperately pass away the time waiting for you, who will not come.

I suppose that <u>futile</u>[1] waiting was the sorrowful background music of our <u>impoverished</u>[2] little community when I was young. The Depression that gripped the nation was no new thing to us, for the black workers of rural Maryland had always been depressed. I don't know what it was that we were waiting for; certainly not for the prosperity that was "just around the corner," for those were white folks' words, which we never believed. Nor did we wait for hard work and thrift to pay off in shining success as the American Dream[3] promised, for we knew better than that, too. Perhaps we waited for a miracle, amorphous in concept but necessary if one were to have the grit to rise before dawn each day and labor in the white man's vineyard until after dark, or to wander about in the September dust offering one's sweat in return for some meager share of bread. But God was *chary* with miracles in those days, and so we waited—and waited.

We children, of course, were only vaguely aware of the extent of our poverty. Having no radios, few newspapers, and no magazines, we were somewhat unaware of the world outside our community. Nowadays we would be called "culturally deprived," and people would write books and hold conferences about us. In those days everybody we knew was just as hungry and ill-clad as we were. Poverty was the cage in which we all were trapped, and our hatred of it was still the vague, undirected restlessness of the zoo-bred flamingo who knows that nature created him to fly free.

---

1. futile (fyo͞ot′ 'l): useless; hopeless; ineffective.
2. impoverished (im päv′ ər ishd): made poor; robbed of strength or power.
3. American Dream: the American ideal of attaining success through equality of opportunity afforded all citizens.

As I think of those days I feel most poignantly[4] the tag end of summer, the bright, dry times when we began to have a sense of shortening days and the imminence of the cold.

By the time I was fourteen my brother Joey and I were the only children left at our house, the older ones having left home for early marriage or the lure of the city, and the two babies having been sent to relatives who might care for them better than we. Joey was three years younger than I, and a boy, and therefore vastly inferior. Each morning our mother and father trudged wearily down the dirt road and around the bend, she to her domestic job, he to his daily unsuccessful quest for work. After a few chores around the tumbledown shanty, Joey and I were free to run wild in the sun with other children similarly situated.

For the most part, those days are ill-defined in my memory, running together and combining like a fresh watercolor painting left out in the rain. I remember squatting in the road, drawing a picture in the dust, a picture that Joey gleefully erased with one sweep of his dirty foot. I remember fishing for minnows in a muddy creek and watching sadly as they eluded my cupped hands, while Joey laughed uproariously. And I remember, that year, a strange restlessness of body and spirit, a feeling that something old and familiar was ending, and something unknown and therefore terrifying was beginning.

One day returns to me with special clarity for some reason, perhaps because it was the beginning of the experience that in some inexplicable way marked the end of innocence. I was loafing under the great oak tree in our yard, deep in some reverie that I have now forgotten except that it involved some secret thoughts of one of the Harris boys across the yard. Joey and a bunch of kids were bored now with the old tire suspended from an oak limb, which had kept them entertained for a while.

"Hey, Lizabeth," Joey yelled. He never talked when he could yell. "Hey, Lizabeth, let's us go somewhere."

I came reluctantly from my private world.

"Where at, Joey?"

The truth was that we were becoming tired of the formlessness of our summer days. The idleness whose prospect had seemed so beautiful during the busy days of spring now had degenerated to an almost desperate effort to fill up the empty midday hours.

"Let's go see can we find us some locusts on the hill," someone suggested.

Joey was scornful. "Ain't no more locusts there. Y'all got 'em all while they was still green."

The argument that followed was brief and not really worth the effort. Hunting locust trees wasn't fun any more by now.

"Tell you what," said Joey finally, his eyes sparkling. "Let's us go over to Miss Lottie's."

The idea caught on at once, for annoying Miss Lottie was always fun. I was still child enough to scamper along with the group over rickety fences and through bushes that tore our already raggedy clothes, back to where Miss Lottie lived. I think now that we must have made a tragicomic spectacle, five or six kids of different ages, each of us clad in only one garment—the girls in faded dresses that were too long or too short, the boys in patchy pants, their sweaty brown chests gleaming in the hot sun. A little cloud of dust followed our thin legs and bare feet as we tramped over the barren land.

When Miss Lottie's house came into view we stopped, ostensibly to plan our strategy but actually to reinforce our courage.

Miss Lottie's house was the most ramshackle of all our ramshackle homes. The sun and rain had long since faded its rickety frame siding

---

4. poignantly (poin′ yənt lē): in a manner that sharply, keenly, or painfully affects the feelings.

from white to a sullen gray. The boards themselves seemed to remain upright not from being nailed together but rather from leaning together like a house that a child might have constructed from cards.

A brisk wind might have blown it down, and the fact that it was still standing implied a kind of enchantment that was stronger than the elements. There it stood, and as far as I know is standing yet—a gray, rotting thing with no porch, no shutters, no steps, set on a cramped lot with no grass, not even weeds—a monument to decay.

In front of the house in a squeaky rocking chair sat Miss Lottie's son, John Burke, completing the impression of decay. John Burke was what was known as "queer-headed." Black and ageless, he sat, rocking day in and day out in a mindless stupor, lulled by the monotonous squeak-squawk of the chair. A battered hat atop his shaggy head shaded him from the sun. Usually John Burke was totally unaware of everything outside his quiet dream world. But if you disturbed him, if you intruded upon his fantasies, he would become enraged, strike out at you, and curse at you in some strange enchanted language which only he could understand. We children made a game of thinking of ways to disturb John Burke and then to elude his violent retribution.

But our real fun and our real fear lay in Miss Lottie herself. Miss Lottie seemed to be at least a hundred years old. Her big frame still held traces of the tall, powerful woman she must have been in youth, although it was now bent and drawn. Her smooth skin was a dark reddish-brown, and her face had Indian-like features and the stern stoicism[5] that one associates with Indian faces.

Miss Lottie didn't like intruders either, especially children. She never left her yard, and nobody ever visited her. We never knew how she managed those necessities that depend on human interaction—how she ate, for example,

or even whether she ate. When we were tiny children, we thought Miss Lottie was a witch, and we made up tales, that we half believed ourselves, about her exploits. We were far too sophisticated now, of course, to believe the witch-nonsense. But old fears have a way of clinging like cobwebs, and so when we sighted the tumbledown shack, we had to stop to reinforce our nerves.

"Look, there she," I whispered, forgetting that Miss Lottie could not possibly have heard me from that distance. "She fooling with them crazy flowers."

"Yeh, look at 'er."

Miss Lottie's marigolds were perhaps the strangest part of the picture. Certainly they did not fit in with the crumbling decay of the rest of her yard. Beyond the dusty brown yard, in front of the sorry gray house, rose suddenly and shockingly a dazzling strip of bright blossoms, clumped together in enormous mounds, warm and passionate and sun-golden. The old black witch-woman worked on them all summer, every summer, down on her creaky knees, weeding and cultivating and arranging, while the house crumbled and John Burke rocked. For some perverse[6] reason, we children hated those marigolds. They interfered with the perfect ugliness of the place; they were too beautiful; they said too much that we could not understand; they did not make sense. There was something in the vigor with which the old woman destroyed the weeds that intimidated us. It should have been a comical sight—the old woman with the man's hat on her cropped white head, leaning over the bright mounds, her big backside in the air—but it wasn't comical; it was something we could not name. We had to annoy her by whizzing a pebble into her

---

5. stoicism (stō′ i siz′ əm): stern control or holding in of emotion.

6. perverse (pər vʉrs′): stubbornly contrary; wrong, harmful, or against one's own interests.

flowers or by yelling a dirty word, then dancing away from her rage, reveling in our youth and mocking her age. Actually, I think it was the flowers we wanted to destroy, but nobody had the nerve to try it, not even Joey, who was usually fool enough to try anything.

"Y'all git some stones," commanded Joey now, and was met with instant giggling obedience as everyone except me began to gather pebbles from the dusty ground. "Come on, Lizabeth."

I just stood there peering through the bushes, torn between wanting to join the fun and feeling that it was all a bit silly.

"You scared, Lizabeth?"

I cursed and spat on the ground—my favorite gesture of phony bravado. "Y'all children get the stones. I'll show you how to use 'em."

I said before that we children were not consciously aware of how thick were the bars of our cage. I wonder now, though, whether we were not more aware of it than I thought. Perhaps we had some dim notion of what we were, and how little chance we had of being anything else. Otherwise, why would we have been so preoccupied with destruction? Anyway, the pebbles were collected quickly, and everybody looked at me to begin the fun.

"Come on, y'all."

We crept to the edge of the bushes that bordered the narrow road in front of Miss Lottie's place. She was working placidly kneeling over the flowers, her dark hand plunged into the golden mound. Suddenly "zing"—an expertly aimed stone cut the head off one of the blossoms.

"Who out there?" Miss Lottie's backside came down and her head came up as her sharp eyes searched the bushes. "You better git!"

We had crouched down out of sight in the bushes, where we stifled the giggles that insisted on coming. Miss Lottie gazed warily across the road for a moment, then cautiously returned to her weeding. "Zing"—Joey sent a pebble into the blooms, and another marigold was beheaded.

Miss Lottie was enraged now. She began struggling to her feet, leaning on a rickety cane and shouting, "Y'all git! Go on home!" Then the rest of the kids let loose with their pebbles, storming the flowers and laughing wildly and senselessly at Miss Lottie's impotent rage. She shook her stick at us and started shakily toward the road crying, "Git 'long! John Burke! John Burke, come help!"

Then I lost my head entirely, mad with the power of inciting such rage, and ran out of the bushes in the storm of pebbles, straight toward Miss Lottie chanting madly, "Old lady witch, fell in a ditch, picked up a penny and thought she was rich!" The children screamed with delight, dropped their pebbles and joined the crazy dance, swarming around Miss Lottie like bees and chanting, "Old lady witch!" while she screamed curses at us. The madness lasted only a moment, for John Burke, startled at last, lurched out of his chair, and we dashed for the bushes just as Miss Lottie's cane went whizzing at my head.

I did not join the merriment when the kids gathered again under the oak in our bare yard. Suddenly I was ashamed, and I did not like being ashamed. The child in me sulked and said it was all in fun, but the woman in me flinched at the thought of the malicious attack that I had led. The mood lasted all afternoon. When we ate the beans and rice that was supper that night, I did not notice my father's silence, for he was always silent these days, nor did I notice my mother's absence, for she always worked until well into evening. Joey and I had a particularly bitter argument after supper; his exuberance got on my nerves. Finally I stretched out upon the pallet in the room we shared and fell into a fitful doze.

When I awoke, somewhere in the middle of the night, my mother had returned, and I vaguely listened to the conversation that was audible through the thin walls that separated our rooms. At first I heard no words, only voices. My mother's voice was like a cool, dark room in summer—peaceful, soothing, quiet. I loved to listen to it; it made things seem all right somehow. But my father's voice cut through hers, shattering the peace.

"Twenty-two years, Maybelle, twenty-two years," he was saying, "and I got nothing for you, nothing, nothing."

"It's all right, honey, you'll get something. Everybody out of work now, you know that."

"It ain't right. Ain't no man ought to eat his woman's food year in and year out, and see his children running wild. Ain't nothing right about that."

"Honey, you took good care of us when you had it. Ain't nobody got nothing nowadays."

"I ain't talking about nobody else, I'm talking about *me*. God knows I try." My mother said something I could not hear, and my father cried out louder. "What must a man do, tell me that?"

"Look, we ain't starving. I git paid every week, and Mrs. Ellis is real nice about giving me things. She gonna let me have Mr. Ellis's old coat for you this winter—"

"Forget Mr. Ellis's coat! And forget his money! You think I want white folks' leavings? Oh, Maybelle"—and suddenly he sobbed, loudly and painfully, and cried helplessly and hopelessly in the dark night. I had never heard a man cry before. I did not know men ever cried. I covered my ears with my hands but could not cut off the sound of my father's harsh, painful, despairing sobs. My father was a strong man who would whisk a child upon his shoulders and go singing through the house. My father whittled toys for us and laughed so loud that the great oak seemed to laugh with him, and taught us how to fish and hunt rabbits. How could it be that my father was crying? But the sobs went on, unstifled, finally

quieting until I could hear my mother's voice, deep and rich, humming softly as she used to hum to a frightened child.

The world had lost its boundary lines. My mother, who was small and soft, was now the strength of the family; my father, who was the rock on which the family had been built, was sobbing like the tiniest child. Everything was suddenly out of tune, like a broken accordion. Where did I fit into this crazy picture? I do not now remember my thoughts, only a feeling of great bewilderment and fear.

Long after the sobbing and the humming had stopped, I lay on the pallet, still as stone with my hands over my ears, wishing that I could cry and be comforted. The night was silent now except for the sound of the crickets and of Joey's soft breathing. But the room was too crowded with fear to allow me to sleep, and finally, feeling the terrible aloneness of 4 A.M., I decided to awaken Joey.

"Ouch! What's the matter with you? What you want?" he demanded disagreeably when I had pinched and slapped him awake.

"Come on, wake up."

"What for? Go 'way."

I was lost for a reasonable reply. I could not say, "I'm scared, and I don't want to be alone," so I merely said, "I'm going out. If you want to come, come on."

The promise of adventure awoke him. "Going out now? Where at, Lizabeth? What you going to do?"

I was pulling my dress over my head. Until now I had not thought of going out. "Just come on," I replied tersely.

I was just out the window and halfway down the road before Joey caught up with me.

"Wait, Lizabeth, where you going?"

I was running as if the Furies[7] were after me,

---

7. Furies (fyo͝or' ēz): in Greek and Roman mythology, female spirits with serpentine hair who punished wrongdoers.

as perhaps they were—running silently and furiously until I came to where I had half known I was headed—to Miss Lottie's yard.

The half-dawn light was more eerie than complete darkness, and in it the old house was like the ruin that my world had become—foul and crumbling, a grotesque creature. It looked haunted, but I was not afraid because I was haunted too.

"Lizabeth, you lost your mind?" panted Joey.

I had indeed lost my mind, for all the smoldering emotions of that summer swelled in me and burst—the great need for my mother who was never there, the hopelessness of our poverty and degradation,[8] the bewilderment of being neither child nor woman and yet both at once, the fear unleashed by my father's tears. And these feelings combined in one great impulse toward destruction.

"Lizabeth!"

I leaped furiously into the mounds of marigolds and pulled madly, trampling and pulling and destroying the perfect yellow blooms. The fresh smell of early morning and of dew-soaked marigolds spurred me on as I went tearing and mangling and sobbing while Joey tugged my dress or my waist crying, "Lizabeth stop, please stop!"

And then I was sitting in the ruined little garden among the uprooted and ruined flowers, crying and crying, and it was too late to undo what I had done. Joey was sitting beside me, silent and frightened, not knowing what to say. Then, "Lizabeth, look."

I opened my swollen eyes and saw in front of me a pair of large calloused feet; my gaze lifted to the swollen legs, the age-distorted body clad in a tight cotton night dress, and then the shadowed Indian face surrounded by stubby white hair. And there was no rage in the face now, now that the garden was destroyed and there was nothing any longer to be protected.

"M-miss Lottie!" I scrambled to my feet and just stood there and stared at her, and that was

the moment when childhood faded and womanhood began. The violent, crazy act was the last act of childhood. For as I gazed at the immobile face with sad, weary eyes, I gazed upon a kind of reality that is hidden to childhood. The witch was no longer a witch but only a broken old woman who had dared to create beauty in the midst of ugliness and sterility. She had been born in squalor and had lived in it all her life. Now at the end of that life she had nothing except a falling-down hut, a wrecked body, and John Burke, the mindless son of her passion. Whatever verve there was left in her, whatever was of love and beauty and joy that had not been squeezed out by life, had been there in the marigolds she had so tenderly cared for.

Of course I could not express the things that I knew about Miss Lottie as I stood there awkward and ashamed. The years have put words to the things I knew in that moment, and as I look back upon it, I know that that moment marked the end of innocence. . . . Innocence involves an unseeing acceptance of things at face value, an ignorance of the area below the surface. In that humiliating moment I looked beyond myself and into the depths of another person. This was the beginning of compassion, and one cannot have both compassion and innocence.

The years have taken me worlds away from that time and that place, from the dust and squalor of our lives and from the bright thing that I destroyed in a blind, childish striking out at God-knows-what. Miss Lottie died long ago, and many years have passed since I last saw her hut, completely barren at last, for despite my wild contrition[9] she never planted marigolds again. Yet, there are

---

8. degradation (deg′ rə dā′ shən): a state of corruption and loss of dignity and humanity.
9. contrition (kən trish′ ən): feeling of sorrow or regret for wrong doing.

times when the image of those passionate yellow mounds returns with a painful poignancy. For one does not have to be ignorant and poor to find that one's life is barren as the dusty yards of one's town. And I too have planted marigolds.

Thinking About the Story

A PERSONAL RESPONSE

sharing impressions

1. What was the strongest emotion you felt as you read this story? Write about this emotion in your journal.

constructing interpretations

2. What does Lizabeth mean when she says that she too has planted marigolds?
Think about
- her interpretation of Miss Lottie's reasons for planting marigolds
- her statement that "one does not have to be ignorant and poor to find that one's life is barren as the dusty yards of one's town"
- the "you" she addresses in the second paragraph of the story

3. Why does Lizabeth destroy the marigolds?
Think about
- why the children like to annoy Miss Lottie
- how Lizabeth describes the unhappiness in her family
- how Lizabeth describes being "fourteen-going-on-fifteen"

4. How does the destruction of the marigolds signal the end of Lizabeth's childhood and the beginning of womanhood?

5. How do different characters in the story suffer unhappiness or loss?

A CRITICAL RESPONSE

6. What does the use of flashback add to the story?
Think about
- flashback as an event that happened before the beginning of the story
- how the story might have been different if it had been told by the child Lizabeth right after it happened
- how the incident continues to affect the adult narrator

7. Analyze the sources of the tensions that lead Lizabeth to destroy the marigolds. Support your analysis with examples from the story.

Analyzing the Writer's Craft

SYMBOL

Reread the description of John Burke sitting in front of his mother's house. What does his presence tell you about Miss Lottie's life?

Building a Literary Vocabulary. A symbol is a person, place, object, or activity that stands for something beyond itself. Usually, a son or daughter represents a parent's hopes and dreams for the future. Because of John Burke's infirmities, he is unable to function outside his own dream world, and in this story he can be seen as a symbol of Miss Lottie's frustrated hopes and desires. The narrator describes him as "completing the impression of decay" associated with Miss Lottie and her house.

Application: Analyzing a Symbol. Work in a small group to make a list of what the marigolds mean to Lizabeth, both as the adult narrator and as the child she remembers. Then make a list of what the marigolds mean to Miss Lottie. Compare the lists to analyze how a single symbol can have complex meaning in a story.

Connecting Reading and Writing

1. Draw or find pictures that illustrate the story. Around the pictures create a **cluster diagram** of words associated with the pictures.

Option: Write a **proposal** to the publisher of this story explaining why your pictures would be the best illustrations.

2. Describe an incident in which you expressed your anger, either constructively or destructively. Create a **word search puzzle** of adjectives and verbs you associate with the incident, which might be used in a book of word games.

Option: Write a **script** for a skit that would portray the incident in flashback.

3. Support or challenge this quotation from the story: "One cannot have both compassion and innocence." Using specific examples from your reading and from real life, argue your opinion in a **sermon.**

Option: Argue your opinion in an **editorial**.

4. Analyze Lizabeth's character at fourteen, exploring both her positive and negative qualities. Present your analysis in a teacher's **note** to Lizabeth's parents.

Option: Create a **dialogue** between two of Lizabeth's close friends.

Initiation

SYLVIA PLATH

A biography of Plath appears on page 426.

Approaching the Story

"Initiation" concerns one girl's experience with a high school sorority, a highly selective social club for girls much like a fraternity for boys. As the story opens, Millicent is participating in the sorority's hazing ceremony, a series of humiliating tasks that girls hoping to become members must complete.

Building Vocabulary

These essential words are footnoted within the story.

initiation (i nish′ ē ā′ shen): She could not think of anyone who had ever been invited into the high school sorority and failed to get through **initiation** time. (page 133)

elect (ē lekt′): What girl would not want to be one of the **elect**? (page 133)

malicious (mə lish′ əs): There was something about her tone that annoyed Millicent. It was almost **malicious**. (page 135)

comradeship (käm′ rəd ship′): Why, this was wonderful, the way she felt a sudden **comradeship** with a stranger. (page 137)

prestige (pres tēzh′): "But it sure gives a girl **prestige** value." (page 139)

Connecting Writing and Reading

Most teenagers feel pressured to behave in certain ways. The pressure may come from adults or from friends and classmates. In your journal, name some pressures that you feel and briefly note your response to these pressures. As you read this story, notice the way Millicent responds to pressure to join a sorority.

THE BASEMENT ROOM was dark and warm, like the inside of a sealed jar, Millicent thought, her eyes getting used to the strange dimness. The silence was soft with cobwebs, and from the small, rectangular window set high in the stone wall there sifted a faint bluish light that must be coming from the full October moon. She could see now that what she was sitting on was a woodpile next to the furnace.

Millicent brushed back a strand of hair. It was stiff and sticky from the egg that they had broken on her head as she knelt blindfolded at the sorority altar a short while before. There had been a silence, a slight crunching sound, and then she had felt the cold, slimy egg-white flattening and spreading on her head and sliding down her neck. She had heard someone smothering a laugh. It was all part of the ceremony.

Then the girls had led her here, blindfolded still, through the corridors of Betsy Johnson's house and shut her in the cellar. It would be an hour before they came to get her, but then Rat Court would be all over and she would say what she had to say and go home.

For tonight was the grand finale, the trial by fire. There really was no doubt now that she would get in. She could not think of anyone who had ever been invited into the high school sorority and failed to get through initiation[1] time. But even so, her case would be quite different. She would see to that. She could not exactly say what had decided her revolt, but it definitely had something to do with Tracy and something to do with the heather birds.

What girl at Lansing High would not want to be in her place now? Millicent thought, amused. What girl would not want to be one of the elect,[2] no matter if it did mean five days of initiation before and after school, ending in the climax of Rat Court on Friday night when they made the new girls members? Even Tracy had been wistful when she heard that Millicent had been one of the five girls to receive an invitation.

"It won't be any different with us, Tracy," Millicent had told her. "We'll still go around together like we always have, and next year you'll surely get in."

"I know, but even so," Tracy had said quietly, "you'll change, whether you think you will or not. Nothing ever stays the same."

And nothing does, Millicent had thought. How horrible it would be if one never changed . . . if she were condemned to be the plain, shy Millicent of a few years back for the rest of her life. Fortunately there was always the changing, the growing, the going on.

It would come to Tracy, too. She would tell Tracy the silly things the girls had said, and Tracy would change also, entering eventually into the magic circle. She would grow to know the special ritual as Millicent had started to last week.

"First of all," Betsy Johnson, the vivacious blonde secretary of the sorority, had told the five new candidates over sandwiches in the school cafeteria last Monday, "first of all, each of you has a big sister. She's the one who bosses you around, and you just do what she tells you."

"Remember the part about talking back and smiling," Louise Fullerton had put in, laughing. She was another celebrity in high school, pretty and dark and vice-president of the student council. "You can't say anything unless your big sister asks you something or tells you to talk to someone. And you can't smile, no matter how you're dying to." The girls had laughed a little nervously, and then the bell

---

1. **initiation** (i nish′ ē ā′ shən): a ceremony by which one is admitted as a member into a group or organization.
2. **elect** (ē lekt′): the one, or few, chosen.

had rung for the beginning of afternoon classes.

It would be rather fun for a change, Millicent mused, getting her books out of her locker in the hall, rather exciting to be part of a closely knit group, the exclusive set at Lansing High. Of course, it wasn't a school organization. In fact, the principal, Mr. Cranton, wanted to do away with initiation week altogether, because he thought it was undemocratic and disturbed the routine of school work. But there wasn't really anything he could do about it. Sure, the girls had to come to school for five days without any lipstick on and without curling their hair, and of course everybody noticed them, but what could the teachers do?

Millicent sat down at her desk in the big study hall. Tomorrow she would come to school, proudly, laughingly, without lipstick, with her brown hair straight and shoulder length, and then everybody would know, even the boys would know, that she was one of the elect. Teachers would smile helplessly, thinking perhaps: So now they've picked Millicent Arnold. I never would have guessed it.

A year or two ago, not many people would have guessed it. Millicent had waited a long time for acceptance, longer than most. It was as if she had been sitting for years in a pavilion outside a dance floor, looking in through the windows at the golden interior, with the lights clear and the air like honey, wistfully watching the couples waltzing to the never-ending music, laughing in pairs and groups together, no one alone.

But now at last, amid a week of fanfare and merriment, she would answer her invitation to enter the ballroom through the main entrance marked "Initiation." She would gather up her velvet skirts, her silken train, or whatever the disinherited princesses wore in the story books, and come into her rightful kingdom. . . . The bell rang to end study hall.

"Millicent, wait up!" It was Louise Fullerton behind her, Louise who had always before been very nice, very polite, friendlier than the rest, even long ago, before the invitation had come.

"Listen," Louise walked down the hall with her to Latin, their next class, "are you busy right after school today? Because I'd like to talk to you about tomorrow."

"Sure. I've got lots of time."

"Well, meet me in the hall after homeroom then, and we'll go down to the drugstore or something."

Walking beside Louise on the way to the drugstore, Millicent felt a surge of pride. For all anyone could see, she and Louise were the best of friends.

"You know, I was so glad when they voted you in," Louise said.

Millicent smiled. "I was really thrilled to get the invitation," she said frankly, "but kind of sorry that Tracy didn't get in, too."

Tracy, she thought. If there is such a thing as a best friend, Tracy has been just that this last year.

"Yes, Tracy," Louise was saying, "she's a nice girl, and they put her up on the slate, but . . . well, she had three blackballs against her."

"Blackballs? What are they?"

"Well, we're not supposed to tell anybody outside the club, but seeing as you'll be in at the end of the week I don't suppose it hurts." They were at the drugstore now.

"You see," Louise began explaining in a low voice after they were seated in the privacy of the booth, "once a year the sorority puts up all the likely girls that are suggested for membership. . . ."

Millicent sipped her cold, sweet drink slowly, saving the ice cream to spoon up last. She listened carefully to Louise who was going on," . . . and then there's a big meeting, and all the girls' names are read off and each girl is discussed."

"Oh?" Millicent asked mechanically, her voice sounding strange.

"Oh, I know what you're thinking," Louise laughed. "But it's really not as bad as all that. They keep it down to a minimum of catting.[3] They just talk over each girl and why or why not they think she'd be good for the club. And then they vote. Three blackballs eliminate a girl."

"Do you mind if I ask you what happened to Tracy?" Millicent said.

Louise laughed a little uneasily. "Well, you know how girls are. They notice little things. I mean, some of them thought Tracy was just a bit *too* different. Maybe you could suggest a few things to her."

"Like what?"

"Oh, like maybe not wearing knee socks to school, or carrying that old bookbag. I know it doesn't sound like much, but well, it's things like that which set someone apart. I mean, you know that no girl at Lansing would be seen dead wearing knee socks, no matter how cold it gets, and it's kiddish and kind of green[4] to carry a bookbag."

"I guess so," Millicent said.

"About tomorrow," Louise went on. "You've drawn Beverly Mitchell for a big sister. I wanted to warn you that she's the toughest, but if you get through all right it'll be all the more credit for you."

"Thanks, Lou," Millicent said gratefully, thinking, this is beginning to sound serious. Worse than a loyalty test, this grilling over the coals. What's it supposed to prove anyway? That I can take orders without flinching? Or does it just make them feel good to see us run around at their beck and call?

"All you have to do really," Louise said, spooning up the last of her sundae, "is be very meek and obedient when you're with Bev and do just what she tells you. Don't laugh or talk back or try to be funny, or she'll just make it harder for you, and believe me, she's a great

one for doing that. Be at her house at seven-thirty."

And she was. She rang the bell and sat down on the steps to wait for Bev. After a few minutes the front door opened and Bev was standing there, her face serious.

"Get up, gopher,"[5] Bev ordered.

There was something about her tone that annoyed Millicent. It was almost <u>malicious</u>.[6] And there was an unpleasant anonymity about the label "gopher," even if that was what they always called the girls being initiated. It was degrading, like being given a number. It was a denial of individuality.

Rebellion flooded through her.

"I said get up. Are you deaf?"

Millicent got up, standing there.

"Into the house, gopher. There's a bed to be made and a room to be cleaned at the top of the stairs."

Millicent went up the stairs mutely. She found Bev's room and started making the bed. Smiling to herself, she was thinking: How absurdly funny, me taking orders from this girl like a servant.

Bev was suddenly there in the doorway. "Wipe that smile off your face," she commanded.

There seemed something about this relationship that was not all fun. In Bev's eyes, Millicent was sure of it, there was a hard, bright spark of exultation.

On the way to school, Millicent had to walk behind Bev at a distance of ten paces, carrying her books. They came up to the drugstore where

---

3. catting (kat' iŋ): making mean and spiteful remarks.

4. green: unsophisticated, inexperienced, naive.

5. gopher (gō' fər), also spelled **gofer:** a person expected to run errands and cater to others; a "go for."

6. malicious (mə lish' əs): having, showing, or caused by the desire to harm another or do mischief.

there already was a crowd of boys and girls from Lansing High waiting for the show.

The other girls being initiated were there, so Millicent felt relieved. It would not be so bad now, being part of the group.

"What'll we have them do?" Betsy Johnson asked Bev. That morning Betsy had made her "gopher" carry an old colored parasol through the square and sing "I'm Always Chasing Rainbows."

"I know," Herb Dalton, the good-looking basketball captain, said.

A remarkable change came over Bev. She was all at once very soft and coquettish.

"You can't tell them what to do," Bev said sweetly. "Men have nothing to say about this little deal."

"All right, all right," Herb laughed, stepping back and pretending to fend off a blow.

"It's getting late," Louise had come up. "Almost eight-thirty. We'd better get them marching on to school."

The "gophers" had to do a Charleston[7] step all the way to school, and each one had her own song to sing, trying to drown out the other four. During school, of course, you couldn't fool around, but even then, there was a rule that you mustn't talk to boys outside of class or at lunchtime . . . or any time at all after school. So the sorority girls would get the most popular boys to go up to the "gophers" and ask them out, or try to start them talking, and sometimes a "gopher" was taken by surprise and began to say something before she could catch herself. And then the boy reported her and she got a black mark.

Herb Dalton approached Millicent as she was getting an ice cream at the lunch counter that noon. She saw him coming before he spoke to her, and looked down quickly, thinking: He is too princely, too dark and smiling. And I am much too vulnerable. Why must he be the one I have to be careful of?

I won't say anything, she thought, I'll just smile very sweetly.

She smiled up at Herb very sweetly and mutely. His return grin was rather miraculous. It was surely more than was called for in the line of duty.

"I know you can't talk to me," he said, very low. "But you're doing fine, the girls say. I even like your hair straight and all."

Bev was coming toward them, then, her red mouth set in a bright, calculating smile. She ignored Millicent and sailed up to Herb.

"Why waste your time with gophers?" she caroled gaily. "Their tongues are tied, but completely."

Herb managed a parting shot. "But that one keeps *such* an attractive silence."

Millicent smiled as she ate her sundae at the counter with Tracy. Generally, the girls who were outsiders now, as Millicent had been, scoffed at the initiation antics as childish and absurd to hide their secret envy. But Tracy was understanding, as ever.

"Tonight's the worst, I guess, Tracy," Millicent told her. "I hear that the girls are taking us on a bus over to Lewiston and going to have us performing in the square."

"Just keep a poker face outside," Tracy advised. "But keep laughing like mad inside."

Millicent and Bev took a bus ahead of the rest of the girls; they had to stand up on the way to Lewiston Square. Bev seemed very cross about something. Finally she said, "You were talking with Herb Dalton at lunch today."

"No," said Millicent honestly.

"Well, I *saw* you smile at him. That's practically as bad as talking. Remember not to do it again."

Millicent kept silent.

---

7. **Charleston** (chärls′ tən): a lively dance popular during the 1920's.

"It's fifteen minutes before the bus gets into town," Bev was saying then. "I want you to go up and down the bus asking people what they eat for breakfast. Remember, you can't tell them you're being initiated."

Millicent looked down the aisle of the crowded bus and felt suddenly quite sick. She thought: How will I ever do it, going up to all those stony-faced people who are staring coldly out of the window. . . .

"You heard me, gopher."

"Excuse me, madam," Millicent said politely to the lady in the first seat of the bus, "but I'm taking a survey. Could you please tell me what you eat for breakfast?"

"Why . . . er . . . just orange juice, toast, and coffee," she said.

"Thank you very much." Millicent went on to the next person, a young business man. He ate eggs sunny side up, toast and coffee.

By the time Millicent got to the back of the bus, most of the people were smiling at her. They obviously know, she thought, that I'm being initiated into something.

Finally, there was only one man left in the corner of the back seat. He was small and jolly, with a ruddy, wrinkled face that spread into a beaming smile as Millicent approached. In his brown suit with the forest-green tie he looked something like a gnome or a cheerful leprechaun.

"Excuse me, sir," Millicent smiled, "but I'm taking a survey. What do you eat for breakfast?"

"Heather birds' eyebrows on toast," the little man rattled off.

"*What?*" Millicent exclaimed.

"Heather birds' eyebrows," the little man explained. "Heather birds live on the mythological moors and fly about all day long, singing wild and sweet in the sun. They're bright purple and have *very* tasty eyebrows."

Millicent broke out into spontaneous laugh-ter. Why, this was wonderful, the way she felt a sudden comradeship[8] with a stranger.

"Are you mythological, too?"

"Not exactly," he replied, "but I certainly hope to be someday. Being mythological does wonders for one's ego."

The bus was swinging into the station now; Millicent hated to leave the little man. She wanted to ask him more about the birds.

And from that time on, initiations didn't bother Millicent at all. She went gaily about Lewiston Square from store to store asking for broken crackers and mangoes, and she just laughed inside when people stared and then brightened, answering her crazy ques-tions as if she were quite serious and really a person of consequence.[9] So many people were shut up tight inside themselves like boxes, yet they would open up, unfolding quite wonderfully, if only you were interest-ed in them. And really, you didn't have to belong to a club to feel related to other human beings.

One afternoon Millicent had started talk-ing with Liane Morris, another of the girls being initiated, about what it would be like when they were finally in the sorority.

"Oh, I know pretty much what it'll be like," Liane had said. "My sister belonged before she graduated from high school two years ago."

"Well, just what *do* they do as a club?" Millicent wanted to know.

"Why, they have a meeting once a week . . . each girl takes turns entertaining at her house. . . ."

"You mean it's just a sort of exclusive social group. . . ."

"I guess so . . . though that's a funny way of

---

8. **comradeship** (käm′ rəd ship′): a relationship aris-ing from the sharing of mutual interests and activities.
9. **consequence:** importance or influence.

The Adolescent, 1956, RAPHAEL SOYER.
By permission of the Soyer family.

putting it. But it sure gives a girl prestige[10] value. My sister started going steady with the captain of the football team after she got in. Not bad, I say."

No, it wasn't bad, Millicent had thought, lying in bed on the morning of Rat Court and listening to the sparrows chirping in the gutters. She thought of Herb. Would he ever have been so friendly if she were without the sorority label? Would he ask her out (if he ever did) just for herself, no strings attached?

Then there was another thing that bothered her. Leaving Tracy on the outskirts. Because that is the way it would be; Millicent had seen it happen before.

Outside, the sparrows were still chirping, and as she lay in bed Millicent visualized them, pale gray-brown birds in a flock, one like the other, all exactly alike.

And then, for some reason, Millicent thought of the heather birds. Swooping carefree over the moors, they would go singing and crying out across the great spaces of air, dipping and darting, strong and proud in their freedom and their sometime loneliness. It was then that she made her decision.

Seated now on the woodpile in Betsy Johnson's cellar, Millicent knew that she had come triumphant through the trial of fire, the searing period of the ego which could end in two kinds of victory for her. The easiest of which would be her coronation as a princess, labeling her conclusively as one of the select flock.

The other victory would be much harder, but she knew that it was what she wanted. It was not that she was being noble or anything. It was just that she had learned there were other ways of getting into the great hall, blazing with lights, of people and of life.

It would be hard to explain to the girls tonight, of course, but she could tell Louise later just how it was. How she had proved something to herself by going through everything, even Rat Court, and then deciding not to join the sorority after all. And how she could still be friends with everybody. Sisters with everybody. Tracy, too.

The door behind her opened and a ray of light sliced across the soft gloom of the basement room.

"Hey Millicent, come on out now. This is it." There were some of the girls outside.

"I'm coming," she said, getting up and moving out of the soft darkness into the glare of light, thinking: This is it, all right. The worst part, the hardest part, the part of initiation that I figured out myself.

But just then, from somewhere far off, Millicent was sure of it, there came a melodic fluting, quite wild and sweet, and she knew that it must be the song of the heather birds as they went wheeling and gliding against wide blue horizons through vast spaces of air, their wings flashing quick and purple in the bright sun.

Within Millicent another melody soared, strong and exuberant, a triumphant answer to the music of the darting heather birds that sang so clear and lilting over the far lands. And she knew that her own private initiation had just begun.

---

10. prestige (pres tēzh′): status or reputation.

Thinking About the Story

A PERSONAL RESPONSE

sharing impressions

1. What are your thoughts about Millicent's decision? Briefly note your thoughts in your journal.

constructing interpretations

2. How would you explain the meaning of the last sentence in the story?

3. Why does Millicent make the decision she does?

Think about
- her relationships with Tracy and Bev
- the things she has to do during initiation week
- what she finds out about being in a sorority
- the effect of her conversation with the older man on the bus

4. Compare Millicent's situation with the pressures you wrote about in your prereading journal entry.

5. How does Millicent change during the story?

A CREATIVE RESPONSE

6. If Herb Dalton had told Millicent that he would take her out as soon as she was in the sorority, how might her final decision have been affected?

A CRITICAL RESPONSE

7. Go back through the story and find the point at which you think Millicent begins to change her mind about initiations. Be prepared to explain your answer.

8. What do you think heather birds symbolize for Millicent?

Think about
- how she felt when the man on the bus first spoke of them
- how they are described toward the end of the story
- how they differ from the sparrows she hears outside her window

9. Analyze the way the description in the first two paragraphs prepares the reader for the rest of the story.

Think about
- the feelings you have as you read the paragraphs
- the sights, sounds, and physical sensations that the language conveys
- the comparisons made

Analyzing the Writer's Craft

PSYCHOLOGICAL REALISM

Do you think Millicent's decision is a difficult one for her to make? Think about how you learn about her decision.

Building a Literary Vocabulary. The literary technique in which a writer explores the thoughts of a character confronted by a difficult moral choice is called psychological realism. Sylvia Plath used this technique in portraying Millicent's experience during initiation week. The reader knows what Millicent is thinking and feeling throughout the week and so can follow the way she gradually reaches her decision.

Application: Understanding Psychological Realism. With a partner go through the first half of the story and look for passages that help explain Millicent's reasons for wanting to join a sorority in the first place. List those reasons on a sheet of paper. Then look for passages in the second half that show Millicent beginning to change her mind, and jot down her reasons for not joining a sorority. These two lists give you examples of some of Millicent's needs and desires. Now imagine what she might say in any one of the following situations:

- her appearance before Rat Court
- the next time she meets Herb Dalton
- the next time she meets Bev Mitchell

With your partner act out any one of these scenes in front of the class.

Connecting Reading and Writing

1. Consider how Millicent might feel about her decision after ten years have passed. In an **interview** with Millicent, indicate her thoughts on the subject and the shape her life has taken.

Option: Have Millicent write a **letter** to Tracy recalling her decision.

2. Millicent learns that there are "other ways of getting into the great hall, blazing with lights, of people and of life." Explain what she has learned in a **poem.**

Option: Present her views in a brief **essay** that she might write on a college application.

3. Should sororities and fraternities be allowed in high schools, as they were in the 1950's? Take a position and argue it in a **speech.**

Option: Write a **newspaper editorial** arguing your position.

Through the Tunnel

DORIS LESSING

A biography of Lessing appears on page 424.

Approaching the Story

Jerry, the main character of "Through the Tunnel," is an English boy of eleven on a seaside vacation with his widowed mother. This story takes place in a foreign country, but Jerry's experience is something all young people can understand.

Building Vocabulary

These essential words are footnoted within the story.

contrition (kən trish′ ən): **Contrition** sent him running after her. (page 143)

supplication (sup′ lə kā′ shən): He had swum in and was on the rocks beside them, smiling with a desperate, nervous **supplication**. (page 144)

defiant (dē fī′ ənt), **beseeching** (bē sēch′ iŋ): "I want some swimming goggles," he panted, **defiant** and **beseeching**. (page 145)

incredulous (in krej′ o͞o ləs): He was **incredulous** and then proud to find he could hold his breath without strain for two minutes. (page 146)

Connecting Writing and Reading

Think about times in your life when you took risks to achieve something. What did you risk losing? In your journal, list risks that you have taken and evaluate whether each risk was worth taking. As you read this story, compare Jerry's risks with yours.

GOING TO THE shore on the first morning of the vacation, the young English boy stopped at a turning of the path and looked down at a wild and rocky bay, and then over the crowded beach he knew so well from other years. His mother walked on in front of him, carrying a bright striped bag in one hand. Her other arm, swinging loose, was very white in the sun. The boy watched that white, naked arm, and turned his eyes, which had a frown behind them, toward the bay and back again to his mother. When she felt he was not with her, she swung around. "Oh, there you are, Jerry!" she said. She looked impatient, then smiled. "Why, darling, would you rather not come with me? Would you rather—" She frowned, conscientiously worrying over what amusements he might secretly be longing for, which she had been too busy or too careless to imagine. He was very familiar with that anxious, apologetic smile. Contrition[1] sent him running after her. And yet, as he ran, he looked back over his shoulder at the wild bay; and all morning, as he played on the safe beach, he was thinking of it.

Next morning, when it was time for the routine of swimming and sunbathing, his mother said, "Are you tired of the usual beach, Jerry? Would you like to go somewhere else?"

"Oh, no!" he said quickly, smiling at her out of that unfailing impulse of contrition—a sort of chivalry. Yet, walking down the path with her, he blurted out, "I'd like to go and have a look at those rocks down there."

She gave the idea her attention. It was a wild-looking place, and there was no one there; but she said, "Of course, Jerry. When you've had enough, come to the big beach. Or just go straight back to the villa, if you like." She walked away, that bare arm, now slightly reddened from yesterday's sun, swinging. And he almost ran after her again, feeling it unbearable that she should go by herself, but he did not.

She was thinking, Of course he's old enough to be safe without me. Have I been keeping him too close? He mustn't feel he ought to be with me. I must be careful.

He was an only child, eleven years old. She was a widow. She was determined to be neither possessive nor lacking in devotion. She went worrying off to her beach.

As for Jerry, once he saw that his mother had gained her beach, he began the steep descent to the bay. From where he was, high up among red-brown rocks, it was a scoop of moving bluish green fringed with white. As he went lower, he saw that it spread among small promontories and inlets of rough, sharp rock, and the crisping, lapping surface showed stains of purple and darker blue. Finally, as he ran sliding and scraping down the last few yards, he saw an edge of white surf and the shallow, luminous movement of water over white sand and, beyond that, a solid, heavy blue.

He ran straight into the water and began swimming. He was a good swimmer. He went out fast over the gleaming sand, over a middle region where rocks lay like discolored monsters under the surface, and then he was in the real sea—a warm sea where irregular cold currents from the deep water shocked his limbs.

When he was so far out that he could look back not only on the little bay but past the promontory that was between it and the big beach, he floated on the buoyant surface and looked for his mother. There she was, a speck of yellow under an umbrella that looked like a slice of orange peel. He swam back to shore, relieved at being sure she was there, but all at once very lonely.

On the edge of a small cape that marked the side of the bay away from the promontory was a loose scatter of rocks. Above them, some boys were stripping off their clothes. They

---

1. contrition (kən trish′ ən): a feeling of sorrow for doing wrong.

came running, naked, down to the rocks. The English boy swam toward them, but kept his distance at a stone's throw. They were of that coast; all of them were burned smooth dark brown and speaking a language he did not understand. To be with them, of them, was a craving that filled his whole body. He swam a little closer; they turned and watched him with narrowed, alert dark eyes. Then one smiled and waved. It was enough. In a minute, he had swum in and was on the rocks beside them, smiling with a desperate, nervous supplication.[2] They shouted cheerful greetings at him; and then, as he preserved his nervous, uncomprehending smile, they understood that he was a foreigner strayed from his own beach, and they proceeded to forget him. But he was happy. He was with them.

They began diving again and again from a high point into a well of blue sea between rough, pointed rocks. After they had dived and come up, they swam around, hauled themselves up, and waited their turn to dive again. They were big boys—men, to Jerry. He dived, and they watched him; and when he swam around to take his place, they made way for him. He felt he was accepted and he dived again, carefully, proud of himself.

Soon the biggest of the boys poised himself, shot down into the water, and did not come up. The others stood about, watching. Jerry, after waiting for the sleek brown head to appear, let out a yell of warning; they looked at him idly and turned their eyes back toward the water. After a long time, the boy came up on the other side of a big dark rock, letting the air out of his lungs in a sputtering gasp and a shout of triumph. Immediately the rest of them dived in. One moment, the morning seemed full of chattering boys; the next, the air and the surface of the water were empty. But through the heavy blue, dark shapes could be seen moving and groping.

Jerry dived, shot past the school of under-water swimmers, saw a black wall of rock looming at him, touched it, and bobbed up at once to the surface, where the wall was a low barrier he could see across. There was no one visible; under him, in the water, the dim shapes of the swimmers had disappeared. Then one, and then another of the boys came up on the far side of the barrier of rock, and he understood that they had swum through some gap or hole in it. He plunged down again. He could see nothing through the stinging salt water but the blank rock. When he came up the boys were all on the diving rock, preparing to attempt the feat again. And now, in a panic of failure, he yelled up, in English, "Look at me! Look!" and he began splashing and kicking in the water like a foolish dog.

They looked down gravely, frowning. He knew the frown. At moments of failure, when he clowned to claim his mother's attention, it was with just this grave, embarrassed inspection that she rewarded him. Through his hot shame, feeling the pleading grin on his face like a scar that he could never remove, he looked up at the group of big brown boys on the rock and shouted, *"Bonjour! Merci! Au revoir! Monsieur, monsieur!"*[3] while he hooked his fingers round his ears and waggled them.

Water surged into his mouth; he choked, sank, came up. The rock, lately weighted with boys, seemed to rear up out of the water as their weight was removed. They were flying down past him, now, into the water; the air was full of falling bodies. Then the rock was empty in the hot sunlight. He counted one, two, three. . . .

At fifty, he was terrified. They must all be drowning beneath him, in the watery caves of

---

2. supplication (sup′ lə kā′ shən): a humble request, prayer, or petition.

3. *Bonjour! Merci! Au revoir! Monsieur, monsieur!* (bon zh‾o‾or′ mer sē′ ō′ rə vwär′ mə syʉr′) *French:* Good day! Thank you! Goodbye! Sir, sir!

the rock! At a hundred, he stared around him at the empty hillside, wondering if he should yell for help. He counted faster, faster, to hurry them up, to bring them to the surface quickly, to drown them quickly—anything rather than the terror of counting on and on into the blue emptiness of the morning. And then, at a hundred and sixty, the water beyond the rock was full of boys blowing like brown whales. They swam back to the shore without a look at him.

He climbed back to the diving rock and sat down, feeling the hot roughness of it under his thighs. The boys were gathering up their bits of clothing and running off along the shore to another promontory. They were leaving to get away from him. He cried openly, fists in his eyes. There was no one to see him, and he cried himself out.

It seemed to him that a long time had passed, and he swam out to where he could see his mother. Yes, she was still there, a yellow spot under an orange umbrella. He swam back to the big rock, climbed up, and dived into the blue pool among the fanged and angry boulders. Down he went, until he touched the wall of rock again. But the salt was so painful in his eyes that he could not see.

He came to the surface, swam to shore, and went back to the villa to wait for his mother. Soon she walked slowly up the path, swinging her striped bag, the flushed, naked arm dangling beside her. "I want some swimming goggles," he panted, defiant[4] and beseeching.[5]

She gave him a patient, inquisitive look as she said casually, "Well, of course, darling."

But now, now, now! He must have them this minute, and no other time. He nagged and pestered until she went with him to a shop. As soon as she had bought the goggles, he grabbed them from her hand, as if she were going to claim them for herself, and was off, running down the steep path to the bay.

Jerry swam out to the big barrier rock, adjusted the goggles, and dived. The impact of the water broke the rubber-enclosed vacuum, and the goggles came loose. He understood that he must swim down to the base of the rock from the surface of the water. He fixed the goggles tight and firm, filled his lungs, and floated, face down, on the water. Now, he could see. It was as if he had eyes of a different kind—fish eyes that showed everything clear and delicate and wavering in the bright water.

Under him, six or seven feet down, was a floor of perfectly clean, shining white sand, rippled firm and hard by the tides. Two grayish shapes steered there, like long, rounded pieces of wood or slate. They were fish. He saw them nose toward each other, poise motionless, make a dart forward, swerve off, and come around again. It was like a water dance. A few inches above them the water sparkled as if sequins were dropping through it. Fish again—myriads of minute fish, the length of his fingernail, were drifting through the water, and in a moment he could feel the innumerable tiny touches of them against his limbs. It was like swimming in flaked silver. The great rock the big boys had swum through rose sheer out of the white sand—black, tufted lightly with greenish weed. He could see no gap in it. He swam down to its base.

Again and again he rose, took a big chestful of air, and went down. Again and again he groped over the surface of the rock, feeling it, almost hugging it in the desperate need to find the entrance. And then, once, while he was clinging to the black wall, his knees came up and he shot his feet out forward and they met no obstacle. He had found the hole.

He gained the surface, clambered about the stones that littered the barrier rock until he found a big one, and, with this in his arms, let himself down over the side of the rock. He

---

4. defiant (dē fī′ ənt): with bold opposition and willingness to challenge or fight.

5. beseeching (bē sēch′ iŋ): earnestly asking, begging.

dropped, with the weight, straight to the sandy floor. Clinging tight to the anchor of stone, he lay on his side and looked in under the dark shelf at the place where his feet had gone. He could see the hole. It was an irregular, dark gap; but he could not see deep into it. He let go of his anchor, clung with his hands to the edge of the hole, and tried to push himself in.

He got his head in, found his shoulders jammed, moved them in sidewise, and was inside as far as his waist. He could see nothing ahead. Something soft and clammy touched his mouth; he saw a dark frond moving against the grayish rock, and panic filled him. He thought of octopuses, of clinging weed. He pushed himself out backward and caught a glimpse, as he retreated, of a harmless tentacle of seaweed drifting in the mouth of the tunnel. But it was enough. He reached the sunlight, swam to shore, and lay on the diving rock. He looked down into the blue well of water. He knew he must find his way through that cave, or hole, or tunnel, and out the other side.

First, he thought, he must learn to control his breathing. He let himself down into the water with another big stone in his arms, so that he could lie effortlessly on the bottom of the sea. He counted. One, two, three. He counted steadily. He could hear the movement of blood in his chest. Fifty-one, fifty-two. . . . His chest was hurting. He let go of the rock and went up into the air. He saw that the sun was low. He rushed to the villa and found his mother at her supper. She said only "Did you enjoy yourself?" and he said "Yes."

All night the boy dreamed of the water-filled cave in the rock, and as soon as breakfast was over he went to the bay.

That night, his nose bled badly. For hours he had been under water, learning to hold his breath, and now he felt weak and dizzy. His mother said, "I shouldn't overdo things, darling, if I were you."

That day and the next, Jerry exercised his lungs as if everything, the whole of his life, all that he would become, depended upon it. Again his nose bled at night, and his mother insisted on his coming with her the next day. It was a torment to him to waste a day of his careful self-training, but he stayed with her on that other beach, which now seemed a place for small children, a place where his mother might lie safe in the sun. It was not his beach.

He did not ask for permission, on the following day, to go to his beach. He went, before his mother could consider the complicated rights and wrongs of the matter. A day's rest, he discovered, had improved his count by ten. The big boys had made the passage while he counted a hundred and sixty. He had been counting fast, in his fright. Probably now, if he tried, he could get through the long tunnel, but he was not going to try yet. A curious, most unchildlike persistence, a controlled impatience, made him wait. In the meantime, he lay underwater on the white sand, littered now by stones he had brought down from the upper air, and studied the entrance to the tunnel. He knew every jut and corner of it, as far as it was possible to see. It was as if he already felt its sharpness about his shoulders.

He sat by the clock in the villa, when his mother was not near, and checked his time. He was incredulous[6] and then proud to find he could hold his breath without strain for two minutes. The words "two minutes," authorized by the clock, brought close the adventure that was so necessary to him.

In another four days, his mother said casually one morning, they must go home. On the day before they left, he would do it. He would do it if it killed him, he said defiantly to himself. But two days before they were to leave—a day of triumph when he increased his count by fifteen—his nose bled so badly that he turned dizzy and had to lie limply over the big rock like a bit of seaweed, watching the thick red blood flow on to the rock and trickle slowly

---

6. **incredulous** (in krej′ o͞o ləs): doubtful, disbelieving.

down to the sea. He was frightened. Supposing he turned dizzy in the tunnel? Supposing he died there, trapped? Supposing—his head went around, in the hot sun, and he almost gave up. He thought he would return to the house and lie down, and next summer, perhaps, when he had another year's growth in him—*then* he would go through the hole.

But even after he had made the decision, or thought he had, he found himself sitting up on the rock and looking down into the water; and he knew that now, this moment, when his nose had only just stopped bleeding, when his head was still sore and throbbing—this was the moment when he would try. If he did not do it now, he never would. He was trembling with fear that he would not go; and he was trembling with horror at that long, long tunnel under the rock, under the sea. Even in the open sunlight, the barrier rock seemed very wide and very heavy; tons of rock pressed down on where he would go. If he died there, he would lie until one day—perhaps not before next year—those big boys would swim into it and find it blocked.

He put on his goggles, fitted them tight, tested the vacuum. His hands were shaking. Then he chose the biggest stone he could carry and slipped over the edge of the rock until half of him was in the cool, enclosing water and half in the hot sun. He looked up once at the empty sky, filled his lungs once, twice, and then sank fast to the bottom with the stone. He let it go and began to count. He took the edges of the hole in his hands and drew himself into it, wriggling his shoulders in sidewise as he remembered he must, kicking himself along with his feet.

Soon he was clear inside. He was in a small rockbound hole filled with yellowish-gray water. The water was pushing him up against the roof. The roof was sharp and pained his back. He pulled himself along with his hands—fast, fast—and used his legs as levers.

His head knocked against something; a sharp pain dizzied him. Fifty, fifty-one, fifty-two. . . . He was without light, and the water seemed to press upon him with the weight of rock. Seventy-one, seventy-two. . . . There was no strain on his lungs. He felt like an inflated balloon, his lungs were so light and easy, but his head was pulsing.

He was being continually pressed against the sharp roof, which felt slimy as well as sharp. Again he thought of octopuses, and wondered if the tunnel might be filled with weed that could tangle him. He gave himself a panicky, convulsive kick forward, ducked his head, and swam. His feet and hands moved freely, as if in open water. The hole must have widened out. He thought he must be swimming fast, and he was frightened of banging his head if the tunnel narrowed.

A hundred, a hundred and one. . . . The water paled. Victory filled him. His lungs were beginning to hurt. A few more strokes and he would be out. He was counting wildly; he said a hundred and fifteen, and then, a long time later, a hundred and fifteen again. The water was a clear jewel-green all around him. Then he saw, above his head, a crack running up through the rock. Sunlight was falling through it, showing the clean, dark rock of the tunnel, a single mussel shell, and darkness ahead.

He was at the end of what he could do. He looked up at the crack as if it were filled with air and not water, as if he could put his mouth to it to draw in air. A hundred and fifteen, he heard himself say inside his head—but he had said that long ago. He must go on into the blackness ahead, or he would drown. His head was swelling, his lungs cracking. A hundred and fifteen, a hundred and fifteen pounded through his head, and he feebly clutched at rocks in the dark, pulling himself forward, leaving the brief space of sunlit water behind. He felt he was dying. He was no longer quite conscious. He struggled on in the darkness between lapses into unconsciousness. An immense, swelling pain filled his head, and then the darkness cracked with an explosion of green light. His hands, groping forward, met nothing; and his feet, kicking back, propelled him out into the open sea.

He drifted to the surface, his face turned up to the air. He was gasping like a fish. He felt he would sink now and drown; he could not swim the few feet back to the rock. Then he was clutching it and pulling himself up onto it. He lay face down, gasping. He could see nothing but a red-veined, clotted dark. His eyes must have burst, he thought; they were full of blood. He tore off his goggles and a gout of blood went into the sea. His nose was bleeding, and the blood had filled the goggles.

He scooped up handfuls of water from the cool, salty sea, to splash on his face, and did not know whether it was blood or salt water he tasted. After a time, his heart quieted, his eyes cleared, and he sat up. He could see the local boys diving and playing half a mile away. He did not want them. He wanted nothing but to get back home and lie down.

In a short while, Jerry swam to shore and climbed slowly up the path to the villa. He flung himself on his bed and slept, waking at the sound of feet on the path outside. His mother was coming back. He rushed to the bathroom, thinking she must not see his face with bloodstains, or tearstains, on it. He came out of the bathroom and met her as she walked into the villa, smiling, her eyes lighting up.

"Have a nice morning?" she asked, laying her hand on his warm brown shoulder.

"Oh, yes, thank you," he said.

"You look a bit pale." And then, sharp and anxious, "How did you bang your head?"

"Oh, just banged it," he told her.

She looked at him closely. He was strained; his eyes were glazed-looking. She was worried. And then she said to herself, Oh, don't fuss! Nothing can happen. He can swim like a fish.

They sat down to lunch together.

"Mummy," he said, "I can stay under water for two minutes—three minutes, at least." It came bursting out of him.

"Can you, darling?" she said. "Well, I shouldn't overdo it. I don't think you ought to swim any more today."

She was ready for a battle of wills, but he gave in at once. It was no longer of the least importance to go to the bay.

Thinking About the Story

A PERSONAL RESPONSE

sharing impressions

1. In your journal record your reaction to Jerry's swim through the tunnel.

constructing interpretations

2. How does Jerry seem to feel about himself and his swim at the end of the story?

3. Why do you think it is so important to Jerry to swim through the tunnel?

Think about
- his age and family situation
- his interactions with the older boys
- the risks involved

4. How would you describe Jerry's relationship with his mother?

Think about
- the concerns his mother has
- why Jerry is described as both "defiant and beseeching"
- why Jerry doesn't tell his mother about the risk he has taken

A CREATIVE RESPONSE

5. If Jerry had failed to make it through the tunnel (yet had survived the attempt), how might the story have ended?

A CRITICAL RESPONSE

6. What elements of psychological realism do you see in the portrayal of Jerry's struggle?

Think about
- psychological realism as a technique in which the writer reveals the thoughts of a character confronted by a difficult moral choice
- what you know of Jerry's fears and desires at various points in the story
- what, if any, moral choice Jerry makes

7. Describe some rites of passage common today among adolescents and explain what risks are involved.

Analyzing the Writer's Craft

SETTING AND SYMBOL

Jerry notices the contrast between the beach where he and his mother usually swim and the bay where the boys swim. What might these two locations represent to Jerry?

Building a Literary Vocabulary. Setting is the time and place of the action of a story. A symbol is a person, place, object, or activity that stands for something beyond itself. In "Through the Tunnel" key parts of the setting have symbolic meaning. For example, the beach where Jerry and his mother usually go is described as "a place for small children, a place where his mother might lie safe in the sun." This sheltered beach, with its sense of security, seems to represent Jerry's ties to childhood

and dependency—both of which he longs to shed. In contrast, the bay where the older boys swim is bounded by "small promontories and inlets of rough, sharp rock." Jerry is drawn to the wild, rocky bay because for him it represents the danger and mystery of the older, masculine world he wants to be part of.

Application: Interpreting Symbol. Working with two or three classmates, reread the descriptions of the tunnel and of Jerry's feelings about it. On a sheet of paper, list possible symbolic interpretations of the tunnel, supported by evidence from the story. Then present your group's interpretations to the class as an oral presentation.

Connecting Reading and Writing

1. The line between courage and foolishness is often a thin one. Decide whether Jerry's action is brave or foolish and argue your position in a **letter** to Jerry.

Option: Interview twelve classmates and write a **report** summarizing their opinions about the wisdom of Jerry's action.

2. Think of several prominent symbols of maturity and status for teenagers today. Explore the meanings of these symbols in a short **pamphlet** for incoming freshmen.

Option: Write about these symbols in **notes** for a speech for freshmen orientation.

3. Does Jerry's mother allow him too little, just enough, or too much freedom? Explain your response in a **note** to Jerry's mother.

Option: Write a **diary entry** for Jerry in which he gives his opinion about this issue.

4. How do you think Jerry would react if, twenty years from the time of this story, his own son seemed to be drawn to risky behavior? Describe Jerry's response in a **letter** to an advice columnist.

Option: Write a **script** for a conversation between Jerry and his son.

The Cave

JEAN McCORD

A biography of McCord appears on page 425.

Approaching the Story

Like "The Secret Lion," "The Cave" is told in the main character's own words. Charley recounts the central events in the story after having spent three days thinking about them. He speaks directly and conversationally, mentioning names and places as though he assumes the reader will be able to follow his train of thought. In the opening paragraphs, Charley refers to George, whose acquaintance with Charley is the basis for the story.

GEORGE IS GONE. He's either dead, or he's crawled off into one of the deep caves and laid himself down in darkness and silence to die. How long do you think it will take for an old man to die of a broken heart?

I know I'm to blame. I had my part in what happened, except right at the last when the guys went and did what they did. I wasn't in on that, but I might as well have been. It was the same in the end, anyway. When the work and the glory was gone, there was simply no reason for George to go on living.

Why do things happen like that in life? Things you do or cause to be done like me, and you don't even know what's going on, what it really means, at the time.

I was the only one who knew about him at first.

One Saturday morning in early spring, I'd left the house for a run. My bones are growing fast, and sometimes I get these aches in my knees. When I'm all scrunched up behind my desk in school, they ache all the more. The only thing that helps is to get away by myself and run along the banks of the Godalming River. My mother frequently says, "Charles, you eat like a horse these days." What she doesn't know is that I feel like a horse, too. I run along the trails on the riverbank for miles, the blood pounding in my throat, the clap of my hooves beating against the dirt, the wind tickling through my mane, before I finally collapse and throw myself down on the ground, and my hooves turn back into smelly canvas sneakers.

That morning I'd been galloping long and hard to get the kinks out of my knees. The riverbanks are high and steep where we live, overgrown with trees that lean outward and trails that wind along for miles. Once they were animal trails, I think; then the Chippewa Indians lived here and must have used them. Nobody knows all the trails; they run at different levels, dipping and rising with the contour of the banks. I'd gotten a little further than I'd ever been before, changing levels, first up high near the top of the cliffs, then running swiftly downhill by a crosstrail. I'd suddenly seen a new path angling up from the river road, had swung into it, and loped along uphill as far as I could until a stitch in my side made me stop.

There was a spring there, bubbling up into a little pool under the roots of a tree. I leaned over and drank like a horse drinks, lips barely touching water, sucking it up noisily. The water was as clear as sunlight, and cold, and tasted slightly brown from the leaves lying in it.

When I raised my head I was looking up the hill about twenty feet, and I saw something hidden behind some brush. I wish now I'd gone on and let it be, but my curiosity always drives me like I was some snoopy girl, fingering something in her best friend's dresser drawer. I went soundlessly up the hill in my sneakers, noticing there were no steps or trail to give this away, whatever it was. I got up to it and found it was the mouth of a cave, high on the hill with a perfect view up and down the river. It had been boarded over with two-by-fours and some rough, river-washed planks. A skinny door hung slightly open on leather hinges.

I started to stick my nose in the crack when, just then, a voice remarked behind my back, "Looking for something?" and I spun around so fast and so guilty I almost fell down the hill.

There was an old man sitting casually under a tree and keeping so still that I hadn't even seen him. But he had been watching me, probably since the moment I'd stopped to drink.

He looked so weird I recognized him right away for what he was, a bum, yet he wasn't like any other bum I'd ever seen. His hair was long and tangled, falling almost to his shoulders like a Bible prophet's, and his face was a mass of porcupine bristles, not having been shaved in weeks. His nose was a narrow, anxious-looking beak, but his brown eyes were as soft as the spring water, and his mouth was clamped on the broken stub of a pipe, unlit. I

took time to look him over instead of bolting as had been my first intention since there was that look in his eye that told me he was harmless. Besides, what was there to be afraid of? I hadn't done anything.

"Sit down, boy, if you like." He motioned me over.

I went and squatted, looking up and down at the view companionably.

After a while he spoke again. "Got a name?"

I almost said, "Yes, sir, Charles," but I stopped myself. "Charley," I grunted.

"Good name," he said. "Long lineage;[1] way back. You heard of Charlemagne?"[2]

"Yes." I looked at him curiously. I'd studied that in history class, but where had he heard about the guy?

"Same name. Means Charley the Greatest. A royal name. Dozens of crowned heads answered to it."

"Oh yeah?" I was interested in spite of myself. Now why hadn't the teacher mentioned that? It might have made that history class a little easier to take. But our history teacher always droned on, reading from our textbook like he was a hive of bees on a warm day. After a while, your ears got hypnotized and heard what he was saying, but the meaning was completely gone.

"Got a pretty royal name myself," the old bum was saying. "George. Same as six kings of England, two of Greece, a Pres. of the U.S. of A., and a saint who was quite a dragon hunter.[3] Not that it's ever brought me much."

---

1. **lineage** (lin′ ē ij): descent from an ancestor; family line.
2. **Charlemagne** (shär′ lə mān′): King of the Franks and emperor of the Roman Empire who lived from A.D. 742 to 814.
3. **a saint . . . dragon hunter:** the patron saint of England, a reference to St. George, a legendary dragon slayer.

He was looking ruefully at his pipe, which was quite empty. And then to make it look funny and make me laugh, which I did, he wriggled his big toe, which was sticking clean out of the tip of one shoe. I wished I had some tobacco to give him, but I didn't. Maybe another time.

"You live in there?" I jerked my thumb at the boards hiding the cave.

"Well, let's just say it's my Passport to Paradise."

Urrgh, I thought, this old boy's got a few bats flying round in his belfry. But he had my curiosity aroused again, just the same. I'll come back tomorrow and bring him some tobacco, I thought. I can take some from my Dad and he'll never miss it.

As it happened, I didn't return the next day because my folks made me go with them to visit Aunt Margaret.

A week later, Saturday again, I wrapped some tobacco in a handkerchief and headed back to see old George. Usually I would have gone to the clubhouse and spent the day with my gang. I belong to the Jesse James[4] gang. When you live in a city like ours where all the tough kids seem jammed together on the South Side, you either join a gang or get your head knocked off. We're not really fierce guys, not like some of the gangs you read about in other parts of the country. We don't have police records, and we don't go in for mugging or robbery or any of that stuff. We just got together for protection, you might say, and it depends mostly on where a guy lives as to what gang he'll belong to. The toughest gang of all live down on the river flats and call themselves the River Rats. We all stay away from them, much as we can. The River Rats are . . . well, I just wouldn't have wanted to belong to them, not then.

I was walking on the new trail leading to George's place, going slowly so I could look at the sun shining through the trees with a green light. I felt a sudden prickle of cold air on my neck, and the coolness led me like the flow of a little stream falling downhill, right to a small opening that slanted down into the ground. I knew it was the air hole for some cave, a new one, one I'd never been in. You see, the cliffs are made of limestone, and waters trickling down through them for millions of years have cut out many caves. The mouths of the large ones are down at the present river level, and they are mostly all in use as mushroom caves. There are huge steel doors blocking them off, and the mushroom growers have made long beds inside of dirt and manure. Dim electric lights swing down the middle, and the temperature is always a cool 55° which is perfect for mushrooms but chilly for a person.

My gang had been in lots of mushroom caves, but we had to sneak in by the air holes and stand a chance of getting caught by the mushroom growers. They would shout at us, threatening to call the police if they saw us in the shadowy darkness of their stinking caves, thinking we were going to steal their old toadstools. Who wanted them? We never even touched them, except to kick over a few once in a while. The stuff they grew in was too much for us. Outside the caves were big banks of manure, steaming in the cool drafts and smelling like something you'd rather not even get close to.

For a long time now we'd been looking for an unused cave, one we could keep secret for ourselves. We wanted to hold meetings there, safe from the other neighborhood gangs, have initiations, and just sit around in the darkness lit up by a warm fire and chew the fat. We were pretty sure there were a few caves not grabbed off by the mushroom tycoons if we could just find them.

This was it. I knew when I brushed the dirt

---

4. **Jesse James:** U.S. outlaw who lived from 1847 to 1882.

away a little and peered down into the darkness leading into the hillside like a large animal's burrow, that this would be our own cave. I would go tell the gang about it.

I ran all the way back, putting my best into being one of the greatest, Man O'War,[5] and made about as good a time as possible for a horse with only two legs.

The gang was all gathered at the usual place, an abandoned coal shed. They were itchy with restlessness, and it made the perfect announcement.

"You're late, Charley," Pat Dalloway, our leader, said out of the side of his mouth. He likes to act like John Dillinger[6] or the head of the Mafia. He narrowed his eyes while I was giving the details of my discovery.

"What are we waiting for?" Butts yelped. He's a barky type, like a scared dog, and lives on the far side of town. He's only in our Jesse James gang because he's Pat Dalloway's cousin.

"Lead on, boy!" "Let's go!" Chunky and Ted and the others were yelling.

They followed me, a pounding troop at my heels, though we had to stop several times for Chunky to catch his breath.

We clustered round at the spot, and Pat fell on his knees and stuck his head into the hole. He pulled it out again quickly. "It's a good one, Charley," he said with a grin at the gang, "and since you were the finder, to you goes the honor."

I opened my mouth to protest because going into a cave for the first time is always scary. You know such things as saber-toothed tigers and floating ghosts don't really exist, but when you are in total darkness in an unknown place with only a small flashlight, you become suddenly positive they not only do, they are breathing down your neck that instant.

"No, no, we can't have it any other way, can we, boys?" Pat said as he saw my face.

I could only swallow and shrug, but I thought to myself, OK Dalloway, but a couple

more times like this and I'll be ready to take over the gang. It takes guts to be the leader, and Pat seemed to be slacking up a bit.

I took one flashlight in my hand and dropped another inside my shirt. Then I stuck my head in the hole and lay down on my stomach. I was prepared for a gentle, short drop that would end in a small cave from which I'd holler back at the others to "come on in."

Only, after wriggling in till my feet were out of sight of the gang, this little hole took me by surprise and suddenly slanted down at a swift angle. There was nothing to grab at along the way, just the soft sandstone walls worn into smoothness by the ancient waters. I slid down the hole like I was on one of those little tin chutes at a kid's playground, and it occurred to me, sliding like an otter, trying to drag my elbows and toes into the unyielding walls, that I could pop out of this into a really big cave with a nice little drop of maybe a couple hundred feet. I groaned. Why hadn't I had the sense to tie a rope around my waist and have the gang lower me easy? I'd never make a leader because I didn't have any brains, and a voice seemed to tell me I was going to have even fewer in a couple seconds.

I dropped on into what seemed the center of the earth and, when I'd given up hope, rolled out of that chute like a marble and fell about three feet to bounce on soft, cool sand. The flashlight shot out of my hand pointing away from me, its puny beam lost in the vastness of this black cavern. I sat there rubbing my hands and stomach to ease the smarting and feeling myself, but I was OK. However, the thought occurred to me before I even reached for the light, how was I going to get out? That hole was too steep and smooth to

---

5. **Man O' War:** a famous racehorse.
6. **John Dillinger** (dil′ in jər): U.S. gangster and bank robber who lived from 1903 to 1934.

climb back up, and something told me the gang wasn't going to follow me in.

I crawled over to the flashlight. When I turned it up towards the ceiling its beam just got lost in the blackness. There was no sound in the cave. It felt as if there had never been a single sound ever in there. I went over to the hole I'd dropped out of and listened up it for the gang. I couldn't hear them. It was so spooky in that huge cave that it felt like I was down among the dead, like in the catacombs[7] I'd read about, and I even looked around a bit, but not too much. I couldn't see anything, just creamy yellow walls and white sand underfoot. I wondered if I was the first person who had ever been in here. It sure looked like it. There wasn't a mark on the walls, and I couldn't see any footprints. My light was wavering around, and I got a <u>desolate</u>[8] feeling that it was going to go out on me.

I knew the guys outside would notify somebody sooner or later, the firemen or police. Even my Dad. Or would they? I began to doubt even that, thinking maybe they might all go on home and be too scared to get themselves into any trouble with the police and might just decide to forget about me. Well, in a place like that, your mind just seems to run away from you.

I had to get out. I turned and started walking, hurrying for what seemed like miles, but there's nothing to judge by, so you don't really know how far. A few steps even seems like a long ways. My flashlight was dimming down, and my fear was growing. I started running, not even watching for anything, just trying to find some new hole, or an end of any kind. The back of my mind kept telling me that most of these big caves had open mouths down on the river level, but I had also heard that some of them emptied out beneath the water. And that would be just great!

The cave was so long and black I felt like Jonah[9] inside his whale. I felt I was going deeper into the earth all the time, but I couldn't tell about that, either. And just when my light was about to go out for good, and I was going to throw myself down and yell in terror for help, I saw a paleness around a bend.

I shot around the corner and found myself in a room about as big as our living room at home. It was still a cave, but someone was living in it. A few scraps of furniture sat around, made-up furniture of boxes and planks and junk. The front of the cave was boarded over with old planks, and a small door swung lazily on leather hinges.

I stopped right in the middle of it and looked around. And then I saw what was really so different from anyone's living room in a house. The walls were covered with statues. Not the kind carved from wood; these statues were cut right out of the walls in what our art teacher calls bas-relief.[10] They seemed almost to be living beings who were growing out of the rock, and all of them were watching me carefully. I was so glad to see the sunlight through the door, I could only sob with relief. But as usual my curiosity was still with me, so I looked around. On one wall I could recognize certain figures. One was Lincoln, surely, with his big nose and sad eyes. Next to him was George Washington, I thought. Another wall held a crucifixion scene with bent-over people seeming to writhe at the foot of it. Next to that was, holy cow, a real masterpiece, I thought in slow admiration. A guy on a horse, both of them wearing armor, was spearing a

---

7. **catacombs** (kat′ ə kōmz′): a series of galleries in an underground burial place.

8. **desolate** (des′ ə lit): miserable; comfortless.

9. **Jonah** (jō′ nə): a Hebrew prophet who was tossed overboard during a storm and was swallowed by a great fish.

10. **bas-relief** (bä′ ri lēf′) *French*: sculpture in which figures are carved in a flat surface so that they project only a little from the background.

dragon who was lashing around with claws and scales all over him. They were all big, more than life-size, and you could see that somebody had put an awful lot of work into them.

As I walked towards the swinging door, it struck me then. I'd seen that door before. I stepped through it, looked around feeling terribly foolish, and found myself staring right into George's startled eyes. I guess he'd never seen anyone walk out of his cave before.

"Hey!" he said.

"Yeah, I know." I waved my hand backwards. "I got lost." I grinned feebly. "A wicked witch changed me into a rabbit, and a dog chased me down a hole, and, well, here I am. . . ."

It was the best I could do, seeing I was so happy I wanted to run over and shake both his hands.

George looked at me a minute, then he laughed. "You're all right, kid," he said. "I told you Charley was a lucky name. Come and sit. You look pretty fagged out."

I stretched out beside him in the sun and squirmed with the pure pleasure of it on my body. Somewhere back in there I had thought I was doomed to wander in darkness for the rest of my life, which in that dry cave didn't seem to be too long to go. It was only when I rolled over on my stomach, wanting to hug the ground, that I felt the extra flashlight biting into me.

"What time is it?" I asked, my face against the dirt.

George squinted at the sun. "Mebbe two o'clock, or so."

I sighed. I'd been in the cave less than half an hour. It had seemed like days.

"That's pretty good stuff in there," I said cautiously. "It looks like . . . well . . . like a regular art gallery."

George looked down at his hands. They were square and blocky with dirt under the nails. "It fills my time," he said. He stared at

them for a long time. Finally, gazing down the river, he said quietly, "Look, Charley. I don't pay no rent on that cave, but it's mine just the same. I found it first. I fixed it up. Been here over five years now, and I got a lot more work to do. I'm just beginning to get good." He looked at me, and I could actually see the pleading in his eyes. "If people knew about me, they'd come and drive me out. Against the law, or if it ain't, they'd make one. Now why don't you just go on home and keep your mouth shut. Here. Take this." He handed me a little bit of wood that he had been working on when I'd stepped out of his home. It was a tiny carved fawn, its legs folded under itself and its head bent like it was hiding from dogs who were hunting it.

"Well, gee. Thanks. Thanks a lot." I got up and stood there, tongue-tied. I wanted to say I was sorry I'd intruded, that it was just to save my neck, that I had to come out that way. But he must have known. After all, he knew that cave better than I did, and right then he was welcome to it, all of it. I had no intention of telling anyone; certainly not the gang, but I had to get back to them before they got up a lot of people looking for me.

I plunged down George's hill and onto the trail leading back to where I'd left the others. I ran pretty well. Maybe I'd never beat Man O'War in a straightaway, but I could sure make him blow a little on the curves. If he was still around, that is.

When I got to where I'd left the gang, I slowed down and sauntered up to them. They were all in a knot with serious looks on their faces, and when they turned around, their jaws dropped.

"You lily-livered chickens doing anything to get me out of there?" I blustered at them.

"Hey, Charley! Charley, old boy. We thought you were a goner, sure!" They were all shouting at once and pounding me on the back.

"You been in there before, wise guy, ain't you?" Pat scowled at me. "Tried to be smart. Snuck out another way and let us think you were lost." He was really mad. Some of the guys must have been riding him about getting some help to rescue me. His leadership was toppling, all right. Any day soon, now, Dalloway, I thought, I'm gonna fight you and win. I flexed my arm muscles. They felt good and tight to me.

But at the same time I was thinking desperately. What was I going to tell them to make them stay out of the cave? I had to think up a story, and a good one, quick. "Look," I said. "It ain't even a cave. It's just a kind of tunnel, not big enough for a cat. It goes down a long ways, straight, and then winds around and comes out behind the bend over there, somewhere. I didn't even mark it."

"You were gone too long," Pat said, shoving his face next to mine.

"I was scrabbling along on my belly, the whole way. See?" I showed them the raw marks on my arms and stomach. "It never gets more than two feet high, or wide. It ain't worth beans." I turned. "Come on. Let's go home. I'm starved."

"What you got in your hand, Charley? You must have found something."

I stared at my own hand like I'd never seen it before. I hadn't thought to put the little carving in my pocket. Then I did a stupid thing, which makes me think I'll never be fit to be a leader for a pack of mangy dogs. Instead of blustering it out, I gave a leap downhill and started running hard. With a head start none of them could catch me, and I raced along as fast as I'd ever run in my life before. I could hear them for a while pounding along almost at my back, but one by one, I outran them and got to my home.

I sped up to my bedroom, and in a couple minutes I could hear them all outside, hollering at me, "Charley, hey, come on out. We want to talk to you." But I wouldn't go.

Then I stayed away from the gang for a while. I'd see the fellows in school since we were in the same classes, but I didn't go to the clubhouse nor join them at the drugstore like I always had. And that seemed funny. To me, who had been thinking of taking over the gang any day, and to them, too, because they couldn't figure it out. There was no real reason except I thought I'd try being an individual for a change, instead of just one of a group who all did and thought the same things. And that mostly what Pat Dalloway said to do and think.

I took to visiting old George as often as I had time for it. He was a pretty smart old buzzard, and he seemed to know some secret about life. What I mean is, he had kind of come to terms with life, and he had made all the conditions. He sure didn't work, since every time I ever went there, except once, he was either outside looking at his view, possessing it, kind of, or in his cave doing a carving. He had started a new one of Knute Rockne,[11] which was going to be really great. He let me come into his place now and sit on the bunch of planks and old rags that was his bed. If I just sat and watched him and didn't ask a lot of nosy questions, he ignored me and went on with his work. I usually brought him some tobacco and whatever I could sneak out of the refrigerator behind my Mom's back. I guess she thought I'd suddenly developed a tapeworm because she'd look funny at me and frown once in a while, but never said anything.

At first I pried him a little. "Say, George, what you been doing all your life?"

"My life, boy? I lost it. Laid it down for a little and when I went back looking for it, it was too late. Gone. Just like that." He snapped his fingers.

---

11. Knute Rockne (nō͞ot räk' nē): a famous U.S. football player and coach who lived from 1888 to 1931.

"Where were you the other day?"

"Well, occasionally even an old hermit's got to go down into the morass[12] of humanity." He stepped back viewing his work. "If you can find me another picture of Knute here, why, I'd be might obliged."

"Sure." I knew where there was one. In my Dad's picture album. He'd played football when he was in college and was still crazy about the game.

George looked over at me. His beard was only about a half-inch long now because he'd shaved last week. It must have been the day he was gone, I thought. Wonder where he goes and for what? Maybe he's got some money stashed away in a bank and he goes for some every once in a while. I could see he'd bought a few groceries because they stood out in clear sight on a couple orange crates piled up, but I didn't know how he cooked or if he even bothered to. I knew he got his water from the little spring and kept several cans of it in the cave, which he used to throw on his new carving. It softened up the rock a little.

"You ever going to let people see all this someday?" I asked. "When you're ready, I mean?"

"Maybe I should have done drawings with burnt sticks and red ochre.[13] Of ancient bison and vanished deer. That would have confused a few experts, I'll bet," he answered, almost to himself. If you could call that an answer. That's how George was. I liked being with George. He didn't expect anything of me like my Dad always did, and by now, I was getting pretty fond of the old guy. Oh, I knew he wasn't any Michelangelo,[14] but considering everything, he was pretty good. Lincoln and Washington and St. George and Christ and Knute Rockne and others. I loved the way he mixed them up like they were all friends of each other. Maybe they were.

"You know, Charley boy, " George seemed to be talking to Knute, but I was listening. "I been thinking. That's a big cave in behind

there. Lots of beautiful walls. Nothing ever been done to them. My time . . . my grains of sand . . . are running through pretty fast now." He was silent till I thought he'd forgotten what he was talking about. Then he said, "You ever have a hankering to do a little carving?"

I shook my head "no," but his back was turned and he didn't see me.

"Old, old," he was muttering to Knute, "seventy-five, and that's the full allotment. Might not even get to finish this one." He jabbed at Knute's jaw. "It's a way of life, Charley my boy. The only way; creating things. Let others build the cars and roads and wooden houses. You know how long the cave drawings, the ones in southern France, been around?" He whirled on me with a fierce light in his eye.

I shook my head again.

"Fifteen, maybe twenty thousand years." He glared at me. "How do you like that for beating old Mister Time?"

I got up to go. It was getting late, and I didn't have anything to say to him.

"See you, George."

"Yuh," he grunted.

I didn't go back for three weeks. It was late Spring now, and final exams were coming up. Every time it looked like I was going to stick my nose out the door, either my Mom or Dad pounced on me and made me get to studying. The cave was too far to go to after school and still get home in time for supper, and weekends, like I say, I was kept hopping.

Finally school was out. I'd passed everything, and it was a real relief. I couldn't even stay mad at my parents for making me work

---

12. morass (mə ras'): swamp or bog: often used figuratively.

13. ochre (ō' kər), also spelled **ocher:** clay used as a pigment.

14. Michelangelo (mī' kəl an' jə lō'): an Italian sculptor, painter, and architect who lived from 1475 to 1564.

because otherwise I probably wouldn't have made it.

But now I was free for the whole summer. Maybe next year when I'd be sixteen, I'd get a job of some sort, but this summer was still mine, to use as I wanted. I'd been thinking over the last few weeks that I'd spend most of it with old George. Secretly, I'd begun to think about carving. The old boy had something there. I knew he'd teach me. I thought of that long, beautiful, empty cave. We'd haul in firewood and build us a nice, warming fire which would give us light to work by. Maybe someday we could run in an electric line like the mushroom growers. People would come from all around.

My folks would be so surprised they'd be speechless. "Do you mean our boy Charles did this?" they'd say to George, and old George would grin and say, "Yep."

I took a loaf of bread, a half pound of salami from the cupboard, a pocketful of tobacco from my Dad's stock, and slipped off to the cliffs. Over the edge onto the trails and boy, it sure felt good to be running along them again. The trees were solid green now, and the river was running clean like a band of silver far below. Mourning doves were moaning their sad calls, and spiders had flung their lines across the trails overnight.

Coming up to George's cave, I slowed to catch my breath. When I looked up there, something was terribly wrong. The boards hiding the mouth of the cave were all knocked out, though you still couldn't see it from the trail unless you knew it was there. I stopped to listen a minute, and then I heard voices. I knew those voices.

I burst into George's living room, and the shock of it made me sick to my stomach. The whole cave was a mess, completely torn up. The furniture was busted so it was nothing now but old driftwood boards. A fire had been built right in the middle of the cave out of the orange crates. But worse than that, the statues had been destroyed. The delicate ones, the ones that had been carved out almost full, were knocked completely loose and lay on the cave floor as a pile of broken rubbish. The others had heads and arms missing and could never be fixed. "Looey," cross-eyed and stupid, was lounging on what was left of the beautiful horse; St. George had been scraped out of his saddle completely. The place was dirty. And George was nowhere around.

The gang, my gang, was sitting around smoking and looking smug.[15]

"Welcome to our new clubhouse, Charley old boy," Pat Dalloway said.

"Where's George?" My tongue seemed too thick to talk.

"You mean that old bum?" Pat chuckled. "He cleared out after we knocked up the place."

I stepped forward and kicked aside Knute Rockne's face. My fists were cocked.

"You dirty rats," I screamed. "You dirty, filthy no-good rats! Who gave you the right?"

"Aw, come on, Charley," big fat Chunky was saying. "That old bum didn't own this cave. We got as much right to it. We just chased him out and took over, that's all. You helped. We all went in that air hole and found out it ended here."

And that did it. Inside I was all broken up into little pieces. I knew what the outcome would be before I started, but from where I stood, I leaped at Pat and crashed him to the floor. We fought, slugging each other, biting and gouging, rolling over on top of broken statues. Pat was a pretty dirty fighter. He fought to win; no rules. Once I had him on his back and was choking him, but his hand came up with a fistful of sand right into my eyes. From there on he had it all his way. He fin-

15. **smug** (smug): self-satisfied; convinced of one's own superiority.

ished me off and for good measure gave me a couple extra kicks. No one else interfered. They knew it was between Pat and me.

"Get out," he panted. "You don't belong no more."

Butts and Jim dragged me out and threw me down the hill. My bread and salami had scattered all over. They tossed it after me. "So long, Charley," they said.

When I could move, I picked myself up and hobbled away. I took the trail going downhill. Tomorrow I would have two black eyes. A pretty way to start summer vacation. And my folks were in for a big surprise, all right, a big, fat dentist bill.

But it isn't over yet. In fact, it's just started.

I been lying up in my bedroom for three days now, thinking. My mother brings me hot soup and cries a little when she looks at me. My father wanted to go to the police and prosecute, but I wouldn't tell him anything. This is between me and my old gang.

To do a thing like that . . . to destroy an old man's dream of immortality[16] . . . to tear up what he called his Passport to Paradise . . . well . . . they're going to pay for it, all right.

Tomorrow I'm getting out of bed. I'm going down to the river flats and join that gang that calls themselves the River Rats. I'm going to fight every guy in it till I'm the leader.

Then I'm going to lead them to that cave.

Pat Dalloway . . . you are going to get what's coming to you!

Bill and Ted and Chunky. Jim and Butts and Looey . . . you are in for a big surprise. . . . When we descend on you . . . when we get through with you . . . you are going to feel just like those statues . . . .

---

16. immortality (im' môr tal' i tē): living or lasting forever.

Reviewing Concepts

CHARACTER AND CONFLICT: THE STRUGGLES OF YOUTH

making
connections

In the stories in this unit, young characters struggle against different forces in their lives. Sometimes they struggle against other people—people such as their parents, teachers or neighbors, siblings, or peers of the same age. Sometimes they struggle against themselves, wrestling with troublesome fears or desires. Sometimes the characters are pitted not against individuals but against social conditions, such as poverty or prejudice.

Several conflicts with people emerge in "The Secret Lion." The narrator and his friend Sergio are in conflict with their mothers, who forbid them to go to the places that are most interesting to them and who see no value in the treasures they discover. They are at odds with their teachers, who will not answer the questions they want answered, and with the girls they know, whom they can no longer talk to. They are also in conflict with the golfers, who drive them away from their green "heaven." These conflicts can be categorized on a chart like the one below.

Story	Character(s)	Conflict with Parents	Conflict with Nonrelated Adults	Conflict with Siblings	Conflict with Peers	Conflict with Self	Conflict with Social Conditions
"The Secret Lion"	narrator and Sergio	X	X		X		

Think about the characters and conflicts in the other stories in this unit. Complete the chart begun above, naming the main character in each story and categorizing the conflicts he or she faces.

describing
connections

As you look over your completed chart, you will notice that various characters experience conflicts within the same category. You will find that several characters struggle with their peers, for example. Choose one category of conflict present in two or more stories. Further analyze the struggles faced by the characters, noting whether these struggles have similar causes or similar outcomes. Outline a **speech** that you would make to young people about a particular category of conflict, using the experiences of characters in this unit to illustrate your points.

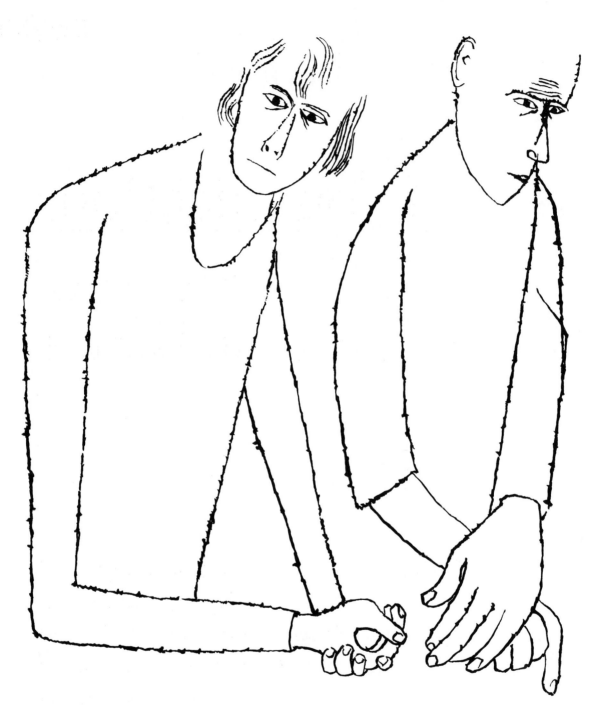

To Parents One Had to Hurt (Rilke Portfolio), 1968, BEN SHAHN.
New Jersey State Museum Collection,
Purchase, FA1968.192m.

Complications:

Stories of Human Nature

"To say that man is made up of strength and weakness, of insight and blindness, of pettiness and grandeur, is not to draw up an indictment against him: it is to define him."

DENIS DIDEROT, 1713-1784
French encyclopedist and philosopher

Complications: Stories of Human Nature

There is a human tendency to make pronouncements about human tendencies: "To err is human," "People are strange," "Woman is a contradiction," "Only man is vile." Rarely do people attribute goodness and wisdom to human nature; more often, they invoke "human nature" to explain greed, envy, stupidity, and countless other weaknesses. "That's just the way folks are" you may have heard someone say, with a helpless shake of the head—certainly fallible, perhaps incomprehensible.

The stories in this unit focus on the irrational, unpredictable, and sometimes twisted side of human nature. The characters, who are often dishonest with themselves and others, get into difficult situations and sometimes make them worse. You will read about aimless young men in India and Brooklyn, proper matrons in Japan, a zealous man in a Greek-American community, a jealous husband in Brazil, and a mysterious Irish landowner in a distant land. As you meet these characters from around the world, you may marvel at what Oscar Wilde once called "that dreadful universal thing called human nature."

Literary Vocabulary

INTRODUCED IN THIS UNIT

Satire. Satire is a literary technique in which ideas, customs, or institutions are ridiculed for the purpose of improving society. Often satire exaggerates a wrong, forcing the reader to see the subject of the satire in a more critical light. One story in this unit, "The Pearl," satirizes the mores, or expected ways of behaving, of modern Japanese society.

Tone. Tone is the attitude a writer takes toward a subject. Style and description in a work of literature help create tone, which might be formal, informal, ironic, angry, serious, or playful. The tone of "The Secret Lion," for example, might be described as both playful and nostalgic, reflecting the writer's ability to recapture events through the eyes of a child.

Character. Characters are the people (and occasionally animals or fantasy creatures) who participate in the action of a literary work. Characters are either main or minor, depending upon the extent of their development and upon their importance in the literary work. In "Marigolds," for example, Elizabeth and Miss Lottie are the main characters; Joey, Elizabeth's parents, and John Burke could be considered minor characters. In any story, one of the main characters is the protagonist, or central character—the one who most arouses the reader's interest and sympathy. Often another main character acts as the antagonist, the force pitted against the protagonist. In "Marigolds" Elizabeth is the protagonist and Miss Lottie is the antagonist. Sometimes a minor character in a story will be a foil, a character who provides a striking contrast to a main character. In "Seventeen Syllables," for example, the refined Mr. Kuroda is a foil for Rosie's work-worn father.

Foreshadowing. Foreshadowing is a writer's use of hints or clues to point to events that will occur later in the plot of a story. Use of this technique creates suspense while preparing the reader for what is to come. At the beginning of "The Heir," for example, Sŏgun, reading to his cousin Sŏkhŭi, is asked by her, "Why did the man leave his home?" Sŏgun does not answer; instead, he blushes and tries to discontinue their reading. The cousin's question and Sŏgun's apparent discomfort foreshadow his own eventual departure from the house of his relatives.

REVIEWED IN THIS UNIT

Theme   **Point of View**

The Pearl

YUKIO MISHIMA

A biography of Mishima appears on page 425.

Approaching the Story

The controversial author of "The Pearl," Yukio Mishima (yōō′ kē ō′ mish′ i mä′), is best known for his commentary on the complex social mores, or accepted ways of behaving, that govern a society's behavior. In Japanese society, for example, the need to "save face" by maintaining dignity in an awkward situation often motivates an individual's actions. This story is set in contemporary Japan and portrays an episode in the lives of five friends from middle-class society.

Building Vocabulary

These essential words are footnoted within the story.

implicitly (im plis′ it lē): [They] could be trusted **implicitly** not to divulge . . . the number of candles on today's cake. (page 167)

incensed (in sensd′): She was **incensed** at a hostess who could create such an impossible situation. (page 168)

loquacious (lō kwā′ shəs): Though normally relaxed and **loquacious** in each other's company, they now lapsed into a long silence. (page 171)

modicum (mäd′ i kəm): There might be a **modicum** of truth even in the assertions of Mrs. Yamamoto. (page 173)

castigation (kas′ ti gā′ shən): There had been times in her **castigation** of that lady when she had allowed herself to be blinded by emotion. (page 173)

Connecting Writing and Reading

Picture yourself in the following situations: (1) You are giving an assigned speech to your class when you realize that your shirt is on inside out. What do you do or say? (2) You are invited to a party that you do not want to attend. How do you get out of going without offending anyone? (3) You attend a social event with the family of a friend. You discover that they expect you to pay your own way, but you have brought no money. What do you do?

What you do in an awkward situation depends in part on the social mores of your society. In this story, too, social expectations influence the actions of characters. As you read, notice the degree to which mores determine behavior.

ECEMBER 10 WAS Mrs. Sasaki's[1] birthday, but since it was Mrs. Sasaki's wish to celebrate the occasion with the minimum of fuss, she had invited to her house for afternoon tea only her closest friends. Assembled were Mesdames Yamamoto, Matsumura, Azuma, and Kasuga[2] —all four being forty-three years of age, exact contemporaries of their hostess.

These ladies were thus members, as it were, of a Keep-Our-Ages-Secret Society and could be trusted <u>implicitly</u>[3] not to divulge to outsiders the number of candles on today's cake. In inviting to her birthday party only guests of this nature, Mrs. Sasaki was showing her customary prudence.

On this occasion Mrs. Sasaki wore a pearl ring. Diamonds at an all-female gathering had not seemed in the best of taste. Furthermore, pearls better matched the color of the dress she was wearing on this particular day.

Shortly after the party had begun, Mrs. Sasaki was moving across for one last inspection of the cake when the pearl in her ring, already a little loose, finally fell from its socket. It seemed a most inauspicious event for this happy occasion, but it would have been no less embarrassing to have everyone aware of the misfortune, so Mrs. Sasaki simply left the pearl close by the rim of the large cake dish and resolved to do something about it later. Around the cake were set out the plates, forks, and paper napkins for herself and the four guests. It now occurred to Mrs. Sasaki that she had no wish to be seen wearing a ring with no stone while cutting this cake, and accordingly she removed the ring from her finger and very deftly, without turning around, slipped it into a recess in the wall behind her back.

Amid the general excitement of the exchange of gossip, and Mrs. Sasaki's surprise and pleasure at the thoughtful presents brought by her guests, the matter of the pearl was very quickly forgotten. Before long it was time for the customary ceremony of lighting and extinguishing the candles on the cake. Everyone crowded excitedly about the table, lending a hand in the not untroublesome task of lighting forty-three candles.

Mrs. Sasaki, with her limited lung capacity, could hardly be expected to blow out all that number at one puff, and her appearance of utter helplessness gave rise to a great deal of hilarious comment.

The procedure followed in serving the cake was that, after the first bold cut, Mrs. Sasaki carved for each guest individually a slice of whatever thickness was requested and transferred this to a small plate, which the guest then carried back with her to her own seat. With everyone stretching out hands at the same time, the crush and confusion around the table was considerable.

On top of the cake was a floral design executed in pink icing and liberally interspersed with small silver balls. These were silver-painted crystals of sugar—a common enough decoration on birthday cakes. In the struggle to secure helpings, moreover, flakes of icing, crumbs of cake, and a number of these silver balls came to be scattered all over the white tablecloth. Some of the guests gathered these stray particles between their fingers and put them on their plates. Others popped them straight into their mouths.

In time all returned to their seats and ate their portions of cake at their leisure, laughing. It was not a homemade cake, having been

---

1. **Sasaki** (sä sä′ kē).
2. **Mesdames Yamamoto, Matsumura, Azuma, and Kasuga** (mā däm′, yä mä mô′ tô, mät soo moo′ rä, ä′ zoo mä, kä′ soo gä): *Mesdames* is the plural form of the French title for a married woman, *Madame*, equivalent to *Mrs.*
3. **implicitly** (im plis′ it lē): absolutely; unquestioningly.

ordered by Mrs. Sasaki from a certain high-class confectioner's, but the guests were unanimous in praising its excellence.

Mrs. Sasaki was bathed in happiness. But suddenly, with a tinge of anxiety, she recalled the pearl she had abandoned on the table, and rising from her chair as casually as she could, she moved across to look for it. At the spot where she was sure she had left it, the pearl was no longer to be seen.

Mrs. Sasaki abhorred losing things. At once and without thinking, right in the middle of the party, she became wholly engrossed in her search, and the tension in her manner was so obvious that it attracted everyone's attention.

"Is there something the matter?" someone asked.

"No, not at all, just a moment. . . ."

Mrs. Sasaki's reply was ambiguous, but before she had time to decide to return to her chair, first one, then another, and finally every one of her guests had risen and was turning back the tablecloth or groping about on the floor.

Mrs. Azuma, seeing this commotion, felt that the whole thing was just too deplorable for words. She was incensed[4] at a hostess who could create such an impossible situation over the loss of a solitary pearl.

Mrs. Azuma resolved to offer herself as a sacrifice and to save the day. With a heroic smile she declared: "That's it then! It must have been a pearl I ate just now! A silver ball dropped on the tablecloth when I was given my cake, and I just picked it up and swallowed it without thinking. It *did* seem to stick in my throat a little. Had it been a diamond, now, I would naturally return it—by an operation, if necessary—but as it's a pearl, I must simply beg your forgiveness."

This announcement at once resolved the company's anxieties, and it was felt, above all, that it had saved the hostess from an embarrassing predicament. No one made any

attempt to investigate the truth or falsity of Mrs. Azuma's confession. Mrs. Sasaki took one of the remaining silver balls and put it in her mouth.

"Mm," she said. "Certainly tastes like a pearl, this one!"

Thus, this small incident, too, was cast into the crucible of good-humored teasing, and there—amid general laughter—it melted away.

When the party was over, Mrs. Azuma drove off in her two-seater sportscar, taking with her in the other seat her close friend and neighbor Mrs. Kasuga. Before two minutes had passed, Mrs. Azuma said, "Own up! It was you who swallowed the pearl, wasn't it? I covered up for you and took the blame on myself."

This unceremonious manner of speaking concealed deep affection, but however friendly the intention may have been, to Mrs. Kasuga a wrongful accusation was a wrongful accusation. She had no recollection whatsoever of having swallowed a pearl in mistake for a sugar ball. She was—as Mrs. Azuma too must surely know—fastidious in her eating habits, and if she so much as detected a single hair in her food, whatever she happened to be eating at the time immediately stuck in her gullet.

"Oh, really now!" protested the timid Mrs. Kasuga in a small voice, her eyes studying Mrs. Azuma's face in some puzzlement. "I just couldn't do a thing like that!"

"It's no good pretending. The moment I saw that green look on your face, I knew."

The little disturbance at the party had seemed closed by Mrs. Azuma's frank confession, but even now it had left behind it this strange awkwardness. Mrs. Kasuga, wondering how best to demonstrate her innocence, was at the same time seized by the fantasy that a solitary pearl was lodged somewhere in her

---

4. **incensed** (in sensd'): extremely angered.

168 Stories of Human Nature

intestines. It was unlikely, of course, that she should mistakenly swallow a pearl for a sugar ball, but in all that confusion of talk and laughter, one had to admit that it was at least a possibility. Though she thought back over the events of the party again and again, no moment in which she might have inserted a pearl into her mouth came to mind—but after all, if it was an unconscious act, one would not expect to remember it.

Mrs. Kasuga blushed deeply as her imagination chanced upon one further aspect of the matter. It had occurred to her that when one accepted a pearl into one's system, it almost certainly—its luster a trifle dimmed, perhaps, by gastric juices—reemerged intact within a day or two.

And with this thought the design of Mrs. Azuma, too, seemed to have become transparently clear. Undoubtedly Mrs. Azuma had viewed this same prospect with embarrassment and shame and had therefore cast her responsibility onto another, making it appear that she had considerately taken the blame to protect a friend.

Meanwhile, Mrs. Yamamoto and Mrs. Matsumura, whose homes lay in a similar direction, were returning together in a taxi. Soon after the taxi had started, Mrs. Matsumura opened her handbag to make a few adjustments to her make-up. She remembered that she had done nothing to her face since all that commotion at the party.

As she was removing the powder compact, her attention was caught by a sudden dull gleam as something tumbled to the bottom of the bag. Groping about with the tips of her fingers, Mrs. Matsumura retrieved the object and saw to her amazement that it was a pearl.

Mrs. Matsumura stifled an exclamation of surprise. Recently her relationship with Mrs. Yamamoto had been far from cordial, and she had no wish to share with that lady a discovery with such awkward implications for herself.

Fortunately, Mrs. Yamamoto was gazing out the window and did not appear to have noticed her companion's momentary start of surprise.

Caught off balance by this sudden turn of events, Mrs. Matsumura did not pause to consider how the pearl had found its way into her bag but immediately became a prisoner of her own private brand of school-captain morality. It was unlikely—she thought—that she would do a thing like this, even in a moment of abstraction. But since, by some chance, the object had found its way into her handbag, the proper course was to return it at once. If she failed to do so, it would weigh heavily upon her conscience. The fact that it was a pearl, too—an article you could call neither all that expensive nor yet all that cheap—only made her position more ambiguous.

At any rate, she was determined that her companion, Mrs. Yamamoto, should know nothing of this incomprehensible development—especially when the affair had been so nicely rounded off, thanks to the selflessness of Mrs. Azuma. Mrs. Matsumura felt she could remain in the taxi not a moment longer, and on the pretext of remembering a promise to visit a sick relative on her way back, she made the driver set her down at once, in the middle of a quiet residential district.

Mrs. Yamamoto, left alone in the taxi, was a little surprised that her practical joke should have moved Mrs. Matsumura to such abrupt action. Having watched Mrs. Matsumura's reflection in the window just now, she had clearly seen her draw the pearl from her bag.

At the party Mrs. Yamamoto had been the very first to receive a slice of cake. Adding to her plate a silver ball which had spilled onto the table, she had returned to her seat—again before any of the others—and there had noticed that the silver ball was a pearl. At this discovery she had at once conceived a malicious plan. While all the others were preoccupied with the cake, she had quickly slipped the pearl into the handbag left on the next chair by that insufferable hypocrite Mrs. Matsumura.

Stranded in the middle of a residential district where there was little prospect of a taxi, Mrs. Matsumura fretfully gave her mind to a number of reflections on her position.

First, no matter how necessary it might be for the relief of her own conscience, it would be a shame, indeed, when people had gone to such lengths to settle the affair satisfactorily, to go and stir up things all over again; and it would be even worse if in the process—because of the inexplicable nature of the circumstances—she were to direct unjust suspicions upon herself.

Secondly—notwithstanding these considerations—if she did not make haste to return the pearl now, she would forfeit her opportunity forever. Left till tomorrow (at the thought Mrs. Matsumura blushed), the returned pearl would be an object of rather disgusting speculation and doubt. Concerning this possibility, Mrs. Azuma herself had dropped a hint.

It was at this point that there occurred to Mrs. Matsumura, greatly to her joy, a master scheme which would both salve her conscience and at the same time involve no risk of exposing her character to any unjust suspicion. Quickening her step, she emerged at length onto a comparatively busy thoroughfare, where she hailed a taxi and told the driver to take her quickly to a certain celebrated pearl shop on the Ginza. There she took the pearl from her bag and showed it to the attendant, asking to see a pearl of slightly larger size and clearly superior quality. Having made her purchase, she proceeded once more, by taxi, to Mrs. Sasaki's house.

Mrs. Matsumura's plan was to present this newly purchased pearl to Mrs. Sasaki, saying she had found it in her jacket pocket. Mrs. Sasaki would accept it and later attempt to fit it into the ring. However, being a pearl of a different size, it would not fit into the ring, and Mrs. Sasaki—puzzled—would try to return it to Mrs. Matsumura, but Mrs. Matsumura would refuse to have it returned. Thereupon Mrs. Sasaki would have no choice but to reflect as follows: The woman has behaved in this way in order to protect someone else. Such being the case, it is perhaps safest simply to accept the pearl and forget the matter. Mrs. Matsumura has doubtless observed one of the three ladies in the act of stealing the pearl. But at least, of my four guests, I can now be sure that Mrs. Matsumura, if no one else, is completely without guilt. Whoever heard of a thief stealing something and then replacing it with a similar article of greater value?

By this device Mrs. Matsumura proposed to escape forever the infamy of suspicion and equally—by a small outlay of cash—the pricks of an uneasy conscience.

To return to the other ladies. After reaching home, Mrs. Kasuga continued to feel painfully upset by Mrs. Azuma's cruel teasing. To clear herself of even a ridiculous charge like this—she knew—she must act before tomorrow or it would be too late. That is to say, in order to offer positive proof that she had not eaten the pearl, it was above all necessary for the pearl itself to be somehow produced. And, briefly, if she could show the pearl to Mrs. Azuma immediately, her innocence on the gastronomic count (if not on any other) would be firmly established. But if she waited until tomorrow, even though she managed to produce the pearl, the shameful and hardly mentionable suspicion would inevitably have intervened.

The normally timid Mrs. Kasuga, inspired with the courage of impetuous action, burst from the house to which she had so recently returned, sped to a pearl shop in the Ginza, and selected and bought a pearl which, to her eye, seemed of roughly the same size as those silver balls on the cake. She then telephoned Mrs. Azuma. On returning home, she explained, she had discovered in the folds of the bow of her sash the pearl which Mrs. Sasaki had lost, but since she felt too ashamed to return it by herself, she wondered if Mrs. Azuma would be so kind as to go with her, as soon as possible. Inwardly Mrs. Azuma considered the story a little unlikely, but since it was the request of a good friend, she agreed to go.

Mrs. Sasaki accepted the pearl brought to her by Mrs. Matsumura and, puzzled at its failure to fit the ring, fell obligingly into that very train of thought for which Mrs. Matsumura had prayed; but it was a surprise to her when Mrs. Kasuga arrived about an hour later, accompanied by Mrs. Azuma, and returned another pearl.

Mrs. Sasaki hovered perilously on the brink of discussing Mrs. Matsumura's prior visit but checked herself at the last moment and accepted the second pearl as unconcernedly as she could. She felt sure that this one at any rate would fit, and as soon as the two visitors had taken their leave, she hurried to try it in the ring. But it was too small and wobbled loosely in the socket. At this discovery Mrs. Sasaki was not so much surprised as dumbfounded.

On the way back in the car, both ladies found it impossible to guess what the other might be thinking, and though normally relaxed and <u>loquacious</u>[5] in each other's company, they now lapsed into a long silence.

Mrs. Azuma, who believed she could do nothing without her own full knowledge, knew for certain that she had not swallowed the pearl herself. It was simply to save everyone from embarrassment that she had cast shame aside and made that declaration at the party—more particularly, it was to save the situation for her friend, who had been fidgeting

about and looking conspicuously guilty. But what was she to think now? Beneath the peculiarity of Mrs. Kasuga's whole attitude, and beneath this elaborate procedure of having herself accompany her as she returned the pearl, she sensed that there lay something much deeper. Could it be that Mrs. Azuma's intuition had touched upon a weakness in her friend's make-up which it was forbidden to touch upon and that by thus driving her friend into a corner, she had transformed an unconscious, impulsive kleptomania into a deep mental derangement beyond all cure?

Mrs. Kasuga, for her part, still retained the suspicion that Mrs. Azuma had genuinely swallowed the pearl and that her confession at the party had been the truth. If that was so, it had been unforgivable of Mrs. Azuma, when everything was smoothly settled, to tease her so cruelly on the way back from the party, shifting the guilt onto herself. As a result, timid creature that she was, she had been panic-striken and, besides spending good money, had felt obliged to act out that little play—and was it not exceedingly ill-natured of Mrs. Azuma that even after all this, she still refused to confess it was she who had eaten the pearl? And if Mrs. Azuma's innocence was all pretense, she herself—acting her part so painstakingly—must appear in Mrs. Azuma's eyes as the most ridiculous of third-rate comedians.

To return to Mrs. Matsumura: That lady, on her way back from obliging Mrs. Sasaki to accept the pearl, was feeling now more at ease in her mind and had the notion to make a leisurely reinvestigation, detail by detail, of the events of the recent incident. When going to collect her portion of the cake, she had most

---

5. loquacious (lō kwā′ shəs): talkative, especially in a fluently expressive way.

certainly left her handbag on the chair. Then, while eating the cake, she had made liberal use of the paper napkin—so there could have been no necessity to take a handkerchief from her bag. The more she thought about it, the less she could remember having opened her bag until she touched up her face in the taxi on the way home. How was it, then, that a pearl had rolled into a handbag which was always shut?

She realized now how stupid she had been not to have remarked this simple fact before, instead of flying into a panic at the mere sight of the pearl. Having progressed this far, Mrs. Matsumura was struck by an amazing thought. Someone must purposely have placed the pearl in her bag in order to incriminate her. And of the four guests at the party, the only one who would do such a thing was, without doubt, the detestable Mrs. Yamamoto. Her eyes glinting with rage, Mrs. Matsumura hurried toward the house of Mrs. Yamamoto.

From her first glimpse of Mrs. Matsumura standing in the doorway, Mrs. Yamamoto knew at once what had brought her. She had already prepared her line of defense.

However, Mrs. Matsumura's cross-examination was unexpectedly severe, and from the start it was clear that she would accept no evasions.

"It was you, I know. No one but you could do such a thing," began Mrs. Matsumura, deductively.

"Why choose me? What proof have you? If you can say a thing like that to my face, I suppose you've come with pretty conclusive proof, have you?" Mrs. Yamamoto was at first icily composed.

To this Mrs. Matsumura replied that Mrs. Azuma, having so nobly taken the blame on herself, clearly stood in an incompatible relationship with mean and despicable behavior of this nature; and as for Mrs. Kasuga, she was much too weak-kneed for such dangerous work; and that left only one person—herself.

Mrs. Yamamoto kept silent, her mouth shut tight like a clamshell. On the table before her gleamed the pearl which Mrs. Matsumura had set there. In the excitement she had not even had time to raise a teaspoon, and the Ceylon tea she had so thoughtfully provided was beginning to get cold.

"I had no idea that you hated me so." As she said this, Mrs. Yamamoto dabbed at the corners of her eyes, but it was plain that Mrs. Matsumura's resolve not to be deceived by tears was as firm as ever.

"Well, then," Mrs. Yamamoto continued, "I shall say what I had thought I must never say. I shall mention no names, but one of the guests . . . "

"By that, I suppose, you can only mean Mrs. Azuma or Mrs. Kasuga?"

"Please, I beg at least that you allow me to omit the name. As I say, one of the guests had just opened your bag and was dropping something inside when I happened to glance in her direction. You can imagine my amazement! Even if I had felt *able* to warn you, there would have been no chance. My heart just throbbed and throbbed, and on the way back in the taxi—oh, how awful not to be able to speak even then! If we had been good friends, of course, I could have told you quite frankly, but since I knew of your apparent dislike for me . . . "

"I see. You have been very considerate, I'm sure. Which means, doesn't it, that you have now cleverly shifted the blame onto Mrs. Azuma and Mrs. Kasuga?"

"Shifted the blame! Oh, how can I get you to understand my feelings? I only wanted to avoid hurting anyone."

"Quite. But you didn't mind hurting me, did you? You might at least have mentioned this in the taxi."

"And if you had been frank with me when you found the pearl in your bag, I would probably have told you, at that moment, everything

I had seen—but no, you chose to leave the taxi at once, without saying a word!"

For the first time, as she listened to this, Mrs. Matsumura was at a loss for a reply.

"Well, then. Can I get you to understand? I wanted no one to be hurt."

Mrs. Matsumura was filled with an even more intense rage.

"If you are going to tell a string of lies like that," she said, "I must ask you to repeat them, tonight if you wish, in my presence, before Mrs. Azuma and Mrs. Kasuga."

At this Mrs. Yamamoto started to weep.

"And thanks to you," she sobbed reprovingly, "all my efforts to avoid hurting anyone will have come to nothing."

It was a new experience for Mrs. Matsumura to see Mrs. Yamamoto crying, and though she kept reminding herself not to be taken in by tears, she could not altogether dismiss the feeling that perhaps somewhere, since nothing in this affair could be proved, there might be a modicum[6] of truth even in the assertions of Mrs. Yamamoto.

In the first place—to be a little more objective—if one accepted Mrs. Yamamoto's story as true, then her reluctance to disclose the name of the guilty party, whom she had observed in the very act, argued some refinement of character. And just as one could not say for sure that the gentle and seemingly timid Mrs. Kasuga would never be moved to an act of malice, so even the undoubtedly bad feeling between Mrs. Yamamoto and herself could, by one way of looking at things, be taken as actually lessening the likelihood of Mrs. Yamamoto's guilt. For if she was to do a thing like this, with their relationship as it was, Mrs. Yamamoto would be the first to come under suspicion.

"We have differences in our natures," Mrs. Yamamoto continued tearfully, "and I cannot deny that there are things about yourself which I dislike. But for all that, it is really too

bad that you should suspect me of such a petty trick to get the better of you. . . . Still, on thinking it over, to submit quietly to your accusations might well be the course most consistent with what I have felt in this matter all along. In this way I alone shall bear the guilt, and no other will be hurt."

After this pathetic pronouncement, Mrs. Yamamoto lowered her face to the table and abandoned herself to uncontrolled weeping.

Watching her, Mrs. Matsumura came, by degrees, to reflect upon the impulsiveness of her own behavior. Detesting Mrs. Yamamoto as she had, there had been times in her castigation[7] of that lady when she had allowed herself to be blinded by emotion.

When Mrs. Yamamoto raised her head again after this prolonged bout of weeping, the look of resolution on her face, somehow remote and pure, was apparent even to her visitor. Mrs. Matsumura, a little frightened, drew herself upright in her chair.

"This thing should never have been. When it is gone, everything will be as before." Speaking in riddles, Mrs. Yamamoto pushed back her disheveled hair and fixed a terrible, yet hauntingly beautiful, gaze upon the top of the table. In an instant she had snatched up the pearl from before her and, with a gesture of no ordinary resolve, tossed it into her mouth. Raising her cup by the handle, her little finger elegantly extended, she washed the pearl down her throat with one gulp of cold Ceylon tea.

Mrs. Matsumura watched in horrified fascination. The affair was over before she had time to protest. This was the first time in her life she had seen a person swallow a pearl, and

---

6. modicum (mäd′ i kəm): a small amount.

7. castigation (kas′ ti ga′ shən): the act of punishing or scolding severely, especially by criticizing publicly.

there was in Mrs. Yamamoto's manner something of that desperate finality one might expect to see in a person who had just drunk poison.

However, heroic though the action was, it was above all a touching incident, and not only did Mrs. Matsumura find her anger vanished into thin air, but so impressed was she by Mrs. Yamamoto's simplicity and purity that she could only think of that lady as a saint. And now Mrs. Matsumura's eyes too began to fill with tears, and she took Mrs. Yamamoto by the hand.

"Please forgive me, please forgive me," she said. "It was wrong of me."

For a while they wept together, holding each other's hands and vowing to each other that henceforth they would be the firmest of friends.

When Mrs. Sasaki heard rumors that the relationship between Mrs. Yamamoto and Mrs. Matsumura, which had been so strained, had suddenly improved, and that Mrs. Azuma and Mrs. Kasuga, who had been such good friends, had suddenly fallen out, she was at a loss to understand the reasons and contented herself with the reflection that nothing was impossible in this world.

However, being a woman of no strong scruples, Mrs. Sasaki requested a jeweler to refashion her ring and to produce a design into which two new pearls could be set, one large and one small, and this she wore quite openly, without further mishap.

Soon she had completely forgotten the small commotion on her birthday, and when anyone asked her age, she would give the same untruthful answers as ever.

Thinking About the Story

A PERSONAL RESPONSE

sharing impressions

1. What do you think about the behavior of the four women? In your journal briefly describe your impressions.

constructing interpretations

2. Why do you think these women behave as they do?

Think about
- personal characteristics attributed to each of them
- how they interact with each other
- the position they are placed in when it appears that the pearl is missing
- ways in which they try to save face
- the social mores that can be inferred from this story

3. Explain whether you think Mrs. Yamamoto's swallowing of the pearl is a good resolution to the situation.

4. Which of the characters do you think is most responsible for the confusion resulting from the loss of the pearl? Why?

A CREATIVE RESPONSE

5. If Mrs. Azuma had not claimed to have swallowed the pearl, how might the outcome of the story be different?

A CRITICAL RESPONSE

6. What message do you think Mishima conveys about the society in which the characters live? Use examples from the story to support your opinion.

7. Do you think the incidents described in the story could happen in contemporary American society? Why or why not?

Analyzing the Writer's Craft

SATIRE AND TONE

How do you think Mishima wants readers to feel about the characters and their problems?

Building a Literary Vocabulary. Satire is a literary technique in which ideas or customs are ridiculed for the purpose of improving society. The tone, or writer's attitude, that comes through in a satire may be gently witty, mildly abrasive, or bitterly critical. In "The Pearl" the rather trivial misplacing of a pearl drives four friends into a complicated and ridiculous series of maneuvers. The characters end up looking foolish because of the lengths to which they go to avoid having anyone think unsuitable thoughts about them. Mishima's satire depends on the mildly ironic or sarcastic tone with which he describes the reactions of the characters to the loss of the pearl. For example, when the narrator says "Mrs. Azuma resolved to offer herself as a sacrifice and to save the day," he does not expect the reader to take the statement literally.

Application: Understanding Satire and Tone. Working with a partner, list phrases or lines from the story that reveal Mishima's tone in the story. After identifying these examples, explain in writing what you think is being satirized. Be prepared to share your opinion with the class.

Connecting Reading and Writing

1. Read another story from Mishima's *Death in Midsummer and Other Stories*, from which "The Pearl" was taken. Based on these two stories, write a **review** of Mishima's work for a school literary magazine. Make sure to comment on elements such as character, theme, and tone in both stories.

Option: Write a **letter** to the head of the English department at your school, comparing the two works and recommending one of them for inclusion in next year's curriculum.

2. Create a **poster** announcing auditions for the stage version of "The Pearl." Be sure your poster includes specific details about the cast of characters.

Option: Write **stage directions** for one scene from the story, for example the scene in which the pearl first disappears or the final scene between Mrs.

Matsumura and Mrs. Yamamoto.

3. Write a brief **satirical sketch** for the school newspaper, exposing a social situation in your school that you believe needs improvement.

Option: Write an **editorial** stating your opinion about that same situation for your school newspaper.

4. Create an **annotated map** to share with a classmate who is confused about events in "The Pearl." Show the various locations—for example, the women's homes and the jewelry stores—and what event(s) happen in each.

Option: Write a **time line** of events to help a classmate organize information from the story. Indicate the characters that are involved in each event.

The Wooing of Ariadne

HARRY MARK PETRAKIS

A biography of Petrakis appears on page 426.

*A*pproaching the Story

"The Wooing of Ariadne" (ar′ ē ad′ nē) is set in the Greek community of a large American city. Like other closely knit ethnic groups, Greek immigrants to America have often maintained their culture and customs. The narrator of this story exhibits certain "macho" qualities that are frequently associated with Old World beliefs and practices.

*B*uilding Vocabulary

These essential words are footnoted within the story.

protestations (prät′ es tā′ shənz): I knew from the beginning she must accept my love—put aside foolish female **protestations.** (page 178)

wiles (wīlz): I am wise to these **wiles.** (page 178)

subterfuge (sub′ tər fyo͞oj′): Her **subterfuge** so apparent. Trying to conceal her pleasure at my interest. (page 178)

venerable (ven′ ər ə bəl): But my Ariadne, worthy and **venerable,** hurled her spirit into my teeth. (page 179)

paragon (par′ ə gän′): I marveled at how he could have produced such a **paragon** of women. (page 181)

*C*onnecting Writing and Reading

Think about the dating practices in your school. In your journal describe the following:
- how a boy or girl first shows romantic interest
- whether the boy or the girl asks for the first date
- where a couple goes on a first date

As you read, compare the dating practices you are familiar with to those practiced by the characters in the story.

The Wooing of Ariadne

I KNEW FROM the beginning she must accept my love—put aside foolish female protestations.[1] It is the distinction of the male to be the aggressor and the cloak of the female to lend grace to the pursuit. Aha! I am wise to these wiles.[2]

I first saw Ariadne at a dance given by the Spartan brotherhood in the Legion Hall on Laramie Street. The usual assemblage of prune-faced and banana-bodied women smelling of virtuous anemia. They were an outrage to a man such as myself.

Then I saw her! A tall, stately woman, perhaps in her early thirties. She had firm and slender arms bare to the shoulders and a graceful neck. Her hair was black and thick and piled in a great bun at the back of her head. That grand abundance of hair attracted me at once. This modern aberration women have of chopping their hair close to the scalp and leaving it in fantastic disarray I find revolting.

I went at once to my friend Vasili, the baker, and asked him who she was.

"Ariadne Langos," he said. "Her father is Janco Langos, the grocer."

"Is she engaged or married?"

"No," he said slyly. "They say she frightens off the young men. They say she is very spirited."

"Excellent," I said and marveled at my good fortune in finding her unpledged. "Introduce me at once."

"Marko," Vasili said with some apprehension. "Do not commit anything rash."

I pushed the little man forward. "Do not worry, little friend," I said. "I am a man suddenly possessed by a vision. I must meet her at once."

We walked together across the dance floor to where my beloved stood. The closer we came the more impressive she was. She towered over the insignificant apple-core women around her. Her eyes, dark and thoughtful, seemed to be restlessly searching the room.

Be patient, my dove! Marko is coming.

"Miss Ariadne," Vasili said. "This is Mr. Marko Palamas. He desires to have the honor of your acquaintance."

She looked at me for a long and piercing moment. I imagined her gauging my mighty strength by the width of my shoulders and the circumference of my arms. I felt the tips of my mustache bristle with pleasure. Finally she nodded with the barest minimum of courtesy. I was not discouraged.

"Miss Ariadne," I said, "may I have the pleasure of this dance?"

She stared at me again with her fiery eyes. I could imagine more timid men shriveling before her fierce gaze. My heart flamed at the passion her rigid exterior concealed.

"I think not," she said.

"Don't you dance?"

Vasili gasped beside me. An old prune-face standing nearby clucked her toothless gums.

"Yes, I dance," Ariadne said coolly. "I do not wish to dance with you."

"Why?" I asked courteously.

"I do not think you heard me," she said. "I do not wish to dance with you."

Oh, the sly and lovely darling. Her subterfuge[3] so apparent. Trying to conceal her pleasure at my interest.

---

1. protestations (prät′ es tā′ shənz): objections or protests.
2. wiles (wīlz): tricks or strategies intended to deceive.
3. subterfuge (sub′ tər fyo͞oj′): an action used to hide one's true purpose; scheme, excuse, trick.

"Why?" I asked again.

"I am not sure," she said. "It could be your appearance, which bears considerable resemblance to a gorilla, or your manner, which would suggest closer alliance to a pig."

"Now that you have met my family," I said engagingly, "let us dance."

"Not now," she said, and her voice rose. "Not this dance or the one after. Not tonight or tomorrow night or next month or next year. Is that clear?"

Sweet, sweet Ariadne. Ancient and eternal game of retreat and pursuit. My pulse beat more quickly.

Vasili pulled at my sleeve. He was my friend, but without the courage of a goat. I shook him off and spoke to Ariadne.

"There is a joy like fire that consumes a man's heart when he first sets eyes on his beloved," I said. "This I felt when I first saw you." My voice trembled under a mighty passion. "I swear before God from this moment that I love you."

She stared shocked out of her deep dark eyes and, beside her, old prune-face staggered as if she had been kicked. Then my beloved did something that proved indisputably that her passion was as intense as mine.

She doubled up her fist and struck me in the eye. A stout blow for a woman that brought a haze to my vision, but I shook my head and moved a step closer.

"I would not care," I said, "if you struck out both my eyes. I would cherish the memory of your beauty forever."

By this time the music had stopped, and the dancers formed a circle of idiot faces about us. I paid them no attention and ignored Vasili, who kept whining and pulled at my sleeve.

"You are crazy!" she said. "You must be mad! Remove yourself from my presence or I will tear out both your eyes and your tongue besides!"

You see! Another woman would have cried, or been frightened into silence. But my Ariadne, worthy and <u>venerable</u>,[4] hurled her spirit into my teeth.

"I would like to call on your father tomorrow," I said. From the assembled dancers who watched there rose a few vagrant whispers and some rude laughter. I stared at them carefully and they hushed at once. My temper and strength of arm were well known.

Ariadne did not speak again, but in a magnificent spirit stamped from the floor. The music began, and men and women began again to dance. I permitted Vasili to pull me to a corner.

"You are insane!" he said. He wrung his withered fingers in anguish. "You assaulted her like a Turk![5] Her relatives will cut out your heart!"

"My intentions were honorable," I said. "I saw her and loved her and told her so." At this point I struck my fist against my chest. Poor Vasili jumped.

"But you do not court a woman that way," he said.

"*You* don't, my anemic friend," I said. "Nor do the rest of these sheep. But I court a woman that way!"

He looked to heaven and helplessly shook his head. I waved goodbye and started for my hat and coat.

"Where are you going?" he asked.

"To prepare for tomorrow," I said. "In the morning I will speak to her father."

I left the hall and in the street felt the night wind cold on my flushed cheeks. My blood was inflamed. The memory of her loveliness fed fuel to the fire. For the first time I understood with a terrible clarity the driven heroes of the

---

4. **venerable** (ven′ ər ə bəl): worthy of respect because of age, dignity, or character.

5. **Turk:** among Greeks, sometimes a negative term because of historical animosity between Greeks and Turks.

Bust of a Woman, date unknown, ANDRÉ DERAIN.
Copyright 1991 ARS, New York/ADAGP.

past performing mighty deeds in love, Paris stealing Helen in passion, and Menelaus pursuing with a great fleet.[6] In that moment, if I knew the whole world would be plunged into conflict, I would have followed Ariadne to Hades.[7]

I went to my rooms above my tavern. I could not sleep. All night I tossed in restless frenzy. I touched my eye that she had struck with her spirited hand.

Ariadne! Ariadne! my soul cried out.

In the morning I bathed and dressed carefully. I confirmed the address of Langos, the grocer, and started to his store. It was a bright cold November morning, but I walked with spring in my step.

---

6. Paris . . . fleet: a reference to the Greek legend in which the Trojan War was started because Paris, prince of Troy, kidnapped Helen, whose husband, Menelaus (men′ ə lā′ əs), was king of Sparta.

7. Hades (hā′ dēz): in Greek mythology, the kingdom of the dead.

When I opened the door of the Langos grocery, a tiny bell rang shrilly. I stepped into the store piled with fruits and vegetables and smelling of cabbages and greens.

A stooped little old man with white bushy hair and owlish eyes came toward me. He looked as if his veins contained vegetable juice instead of blood, and if he were, in truth, the father of my beloved, I marveled at how he could have produced such a paragon[8] of women.

"Are you Mr. Langos?"

"I am," he said, and he came closer. "I am."

"I met your daughter last night," I said. "Did she mention I was going to call?"

He shook his head somberly.

"My daughter mentioned you," he said. "In thirty years I have never seen her in such a state of agitation. She was possessed."

"The effect on me was the same," I said. "We met for the first time last night, and I fell passionately in love."

"Incredible," the old man said.

"You wish to know something about me," I said. "My name is Marko Palamas. I am a Spartan emigrated to this country eleven years ago. I am forty-one years old. I have been a wrestler and a sailor and fought with the resistance movement in Greece in the war.[9] For this service I was decorated by the king. I own a small but profitable tavern on Dart Street. I attend church regularly. I love your daughter."

As I finished he stepped back and bumped a rack of fruit. An orange rolled off to the floor. I bent and retrieved it to hand it to him, and he cringed as if he thought I might bounce it off his old head.

"She is a bad-tempered girl," he said. "Stubborn, impatient, and spoiled. She has been the cause of considerable concern to me. All the eligible young men have been driven away by her temper and disposition."

"Poor girl," I said. "Subjected to the courting of calves and goats."

The old man blinked his owlish eyes. The front door opened and a battleship of a woman sailed in.

"Three pounds of tomatoes, Mr. Langos," she said. "I am in a hurry. Please to give me good ones. Last week two spoiled before I had a chance to put them into Demetri's salad."

"I am very sorry," Mr. Langos said. He turned to me. "Excuse me, Mr. Poulmas."

"Palamas," I said. "Marko Palamas."

He nodded nervously. He went to wait on the battleship, and I spent a moment examining the store. Neat and small. I would not imagine he did more than hold his own. In the rear of the store there were stairs leading to what appeared to be an apartment above. My heart beat faster.

When he had bagged the tomatoes and given change, he returned to me and said, "She is also a terrible cook. She cannot fry an egg without burning it." His voice shook with woe. "She cannot make pilaf or lamb with squash." He paused. "You like pilaf and lamb with squash?"

"Certainly."

"You see?" he said in triumph. "She is useless in the kitchen. She is thirty years old, and I am resigned she will remain an old maid. In a way I am glad because I know she would drive some poor man to drink."

"Do not deride her to discourage me," I said. "You need have no fear that I will mistreat her or cause her unhappiness. When she is married to me she will cease being a problem to you." I paused. "It is true that I am not pretty by the foppish standards that prevail today. But I am a man. I wrestled Zahundos and pinned him two straight falls in Baltimore. A giant of a man. Afterward he conceded he had met his master.

---

8. paragon (par′ ə gän′): a model of perfection or excellence.

9. the war: World War II, when organized underground movements resisted Nazi occupation.

This from Zahundos was a mighty compliment."

"I am sure," the old man said without enthusiasm. "I am sure."

He looked toward the front door as if hoping for another customer.

"Is your daughter upstairs?"

He looked startled and tugged at his apron. "Yes," he said. "I don't know. Maybe she has gone out."

"May I speak to her? Would you kindly tell her I wish to speak with her."

"You are making a mistake," the old man said. "A terrible mistake."

"No mistake," I said firmly.

The old man shuffled toward the stairs. He climbed them slowly. At the top he paused and turned the knob of the door. He rattled it again.

"It is locked," he called down. "It has never been locked before. She has locked the door."

"Knock," I said. "Knock to let her know I am here."

"I think she knows," the old man said. "I think she knows."

He knocked gently.

"Knock harder," I suggested. "Perhaps she does not hear."

"I think she hears," the old man said. "I think she hears."

"Knock again," I said. "Shall I come up and knock for you?"

"No, no," the old man said quickly. He gave the door a sound kick. Then he groaned as if he might have hurt his foot.

"She does not answer," he said in a quavering voice. "I am very sorry she does not answer."

"The coy darling," I said and laughed. "If that is her game." I started for the front door of the store.

I went out and stood on the sidewalk before the store. Above the grocery were the front windows of their apartment. I cupped my hands about my mouth.

"Ariadne!" I shouted. "Ariadne!"

The old man came out of the door running disjointedly. He looked frantically down the street.

"Are you mad?" he asked shrilly. "You will cause a riot. The police will come. You must be mad!"

"Ariadne!" I shouted. "Beloved!"

A window slammed open, and the face of Ariadne appeared above me. Her dark hair tumbled about her ears.

"Go away!" she shrieked. "Will you go away!"

"Ariadne," I said loudly. "I have come as I promised. I have spoken to your father. I wish to call on you."

"Go away!" she shrieked. "Madman! Imbecile! Go away!"

By this time a small group of people had assembled around the store and were watching curiously. The old man stood wringing his hands and uttering what sounded like small groans.

"Ariadne," I said. "I wish to call on you. Stop this nonsense and let me in."

She pushed farther out the window and showed me her teeth.

"Be careful, beloved," I said. "You might fall."

She drew her head in quickly, and I turned then to the assembled crowd.

"A misunderstanding," I said. "Please move on."

Suddenly old Mr. Langos shrieked. A moment later something broke on the sidewalk a foot from where I stood. A vase or a plate. I looked up, and Ariadne was preparing to hurl what appeared to be a water pitcher.

"Ariadne!" I shouted. "Stop that!"

The water pitcher landed closer than the vase, and fragments of glass struck my shoes. The crowd scattered, and the old man raised his hands and wailed to heaven.

Ariadne slammed down the window.

The crowd moved in again a little closer, and somewhere among them I heard laughter.

I fixed them with a cold stare and waited for some one of them to say something offensive. I would have tossed him around like a sardine, but they slowly dispersed and moved on. In another moment the old man and I were alone.

I followed him into the store. He walked an awkward dance of agitation. He shut the door and peered out through the glass.

"A disgrace," he wailed. "A disgrace. The whole street will know by nightfall. A disgrace."

"A girl of heroic spirit," I said. "Will you speak to her for me? Assure her of the sincerity of my feelings. Tell her I pledge eternal love and devotion."

The old man sat down on an orange crate and weakly made his cross.[10]

"I had hoped to see her myself," I said. "But if you promise to speak to her, I will return this evening."

"That soon?" the old man said.

"If I stayed now," I said, "it would be sooner."

"This evening," the old man said and shook his head in resignation. "This evening."

I went to my tavern for a while and set up the glasses for the evening trade. I made arrangements for Pavlakis to tend bar in my place. Afterward I sat alone in my apartment and read a little majestic Pindar[11] to ease the agitation of my heart.

Once in the mountains of Greece when I fought with the guerrillas in the last year of the great war, I suffered a wound from which it seemed I would die. For days, high fever raged in my body. My friends brought a priest at night secretly from one of the captive villages to read the last rites. I accepted the coming of death and was grateful for many things. For the gentleness and wisdom of my old grandfather, the loyalty of my companions in war, the years I sailed between the wild ports of the seven seas, and the strength that flowed to me from the Spartan earth. For one thing only did I weep when it seemed I would leave life, that I had

never set ablaze the world with a burning song of passion for one woman. Women I had known, but I had been denied mighty love for one woman. For that I wept.

In Ariadne I swore before God I had found my woman. I knew by the storm-lashed hurricane that swept within my body. A woman whose majesty was in harmony with the earth, who would be faithful and beloved to me as Penelope had been to Ulysses.[12]

That evening near seven I returned to the grocery. Deep twilight had fallen across the street, and the lights in the window of the store had been dimmed. The apples and oranges and pears had been covered with brown paper for the night.

I tried the door and found it locked. I knocked on the glass, and a moment later the old man came shuffling out of the shadows and let me in.

"Good evening, Mr. Langos."

He muttered some greeting in answer. "Ariadne is not here," he said. "She is at the church. Father Marlas wishes to speak with you."

"A fine young priest," I said. "Let us go at once."

I waited on the sidewalk while the old man locked the store. We started the short walk to the church.

"A clear and ringing night," I said. "Does it not make you feel the wonder and glory of being alive?"

The old man uttered what sounded like a groan, but a truck passed on the street at that moment and I could not be sure.

---

10. **made his cross:** made the sign of the cross.

11. **Pindar** (pin′ dər): a Greek lyric poet who lived from 522 to 443 B.C.

12. **Penelope** (pə nel′ ə pē) . . . **Ulysses** (yoo lis′ ēz′): a reference to the story of Penelope, who waited faithfully for the return of her husband, Ulysses, from the Trojan War.

At the church we entered by a side door leading to the office of Father Marlas. I knocked on the door, and when he called to us to enter we walked in.

Young Father Marlas was sitting at his desk in his black cassock and with his black goatee trim and imposing beneath his cleanshaven cheeks. Beside the desk, in a dark blue dress, sat Ariadne, looking somber and beautiful. A baldheaded, big-nosed old man with flint and fire in his eyes sat in a chair beside her.

"Good evening, Marko," Father Marlas said and smiled.

"Good evening, Father," I said.

"Mr. Langos and his daughter you have met," he said, and he cleared his throat. "This is Uncle Paul Langos."

"Good evening, Uncle Paul," I said. He glared at me and did not answer. I smiled warmly at Ariadne in greeting, but was watching the priest.

"Sit down," Father Marlas said.

I sat down across from Ariadne, and old Mr. Langos took a chair beside Uncle Paul. In this way we were arrayed in battle order as if we were opposing armies.

A long silence prevailed, during which Father Marlas cleared his throat several times. I observed Ariadne closely. There were grace and poise even in the way her slim-fingered hands rested in her lap. She was a dark and lovely flower, and my pulse beat more quickly at her nearness.

"Marko," Father Marlas said finally. "Marko, I have known you well for the three years since I assumed duties in this parish. You are most regular in your devotions and very generous at the time of the Christmas and Easter offerings. Therefore, I find it hard to believe this complaint against you."

"My family are not liars!" Uncle Paul said, and he had a voice like hunks of dry, hard cheese being grated.

"Of course not," Father Marlas said quickly.

He smiled benevolently at Ariadne. "I only mean to say—"

"Tell him to stay away from my niece," Uncle Paul burst out.

"Excuse me, Uncle Paul," I said very politely. "Will you kindly keep out of what is not your business?"

Uncle Paul looked shocked. "Not my business?" He looked from Ariadne to Father Marlas and then to his brother. "Not my business?"

"This matter concerns Ariadne and me," I said. "With outside interference it becomes more difficult."

"Not my business!" Uncle Paul said. He couldn't seem to get that through his head.

"Marko," Father Marlas said, and his composure was slightly shaken. "The family feels you are forcing your attention upon this girl. They are concerned."

"I understand, Father," I said. "It is natural for them to be concerned. I respect their concern. It is also natural for me to speak of love to a woman I have chosen for my wife."

"Not my business!" Uncle Paul said again, and shook his head violently.

"My daughter does not wish to become your wife," Mr. Langos said in a squeaky voice.

"That is for your daughter to say," I said courteously.

Ariadne made a sound in her throat, and we all looked at her. Her eyes were deep and cold, and she spoke slowly and carefully, as if weighing each word on a scale in her father's grocery.

"I would not marry this madman if he were one of the Twelve Apostles,"[13] she said.

"See!" Mr. Langos said in triumph.

"Not my business!" Uncle Paul snarled.

"Marko," Father Marlas said. "Try to understand."

---

13. Twelve Apostles (ə päs′ əls): the twelve disciples sent out by Christ to teach the gospel.

"We will call the police!" Uncle Paul raised his voice. "Put this hoodlum under a bond!"

"Please!" Father Marlas said. "Please!"

"Today he stood on the street outside the store," Mr. Langos said excitedly. "He made me a laughingstock."

"If I were a younger man," Uncle Paul growled, "I would settle this without the police. Zi-ip!" He drew a calloused finger violently across his throat.

"Please," Father Marlas said.

"A disgrace!" Mr. Langos said.

"An outrage!" Uncle Paul said.

"He must leave Ariadne alone!" Mr. Langos said.

"We will call the police!" Uncle Paul said.

"Silence!" Father Marlas said loudly.

With everything suddenly quiet he turned to me. His tone softened.

"Marko," he said, and he seemed to be pleading a little. "Marko, you must understand."

Suddenly a great bitterness assailed me, and anger at myself, and a terrible sadness that flowed like night through my body because I could not make them understand.

"Father," I said quietly, "I am not a fool. I am Marko Palamas, and once I pinned the mighty Zahundos in Baltimore. But this battle, more important to me by far, I have lost. That which has not the grace of God is better far in silence."

I turned to leave, and it would have ended there.

"Hoodlum!" Uncle Paul said. "It is time you were silent!"

I swear in that moment if he had been a younger man I would have flung him to the dome of the church. Instead I turned and spoke to them all in fire and fury.

"Listen," I said. "I feel no shame for the violence of my feelings. I am a man bred of the Spartan earth, and my emotions are violent. Let those who squeak of life feel shame. Nor

do I feel shame because I saw this flower and loved her. Or because I spoke at once of my love."

No one moved or made a sound.

"We live in a dark age," I said. "An age where men say one thing and mean another. A time of dwarfs afraid of life. The days are gone when mighty Pindar sang his radiant blossoms of song. When the noble passions of men set ablaze cities, and the heroic deeds of men rang like thunder to every corner of the earth."

I spoke my final words to Ariadne. "I saw you and loved you," I said gently. "I told you of my love. This is my way—the only way I know. If this has proved offensive to you, I apologize to you alone. But understand clearly that for none of this do I feel shame."

I turned then and started to the door. I felt my heart weeping as if waves were breaking within my body.

"Marko Palamas," Ariadne said. I turned slowly. I looked at her. For the first time the warmth I was sure dwelt in her body radiated within the circles of her face. For the first time she did not look at me with her eyes like glaciers.

"Marko Palamas," she said, and there was a strange, moving softness in the way she spoke my name. "You may call on me tomorrow."

Uncle Paul shot out of his chair. "She is mad too!" he shouted. "He has bewitched her!"

"A disgrace!" Mr. Langos said.

"Call the police!" Uncle Paul shouted. "I'll show him if it's my business!"

"My poor daughter!" Mr. Langos wailed.

"Turk!" Uncle Paul shouted. "Robber!"

"Please!" Father Marlas said. "Please!"

I ignored them all. In that winged and zestful moment I had eyes only for my beloved, for Ariadne, blossom of my heart and black-eyed flower of my soul!

Thinking About the Story

sharing
impressions

1. How did you react to the turn of events at the end of the story? Write your thoughts in your journal.

constructing
interpretations

2. How do you account for Ariadne's change of heart?
Think about
- the kind of person she seems to be
- Marko's speech beginning, "I feel no shame for the violence of my feelings." (page 185)

3. Some people might say that Marko is stubborn and conceited, others that he is honest and determined. How would you characterize Marko as a person? Cite details to explain your response.

4. How do you explain the reaction of Ariadne's family to Marko?
Think about
- Mr. Langos's attempts to discourage Marko with unflattering descriptions of his daughter
- Uncle Paul's violent objections to Marko
- what appear to be the expected dating practices within the community

A CREATIVE RESPONSE

5. If Marko is successful in developing a relationship with Ariadne and they marry, what kind of life do you think they will have together?

A CRITICAL RESPONSE

6. Think about how Marko views relationships between men and women. In your opinion, how would most of the people you know respond to Marko's attitude?

7. In your opinion, what makes this story humorous? Point out any passages that you thought were funny as you read the story.

Analyzing the Writer's Craft

CHARACTER

What role is played by each person in this story?

Building a Literary Vocabulary. Characters are the people (and occasionally animals or fantasy creatures) who participate in the action of a literary work. Characters are either main or minor, depending on the extent of their development and on their importance in the literary work. Of the main characters, one is the protagonist, or central character, who most arouses the reader's interest and sympathy. In "Initiation," the main characters are Millicent, Louise, Tracy, Bev, and Herb Dalton. Millicent is the protagonist. Often, another character in the story acts as the antagonist, the force pitted against the protagonist. Millicent's antagonist is Bev, who enjoys making her perform demeaning tasks. Sometimes a minor character in a story will be a foil, a character who provides a striking contrast to a main character, thus calling attention to certain traits of the main character. The cheerfully eccentric man on the bus is a foil for the cruel, rigid Bev.

Application: Analyzing the Functions of Characters. Choose students to represent each character named in the story, having them wear or hold large name tags. Ask the main characters to stand in the center of the room and the minor characters to stand at the sides. Decide which of the main characters is the protagonist and which is the antagonist, and pin a *P* and an *A* to their backs. Then ask these two to pantomime their relationship to each other. Finally, decide whether any of the minor characters acts as a foil for a main character. If so, have these two characters stand next to each other and describe or pantomime their contrasting qualities.

Connecting Reading and Writing

1. What will happen when Marko calls on Ariadne? Write their dialogue in the form of a brief **dramatic scene** to be performed for another English class that has read this story.

Option: Write the scene as a **final episode** of "The Wooing of Ariadne," to be shared with others who have read the story.

2. Write **director's notes** to be used by an actress preparing for the role of Ariadne.

Option: Using Ariadne as a model of the kind of woman Marko admires, compose an **ad** that Marko might place in the personals column of a community newspaper.

3. Compose Ariadne's **diary entries** describing her initial meeting with Marko at the dance, his visit the next day, and the scene in the priest's office.

Option: Create a series of **telephone conversations** between Ariadne and a friend in which Ariadne describes her encounters with Marko.

4. Research the name Ariadne and write an explanatory **footnote** for the name, for use in a textbook such as this one.

Option: Write a brief **hypothesis** for your teacher and your class, suggesting why Petrakis might have chosen this name for his character.

The Interview

RUTH PRAWER JHABVALA

A biography of Jhabvala appears on page 423.

Approaching the Story

The narrator of this story by Ruth Prawer Jhabvala (prä′ wer jäb wä′ lä) is a young Indian man who belongs to a typical urban Indian family. Marriages in India are generally arranged for young people, who, after marrying, live with the husband's parents. In this highly traditional society, women are taught to be subservient to men, and women's roles outside the home are few. Within the home, the mother or the wife of an oldest son dominates the extended family, supervising the cooking, making decisions, and keeping the keys. Many educated Indian men seek work at government jobs that require fluent English, a lingering effect of the long British occupation of India.

Connecting Writing and Reading

Make a list of things that you do only because they are expected of you, not because you really want to do them. In your journal describe how it feels to be forced to meet someone else's expectations for you. As you read, compare your feelings to the narrator's feelings about his family's expectations for him.

I AM ALWAYS very careful of my appearance, so you could not say that I spent much more time than usual over myself that morning. I trimmed and oiled my mustache, but then I often do that; I always like it to look very neat, like Raj Kapoor's,[1] the film star's. My sister-in-law and my wife were watching me, my sister-in-law smiling and resting one hand on her hip and my wife only looking anxious. I knew why she was anxious. All night she had been whispering to me, saying, "Get this job and take me away to live somewhere alone—only you and I and the children." I had answered, "Yes," because I wanted to go to sleep. I don't know where and why she has taken this notion that we should go and live alone.

When I had finished combing my hair, I sat on the floor, and my sister-in-law brought me my food on a tray. It may sound strange that my sister-in-law, and not my wife, should serve me, but it is so in our house. It used to be my mother who brought me my food, even after I was married; she would never allow my wife to do this for me, though my wife wanted to very much. Then, when my mother got so old, my sister-in-law began to serve me. I know that my wife feels deeply hurt by this, but she doesn't dare say anything. My mother really doesn't notice things anymore; otherwise, she certainly would not allow my sister-in-law to serve me. She always used to be very jealous of this privilege, though she never cared who served my brother. Now she has become so old that she can hardly see anything, and most of the time she sits in the corner by the family trunks and folds and strokes her pieces of cloth. For years now she has been collecting pieces of cloth. Some of them are very old and dirty, but she doesn't care. Nobody else is allowed to touch them, and once, I remember, there was a great quarrel because my wife had taken one of them to make a dress for our child. My mother shouted at her—it was terrible to hear her, but then she has never liked my wife—and my wife was very much afraid and cried and tried to excuse herself. I hit her across the face, not very hard and not because I wanted to, but only to satisfy my mother. It seemed to quiet the old woman, and she went back to folding and stroking her pieces of cloth.

All the time I was eating, I could feel my sister-in-law looking at me and smiling. It made me uncomfortable. I thought she might be smiling because she knew I wouldn't get the job for which I had to go and be interviewed that day. I also knew I wouldn't get it, but I didn't like her smiling like that, as if she were saying, "You see, you will always have to be dependent on us." It is clearly my brother's duty to keep me and my family until I can get work and contribute my own earnings to the household, so there is no need for smiling. But it is true that I am more dependent on her now than on anyone else. Lately, my sister-in-law has become more and more the most important person in the house, and now she even keeps the keys and the household stores. At first, I didn't like this. As long as my mother was managing the household, I was sure of getting many extra tidbits. But now I find that my sister-in-law is also very kind to me—much more kind than she is to her husband. It is not for him that she saves the tidbits or for her children. She never says anything when she gives them to me, but she smiles, and then I feel confused and rather embarrassed. My wife has noticed what she does for me.

I have found that women are usually kind to me. I think they realize that I am a rather sensitive person and that therefore I must be treated gently. My mother has always treated me very gently. I am her youngest child, and I am fifteen years younger than my brother, who

---

1. Raj Kapoor's (räj ku pōōrz′).

is next to me. (She did have several children in between us, but they all died.) Right from the time when I was a tiny baby, she understood that I needed greater care and tenderness than other children. She always made me sleep close beside her in the night, and in the day I usually sat with her and my grandmother and my widowed aunt, who were also very fond of me. When I got bigger, my father sometimes wanted to take me to help in his stall (he had a little grocer's stall, where he sold lentils and rice and cheap cigarettes and colored drinks in bottles), but my mother and grandmother and aunt never liked to let me go. Once, I remember, he did take me with him, and he made me pour some lentils out of paper bags into a tin. I rather liked pouring the lentils—they made such a nice noise as they landed in the tin—but suddenly my mother came and was very angry with my father for making me do this work. She took me home at once, and when she told my grandmother and aunt what had happened, they stroked me and kissed me, and then they gave me a beautiful hot fritter to eat. The fact is, right from childhood I have been a person who needs a lot of peace and rest, and my food, too, has to be rather more delicate than that of other people. I have often tried to explain this to my wife, but as she is not very intelligent, she doesn't seem to understand.

Now my wife was watching me while I ate. She was squatting on the floor, washing our youngest baby; the child's head was in her lap, and all one could see of it was the back of its naked legs. My wife did not watch me as openly as my sister-in-law did, but from time to time she raised her eyes to me, looking very worried and troubled. She, too, was thinking about the job for which I was going to be interviewed, but she was anxious that I should get it. I cannot imagine why she wanted us to go and live alone, when she knew that it was not possible and never would be.

And even if it were possible, I would not like it. I cannot leave my mother, and I do not think I would like to live away from my sister-in-law. I often look at her, and it makes me happy. Even though she is not young anymore, she is still beautiful. She is tall, with big hips and eyes that flash. She often gets angry, and then she is the most beautiful of all. Her eyes look like fire, and she shows all her teeth, which are very strong and white, and her head is proud, with the black hair flying loose. My wife is not beautiful at all. I was very disappointed in her when they first married me to her. Now I have grown used to her, and I even like her because she is so good and quiet and never troubles me at all. But I don't think anybody else in our house likes her. My sister-in-law always calls her "that beauty," and she makes her do all the most difficult household tasks. She shouts at her and abuses her, which is not right because my wife has never done anything to her and has always treated her with respect. But I cannot interfere in their quarrels.

I finished my meal and then I was ready to go, though I did not want to. My mother blessed me, and my sister-in-law looked at me over her shoulder, and her great eyes flashed with laughter. I did not look at my wife, who was still squatting on the floor, but I knew she was pleading with me to get the job. Even as I walked down the stairs, I knew what would happen at the interview. I had been to so many during the past few months, and the same thing always happened. Of course, I know I have to work. My last position was in an insurance office, and all day they made me sit at a desk and write figures. What pleasure could there be for me in that? I am a very thoughtful person, and I always like to sit and think my own thoughts. But in that office, my thinking sometimes caused me to make mistakes over the figures, and then they were very angry with me. I was always afraid of their anger, and I begged their forgiveness and admitted that I was much at fault. But the last time they would not forgive me again, although I begged many times and cried what a faulty, bad man I was and what good men they were, and how they were my mother and my father, and how I looked only to them for my life and the lives of my children. But when they still said I must go, I saw that the work there was really finished, so I stopped crying. I went into the cloakroom and combed my hair and folded my soap in my towel, and then I took my money from the accountant without a word and left the office with my eyes lowered. But I was no longer afraid, because what is finished is finished, and my brother still had work and probably one day I would get another job.

Ever since then, my brother has been trying to get me into government service. He himself is a clerk in government service and enjoys many advantages. Every five years, he gets an increase of ten rupees[2] in his salary. He has ten days' sick leave in the year, and when he retires he will get a pension. It would be good for me to have such a job, but it is difficult to get, because first there is an interview, at which important people sit at a desk and ask many questions. Because I am afraid of them, I cannot understand properly what they are saying, but I answer what I think they want me to answer. But it seems that my answers are somehow not the right ones, because they have not given me a job.

Now, as I walked down the stairs, I wished I could go to the cinema instead. If I had had ten annas,[3] perhaps I would have gone; it was just time for the morning show. The young clerks and the students would be collecting in a queue outside the cinema now. They would be standing and not talking much, holding their ten annas and waiting for the box office to open. I enjoy those morning shows, perhaps because the people who come to them are all young men, like myself—all silent and rather sad. I am often sad; it would even be right to say that I am sad most of the time. But when the film begins, I am happy. I love to see the beautiful women dressed in golden clothes, with heavy earrings, and necklaces, and bracelets covering their arms, and to see their handsome lovers, who are all the things I would like to be. And when they sing their love songs, so full of deep feelings, the tears sometimes come into my eyes because I am so happy. After the film is over, I never go home straightway, but I walk around the streets and think about how wonderful life could be.

When I arrived at the place where the interview was, I had to walk down many corridors and ask directions from many peons before I could find the right room. The peons were all rude to me because they knew what I had come for. They lounged back on benches outside the offices, and when I asked them, they looked me up and down before answering and sometimes made jokes about me to one another. But I was very polite to them, for even though they were only peons, they had uniforms and jobs and belonged here, whereas I did not. At last I came to the room where I had to wait. Many others were already sitting there, on chairs drawn up against the wall all around the room. No one was talking. I found a chair, and after a while an official came in with a list and asked if anyone else had come. I got up and he asked my name, and then he looked down the list and made a tick with a pencil. "Why are you late?" he asked me very sternly. I begged pardon and told him the bus in which I had come had had an accident. He said, "When you are called for an interview, you have to be here exactly on time or your

2. **rupees** (r$\overline{oo}$ pēz′): The rupee is the basic monetary unit of India.
3. **annas** (a′ nəz): The anna is a former monetary unit of India equal to one-sixteenth of a rupee.

name is crossed off the list." I begged pardon again and asked him very humbly please not to cross me off this time. I knew that all the others were listening, even though none of them looked at us. He said some more things to me very scornfully, but in the end he said, "Wait here. When your name is called, you must go in at once."

I didn't count the number of people waiting in the room, but there were a great many. Perhaps there was one job free, perhaps two or three. As I sat there, I began to feel the others all hoping anxiously that they might get the job, so I became worried and anxious, too. I stared around and tried to put my mind on something else. The walls of the room were painted green halfway up and white above that, and were quite bare. There was a fan turning from the ceiling, but it didn't give much breeze. An interview was going on behind the big door. One by one, we would all be called in there and have the door closed behind us.

I began to worry desperately. It always happens like this. When I come to an interview, I never want the job at all, but when I see all the others waiting and worrying, I want it terribly. Yet at the same time I know, deep down, that I don't want it. I know it would only be the same thing over again: writing figures and making mistakes and then being afraid when they found out. And there would be a superior officer in my office to whom I would have to be very deferential, and every time I saw him or heard his voice, I would begin to be afraid that he had found out something against me. For weeks and months I would sit and write figures, getting wearier of it and wearier, and thinking my own thoughts more and more. Then the mistakes would come, and my superior officer would be angry.

My brother never makes mistakes. For years he has been sitting in the same office, writing figures, being deferential to his superior officer, and concentrating very hard on his work. But, nevertheless, he is afraid of the same thing—a mistake that will make them angry with him and cost him his job. I think it is right for him to be afraid, for what would become of us all if he also lost his job? It is not the same with me. I believe I am afraid to lose my job only because that is a thing of which one is expected to be afraid. When I have actually lost it, I am really relieved. But this is not surprising, because I *am* very different from my brother; even in appearance I am different. As I have said, he is fifteen years older than I, but even when he was my age, he never looked as I do. My appearance has always attracted others; and right up to the time I was married, my mother used to stroke my hair and my face and say many tender things to me. Once when I was walking on my way to school through the bazaar, a man called to me very softly; and when I came, he gave me a ripe mango and said, "You are beautiful, beautiful." He looked at me in an odd, kind way and wanted me to go with him to his house, in another part of the city. I love wearing fine clothes—especially very thin white muslin kurtas[4] that have been freshly washed and starched and are embroidered at the shoulders. Sometimes I also use scent—a fine khas[5] smell—and my hair oil also smells of khas. Several years ago, just after I was married, there was a handsome teenage girl who lived in the tailor's shop opposite our house and who used to wait for me and follow me whenever I went out. But it is my brother, not I, who is married to a beautiful wife, and this has always seemed most unfair.

The big closed door opened, and the man who had been in there for an interview came out. We all looked at him, but he walked out

---

4. kurtas (kʉrt′ əz): knee-length collarless shirts worn over pajamas by men in India.

5. khas (kus): fragrant grass used in scented oil.

in a great hurry, with a preoccupied expression on his face. I could feel the anxiety in the other men getting stronger, and mine, too. The official with the list came, and we all looked up at him. He read off another name, and the man whose name was called jumped up from his chair. He started forward, but then he was brought up short by his dhoti,[6] which had got caught on a nail in the chair. As soon as he realized what had happened, he became very agitated, and when he tried to disentangle himself, his fingers shook so much that he could not get the dhoti off the nail. The official watched him coldly and said, "Hurry, now! Do you think the gentlemen will wait for as long as you please?" In his confusion, the man dropped his umbrella, and then he tried to disentangle the dhoti and pick up the umbrella at the same time. When he could not get the dhoti loose, he became so desperate that he pulled at the cloth and ripped it free. It was a pity to see the dhoti torn, because it was a new one, which he was probably wearing for the first time and had put on specially for the interview. He clasped his umbrella to his chest and scurried into the interviewing room with his dhoti hanging about his legs and his face swollen with embarrassment and confusion.

We all sat and waited. The fan, which seemed to be a very old one, made a creaking noise. One man kept cracking his finger joints—*tik*, we heard, *tik*. All the rest of us kept very still. From time to time, the official with the list came in and walked around the room very slowly, tapping his list, and then we all looked down at our feet, and the man even stopped cracking his fingers. A faint and muffled sound of voices came from behind the closed door. Sometimes a voice was raised, but even then I could not make out what was being said, though I strained hard.

My previous interview was very unpleasant for me. One of the people who were interviewing took a dislike to me and shouted at me

very loudly. He was a large, fat man who wore an English suit. His teeth were quite yellow, and when he became angry and shouted he showed them all, and even though I was very upset, I couldn't help looking at them and wondering how they had become so yellow. I don't know why he was angry. He shouted, "Good God, man! Can't you understand what's said to you?" It was true I could not understand, but I had been trying hard to answer well. What else did he expect of me? Probably there was something in my appearance he did not like. It happens that way sometimes—they take a dislike to you, and then, of course, there is nothing you can do.

Now the thought of the man with the yellow teeth made me more anxious than ever. I need great calm in my life. Whenever anything worries me too much, I have to cast the thought of it off immediately; otherwise, there is a danger that I may become ill. I felt now as if I were about to become very ill. All my limbs were itching, so that it was difficult for me to sit still, and I could feel blood rushing into my brain. I knew it was this room that was doing me so much harm—the waiting, silent men; the noise from the fan; the official with the list, walking up and down, tapping his list or striking it against his thigh; and the big closed door behind which the interview was going on. I felt a great need to get up and go away. I *didn't* want the job. I wasn't even thinking about it anymore—only about how to avoid having to sit here and wait.

Now the door opened again, and the man with the torn dhoti came out. He was biting his lip and scratching the back of his neck, and he, too, walked straight out without looking at us at all. The big door of the interviewing room was left slightly open for a moment, and

---

6. dhoti (dō′ tē): typical garment worn by Indian men, consisting of cloth tied around the waist and extending down to the ankles.

I could see a man's arm in a white shirt sleeve and part of the back of his head. His shirt was very white and of good material, and his ears stood away from his head so that one could see how his spectacles fitted over the backs of his ears. I suddenly realized that this man would be my enemy and that he would make things very difficult for me and perhaps even shout at me. Then I knew it was no use for me to stay there. The official with the list came back, and a panic seized me that he would read out my name. I rose quickly, murmuring, "Please excuse me—bathroom," and went out. I heard the official with the list call after me, "Hey, Mister, where are you going?" so I lowered my head and walked faster. I would have started to run, but that might have caused some kind of suspicion, so I just walked as fast as I could down the stairs and right out of the building. There, at last, I was able to stop and take a deep breath, and I felt much better.

I stood still only for a minute, and then I started off again, though not in any particular direction. There were a great many clerks and peons moving past me in the street, hurrying from one office building to another, with files and papers under their arms. Everyone seemed to have something to do. In the next block, I found a little park, and I was glad to see people like myself, who had nothing to do, sitting under the trees or in any other patch of shade they could find. But I couldn't sit there; it was too close to the office blocks, and any moment someone might come up and say to me, "Why did you go away?" So I walked farther. I was feeling quite lighthearted with relief over having escaped the interview.

At last I came to a row of eating stalls, and I sat down on a wooden bench outside one of them, which was called the Paris Hotel, and asked for tea. I felt badly in need of tea, and since I intended to walk part of the way home, I was in a position to pay for it. There were two Sikhs[7] sitting at the end of my bench who were eating with great appetite, dipping their hands very rapidly into brass bowls. Between mouthfuls, they exchanged remarks with the proprietor of the Paris Hotel, who sat high up inside his stall, stirring a big brass pot in which he was cooking the day's food. He was chewing a betel leaf, and from time to time he very skillfully spat the red betel juice far over the cooking pot and onto the ground between the wooden benches and tables.

I sat quietly at my end of the bench and drank my tea. The food smelled good, and it made me realize that I was hungry. I made a calculation and decided that if I walked all the way home, I could afford a little cake. (I am very fond of sweet things.) The cake was not very new, but it had a beautiful piece of bright orange peel inside it. What I wanted to do when I got home was to lie down at once and not wake up again until the next morning. That way, no one would be able to ask me any questions. By not looking at my wife at all I would be able to avoid the question in her eyes. I would not look at my sister-in-law, either, but she would be smiling—that I knew—leaning against the wall, with her hand on her hip, and looking at me and smiling. She would know that I had run away, but she would not say anything.

Let her know! What did it matter? It was true I had no job and no immediate prospect of getting one. It was true that I was dependent on my brother. Everybody knew that. There is no shame in it; there are many people without jobs. And she had been so kind to me up till now that there was no reason she should not continue to be kind to me.

The Sikhs at the end of the bench had finished eating. They licked their fingers and

---

7. Sikhs (sēks): members of a Hindu religious sect based on belief in one God and on rejection of the caste system, a rigid system of class distinctions.

belched deeply, the way one does after a good meal. They started to joke and laugh with the proprietor. I sat quiet and alone at my end of the bench. Of course, they did not laugh and joke with me, for they knew that I was superior to them; they work with their hands, whereas I am a lettered man who does not have to sweat for a living but sits on a chair in an office and writes figures and can speak in English. My brother is very proud of his superiority, and he has great contempt for carpenters and mechanics and such people. I, too, am proud of being a lettered man, but when I listened to the Sikhs laughing and joking, it occurred to me that perhaps their life was happier than mine. It was a thought that had come to me before. There is a carpenter who lives downstairs in our house, and though he is poor, there is always great eating in his house, and many people come, and I hear them laughing and singing and even dancing. The carpenter is a big, strong man, and he always looks happy, never anxious and sick with worry the way my brother does. To be sure, he doesn't wear shoes and clean, white clothes as my brother and I do, nor does he speak any English, but all the same he is happy. I don't think he gets weary of his work, and he doesn't look like a man who is afraid of his superior officers.

I put the ignorant carpenter out of my mind and thought again of my sister-in-law. If I were kind to her, I decided, she would really be kind to me someday. I became quite excited at this idea. Then I would know whether she is as soft and yet as strong as she looks. And I would know about her mouth, with the big, strong teeth. Her tongue and palate are very pink—just the color of the pink satin blouse she wears on festive occasions. And this satin has often made me think also of how smooth and warm her skin would feel. Her eyes would be shut and perhaps there would be tears on the lashes, and she would be smiling but in a different sort of way. I became very excited when I thought of it, but then the excitement passed and I was sad. I thought of my wife, who is thin and not beautiful and is without excitement. But she does whatever I want and always tries to please me. I thought of her whispering to me in the night, "Take me away to live somewhere alone—only you and I and the children." That can never be, and so always she will have to be unhappy.

Sitting on that bench, I grew more and more sad when I thought of her being unhappy, because it is not only she who is unhappy but I also and many others. Everywhere there is unhappiness. I thought of the man whose new dhoti had been torn and who would now have to go home and sew it carefully, so that the tear would not be seen. I thought of all those other men sitting and waiting to be interviewed, all but one or two of whom would not get the job for which they had come and so would have to go on to another interview and another and another, to sit and wait and be anxious. And my brother, who has a job but is frightened that he will lose it—and my mother, who is so old that she can only sit on the floor and stroke her pieces of cloth—and my sister-in-law, who is warm and strong and does not care for her husband. Yet life could be so different. When I go to the cinema and hear the beautiful songs they sing, I know how different it could be; and also sometimes, when I sit alone and think my thoughts, I have a feeling that everything could be truly beautiful. But now my tea was finished and also my cake, and I wished I had not bought them, because it was a long way to walk home and I was tired.

Thinking About the Story

A PERSONAL RESPONSE

sharing impressions

1. How do you feel about the narrator of the story? Jot down your reaction in your journal.

constructing interpretations

2. How well do you think the narrator understands himself?
Think about
- qualities he directly ascribes to himself
- qualities indirectly revealed in his internal monologue
- the reasons he gives for avoiding the interview
- the things that give him pleasure

3. Evaluate the narrator's family relationships.
Think about
- the expectations of his family
- his role as a dependent brother in the household
- the nature of his relationship with his wife
- his comments about his sister-in-law

4. How do you account for the narrator's fascination with movies? Cite examples to support your response.

5. Is the narrator's tendency to be a "thoughtful person" a strength or weakness in his case?

A CREATIVE RESPONSE

6. If the narrator had gone through the interview and been hired for the job, how might the story have ended?

A CRITICAL RESPONSE

7. Use details from "The Interview" to explain the story's message about human nature.

8. What differences and similarities do you see between the narrator of this story and Marko in "The Wooing of Ariadne"?

Analyzing the Writer's Craft

POINT OF VIEW AND NARRATOR

Think about the information the narrator provides about himself and his family and whether his observations seem accurate.

Building a Literary Vocabulary. Point of view refers to the narrative method, or kind of narrator, used in a short story, novel, or nonfiction selection. "The Interview" is written from the first-person point of view. The narrator is the main character in the story, and the events in the story are seen through his eyes. Because the first-person point of view reveals only the narrator's view—of himself, his family relationships, and events in the story—the reader may find that the observations are colored or distorted by his perspective.

Application: Understanding Point of View and Narrator. Read the following statements that the narrator makes. With a classmate, discuss how the narrator's perceptions in each statement compare with your own.

1. "I am always very careful of my appearance. . . . I always like it [my mustache] to look very neat, like Raj Kapoor's, the film star's."

2. "I think they [women] realize that I am a rather sensitive person and that therefore I must be treated gently."

3. "I believe I am afraid to lose my job only because that is a thing of which one is expected to be afraid. When I have actually lost it, I am really relieved."

4. "I, too, am proud of being a lettered man, but when I listened to the Sikhs laughing and joking, it occurred to me that perhaps their life was happier than mine."

Connecting Reading and Writing

1. Put yourself in the role of an employment counselor to whom the young man in the story comes for advice. Write a **dialogue** to share with the class in which you and the young man discuss his interests, skills, and goals.

Option: Imagine that the young man has decided to apply for a vocational program and needs a reference. Write a **recommendation** for him.

2. Write a **narrative** for your teacher and classmates from the point of view of the wife in the story. Include such information as her thoughts and feelings about being in that household, her goals for her husband, and her own dreams.

Option: Record the thoughts and feelings of the narrator's wife in a **diary entry** that she might write.

3. Read more about contemporary Indian society and write an **expository essay** for publication in a travel magazine in which you discuss the impact of Western values, such as ambition, on traditional Indian life.

Option: Write **notes** for an oral presentation on this subject for your class.

A Summer's Reading

BERNARD MALAMUD

A biography of Malamud appears on page 424.

Approaching the Story

Bernard Malamud once described himself as a chronicler of "simple people struggling to make their lives better in a world of bad luck." In writing about these people, Malamud explored basic issues such as commitment, responsibility, moral choice, suffering, and love. In "A Summer's Reading," the main character is a lonely young man who has quit school and scorns worthwhile reading. The story is set in a working-class neighborhood of New York City during the 1940's.

Building Vocabulary

These essential words are footnoted within the story.

unobtrusively (un əb troo′ siv lē): George **unobtrusively** crossed the street. (page 201)

railed (rāld): Sophie **railed** at him, then begged him to come out. (page 203)

Connecting Writing and Reading

In your journal, list several good books that you have read. Then briefly explain what motivated you to read each one. Did you read primarily for pleasure? for self-improvement? to impress someone else? to fill up idle time? to complete an assignment? As you read this story, consider what might motivate the main character to read good books.

GEORGE STOYONOVICH was a neighborhood boy who had quit high school on an impulse when he was sixteen, run out of patience, and though he was ashamed every time he went looking for a job, when people asked him if he had finished and he had to say no, he never went back to school. This summer was a hard time for jobs and he had none. Having so much time on his hands, George thought of going to summer school, but the kids in his classes would be too young. He also considered registering in a night high school, only he didn't like the idea of the teachers always telling him what to do. He felt they had not respected him. The result was he stayed off the streets and in his room most of the day. He was close to twenty and had needs with the neighborhood girls, but no money to spend, and he couldn't get more than an occasional few cents because his father was poor, and his sister Sophie, who resembled George, a tall bony girl of twenty-three, earned very little and what she had she kept for herself. Their mother was dead, and Sophie had to take care of the house.

Very early in the morning George's father got up to go to work in a fish market. Sophie left at about eight for her long ride in the subway to a cafeteria in the Bronx.[1] George had his coffee by himself, then hung around in the house. When the house, a five-room railroad flat[2] above a butcher store, got on his nerves he cleaned it up—mopped the floors with a wet mop and put things away. But most of the time he sat in his room. In the afternoons he listened to the ball game. Otherwise he had a couple of old copies of the *World Almanac* he had bought long ago, and he liked to read in them and also the magazines and newspapers that Sophie brought home, that had been left on the tables in the cafeteria. They were mostly picture magazines about movie stars and sports figures, also usually the *News* and

Mirror. Sophie herself read whatever fell into her hands, although she sometimes read good books.

She once asked George what he did in his room all day and he said he read a lot too.

"Of what besides what I bring home? Do you ever read any worthwhile books?"

"Some," George answered, although he really didn't. He had tried to read a book or two that Sophie had in the house but found he was in no mood for them. Lately he couldn't stand made-up stories; they got on his nerves. He wished he had some hobby to work at—as a kid he was good in carpentry, but where could he work at it? Sometimes during the day he went for walks, but mostly he did his walking after the hot sun had gone down and it was cooler in the streets.

In the evening after supper George left the house and wandered in the neighborhood. During the sultry days some of the storekeepers and their wives sat in chairs on the thick, broken sidewalks in front of their shops, fanning themselves, and George walked past them and the guys hanging out on the candy-store corner. A couple of them he had known his whole life, but nobody recognized each other. He had no place special to go, but generally, saving it till the last, he left the neighborhood and walked for blocks till he came to a darkly lit little park with benches and trees and an iron railing, giving it a feeling of privacy. He sat on a bench here, watching the leafy trees and the flowers blooming on the inside of the railing, thinking of a better life for himself. He thought of the jobs he had had since he had quit school—delivery boy, stock clerk, runner, lately working in a factory—and he was dissatisfied with all of them. He felt he would some-

---

1. **the Bronx:** one of the five boroughs composing New York City.
2. **railroad flat:** an apartment with rooms arranged one behind another.

day like to have a good job and live in a private house with a porch, on a street with trees. He wanted to have some dough in his pocket to buy things with, and a girl to go with, so as not to be so lonely, especially on Saturday nights. He wanted people to like and respect him. He thought about these things often but mostly when he was alone at night. Around midnight he got up and drifted back to his hot and stony neighborhood.

One time while on his walk George met Mr. Cattanzara coming home very late from work. He wondered if he was drunk but then could tell he wasn't. Mr. Cattanzara, a stocky, baldheaded man who worked in a change booth on an IRT station,[3] lived on the next block after George's, above a shoe repair store. Nights, during the hot weather, he sat on his stoop in an undershirt, reading the *New York Times* in the light of the shoemaker's window. He read it from the first page to the last, then went up to sleep. And all the time he was reading the paper, his wife, a fat woman with a white face, leaned out of the window, gazing into the street, her thick white arms folded under her loose breasts, on the window ledge.

Once in a while Mr. Cattanzara came home drunk, but it was a quiet drunk. He never made any trouble, only walked stiffly up the street and slowly climbed the stairs into the hall. Though drunk, he looked the same as always, except for his tight walk, the quietness, and that his eyes were wet. George liked Mr. Cattanzara because he remembered him giving him nickels to buy lemon ice with when he was a squirt. Mr. Cattanzara was a different type than those in the neighborhood. He asked different questions than the others when he met you, and he seemed to know what went on in all the newspapers. He read them, as his fat sick wife watched from the window.

"What are you doing with yourself this summer, George?" Mr. Cattanzara asked. "I see you walkin' around at nights."

George felt embarrassed. "I like to walk."

"What are you doin' in the day now?"

"Nothing much just right now. I'm waiting for a job." Since it shamed him to admit he wasn't working, George said, "I'm staying home—but I'm reading a lot to pick up my education."

Mr. Cattanzara looked interested. He mopped his hot face with a red handkerchief.

"What are you readin'?"

George hesitated, then said, "I got a list of books in the library once, and now I'm gonna read them this summer." He felt strange and a little unhappy saying this, but he wanted Mr. Cattanzara to respect him.

"How many books are there on it?"

"I never counted them. Maybe around a hundred."

Mr. Cattanzara whistled through his teeth.

"I figure if I did that," George went on earnestly, "it would help me in my education. I don't mean the kind they give you in high school. I want to know different things than they learn there, if you know what I mean."

The change maker nodded. "Still and all, one hundred books is a pretty big load for one summer."

"It might take longer."

"After you're finished with some, maybe you and I can shoot the breeze about them?" said Mr. Cattanzara.

"When I'm finished," George answered.

Mr. Cattanzara went home and George continued on his walk. After that, though he had the urge to, George did nothing different from usual. He still took his walks at night, ending up in the little park. But one evening the shoemaker on the next block stopped George to say he was a good boy, and George figured that Mr. Cattanzara had told him all about the books he was reading. From the shoemaker it must have gone down the street,

---

3. IRT station: a New York City subway station.

because George saw a couple of people smiling kindly at him, though nobody spoke to him personally. He felt a little better around the neighborhood and liked it more, though not so much he would want to live in it forever. He had never exactly disliked the people in it, yet he had never liked them very much either. It was the fault of the neighborhood. To his surprise, George found out that his father and Sophie knew about his reading too. His father was too shy to say anything about it—he was never much of a talker in his whole life—but Sophie was softer to George, and she showed him in other ways she was proud of him.

As the summer went on George felt in a good mood about things. He cleaned the house every day, as a favor to Sophie, and he enjoyed the ball games more. Sophie gave him a buck a week allowance, and though it still wasn't enough and he had to use it carefully, it was a helluva lot better than just having two bits now and then. What he bought with the money—cigarettes mostly, an occasional beer or movie ticket—he got a big kick out of. Life wasn't so bad if you knew how to appreciate it. Occasionally he bought a paperback book from the newsstand, but he never got around to reading it, though he was glad to have a couple of books in his room. But he read thoroughly Sophie's magazines and newspapers. And at night was the most enjoyable time, because when he passed the storekeepers sitting outside their stores, he could tell they regarded him highly. He walked erect, and though he did not say much to them, or they to him, he could feel approval on all sides. A couple of nights he felt so good that he skipped the park at the end of the evening. He just wandered in the neighborhood, where people had known him from the time he was a kid playing punchball whenever there was a game of it going; he wandered there, then came home and got undressed for bed, feeling fine.

For a few weeks he had talked only once with Mr. Cattanzara, and though the change maker had said nothing more about the books, asked no questions, his silence made George a little uneasy. For a while George didn't pass in front of Mr. Cattanzara's house any more, until one night, forgetting himself, he approached it from a different direction than he usually did when he did. It was already past midnight. The street, except for one or two people, was deserted, and George was surprised when he saw Mr. Cattanzara still reading his newspaper by the light of the streetlamp overhead. His impulse was to stop at the stoop and talk to him. He wasn't sure what he wanted to say, though he felt the words would come when he began to talk; but the more he thought about it, the more the idea scared him, and he decided he'd better not. He even considered beating it home by another street, but he was too near Mr. Cattanzara, and the change maker might see him as he ran, and get annoyed. So George unobtrusively[4] crossed the street, trying to make it seem as if he had to look in a store window on the other side, which he did, and then went on, uncomfortable at what he was doing. He feared Mr. Cattanzara would glance up from his paper and call him a dirty rat for walking on the other side of the street, but all he did was sit there, sweating through his undershirt, his bald head shining in the dim light as he read his *Times,* and upstairs his fat wife leaned out of the window, seeming to read the paper along with him. George thought she would spy him and yell out to Mr. Cattanzara, but she never moved her eyes off her husband.

George made up his mind to stay away from the change maker until he had got some of his softback books read, but when he started them and saw they were mostly

---

4. unobtrusively (un əb tro͞o′ siv lē): in a way that does not call attention to itself.

storybooks, he lost his interest and didn't bother to finish them. He lost his interest in reading other things too. Sophie's magazines and newspapers went unread. She saw them piling up on a chair in his room and asked why he was no longer looking at them, and George told her it was because of all the other reading he had to do. Sophie said she had guessed that was it. So for most of the day, George had the radio on, turning to music when he was sick of the human voice. He kept the house fairly neat, and Sophie said nothing on the days when he neglected it. She was still kind and gave him his extra buck, though things weren't so good for him as they had been before.

But they were good enough, considering. Also his night walks invariably picked him up, no matter how bad the day was. Then one night George saw Mr. Cattanzara coming down the street toward him. George was about to turn and run but he recognized from Mr. Cattanzara's walk that he was drunk, and if so, probably he would not even bother to notice him. So George kept on walking straight ahead until he came abreast of Mr. Cattanzara and though he felt wound up enough to pop into the sky, he was not surprised when Mr. Cattanzara passed him without a word, walking slowly, his face and body stiff. George drew a breath in relief at his narrow escape, when he heard his name called, and there stood Mr. Cattanzara at his elbow, smelling like the inside of a beer barrel. His eyes were sad as he gazed at George, and George felt so intensely uncomfortable he was tempted to shove the drunk aside and continue on his walk.

But he couldn't act that way to him, and, besides, Mr. Cattanzara took a nickel out of his pants pocket and handed it to him.

"Go buy yourself a lemon ice, Georgie."

"It's not that time any more, Mr. Cattanzara," George said, "I am a big guy now."

"No, you ain't," said Mr. Cattanzara, to which George made no reply he could think of.

"How are all your books comin' along now?" Mr. Cattanzara asked. Though he tried to stand steady, he swayed a little.

"Fine, I guess," said George, feeling the red crawling up his face.

"You ain't sure?" The change maker smiled slyly, a way George had never seen him smile.

"Sure I'm sure. They're fine."

Though his head swayed in little arcs, Mr. Cattanzara's eyes were steady. He had small blue eyes which could hurt if you looked at them too long.

"George," he said, "name me one book on that list that you read this summer, and I will drink to your health."

"I don't want anybody drinking to me."

"Name me one so I can ask you a question on it. Who can tell, if it's a good book maybe I might wanna read it myself."

George knew he looked passable on the outside, but inside he was crumbling apart.

Unable to reply, he shut his eyes, but when —years later—he opened them, he saw that Mr. Cattanzara had, out of pity, gone away, but in his ears he still heard the words he had said when he left, "George, don't do what I did."

The next night he was afraid to leave his room, and though Sophie argued with him he wouldn't open the door.

"What are you doing in there?" she asked.

"Nothing."

"Aren't you reading?"

"No."

She was silent a minute, then asked, "Where do you keep the books you read? I never see any in your room outside of a few cheap trashy ones."

He wouldn't tell her.

"In that case you're not worth a buck of my hard-earned money. Why should I break my back for you? Go on out, you bum, and get a job."

He stayed in his room for almost a week, except to sneak into the kitchen when nobody was home. Sophie railed[5] at him, then begged him to come out, and his old father wept, but George wouldn't budge, though the weather was terrible and his small room stifling. He found it very hard to breathe, each breath was like drawing a flame into his lungs.

One night, unable to stand the heat anymore, he burst into the street at one A.M., a shadow of himself. He hoped to sneak to the park without being seen, but there were people all over the block, wilted and listless, waiting for a breeze. George lowered his eyes and walked, in disgrace, away from them, but before long he discovered they were still friendly to him. He figured Mr. Cattanzara hadn't told on him. Maybe when he woke up out of his drunk the next morning, he had forgotten all about meeting George. George felt his confidence slowly come back to him.

That same night a man on a street corner asked him if it was true that he had finished reading so many books, and George admitted he had. The man said it was a wonderful thing for a boy his age to read so much.

"Yeah," George said, but he felt relieved. He hoped nobody would mention the books any more, and when, after a couple of days, he accidentally met Mr. Cattanzara again, *he* didn't, though George had the idea he was the one who had started the rumor that he had finished all the books.

One evening in the fall, George ran out of his house to the library, where he hadn't been in years. There were books all over the place, wherever he looked, and though he was struggling to control an inward trembling, he easily counted off a hundred, then sat down at a table to read.

---

5. railed (rāld): spoke bitterly or complained violently.

Thinking About the Story

A PERSONAL RESPONSE

sharing impressions

1. What do you think about George after reading this story? In your journal, record your impressions of him.

constructing interpretations

2. In your opinion, what finally motivates George to start reading good books?

Think about
- the influence of Mr. Cattanzara, a change maker
- the influence of his sister Sophie
- the values of the neighborhood people
- George's situation this particular summer

3. How would you explain the changes that take place in George's relationship to his family and neighbors?

4. Why do you think Mr. Cattanzara lies to the neighbors about George's completion of the reading?
> ***Think about***
> - how he reacts when George first tells him about reading
> - why he tells the neighbors about George's reading in the first place
> - how he reacts when he finds out George is lying about his reading

A CREATIVE RESPONSE

5. How might this story be different if George did not value the respect of Mr. Cattanzara?

6. What effect do you think reading the hundred books will have on George?

A CRITICAL RESPONSE

7. Do you agree with Malamud's view that one person can make a difference in the life of someone else? Explain your answer by citing examples from this story and your own experiences.

8. To what extent, if any, do you think George is like a typical teenager?
> ***Think about***
> - his attitude toward adults
> - his relationships with other members of his family
> - the way he uses his free time
> - his needs and aspirations
> - his reaction to reading made-up stories
> - his motivation to read good books

9. How would you compare George's situation to the situation of the young man in "The Interview"?

Analyzing the Writer's Craft

Consider how much you know about George and how little you know about Mr. Cattanzara.

Building a Literary Vocabulary. Point of view refers to the narrative method, or the kind of narrator, used in a literary work. Third-person point of view means that a story is told by a narrative voice outside the action, not by one of the characters. If a story is told from an omniscient, or all-knowing, third-person point of view, the narrator sees into the mind of more than one character. For example, in "The Pearl" the narrator reveals the thoughts and feelings not only of Mrs. Sasaki but also of Mrs. Azuma and the other guests at the party. If a story is told from a limited third-person point of view, the narrator tells only what one character thinks, feels, and observes. In "A Summer's Reading," the reader's understanding of the story is limited to George's understanding and perceptions; the narrator does not reach into the mind of any other character.

Application: Analyzing Point of View. Go back through the story and reread the passages describing the encounters between George and Mr. Cattanzara. Rewrite one of these passages from the omniscient third-person point of view so that Mr. Cattanzara's thoughts are also revealed. Then, in a small group, discuss the different effects of the limited and the omniscient points of view. Speculate about why Bernard Malamud might have chosen the limited third-person point of view for his story.

Connecting Reading and Writing

1. What books would you recommend George read? Create a **reading list** of from five to ten titles and for each, briefly explain why you think the book might appeal to George.

Option: Survey twenty of your classmates and write a **report** about their recommended books.

2. Imagine that George has applied for admission to a college and needs a reference. Write a **recommendation** for him to the dean of admissions, indicating what kind of student you think he will be.

Option: Write an **application essay** that George might submit to a college.

3. If you were going to address a meeting of teachers on the best ways to motivate students to read, what would you say? Using your prereading notes to get started, write **note cards** containing the main points you would cover in your address.

Option: Write an **editorial** for your school paper to persuade students to read good books.

4. The critic Jeffrey Helterman wrote the following assessment of Malamud's short stories: "The surprising thing about Malamud's short fiction is that we recognize ourselves in his characters. . . . They are us." Write a **letter** to Helterman, explaining your reasons for agreeing or disagreeing with his opinion.

Option: In your journal write a **personal response** to "A Summer's Reading," commenting on how closely you identify with the main characters.

Metonymy,
or The Husband's Revenge

RACHEL DE QUEIROZ

A biography of de Queiroz appears on page 426.

Approaching the Story

In her novels, plays, and short stories, Brazilian writer Rachel de Queiroz (rä chel′ de ke′ ē rôs) has written richly of the Latin American world. The situation she describes in this short story, however, could happen anywhere. The narrator of "Metonymy" begins by discussing a figure of speech and from there launches into a compelling tale with an unexpected twist.

Building Vocabulary

These essential words are footnoted within the story.

rebuke (ri byo͞ok′): I accepted his **rebuke** with humility. (page 207)

rhetoric (ret′ ər ik): Ever since, I have been using metonymy—my only bond with classical **rhetoric**. (page 207)

illicit (il lis′ it): Fate . . . does not like **illicit** love. (page 208)

Connecting Writing and Reading

Imagine that you have been cheated, have had something valuable stolen from you, have had a friend break an important promise, or have become very, very jealous. Which of these things would you feel like doing?

smashing dishes	plotting to get back at the person
picking a fight with the person	trying to forget the incident
crying	writing a hate letter
attempting a reconciliation	lashing out at anybody who got in your way

Describe briefly in your journal how you might express your anger or seek revenge. Then compare your reactions with the reaction of the main character.

METONYMY. I LEARNED the word in 1930 and shall never forget it. I had just published my first novel. A literary critic had scolded me because my hero went out into the night "chest unbuttoned."

"What deplorable nonsense!" wrote this eminently sensible gentleman. "Why does she not say what she means? Obviously, it was his shirt that was unbuttoned, not his chest."

I accepted his rebuke[1] with humility, indeed with shame. But my illustrious Latin professor, Dr. Matos Peixoto,[2] came to my rescue. He said that what I had written was perfectly correct; that I had used a respectable figure of speech known as metonymy; and that this figure consisted in the use of one word for another word associated with it—for example, a word representing a cause instead of the effect, or representing the container when the content is intended. The classic instance, he told me, is "the sparkling cup"; in reality, not the cup but the wine in it is sparkling.

The professor and I wrote a letter, which was published in the newspaper where the review had appeared. It put my unjust critic in his place. I hope he learned a lesson. I know I did. Ever since, I have been using metonymy—my only bond with classical rhetoric.[3]

Moreover, I have devoted some thought to it, and I have concluded that metonymy may be more than a figure of speech. There is, I believe, such a thing as practical or applied metonymy. Let me give a crude example, drawn from my own experience. A certain lady of my acquaintance suddenly moved out of the boardinghouse where she had been living for years and became a mortal enemy of the woman who owned it. I asked her why. We both knew that the woman was a kindly soul; she had given my friend injections when she needed them, had often loaned her a hot water

bottle, and had always waited on her when she had her little heart attacks. My friend replied: "It's the telephone in the hall. I hate her for it. Half the time when I answered it, the call was a hoax or joke of some sort."

"But the owner of the boardinghouse didn't perpetrate these hoaxes. She wasn't responsible for them."

"No. But whose telephone was it?"

I know another case of applied metonymy, a more disastrous one, for it involved a crime. It happened in a city of the interior, which I shall not name for fear that someone may recognize the parties and revive the scandal. I shall narrate the crime but conceal the criminal.

Well, in this city of the interior there lived a man. He was not old, but he was spent, which is worse than being old. In his youth he had suffered from beriberi.[4] His legs were weak, his chest was tired and asthmatic, his skin was yellowish, and his eyes were rheumy. He was, however, a man of property; he owned the house in which he lived and the one next to it, in which he had set up a grocery store. Therefore, although so unattractive personally, he was able to find himself a wife. In all justice to him, he did not tempt fate by marrying a beauty. Instead, he married a poor, emaciated girl who worked in a men's clothing factory. By her face one would have thought that she had consumption.[5] So our friend felt safe. He did not foresee the effects of good nutrition and a healthful life on a woman's appearance. The

---

1. rebuke (ri byōōk′): sharp scolding or reprimand.
2. Matos Peixoto (mä′ tôs pā zhô′ tô).
3. rhetoric (ret′ ər ik): the art of using words effectively in speaking or writing.
4. beriberi (ber′ ē ber′ ē): a disease caused by poor diet that results in nerve disorders and sometimes swelling of the body.
5. consumption (kən sump′ shən): tuberculosis.

girl no longer spent eight hours a day at a sewing table. She was the mistress of her house. She ate well: fresh meat, cucumber salad, pork fat with beans and manioc[6] mush, all kinds of sweets, and oranges, which her husband bought by the gross for his customers. The effects were like magic. Her body filled out, especially in the best places. She even seemed to grow taller. And her face—what a change! I may have forgotten to mention that her features, in themselves, were good to begin with. Moreover, money enabled her to embellish her natural advantages with art; she began to wear make-up, to wave her hair, and to dress well.

Lovely, attractive, she now found her sickly, prematurely old husband a burden and a bore. Each evening, as soon as the store was closed, he dined, mostly on milk (he could not stomach meat), took his newspaper, and rested on his chaise longue[7] until time to go to bed. He did not care for movies or for soccer or for radio. He did not even show much interest in love. Just a sort of tepid, tasteless cohabitation.

And then Fate intervened: it produced a sergeant.

Granted, it was unjust for a young wife, after being reconditioned at her husband's expense, to employ her charms against the aforesaid husband. Unjust; but, then, this world thrives on injustice, doesn't it? The sergeant—I shall not say whether he was in the army, the air force, the marines, or the fusiliers,[8] for I still mean to conceal the identities of the parties—the sergeant was muscular, young, ingratiating, with a manly, commanding voice and a healthy spring in his walk. He looked gloriously martial in his high-buttoned uniform.

One day, when the lady was in charge of the counter (while her husband lunched), the sergeant came in. Exactly what happened and what did not happen is hard to say. It seems that the sergeant asked for a pack of cigarettes.

Then he wanted a little vermouth. Finally he asked permission to listen to the sports broadcast on the radio next to the counter. Maybe it was just an excuse to remain there awhile. In any case, the girl said it would be all right. It is hard to refuse a favor to a sergeant, especially a sergeant like this one. It appears that the sergeant asked nothing more that day. At most, he and the girl exchanged expressive glances and a few agreeable words, murmured so softly that the customers, always alert for something to gossip about, could not hear them.

Three times more the husband lunched while his wife chatted with the sergeant in the store. The flirtation progressed. Then the husband fell ill with a grippe,[9] and the two others went far beyond flirtation. How and where they met, no one was able to discover. The important thing is that they were lovers and that they loved with a forbidden love, like Tristan and Isolde or Paolo and Francesca.[10]

Then Fate, which does not like illicit[11] love and generally punishes those who engage in it, transferred the sergeant to another part of the country.

It is said that only those who love can really know the pain of separation. The girl cried so

---

6. manioc (man′ ē äk′): a tropical plant with edible roots.

7. chaise longue (shāz′ lôn′): a couchlike chair with support for the back and a seat long enough to support a person's outstretched legs.

8. fusiliers (fyoo′ zi lirz′): special regiment of soldiers.

9. grippe (grip): the flu.

10. Tristan and Isolde or Paolo and Francesca (tris′ tən, i sōl′ də, pä′ ô lô, frän ches′ kä): two legendary pairs of lovers whose affairs ended in tragedy.

11. illicit (il lis′ it): not allowed by law or custom; improper.

much that her eyes grew red and swollen. She lost her appetite. Beneath her rouge could be seen the consumptive complexion of earlier times. And these symptoms aroused her husband's suspicion, although, curiously, he had never suspected anything when the love affair was flourishing and everything was wine and roses.

He began to observe her carefully. He scrutinized her in her periods of silence. He listened to her sighs and to the things she murmured in her sleep. He snooped around and found a postcard and a book, both with a man's name in the same handwriting. He found the insignia of the sergeant's regiment and concluded that the object of his wife's murmurs, sighs, and silences was not only a man but a soldier. Finally he made the supreme discovery: that they had indeed betrayed him. For he discovered the love letters, bearing airmail stamps, a distant postmark, and the sergeant's name. They left no reasonable doubt.

For five months the poor fellow twisted the poisoned dagger of jealousy inside his own thin, sickly chest. Like a boy who discovers a bird's nest and, hiding nearby, watches the eggs increasing in number every day, so the husband, using a duplicate key to the wood chest where his wife put her valuables, watched the increase in the number of letters concealed there. He had given her the chest during their honeymoon, saying, "Keep your secrets here." And the ungrateful girl had obeyed him.

Every day at the fateful hour of lunch, she replaced her husband at the counter. But he was not interested in eating. He ran to her room, pulled out a drawer in her bureau, removed the chest from under a lot of panties, slips, and such, took the little key out of his pocket, opened the chest, and anxiously read the new letter. If there was no new letter, he reread the one dated August 21; it was so full of realism that it sounded like dialogue from a French movie. Then he put everything away and hurried to the kitchen, where he swallowed a few spoonfuls of broth and gnawed at a piece of bread. It was almost impossible to swallow with the passion of those two thieves sticking in his throat.

When the poor man's heart had become utterly saturated with jealousy and hatred, he took a revolver and a box of bullets from the counter drawer; they had been left, years before, by a customer as security for a debt which had never been paid. He loaded the revolver.

One bright morning at exactly ten o'clock, when the store was full of customers, he excused himself and went through the doorway that connected the store with his home. In a few seconds the customers heard the noise of a row, a woman's scream, and three shots. On the sidewalk in front of the shopkeeper's house they saw his wife on her knees, still screaming, and him, with the revolver in his trembling hand, trying to raise her. The front door of the house was open. Through it, they saw a man's legs, wearing khaki trousers and boots. He was lying face down, with his head and torso in the parlor, not visible from the street.

The husband was the first to speak. Raising his eyes from his wife, he looked at the terror-stricken people and spotted among them his favorite customer. He took a few steps, stood in the doorway, and said:

"You may call the police."

At the police station he explained that he was a deceived husband. The police chief remarked, "Isn't this a little unusual? Ordinarily you kill your wives. They're weaker than their lovers."

The man was deeply offended.

"No," he protested. "I would be utterly incapable of killing my wife. She is all that I have in the world. She is refined, pretty, and hard-working. She helps me in the store, she understands bookkeeping, she writes the letters to the wholesalers. She is the only person who knows how to prepare my food. Why should I want to kill my wife?"

"I see," said the chief of police. "So you killed her lover."

The man shook his head.

"Wrong again. The sergeant—her lover—was transferred to a place far from here. I discovered the affair only after he had gone. By reading his letters. They tell the whole story. I know one of them by heart, the worst of them. . . ."

The police chief did not understand. He said nothing and waited for the husband to continue, which he presently did:

"Those letters! If they were alive, I would kill them, one by one. They were shameful to read—almost like a book. I thought of taking an airplane trip. I thought of killing some other sergeant here, so that they would all learn a lesson not to fool around with another man's wife. But I was afraid of the rest of the regiment; you know how these military men stick together. Still, I had to do something. Otherwise I would have gone crazy. I couldn't get those letters out of my head. Even on days when none arrived, I felt terrible, worse than my wife. I had to put an end to it, didn't I? So today, at last, I did it. I waited till the regular time and, when I saw the wretch appear on the other side of the street, I went into the house, hid behind a door, and lay there waiting for him."

"The lover?" asked the police chief stupidly.

"No, of course not. I told you I didn't kill her lover. It was those letters. The sergeant sent them—but *he* delivered them. Almost every day, there he was at the door, smiling, with the vile envelope in his hand. I pointed the revolver and fired three times. He didn't say a word; he just fell. No, Chief, it wasn't her lover. It was the mailman."

Thinking About the Story

A PERSONAL RESPONSE

sharing impressions

1. How do you feel about the husband's action at the end of the story? Express your feelings briefly in your journal.

constructing interpretations

2. Which character do you sympathize with most, and why?

A CREATIVE RESPONSE

3. How might the story be different if the sergeant had not been transferred?

A CRITICAL RESPONSE

4. How would you describe the tone of this story?

    Think about
- the definition of tone as the attitude a writer takes toward a subject
- the narrator's introductory anecdote about the word *metonymy*
- the narrator's commentary interspersed throughout the story
- who, if anyone, is treated as a sympathetic character
- the outcome of the story

5. Do you think this story has a message? Explain your view.

6. Of the stories you have read in this unit, which one best illustrates "the irrational, unpredictable, and twisted side of human nature"? Explain why you think so.

Analyzing the Writer's Craft

FORESHADOWING

Did the ending of this story surprise you? What clues in the story could have helped prepare you for the way it ended?

Building a Literary Vocabulary. Foreshadowing is a writer's use of hints or clues to indicate events that will occur later in a narrative. This technique creates suspense and at the same time prepares the reader for what is to come. In "Metonymy, or The Husband's Revenge," for instance, the second part of the title provides a clue that the husband will seek some kind of revenge. Readers may easily overlook this clue, however, and the actual ending may still come as a surprise, especially since it is contrary to what readers would ordinarily expect.

Application: Recognizing Foreshadowing. Working with a partner, read the story again and identify passages that foreshadow an unfortunate or violent outcome of some kind. Then look for clues that lay the groundwork for the ending that takes place. Compare your findings with those of other groups in the class.

Connecting Reading and Writing

1. Consider what the wife's reflections might be concerning this event and express them in the form of a **first-person account** that she writes for herself.

Option: Imagine the exchange that might take place between the police officer and the wife following the murder. Write down what they say in a set of **questions and answers.** Make a recording of the exchange and play it for your class.

2. Write a **letter** that you think the wife might send to the sergeant, telling him what has happened and what she has decided to do.

Option: Write a brief **summary** of what might happen next in the story if it were continued.

3. Think back to the "chest unbuttoned" and "the sparkling cup," the examples of metonymy provided at the beginning of the story. List additional examples of this **figure of speech.** Some examples may be ones you have heard or read; others can be your creation. Share your list with the class.

Option: Create several **cartoons** for your classmates that illustrate literally your examples of metonymy.

The Form of the Sword

JORGE LUIS BORGES

A biography of Borges appears on page 420.

Approaching the Story

Jorge Luis Borges (hôr′ hə lōō ēs′ bôr′ hes) is an Argentine writer whose stories often portray high-action adventure in dreamlike settings. The story you are about to read is a frame story. In the "frame" the narrator describes his encounter with an English landowner who has been the subject of curious speculation on the part of his South American neighbors. The Englishman, whose own story forms the central part of "The Form of the Sword," recalls an incident that occurred in Ireland during the civil war some years before.

HIS FACE WAS crossed with a rancorous scar: a nearly perfect ashen arc which sank into his temple on one side and his cheek on the other. His real name is of no importance: in Tacuarembo[1] everyone knew him as the Englishman of La Colorada.[2] The great landowner of these parts, Cardoso,[3] had not been interested in selling; I have heard that the Englishman had recourse to an unexpected argument: he told him the secret history of the scar. The Englishman had come from the frontier, from Rio Grande del Sur;[4] there were those who said he had been a smuggler in Brazil. His fields were overgrown with underbrush; the wells were bitter; to remedy these faults, the Englishman worked alongside his *peones*.[5] They say he was strict to the point of cruelty but scrupulously fair. They also say he was a drinking man: a couple of times a year he would lock himself up in a room in the tower, and two or three days later he would emerge as if from a bout of insanity or from the battlefield, pale, tremulous, abashed—and as authoritarian as ever. I remember his glacial eyes, his energetic thinness, his gray mustache. He had scant dealings with anyone; true, his Spanish was rudimentary, contaminated with Brazilian. Apart from an occasional commercial letter or pamphlet, he received no correspondence.

The last time I made a trip through the northern provinces, a flash flood in the Caraguatá arroyo[6] forced me to spend the night at La Colorada. I was only there a few minutes when I felt that my presence was inopportune. I tried getting into the good

1. **Tacuarembo** (tä kwä *rem*′ bô).
2. **La Colorada** (lä kô lô *rä*′ dä).
3. **Cardoso** (kär dô′ sô).
4. **Rio Grande del Sur** (rē′ ô grän′ dä del sōōr).
5. *peones* (pē ô′ nes) *Spanish:* peasants.
6. **Caraguatá arroyo** (kä rä gwä tä′ ə rɔi′ ō): an arroyo is a narrow ravine.

graces of the Englishman; I resorted to the least acute of all the passions: patriotism. I said that a country with the spirit of England was invincible. My interlocutor[7] agreed, but he added with a smile that he was not English. He was Irish, from Dungarvan. Having said this, he stopped himself, as if he had revealed a secret.

After supper, we went out to look at the sky. It had cleared, but behind the ridge of the mountains, the south, fissured and shot through with lightning flashes, was brewing up another storm. Back in the deserted dining room, the waiter who had served us supper brought out a bottle of rum. We drank steadily, in silence.

I do not know what hour of the night it might have been when I realized that I was drunk; I do not know what inspiration or exultation or tedium made me mention the scar. The Englishman's face changed color. For a few seconds, I thought he was going to ask me to leave. Finally he said, in a normal voice, "I'll tell you the story of my wound on one condition: that you do not minimize the opprobrium[8] it calls forth, that you not belittle a single infamous circumstance."

I agreed. And this, then, is the story he recounted, in a mixture of English, Spanish, and Portuguese:

About 1922, in a city in Connaught,[9] I was one of many men conspiring for Irish independence. Of my comrades, some survived to engage in peaceful pursuits; others, paradoxically, fight in the desert and at sea under the English colors; another, the man of greatest worth, died in the courtyard of a barracks, at dawn, before a firing squad of soldiers drowsy with sleep; still others (not the most unfortunate ones) met their fate in the anonymous and nearly secret battles of the civil war. We were Republicans, Catholics; we were, I suspect, romantics. For us, Ireland was not only

the utopian[10] future and the intolerable present; it was a bitter and loving mythology, it was the circular towers and red bogs, it was the repudiation of Parnell[11] and the enormous epics which sing of the theft of bulls who in a former incarnation were heroes and in others were fish and mountains. . . . On one evening I shall never forget, we were joined by a comrade from Munster: a certain John Vincent Moon.

He was scarcely twenty years old. He was thin and soft at the same time. He gave one the uncomfortable impression of being invertebrate. He had studied, with fervor and vanity, every page of some communist manual or other; dialectic materialism[12] served him as a means to end any and all discussion. The reasons that one man may have to abominate another, or love him, are infinite: Moon reduced universal history to a sordid economic conflict. He asserted that the revolution is predestined to triumph. I told him that only lost causes can interest a gentleman. . . . By then it was nighttime. We continued our disagreements along the corridor, down the stairs, into the vague streets. The judgments emitted by Moon impressed me less than their unattractive and apodictic[13] tone. The new comrade did not argue: he passed judgment with obvious disdain and a certain fury.

As we came to the outlying houses, a sud-

---

7. interlocutor (in' tər läk' yoo tər): one who takes part in a conversation; talker; interpreter.

8. opprobrium (ə prō' brē əm): scorn or contempt, especially involving condemnation.

9. Connaught (kä' nôt).

10. utopian (yoo tō' pē ən): based on ideas of perfection in social and political organization.

11. Parnell: Charles Stewart Parnell, advocate of home rule for Ireland.

12. dialectic materialism (dī ə lek' tik): philosophy developed by Karl Marx.

13. apodictic (ap' ə dik' tik): involving or expressing necessary truth; absolutely certain.

den exchange of gunfire caught us by surprise. (Just before or after, we skirted the blank wall of a factory or barracks.) We took refuge along a dirt road; a soldier, looming gigantic in the glare, rushed out of a burning cabin. He shrieked at us and ordered us to halt. I pressed on; my comrade did not follow me. I turned back; John Vincent Moon was frozen in his tracks, fascinated and eternalized, as it were, by terror. I rushed to his side, brought down the soldier with a single blow, shook and pounded Vincent Moon, berated him, and ordered him to follow me. I was forced to yank him by his arm; a passionate fear paralyzed him. We fled through a night suddenly shot through with blazes. A burst of rifle fire sought us out; a bullet grazed Moon's right shoulder; while we ran among the pines, he broke into feeble sobbing.

During that autumn of 1922, I had taken refuge in a country house belonging to General Berkeley. This officer (whom I had never seen) was carrying out some administrative assignment in Bengal. His house, though it was less than a hundred years old, was dark and deteriorated and abounded in perplexing corridors and vain antechambers. A museum and an enormous library usurped the ground floor: controversial and incompatible books which, somehow, make up the history of the nineteenth century; scimitars from Nishapur,[14] in whose arrested circular arcs the wind and violence of battle seem to last. We entered (I seem to remember) through the back part of the house. Moon, his lips dry and quivering, muttered that the events of the evening had been very interesting. I dressed his wound and brought him a cup of tea. (His "wound," I saw, was superficial.) Suddenly he stammered perplexedly, "But you took a considerable chance."

I told him not to worry. (The routine of the civil war had impelled me to act as I had acted. Besides, the capture of a single one of our men could have compromised our cause.)

The following day Moon had recovered his aplomb.[15] He accepted a cigarette and severely cross-questioned me concerning "the economic resources of our revolutionary party." His questions were quite lucid. I told him (in all truth) that the situation was serious. Shattering volleys of rifle fire reverberated in the south. I told Moon that our comrades expected us. My trench coat and revolver were in my room; when I returned, I found Moon stretched on the sofa, his eyes shut. He thought he had fever; he spoke of a painful shoulder spasm.

I realized then that his cowardice was irreparable. I awkwardly urged him to take care of himself and took my leave. I blushed for this fearful man, as if I, and not Vincent Moon, were the coward. What one man does is something done, in some measure, by all men. For that reason, a disobedience committed in a garden contaminates the human race; for that reason, it is not unjust that the crucifixion of a single Jew suffices to save it. Perhaps Schopenhauer is right: I am all others, any man is all men, Shakespeare is in some way the wretched John Vincent Moon.

We spent nine days in the enormous house of the general. Of the agony and splendor of the battle I shall say nothing: my intention is to tell the story of this scar which affronts me. In my memory, those nine days form a single day; except for the next to the last, when our men rushed a barracks and we were able to avenge, man for man, the sixteen comrades who had been machine-gunned at Elphin. I would slip out of the house toward dawn, in the confusion of the morning twilight. I was back by dusk. My companion would be waiting for me upstairs: his wound did not allow him to come down to meet me. I can see him

---

14. **Nishapur** (ni′ shə pōōr).

15. **aplomb** (ə pläm′): poise; composure.

with some book of strategy in his hand: F. N. Maude or Clausewitz.[16] "The artillery is my preferred arm," he conceded one night. He would inquire into our plans; he liked to censure or revamp them. He was also in the habit of denouncing our "deplorable economic base." Dogmatic and somber, he would prophesy a ruinous end. *C'est une affaire flambee*,[17] he would murmur. In order to show that his being a physical coward made no difference to him, he increased his intellectual arrogance. Thus, for better or for worse, passed nine days.

On the tenth, the city definitively fell into the hands of the Black and Tans. Tall, silent horsemen patrolled the streets. The wind was filled with ashes and smoke. At an intersection in the middle of a square, I saw a corpse—less tenacious in my memory than a manikin— upon which some soldiers interminably practiced their marksmanship. . . . I had left my quarters as the sunrise hung in the sky. I returned before midday. In the library, Moon was talking to someone; by his tone of voice I realized that he was using the telephone. Then I heard my name; then that I would return at seven; then the suggestion that I be arrested as I crossed the garden. My reasonable friend was selling me reasonably. I heard him requesting certain guarantees of personal security.

At this point my story becomes confused, its thread is lost. I know I pursued the informer down the dark corridors of nightmare and the deep stairs of vertigo.[18] Moon had come to know the house very well, much better than I. Once or twice I lost him. I cornered him

before the soldiers arrested me. From one of the general's mounted sets of arms I snatched down a cutlass; with the steel half-moon I sealed his face, forever, with a half-moon of blood. Borges, I have confessed this to you, a stranger. *Your* contempt will not wound me as much.

Here the narrator stopped. I noticed that his hands were trembling.

"And Moon?" I asked him.

"He was paid the Judas-money and fled to Brazil. And that afternoon, he watched some drunks in an impromptu firing squad in the town square shoot down a manikin."

I waited in vain for him to go on with his story. At length I asked him to continue.

A sob shook his body. And then, with feeble sweetness, he pointed to the white arced scar.

"You don't believe me?" he stammered. "Don't you see the mark of infamy[19] written on my face? I told you the story the way I did so that you would hear it to the end. I informed on the man who took me in: I am Vincent Moon. Despise me."

---

16. Clausewitz (klou′ zə wits).

17. *C'est une affaire flambée* (set ün à fer′ flän be′) *French*: idiom meaning "It is a lost cause."

18. vertigo (vʉr′ ti gō′): a condition in which one has the feeling of whirling, causing imbalance; a dizzy, confused state of mind.

19. infamy (in′ fə mē): disgrace, especially when it is widely known and involves well-deserved and extreme contempt; notoriety.

COMPLICATIONS:
STORIES OF
HUMAN NATURE

Reviewing Concepts

CHARACTER AND SETTING: DETERMINANTS OF ACTION

making
connections

In this unit are some memorable characters who make some surprising decisions. Consider whether these characters do what they do because they are who they are or because they are where they are. In other words, to what degree does setting influence characters' actions? Setting is more than just the time and physical location of a story. Setting may also include political and economic conditions, such as war or widespread unemployment. Social expectations, such as the expectation that neighbors greet each other on sight, may also be an element of setting. Even the expectations of a character's family can be considered part of the setting in which he or she is placed.

Think about George from "A Summer's Reading." The bar graph below shows how one reader rated the extent to which George's actions are influenced by his inner desires and influenced by three elements of the external setting: political/economic conditions, social expectations, and family expectations.

George from "A Summer's Reading"

	Influence actions not at all	Influence actions somewhat	Influence actions greatly
Personal desires			
Political/economic conditions			
Social expectations			
Family expectations			

describing
connections

Select a main character from each of the other stories you have read in Unit 3. Complete similar bar graphs for these characters.

Look over your bar graphs and choose two characters that seem strikingly similar or strikingly different. In an **essay,** compare or contrast these characters. Describe in detail the factors influencing their actions; for example, you might name the specific social expectations that a character feels pressured to fulfill. Comment on the relative importance of internal and external factors in determining the characters' behavior. Share your conclusions with your classmates.

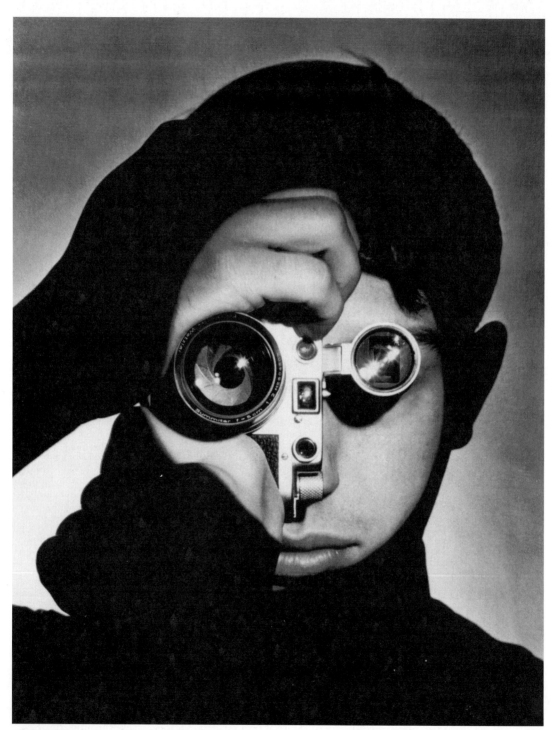

The Photojournalist, 1951, ANDREAS FEININGER.
Andreas Feininger, *Life* Magazine © Time Warner Inc.

Illuminations:
Stories About
Society

*"Literature is one of a society's
instruments of self-awareness."*

ITALO CALVINO, 1923-1985
Italian novelist and short story writer

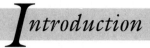

Illuminations: Stories About Society

Imagine that there is a wrong you see in your community—perhaps a policy you would like to see ended or a widespread attitude you would like to see changed. How would you protest this wrong? You might organize a boycott, make a speech, or write a letter to a government official. You might also write a story. Many fiction writers think of themselves as people who shine a light on the flaws of society, pointing out the weak spots so that they may be corrected.

The writers of the works in this unit examine societies in Latin American, South Africa, Germany, Italy, and the United States. They criticize troubling aspects of these societies, such as racial injustice, political assassination, censorship, and commercialism. Some of these writers deliver their message through humorous exaggeration; others, through controlled understatement. Still others rely on straightforward condemnation. As you read the stories, notice what methods the writers use to protest social ills and whether the writers seem optimistic that these ills can be remedied. Consider whether the faults exposed are present in your own community.

Although these stories are meant to make you think critically about society, they are also meant to engage you. Like all good stories, they are rich in character, setting, and suspense. Doubtless you will find them more enjoyable than political tracts; you may even find them more persuasive.

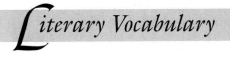 *iterary Vocabulary*

INTRODUCED IN THIS UNIT

Structure. Structure refers to the way that a work of literature is put together. In prose, the structure is the arrangement of larger units, or parts, of a selection. In "Metonymy, or The Husband's Revenge," the narrator begins the story by explaining the term *metonymy,* a figure of speech. Then she tells the tale of a love triangle, which turns out to be a case of applied metonymy. This structure allows the writer to intensify the irony and humor of the tale she relates.

REVIEWED IN THIS UNIT

Satire   **Point of View**   **Conflict**   **Theme**   **Irony**   **Climax**

Santa's Children

ITALO CALVINO

A biography of Calvino appears on page 420.

Approaching the Story

Italo Calvino's (ē′ tä lô käl vē′ nô) clever use of irony and whimsy have made him one of the most popular Italian fiction writers of the twentieth century. "Santa's Children" is from *Marcovaldo, or The Seasons in the City*, a collection of short stories about Marcovaldo, an unskilled worker who lives in an industrial city of northern Italy. The earliest stories in this book are set during a time of poverty after World War II. The later stories, including "Santa's Children," are set in the mid-1960's when, according to Calvino, "the illusions of an economic boom flourished." Calvino attacks such illusions, writing in a satirical tone that is evident as the story begins.

Building Vocabulary

These essential words are footnoted within the story.

placated (plā′ kāt′ id): The heavy conflicts of interest are **placated** and give way to a new rivalry. (page 223)

jaded: After a while they were **jaded** and paid no further attention. (page 225)

Connecting Writing and Reading

What qualities do you think characterize Christmas in the present-day United States? In your journal, make a cluster diagram of words and phrases that you associate with Christmas. Then, as you read "Santa's Children," jot down words and phrases that describe the writer's view of Christmas.

NO PERIOD OF the year is more gentle and good, for the world of industry and commerce, than Christmas and the weeks preceding it. From the streets rises the tremulous sound of the mountaineers' bagpipes; and the big companies, till yesterday coldly concerned with calculating gross product and dividends, open their hearts to human affections and to smiles. The sole thought of Boards of Directors now is to give joy to their fellow man, sending gifts accompanied by messages of goodwill both to other companies and to private individuals; every firm feels obliged to buy a great stock of products from a second firm to serve as presents to third firms; and those firms, for their part, buy from yet another firm further stocks of presents for the others; the office windows remain aglow till late, specially those of the shipping department, where the personnel work overtime wrapping packages and boxes;

beyond the misted panes, on the sidewalks covered by a crust of ice, the pipers advance. Having descended from the dark mysterious mountains, they stand at the downtown intersections, a bit dazzled by the excessive lights, by the excessively rich shop windows; and heads bowed, they blow into their instruments; at that sound, among the businessmen the heavy conflicts of interest are <u>placated</u>[1] and give way to a new rivalry: to see who can present the most conspicuous and original gift in the most attractive way.

At Sbav and Co. that year the Public Relations Office suggested that the Christmas presents for the most important persons should be delivered at home by a man dressed as Santa Claus.

The idea won the unanimous approval of the top executives. A complete Santa Claus outfit was bought: white beard, red cap and

---

1. **placated** (plā′ kāt′ id): pacified; calmed.

tunic edged in white fur, big boots. They had the various delivery men try it on to see whom it fitted best, but one man was too short and the beard touched the ground; another was too stout and couldn't get into the tunic; another was too young; yet another was too old and it wasn't worth wasting make-up on him.

While the head of the Personnel Office was sending for other possible Santas from the various departments, the assembled executives sought to develop the idea: the Human Relations Office wanted the employees' Christmas packages also to be distributed by Santa Claus, at a collective ceremony; the Sales Office wanted Santa to make a round of the shops as well; the Advertising Office was worried about the prominence of the firm's name, suggesting that perhaps they should tie four balloons to a string with the letters S.B.A.V.

All were caught up in the lively and cordial atmosphere spreading through the festive, productive city; nothing is more beautiful than the sensation of material goods flowing on all sides and, with it, the goodwill each feels toward the others; for this, this above all, as the skirling sound of the pipes reminds us, is what really counts.

In the shipping department, goods—material and spiritual—passed through Marcovaldo's hands, since it represented merchandise to load and unload. And it was not only through loading and unloading that he shared in the general festivity but also by thinking that at the end of that labyrinth of hundreds of thousands of packages there waited a package belonging to him alone, prepared by the Human Relations Office—and even more, by figuring how much was due him at the end of the month, counting the Christmas bonus and his overtime hours. With that money, he too would be able to rush to the shops and buy, buy, buy, to give presents, presents, presents, as his

most sincere feelings and the general interests of industry and commerce decreed.

The head of the Personnel Office came into the shipping department with a fake beard in his hand. "Hey, you!" he said to Marcovaldo. "See how this beard looks on you. Perfect! You're Santa then. Come upstairs. Get moving. You'll be given a special bonus if you make fifty home deliveries per day."

Got up as Santa Claus, Marcovaldo rode through the city on the saddle of the motor-bike-truck laden with packages wrapped in varicolored paper, tied with pretty ribbons, and decorated with twigs of mistletoe and holly. The white cotton beard tickled him a little, but it protected his throat from the cold air.

His first trip was to his own home, because he couldn't resist the temptation of giving his children a surprise. At first, he thought, they won't recognize me. Then I bet they'll laugh!

The children were playing on the stairs. They barely looked up. "Hi, Papà."

Marcovaldo was let down. "Hmph . . . Don't you see how I'm dressed?"

"How are you supposed to be dressed?" Pietruccio[2] said. "Like Santa Claus, right?"

"And you recognized me first thing?"

"Easy! We recognized Signor Sigismondo,[3] too; and he was disguised better than you!"

"And the janitor's brother-in-law!"

"And the father of the twins across the street!"

"And the uncle of Ernestina—the girl with the braids!"

"All dressed like Santa Claus?" Marcovaldo asked, and the disappointment in his voice wasn't due only to the failure of the family surprise but also because he felt that the company's prestige had somehow been impaired.

---

2. **Pietruccio** (pē e trōōch' chē ō).

3. **Signor Sigismondo** (sē nyôr' sē gēz môn' dô): *Signor* is the Italian equivalent of *Mr.*

"Of course. Just like you," the children answered. "Like Santa Claus. With a fake beard, as usual." And turning their backs on him, the children became absorbed again in their games.

It so happened that the Public Relations Offices of many firms had had the same idea at the same time; and they had recruited a great number of people, jobless for the most part, pensioners, street vendors, and had dressed them in the red tunic with the cotton-wool beard. The children, the first few times, had been amused, recognizing acquaintances under that disguise, neighborhood figures, but after a while they were jaded[4] and paid no further attention.

The game they were involved in seemed to absorb them entirely. They had gathered on a landing and were seated in a circle. "May I ask what you're plotting?" Marcovaldo inquired.

"Leave us alone, Papà; we have to fix our presents."

"Presents for whom?"

"For a poor child. We have to find a poor child and give him presents."

"Who said so?"

"It's in our school reader."

Marcovaldo was about to say: "You're poor children yourselves!" But during this past week he had become so convinced that he was an inhabitant of the Land of Plenty, where all purchased and enjoyed themselves and exchanged presents, that it seemed bad manners to mention poverty; and he preferred to declare: "Poor children don't exist any more!"

Michelino[5] stood up and asked: "Is that why you don't bring us presents, Papà?"

Marcovaldo felt a pang at his heart. "I have to earn some overtime now," he said hastily, "and then I'll bring you some."

"How do you earn it?"

"Delivering presents," Marcovaldo said.

"To us?"

"No, to other people."

"Why not to us? It'd be quicker."

Marcovaldo tried to explain. "Because I'm not the Human Relations Santa Claus, after all; I'm the Public Relations Santa Claus. You understand?"

"No."

"Never mind." But since he wanted somehow to apologize for coming home empty-handed, he thought he might take Michelino with him on his round of deliveries. "If you're good, you can come and watch your Papà taking presents to people," he said, straddling the seat of the little delivery wagon.

"Let's go. Maybe I'll find a poor child," Michelino said and jumped on, clinging to his father's shoulders.

In the streets of the city Marcovaldo encountered only other red-and-white Santas, absolutely identical with him, who were driving panel trucks or delivery carts or opening the doors of shops for customers laden with packages or helping carry their purchases to the car. And all these Santas seemed concentrated, busy, as if they were responsible for the operation of the enormous machine of the Holiday Season.

And exactly like them, Marcovaldo ran from one address to another, following his list, dismounted from his seat, sorted the packages in the wagon, selected one, presented it to the person opening the door, pronouncing the words: "Sbav and Company wish a Merry Christmas and a Happy New Year," and pocketed the tip.

This tip could be substantial and Marcovaldo might have been considered content, but something was missing. Every time, before ringing at a door, followed by Michelino, he anticipated the wonder of the person who, on opening the door, would see

---

4. **jaded:** dulled by excesses.
5. **Michelino** (mē kā lē′ nō̂).

Santa Claus himself standing there before him; he expected some fuss, curiosity, gratitude. And every time he was received like the postman, who brings the newspaper day after day.

He rang at the door of a luxurious house. A governess answered the door. "Oh, another package. Who's this one from?"

"Sbav and Company wish a . . ."

"Well, bring it in," and she led Santa Claus down a corridor filled with tapestries, carpets, and majolica[6] vases. Michelino, all eyes, followed his father.

The governess opened a glass door. They entered a room with a high ceiling, so high that a great fir tree could fit beneath it. It was a Christmas tree lighted by glass bubbles of every color, and from its branches hung presents and sweets of every description. From the ceiling hung heavy crystal chandeliers, and the highest branches of the fir caught some of the glistening drops. Over a large table were arrayed glass, silver, boxes of candied fruit and cases of bottles. The toys, scattered over a great rug, were as numerous as in a toyshop, mostly complicated electronic devices and model spaceships. On that rug, in an empty corner, there was a little boy about nine years old, lying prone, with a bored, sullen look. He was leafing through an illustrated volume, as if everything around him were no concern of his.

"Gianfranco,[7] look. Gianfranco," the governess said. "You see? Santa Claus has come back with another present."

"Three hundred twelve," the child sighed, without looking up from his book. "Put it over there."

"It's the three hundred and twelfth present that's arrived," the governess said. "Gianfranco is so clever. He keeps count; he doesn't miss one. Counting is his great passion."

On tiptoe Marcovaldo and Michelino left the house.

"Papà, is that little boy a poor child?" Michelino asked.

Marcovaldo was busy rearranging the contents of the truck and didn't answer immediately. But after a moment, he hastened to protest: "Poor? What are you talking about? You know who his father is? He's the president of the Society for the Implementation of Christmas Consumption/Commendatore—"[8]

He broke off, because he didn't see Michelino anywhere. "Michelino! Michelino! Where are you?" He had vanished.

I bet he saw another Santa Claus go by, took him for me, and has gone off after him . . . Marcovaldo continued his rounds, but he was a bit concerned and couldn't wait to get home again.

At home, he found Michelino with his brothers, good as gold.

"Say, where did you go?"

"I came home to collect our presents . . . the presents for that poor child . . ."

"What? Who?"

"The one that was so sad . . . the one in the villa, with the Christmas tree . . ."

"Him? What kind of a present could you give him?"

"Oh, we fixed them up very nice . . . three presents, all wrapped in silver paper."

The younger boys spoke up: "We all went together to take them to him! You should have seen how happy he was!"

"I'll bet!" Marcovaldo said. "That was just what he needed to make him happy: your presents!"

"Yes, ours! . . . He ran over right away to tear off the paper and see what they were . . ."

---

6. **majolica** (mə jäl′ i kə): a variety of richly decorated Italian pottery.

7. **Gianfranco** (jē än fraŋ′ kô).

8. **Commendatore** (kôm men′ dä tō′ rā): a title, used to address or refer to a member of the aristocratic class, that nostalgically recollects the time of knights and chivalry.

"And what were they?"

"The first was a hammer: that big round hammer, the wooden kind . . ."

"What did he do then?"

"He was jumping with joy! He grabbed it and began to use it!"

"How?"

"He broke all the toys! And all the glassware! Then he took the second present . . ."

"What was that?"

"A slingshot. You should have seen him. He was so happy! He hit all the glass balls on the Christmas tree. Then he started on the chandeliers . . ."

"That's enough. I don't want to hear any more! And the . . . third present?"

"We didn't have anything left to give, so we took some silver paper and wrapped up a box of kitchen matches. That was the present that made him happiest of all. He said: They never let me touch matches! He began to strike them, and . . ."

"And?"

". . . and he set fire to everything!"

Marcovaldo was tearing his hair. "I'm ruined!"

The next day, turning up at work, he felt the storm brewing. He dressed again as Santa Claus, in great haste, loaded the presents to be delivered onto the truck, already amazed that no one had said anything to him, and then he saw, coming toward him, the three section chiefs: the one from Public Relations, the one from Advertising, and the one from Sales.

"Stop!" they said to him. "Unload everything. At once!"

This is it, Marcovaldo said to himself, and could already picture himself fired.

"Hurry up! We have to change all the packages!" the three section chiefs said. "The Society for the Implementation of Christmas Consumption has launched a campaign to push the Destructive Gift!"

"On the spur of the moment like this," one of the men remarked. "They might have thought of it sooner . . ."

"It was a sudden inspiration the President had," another chief explained. "It seems his little boy was given some ultramodern gift articles, Japanese, I believe, and for the first time the child was obviously enjoying himself . . ."

"The important thing," the third added, "is that the Destructive Gift serves to destroy articles of every sort: just what's needed to speed up the pace of consumption and give the market a boost . . . All in minimum time and within a child's capacities . . . The President of the Society sees a whole new horizon opening out. He's in seventh heaven, he's so enthusiastic . . ."

"But this child . . ." Marcovaldo asked, in a faint voice: "did he really destroy much stuff?"

"It's hard to make an estimate, even a hazy one, because the house was burned down . . ."

Marcovaldo went back to the street, illuminated as if it were night, crowded with mamas and children and uncles and grannies and packages and balloons and rocking horses and Christmas trees and Santa Clauses and chickens and turkeys and fruit cakes and bottles and bagpipers and chimney sweeps and chestnut vendors shaking pans of chestnuts over round, glowing black stoves.

And the city seemed smaller, collected in a luminous vessel, buried in the dark heart of a forest among the age-old trunks of the chestnut trees and an endless cloak of snow. Somewhere in the darkness the howl of the wolf was heard; the hares had a hole buried in the snow, in the warm red earth under a layer of chestnut burrs.

A jack-hare came out, white, onto the snow; he twitched his ears, ran beneath the moon, but he was white and couldn't be seen, as if he weren't there. Only his little paws left a light print on the snow, like little clover leaves. Nor could the wolf be seen, for he was black and stayed in the black darkness of the forest. Only if he opened his mouth, his teeth were visible, white and sharp.

There was a line where the forest, all black, ended and the snow began, all white. The hare ran on this side, and the wolf on that.

The wolf saw the hare's prints on the snow and followed them, always keeping in the black, so as not to be seen. At the point where the prints ended there should be the hare, and the wolf came out of the black, opened wide his red maw and his sharp teeth, and bit the wind.

The hare was a bit farther on, invisible; he scratched one ear with his paw and escaped, hopping away.

Is he here? There? Is he a bit farther on?

Only the expanse of snow could be seen, white as this page.

Thinking About the Story

A PERSONAL RESPONSE

sharing impressions

1. In your journal record any thoughts, feelings, and questions you have about this story.

constructing interpretations

2. How do you think the episode of the hare and the wolf relates to the rest of the story?

Think about
- why the hare is associated with white and the wolf associated with black
- how the hare disappears into the snow, leaving the wolf to bite the wind
- what the two animals might represent
- what the writer might be saying about Christmas

3. Based on the writer's view of Christmas, what do you think is the most serious fault of the society portrayed in this story?

Think about
- why there are so many Santas around town
- why Gianfranco loves the gifts from Marcovaldo's children more than the other 312 he received
- why The Society for the Implementation of Christmas Consumption exists
- the Destructive Gift campaign

4. To what degree does Marcovaldo share the values of the rest of his society?

A CREATIVE RESPONSE

5. If this story were set in the present-day United States, would it be different? Refer to your prereading cluster diagram to help you formulate a response.

A CRITICAL RESPONSE

6. Based on your interpretation of the story, who do you think are the "Santa's Children" referred to in the title? Explain your answer.

Analyzing the Writer's Craft

SATIRE AND POINT OF VIEW

Reread the opening sentence and explain what view of Christmas the writer expresses.

Building a Literary Vocabulary. Satire is a literary technique in which ideas or customs are ridiculed for the purpose of improving society. "Santa's Children" is satiric from the very first sentence. The phrase "No period of the year is more gentle and good" leads the reader to expect a traditional holiday sentiment of peace and goodwill. Instead, the next phrase "for the world of industry and commerce" ironically undercuts the holiday sentiment by referring to the commercial exploitation of Christmas.

Point of view enhances the satire of this story. Point of view refers to the kind of narrator used in a literary work. Because "Santa's Children" is told from a third-person point of view, the narrator is not a direct participant in the action and is free to comment on it. In the opening paragraphs, the narrator sets the satiric tone by parroting the corporate jargon that praises Christmas for promoting business success. Then the narrator enters Marcovaldo's mind to reveal a well-intentioned but confused man sincerely trying to make his family happy yet influenced by the commercial values around him. By showing Marcovaldo's befuddled attempts to fit into the business world and his inability to explain that world to his children, the narrator implies criticism of a society that seduces yet shuts out the ordinary citizen.

Application: Analyzing Satire. In a group analyze the following paragraphs to determine what ideas or behaviors Calvino is criticizing.

On page 224, beginning "All were caught up in the lively and cordial atmosphere . . ."

On page 225, beginning "Marcovaldo was about to say . . ."

On page 225, beginning "This tip could be substantial . . ."

On page 227, beginning "'The important thing,' the third added . . ."

Share your interpretations with the class.

Connecting Reading and Writing

1. Design **Christmas cards** to be sent by each of the following characters: Marcovaldo, Michelino, Gianfranco, and Gianfranco's father.

Option: Have each character make a **list** of Christmas gifts he would like to give or receive.

2. Imagine that you work for the Society for the Implementation of Christmas Consumption. Write a **press release** announcing, explaining, and praising the Destructive Gift.

Option: Advertise the Destructive Gift in a **catalog** of holiday gifts.

3. Write a **proposal** to the publisher of this story that explains how you would illustrate the story with photos. Be sure to specify which scenes you have in mind.

Option: Write a **character sketch** of Marcovaldo to be used by an artist hired to illustrate the story. Be sure to include a physical description.

Six Feet of the Country

NADINE GORDIMER

A biography of Gordimer appears on page 422.

Approaching the Story

Apartheid is the system of rigid racial segregation adopted as official government policy in South Africa after 1948. Apartheid laws deny full citizenship to blacks and other nonwhites and restrict most aspects of their lives, including where they may live, where they may travel, and what kinds of jobs they may hold. Only recently have apartheid laws begun to be repealed. The novels and short stories of Nadine Gordimer, a white South African and Nobel Prize winner, show the effects of apartheid on personal relationships. In "Six Feet of the Country," Gordimer examines the experiences and attitudes of a British couple—a businessman and a former actress—who have moved to the South African countryside.

Building Vocabulary

These essential words are footnoted within the story.

imbued (im byo̅o̅d'): Lerice . . . has sunk into the business of running the farm with all the serious intensity with which she once **imbued** the shadows in a playwright's mind. (page 232)

histrionical (his' trē än' i kul): I find Lerice's earthy enthusiasms just as irritating as I once found her **histrionical** ones. (page 232)

expostulated (eks päs' chə lāt' id): Now Petrus **expostulated** with him. (page 238)

laconic (lə kän' ik): They were shocked, in a **laconic** fashion, by their own mistake. (page 239)

Connecting Writing and Reading

Based on the title, "Six Feet of the Country," and on the information provided in Approaching the Story, what do you predict about this story? In your journal jot down your ideas. As you read, compare your prediction to what actually happens.

Six Feet of the Country

MY WIFE AND I are not real farmers—not even Lerice, really. We bought our place, ten miles out of Johannesburg on one of the main roads, to change something in ourselves, I suppose; you seem to rattle about so much within a marriage like ours. You long to hear nothing but a deep, satisfying silence when you sound a marriage. The farm hasn't managed that for us, of course, but it has done other things, unexpected, illogical. Lerice, who I thought would retire there in Chekhovian sadness for a month or two and then leave the place to the servants while she tried yet again to get a part she wanted and become the actress she would like to be, has sunk into the business of running the farm with all the serious intensity with which she once imbued[1] the shadows in a playwright's mind. I should have given it up long ago if it had not been for her. Her hands, once small and plain and well kept—she was not the sort of actress who wears red paint and diamond rings—are hard as a dog's pads.

I, of course, am there only in the evenings and at weekends. I am a partner in a travel agency, which is flourishing—needs to be, as I tell Lerice, in order to carry the farm. Still, though I know we can't afford it, and though the sweetish smell of the fowls Lerice breeds sickens me, so that I avoid going past their runs, the farm is beautiful in a way I had almost forgotten—especially on a Sunday morning when I get up and go out into the paddock and see not the palm trees and fishpond and imitation-stone birdbath of the suburbs but white ducks on the dam, the lucerne[2] field brilliant as window-dresser's grass, and the little, stocky, mean-eyed bull, lustful but bored, having his face tenderly licked by one of his ladies. Lerice comes out with her hair uncombed, in her hand a stick dripping with cattle dip. She will stand and look dreamily for a moment, the way she would pretend to look sometimes in those plays. "They'll mate tomorrow," she will say. "This is their second day. Look how she loves him, my little Napoleon." So that when people come to see us on Sunday afternoon, I am likely to hear myself saying as I pour out the drinks, "When I drive back home from the city every day past those rows of suburban houses, I wonder how the devil we ever did stand it . . . Would you care to look around?" And there I am, taking some pretty girl and her husband stumbling down to our riverbank, the girl catching her stockings on the mealie-stooks and stepping over cow turds humming with jewel-green flies while she says, ". . .the *tensions* of the damned city. And you're near enough to get into town to a show, too! I think it's wonderful. Why, you've got it both ways!"

And for a moment I accept the triumph as if I *had* managed it—the impossibility that I've been trying for all my life: just as if the truth was that you could get it "both ways," instead of finding yourself with not even one way or the other but a third, one you had not provided for at all.

But even in our saner moments, when I find Lerice's earthy enthusiasms just as irritating as I once found her histrionical[3] ones and she finds what she calls my "jealousy" of her capac-

---

1. **imbued** (im byo͞od′): filled completely; saturated.
2. **lucerne** (lo͞o surn′): a chiefly British term for alfalfa.
3. **histrionical** (his′ trē än′ i kul): theatrical; dramatic.

ity for enthusiasm as big a proof of my inadequacy for her as a mate as ever it was, we do believe that we have at least honestly escaped those tensions peculiar to the city about which our visitors speak. When Johannesburg people speak of "tension," they don't mean hurrying people in crowded streets, the struggle for money, or the general competitive character of city life. They mean the guns under the white men's pillows and the burglar bars on the white men's windows. They mean those strange moments on city pavements when a black man won't stand aside for a white man.

Out in the country, even ten miles out, life is better than that. In the country, there is a lingering remnant of the pretransitional stage; our relationship with the blacks is almost feudal. Wrong, I suppose, obsolete, but more comfortable all around. We have no burglar bars, no guns. Lerice's farm boys have their wives and their piccanins[4] living with them on the land. They brew their sour beer without the fear of police raids. In fact, we've always rather prided ourselves that the poor devils have nothing much to fear, being with us; Lerice even keeps an eye on their children, with all the competence of a woman who has never had a child of her own, and she certainly doctors them all—children and adults—like babies whenever they happen to be sick.

It was because of this that we were not particularly startled one night last winter when the boy Albert came knocking at our window long after we had gone to bed. I wasn't in our bed but sleeping in the little dressing room-cum-linen room next door because Lerice had annoyed me and I didn't want to find myself softening toward her simply because of the sweet smell of the talcum powder on her flesh after her bath. She came and woke me up. "Albert says one of the boys is very sick," she said. "I think you'd better go down and see. He wouldn't get us up at this hour for nothing."

"What time is it?"

"What does it matter?" Lerice is maddeningly logical.

I got up awkwardly as she watched me—how is it I always feel a fool when I have deserted her bed? After all, I know from the way she never looks at me when she talks to me at breakfast next day that she is hurt and humiliated at my not wanting her—and I went out, clumsy with sleep.

"Which of the boys is it?" I asked Albert as we followed the dance of my torch.

"He's too sick. Very sick," he said.

"But who? Franz?" I remembered Franz had had a bad cough for the past week.

Albert did not answer; he had given me the path and was walking along beside me in the tall, dead grass. When the light of the torch caught his face, I saw that he looked acutely embarrassed. "What's this all about?" I said.

He lowered his head under the glance of the light. "It's not me, baas.[5] I don't know. Petrus he send me."

Irritated, I hurried him along to the huts. And there, on Petrus's iron bedstead, with its brick stilts, was a young man, dead. On his forehead there was still a light, cold sweat; his body was warm. The boys stood around as they do in the kitchen when it is discovered that someone has broken a dish—uncooperative, silent. Somebody's wife hung about in the shadows, her hands wrung together under her apron.

I had not seen a dead man since the war. This was very different. I felt like the others—extraneous, useless. "What was the matter?" I asked.

The woman patted at her chest and shook her head to indicate the painful impossibility of breathing.

---

4. piccanins (pik′ ə ninz): a derogatory term for native African children.

5. baas (bäs): a term of address used in South Africa for a white man.

He must have died of pneumonia.

I turned to Petrus. "Who was this boy? What was he doing here?" The light of a candle on the floor showed that Petrus was weeping. He followed me out the door.

When we were outside, in the dark, I waited for him to speak. But he didn't. "Now, come on, Petrus, you must tell me who this boy was. Was he a friend of yours?"

"He's my brother, baas. He came from Rhodesia to look for work."

The story startled Lerice and me a little. The young boy had walked down from Rhodesia to look for work in Johannesburg, had caught a chill from sleeping out along the way, and had lain ill in his brother Petrus's hut since his arrival three days before. Our boys had been frightened to ask us for help for him because we had never been intended ever to know of his presence. Rhodesian natives are barred from entering the Union unless they have a permit; the young man was an illegal immigrant. No doubt our boys had managed the whole thing successfully several times before; a number of relatives must have walked the seven or eight hundred miles from poverty to the paradise of zoot suits,[6] police raids, and black slum townships that is their Egoli,[7] City of Gold—the African name for Johannesburg. It was merely a matter of getting such a man to lie low on our farm until a job could be found with someone who would be glad to take the risk of prosecution for employing an illegal immigrant in exchange for the services of someone as yet untainted by the city.

Well, this was one who would never get up again.

"You would think they would have felt they could tell *us*," said Lerice next morning. "Once the man was ill. You would have thought at least—" When she is getting intense over something, she has a way of standing in the middle of a room as people do when they are shortly to leave on a journey, looking searchingly about her at the most familiar objects as if she had never seen them before. I had noticed that in Petrus's presence in the kitchen, earlier, she had had the air of being almost offended with him, almost hurt.

In any case, I really haven't the time or inclination any more to go into everything in our life that I know Lerice, from those alarmed and pressing eyes of hers, would like us to go into. She is the kind of woman who doesn't mind if she looks plain, or odd; I don't suppose she would even care if she knew how strange she looks when her whole face is out of proportion with urgent uncertainty. I said, "Now I'm the one who'll have to do all the dirty work, I suppose."

She was still staring at me, trying me out with those eyes—wasting her time, if she only knew.

"I'll have to notify the health authorities," I said calmly. "They can't just cart him off and bury him. After all, we don't really know what he died of."

She simply stood there, as if she had given up—simply ceased to see me at all.

I don't know when I've been so irritated. "It might have been something contagious," I said. "God knows." There was no answer.

I am not enamored of holding conversations with myself. I went out to shout to one of the boys to open the garage and get the car ready for my morning drive to town.

As I had expected, it turned out to be quite a business. I had to notify the police as well as the health authorities and answer a lot of tedious questions: How was it I was ignorant of the boy's presence? If I did not supervise my native quarters, how did I know that that sort

---

6. **zoot suits:** men's flashy suits of a once-popular style, with broadly padded shoulders and baggy trousers.
7. **Egoli** (ē gô′ lē).

of thing didn't go on all the time? And when I flared up and told them that so long as my natives did their work, I didn't think it my right or concern to poke my nose into their private lives, I got from the coarse, dull-witted police sergeant one of those looks that come not from any thinking process going on in the brain but from that faculty common to all who are possessed by the master-race theory—a look of insanely inane certainty. He grinned at me with a mixture of scorn and delight at my stupidity.

Then I had to explain to Petrus why the health authorities had to take away the body for a post-mortem—and, in fact, what a post-mortem was. When I telephoned the health department some days later to find out the result, I was told that the cause of death was, as we had thought, pneumonia and that the body had been suitably disposed of. I went out to where Petrus was mixing a mash for the fowls and told him that it was all right, there would be no trouble; his brother had died from that pain in his chest. Petrus put down the paraffin tin and said, "When can we go to fetch him, baas?"

"To fetch him?"

"Will the baas please ask them when we must come?"

I went back inside and called Lerice, all over the house. She came down the stairs from the spare bedrooms, and I said, "*Now* what am I going to do? When I told Petrus, he just asked calmly when they could go and fetch the body. They think they're going to bury him themselves."

"Well, go back and tell him," said Lerice. "You must tell him. Why didn't you tell him then?"

When I found Petrus again, he looked up politely. "Look, Petrus," I said. "You can't go to fetch your brother. They've done it already— they've *buried* him, you understand?"

"Where?" he said slowly, dully, as if he thought that perhaps he was getting this wrong.

"You see, he was a stranger. They knew he wasn't from here, and they didn't know he had some of his people here, so they thought they must bury him." It was difficult to make a pauper's grave sound like a privilege.

"Please, baas, the baas must ask them." But he did not mean that he wanted to know the burial place. He simply ignored the incomprehensible machinery I told him had set to work on his dead brother; he wanted the brother back.

"But, Petrus," I said, "how can I? Your brother is buried already. I can't ask them now."

"Oh, baas!" he said. He stood with his bran-smeared hands uncurled at his sides, one corner of his mouth twitching.

"Good God, Petrus, they won't listen to me! They can't, anyway. I'm sorry, but I can't do it. You understand?"

He just kept on looking at me, out of his knowledge that white men have everything, can do anything; if they don't, it is because they won't.

And then, at dinner, Lerice started. "You could at least phone," she said.

"Christ, what d'you think I am? Am I supposed to bring the dead back to life?"

But I could not exaggerate my way out of this ridiculous responsibility that had been thrust on me. "Phone them up," she went on. "And at least you'll be able to tell him you've done it and they've explained that it's impossible."

She disappeared somewhere into the kitchen quarters after coffee. A little later she came back to tell me, "The old father's coming down from Rhodesia to be at the funeral. He's got a permit and he's already on his way."

Unfortunately, it was not impossible to get the body back. The authorities said that it was somewhat irregular but that since the hygiene conditions had been fulfilled, they could not refuse permission for exhumation. I found out that, with the undertaker's charges, it would cost twenty pounds. Ah, I thought, that settles it. On five pounds a month, Petrus won't have twenty pounds—and just as well, since it couldn't do the dead any good. Certainly I should not offer it to him myself. Twenty pounds—or anything else within reason, for that matter—I would have spent without grudging it on doctors or medicines that might have helped the boy when he was alive. Once he was dead, I had no intention of encouraging Petrus to throw away, on a gesture, more than he spent to clothe his whole family in a year.

When I told him, in the kitchen that night, he said, "Twenty pounds?"

I said, "Yes, that's right, twenty pounds."

For a moment, I had the feeling, from the look on his face, that he was calculating. But when he spoke again I thought I must have imagined it. "We must pay twenty pounds!" he said in the faraway voice in which a person speaks of something so unattainable it does not bear thinking about.

"All right, Petrus," I said and went back to the living room.

The next morning before I went to town, Petrus asked to see me. "Please, baas," he said, awkwardly, handing me a bundle of notes. They're so seldom on the giving rather than the receiving side, poor devils, they don't really know how to hand money to a white man. There it was, the twenty pounds, in ones and halves, some creased and folded until they were soft as dirty rags, others smooth and fairly new—Franz's money, I suppose, and Albert's, and Dora the cook's, and Jacob the gardener's, and God knows who else's besides, from all the farms and small holdings round about. I took it in irritation more than in astonishment, really—irritation at the waste, the uselessness of this sacrifice by people so poor. Just like the poor everywhere, I thought, who stint themselves the decencies of life in order to ensure themselves the decencies of death. So incomprehensible to people like Lerice and me, who regard life as something to be spent extravagantly and, if we think about death at all, regard it as the final bankruptcy.

The farmhands don't work on Saturday afternoon anyway, so it was a good day for the funeral. Petrus and his father had borrowed our donkey cart to fetch the coffin from the city, where, Petrus told Lerice on their return, everything was "nice"—the coffin waiting for them, already sealed up to save them from what must have been a rather unpleasant sight after two weeks' interment. (It had taken all that time for the authorities and the undertaker to make the final arrangements for moving the body.) All morning, the coffin lay in Petrus's hut, awaiting the trip to the little old burial ground, just outside the eastern boundary of our farm, that was a relic of the days when this was a real farming district rather than a fashionable rural estate. It was pure chance that I happened to be down there near the fence when the procession came past; once again Lerice had forgotten her promise to me and had made the house uninhabitable on a Saturday afternoon. I had come home and been infuriated to find her in a pair of filthy old slacks and with her hair uncombed since the night before, having all the varnish scraped from the living-room floor, if you please. So I had taken my No. 8 iron and gone off to practice my approach shots. In my annoyance, I had forgotten about the funeral, and was reminded only when I saw the procession coming up the path along the outside of the fence toward me; from where I was standing, you can see the graves quite clearly, and that day the sun glinted on bits of broken pottery, a lopsided homemade cross, and jam jars brown with rainwater and dead flowers.

I felt a little awkward and did not know whether to go on hitting my golf ball or stop at least until the whole gathering was decently

Man, 1959, CHARLES WHITE. Heritage Gallery, Los Angeles.

past. The donkey cart creaks and screeches with every revolution of the wheels, and it came along in a slow, halting fashion somehow peculiarly suited to the two donkeys who drew it, their little potbellies rubbed and rough, their heads sunk between the shafts, and their ears flattened back with an air submissive and downcast; peculiarly suited, too, to the group of men and women who came along slowly behind. The patient ass. Watching, I thought, you can see now why the creature became a Biblical symbol. Then the procession drew level with me and stopped, so I had to put down my club. The coffin was taken down off the cart—it was a shiny, yellow-varnished wood, like cheap furniture—and the donkeys twitched their ears against the flies. Petrus, Franz, Albert, and the old father from Rhodesia hoisted it on their shoulders, and the procession moved on, on foot. It was really a very awkward moment. I stood there rather foolishly at the fence, quite still, and slowly they filed past, not looking up, the four men bent beneath the shiny wooden box, and the straggling troop of mourners. All of them were servants or neighbors' servants whom I knew as casual, easygoing gossipers about our lands or kitchen. I heard the old man's breathing.

I had just bent to pick up my club again when there was a sort of jar in the flowing solemnity of their processional mood; I felt it at once, like a wave of heat along the air or one of those sudden currents of cold catching at your legs in a placid stream. The old man's voice was muttering something; the people had stopped, confused, and they bumped into one another, some pressing to go on, others hissing them to be still. I could see that they were embarrassed, but they could not ignore the voice; it was much the way that the mumblings of a prophet, though not clear at first, arrest the mind. The corner of the coffin the old man carried was sagging at an angle; he seemed to be trying to get out from under the

weight of it. Now Petrus expostulated[8] with him.

The little boy who had been left to watch the donkeys dropped the reins and ran to see. I don't know why—unless it was for the same reason people crowd around someone who has fainted in a cinema—but I parted the wires of the fence and went through, after him.

Petrus lifted his eyes to me—to anybody—with distress and horror. The old man from Rhodesia had let go of the coffin entirely, and the three others, unable to support it on their own, had laid it on the ground, in the pathway. Already there was a film of dust lightly wavering up its shiny sides. I did not understand what the old man was saying; I hesitated to interfere. But now the whole seething group turned on my silence. The old man himself came over to me, with his hands outspread and shaking, and spoke directly to me, saying something that I could tell from the tone, without understanding the words, was shocking and extraordinary.

"What is it, Petrus? What's wrong?" I appealed.

Petrus threw up his hands, bowed his head in a series of hysterical shakes, then thrust his face up at me suddenly. "He says, 'My son was not so heavy.'"

Silence. I could hear the old man breathing; he kept his mouth a little open, as old people do.

"My son was young and thin," he said at last, in English.

Again silence. Then babble broke out. The old man thundered against everybody; his teeth were yellowed and few, and he had one of those fine, grizzled, sweeping mustaches one doesn't often see nowadays, which must have been grown in emulation of early Empire builders. It seemed to frame all his utterances

---

8. expostulated (eks päs′ chə lāt′ id): reasoned earnestly about improper conduct; protested.

with a special validity. He shocked the assembly; they thought he was mad, but they had to listen to him. With his own hands he began to prize the lid off the coffin, and three of the men came forward to help him. Then he sat down on the ground; very old, very weak, and unable to speak, he merely lifted a trembling hand toward what was there. He abdicated, he handed it over to them; he was no good anymore.

They crowded round to look (and so did I), and now they forgot the nature of this surprise and the occasion of grief to which it belonged and for a few minutes were carried up in the astonishment of the surprise itself. They gasped and flared noisily with excitement. I even noticed the little boy who had held the donkeys jumping up and down, almost weeping with rage because the backs of the grownups crowded him out of his view.

In the coffin was someone no one had ever seen before: a heavily built, rather light-skinned native with a neatly stitched scar on his forehead—perhaps from a blow in a brawl that had also dealt him some other, slower-working injury that had killed him.

I wrangled with the authorities for a week over that body. I had the feeling that they were shocked, in a <u>laconic</u>[9] fashion, by their own mistake but that in the confusion of their anonymous dead they were helpless to put it right. They said to me, "We are trying to find out" and "We are still making inquiries." It was as if at any moment they might conduct me into their mortuary and say, "There! Lift up the sheets; look for him—your poultry boy's brother. There are so many black faces—surely one will do?"

And every evening when I got home, Petrus was waiting in the kitchen. "Well, they're trying. They're still looking. The baas is seeing to it for you, Petrus," I would tell him. "God, half the time I should be in the office I'm driving around the back end of town chasing after this affair," I added aside, to Lerice, one night.

She and Petrus both kept their eyes turned on me as I spoke, and, oddly, for those moments they looked exactly alike, though it sounds impossible: my wife, with her high, white forehead and her attenuated Englishwoman's body, and the poultry boy, with his horny bare feet below khaki trousers tied at the knee with string and the peculiar rankness of his nervous sweat coming from his skin.

"What makes you so indignant, so determined about this now?" said Lerice suddenly.

I stared at her. "It's a matter of principle. Why should they get away with a swindle? It's time these officials had a jolt from someone who'll bother to take the trouble."

She said, "Oh." And as Petrus slowly opened the kitchen door to leave, sensing that the talk had gone beyond him, she turned away, too.

I continued to pass on assurances to Petrus every evening, but although what I said was the same and the voice in which I said it was the same, every evening it sounded weaker. At last, it became clear that we would never get Petrus's brother back, because nobody really knew where he was. Somewhere in a graveyard as uniform as a housing scheme, somewhere under a number that didn't belong to him, or in the medical school, perhaps, laboriously reduced to layers of muscle and strings of nerve? Goodness knows. He had no identity in this world anyway.

It was only then, and in a voice of shame, that Petrus asked me to try and get the money back.

"From the way he asks, you'd think he was robbing his dead brother," I said to Lerice later. But as I've said, Lerice had got so intense

---

9. laconic (lə kän′ ik): sparing of words; terse.

about this business that she couldn't even appreciate a little ironic smile.

I tried to get the money; Lerice tried. We both telephoned and wrote and argued, but nothing came of it. It appeared that the main expense had been the undertaker, and after all he had done his job. So the whole thing was a complete waste, even more of a waste for the poor devils than I had thought it would be.

The old man from Rhodesia was about Lerice's father's size, so she gave him one of her father's old suits, and he went back home rather better off, for the winter, than he had come.

Thinking About the Story

A PERSONAL RESPONSE

sharing impressions

1. How do you feel about the ending of this story? Jot down your impressions in your journal.

constructing interpretations

2. What do you think of the narrator's comment at the end of the story that the old man "went back home rather better off . . . than he had come"?

3. Whose values appeal to you the most in this story? Support your response with examples from the story.

4. Analyze the relationship between the narrator and Lerice.
Think about
- how the narrator describes their marriage
- each person's values
- the effect of the incident on their relationship

5. How do your prereading predictions compare with the actual story? Use examples to explain your response.

A CREATIVE RESPONSE

6. Could the narrator have done anything differently about the mix-up of the corpses? Explain.

A CRITICAL RESPONSE

7. What do you consider the strongest conflict in this story, and why?

8. How would you explain the main message about South African society communicated in this story?

> ***Think about***
> - the picture of the black people that you formed from reading this story
> - the narrator's final remarks about Petrus's dead brother
> - the significance of the title of this story
> - which character is portrayed most sympathetically

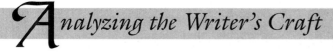

Analyzing the Writer's Craft

POINT OF VIEW

Think about the voice in which the writer relates the events of this story.

Building a Literary Vocabulary. Point of view refers to the narrative method, or the kind of narrator, used in a literary work. In the first-person point of view, the narrator is a character in the work who tells everything in his or her own words. In "Six Feet of the Country," Nadine Gordimer uses the first-person point of view. All the events are recounted by Lerice's husband, a narrator who participates in the action of the story.

Application: Analyzing Point of View. Go back through the story and identify the passages that have a strong effect on you. Rewrite one passage from the third-person point of view. Then in a small group discuss the two versions and their effects. Speculate about why Nadine Gordimer might have chosen the first-person point of view.

Connecting Reading and Writing

1. How do you think Petrus feels about the mistakes that happen in this story? Write a **journal entry** in which he expresses his feelings.

Option: Have Petrus reveal his feelings in a **poem** to be published along with this story.

2. Write a **memo** to a social studies teacher recommending that Gordimer's story be required reading for a unit on South Africa.

Option: Write a **letter** to the parents of the students, explaining your recommendation.

3. If you were a marriage counselor, what would you tell the narrator and Lerice about their relationship? In a **case study,** analyze their relationship and suggest improvements.

Option: Explore their relationship in an **advice column** for a popular magazine.

The Prisoner Who Wore Glasses

BESSIE HEAD

A biography of Head appears on page 422.

Approaching the Story

In the 1960's Bessie Head fled from South Africa to neighboring Botswana to escape the discrimination she suffered because her parents were of different races. At the time Head was writing, the South African policy of apartheid decreed that the races must be kept strictly separate. The white minority controlled the government and used its power to enforce apartheid and maintain dominance over the black majority. Those who resisted apartheid were jailed. The two main characters of "The Prisoner Who Wore Glasses," which is set on a South African prison farm, are a black political prisoner and a prison guard, or warder. The warder is an Afrikaner, a white South African of Dutch descent, and speaks English with a heavy accent.

Building Vocabulary

These essential words are footnoted within the story.

bedlam (bed′ ləm): His mind travelled back . . . through the . . . **bedlam** in which he had lived. (page 244)

ruefully (rōō′ fəl ē): "Let's face it," he thought **ruefully**. "I'm only learning right now what it means to be a politician." (page 244)

tirade (tī′ rād′): All throughout the **tirade** from his chief, Warder Hannetjie failed to defend himself. (page 245)

Connecting Writing and Reading

In your journal define what you think it means to be assertive. On a scale of 1 to 10, rate how important it is to be assertive in order to get what you want at home and at school. As you read the story, compare your ideas about assertiveness to the assertiveness displayed by the two main characters.

S CARCELY A BREATH of wind disturbed the stillness of the day, and the long rows of cabbages were bright green in the sunlight. Large white clouds drifted slowly across the deep blue sky. Now and then they obscured the sun and caused a chill on the backs of the prisoners who had to work all day long in the cabbage field. This trick the clouds were playing with the sun eventually caused one of the prisoners who wore glasses to stop work, straighten up and peer shortsightedly at them. He was a thin little fellow with a hollowed-out chest and comic knobbly knees. He also had a lot of fanciful ideas, because he smiled at the clouds.

"Perhaps they want me to send a message to the children," he thought tenderly, noting that the clouds were drifting in the direction of his home some hundred miles away. But before he could frame the message, the warder in charge of his work span[1] shouted:

"Hey, what you tink you're doing, Brille?"

The prisoner swung round, blinking rapidly, yet at the same time sizing up the enemy. He was a new warder, named Jacobus Stephanus Hannetjie.[2] His eyes were the color of the sky, but they were frightening. A simple, primitive, brutal soul gazed out of them. The prisoner bent down quickly, and a message was quietly passed down the line:

"We're in for trouble this time, comrades."

"Why?" rippled back up the line.

"Because he's not human," the reply rippled down, and yet only the crunching of the spades as they turned over the earth disturbed the stillness.

This particular work span was known as Span One. It was composed of ten men, and they were all political prisoners. They were grouped together for convenience, as it was one of the prison regulations that no black warder should be in charge of a political prisoner lest this prisoner convert him to his views. It never seemed to occur to the authorities that this very reasoning was the strength of Span One and a clue to the strange terror they aroused in the warders. As political prisoners they were unlike the other prisoners in the sense that they felt no guilt, nor were they outcasts of society. All guilty men instinctively cower, which was why it was the kind of prison where men got knocked out cold with a blow at the back of the head from an iron bar. Up until the arrival of Warder Hannetjie, no warder had dared beat any member of Span One and no warder had lasted more than a week with them. The battle was entirely psychological. Span One was assertive, and it was beyond the scope of white warders to handle assertive black men. Thus, Span One had got out of control. They were the best thieves and liars in the camp. They lived all day on raw cabbages. They chatted and smoked tobacco. And since they moved, thought and acted as one, they had perfected every technique of group concealment.

Trouble began that very day between Span One and Warder Hannetjie. It was because of the shortsightedness of Brille. That was the nickname he was given in prison and is the Afrikaans[3] word for someone who wears glasses. Brille could never judge the approach of the prison gates, and on several previous occasions he had munched on cabbages and dropped them almost at the feet of the warder, and all previous warders had overlooked this. Not so Warder Hannetjie.

"Who dropped that cabbage?" he thundered.

Brille stepped out of line.

"I did," he said meekly.

---

1. **work span:** work brigade or work group.

2. **Jacobus Stephanus Hannetjie** (yä′ kô boos ste′ fä noos hä′ net ye).

3. **Afrikaans** (af′ ri käns′): the dialect of Dutch spoken by South Africans of Dutch descent.

"All right," said Hannetjie. "The whole Span goes three meals off."

"But I told you I did it," Brille protested.

The blood rushed to Warder Hannetjie's face.

"Look 'ere," he said. "I don't take orders from a kaffir. I don't know what kind of kaffir you tink you are. Why don't you say baas. I'm your baas. Why don't you say baas, hey?"

Brille blinked his eyes rapidly, but by contrast his voice was strangely calm.

"I'm twenty years older than you," he said. It was the first thing that came to mind, but the comrades seemed to think it a huge joke. A titter swept up the line. The next thing, Warder Hannetjie whipped out a knobkerrie[4] and gave Brille several blows about the head. What surprised his comrades was the speed with which Brille had removed his glasses, or else they would have been smashed to pieces on the ground.

That evening in the cell Brille was very apologetic.

"I'm sorry, comrades," he said. "I've put you into a hell of a mess."

"Never mind, brother, they said. What happens to one of us, happens to all."

"I'll try to make up for it, comrades," he said. "I'll steal something so that you don't go hungry."

Privately, Brille was very philosophical about his head wounds. It was the first time an act of violence had been perpetrated against him, but he had long been a witness of extreme, almost unbelievable human brutality. He had twelve children, and his mind travelled back that evening through the sixteen years of bedlam[5] in which he had lived. It had all happened in a small, drab little three-bedroom house in a small, drab little street in the Eastern Cape and the children kept coming year after year because neither he nor Martha managed the contraceptives the right way and a teacher's salary never allowed moving to a

bigger house and he was always taking exams to improve this salary only to have it all eaten up by hungry mouths. Everything was pretty horrible, especially the way the children fought. They'd get hold of each other's heads and give them a good bashing against the wall. Martha gave up somewhere along the line, so they worked out a thing between them. The bashings, biting and blood were to operate in full swing until he came home. He was to be the bogeyman, and when it worked, he never failed to have a sense of godhead at the way in which his presence could change savages into fairly reasonable human beings.

Yet somehow it was this chaos and mismanagement at the center of his life that drove him into politics. It was really an ordered, beautiful world with just a few basic slogans to learn along with the rights of mankind. At one stage, before things became very bad, there were conferences to attend, all very far away from home.

"Let's face it," he thought ruefully.[6] "I'm only learning right now what it means to be a politician. All this while I've been running away from Martha and the kids."

And the pain in his head brought a hard lump to his throat. That was what the children did to each other daily and Martha wasn't managing and if Warder Hannetjie had not interrupted him that morning he would have sent the following message:

"Be good comrades, my children. Cooperate, then life will run smoothly."

The next day Warder Hannetjie caught this old man with twelve children stealing grapes from the farm shed. They were an enormous quantity of grapes in a ten-gallon tin, and for this misdeed the old man spent a

---

4. **knobkerrie:** a short club with a knobbed end.

5. **bedlam** (bed′ ləm): a condition of noise and confusion.

6. **ruefully** (rōō′ fəl ē): regretfully.

week in the isolation cell. In fact, Span One as a whole was in constant trouble. Warder Hannetjie seemed to have eyes at the back of his head. He uncovered the trick about the cabbages, how they were split in two with the spade and immediately covered with earth and then unearthed again and eaten with split-second timing. He found out how tobacco smoke was beaten into the ground, and he found out how conversations were whispered down the wind.

For about two weeks Span One lived in acute misery. The cabbages, tobacco and conversations had been the pivot of jail life to them. Then one evening they noticed that their good old comrade who wore the glasses was looking rather pleased with himself. He pulled out a four-ounce packet of tobacco by way of explanation and the comrades fell upon it with great greed. Brille merely smiled. After all, he was the father of many children. But when the last shred had disappeared, it occurred to the comrades that they ought to be puzzled. Someone said:

"I say, brother. We're watched like hawks these days. Where did you get the tobacco?"

"Hannetjie gave it to me," said Brille.

There was a long silence. Into it dropped a quiet bombshell.

"I saw Hannetjie in the shed today," and the failing eyesight blinked rapidly. "I caught him in the act of stealing five bags of fertilizer, and he bribed me to keep my mouth shut."

There was another long silence.

"Prison is an evil life," Brille continued, apparently discussing some irrelevant matter. "It makes a man contemplate all kinds of evil deeds."

He held out his hand and closed it.

"You know, comrades," he said. "I've got Hannetjie. I'll betray him tomorrow."

Everyone began talking at once.

"Forget it, brother. You'll get shot."

Brille laughed.

"I won't," he said. "That is what I mean about evil. I am a father of children and I saw today that Hannetjie is just a child and stupidly truthful. I'm going to punish him severely because we need a good warder."

The following day, with Brille as witness, Hannetjie confessed to the theft of the fertilizer and was fined a large sum of money. From then on Span One did very much as they pleased while Warder Hannetjie stood by and said nothing. But it was Brille who carried this to extremes. One day, at the close of work Warder Hannetjie said:

"Brille, pick up my jacket and carry it back to the camp."

"But nothing in the regulations says I'm your servant, Hannetjie," Brille replied coolly.

"I've told you not to call me Hannetjie. You must say, baas," but Warder Hannetjie's voice lacked conviction. In turn, Brille squinted up at him.

"I'll tell you something about this baas business, Hannetjie," he said. "One of these days we are going to run the country. You are going to clean my car. Now, I have a fifteen-year-old son and I'd die of shame if you had to tell him that I ever called you baas."

Warder Hannetjie went red in the face and picked up his coat.

On another occasion Brille was seen to be walking about the prison yard, openly smoking tobacco. On being taken before the prison commander, he claimed to have received the tobacco from Warder Hannetjie. All throughout the <u>tirade</u>[7] from his chief, Warder Hannetjie failed to defend himself, but his nerve broke completely. He called Brille to one side.

"Brille," he said. "This thing between you and me must end. You may not know it, but I have a wife and children and you're driving me to suicide."

---

7. tirade (ti′ rād′): a long angry or scolding speech.

"Why don't you like your own medicine, Hannetjie?" Brille asked quietly.

"I can give you anything you want," Warder Hannetjie said in desperation.

"It's not only me but the whole of Span One," said Brille cunningly. "The whole of Span One wants something from you."

Warder Hannetjie brightened with relief.

"I tink I can manage if it's tobacco you want," he said.

Brille looked at him, for the first time struck with pity and guilt. He wondered if he had carried the whole business too far. The man was really a child.

"It's not tobacco we want, but you," he said. "We want you on our side. We want a good warder because without a good warder we won't be able to manage the long stretch ahead."

Warder Hannetjie interpreted this request in his own fashion, and his interpretation of what was good and human often left the prisoners of Span One speechless with surprise. He had a way of slipping off his revolver and picking up a spade and digging alongside Span One. He had a way of producing unheard-of luxuries like boiled eggs from his farm nearby and things like cigarettes, and Span One responded nobly and got the reputation of being the best work span in the camp. And it wasn't only take from their side. They were awfully good at stealing certain commodities like fertilizer which were needed on the farm of Warder Hannetjie.

Thinking About the Story

A PERSONAL RESPONSE

sharing impressions

1. How do you feel about the relationship between Brille and Hannetjie? Describe your feelings in your journal.

constructing interpretations

2. Why do you think Hannetjie becomes such a "good warder" at the end of the story?

3. In your opinion, what is this story saying about assertiveness and cooperation?
Think about
- why each man thinks he has the right to be assertive
- how effective each man's assertiveness is
- how the men cooperate at the end of the story

4. What connections do you see between Brille's relationship with his children and his relationship with Hannetjie? Use details from the story to support your answer.

A CREATIVE RESPONSE

5. If Brille had not caught Hannetjie stealing fertilizer, how might the relationship between the two have been different?

A CRITICAL RESPONSE

6. Do you think the descriptions of the two characters make them seem like real people or more like the stereotypes of cruel oppressor and noble victim? Go back through the story to find specific details to support your answer.

7. In your opinion, which story sends a stronger message—"Six Feet of the Country" or "The Prisoner Who Wore Glasses"?

8. How much relevance do you think this story has to life in the present-day United States? Explain your answer.

Analyzing the Writer's Craft

CONFLICT AND THEME

Why do you think Brille gets in trouble with Hannetjie so often at the beginning of the story?

Building a Literary Vocabulary. The struggle between opposing forces that is the basis for the plot of a story is called the conflict. An external conflict can occur between characters, between a character and society, or between a character and nature. In "The Prisoner Who Wore Glasses," a series of minor conflicts occurs between Brille and Hannetjie that expresses the more fundamental conflicts between the two men. On one level their conflict is personal—Brille fights Hannetjie because the warder tries to take away the prisoner's self-respect. On another level their conflict might be seen as representing a clash of social forces: Hannetjie represents the white political structure in South Africa, trying to hang onto its power, while Brille represents the black political movement, demanding equality and humane treatment. Each man is motivated by deeply ingrained social and political beliefs. By examining their motives and determining which beliefs the writer portrays sympathetically, the reader can determine the theme of the story.

Application: Analyzing Conflict and Theme. In a group of three or four, go back through the story and identify the different instances of conflict between Brille and Hannetjie. Create a chart in which you list each incident and identify the nature of the conflict, the beliefs that motivate Brille and Hannetjie, which character is in control when the incident ends, and what the incident might represent in terms of the larger conflict between whites and blacks. Then as a group decide on the main theme, or perception about life, that Bessie Head wants to share with her readers. Discuss your conclusions with the class.

Connecting Reading and Writing

1. Imagine that you are Hannetjie at the end of the story. Write a **report** analyzing Brille's character for a parole hearing.

Option: Create a **petition** for parole that Brille might write on his own behalf.

2. Write a **letter** from Brille to his children in which he gives them fatherly advice about assertiveness and cooperation in politics and in daily relationships.

Option: Write the outline for a **lecture** on assertiveness and cooperation that Brille might deliver to a group of young black students.

3. On a **book jacket** for an anthology that contains the Nadine Gordimer and Bessie Head stories you have just read, compare and contrast the way the stories portray apartheid and race relations.

Option: In an **expository essay**, compare and contrast the relationship between Petrus and the narrator in "Six Feet of the Country" with the relationship between Brille and Hannetjie.

Action Will Be Taken
An Action-Packed Story

HEINRICH BÖLL

A biography of Böll appears on page 419.

Approaching the Story

In many of his short stories, German writer Heinrich Böll turns a critical eye on modern German society. During the 1950's West Germany was rapidly rebuilding its economy following the devastation of World War II. "Action Will Be Taken" is set against this background of feverish activity.

Building Vocabulary

These essential words are footnoted within the story.

pensiveness (pen' siv nis): By nature I am inclined more to **pensiveness** and inactivity than to work. (page 250)

aversion (ə vʉr' zhən): My **aversion** to . . . well-lit rooms is as strong as my aversion to work. (page 250)

imperative (im per' ə tiv): But as a rule—for I felt that was in keeping with the tone of the place—I used the **imperative.** (page 251)

penchant (pen' chənt): I am equipped with not only a **penchant** for pensiveness and inactivity but also a face and figure that go extremely well with dark suits. (page 253)

vocation (vō kā' shən): I discovered my true **vocation,** a vocation in which pensiveness is essential and inactivity my duty. (page 253)

Connecting Writing and Reading

Imagine yourself twenty years from now. What kind of job would you like to have? Why does this type of work appeal to you? Respond in your journal. As you read this story, compare your thoughts about a future job with the narrator's experiences in the work world.

Action Will Be Taken

PROBABLY ONE OF the strangest interludes in my life was the time I spent as an employee in Alfred Wunsiedel's[1] factory. By nature I am inclined more to <u>pensiveness</u>[2] and inactivity than to work, but now and again prolonged financial difficulties compel me—for pensiveness is no more profitable than inactivity—to take on a so-called job. Finding myself once again at a low ebb of this kind, I put myself in the hands of the employment office and was sent with seven other fellow sufferers to Wunsiedel's factory, where we were to undergo an aptitude test.

The exterior of the factory was enough to arouse my suspicions: the factory was built entirely of glass brick, and my <u>aversion</u>[3] to well-lit buildings and well-lit rooms is as strong as my aversion to work. I became even more suspicious when we were immediately served breakfast in the well-lit, cheerful coffee shop: pretty waitresses brought us eggs, coffee, and toast, orange juice was served in tastefully designed jugs, goldfish pressed their bored faces against the sides of pale-green aquariums.

The waitresses were so cheerful that they appeared to be bursting with good cheer. Only a strong effort of will—so it seemed to me—restrained them from singing away all day long. They were as crammed with unsung songs as chickens with unlaid eggs.

Right away I realized something that my fellow sufferers evidently failed to realize: that this breakfast was already part of the test; so I chewed away reverently, with the full appreciation of a person who knows he is supplying his body with valuable elements. I did something which normally no power on earth can make me do: I drank orange juice on an empty stomach, left the coffee and egg untouched, as well as most of the toast, got up, and paced up and down in the coffee shop, pregnant with action.

As a result I was the first to be ushered into the room where the questionnaires were spread out on attractive tables. The walls were done in a shade of green that would have summoned the word "delightful" to the lips of interior decoration enthusiasts. The room appeared to be empty, and yet I was so sure of being observed that I behaved as someone pregnant with action behaves when he believes himself unobserved: I ripped my pen impatiently from my pocket, unscrewed the top, sat down at the nearest table, and pulled the questionnaire toward me, the way irritable customers snatch at the bill in a restaurant.

Question No. 1: Do you consider it right for a human being to possess only two arms, two legs, eyes, and ears?

Here for the first time I reaped the harvest of my pensive nature and wrote without hesitation: "Even four arms, legs, eyes, and ears would not be adequate for my driving energy. Human beings are very poorly equipped."

Question No. 2: How many telephones can you handle at one time?

Here again the answer was as easy as simple arithmetic: "When there are only seven telephones," I wrote, "I get impatient; there have to be nine before I feel I am working to capacity."

Question No. 3: How do you spend your free time?

---

1. **Wunsiedel:** (vo͞on′ sē dəl).
2. **pensiveness** (pen′ siv nis): deep thoughtfulness, often with some sadness.
3. **aversion** (ə vʉr′ zhən): a strong or definite dislike.

My answer: "I no longer acknowledge the term free time—on my fifteenth birthday I eliminated it from my vocabulary, for in the beginning was the act."

I got the job. Even with nine telephones I really didn't feel I was working to capacity. I shouted into the mouthpieces: "Take immediate action!" or: "Do something!—We must have some action—Action will be taken— Action has been taken—Action should be taken." But as a rule—for I felt that was in keeping with the tone of the place—I used the imperative.[4]

Of considerable interest were the noon-hour breaks, when we consumed nutritious foods in an atmosphere of silent good cheer. Wunsiedel's factory was swarming with people who were obsessed with telling you the story of their lives, as indeed vigorous personalities are fond of doing. The story of their lives is more important to them than their lives; you have only to press a button, and immediately it is covered with spewed-out exploits.

Wunsiedel had a right-hand man called Broschek,[5] who had in turn made a name for himself by supporting seven children and a paralyzed wife by working night shifts in his student days, and successfully carrying on four business agencies, besides which he had passed two examinations with honors in two years. When asked by reporters: "When do you sleep, Mr. Broschek?" he had replied: "It's a crime to sleep!"

Wunsiedel's secretary had supported a paralyzed husband and four children by knitting, at the same time graduating in psychology and German history as well as breeding shepherd dogs, and she had become famous as a nightclub singer where she was known as *Vamp Number Seven*.

Wunsiedel himself was one of those people who every morning, as they open their eyes, make up their minds to act. "I must act," they think as they briskly tie their bathrobe belts around them. "I must act," they think as they

shave, triumphantly watching their beard hairs being washed away with the lather: these hirsute vestiges are the first daily sacrifices to their driving energy. The most intimate functions also give these people a sense of satisfaction; water swishes, paper is used. Action has been taken. Bread gets eaten, eggs are decapitated.

With Wunsiedel, the most trivial activity looked like action: the way he put on his hat, the way—quivering with energy—he buttoned up his overcoat, the kiss he gave his wife, everything was action.

When he arrived at his office he greeted his secretary with a cry of "Let's have some action!" And in ringing tones she would call back: "Action will be taken!" Wunsiedel then went from department to department, calling out his cheerful: "Let's have some action!" Everyone would answer: "Action will be taken!" And I would call back to him, too, with a radiant smile, when he looked into my office: "Action will be taken!"

Within a week I had increased the number of telephones on my desk to eleven, within two weeks to thirteen, and every morning on the streetcar I enjoyed thinking up new imperatives, or chasing the words *take action* through various tenses and modulations: for two whole days I kept saying the same sentence over and over again because I thought it sounded so marvelous: "Action ought to have been taken"; for another two days it was: "Such action ought not to have been taken."

So I was really beginning to feel I was working to capacity when there actually was some action. One Tuesday morning—I had hardly settled down at my desk—Wunsiedel rushed into my office crying his "Let's have some action!" But an inexplicable something in his

---

4. imperative (im per′ ə tiv); the grammatical form that expresses a command or strong request.

5. Broschek (brô′ shək).

face made me hesitate to reply, in a cheerful voice as the rules dictated: "Action will be taken!" I must have paused too long, for Wunsiedel, who seldom raised his voice, shouted at me: "Answer! Answer, you know the rules!" And I answered, under my breath, reluctantly, like a child who is forced to say: I am a naughty child. It was only by a great effort that I managed to bring out the sentence: "Action will be taken," and hardly had I

Untitled, 1983, KEITH HARING.
© The Estate of Keith Haring, 1991.

uttered it when there really was some action: Wunsiedel dropped to the floor. As he fell he rolled over onto his side and lay right across the open doorway. I knew at once, and I confirmed it when I went slowly around my desk and approached the body on the floor: he was dead.

Shaking my head I stepped over Wunsiedel, walked slowly along the corridor to Broschek's office, and entered without knocking. Broschek was sitting at his desk, a telephone receiver in each hand, between his teeth a ballpoint pen with which he was making notes on a writing pad, while with his bare feet he was operating a knitting machine under the desk. In this way he helps to clothe his family. "We've had some action," I said in a low voice.

Broschek spat out the ballpoint pen, put down the two receivers, reluctantly detached his toes from the knitting machine.

"What action?" he asked.

"Wunsiedel is dead," I said.

"No," said Broschek.

"Yes," I said, "come and have a look!"

"No," said Broschek, "that's impossible," but he put on his slippers and followed me along the corridor.

"No," he said, when we stood besides Wunsiedel's corpse, "no, no!" I did not contradict him. I carefully turned Wunsiedel over onto his back, closed his eyes, and looked at him pensively.

I felt something like tenderness for him and realized for the first time that I had never hated him. On his face was that expression which one sees on children who obstinately refuse to give up their faith in Santa Claus, even though the arguments of their playmates sound so convincing.

"No," said Broschek, "no."

"We must take action," I said quietly to Broschek.

"Yes," said Broschek, "we must take action."

Action was taken: Wunsiedel was buried, and I was delegated to carry a wreath of artificial roses behind his coffin, for I am equipped with not only a penchant[6] for pensiveness and inactivity but also a face and figure that go extremely well with dark suits. Apparently as I walked along behind Wunsiedel's coffin carrying the wreath of artificial roses, I looked superb. I received an offer from a fashionable firm of funeral directors to join their staff as a professional mourner. "You are a born mourner," said the manager, "your outfit would be provided by the firm. Your face—simply superb!"

I handed in my notice to Broschek, explaining that I had never really felt I was working to capacity there; that, in spite of the thirteen telephones, some of my talents were going to waste. As soon as my first professional appearance as a mourner was over I knew: This is where I belong, this is what I am cut out for.

Pensively I stand behind the coffin in the funeral chapel, holding a simple bouquet, while the organ plays Handel's *Largo*,[7] a piece that does not receive nearly the respect it deserves. The cemetery café is my regular haunt; there I spend the intervals between my professional engagements, although sometimes I walk behind coffins which I have not been engaged to follow, I pay for flowers out of my own pocket and join the welfare worker who walks behind the coffin of some homeless person. From time to time I also visit Wunsiedel's grave, for after all I owe it to him that I discovered my true vocation,[8] a vocation in which pensiveness is essential and inactivity my duty.

It was not till much later that I realized I had never bothered to find out what was being produced in Wunsiedel's factory. I expect it was soap.

---

6. penchant (pen′ chənt): a strong liking or fondness.

7. *largo* (lär′ gō): in music, a piece or movement to be performed in a slow and stately manner.

8. vocation (vō kā′ shən): the work or career to which one feels called.

Thinking About the Story

A PERSONAL RESPONSE

sharing impressions

1. How did you react to this story? Describe your reaction in your journal.

constructing interpretations

2. What is your impression of the work world portrayed in this story?

Think about
- the emphasis on action
- the description of the narrator's fellow workers
- the questionnaire that the narrator fills out
- why the narrator is chosen for the job
- the description of the factory coffee shop

3. How would you describe the narrator?

Think about
- how he performs his job at Wunsiedel's factory
- his sudden reluctance to answer Wunsiedel
- what he chooses as his "true vocation"

A CREATIVE RESPONSE

4. The narrator never finds out what Wunsiedel's factory actually produces. Identify some product that you think would be appropriate for this factory and explain your reasoning.

A CRITICAL RESPONSE

5. Explain the ironies in this story.

Think about
- irony defined as a contrast between what is expected and what actually happens or between what seems real and what is real
- the repetition of the word *action*
- the narrator's realization that he never knew what the factory produced

6. To what extent is this story relevant to present-day society? Explain.

Analyzing the Writer's Craft

SATIRE

Think about the routine in a normal factory or office. Now think about the narrator's daily routine at Wunsiedel's factory. What aspects of the workplace in this story seem exaggerated or ridiculous?

Building a Literary Vocabulary. Satire is a literary technique in which ideas, customs, or institutions are ridiculed for the purpose of improving society. Often, satire exaggerates a wrong, forcing the reader to see the subject of the satire in a more critical light. For example, the narrator in this story finds fault with the extreme cheerfulness of the waitresses in the coffee shop, describing them as barely able to keep from "singing away all day long . . . as crammed with unsung songs as chickens with unlaid eggs."

Application: Analyzing Satire. With a small group of students, look for four or five ridiculous or exaggerated details either in the description of daily life in Wunsiedel's factory or elsewhere in the story. Then identify what it is that Böll seems to be criticizing or ridiculing in each case. Finally, describe in a sentence or two what you think is the general satirical purpose of the story. If possible, also suggest changes or reforms that Böll might recommend in German life. After you agree among yourselves, share your examples and conclusions with the rest of the class.

Connecting Reading and Writing

1. Using Böll's story as a model, write a **satire** of a custom or institution in your school or community for publication in a humor magazine.

Option: Write a **letter to the editor** of a humor magazine asking that more satire be published, including Böll's story.

2. Imagine that you are a government or factory official. Write a **rebuttal** to this story to appear on the editorial page of a daily newspaper.

Option: Write your response to the story as an **interoffice memo** at Wunsiedel's factory.

3. Now that the narrator has resigned from Wunsiedel's factory, write a **help-wanted notice** to find someone to replace him.

Option: Create a **job application** for the mourner position and fill it out as though you were the narrator.

4. Read one or two other stories by Böll, such as "The Laugher." Then compare "Action Will Be Taken" with one of these in a **comparison/contrast essay** for your teacher.

Option: Summarize your conclusions in a **chart** to be used by students studying for a test on these stories.

Lather and Nothing Else

HERNANDO TÉLLEZ

A biography of Téllez appears on page 428.

Approaching the Story

"Lather and Nothing Else" takes place in a Latin American country where an underground revolutionary movement is pitted against the existing government. Usually, revolutionaries use guerrilla warfare, or surprise attacks. When rebel forces work secretly for change in this way, it is difficult for any one person to know who the enemy is.

In this story, the action takes place in an old-fashioned barber shop where the barber uses a straight razor sharpened on a strop, or thick band of leather.

Building Vocabulary

These essential words are footnoted within the story.

foray (fôr´ ā): I estimated he had a four-days' growth of beard, the four days he had been gone on the last **foray** after our men. (page 257)

nape (nāp): I finished tying the knot against his **nape**. (page 257)

rejuvenated (ri jōō´ və nāt´ ed): Torres was **rejuvenated**. (page 258)

indelible (in del´ ə bəl), **stanched** (stôncht): The blood would go flowing, along the floor, warm, **indelible,** not to be **stanched,** until it reached the street. (page 259)

avenger (ə venj´ ər): And others would say, "The **avenger** of our people. A name to remember." (page 259)

Connecting Writing and Reading

In your journal, copy the following situations that require a decision:
- choosing the three people who should be cut from a school team
- deciding the winner in a talent competition
- deciding how to punish someone who has vandalized the school

For each situation, indicate whether you would want to make the decision yourself or whether you would want someone else to make it for you, and why. As you read "Lather and Nothing Else," think carefully about the complex decision the barber, who is telling the story, must make.

HE CAME IN without a word. I was stropping my best razor. And when I recognized him, I started to shake. But he did not notice. To cover my nervousness, I went on honing the razor. I tried the edge with the tip of my thumb and took another look at it against the light.

Meanwhile, he was taking off his cartridge-studded belt with the pistol holster suspended from it. He put it on a hook in the wardrobe and hung his cap above it. Then he turned full around toward me and, loosening his tie, remarked, "It's hot as the devil. I want a shave." With that he took his seat.

I estimated he had a four-days' growth of beard, the four days he had been gone on the last foray[1] after our men. His face looked burnt, tanned by the sun.

I started to work carefully on the shaving soap. I scraped some slices from the cake, dropped them into the mug, then added a little lukewarm water, and stirred with the brush. The lather soon began to rise.

"The fellows in the troop must have just about as much beard as I." I went on stirring up lather.

"But we did very well, you know. We caught the leaders. Some of them we brought back dead; others are still alive. But they'll all be dead soon."

"How many did you take?" I asked.

"Fourteen. We had to go pretty far in to find them. But now they're paying for it. And not one will escape; not a single one."

He leaned back in the chair when he saw the brush in my hand, full of lather. I had not yet put the sheet on him. I was certainly flustered. Taking a sheet from the drawer, I tied it around my customer's neck.

He went on talking. He evidently took it for granted that I was on the side of the existing regime.

"The people must have gotten a scare with what happened the other day," he said.

"Yes," I replied, as I finished tying the knot against his nape,[2] which smelt of sweat.

"Good show, wasn't it?"

"Very good," I answered, turning my attention now to the brush. The man closed his eyes wearily and awaited the cool caress of the lather.

I had never had him so close before. The day he ordered the people to file through the schoolyard to look upon the four rebels hanging there, my path had crossed his briefly. But the sight of those mutilated bodies kept me from paying attention to the face of the man who had been directing it all and whom I now had in my hands.

It was not a disagreeable face, certainly. And the beard, which aged him a bit, was not unbecoming. His name was Torres. Captain Torres.

I started to lay on the first coat of lather. He kept his eyes closed.

"I would love to catch a nap," he said, "but there's a lot to be done this evening."

I lifted the brush and asked, with pretended indifference: "A firing party?"

"Something of the sort," he replied, "but slower."

"All of them?"

"No, just a few."

I went on lathering his face. My hands began to tremble again. The man could not be aware of this, which was lucky for me. But I wished he had not come in. Probably many of our men had seen him enter the shop. And with the enemy in my house I felt a certain responsibility.

I would have to shave his beard just like any other, carefully, neatly, just as though he were a good customer, taking heed that not a single pore should emit a drop of blood. Seeing to it

---

1. **foray** (fôr′ ā): a sudden attack or raid.
2. **nape** (nāp): back part of the neck.

that the blade did not slip in the small whorls. Taking care that the skin was left clean, soft, shining, so that when I passed the back of my hand over it not a single hair should be felt. Yes. I was secretly a revolutionary, but at the same time I was a conscientious barber, proud of the way I did my job. And that four-day beard presented a challenge.

I took up the razor, opened the handle wide, releasing the blade, and started to work, downward from one sideburn. The blade responded to perfection. The hair was tough and hard; not very long, but thick. Little by little the skin began to show through. The razor gave out its usual sound as it gathered up layers of soap mixed with bits of hair. I paused to wipe it clean, and taking up the strop once more went about improving its edge, for I am a painstaking barber.

The man, who had kept his eyes closed, now opened them, put a hand out from under the sheet, felt of the part of his face that was emerging from the lather, and said to me, "Come at six o'clock this evening to the school."

"Will it be like the other day?" I asked, stiff with horror.

"It may be even better," he replied.

"What are you planning to do?"

"I'm not sure yet. But we'll have a good time."

Once more he leaned back and shut his eyes. I came closer, the razor on high.

"Are you going to punish all of them?" I timidly ventured.

"Yes, all of them."

The lather was drying on his face. I must hurry. Through the mirror, I took a look at the street. It appeared about as usual; there was the grocery shop with two or three customers. Then I glanced at the clock, two-thirty.

The razor kept descending. Now from the other sideburn downward. It was a blue beard, a thick one. He should let it grow like some poets, or some priests. It would suit him well. Many people would not recognize him. And that would be a good thing for him, I thought, as I went gently over all the throat line. At this point you really had to handle your blade skillfully, because the hair, while scantier, tended to fall into small whorls. It was a curly beard. The pores might open, minutely, in this area and let out a tiny drop of blood. A good barber like myself stakes his reputation on not permitting that to happen to any of his customers.

And this was indeed a special customer. How many of ours had he sent to their death? How many had he mutilated? It was best not to think about it. Torres did not know I was his enemy. Neither he nor the others knew it. It was a secret shared by very few, just because that made it possible for me to inform the revolutionaries about Torres's activities in the town and what he planned to do every time he went on one of his raids to hunt down rebels. So it was going to be very difficult to explain how it was that I had him in my hands and then let him go in peace, alive, cleanshaven.

His beard had now almost entirely disappeared. He looked younger, several years younger than when he had come in. I suppose that always happens to men who enter and leave barbershops. Under the strokes of my razor, Torres was rejuvenated;[3] yes, because I am a good barber, the best in this town, and I say this in all modesty.

A little more lather here under the chin, on the Adam's apple, right near the great vein. How hot it is! Torres must be sweating just as I am. But he is not afraid. He is a tranquil man, who is not even giving thought to what he will do to his prisoners this evening. I, on the other hand, polishing his skin with this razor but avoiding the drawing of blood, careful with every stroke—I cannot keep my thoughts in order.

---

3. **rejuvenated** (ri jo͞o′ və nāt′ ed): brought back to youthful strength or appearance.

Confound the hour he entered my shop! I am a revolutionary but not a murderer. And it would be so easy to kill him. He deserves it. Or does he? No! No one deserves the sacrifice others make in becoming assassins. What is to be gained by it? Nothing. Others and still others keep coming, and the first kill the second, and then these kill the next, and so on until everything becomes a sea of blood. I could cut his throat, so, swish, swish! He would not even have time to moan, and with his eyes shut he would not even see the shine of the razor or the gleam in my eye.

But I'm shaking like a regular murderer. From his throat a stream of blood would flow on the sheet, over the chair, down on my hands, onto the floor. I would have to close the door. But the blood would go flowing, along the floor, warm, <u>indelible</u>,[4] not to be <u>stanched</u>,[5] until it reached the street like a small scarlet river.

I'm sure that with a good strong blow, a deep cut, he would feel no pain. He would not suffer at all. And what would I do then with the body? Where would I hide it? I would have to flee, leave all this behind, take shelter far away, very far away. But they would follow until they caught up with me. "The murderer of Captain Torres. He slit his throat while he was shaving him. What a cowardly thing to do." And others would say, "The <u>avenger</u>[6] of our people. A name to remember"—my name here. "He was the town barber. No one knew he was fighting for our cause."

And so, which will it be? Murderer or hero? My fate hangs on the edge of this razor blade. I can turn my wrist slightly, put a bit more pressure on the blade, let it sink in. The skin will yield like silk, like rubber, like the strop. There is nothing more tender than a man's skin, and the blood is always there, ready to burst forth. A razor like this cannot fail. It is the best one I have.

But I don't want to be a murderer. No, sir. You came in to be shaved. And I do my work honorably. I don't want to stain my hands with blood. Just with lather, and nothing else. You are an executioner; I am only a barber. Each one to his job. That's it. Each one to his job.

The chin was now clean, polished, soft. The man got up and looked at himself in the glass. He ran his hand over the skin and felt its freshness, its newness.

"Thanks," he said. He walked to the wardrobe for his belt, his pistol, and his cap. I must have been very pale, and I felt my shirt soaked with sweat. Torres finished adjusting his belt buckle, straightened his gun in its holster, and, smoothing his hair mechanically, put on his cap. From his trousers pocket he took some coins to pay for the shave. And he started toward the door. On the threshold he stopped for a moment, and turning toward me he said,

"They told me you would kill me. I came to find out if it was true. But it's not easy to kill. I know what I'm talking about."

---

4. indelible (in del′ ə bəl): unable to be erased or blotted out.

5. stanched (stôncht): stopped.

6. avenger (ə venj′ ər): one who gets revenge for; one who punishes someone who has done wrong.

Thinking About the Story

A PERSONAL RESPONSE

sharing
impressions

1. Which character do you have the strongest feeling about, Torres or the barber? Describe your reaction in your journal.

constructing
interpretations

2. In your view, does the barber make the right decision? Explain why or why not.

3. Why does the barber decide not to kill Torres?
Think about
- how the barber performs his work
- his involvement in the revolutionary movement
- his thoughts about murder

4. What kind of person do you think Torres is?
Think about
- the barber's description of him
- what he tells the barber during the shave
- why he puts himself into the barber's hands
- his final words before leaving

A CREATIVE RESPONSE

5. What if the barber had killed Captain Torres? Imagine what the barber's thoughts and actions would be after doing so.

A CRITICAL RESPONSE

6. What do you think is the climax of this story? Be ready to defend your choice.
Think about
- the definition of climax as a turning point and the moment when interest and intensity reach a peak
- the point in the story when the outcome became clear to you

7. Both the barber in this story and Brille in "The Prisoner Who Wore Glasses" are ordinary men who oppose a government they believe is unjust. Which character do you admire more? Give reasons for your answer.

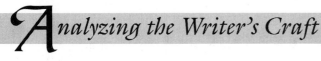

nalyzing the Writer's Craft

CONFLICT

What kinds of problems does the barber face?

Building a Literary Vocabulary. The struggle between opposing forces that is the basis for the plot of a story is called conflict. External conflicts can occur between characters, between a character and society, or between a character and nature. Brille in "The Prisoner Who Wore Glasses" faces an external conflict with a single character, Warder Hannetjie, as well as with a society that deprives him of freedom and dignity. Internal conflicts occur between opposing tendencies within a character. For example, in "Action Will Be Taken" the narrator needs to earn money, but his job at Wunsiedel's factory is unsuited to his pensive nature.

Application: Evaluating Conflicts. Get together in a group and go back through the story to look for passages that indicate conflicts that the barber faces. Make a list of the conflicts and circle the ones that are internal. Then evaluate which of the conflicts is the most important one in the story.

onnecting Reading and Writing

1. How would this episode be different if Captain Torres had told the story? Let him give his interpretation of the episode in a **report** to his commander.

Option: Write a **scene** from the story as told by Torres.

2. Write about a difficult decision that you had to make and compare your decision to the barber's. Present your comparison in a **diary entry.**

Option: Write your comparison in the form of a news reporter's **interview** with you.

3. Analyze the different aspects of the story that make it suspenseful, such as the references to blood. Present your analysis in a **poster** for a film version of the story.

Option: Explain your analysis in an **exposition** written for someone who has not read the story.

4. If the barber of this story, the narrator of "Action Will Be Taken," and Brille of "The Prisoner Who Wore Glasses" were to have a conversation about integrity, what do you think they would say? Present this conversation as a **dramatic skit.**

Option: Draw a **comic strip** showing the imagined conversation.

Blues Ain't No Mockin Bird

TONI CADE BAMBARA

A biography of Bambara appears on page 419.

Approaching the Story

This story is one of many that Toni Cade Bambara has written about the experiences of African Americans. Like much of her work, the story presents the perceptions of children in a dialect appropriate to the narrator. The reader must make an effort to understand the implications of the details given and to become attuned to the rhythms of African-American speech.

Connecting Writing and Reading

Which of the following situations would you find intrusive? Copy this chart in your journal and indicate your responses.

	Yes	No
• someone smiles at you	☐	☐
• someone gives you a gift	☐	☐
• someone pays you a compliment	☐	☐
• someone photographs you	☐	☐
• someone interviews you	☐	☐
• someone enters your home	☐	☐
• someone goes through your dresser drawers or luggage	☐	☐

For every "yes" answer, explain the circumstances in which the situation would seem intrusive. Continue to consider what makes an action intrusive as you read about one family's encounter with strangers.

THE PUDDLE HAD frozen over, and me and Cathy went stompin in it. The twins from next door, Tyrone and Terry, were swingin so high out of sight we forgot we were waitin our turn on the tire. Cathy jumped up and came down hard on her heels and started tap-dancin. And the frozen patch splinterin every which way underneath kinda spooky. "Looks like a plastic spider web," she said. "A sort of weird spider, I guess, with many mental problems." But really it looked like the crystal paperweight Granny kept in the parlor. She was on the back porch Granny was, making the cakes drunk. The old ladle dripping rum into the Christmas tins, like it used to drip maple syrup into the pails when we lived in the Judsons' woods, like it poured cider into the vats when we were on the Cooper place, like it used to scoop buttermilk and soft cheese when we lived at the dairy.

"Go tell that man we ain't a bunch of trees."

"Ma'am?"

"I said to tell that man to get away from here with that camera." Me and Cathy look over toward the meadow where the men with the station wagon'd been roamin around all mornin. The tall man with a huge camera lassoed to his shoulder was buzzin our way.

"They're makin movie pictures," yelled Tyrone, stiffenin his legs and twistin so the tire'd come down slow so they could see.

"They're makin movie pictures," sang out Terry.

"That boy don't never have anything original to say," say Cathy grown-up.

By the time the man with the camera had cut across our neighbor's yard, the twins were out of the trees swingin low and Granny was onto the steps, the screen door bammin soft and scratchy against her palms. "We thought we'd get a shot or two of the house and everything and then—"

"Good mornin," Granny cut him off. And smiled that smile.

"Good mornin," he said, head all down the way Bingo does when you yell at him about the bones on the kitchen floor. "Nice place you got here, aunty. We thought we'd take a—"

"Did you?" said Granny with her eyebrows. Cathy pulled up her socks and giggled.

"Nice things here," said the man, buzzin his camera over the yard. The pecan barrels, the sled, me and Cathy, the flowers, the printed stones along the driveway, the trees, the twins, the toolshed.

"I don't know about the thing, the it, and the stuff," said Granny, still talkin with her eyebrows. "Just people here is what I tend to consider."

Camera man stopped buzzin. Cathy giggled into her collar.

"Mornin, ladies," a new man said. He had come up behind us when we weren't lookin. "And gents," discoverin the twins givin him a nasty look. "We're filmin for the county," he said with a smile. "Mind if we shoot a bit around here?"

"I do indeed," said Granny with no smile. Smilin man was smiling up a storm. So was Cathy. But he didn't seem to have another word to say, so he and the camera man backed on out of the yard, but you could hear the camera buzzin still. "Suppose you just shut that machine off," said Granny real low through her teeth, and took a step down off the porch and then another.

"Now, aunty," Camera said, pointin the thing straight at her.

"Your mama and I are not related."

Smilin man got his notebook out and a chewed-up pencil. "Listen," he said, movin back into our yard, "we'd like to have a statement from you . . . for the film. We're filmin for the county, see. Part of the food stamp[1] campaign. You know about the food stamps?"

Granny said nuthin.

"Maybe there's somethin you want to say for the film. I see you grow your own vegetables," he smiled real nice. "If more folks did that, see, there'd be no need—"

Granny wasn't sayin nuthin. So they backed on out, buzzin at our clothesline and the twins' bicycles, then back on down to the meadow. The twins were danglin in the tire, lookin at Granny. Me and Cathy were waitin, too, cause Granny always got something to say. She teaches steady with no let-up. "I was on this bridge one time," she started off. "Was a crowd cause this man was goin to jump, you understand. And a minister was there and the police and some other folks. His woman was there, too."

"What was they doin?" asked Tyrone.

"Tryin to talk him out of it was what they was doin. The minister talkin about how it was a mortal sin, suicide. His woman takin bites out of her own hand and not even knowin it, so nervous and cryin and talkin fast."

"So what happened?" asked Tyrone.

"So here comes . . . this person . . . with a camera, takin pictures of the man and the minister and the woman. Takin pictures of the man in his misery about to jump, cause life so bad and people been messin with him so bad. This person takin up the whole roll of film practically. But savin a few, of course."

"Of course," said Cathy, hatin the person. Me standin there wonderin how Cathy knew it was "of course" when I didn't and it was *my* grandmother.

After a while Tyrone say, "Did he jump?"

"Yeh, did he jump?" say Terry all eager.

And Granny just stared at the twins till their faces swallow up the eager and they don't even care any more about the man jumpin. Then she goes back onto the porch and lets the screen door go for itself. I'm lookin to

Cathy to finish the story cause she knows Granny's whole story before me even. Like she knew how come we move so much and Cathy ain't but a third cousin we picked up on the way last Thanksgivin visitin. But she knew it was on account of people drivin Granny crazy till she'd get up in the night and start packin. Mumblin and packin and wakin everybody up sayin, "Let's get away from here before I kill me somebody." Like people wouldn't pay her for things like they said they would. Or Mr. Judson bringin us boxes of old clothes and raggedy magazines. Or Mrs. Cooper comin in our kitchen and touchin everything and sayin how clean it all was. Granny goin crazy, and Granddaddy Cain pullin her off the people, sayin, "Now, now, Cora." But next day loadin up the truck, with rocks all in his jaw, madder than Granny in the first place.

"I read a story once," said Cathy, soundin like Granny teacher. "About this lady Goldilocks who barged into a house that wasn't even hers. And not invited, you understand. Messed over the people's groceries and broke up the people's furniture. Had the nerve to sleep in the folks' bed."

"Then what happened?" asked Tyrone. "What they do, the folks, when they come in to all this mess?"

"Did they make her pay for it?" asked Terry, makin a fist. "I'd've made her pay me."

I didn't even ask. I could see Cathy actress was very likely to just walk away and leave us in mystery about this story which I heard was about some bears.

"Did they throw her out?" asked Tyrone, like his father sounds when he's bein extra nasty-plus to the washin-machine man.

"Woulda," said Terry. "I woulda gone upside her head with my fist and—"

"You woulda done whatcha always do—go cry to Mama, you big baby," said Tyrone. So

---

1. **food stamp:** federal coupons given to qualifying low-income persons for use in buying food.

naturally Terry starts hittin on Tyrone and next thing you know they tumblin out the tire and rollin on the ground. But Granny didn't say a thing or send the twins home or step out on the steps to tell us about how we can't afford to be fightin among ourselves. She didn't say nuthin. So I get into the tire to take my turn. And I could see her leanin up against the pantry table, starin at the cakes she was puttin up for the Christmas sale, mumblin real low and grumpy and holdin her forehead like it wanted to fall off and mess up the rum cakes.

Behind me I hear before I can see Granddaddy Cain comin through the woods in his field boots. Then I twist around to see the shiny black oilskin[2] cuttin through what little left there was of yellows, reds, and oranges. His great white head not quite round cause of this bloody thing high on his shoulder, like he was wearin a cap sideways. He takes the shortcut through the pecan grove, and the sound of twigs snappin overhead and underfoot travels clear and cold all the way up to us. And here comes Smilin and Camera up behind him like they was goin to do somethin. Folks like to go for him sometimes. Cathy say it's because he's so tall and quiet and like a king. And people just can't stand it. But Smilin and Camera don't hit him in the head or nuthin. They just buzz on him as he stalks by with the chicken hawk slung over his shoulder, squawkin, drippin red down the back of the oilskin. He passes the porch and stops a second for Granny to see he's caught the hawk at last, but she's just starin and mumblin, and not at the hawk. So he nails the bird to the toolshed door, the hammerin crackin through the eardrums. And the bird flappin himself to death and droolin down the door to paint the gravel in the driveway red, then brown, then black. And the two men movin up on tiptoe like they was invisible or we were blind, one.

"Get them persons out of my flower bed, Mister Cain," says Granny, moanin real low like at a funeral.

"How come your grandmother calls her husband 'Mister Cain' all the time?" Tyrone whispers all loud and noisy and from the city and don't know no better. Like his mama, Miss Myrtle, tell us never mind the formality as if we had no better breedin than to call her Myrtle, plain. And then this awful thing—a giant hawk—come wailin up over the meadow, flyin low and tilted and screamin, zigzaggin through the pecan grove, breakin branches and hollerin, snappin past the clothesline, flyin every which way, flyin into things reckless with crazy.

"He's come to claim his mate," say Cathy fast, and ducks down. We all fall quick and flat into the gravel driveway, stones scrapin my face. I squinch my eyes open again at the hawk on the door, tryin to fly up out of her death like it was just a sack flown into by mistake. Her body holdin her there on that nail, though. The mate beatin the air overhead and clutchin for hair, for heads, for landin space.

The camera man duckin and bendin and runnin and fallin, jigglin the camera and scared. And Smilin jumpin up and down swipin at the huge bird, tryin to bring the hawk down with just his raggedy ole cap. Granddaddy Cain straight up and silent, watchin the circles of the hawk, then aimin the hammer off his wrist. The giant bird -fallin, silent and slow. Then here comes Camera and Smilin all big and bad now that the awful screechin thing is on its back and broken, here they come. And Granddaddy Cain looks up at them like it was the first time noticin, but not payin them too much mind cause he's listenin, we all listenin, to that low groanin music comin from the porch. And we figure any minute now,

---

2. **oilskin:** a garment made waterproof by treatment with oil.

Granny gonna bust through that screen with somethin in her hand and murder on her mind. So Granddaddy say above the buzzin, but quiet, "Good day, gentlemen." Just like that. Like he's invited them in to play cards and they'd stayed too long and all the sandwiches were gone and Reverend Webb was droppin by and it was time to go.

They didn't know what to do. But like Cathy say, folks can't stand Granddaddy tall and silent and like a king. They can't neither. The smile the men smilin is pullin the mouth back and showin the teeth. Lookin like the wolf man, both of them. Then Granddaddy holds his hand out—this huge hand I used to sit in when I was a baby and he'd carry me through the house to my mother like I was a gift on a tray. Like he used to on the trains. They called the other men just waiters. But they spoke of Granddaddy separate and said, The Waiter. And said he had engines in his feet and motors in his hands and couldn't no train throw him off and couldn't nobody turn him round. They were big enough for motors, his hands were. He held that one hand out all still and it gettin to be not at all a hand but a person in itself.

"He wants you to hand him the camera," Smilin whispers to Camera, tiltin his head to talk secret like they was in the jungle or somethin and come upon a native that don't speak the language. The men start untyin the straps, and the put the camera into that great hand speckled with the hawk's blood all black and crackly now. And the hand don't even drop with the weight, just the fingers move, curl up around the machine. But Granddaddy lookin straight at the men. They lookin at each other and everywhere but at Granddaddy's face.

"We filmin for the county, see," say Smilin. "We puttin together a movie for the food stamp program . . . filmin all around these parts. Uhh, filmin for the county."

"Can I have my camera back?" say the tall man with no machine on his shoulder, but still keepin it high like the camera was still there or needed to be. "Please, sir."

Then Granddaddy's other hand flies up like a sudden and gentle bird, slaps down fast on top of the camera and lifts off half like it was a calabash[3] cut for sharing.

"Hey," Camera jumps forward. He gathers up the parts into his chest and everything unrollin and fallin all over. "Whatcha tryin to do? You'll ruin the film." He looks down into his chest of metal reels and things like he protectin a kitten from the cold.

"You standin in the missis' flower bed," say Granddaddy. "This is our own place."

The two men look at him, then at each other, then back at the mess in the camera man's chest, and they just back off. One sayin over and over all the way down to the meadow, "Watch it, Bruno. Keep ya fingers off the film." Then Granddaddy picks up the hammer and jams it into the oilskin pocket, scrapes his boots, and goes into the house. And you can hear the squish of his boots headin though the house. And you can see the funny shadow he throws from the parlor window onto the ground by the string bean patch. The hammer draggin the pocket of the oilskin out so Granddaddy looked even wider. Granny was hummin now—high, not low and grumbly. And she was doin the cakes again, you could smell the molasses from the rum.

"There's this story I'm goin to write one day," say Cathy dreamer. "About the proper use of the hammer."

"Can I be in it?" Tyrone say, with his hand up like it was a matter of first come, first served.

"Perhaps," say Cathy, climbin onto the tire to pump us up. "If you there and ready."

---

3. **calabash** (kal′ ə bash′): a gourdlike fruit.

Thinking About the Story

A PERSONAL RESPONSE

sharing impressions

1. Jot down words and phrases in your journal that describe your impression of Granny, Granddaddy, and the other members of the family.

constructing interpretations

2. What do you suppose is Cathy's idea of "the proper use of the hammer"?
Think about
- how Granddaddy Cain uses the hammer in dealing with the chicken hawks
- what this incident reveals to the filmmakers about Granddaddy's character

3. Do you think Granny and Granddaddy Cain are right to react to the filmmakers as they do? Explain.
Think about
- how the filmmakers address them and treat their property
- why the film is being made
- whether you consider the filmmakers' actions intrusive

4. Summarize the Cains' beliefs about the proper way to treat people.
Think about
- the point of Granny's story about the man on the bridge
- the reasons the family has moved so often
- how Granny addresses her husband and how the narrator and Cathy address the twins' mother

A CREATIVE RESPONSE

5. What might have happened if Granddaddy Cain had not come home when he did?

A CRITICAL RESPONSE

6. Based on what you know about the narrator, explain why this person is or is not a good choice to tell the story.

7. How do you think the title relates to the story?
Think about
- blues as a type of African-American folk music characterized by a slow tempo and melancholy words
- characteristics one might associate with mockingbirds

8. Of all the stories you have read in the unit, which do you think has the most important message for your community? Explain.

Analyzing the Writer's Craft

THEME AND STRUCTURE

Think about the brief stories embedded within the main story in "Blues Ain't No Mockin Bird." What might be the point of including these stories?

Building a Literary Vocabulary. Theme is the central idea or message in a work of literature. Theme should not be confused with subject, or what the work is about. Rather, theme is a perception about life or human nature that the writer shares with the reader. For example, one theme of "Lather and Nothing Else" is that to kill an enemy is to degrade oneself. Theme can be emphasized through the structure of a work of literature—that is, through the way its parts are arranged. Consider the structure of "Santa's Children." The narration of Marcovaldo's experiences during the Christmas season is followed by a brief description of a wolf pursuing a hare. The wolf and hare episode emphasizes the idea, expressed in the main story, of innocence endangered by greedy predators.

Application: Relating Structure and Theme. Working in small groups, decide what themes are conveyed by these brief stories or incidents within "Blues Ain't No Mockin Bird": the story Granny tells about the man on the bridge, Cathy's retelling of the Goldilocks tale, and the episode involving the chicken hawks.

Consider how these themes relate to the family's encounter with the filmmakers and try to determine the theme of the story as a whole. Present your ideas in a diagram similar to the one below.

Blues Ain't No Mockin Bird

Story of man on bridge	Goldilocks tale	Hawk incident
Theme:_____	Theme:_____	Theme: _____
_____	_____	_____
_____	_____	_____

Overall theme: _____

_____

_____

_____

Connecting Reading and Writing

1. Add another **episode** to the story, describing the incident that made the family leave the Judsons' woods or the Cooper place. Read your episode to classmates.

Option: Perform the incident as a **dramatic scene** for the class.

2. Use the Cains' experience to create a set of **guidelines** for reporters and for directors of documentary films.

Option: Write a **letter of complaint** that you would send to the county on the Cains' behalf.

3. Toni Cade Bambara defines her reasons for writing as follows: "Through writing, I attempt to celebrate the tradition of resistance, attempt to tap Black potential, and try to join the chorus of voices that argues exploitation and misery are neither inevitable nor necessary." In an **evaluation** that you would send to Bambara, comment on how these purposes are reflected in her story.

Option: Write a **recommendation** for including this story in a forthcoming anthology of resistance literature.

Out of Place

JOYCE CAROL OATES

A biography of Oates appears on page 426.

Approaching the Story

In her novels and short stories, Joyce Carol Oates often writes about ordinary people struggling to find a place in a changing world. In this short story the main character, Jack Furlong, a wounded Vietnam veteran, struggles to adjust to a new life. He must learn to live with his injuries and memories and with the attitudes of others toward him. As the story begins, Jack, confined in a hospital, recalls an experience from his youth.

I HAVE THIS memory: I am waiting in line for a movie. The line is long, noisy, restless, mostly kids my age (I seem to be about thirteen). The movie must be . . . a Western, I think. I can almost see the posters and I think I see a man with a cowboy hat. Good. I do see this man and I see a horse on the poster, it is all becoming clear. A Western. I am a kid, thirteen, but not like the thirteen-year-olds who pass by the hospital here on their way home from school—they are older than I was at that age, everyone seems older. I am nineteen now, I think. I will be twenty in a few weeks and my mother talks about how I will be home, then, in time for my birthday. That gives her pleasure and so I like to hear her talk about it. But my memory is more important: the movie house, yes, and the kids, and I am one of them. We are all jostling together, moving forward in surges, a bunch of us from St. Ann's Junior High. Other kids are there from Clinton, which is a tough school. We are all in line waiting and no one is out of line. I am

there, with them. We shuffle up to the ticket window and buy our tickets (fifty cents) and go inside, running.

There is something pleasant about this memory, but dwelling upon memories is unhealthy. They tell me that. They are afraid I will remember the explosion, and my friend who died, but I have already forgotten these things. There is no secret about it, of course. Everything is open. We were caught in a land mine explosion and some of us were luckier than others; we weren't killed, that's all. I am very lucky to be alive. I am not being sarcastic but quite truthful, because in the end it is only truth you can stand. In camp, and for a while when we fooled around for so long without ever seeing the enemy, then some of the guys were sarcastic—but that went away. Everything falls away except truth and that is what you hang onto.

The truth is that my right leg is gone and that I have some trouble with my "vision." My eyes.

On sunny days we are wheeled outside, so that we can watch the school children playing across the street. The hospital is very clean and white, and there is a kind of patio or terrace or wide walk around the front and sides, where we can sit. Next door, some distance away, is a school that is evidently a grade school. The children play at certain times— ten-fifteen in the morning, at noon, and two in the afternoon. I don't know if they are always the same children. I have trouble with my "vision," it isn't the way it used to be and yet in a way I can't remember what it used to be like. My glasses are heavy and make red marks on my nose, and sometimes my skin is sore around my ears, but that is the only sign that the glasses are new. In a way nothing is new but has always been with me. That is why I am pleased with certain memories, like the memory of the Western movie. Though I do not remember the movie itself, but only waiting in line to get in the theater.

There is a boy named Ed here, a friend of mine. He was hurt at about the same time I was, though in another place. He is about twenty too. His eyes are as good as ever and he can see things I can't; I sometimes ask him to tell me about the playground and the children there. The playground is surrounded by a high wire fence and the children play inside this fence, on their swings and slides and teeter-totters, making a lot of noise. Their voices are very high and shrill. We don't mind the noise, we like it, but sometimes it reminds me of something—I can almost catch the memory but not quite. Cries and screams by themselves are not bad. I mean the sounds are not bad. But if you open your eyes wide you may have latched onto the wrong memory and might see the wrong things—screams that are not happy screams, etc. There was a boy somewhere who was holding onto the hand of his "buddy." ("Buddy" is a word I would not have used before, I don't know where I got it from exactly.) That boy was crying, because the other boy was dead—but I can't quite remember who they were. The memory comes and goes silently. It is nothing to be upset about. The doctor told us all that it is healthier to think about our problems, not to push them back. He is a neat, clean man dressed in white, a very kind man. Sometimes his face looks creased, there are too many wrinkles in it, and he looks like my father—they are about the same age.

I like the way my father calls him "Dr. Pritchard." You can tell a man's worth by the way my father speaks to him. I know that sounds egotistical but it's true, and my father trusts Dr. Pritchard. It is different when he speaks to someone he doesn't quite trust, oh, for example, certain priests who look too young, too boyish; he hesitates before he calls them "Father." He hesitates before he says hello to Father Presson, who comes here to see me and hear my confession and all, and then the words "Father Presson" come out a little forced.

"Look at that big kid, by the slide. See?" Ed says nervously.

I think I see him—a short blur of no-color by the slide. "What is he doing?"

"I don't know. I thought he was . . . No, I don't know," Ed says.

There is hesitation in Ed's voice too. Sometimes he seems not to know what he is saying, whether he should say it. I can hear the distance in his voice, the distance between the school children over there and us up here on the ledge, in the sun. When the children fight we feel nervous and we don't know what to do. Not that they really fight, not exactly. But sometimes the mood of the playground breaks and a new mood comes upon it. It's hard to explain. Ed keeps watching for that though he doesn't want to see it.

Ed has a short, muscular body, and skin that always looks tanned. His hair is black, shaved off close, and his eyebrows of course are black and very thick. He looks hunched up in the wheelchair, about to spring off and run away. His legs just lie there, though, and never move. They are both uninjured. His problem is something else, in his spine—it is a mysterious thing, how a bullet strikes in one place and damages another. We have all learned a lot about the body, here. I think I would like to be a doctor. I think that, to be a doctor like Dr. Pritchard, you must have a great reverence for the body and its springs and wires and tubes, I mean, you must understand how they work together, all together. It is a strange thing. When I tried to talk to my parents about this they acted strange. I told them that Ed and I would like to be doctors, if things got better.

"Yes," my father said slowly, "the study of medicine is—is—"

"Very beneficial," my mother said.

"Yes, beneficial—"

Then they were silent. I said, "I mean if things get better. I know I couldn't get through medical school, the way I am now."

"I wouldn't be too sure about that," my father said. "You know how they keep discovering all these extraordinary things—"

(My father latches onto special words occasionally. Now it is the word *extraordinary*. I don't know where he got it from, from a friend probably. He is a vice-president for a company that makes a certain kind of waxed paper and waxed cardboard.)

"But you will get better," my mother said. "You know that."

I am seized with a feeling of happiness. Not because of what my mother said, maybe it's true and maybe not, I don't know, but because of—the fact of doctors, the fact of the body itself which is such a mystery. I can't explain it. I said, groping for my words, "If this hadn't happened then—then—I guess I'd just be the

way I was, I mean, I wouldn't know—what it's like to be like this." But that was a stupid thing to say. Mother began crying again; it was embarrassing. With my glasses off, lying back against the pillow, I could pretend that I didn't notice; so I said, speaking in my new voice which is a little slow and stumbling, "I mean —there are lots of things that are mysteries —like the way the spine hooks up with things—and the brain—and—and by myself I wouldn't know about these things—"

But it's better to talk about other matters. In my room, away from the other patients, the talk brought to me by my parents and relatives and friends is like a gift from the outside, and it has the quality of the spring days that are here now: sunny and fragrant but very delicate. My visitors' words are like rays of sunlight. It might seem that you could grab hold of them and sit up, but you can't, they're nothing, they don't last—they are gifts, that's all, like the other gifts I have. For instance, my mother says: "Betty is back now. She wants to know when she can see you, but I thought that could wait."

"Oh, is she back?"

"She didn't have a very happy time, you know,"

"What's she doing now?"

"Oh, nothing, I don't know. She might go to school."

"Where?"

"A community college, nothing much."

"That's nice."

This conversation is about a cousin of mine who married some jerk and ran away to live in Mexico. But the conversation is not really about her. I don't know what it is about. It is "about" the words themselves. When my mother says, "Betty is back now," that means "Betty-is-back-now" is being talked about, not the girl herself. We hardly know the girl herself. Then we move on to talk about Harold

Spender, who is a bachelor friend of my father's. Harold Spender has a funny name and Mother likes him for his name. He is always "spending" too much money. I think he has expensive parties or something, I don't know. But "Harold Spender" is another gift, and I think this gift means: "You see, everything is still the same, your cousin is still a dope and Harold Spender is still with us, spending money. Nothing has changed."

Sometimes when they are here, visiting, and Mother chatters on like that, a terrible door opens in my mind and I can't hear her. It is like waking up at night when you don't know it is night. A door opens and though I know Mother is still talking, I can't hear her. This lasts a few seconds, no more. I go into it and come out of it and no one notices. The door opens by itself, silently, and beyond it everything is black and very quiet, just nothing.

But sometimes I am nervous and feel very sharp. That is a peculiar word, *sharp*. I mean my body tenses and I seem to be sitting forward and my hands grip the arms of the chair, as if I'm about to throw myself out of it and demand something. Demand something! Ed's voice gets like that too. It gets very thin and demanding and sometimes he begins to cry. It's better to turn away from that, from a boy of twenty crying. I don't know why I get nervous. There is no relationship between what my body feels and what is going on outside, and this is what frightens me.

Dr. Pritchard says there is nothing to be frightened about any longer. Nothing.

He is right, of course. I think it will be nice when I am home again and the regular routine begins. My nervousness will go away and there will not be the strange threat of that door, which opens so silently and invites me in. And Father won't take so much time off from work, and Mother will not chatter so. It will be nice to get back into place and decide what I will

do, though there is no hurry about that. When I was in high school I fooled around too much. It wasn't because of basketball either, that was just an excuse; I wasted time and so did the other kids. I wore trousers the color of bone that were pretty short and tight, and I fooled around with my hair, nothing greasy but pretty long in front, flipped down onto my forehead. Mr. Palisano, the physics teacher, was also the basketball coach and he always said: "Hey, Furlong, what's your hurry? Just what's your hurry?" He had a teasing singsong voice he used only on kids he liked. He was a tall, skinny man, a very intelligent man. "Just what's your hurry?" he said when I handed in my physics problems half-finished, or made a fool of myself in basketball practice. He was happy when I told him I was going into physics, but when I failed the first course I didn't want to go back and tell him—the hell with it. So I switched into math because I had to take math anyway. And then what happened? I don't remember. I was just a kid then, I fooled around too much. The kids at the school—it was a middle-sized school run by the Holy Cross fathers, who also ran Notre Dame—just fooled around too much, some of them flunked out. I don't think I flunked out. It gives me a headache to think about it—

To think about the kids in my calculus class, that gives me a headache. I don't know why. I can remember my notebook, and the rows of desks, and the blackboard (though it was green), and the bell striking the hour from outside (though it was always a little off), and I think of it all like a bubble with the people still inside. All the kids and me among them, still in the same room, still there. I like to think of that.

But they aren't still there in that room. Everything has moved on. They have moved on to other rooms and I am out here, at this particular hospital. I wonder if I will be able to catch up with them. If I can read, if my eyes get better, I don't see why not. Father talks about me returning. It's no problem with a wheelchair these days, he says, and there is the business about the artificial "limb," etc. I think it will be nice to get back to books and reading and regular assignments.

I am thinking about high school, about the halls and the stairways. Mr. Palisano, and the physics class, and the afternoon basketball games. I am thinking about the excitement of those games, which was not quite fear, and about the drive back home, in my car or someone else's. I went out a lot. And one night, coming home from a dance, I saw a car parked and a man fooling around by it so I stopped to help him. "Jesus Christ," he kept saying. He had a flat tire and he was very angry. He kept snuffling and wiping his nose on his shoulder, very angry, saying "Jesus Christ" and other things, other words, not the way kids said them but in a different way—hard to explain. It made me understand that adults had made up those words, not in play but out of hatred. He was not kidding. The way he said those words frightened me. Fear comes up from the earth, the coldness of the earth, flowing up from your feet up your legs and into your bowels, like the clay of the earth itself, and your heart begins to hammer. . . .

I never told anyone about that night, what a fool I was to stop. What if something had happened to me?

I was ashamed of being such a fool. I always did stupid things, always went out of my way and turned out looking like a fool. Then I'd feel shame and not tell anyone. For instance, I'm ashamed about something that happened here in the hospital a few days ago. I think it will be nice when I am home again, back in my room, where these things can't happen. There was myself and Ed and another man, out on the terrace by the side entrance, in the sun, and these kids came along. It was funny because they caught my eye when they drove past in a convertible, and they must have turned into the parking lot and got out. They were visiting someone in the hospital. The girl was carrying a grocery bag that probably had fruit in it or something. She had long dark hair and bangs that fell down to her eyebrows, and she wore sunglasses, and bright blue stretch pants of the kind that have stirrups for the feet to keep them stretched down tight. The boy wore sunglasses too, slacks and a sweater, and sandals without socks. He had the critical, surprised look of kids from the big university downtown.

They came up the steps, talking. The girl swung her hair back like a horse, a pony—I mean, the motion reminded me of something like that. She looked over at us and stopped talking, and the boy looked too. They were my age. The girl hesitated but the boy kept walking fast. He frowned. He seemed embarrassed. The girl came toward me, not quite walking directly toward me, and her mouth moved in an awkward smile. She said, "I know you, don't I? Don't I know you?"

I was very excited. I tried to tell her that with her sunglasses on I couldn't see her well. But when I tried to talk the words came out jumbled. She licked her lips nervously. She said, "Were you in the war? Vietnam?"

I nodded.

She stared at me. It was strange that her face showed nothing, unlike the other faces that are turned toward me all the time. The boy, already at the door, said in an irritated sharp voice: "Come on, we're late." The girl took a vague step backward, the way girls swing slowly away from people—you must have seen them often on sidewalks before ice cream parlors or schools? They stare as if fascinated at one person, while beginning the slow inevitable swing toward another who stands behind them. The boy said, opening the door: "Come on! He deserves it!"

They went inside. And then the shame began, an awful shame. I did not understand this though I thought about it a great deal. Someone came out to help me, a nurse. When I cry most people look away in embarrassment but the nurses show nothing, nothing at all. They boss me around a little. Crying makes me think of somebody else crying, a soldier holding another soldier's hand, sitting in some rubble. One soldier is alive and the other dead, the one who is alive is holding the other's hand and crying, like a baby. Like a puppy, a kitten, a baby, something small and helpless, when the crying does no good and is not meant for any good.

I think that my name is Jack Furlong. There was another person named Private Furlong, evidently myself. Now I am back home and I am Jack Furlong again. I can imagine many parts of this city without really seeing them, and what is surprising—and very pleasant—is the way these memories come to me, so unexpected. Lying in bed with no thoughts at all I suddenly find myself thinking of a certain dime store where we hung out, by the comic racks, many years ago; or I think of a certain playground on the edge of a ravine made by a glacier, many thousands of years ago. I don't know what makes these memories come to me but they exert a kind of tug—on my heart, I suppose. It's very strange. My eyes sometimes fill with tears, but a different kind of tears. I was never good at understanding feelings but now, in the hospital, I have a lot of time for thinking. I think that I am a kind of masterpiece. I mean, a miracle. My body and my brain. It is like a little world inside, or a factory, with everything functioning and the dynamo at the very center—my heart—pumping and pumping with no source of energy behind it. I think about that a lot. What keeps it going? And the eyes. Did you know that the eye is strong, very strong? That the muscles are like steel? Yes.

Eyes are very strong, I mean the substance of the eyes is strong. It takes a lot to destroy them.

At last they check me out and bring me home—a happy day. It is good to be back home where everything is peaceful and familiar. When I lived in this house before, I did not think about "living" in it, or about the house at all. Now, looking out of my window, I can see the front lawn and the street and the other houses facing us, all ranch houses, and I am aware of being very fortunate. A few kids are outside, racing past on bicycles. It is a spring day, very warm. The houses on the block make a kind of design if you look right. I am tired from all the exertion involved getting me here, and so it is difficult to explain what I mean—a design, a setting. Everything in place. It has not changed and won't change. It is a very pleasant neighborhood, and I think I remember hearing Mother once say that our house had cost forty-five thousand dollars. I had "heard" this remark years ago but never paid any attention to it. Now I keep thinking about it, I don't know why. There is something wonderful about that figure: it means something. Is it secret? It is the very opposite of rubble, yes. There are no screams here, no sudden explosions. Yes, I think that is why it pleases me so. I fall asleep thinking of forty-five thousand dollars.

My birthday. It is a few days later. I have been looking through the books in my room, a history textbook, a calculus textbook, and something called *College Rhetoric*. Those were my books and I can recognize my handwriting in the margins, but I have a hard time reading them now. To get away from the reading I look around—or the door in my mind begins to open slowly, scaring me, and so I wheel myself over to the window to look out. Father has just flown back from Boston. Yes, it is my birthday and I am twenty. We have a wheelchair of our own now, not the hospital's chair but our own. There is a wooden ramp from our side door right into the garage, and when they push me out I have a sudden sensation of panic right in my heart—do they know how to handle me? What if they push me too hard? They are sometimes clumsy and a little rough, accidentally. Whenever Father does something wrong, I think at once, not meaning to, *They wouldn't do that at the hospital.*

My uncle and my aunt are coming too. We are going out to Skyway for dinner. This is the big restaurant and motel near the airport. There is the usual trouble getting me in and out of the car, but Father is getting used to it. My uncle Floyd keeps saying, "Well, it's great to have you back. I mean it. It's just great, it's just wonderful to have you back." My aunt is wearing a hat with big droopy flowers on it, a pretty hat. But something about the flowers makes me think of giant leaves in the jungle, coated with dust and sweat, and the way the air tasted—it made your throat and lungs ache, the dust in the air. Grit. Things were flying in the air. Someone was screaming, "Don't leave me!" A lot of them were screaming that. But my father said, "We'd better hurry, our reservations are for six."

Six is early to eat, I know. They are hurrying up the evening because I get tired so fast. My uncle opens the door and my father wheels me inside, all of it done easily. My father says to a man, "Furlong, for five—" This restaurant is familiar. On one side there is a stairway going down, carpeted in blue, and down there are rooms for—oh, banquets and meetings and things. Ahead of us is a cocktail lounge, very dark. Off to the left, down a corridor lined with paintings (they are by local artists, for sale), is the restaurant we are going to, the Grotto Room. But the man is looking through his ledger. My mother says to my aunt, "I bought that watercolor here, you know, the one over the piano." The women talk about

something but my uncle stares at my father and the manager, silent. Something is wrong. The manager looks through his book and his face is red and troubled. Finally he looks up and says, "Yes, all right. Down this way." He leads us down to the Grotto Room.

We are seated. The table is covered with a white tablecloth, a glaring white. A waitress is already at Father's elbow. She looks at us, her eyes darting around the table and lingering no longer on me than on anyone else. I know that my glasses are thick and that my face is not pleasant to look at, not the same face as before. But still she does not look at me more than a second, maybe two seconds. Father orders drinks. It is my birthday. He glances over to the side, and I see that some people at the next table, some men and women, are watching us. A woman in red—I think it is red—does something with her napkin, putting it on the table. Father picks up his menu, which is very large. My mother and aunt chatter about something; my mother hands me a menu. At the next table a man stands. He changes places with the woman, and now her back is to our table. I understand this but pretend to notice nothing, look down at the menu with a pleased, surprised expression, because it is better this way. It is better for everyone.

"What do think you'll order? Everything looks so tempting," she says.

They were in a hurry and the wounded and the dead were stacked together, brought back together in a truck. But not carried at the end of a nylon cord, from a helicopter, not that. This memory comes to me in a flash, then fades. I was driving the truck, I think. Wasn't I? I was on the truck. I did not hover at the end of a line, in a plastic sack. Those were the others—I didn't know them, only saw them at a distance. They screamed, "Don't leave me!"

"Lobster," Father says. He speaks with certainty: he is predicting my choice for dinner. "I bet it's lobster, eh?"

"Lobster."

My mother squeezes my arm, pleased that I have given the right answer. "My choice too," she says. "Always have fish on Fridays . . . the old customs . . . I like the old customs, no matter what people say. The Mass in Latin, and . . . and priests who know what their vocations are. . . . How do you want your lobster, dear? Broiled?"

"Yes."

"Or this way—here—the Skyway Lobster?"

She leans over to help me with the menu, pointing at the words. There is a film, a gauzy panel between me and the words, and I keep waiting for it to disappear. The faces around the table, the voices . . . the smiling mouths and eyes . . . I keep glancing up at them, waiting for the veil to be yanked away. *He deserves it. Don't leave me!* In the meantime I think I will have the Skyway Lobster.

"You're sure?"

"Yes."

"My own choice also," my mother says. She looks around the table, in triumph, and the faces smile back at her and me.

Vietnam Veterans Memorial, Washington, D.C.
AP / Wide World Photos, Inc., New York.

The Censors

LUISA VALENZUELA

A biography of Valenzuela appears on page 428.

Approaching the Story

Have you ever become so engrossed in a challenge, such as surpassing your best score on a video game, that nothing else seemed important? If so, you might identify with Juan, the main character in "The Censors," a story by Argentine writer Luisa Valenzuela (lōō ē′ sä vä len zwe′ lä). In this story, set in a fictitious Latin American country, censorship has reached new bureaucratic heights.

Note as you read that the names Juan and Juancito, the diminutive form of Juan, refer to the same person.

OOR JUAN! ONE day they caught him with his guard down before he could even realize that what he had taken as a stroke of luck was really one of fate's dirty tricks. These things happen the minute you're careless and you let down your guard, as one often does. Juancito let happiness—a feeling you can't trust— get the better of him when he received from a confidential source Mariana's new address in Paris and he knew that she hadn't forgotten him. Without thinking twice, he sat down at his table and wrote her a letter. *The* letter that keeps his mind off his job during the day and won't let him sleep at night (what had he scrawled, what had he put on that sheet of paper he sent to Mariana?).

Juan knows there won't be a problem with the letter's contents, that it's irreproachable, harmless. But what about the rest? He knows that they examine, sniff, feel, and read between the lines of each and every letter, and check its tiniest comma and most accidental stain. He knows that all letters pass from hand to hand and go through all sorts of tests in the huge censorship offices and that, in the end, very few continue on their way. Usually it takes months, even years, if there aren't any snags; all this time the freedom, maybe even the life, of both sender and receiver is in jeopardy. And that's why Juan's so down in the dumps: thinking that something might happen to Mariana because of his letters. Of all people, Mariana, who must finally feel safe there where she always dreamed she'd live. But he knows that the Censor's Secret Command operates all over the world and cashes in on the discount in air rates; there's nothing to stop them from going as far as that hidden Paris neighborhood, kidnapping Mariana, and returning to their cozy homes, certain of having fulfilled their noble mission.

Well, you've got to beat them to the punch, do what everyone tries to do: sabotage the machinery, throw sand in its gears, get to the bottom of the problem so as to stop it.

This was Juan's sound plan when he, like many others, applied for a censor's job—not because he had a calling or needed a job: no, he applied simply to intercept his own letter, a consoling but unoriginal idea. He was hired immediately, for each day more and more censors are needed and no one would bother to check on his references.

Ulterior motives couldn't be overlooked by the Censorship Division, but they needn't be too strict with those who applied. They knew how hard it would be for those poor guys to find the letter they wanted and even if they did, what's a letter or two when the new censor would snap up so many others? That's how Juan managed to join the Post Office's Censorship Division, with a certain goal in mind.

The building had a festive air on the outside which contrasted with its inner staidness. Little by little, Juan was absorbed by his job and he felt at peace since he was doing everything he could to get his letter for Mariana. He didn't even worry when, in his first month, he was sent to Section K where envelopes are very carefully screened for explosives.

It's true that on the third day, a fellow worker had his right hand blown off by a letter, but the division chief claimed it was sheer negligence on the victim's part. Juan and the other employees were allowed to go back to their work, albeit feeling less secure. After work, one of them tried to organize a strike to demand higher wages for unhealthy work, but Juan didn't join in; after thinking it over, he report-

ed him to his superiors and thus got promoted.

You don't form a habit by doing something once, he told himself as he left his boss's office. And when he was transferred to Section J, where letters are carefully checked for poison dust, he felt he had climbed a rung in the ladder.

By working hard, he quickly reached Section E where the work was more interesting, for he could now read and analyze the letters' contents. Here he could even hope to get hold of his letter which, judging by the time that had elapsed, had gone through the other sections and was probably floating around in this one.

Soon his work became so absorbing that his noble mission blurred in his mind. Day after day he crossed out whole paragraphs in red ink, pitilessly chucking many letters into the censored basket. These were horrible days when he was shocked by the subtle and conniving ways employed by people to pass on subversive messages; his instincts were so sharp that he found behind a simple "the weather's unsettled" or "prices continue to soar" the wavering hand of someone secretly scheming to overthrow the Government.

His zeal brought him swift promotion. We don't know if this made him happy. Very few letters reached him in Section B—only a handful passed the other hurdles—so he read them over and over again, passed them under a magnifying glass, searched for microprint with an electronic microscope, and tuned his sense of smell so that he was beat by the time he made it home. He'd barely manage to warm up his soup, eat some fruit, and fall into bed, satisfied with having done his duty. Only his darling mother worried, but she couldn't get him back on the right road. She'd say, though it wasn't always true: Lola called, she's at the bar with the girls, they miss you, they're waiting for you. Or else she'd leave a bottle of red wine on the table. But Juan wouldn't overdo it: any distraction could make him lose his edge and the perfect censor had to be alert, keen, attentive, and sharp to nab cheats. He had a truly patriotic task, both self-denying and uplifting.

His basket for censored letters became the best fed as well as the most cunning basket in the whole Censorship Division. He was about to congratulate himself for having finally discovered his true mission, when his letter to Mariana reached his hands. Naturally, he censored it without regret. And just as naturally, he couldn't stop them from executing him the following morning, another victim of his devotion to his work.

Reviewing Concepts

THEME AND STYLE: DELIVERING SOCIAL CRITICISM

making
connections

The writers in this unit all criticize society, but they choose different stylistic methods to express their criticisms. In "Santa's Children," Italo Calvino used exaggeration to call attention to commercialism and greed in modern Italy. The Society for the Implementation of Christmas Consumption does not really exist, and a marketing plan as cynical as the Destructive Gift campaign has never been implemented. Calvino is warning, however, that the unhealthy society he depicts could become a reality if certain trends continue. Calvino did not necessarily have to use humorous overstatement to protest commercialism. He could have painted a realistic portrait of a society with commercialistic, greedy tendencies and had the narrator or a character make a direct statement protesting these tendencies. Alternatively, Calvino could have employed understatement, never directly expressing a criticism but allowing readers to draw their own conclusions about the society depicted. For this approach he might have made the narrator a child or another person who would not recognize a social fault as readily as readers might.

Think about the style of each story in this unit. For each selection, indicate whether the writer predominantly uses overstatement, direct statement, or understatement to express his or her criticisms of society. Mark an **X** at the appropriate point on a scale like the one below.

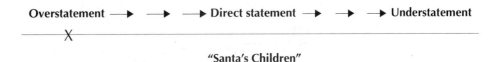

Overstatement → → → Direct statement → → → Understatement
X
"Santa's Children"

describing
connections

Look over the scales you have marked to see which stories use similar techniques to call attention to social flaws. Decide which technique, overstatement, understatement, or direct statement, seems most effective to you and why. Create **notes** for an oral presentation in which you defend your opinion. Use specific examples from the stories.

Flower and Water, date unknown, REIKA IWAMI.

Woodcut on paper. National Museum of Women in the Arts, Washington, D.C.; gift of Kappy Hendricks.

Transformations:

Stories of the Fantastic

"[Fantasy]. . .must be understood not as an escape from reality but as an investigation of it."

T. E. APTER
American-born British novelist and literary critic

Transformations: Stories of the Fantastic

Think about the meaning of the phrase "a flight of fantasy." Where can fantasy take you that real life cannot? Ordinary life may be limited by rules and regulations, but the life of the imagination is bound only by the limits of the human mind. Through the imagination, you can go beyond the world that you know to be real and investigate a world of possibilities—a world of wishes, dreams, and nightmares.

The stories in this section can be classified as fantasy, a kind of literature that, like dreams, disregards the restraints of reality. Some works of fantasy actually create weird dream worlds; others introduce bizarre or magical elements into a mostly realistic world. Fantasy presents a challenge to readers, who are asked to accept, without question, impossible occurrences. In a fantasy, narration is often ambiguous, leaving readers unsure of what happens at the end of a story or even what is happening throughout. Part of the pleasure of reading fantasy literature comes from trying to determine what is going on and what it all means.

The value of good fantasy literature is that it sidesteps questions about accuracy and lifelike representation to explore more tantalizing questions: What is reality? How do humans respond to mysterious occurrences? What if dreams come true? By addressing such questions, fantasy literature can actually bring us closer to an understanding of ourselves, of our secret desires and capabilities.

Literary Vocabulary

Imagery. Imagery refers to words and phrases that re-create sensory experiences for a reader. Images can appeal to any of the five senses: sight, hearing, taste, smell, and touch. The majority of images are visual, stimulating pictures in the reader's mind. In "Blues Ain't No Mockin Bird" images that appeal to both sight and touch help the reader imagine the setting and the characters: "The puddle had frozen over, and me and Cathy went stompin in it. The twins from next door, Tyrone and Terry, were swingin so high out of sight we forgot we were waitin our turn on the tire."

Style: Magical Realism. Style is the particular way that a piece of literature is written. Style refers not so much to what is said but to how it is said. Magical realism is a style of writing that often includes exaggeration, unusual humor, magical and bizarre events, dreams that come true, and superstitions that prove warranted. Magical realism differs from pure fantasy in combining fantastic elements with realistic elements, such as recognizable characters, believable dialogue, a true-to-life setting, a matter-of-fact tone, and a plot that sometimes contains historic events.

Style: Diction. A significant component of style is diction, or a writer's choice of words. Diction encompasses both vocabulary (individual words) and syntax (the order and arrangement of words). Diction can be described in terms such as formal or informal, technical or common, abstract or concrete. In "Six Feet of the Country," for example, Nadine Gordimer uses informal diction to help portray the attitude of the narrator.

Plot Structure	**Mood**	**Symbol**	**Tone**	**Theme**	**Dialogue**

The Night Face Up

JULIO CORTÁZAR

A biography of Cortázar appears on page 421.

Approaching the Story

Argentine writer Julio Cortázar (hoo′ lē ō kôr tä′ zər) is known for writing fantastic literature—fantastic in the sense of supernatural, uncanny, or weird. "Fantastic literature," he said, "is the most fictional of all literatures, given that by its own definition it consists of turning one's back on a reality universally accepted as normal." If "The Night Face Up" does not turn its back on reality, it certainly views reality with suspicion. Expect to feel unsure of your bearings as you read this story.

Building Vocabulary

These essential words are footnoted within the story.

solace (säl′ is): His single **solace** was to hear someone else confirm that the lights indeed had been in his favor. (page 287)

lucid (loo′ sid): Completely **lucid,** . . . he gave his information to the officer. (page 287)

oblivion (ə bliv′ ē ən): He panted, looking for . . . **oblivion** for those images still glued to his eyelids. (page 291)

Connecting Writing and Reading

In your journal describe an experience of waking up from a vivid nightmare. What was frightening you in your dream? What made you realize that it was a dream and not reality? What were your feelings afterward? As you read this story, see whether the same sensations are felt by the main character as he moves between dream and reality.

_H_ ALFWAY DOWN THE long hotel vestibule, he thought that probably he was going to be late, and hurried on into the street to get out his motorcycle from the corner where the next-door superintendent let him keep it. On the jewelry store at the corner, he read that it was ten to nine; he had time to spare. The sun filtered through the tall downtown buildings, and he—because for himself, for just going along thinking, he did not have a name—he swung onto the machine, savoring the idea of the ride. The motor whirred between his legs, and a cool wind whipped his pants legs.

He let the ministries[1] zip past (the pink, the white), and a series of stores on the main street, their windows flashing. Now he was beginning the most pleasant part of the run, the real ride: a long street bordered with trees, very little traffic, with spacious villas whose gardens rambled all the way down to the sidewalks, which were barely indicated by low hedges. A bit inattentive perhaps, but tooling along on the right side of the street, he allowed himself to be carried away by the freshness, by the weightless contraction of this hardly begun day. This involuntary relaxation, possibly, kept him from preventing the accident. When he saw that the woman standing on the corner had rushed into the crosswalk while he still had the green light, it was already somewhat too late for a simple solution. He braked hard with foot and hand, wrenching himself to the left; he heard the woman scream, and at the collision his vision went. It was like falling asleep all at once.

He came to abruptly. Four or five young men were getting him out from under the cycle. He felt the taste of salt and blood; one knee hurt, and when they hoisted him up, he yelped; he couldn't bear the pressure on his right arm. Voices which did not seem to belong to the faces hanging above him encouraged him cheerfully with jokes and assurances. His single solace[2] was to hear someone else confirm that the lights indeed had been in his favor. He asked about the woman, trying to keep down the nausea which was edging up into his throat. While they carried him face up to a nearby pharmacy, he learned that the cause of the accident had gotten only a few scrapes on the legs. "Nah, you barely got her at all, but when ya hit, the impact made the machine jump and flop on its side. . . ." Opinions, recollections of other smashups, take it easy, work him in shoulders first, there, that's fine, and someone in a dustcoat giving him a swallow of something soothing in the shadowy interior of the small local pharmacy.

Within five minutes the police ambulance arrived, and they lifted him onto a cushioned stretcher. It was a relief for him to be able to lie out flat. Completely lucid[3] but realizing that he was suffering the effects of a terrible shock, he gave his information to the officer riding in the ambulance with him. The arm almost didn't hurt; blood dripped down from a cut over the eyebrow all over his face. He licked his lips once or twice to drink it. He felt pretty good; it had been an accident, tough luck; stay quiet a few weeks, nothing worse. The guard said that the motorcycle didn't seem badly racked up. "Why should it," he replied. "It all landed on top of me." They both laughed, and when they got to the hospital, the guard shook his hand and wished him luck. Now the nausea was coming back little by little; meanwhile they were pushing him on a wheeled stretcher toward a pavilion farther back; rolling along under trees full of birds, he shut his eyes and

---

1. **ministries** (min′ is trēz): the headquarters for various government departments.
2. **solace** (säl′ is): something that comforts or relieves.
3. **lucid** (lo͞o′ sid): clearheaded; rational.

wished he were asleep or chloroformed. But they kept him for a good while in a room with that hospital smell, filling out a form, getting his clothes off, and dressing him in a stiff, grayish smock. They moved his arm carefully; it didn't hurt him. The nurses were constantly making wisecracks, and if it hadn't been for the stomach contractions, he would have felt fine, almost happy.

They got him over to X-ray, and twenty minutes later, with the still-damp negative lying on his chest like a black tombstone, they pushed him into surgery. Someone tall and thin in white came over and began to look at the X-rays. A woman's hands were arranging his head; he felt that they were moving him from one stretcher to another. The man in white came over to him again, smiling; something gleamed in his right hand. He patted his cheek and made a sign to someone stationed behind.

It was unusual as a dream because it was full of smells, and he never dreamt smells. First a marshy smell, there to the left of the trail the swamps began already, the quaking bogs[4] from which no one ever returned. But the reek lifted, and instead there came a dark, fresh composite fragrance, like the night under which he moved, in flight from the Aztecs. And it was all so natural, he had to run from the Aztecs who had set out on their manhunt, and his sole chance was to find a place to hide in the deepest part of the forest, taking care not to lose the narrow trail which only they, the Motecas,[5] knew.

What tormented him the most was the odor, as though, notwithstanding the absolute acceptance of the dream, there was something which resisted that which was not habitual, which until that point had not participated in the game. "It smells of war," he thought, his hand going instinctively to the stone knife which was tucked at an angle into his girdle of

woven wool. An unexpected sound made him crouch suddenly stock-still and shaking. To be afraid was nothing strange, there was plenty of fear in his dreams. He waited, covered by the branches of a shrub and the starless night. Far off, probably on the other side of the big lake, they'd be lighting the bivouac fires; that part of the sky had a reddish glare. The sound was not repeated. It had been like a broken limb. Maybe an animal that, like himself, was escaping from the smell of war. He stood erect slowly, sniffing the air. Not a sound could be heard, but the fear was still following, as was the smell, that cloying incense of the war of the blossom.[6] He had to press forward, to stay out of the bogs and get to the heart of the forest. Groping uncertainly through the dark, stooping every other moment to touch the packed earth of the trail, he took a few steps. He would have liked to have broken into a run, but the gurgling fens[7] lapped on either side of him. On the path and in darkness, he took his bearings. Then he caught a horrible blast of that foul smell he was most afraid of, and leaped forward desperately.

"You're going to fall off the bed," said the patient next to him. "Stop bouncing around, old buddy."

He opened his eyes and it was afternoon, the sun already low in the oversized windows of the long ward. While trying to smile at his neighbor, he detached himself almost physically from the final scene of the nightmare. His arm, in a plaster cast, hung suspended from an apparatus with weights and pulleys. He felt thirsty, as though he'd been running for miles, but they didn't want to give him much water,

---

4. **quaking bogs:** areas of wet, spongy ground, probably containing quicksand.

5. **Motecas** (mō te′ käs).

6. **war of the blossom:** the name the Aztecs gave to a ritual war in which they took prisoners for sacrifice.

7. **fens:** low, flat, marshy lands.

barely enough to moisten his lips and make a mouthful. The fever was winning slowly and he would have been able to sleep again, but he was enjoying the pleasure of keeping awake, eyes half-closed, listening to the other patients' conversation, answering a question from time to time. He saw a little white push-cart come up beside the bed; a blond nurse rubbed the front of his thigh with alcohol and stuck him with a fat needle connected to a tube which ran up to a bottle filled with milky, opalescent liquid. A young intern arrived with some metal and leather apparatus which he adjusted to fit onto the good arm to check something or other. Night fell, and the fever went along dragging him down softly to a state in which things seemed embossed as through opera glasses;[8] they were real and soft and, at the same time, vaguely distasteful; like sitting in a boring movie and thinking that, well, still, it'd be worse out in the street, and staying.

A cup of marvelous golden broth came, smelling of leeks, celery, and parsley. A small hunk of bread, more precious than a whole banquet, found itself crumbling little by little. His arm hardly hurt him at all, and only in the eyebrow where they'd taken stitches a quick, hot pain sizzled occasionally. When the big windows across the way turned to smudges of dark blue, he thought it would not be difficult for him to sleep. Still on his back so a little uncomfortable, running his tongue out over his hot, too-dry lips, he tasted the broth still, and with a sigh of bliss, he let himself drift off.

First there was a confusion, as of one drawing all his sensations, for that moment blunted or muddled, into himself. He realized that he was running in pitch darkness, although, above, the sky crisscrossed with treetops was less black than the rest. "The trail," he thought. "I've gotten off the trail." His feet sank into a bed of leaves and mud, and then he couldn't take a step that the branches of shrubs did not whiplash against his ribs and legs. Out of breath, knowing despite the darkness and silence that he was surrounded, he crouched down to listen. Maybe the trail was very near, with the first daylight he would be able to see it again. Nothing now could help him to find it. The hand that unconsciously gripped the haft of the dagger climbed like a fen scorpion up to his neck, where the protecting amulet hung. Barely moving his lips, he mumbled the supplication of the corn which brings about the beneficent moons, and the prayer to Her Very Highness, to the distributor of all Motecan possessions. At the same time he felt his ankles sinking deeper into the mud, and the waiting in the darkness of the obscure grove of live oak grew intolerable to him. The war of the blossom had started at the beginning of the moon and had been going on for three days and three nights now. If he managed to hide in the depths of the forest, getting off the trail farther up past the marsh country, perhaps the warriors wouldn't follow his track. He thought of the many prisoners they'd already taken. But the number didn't count, only the consecrated period. The hunt would continue until the priests gave the sign to return. Everything had its number and its limit, and it was within the sacred period, and he on the other side from the hunters.

He heard the cries and leaped up, knife in hand. As if the sky were aflame on the horizon, he saw torches moving among the branches, very near him. The smell of war was unbearable, and when the first enemy jumped him, leaped at his throat, he felt an almost-pleasure in sinking the stone blade flat to the haft[9] into his chest. The lights were already around him, the happy cries. He managed to cut the air once or twice, then a rope snared him from behind.

---

8. **opera glasses:** small binoculars.
9. **haft:** the hilt, or handle, of a knife.

"It's the fever," the man in the next bed said. "The same thing happened to me when they operated on my duodenum. Take some water; you'll see, you'll sleep all right."

Laid next to the night from which he came back, the tepid shadow of the ward seemed delicious to him. A violet lamp kept watch high on the far wall like a guardian eye. You could hear coughing, deep breathing, once in a while a conversation in whispers. Everything was pleasant and secure, without the chase, no . . . But he didn't want to go on thinking about the nightmare. There were lots of things to amuse himself with. He began to look at the cast on his arm, and the pulleys that held it so comfortably in the air. They'd left a bottle of mineral water on the night table beside him. He put the neck of the bottle to his mouth and drank it like a precious liqueur. He could now make out the different shapes in the ward, the thirty beds, the closets with glass doors. He guessed that his fever was down, his face felt cool. The cut over the eyebrow barely hurt at all, like a recollection. He saw himself leaving the hotel again, wheeling out the cycle. Who'd have thought that it would end like this? He tried to fix the moment of the accident exactly, and it got him very angry to notice that there was a void there, an emptiness he could not manage to fill. Between the impact and the moment that they picked him up off the pavement, the passing out or what went on, there was nothing he could see. And at the same time he had the feeling that this void, this nothingness, had lasted an eternity. No, not even time, more as if, in this void, he had passed across something, or had run back immense distances. The shock, the brutal dashing against the pavement. Anyway, he had felt an immense relief in coming out of the black pit while the people were lifting him off the ground. With pain in the broken arm, blood from the split eyebrow, contusion on the knee; with all that, a relief in returning to daylight, to the day, and to feel sustained and attended. That was weird. Someday he'd ask the doctor at the office about that. Now sleep began to take over again, to pull him slowly down. The pillow was so soft, and the coolness of the mineral water soothed his fevered throat. The violet light of the lamp up there was beginning to get dimmer and dimmer.

As he was sleeping on his back, the position in which he came to did not surprise him, but on the other hand the damp smell, the smell of oozing rock, blocked his throat and forced him to understand. Open the eyes and look in all directions, hopeless. He was surrounded by an absolute darkness. Tried to get up and felt ropes pinning his wrists and ankles. He was staked to the ground on a floor of dank, icy stone slabs. The cold bit into his naked back, his legs. Dully, he tried to touch the amulet with his chin and found they had stripped him of it. Now he was lost; no prayer could save him from the final . . . From afar off, as though filtering through the rock of the dungeon, he heard the great kettledrums of the feast. They had carried him to the temple, he was in the underground cells of Teocalli[10] itself, awaiting his turn.

He heard a yell, a hoarse yell that rocked off the walls. Another yell, ending in a moan. It was he who was screaming in the darkness; he was screaming because he was alive, his whole body with that cry fended off what was coming, the inevitable end. He thought of his friends filling up the other dungeons and of those already walking up the stairs of the sacrifice. He uttered another choked cry; he could barely open his mouth, his jaws were twisted back as if with a rope and a stick, and once in a while they would open slowly with an endless exertion, as if they were made of rubber. The creaking of the wooden latches jolted him

---

10. Teocalli (tā ô̄ kä′ yē): the great temple of the Aztecs.

like a whip. Rent, writhing, he fought to rid himself of the cords sinking into his flesh. His right arm, the strongest, strained until the pain became unbearable, and he had to give up. He watched the double door open, and the smell of the torches reached him before the light did. Barely girdled by the ceremonial loincloths, the priests' acolytes[11] moved in his direction, looking at him with contempt. Lights reflected off the sweaty torsos and off the black hair dressed with feathers. The cords went slack, and in their place the grappling of hot hands, hard as bronze; he felt himself lifted, still face up, and jerked along by the four acolytes who carried him down the passageway. The torchbearers went ahead, indistinctly lighting up the corridor with its dripping walls and a ceiling so low that the acolytes had to duck their heads. Now they were taking him out, taking him out, it was the end. Face up under a mile of living rock which, for a succession of moments, was lit up by a glimmer of torchlight. When the stars came out up there instead of the roof and the great terraced steps rose before him, on fire with cries and dances, it would be the end. The passage was never going to end, but now it was beginning to end, he would see suddenly the open sky full of stars, but not yet, they trundled him along endlessly in the reddish shadow, hauling him roughly along and he did not want that, but how to stop it if they had torn off the amulet, his real heart, the life center.

In a single jump he came out into the hospital night, to the high, gentle, bare ceiling, to the soft shadow wrapping him round. He thought he must have cried out, but his neighbors were peacefully snoring. The water in the bottle on the night table was somewhat bubbly, a translucent shape against the dark azure shadow of the windows. He panted, looking for some relief for his lungs, oblivion[12] for those images still glued to his eyelids. Each time he shut his eyes he saw them take shape

instantly, and he sat up, completely wrung out but savoring at the same time the surety that now he was awake, that the night nurse would answer if he rang, that soon it would be daybreak, with the good, deep sleep he usually had at that hour, no images, no nothing . . . It was difficult to keep his eyes open; the drowsiness was more powerful than he. He made one last effort; he sketched a gesture toward the bottle of water with his good hand and did not manage to reach it; his fingers closed again on a black emptiness, and the passageway went on endlessly, rock after rock, with momentary ruddy flares, and face up he choked out a dull moan because the roof was about to end, it rose, was opening like a mouth of shadow, and the acolytes straightened up, and from on high a waning moon fell on a face whose eyes wanted not to see it, were closing and opening desperately, trying to pass to the other side, to find again the bare, protecting ceiling of the ward. And every time they opened, it was night and the moon, while they climbed the great terraced steps, his head hanging down backward now, and up at the top were the bonfires, red columns of perfumed smoke, and suddenly he saw the red stone, shiny with the blood dripping off it, and the spinning arcs cut by the feet of the victim whom they pulled off to throw him rolling down the north steps. With a last hope he shut his lids tightly, moaning to wake up. For a second he thought he had gotten there, because once more he was immobile in the bed, except that his head was hanging down off it, swinging. But he smelled death, and when he opened his eyes he saw the blood-soaked figure of the executioner-priest coming toward him with the stone knife in his hand. He managed to close his eyelids again, although he knew now he was not going to

---

11. acolytes (ak′ ə līts): attendants.

12. oblivion (ə bliv′ ē ən): the condition of being forgotten.

wake up, that he was awake, that the marvelous dream had been the other, absurd as all dreams are—a dream in which he was going through the strange avenues of an astonishing city, with green and red lights that burned without fire or smoke, on an enormous metal insect that whirred away between his legs. In the infinite lie of the dream, they had also picked him up off the ground, someone had approached him also with a knife in his hand, approached him who was lying face up, face up with his eyes closed between the bonfires on the steps.

*T*hinking *About the Story*

A PERSONAL RESPONSE

sharing impressions

1. What one word best describes the ending of this story? Record this word in your journal.

constructing interpretations

2. How do you explain the ending of this story? State what you think is reality.

> **Think about**
> - the possible effects of shock, fever, and pain-killing drugs on the main character's perceptions
> - the main character's feeling that "he had passed across something, or had run back immense distances"
> - his sensation of being again in his hospital bed but with his head hanging down, swinging
> - his belief that he is not going to wake up and that his life in the city had been a dream

3. Recall what you wrote about waking from a nightmare. Compare your sensations to the sensations of the main character as he moves between dream and reality.

4. What parallels do you see between the main character's experiences in the modern world and the Aztec world?

A CREATIVE RESPONSE

5. If the main character's nightmares had begun when he was healthy, before his accident, how would your interpretation of the story have been affected?

6. Evaluate the writer's use of imagery in this story.

Think about
- imagery as words and phrases that appeal to the five senses
- how the imagery affects your perception of the main character
- how the imagery affects your view of the reality of the two worlds

7. Critic Alberto Manguel describes fantastic literature in the following way: "It makes use of our everyday world as a facade through which the undefinable appears. . . . Fantastic literature deals with what can be best defined as the impossible seeping into the possible. . . . Fantastic literature never really explains anything. . . . Fantastic literature thrives on surprise, on the unexpected logic that is born from its own rules." How does "The Night Face Up" illustrate these qualities?

Analyzing the Writer's Craft

PLOT STRUCTURE

Are the events in this story presented in a way that you are accustomed to?

Building a Literary Vocabulary. As you know, plot refers to the actions and events in a literary work. The plot moves forward because of a conflict, or struggle between opposing forces. In a traditional narrative, plot structure consists of the exposition, the rising action, the climax, and the falling action. The exposition lays the groundwork for the narrative and provides necessary background information. During the rising action, complications of the conflict build to a climax, or turning point. Interest and intensity reach their peak at this point. Following the climax is the falling action, which shows the results of the major events and resolves outstanding questions.

Application: Analyzing Plot Structure. As a class, discuss whether this story has a traditional plot structure. Consider the following questions in your discussion: What is the conflict? What do you learn in the exposition? Where does the rising action begin? What is the climax, and where does it occur? Is there falling action that shows how the conflict has been resolved?

Connecting Reading and Writing

1. Rewrite a section of this story as a **screenplay** for an episode of *The Twilight Zone*.

Option: Create a set of **comic-book panels** to retell part of this story.

2. Do research on the Aztec practice of ritual human sacrifice. In a **letter** to Cortázar, discuss how accurately you think he depicts this practice.

Option: Imagine that you are an archaeologist who specializes in ancient Aztec culture. Write a **note** to a fellow archaeologist commenting on the accuracy of Cortázar's portrayal of this culture.

3. Compare this story with another story in which time and reality are distorted—for example Daphne du Maurier's "Split Second," Ray Bradbury's "The Dragon," or Ambrose Bierce's "An Occurrence at Owl Creek Bridge." Evaluate the two stories on a **rating form** with categories for character development, vividness of setting, plot coherence, and thematic richness. Be prepared to support your ratings with specific comments on the two stories.

Option: Compare the stories in a **review** for a magazine devoted to literature of the fantastic.

4. Write a **narrative sketch** based on the experience of dreaming and waking that you wrote about in prereading. You might borrow techniques used in "The Night Face Up." Share your sketch with a friend.

Option: As an assignment for a film class, write a **synopsis** of a film based on your experience.

The Handsomest Drowned Man in the World

GABRIEL GARCÍA MÁRQUEZ

A biography of García Márquez appears on page 421.

Approaching the Story

Winner of the 1982 Nobel Prize in literature, Gabriel García Márquez (gä′ vrē el′ gär sē′ ä mär′ kes) is known throughout the world for a style called magical realism, which blends elements of fantasy with facts of everyday life. In his novels and short stories, anything can happen—angels fall from the sky, pious young women ascend into heaven, dictators live for two hundred years. Yet the works themselves are set in a gritty, realistic world of poverty and violence, salt air and rust. "The Handsomest Drowned Man in the World" starts with an apparently straightforward event: a drowned man washes ashore on the beach of a barren Colombian fishing village. It then moves into a reality that challenges the imagination.

Building Vocabulary

These essential words are footnoted within the story.

destitute (des′ tə tōōt′): They wept so much, for he was the most **destitute**, most peaceful, and most obliging man on earth. (page 299)

promontory (präm′ ən tôr′ ē): Pointing to the **promontory** of roses on the horizon, he would say, . . . *look there.* (page 300)

Connecting Writing and Reading

Think of someone whom you admire but do not know. The person might be someone at school, a historical figure, or a celebrity such as a rock star, a movie star, or a political leader. In your journal list words and phrases that describe what you imagine this person to be like. As you read the story, compare the imagined qualities you identified with the qualities attributed to the drowned man.

The Handsomest Drowned Man in the World

THE FIRST CHILDREN who saw the dark and slinky bulge approaching through the sea let themselves think it was an enemy ship. Then they saw it had no flags or masts and they thought it was a whale. But when it washed up on the beach, they removed the clumps of seaweed, the jellyfish tentacles, and the remains of fish and flotsam, and only then did they see that it was a drowned man.

They had been playing with him all afternoon, burying him in the sand and digging him up again, when someone chanced to see them and spread the alarm in the village. The men who carried him to the nearest house noticed that he weighed more than any dead man they had ever known, almost as much as a horse, and they said to each other that maybe he'd been floating too long and the water had got into his bones. When they laid him on the floor, they said he'd been taller than all other men because there was barely enough room for him in the house, but they thought that maybe the ability to keep on growing after death was part of the nature of certain drowned men. He had the smell of the sea about him, and only his shape gave one to suppose that it was the corpse of a human being, because the skin was covered with a crust of mud and scales.

They did not even have to clean off his face to know that the dead man was a stranger. The village was made up of only twenty-odd wooden houses that had stone courtyards with no flowers and which were spread about on the end of a desertlike cape. There was so little land that mothers always went about with the fear that the wind would carry off their children, and the few dead that the years had caused among them had to be thrown off the cliffs. But the sea was calm and bountiful, and all the men fit into seven boats. So when they found the drowned man they simply had to look at one another to see that they were all there.

That night they did not go out to work at sea. While the men went to find out if anyone was missing in neighboring villages, the women stayed behind to care for the drowned man. They took the mud off with grass swabs, they removed the underwater stones entangled in his hair, and they scraped the crust off with tools used for scaling fish. As they were doing that, they noticed that the vegetation on him came from faraway oceans and deep water and that his clothes were in tatters, as if he had sailed through labyrinths of coral. They noticed too that he bore his death with pride, for he did not have the lonely look of other drowned men who came out of the sea or that haggard, needy look of men who drowned in rivers. But only when they finished cleaning him off did they become aware of the kind of man he was, and it left them breathless. Not only was he the tallest, strongest, most virile, and best-built man they had ever seen, but even though they were looking at him there was no room for him in their imagination.

They could not find a bed in the village large enough to lay him on, nor was there a table solid enough to use for his wake. The tallest men's holiday pants would not fit him, nor the fattest ones' Sunday shirts, nor the shoes of the one with the biggest feet. Fascinated by his huge size and his beauty, the women then decided to make some pants from a large piece of sail and a shirt from some bridal Brabant[1] linen so that he could continue through his death with dignity. As they sewed, sitting in a circle and gazing at the corpse between stitches, it seemed to them that the wind had never been so steady nor the sea so restless as on that night, and they supposed that the change had something to do with the dead man. They thought that if that magnificent man had lived in the village, his house would have had the widest doors, the highest ceiling, and the strongest floor; his bedstead would have been made from a midship frame held together by iron bolts, and his wife would have been the happiest woman. They thought that he would have had so much authority that he could have drawn fish out of the sea simply by calling their names and that he would have put so much work into his land that springs would have burst forth from among the rocks so that he would have been able to plant flowers on the cliffs. They secretly compared him to their own men, thinking that for all their lives theirs were incapable of doing what he could do in one night, and they ended up dismissing them deep in their hearts as the weakest, meanest, and most useless creatures on earth. They were wandering through that maze of fantasy when the oldest woman, who as the oldest had looked upon the drowned man with more compassion than passion, sighed:

"He has the face of someone called Esteban."[2]

It was true. Most of them had only to take another look at him to see that he could not have any other name. The more stubborn among them, who were the youngest, still lived for a few hours with the illusion that when they put his clothes on and he lay among the flowers in patent leather shoes his name might be Lautaro.[3] But it was a vain illusion. There had not been enough canvas, the poorly cut and worse-sewn pants were too tight, and the hidden strength of his heart popped the buttons on his shirt. After midnight the whistling of the wind died down, and the sea fell into its Wednesday drowsiness.[4] The silence put an end to any last doubts: he was Esteban. The women who had dressed him, who had combed his hair, had cut his nails and shaved him were unable to hold back a shudder of pity when they had to resign themselves to his being dragged along the ground. It was then that they understood how unhappy he must have been with that huge body, since it bothered him even after death. They could see him in life, condemned to going through doors sideways, cracking his head on crossbeams, remaining on his feet during visits, not knowing what to do with his soft, pink, sea lion hands while the lady of the house looked for her most resistant chair and begged him, frightened to death, *sit here, Esteban, please*, and he, leaning against the wall, smiling, *don't bother, ma'am, I'm fine where I am*, his heels raw and his back roasted from having done the same thing so many times whenever he paid a visit, *don't bother, ma'am, I'm fine where I am*, just to avoid the embarrassment of breaking up the chair, and

---

1. **Brabant** (brä′ bänt).

2. **Esteban** (es te′ bän).

3. **Lautaro** (lou tä′ *rô*): the name of a Chilean Indian who became a national hero for leading an uprising against the Spanish in the sixteenth century.

4. **Wednesday drowsiness** (and later **Wednesday meat** and **Wednesday dead body**): an idiom peculiar to this type of fishing community. *Wednesday* can be considered to mean roughly "tiresome." The fishermen regularly returned from the sea on Thursday; therefore, by Wednesday people were running out of food, and the day offered little in the way of excitement or interest.

Dead Peasant, 1939, JOSE CHAVEZ MORADO.
The Art Institute of Chicago; William McCallin McKee Memorial Collection.

never knowing perhaps that the ones who said *don't go, Esteban, at least wait till the coffee's ready,* were the ones who later on would whisper *the big boob finally left, how nice, the handsome fool has gone.* That was what the women were thinking beside the body a little before dawn. Later, when they covered his face with a handkerchief so that the light would not bother him, he looked so forever dead, so defenseless, so much like their men that the first furrows of tears opened in their hearts. It was one of the younger ones who began the weeping. The others, coming to, went from sighs to wails, and the more they sobbed, the more they felt like weeping, because the drowned man was becoming all the more Esteban for them, and so they wept so much, for he was the most <u>destitute</u>,[5] most peaceful, and most obliging man on earth, poor Esteban. So when the men returned with the news that the drowned man was not from the neighboring villages either, the women felt an opening of jubilation in the midst of their tears.

"Praise the Lord," they sighed, "he's ours!"

The men thought the fuss was only womanish frivolity. Fatigued because of the difficult nighttime inquiries, all they wanted was to get rid of the bother of the newcomer once and for all before the sun grew strong on that arid, windless day. They improvised a litter with the remains of foremasts and gaffs, tying it together with rigging so that it would bear the weight of the body until they reached the cliffs. They wanted to tie the anchor from a cargo ship to him so that he would sink easily into the deepest waves, where fish are blind and divers die of nostalgia and bad currents would not bring him back to shore, as had happened with other bodies. But the more they hurried, the more the women thought of ways to waste time. They walked about like startled hens, pecking with the sea charms on their breasts, some interfering on one side to put a scapular[6] of the good wind on the drowned man, some on the other side to put a wrist compass on him, and after a great deal of *get away from there, woman, stay out of the way, look, you almost made me fall on top of the dead man,* the men began to feel mistrust in their livers and started grumbling about why so many main-altar decorations for a stranger, because no matter how many nails and holy-water jars he had on him, the sharks would chew him all the same, but the women kept on piling on their junk relics, running back and forth, stumbling, while they released in sighs what they did not in tears, so that the men finally exploded with *since when has there ever been such a fuss over a drifting corpse, a drowned nobody, a piece of cold Wednesday meat.* One of the women, mortified by so much lack of care, then removed the handkerchief from the dead man's face, and the men were left breathless too.

He was Esteban. It was not necessary to repeat it for them to recognize him. If they had been told Sir Walter Raleigh, even they might have been impressed with his gringo[7] accent, the macaw on his shoulder, his cannibal-killing blunderbuss, but there could be only one Esteban in the world, and there he was, stretched out like a sperm whale, shoeless, wearing the pants of an undersized child, and with those stony nails that had to be cut with a knife. They had only to take the handkerchief off his face to see that he was ashamed, that it was not his fault that he was so big or so heavy or so handsome, and if he had known that this was going to happen, he would have

---

5. destitute (des′ tə tōōt′): living in complete poverty.
6. scapular (skap′ yə lər): two pieces of cloth joined together by strings, worn on the chest and back by some Roman Catholics as a token of religious devotion.
7. gringo (griŋ′ gō): in Latin America, that of a foreigner, especially a person from the United States or England.

looked for a more discreet place to drown in; seriously, I even would have tied the anchor off a galleon around my neck and staggered off a cliff like someone who doesn't like things in order not to be upsetting people now with this Wednesday dead body, as you people say, in order not to be bothering anyone with this filthy piece of cold meat that doesn't have anything to do with me. There was so much truth in his manner that even the most mistrustful men, the ones who felt the bitterness of endless nights at sea fearing that their women would tire of dreaming about them and begin to dream of drowned men, even they and others who were harder still shuddered in the marrow of their bones at Esteban's sincerity.

That was how they came to hold the most splendid funeral they could conceive of for an abandoned drowned man. Some women who had gone to get flowers in the neighboring villages returned with other women who could not believe what they had been told, and those women went back for more flowers when they saw the dead man, and they brought more and more until there were so many flowers and so many people that it was hard to walk about. At the final moment it pained them to return him to the waters as an orphan, and they chose a father and mother from among the best people, and aunts and uncles and cousins, so that through him all the inhabitants of the village became kinsmen. Some sailors who heard the weeping from a distance went off course, and people heard of one who had himself tied to the mainmast, remembering ancient fables about sirens.[8]

While they fought for the privilege of carrying him on their shoulders along the steep escarpment by the cliffs, men and women became aware for the first time of the desolation of their streets, the dryness of their courtyards, the narrowness of their dreams as they faced the splendor and beauty of their drowned man. They let him go without an anchor so that he could come back if he wished and whenever he wished, and they all held their breath for the fraction of centuries the body took to fall into the abyss. They did not need to look at one another to realize that they were no longer all present, that they would never be. But they also knew that everything would be different from then on, that their houses would have wider doors, higher ceilings, and stronger floors so that Esteban's memory could go everywhere without bumping into beams and so that no one in the future would dare whisper *the big boob finally died, too bad, the handsome fool has finally died,* because they were going to paint their house fronts gay colors to make Esteban's memory eternal, and they were going to break their backs digging for springs among the stones and planting flowers on the cliffs so that in future years at dawn the passengers on great liners would awaken, suffocated by the smell of gardens on the high seas, and the captain would have to come down from the bridge in his dress uniform, with his astrolabe,[9] his pole star, and his row of war medals and, pointing to the promontory[10] of roses on the horizon, he would say in fourteen languages, *look there, where the wind is so peaceful now that it's gone to sleep beneath the beds, over there, where the sun's so bright that the sunflowers don't know which way to turn, yes, over there, that's Esteban's village.*

---

8. ancient fables about sirens: a reference to Odysseus' having himself tied to the mast to resist the lure of the sweet songs of the sirens, or sea nymphs.

9. astrolabe (as′ trō lāb′): an old-fashioned navigational instrument for finding the altitude of a star.

10. promontory (präm′ ən tôr′ ē): a peak of high land that juts out into a body of water.

Thinking About the Story

A PERSONAL RESPONSE

sharing impressions

1. In your journal list words and phrases that describe your feelings about the villagers.

constructing interpretations

2. In your opinion, why does the village become known as Esteban's village?

3. Why do you think the villagers are changed by their experience with the drowned man?

Think about
- what is so unusual about his physical appearance
- why they give him a splendid funeral and choose a family for him
- how their perception of their own lives changes when they face "the splendor and beauty of their drowned man"
- how they plan to change the physical appearance of their village

4. What do you think the drowned man represents to the villagers?

Think about
- why they think the sea and the wind respond to his presence
- why both the women and the men are left breathless at the sight of his face
- the imagined qualities that both the women and the men attribute to him

A CREATIVE RESPONSE

5. How might the story have been different if the villagers had discovered who the drowned man was and where he came from?

A CRITICAL RESPONSE

6. Novelist and critic Mario Vargas Llosa writes, "Aracataca [García Márquez's birthplace in Colombia]—like so many Latin American towns—lived on remembrances, myths, solitude, and nostalgia. García Márquez's entire literary work is built with this material which fed him throughout childhood." How is the village in this story similar to or different from García Márquez's birthplace as described by Vargas Llosa?

7. The name Esteban is the Spanish form of Stephen, the name of the first Christian martyr. Lautaro was a South American Indian who led an uprising against the Spanish conquerors. Why do you think the women choose to name the drowned man Esteban instead of Lautaro? Use specific details from the story to support your explanation.

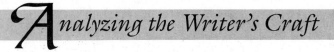

Analyzing the Writer's Craft

STYLE: MAGICAL REALISM

What kind of story did the title lead you to expect?

Building a Literary Vocabulary. Style is the particular way that a piece of literature is written. Style refers not so much to what is said but to how it is said. García Márquez writes in a style called magical realism, which often includes exaggeration, unusual humor, magical and bizarre events, dreams that come true, and superstitions that prove warranted. Magical realism differs from pure fantasy in combining fantastic elements with realistic elements such as recognizable characters, believable dialogue, a true-to-life setting, a matter-of-fact tone, and a plot that sometimes contains historic events.

The first clue that this story exemplifies magical realism comes from the title. Realistically, a drowned person is a gruesome sight. García Márquez nevertheless indicates that although the body spent a long time in the water, the stranger remains extraordinarily handsome. His unexpected handsomeness is the catalyst that awakens the imaginations of the villagers. The fantastic elements of the story enhance and support the theme that imagination can transform otherwise barren lives.

Application: Analyzing Style. As a class divide into four teams to compete in a style-analysis contest. Each team should reread the story up to the sentence "'He has the face of someone called Esteban'" (page 297) and then make a chart with two columns. In the first column list magical elements, such as the villagers' belief that the drowned man continued to grow after death. In the second column list realistic elements, such as the description of the seaweed and jellyfish tentacles that coated the body. Then have a spokesperson from each team read the items on the team's chart to the class. Any examples that are listed by more than one team must be crossed off every team's list. Each team is allowed to keep only the examples that no other team has. The team with the most examples remaining is the winner.

Connecting Reading and Writing

1. Write a **description** of "Esteban's village" that could appear in a tourist guidebook many years after the funeral of the drowned man. Include the name and history of the village in your entry.

Option: For a magazine on home and landscape improvement, write an **article** describing how the village was transformed.

2. To continue the game started in the Writer's Craft exercise, reread the story from "'He has the face of someone called Esteban'" to the end. Make a **chart** listing the magical and realistic elements in the last part of the story. Share your chart.

Option: Define magical realism, using examples in this story, in an **essay** to be printed in a textbook.

3. Write a **fairy tale** for children, using elements of magical realism to enhance the plot.

Option: Prepare a **dramatic script** for your fairy tale and choose classmates to help you perform it.

The Youngest Doll

ROSARIO FERRÉ

A biography of Ferré appears on page 421.

Approaching the Story

"The Youngest Doll" by Rosario Ferré (rô sä′ rē ô fer rä′) is set in Puerto Rico at the beginning of the twentieth century, a period of great change. The island had been controlled by powerful families who owned the sugar cane, coffee, and tobacco plantations on which the economy was based. The wealth and influence of these families declined after the Spanish-American War in 1898, when the island was surrendered to the United States. The economy, dominated by foreign investors, became more industrialized, and a class of newly rich businessmen and professionals arose.

This short story portrays members of the old aristocracy and the rising wealthy classes. Like the previous two stories, this story challenges the reader's expectations with strange turns of events.

Building Vocabulary

These essential words are footnoted within the story.

furtively (fʉr′ tiv lē): They would sit around her and **furtively** lift the starched ruffle of her skirt. (page 304)

ostentatious (äs′ tən tā′ shəs): He would always show up wearing . . . an **ostentatious** tiepin of extravagantly poor taste. (page 306)

exorbitant (eg zor′ bi tənt): The whole town . . . didn't mind paying **exorbitant** fees. (page 307)

Connecting Writing and Reading

In your journal jot down what comes to mind when you hear the term "living doll." What would be the gender, appearance, and personality of someone described by this label? Would you want to be described this way? As you read, be aware of how the term "living doll" changes and takes on new meanings in your mind.

The Youngest Doll

ARLY IN THE morning the maiden aunt took her rocking chair out onto the porch facing the cane fields, as she always did whenever she woke up with the urge to make a doll. As a young woman, she had often bathed in the river, but one day when the heavy rains had fed the dragontail current, she had a soft feeling of melting snow in the marrow of her bones. With her head nestled among the black rocks' reverberations, she could hear the slamming of salty foam on the beach rolled up with the sound of waves, and she suddenly thought that her hair had poured out to sea at last. At that very moment, she felt a sharp bite in her calf. Screaming, she was pulled out of the water and, writhing in pain, was taken home on a stretcher.

The doctor who examined her assured her it was nothing, that she had probably been bitten by an angry river prawn.[1] But days passed and the scab wouldn't heal. A month later the doctor concluded that the prawn had worked its way into the soft flesh of her calf and had nestled there to grow. He prescribed a mustard plaster so that the heat would force it out. The aunt spent a whole week with her leg covered with mustard from thigh to ankle, but when the treatment was over, they found that the ulcer had grown even larger and that it was covered with a slimy, stonelike substance that couldn't be removed without endangering the whole leg. She then resigned herself to living with the prawn permanently curled up in her calf.

She had been very beautiful, but the prawn hidden under the long, gauzy folds of her skirt stripped her of all vanity. She locked herself up in her house, refusing to see any suitors. At first she devoted herself entirely to bringing up her sister's children, dragging her enormous leg around the house quite nimbly. In those days, the family was nearly ruined; they lived surrounded by a past that was breaking up around them with the same impassive musicality with which the dining room chandelier crumbled on the frayed linen cloth of the dining room table. Her nieces adored her. She would comb their hair, bathe and feed them, and when she read them stories, they would sit around her and furtively[2] lift the starched ruffle of her skirt so as to sniff the aroma of ripe sweetsop[3] that oozed from her leg when it was at rest.

As the girls grew up, the aunt devoted herself to making dolls for them to play with. At first they were just plain dolls, with cotton stuffing from the gourd tree and stray buttons sewn on for eyes. As time passed, though, she began to refine her craft, gaining the respect and admiration of the whole family. The birth of a doll was always cause for a ritual celebration, which explains why it never occurred to the aunt to sell them for profit, even when the girls had grown up and the family was beginning to fall into need. The aunt had continued to increase the size of the dolls so that their height and other measurements conformed to those of each of the girls. There were nine of them, and the aunt made one doll for each per year, so it became necessary to set aside a room for the dolls alone. When the eldest turned eighteen, there were one hundred and twenty-

---

1. **prawn** (prôn): a shellfish similar to a large shrimp.
2. **furtively** (fur′ tiv lē): sneakily; not openly.
3. **sweetsop**: a sweet, pungent-smelling, quickly ripening tropical fruit common in Puerto Rico.

six dolls of all ages in the room. Opening the door gave the impression of entering a dovecote or the ballroom in the Czarina's[4] palace or a warehouse in which someone had spread out a row of tobacco leaves to dry. But the aunt did not enter the room for any of these pleasures. Instead, she would unlatch the door and gently pick up each doll, murmuring a lullaby as she rocked it: "This is how you were when you were a year old, this is you at two, and like this at three," measuring out each year of their lives against the hollow they left in her arms.

The day the eldest had turned ten, the aunt sat down in her rocking chair facing the cane fields and never got up again. She would rock away entire days on the porch, watching the patterns of rain shift in the cane fields, coming out of her stupor only when the doctor paid a visit or whenever she awoke with the desire to make a doll. Then she would call out so that everyone in the house would come and help her. On that day, one could see the hired help making repeated trips to town like cheerful Inca messengers, bringing wax, porcelain clay, lace, needles, spools of thread of every color. While these preparations were taking place, the aunt would call the niece she had dreamt about the night before into her room and take her measurements. Then she would make a wax mask of the child's face, covering it with plaster on both sides, like a living face wrapped in two dead ones. She would draw out an endless flaxen thread of melted wax through a pinpoint on its chin. The porcelain of the hands and face was always translucent; it had an ivory tint to it that formed a great contrast with the curdled whiteness of the bisque faces. For the body, the aunt would send out to the garden for twenty glossy gourds. She would hold them in one hand, and with an expert twist of her knife, would slice them up against the railing of the balcony, so that the sun and breeze would dry out the cottony *guano*[5] brains. After a few days, she would scrape off

the dried fluff with a teaspoon and, with infinite patience, feed it into the doll's mouth.

The only items the aunt would agree to use that were not made by her were the glass eyeballs. They were mailed to her from Europe in all colors, but the aunt considered them useless until she had left them submerged at the bottom of the stream for a few days, so that they could learn to recognize the slightest stirring of the prawns' antennae. Only then would she carefully rinse them in ammonia water and place them, glossy as gems and nestled in a bed of cotton, at the bottom of one of her Dutch cookie tins. The dolls were always dressed in the same way, even though the girls were growing up. She would dress the younger ones in Swiss embroidery and the older ones in silk *guipure*,[6] and on each of their heads she would tie the same bow, wide and white and trembling like the breast of a dove.

The girls began to marry and leave home. On their wedding day, the aunt would give each of them their last doll, kissing them on the forehead and telling them with a smile, "Here is your Easter Sunday." She would reassure the grooms by explaining to them that the doll was merely a sentimental ornament, of the kind that people used to place on the lid of grand pianos in the old days. From the porch, the aunt would watch the girls walk down the staircase for the last time. They would carry a modest checkered cardboard suitcase in one hand, the other hand slipped around the waist of the exuberant doll made in their image and likeness, still wearing the same old-fashioned kid slippers and gloves, and with Valenciennes[7] bloomers barely showing under

---

4. Czarina (zä rē′ nə): the wife of a czar, the emperor of Russia.

5. *guano* (gwä′ nō): relating to a type of palm tree.

6. *guipure* (gē pyoor′): a kind of lace.

7. Valenciennes (və len′ sē enz′): a kind of lace originating in the French city of Valenciennes.

their snowy, embroidered skirts. But the hands and faces of these new dolls looked less transparent than those of the old: they had the consistency of skim milk. This difference concealed a more subtle one: the wedding doll was never stuffed with cotton but filled with honey.

All the older girls had married and only the youngest was left at home when the doctor paid his monthly visit to the aunt, bringing along his son, who had just returned from studying medicine up north. The young man lifted the starched ruffle of the aunt's skirt and looked intently at the huge, swollen ulcer which oozed a perfumed sperm from the tip of its greenish scales. He pulled out his stethoscope and listened to her carefully. The aunt thought he was listening for the breathing of the prawn to see if it was still alive, and she fondly lifted his hand and placed it on the spot where he could feel the constant movement of the creature's antennae. The young man released the ruffle and looked fixedly at his father. "You could have cured this from the start," he told him. "That's true," his father answered, "but I just wanted you to come and see the prawn that has been paying for your education these twenty years."

From then on it was the young doctor who visited the old aunt every month. His interest in the youngest was evident from the start, so the aunt was able to begin her last doll in plenty of time. He would always show up wearing a pair of brightly polished shoes, a starched collar, and an ostentatious[8] tiepin of extravagantly poor taste. After examining the aunt, he would sit in the parlor, lean his paper silhouette against the oval frame of the chair and, each time, hand the youngest an identical bouquet of purple forget-me-nots. She would offer him ginger cookies, taking the bouquet squeamishly with the tips of her fingers, as if

she were handling a sea urchin turned inside out. She made up her mind to marry him because she was intrigued by his sleepy profile and also because she was deathly curious to see what the dolphin flesh was like.

On her wedding day, as she was about to leave the house, the youngest was surprised to find that the doll her aunt had given her as a wedding present was warm. As she slipped her arm around its waist, she looked at it curiously, but she quickly forgot about it, so amazed was she at the excellence of its craft. The doll's face and hands were made of the most delicate Mikado porcelain. In the doll's half-open and slightly sad smile she recognized her full set of baby teeth. There was also another notable detail: the aunt had embedded her diamond eardrops inside the doll's pupils.

The young doctor took her off to live in town, in a square house that made one think of a cement block. Each day he made her sit out on the balcony, so that passersby would be sure to see that he had married into high society. Motionless inside her cubicle of heat, the youngest began to suspect that it wasn't only her husband's silhouette that was made of paper, but his soul as well. Her suspicions were soon confirmed. One day, he pried out the doll's eyes with the tip of his scalpel and pawned them for a fancy gold pocket watch with a long embossed chain. From then on the doll remained seated on the lid of the grand piano, but with her gaze modestly lowered.

A few months later, the doctor noticed the doll was missing from her usual place and asked the youngest what she'd done with it. A sisterhood of pious ladies had offered him a healthy sum for the porcelain hands and face, which they thought would be perfect for the image of

---

8. ostentatious (äs′ tən tā′ shəs): showy; flashy.

the Veronica in the next Lenten procession.[9]

The youngest answered that the ants had at last discovered the doll was filled with honey and, streaming over the piano, had devoured it in a single night. "Since its hands and face were of Mikado porcelain," she said, "they must have thought they were made of sugar and at this very moment they are most likely wearing down their teeth, gnawing furiously at its fingers and eyelids in some underground burrow." That night the doctor dug up all the ground around the house, to no avail.

As the years passed, the doctor became a millionaire. He had slowly acquired the whole town as his clientele, people who didn't mind paying exorbitant[10] fees in order to see a genuine member of the extinct sugar cane aristocracy up close. The youngest went on sitting in her rocking chair on the balcony, motionless in her muslin and lace, and always with lowered eyelids. Whenever her husband's patients, draped with necklaces and feathers and carrying elaborate canes, would seat themselves beside her, shaking their self-satisfied rolls of flesh with a jingling of coins, they would notice a strange scent that would involuntarily remind them of a slowly oozing sweetsop. They would then feel an uncomfortable urge to rub their hands together as though they were paws.

There was only one thing missing from the doctor's otherwise perfect happiness. He noticed that although he was aging, the youngest still kept that same firm, porcelained skin she had had when he would call on her at the big house on the plantation. One night he decided to go into her bedroom to watch her as she slept. He noticed that her chest wasn't moving. He gently placed his stethoscope over her heart and heard a distant swish of water. Then the doll lifted her eyelids, and out of the empty sockets of her eyes came the frenzied antennae of all those prawns.

---

9. The Veronica in the next Lenten procession: The Veronica is the image of Jesus' face said in legend to have appeared on the veil or handkerchief used by Saint Veronica to wipe the bleeding face of Jesus. A Lenten procession is a ceremony held during Lent, the period of forty weekdays from Ash Wednesday to Easter held holy by Christian churches.

10. exorbitant (eg zor′ bi tənt): going beyond what is usual; excessive.

Thinking About the Story

A PERSONAL RESPONSE

sharing impressions

1. What questions do you have after reading this story? Note them in your journal.

constructing interpretations

2. How do you explain what the young doctor observes when he enters his wife's bedroom?

3. Does the term "living doll" have different associations for you now that you have read this story?

> **Think about**
> - how the term describes the dolls that the maiden aunt makes
> - how the term describes the women in the story, particularly the youngest niece
> - how positively or negatively you now view the term

4. Speculate about what the aunt hopes to accomplish by making dolls.

> **Think about**
> - what she does when she is not making dolls
> - how closely the dolls resemble her nieces
> - why she submerges the dolls' eyeballs in the stream
> - what she means by telling her nieces, "Here is your Easter Sunday" as she gives them their wedding dolls

5. Which character is most evil and which is most victimized?

> **Think about**
> - the admission the old doctor makes to his son
> - the reasons why the young doctor and the youngest niece marry
> - the young doctor's treatment of his wife and the doll
> - the degree of control the aunt has over her own fate and her youngest niece's fate

A CREATIVE RESPONSE

6. If the aunt had not belonged to an aristocratic family, would the prawn bite have affected her life in the same way?

A CRITICAL RESPONSE

7. How do you think the writer views Puerto Rican society at the turn of the century?

> **Think about**
> - the values of the old doctor, the young doctor, and the young doctor's clientele
> - the values and position of the sugar cane aristocracy
> - the lives led by the women in the story
> - the possible symbolism of the prawn, the hidden ulcer, and the scent of oozing sweetsop

8. What common stylistic elements do you see in "The Youngest Doll," "The Handsomest Drowned Man in the World," and "The Night Face Up"?

Analyzing the Writer's Craft

MOOD

Think about the feeling you get as you read: "the aroma of ripe sweetsop that oozed from her leg."

Building a Literary Vocabulary. Mood is the feeling, or atmosphere, that the writer creates for the reader. One element that contributes strongly to mood is imagery, words and phrases that re-create experiences by appealing to any of the five senses. A literary work may evoke more than one mood, as the descriptions "bittersweet love story" and "tragicomedy" would suggest. In "The Youngest Doll" the image of ripe, oozing sweetsop creates a mood of both richness and decay.

Application: Defining Mood. At the top of a sheet of paper, write two words that describe two different moods you find in "The Youngest Doll." Below these labels list images from the story that help create these two moods. The images may be in different passages or in the same passage. Compare your findings with those of your classmates to see how many moods are evoked by the story and to reinforce your understanding of the relationship between mood and imagery.

Connecting Reading and Writing

1. Suppose a friend turns to you after reading this story and says, "I just don't get it." In an **informal note** to him or her, explain what you think happens in the story.

Option: Write your own **story** relating events from the viewpoint of the aunt, the youngest niece, or the doll itself.

2. Imagine that the doll has been acquired by a prestigious auction house and is being offered for sale. Write **catalog copy** describing the doll.

Option: Advertise the doll in a **TV commercial** for a home shopping network.

3. In an **essay** for your literature class, analyze the writer's comparison of women to dolls in this story

and comment on whether such a comparison is still valid among high school students today.

Option: Present your ideas in a **pamphlet** for distribution at a political rally.

4. Compare "The Youngest Doll" to another story by Rosario Ferré, such as "The Gift" in her collection *Sweet Diamond Dust* or "The Poisoned Tale" in *Short Stories by Latin American Women: The Magic and The Real.* Make some generalizations about Ferré's style and major themes and prepare a **list of questions** to ask her in a radio interview about her writing.

Option: Describe Ferré's style and themes in a brief **profile** intended for a reference book on Latin American writers.

Rhinoceros

EUGÈNE IONESCO

A biography of Ionesco appears on page 422.

Approaching the Story

Audiences attending the plays of Romanian-born Frenchman Eugène Ionesco (yo͞o zhen′ yə nes′ kō), one of the founders of the theater of the absurd, have learned to expect the unexpected. In Ionesco's short stories, too, he often describes bizarre incidents that are comic and yet disturbing. In "Rhinoceros," for example, he presents a series of puzzling transformations while exploring the choice between conformity and individuality.

Building Vocabulary

These essential words are footnoted within the story.

itinerant (ī tin′ ər ənt): The council has forbidden **itinerant** entertainers to stop on municipal territory. (page 311)

paradoxes (par′ ə däks′ əz): "How tiresome you are with your **paradoxes.**" (page 311)

pedant (ped′ 'nt): "You're a **pedant,** who isn't even sure of his own knowledge." (page 312)

mutations (myo͞o tā′ shənz): Were these **mutations** reversible? (page 319)

Connecting Writing and Reading

Are you a conformist? Do you feel pressured to conform to the behavior and attitudes of your fellow students? In your journal create a bar graph that shows the degree to which you conform in areas such as clothing, extracurricular activities, taste in music, and attitude toward school. As you read, think about the issue of conformity in your own life and in the lives of the characters.

*W*E WERE sitting outside the café, my friend Jean and I, peacefully talking about one thing and another, when we caught sight of it on the opposite pavement, huge and powerful, panting noisily, charging straight ahead and brushing against market stalls—a rhinoceros. People in the street stepped hurriedly aside to let it pass. A housewife uttered a cry of terror, her basket dropped from her hands, the wine from a broken bottle spread over the pavement, and some pedestrians, one of them an elderly man, rushed into the shops. It was all over like a flash of lightning. People emerged from their hiding places and gathered in groups which watched the rhinoceros disappear into the distance, made some comments on the incident and then dispersed.

My own reactions are slowish. I absentmindedly took in the image of the rushing beast, without ascribing any very great importance to it. That morning, moreover, I was feeling tired and my mouth was sour, as a result of the previous night's excesses; we had been celebrating a friend's birthday. Jean had not been at the party; and when the first moment of surprise was over, he exclaimed: "A rhinoceros at large in town! Doesn't that surprise you? It ought not to be allowed."

"True," I said, "I hadn't thought of that. It's dangerous."

"We ought to protest to the Town Council."

"Perhaps it's escaped from the zoo," I said.

"You're dreaming," he replied. "There hasn't been a zoo in our town since the animals were decimated by the plague in the seventeenth century."

"Perhaps it belongs to the circus?"

"What circus? The council has forbidden <u>itinerant</u>[1] entertainers to stop on municipal territory. None have come here since we were children."

"Perhaps it has lived here ever since, hidden in the marshy woods round about," I answered with a yawn.

"You're completely lost in a dense alcoholic haze. . . ."

"Which rises from the stomach . . ."

"Yes. And has pervaded your brain. What marshy woods can you think of round about here? Our province is so arid they call it Little Castile."[2]

"Perhaps it sheltered under a pebble? Perhaps it made its nest on a dry branch?"

"How tiresome you are with your <u>paradoxes</u>.[3] You're quite incapable of talking seriously."

"Today, particularly."

"Today and every other day."

"Don't lose your temper, my dear Jean. We're not going to quarrel about that creature. . . ."

We changed the subject of our conversation and began to talk about the weather again, about the rain which fell so rarely in our region, about the need to provide our sky with artificial clouds, and other banal and insoluble questions.

We parted. It was Sunday. I went to bed and slept all day: another wasted Sunday. On Monday morning I went to the office, making a solemn promise to myself never to get drunk again, and particularly not on Saturdays, so as not to spoil the following Sundays. For I had one single free day a week and three weeks' holiday in the summer. Instead of drinking and making myself ill, wouldn't it be better to keep fit and healthy, to spend my precious moments of freedom in a more intelligent fashion: visiting museums, reading literary magazines and listening to lectures? And instead of spending

---

1. itinerant (ī tin′ ər ənt): traveling from place to place, as on a circuit.

2. Castile (kas tēl′): the dry central region of Spain.

3. paradoxes (par′ ə däks′ əz): statements that seem contradictory or absurd but may in fact be true.

all my available money on drink, wouldn't it be preferable to buy tickets for interesting plays? I was still unfamiliar with the avant-garde theater, of which I had heard so much talk; I had never seen a play by Ionesco. Now or never was the time to bring myself up-to-date.

The following Sunday I met Jean once again at the same café.

"I've kept my promise," I said, shaking hands with him.

"What promise have you kept?" he asked.

"My promise to myself. I've vowed to give up drinking. Instead of drinking I've decided to cultivate my mind. Today I am clearheaded. This afternoon I'm going to the Municipal Museum, and this evening I've a ticket for the theater. Won't you come with me?"

"Let's hope your good intentions will last," replied Jean. "But I can't go with you. I'm meeting some friends at the brasserie."[4]

"Oh, my dear fellow, now it's you who are setting a bad example. You'll get drunk!"

"Once in a while doesn't imply a habit," replied Jean irritably. "Whereas you . . . "

The discussion was about to take a disagreeable turn, when we heard a mighty trumpeting, the hurried clatter of some perissodactyl's[5] hoofs, cries, a cat's mewing; almost simultaneously we saw a rhinoceros appear, then disappear, on the opposite pavement, panting noisily and charging straight ahead.

Immediately afterwards a woman appeared holding in her arms a shapeless, bloodstained little object:

"It's run over my cat," she wailed, "it's run over my cat!"

The poor dishevelled woman, who seemed the very embodiment of grief, was soon surrounded by people offering sympathy.

Jean and I got up. We rushed across the street to the side of the unfortunate woman.

"All cats are mortal," I said stupidly, not knowing how to console her.

"It came past my shop last week!" the grocer recalled.

"It wasn't the same one," Jean declared. "It wasn't the same one: last week's had two horns on its nose—it was an Asian rhinoceros; this one had only one—it's an African rhinoceros."

"You're talking nonsense," I said irritably. "How could you distinguish its horns? The animal rushed past so fast that we could hardly see it; you hadn't time to count them. . . ."

"I don't live in a haze," Jean retorted sharply. "I'm clearheaded, I'm quick at figures."

"He was charging with his head down."

"That made it all the easier to see."

"You're a pretentious fellow, Jean. You're a pedant,[6] who isn't even sure of his own knowledge. For in the first place, it's the Asian rhinoceros that has one horn on its nose and the African rhinoceros that has two!"

"You're quite wrong; it's the other way about."

"Would you like to bet on it?"

"I won't bet against you. You're the one who has two horns," he cried, red with fury, "you Asiatic, you!" (He stuck to his guns.)

"I haven't any horns. I shall never wear them. And I'm not an Asiatic, either. In any case, Asiatics are just like other people."

Jean turned his back on me and strode off, cursing.

I felt a fool. I ought to have been more conciliatory and not contradicted him: for I knew he could not bear it. The slightest objection made him foam at the mouth. This was his only fault, for he had a heart of gold and had done me countless good turns. The few people

---

4. brasserie (bràs rē′) *French:* a beer shop or saloon that sells food.
5. perissodactyl (pə ris′ ō dak′ til): an order of hoofed mammals having an uneven number of toes on each foot and including the horse, tapir, and rhinoceros.
6. pedant (ped′ 'nt): a person who shows off his or her learning in a boring way.

who were there and who had been listening to us had, as a result, quite forgotten about the poor woman's squashed cat. They crowded round me, arguing: some maintained that the Asian rhinoceros was indeed one-horned, and that I was right; others maintained that on the contrary the African rhinoceros was one-horned, and that therefore the previous speaker had been right.

"That is not the question," interposed a gentleman (straw boater,[7] small moustache, eyeglass, a typical logician's head) who had hitherto stood silent. "The discussion turned on a problem from which you have wandered. You began by asking yourselves whether today's rhinoceros is the same as last Sunday's or whether it is a different one. That is what must be decided. You may have seen one and the same one-horned rhinoceros on two occasions, or you may have seen one and the same two-horned rhinoceros on two occasions. Or again, you may have seen first one one-horned rhinoceros and then a second one-horned rhinoceros. Or else, first one two-horned rhinoceros and then a second two-horned rhinoceros. If on the first occasion you had seen a two-horned rhinoceros, and on the second a one-horned rhinoceros, that would not be conclusive either. It might be that since last week the rhinoceros had lost one of his horns and that the one you saw today was the same. Or it might be that two two-horned rhinceroses had each lost one of their horns. If you could prove that on the first occasion you had seen a one-horned rhinoceros, whether it was Asian or African, and today a two-horned rhinoceros, whether it was African or Asian—that doesn't matter—then we might conclude that two different rhinoceroses were involved, for it is most unlikely that a second horn could grow in a few days, to any visible extent, on a rhinoceros's nose; this would mean that an Asian, or African, rhinoceros had become an African, or Asian, rhinoceros, which is logically impossible, since the same creature cannot be born in two places at once or even successively."

"That seems clear to me," I said. "But it doesn't settle the question."

"Of course," retorted the gentleman, smiling with a knowledgeable air, "only the problem has now been stated correctly."

"That's not the problem either," interrupted the grocer, who being no doubt of an emotional nature cared little about logic. "Can we allow our cats to be run over under our eyes by two-horned or one-horned rhinoceroses, be they Asian or African?"

"He's right, he's right," everybody exclaimed. "We can't allow our cats to be run over, by rhinoceroses or anything else!"

The grocer pointed with a theatrical gesture to the poor weeping woman, who still held and rocked in her arms the shapeless, bleeding remains of what had once been her cat.

Next day in the paper, under the heading Road Casualties Among Cats, there were two lines describing the death of the poor creature: "crushed underfoot by a pachyderm" it was said, without further details.

On Sunday afternoon I hadn't visited a museum; in the evening I hadn't gone to the theater. I had moped at home by myself, overwhelmed by remorse at having quarrelled with Jean.

"He's so susceptible, I ought to have spared his feelings," I told myself. "It's absurd to lose one's temper about something like that . . . about the horns of a rhinoceros that one had never seen before . . . a native of Africa or of India, such faraway countries, what could it matter to me? Whereas Jean had always been my friend, a friend who . . . to whom I owed so much . . . and who . . ."

---

7. **straw boater:** a stiff hat of braided straw, with a flat crown and brim.

In short, while promising myself to go and see Jean as soon as possible and to make it up with him, I had drunk an entire bottle of brandy without noticing. But I did indeed notice it the next day: a sore head, a foul mouth, an uneasy conscience; I was really most uncomfortable. But duty before everything: I got to the office on time, or almost. I was able to sign the register just before it was taken away.

"Well, so you've seen rhinoceroses too?" asked the chief clerk, who, to my great surprise, was already there.

"Sure I've seen him," I said, taking off my town jacket and putting on my old jacket with the frayed sleeves, good enough for work.

"Oh, now you see, I'm not crazy!" exclaimed the typist Daisy excitedly. (How pretty she was, with her pink cheeks and fair hair! I found her terribly attractive. If I could fall in love with anybody, it would be with her. . . .) "A one-horned rhinoceros!"

"Two-horned!" corrected my colleague Emile Dudard,[8] Bachelor of Law, eminent jurist, who looked forward to a brilliant future with the firm and, possibly, in Daisy's affections.

"*I've* not seen it! And I don't believe in it!" declared Botard,[9] an ex-schoolmaster who acted as archivist. "And nobody's ever seen one in this part of the world, except in the illustrations to school textbooks. These rhinoceroses have blossomed only in the imagination of ignorant women. The thing's a myth, like flying saucers."

I was about to point out to Botard that the expression "blossomed" applied to a rhinoceros, or to a number of them, seemed to me inappropriate, when the jurist exclaimed: "All the same, a cat was crushed, and before witnesses!"

"Collective psychosis," retorted Botard, who was a freethinker, "just like religion, the opium of the people!"

"I believe in flying saucers myself," remarked Daisy.

The chief clerk cut short our argument:

"That'll do! Enough chatter! Rhinoceros or no rhinoceros, flying saucers or no flying saucers, work's got to be done."

The typist started typing. I sat down at my desk and became engrossed in my documents. Emile Dudard began correcting the proofs of a commentary on the Law for the Repression of Alcoholism, while the chief clerk, slamming the door, retired into his study.

"It's a hoax!" Botard grumbled once more, aiming his remarks at Dudard. "It's your propaganda that spreads these rumors!"

"It's not propaganda," I interposed.

"I saw it myself . . . ," Daisy confirmed simultaneously.

"You make me laugh," said Dudard to Botard. "Propaganda? For what?"

"You know that better than I do! Don't act the simpleton!"

"In any case, *I'm* not paid by the Pontenegrins!"[10]

"That's an insult!" cried Botard, thumping the table with his fist. The door of the chief clerk's room opened suddenly and his head appeared.

"Monsieur Boeuf[11] hasn't come in today."

"Quite true, he's not here," I said.

"Just when I needed him. Did he tell anyone he was ill? If this goes on I shall give him the sack . . . ."

It was not the first time that the chief clerk had threatened our colleague in this way.

"Has one of you got the key to his desk?" he went on.

Just then Madame Boeuf made her appearance. She seemed terrified.

---

8. **Emile Dudard** (ā mēl′ dü där′).

9. **Botard** (bô tär′).

10. **Pontenegrins** (pônt′ ne gran′).

11. **Boeuf** (bëf).

"I must ask you to excuse my husband. He went to spend the weekend with relations. He's had a slight attack of 'flu. Look, that's what he says in his telegram. He hopes to be back on Wednesday. Give me a glass of water . . . and a chair!" she gasped, collapsing onto the chair we offered her.

"It's very tiresome! But it's no reason to get so alarmed!" remarked the chief clerk.

"I was pursued by a rhinoceros all the way from home," she stammered.

"With one horn or two?" I asked.

"You make me laugh!" exclaimed Botard.

"Why don't you let her speak!" protested Dudard.

Madame Boeuf had to make a great effort to be explicit:

"It's downstairs, in the doorway. It seems to be trying to come upstairs."

At that very moment a tremendous noise was heard: the stairs were undoubtedly giving way under a considerable weight. We rushed out onto the landing. And there, in fact, amidst the debris, was a rhinoceros, its head lowered, trumpeting in an agonized and agonizing voice and turning vainly round and round. I was able to make out two horns.

"It's an African rhinoceros . . . ," I said, "or rather an Asian one."

My mind was so confused that I was no longer sure whether two horns were characteristic of the Asian or of the African rhinoceros, whether a single horn was characteristic of the African or of the Asian rhinoceros, or whether on the contrary two horns . . . In short, I was floundering mentally, while Botard glared furiously at Dudard.

"It's an infamous plot!" and, with an orator's gesture, he pointed at the jurist: "It's your fault!"

"It's yours!" the other retorted.

"Keep calm, this is no time to quarrel!" declared Daisy, trying in vain to pacify them.

"For years now I've been asking the board to let us have concrete steps instead of that rick-ety old staircase," said the chief clerk. "Something like this was bound to happen. It was predictable. I was quite right!"

"As usual," Daisy added ironically. "But how shall we get down?"

"I'll carry you in my arms," the chief clerk joked flirtatiously, stroking the typist's cheek, "and we'll jump together!"

"Don't put your horny hand on my face, you pachydermous creature!"

The chief clerk had not time to react. Madame Boeuf, who had got up and come to join us, and who had for some minutes been staring attentively at the rhinoceros, which was turning round and round below us, suddenly uttered a terrible cry:

"It's my husband! Boeuf, my poor dear Boeuf, what has happened to you?"

The rhinoceros, or rather Boeuf, responded with a violent and yet tender trumpeting, while Madame Boeuf fainted into my arms and Botard, raising his to heaven, stormed: "It's sheer lunacy! What a society!"

When we had recovered from our initial astonishment, we telephoned to the fire brigade, who drove up with their ladders and fetched us down. Madame Boeuf, although we advised her against it, rode off on her spouse's back toward their home. She had ample grounds for divorce (but who was the guilty party?), yet she chose rather not to desert her husband in his present state.

At the little bistro where we all went for lunch (all except the Boeufs, of course) we learnt that several rhinoceroses had been seen in various parts of the town: some people said seven, others seventeen, others again said thirty-two. In the face of this accumulated evidence, Botard could no longer deny the rhinoceric facts. But he knew, he declared, what to think about it. He would explain it to us some day. He knew the "why" of things, the "underside" of the story, the names of those responsible, the aim and significance of the outrage. Going back to the office that afternoon, business or no business, was out of the question. We had to wait for the staircase to be repaired.

I took advantage of this to pay a call on Jean, with the intention of making it up with him. He was in bed.

"I don't feel very well!" he said.

"You know, Jean, we were both right. There are two-horned rhinoceroses in the town as well as one-horned ones. It really doesn't matter where either sort comes from. The only significant thing, in my opinion, is the existence of the rhinoceros in itself."

"I don't feel very well," my friend kept on saying without listening to me, "I don't feel very well!"

"What's the matter with you? I'm so sorry!"

"I'm rather feverish, and my head aches."

More precisely, it was his forehead which was aching. He must have had a knock, he said. And in fact a lump was swelling up there, just above his nose. He had gone a greenish color, and his voice was hoarse.

"Have you got a sore throat? It may be tonsillitis."

I took his pulse. It was beating quite regularly.

"It can't be very serious. A few days' rest and you'll be all right. Have you sent for the doctor?"

As I was about to let go of his wrist, I noticed that his veins were swollen and bulging out. Looking closely, I observed that not only were the veins enlarged but the skin all round them was visibly changing color and growing hard.

"It may be more serious than I imagined," I thought. "We must send for the doctor," I said aloud.

"I felt uncomfortable in my clothes, and now my pajamas are too tight," he said in a hoarse voice.

"What's the matter with your skin? It's like

leather. . . ." Then, staring at him: "Do you know what happened to Boeuf? He's turned into a rhinoceros."

"Well, what about it? That's not such a bad thing! After all, rhinoceroses are creatures like ourselves, with just as much right to live. . . ."

"Provided they don't imperil our own lives. Aren't you aware of the difference in mentality?"

"Do you think ours is preferable?"

"All the same, we have our own moral code, which I consider incompatible with that of these animals. We have our philosophy, our irreplaceable system of values . . . ."

"Humanism[12] is out of date! You're a ridiculous old sentimentalist. You're talking nonsense."

"I'm surprised to hear you say that, my dear Jean! Have you taken leave of your senses?"

It really looked like it. Blind fury had disfigured his face and altered his voice to such an extent that I could scarcely understand the words that issued from his lips.

"Such assertions, coming from you . . . ," I tried to resume.

He did not give me a chance to do so. He flung back his blankets, tore off his pajamas, and stood up in bed, entirely naked (he who was usually the most modest of men!), green with rage from head to foot.

The lump on his forehead had grown longer; he was staring fixedly at me, apparently without seeing me. Or, rather, he must have seen me quite clearly, for he charged at me with his head lowered. I barely had time to leap to one side; if I hadn't, he would have pinned me to the wall.

"You are a rhinoceros!" I cried.

"I'll trample on you! I'll trample on you!" I made out these words as I dashed toward the door.

---

12. **humanism:** a philosophical movement that holds that humans can be moral and find meaning in life through reason.

I went downstairs four steps at a time, while the walls shook as he butted them with his horn, and I heard him utter fearful angry trumpetings.

"Call the police! Call the police! You've got a rhinoceros in the house!" I called out to the tenants who, in great surprise, looked out of their flats as I passed each landing.

On the ground floor I had great difficulty in dodging the rhinoceros, which emerged from the concierge's lodge and tried to charge me. At last I found myself out in the street, sweating, my legs limp, at the end of my tether.

Fortunately there was a bench by the edge of the pavement, and I sat down on it. Scarcely had I more or less got back my breath when I saw a herd of rhinoceroses hurrying down the avenue and nearing, at full speed, the place where I was. If only they had been content to stay in the middle of the street! But they were so many that there was not room for them all there, and they overflowed onto the pavement. I leapt off my bench and flattened myself against the wall: snorting, trumpeting, with a smell of leather and of wild animals in heat, they brushed past me and covered me with a cloud of dust. When they had disappeared, I could not go back to sit on the bench; the animals had demolished it, and it lay in fragments on the pavement.

I did not find it easy to recover from such emotions. I had to stay at home for several days. Daisy came to see me and kept me informed as to the changes that were taking place.

The chief clerk had been the first to turn into a rhinoceros, to the great disgust of Botard, who, nevertheless, became one himself twenty-four hours later.

"One must keep up with one's times!" were his last words as a man.

The case of Botard did not surprise me, in spite of his apparent strength of mind. I found it less easy to understand the chief clerk's transformation. Of course it might have been involuntary, but one would have expected him to put up more resistance.

Daisy recalled that she had commented on the roughness of his palms the very day that Boeuf had appeared in rhinoceros shape. This must have made a deep impression on him; he had not shown it, but he had certainly been cut to the quick.

"If I hadn't been so outspoken, if I had pointed it out to him more tactfully, perhaps this would never have happened."

"I blame myself, too, for not having been gentler with Jean. I ought to have been friendlier, shown more understanding," I said in my turn.

Daisy informed me that Dudard, too, had been transformed, as had also a cousin of hers, whom I did not know. And there were others, mutual friends, strangers.

"There are a great many of them," she said, "about a quarter of the inhabitants of our town."

"They're still in the minority, however."

"The way things are going, that won't last long!" she sighed.

"Alas! And they're so much more efficient."

Herds of rhinoceroses rushing at top speed through the streets became a sight that no longer surprised anybody. People would stand aside to let them pass and then resume their stroll, or attend to their business, as if nothing had happened.

"How can anybody be a rhinoceros! It's unthinkable!" I protested in vain.

More of them kept emerging from courtyards and houses, even from windows, and went to join the rest.

There came a point when the authorities proposed to enclose them in huge parks. For humanitarian reasons, the Society for the Protection of Animals opposed this. Besides, everyone had some close relative or friend among the rhinoceroses, which, for obvious reasons, made the project well-nigh impracticable. It was abandoned.

The situation grew worse, which was only to be expected. One day a whole regiment of rhinoceroses, having knocked down the walls of the barracks, came out with drums at their head and poured onto the boulevards.

At the Ministry of Statistics, statisticians produced their statistics: census of animals, approximate reckoning of their daily increase, percentage of those with one horn, percentage of those with two. . . . What an opportunity for learned controversies! Soon there were defections among the statisticians themselves. The few who remained were paid fantastic sums.

One day from my balcony I caught sight of a rhinoceros charging forward with loud trumpetings, presumably to join his fellows; he wore a straw boater impaled on his horn.

"The logician!" I cried. "He's one too? Is it possible?" Just at that moment Daisy opened the door.

"The logician is a rhinoceros!" I told her.

She knew. She had just seen him in the street. She was bringing me a basket of provisions.

"Shall we have lunch together?" she suggested. "You know, it was difficult to find anything to eat. The shops have been ransacked; they devour everything. A number of shops are closed 'on account of transformations,' the notices say."

"I love you, Daisy, please never leave me."

"Close the window, darling. They make too much noise. And the dust comes in."

"So long as we're together, I'm afraid of nothing, I don't mind about anything." Then, when I had closed the window: "I thought I should never be able to fall in love with a woman again."

I clasped her tightly in my arms. She responded to my embrace.

"How I'd like to make you happy! Could you be happy with me?"

"Why not? You declare you're afraid of nothing and yet you're scared of everything! What can happen to us?"

"My love, my joy!" I stammered, kissing her lips with a passion such as I had forgotten, intense and agonizing.

The ringing of the telephone interrupted us.

She broke from my arms, went to pick up the receiver, then uttered a cry: "Listen. . . ."

I put the receiver to my ear. I heard ferocious trumpetings.

"They're playing tricks on us now!"

"Whatever can be happening?" she inquired in alarm.

We turned on the radio to hear the news; we heard more trumpetings. She was shaking with fear.

"Keep calm," I said, "keep calm!"

She cried out in terror, "They've taken over the broadcasting station!"

"Keep calm, keep calm!" I repeated, increasingly agitated myself.

Next day in the street they were running about in all directions. You could watch for hours without catching sight of a single human being. Our house was shaking under the weight of our perissodactylic neighbors' hoofs.

"What must be must be," said Daisy. "What can we do about it?"

"They've all gone mad. The world is sick."

"It's not you and I who'll cure it."

"We shan't be able to communicate with anybody. Can you understand them?"

"We ought to try to interpret their psychology, to learn their language."

"They have no language."

"What do you know about it?"

"Listen to me, Daisy. We shall have children, and then they will have children. It'll take time, but between us we can regenerate humanity. With a little courage . . ."

"I don't want to have children."

"How do you hope to save the world, then?"

"Perhaps after all it's we who need saving. Perhaps we are the abnormal ones. Do you see anyone else like us?"

"Daisy, I can't have you talking like that!"

I looked at her in despair.

"It's we who are in the right, Daisy, I assure you."

"What arrogance! There's no absolute right. It's the whole world that is right—not you or me."

"Yes, Daisy, I *am* right. The proof is that you understand me and that I love you as much as a man can love a woman."

"I'm rather ashamed of what you call love, that morbid thing. . . . It cannot compare with the extraordinary energy displayed by all these beings we see around us."

"Energy? Here's energy for you!" I cried, my powers of argument exhausted, giving her a slap.

Then, as she burst into tears: "I won't give in, no, I won't give in."

She rose, weeping, and flung her sweet-smelling arms round my neck.

"I'll stand fast, with you, to the end."

She was unable to keep her word. She grew melancholy and visibly pined away. One morning when I woke up, I saw that her place in the bed was empty. She had gone away without leaving any message.

The situation became literally unbearable for me. It was my fault if Daisy had gone. Who knows what had become of her? Another burden on my conscience. There was nobody who could help me to find her again. I imagined the worst and felt myself responsible.

And on every side there were trumpetings and frenzied chargings and clouds of dust. In vain did I shut myself up in my own room, putting cotton wool in my ears: at night I saw them in my dreams.

"The only way out is to convince them." But of what? Were these <u>mutations</u>[13] reversible? And in order to convince them, one would have to talk to them. In order for them to relearn my language (which moreover I was beginning to forget), I should first have

to learn theirs. I could not distinguish one trumpeting from another, one rhinoceros from another rhinoceros.

One day, looking at myself in the glass, I took a dislike to my long face: I needed a horn, or even two, to give dignity to my flabby features.

And what if, as Daisy had said, it was they who were in the right? I was out of date; I had missed the boat, that was clear.

I discovered that their trumpetings had after all a certain charm, if a somewhat harsh one. I should have noticed that while there was still time. I tried to trumpet: how feeble the sound was, how lacking in vigor! When I made greater efforts, I only succeeded in howling. Howlings are not trumpetings.

It is obvious that one must not always drift blindly behind events and that it's a good thing to maintain one's individuality. However, one must also make allowances for things; asserting one's own difference, to be sure, but yet . . . remaining akin to one's fellows. I no longer bore any likeness to anyone or to anything, except to ancient, old-fashioned photographs which had no connection with living beings.

Each morning I looked at my hands, hoping that the palms would have hardened during my sleep. The skin remained flabby. I gazed at my too-white body, my hairy legs: oh for a hard skin and that magnificent green color, a decent, hairless nudity, like theirs!

My conscience was increasingly uneasy, unhappy. I felt I was a monster. Alas, I would never become a rhinoceros. I could never change.

I dared no longer look at myself. I was ashamed. And yet I couldn't, no, I couldn't.

---

13. **mutations** (myoō tā′ shənz): changes, as in form, nature, and so on.

Thinking About the Story

A PERSONAL RESPONSE

sharing impressions

1. How do you feel about what happens in this story? Jot down your impressions in your journal.

constructing interpretations

2. What do you predict will happen to the narrator?
Think about
- the role of conformity in the lives of the characters
- what the narrator says about maintaining individuality
- the narrator's feeling like a monster at the end of the story

3. How would you describe the transformations that take place in this story?
Think about
- physical changes and what they might mean
- changes in the relationships between characters
- changes in society

A CREATIVE RESPONSE

4. If you were a character in this story, do you think you would turn into a rhinoceros? Explain your answer.

A CRITICAL RESPONSE

5. What do you think the rhinoceroses in this story symbolize?
Think about
- details about their appearance and behavior
- the narrator's comments about them
- what the writer seems to be saying about the issue of conformity

6. The tone of "Rhinoceros" has been described as both serious and absurdly comical. Explain how both descriptions apply to the story.

7. How might the theme of the story be applied to your own life?
Think about
- what you wrote in your journal about conformity
- what Ionesco is saying about society

Analyzing the Writer's Craft

DIALOGUE

Think about what the conversations in this story suggest about the characters.

Building a Literary Vocabulary. Dialogue is written conversation between two or more characters. The use of dialogue brings characters to life and gives the reader insights into their qualities. For example, in "The Prisoner Who Wore Glasses," Brille's concern for his fellow prisoners and their compassion for him is revealed in the following dialogue: "I'm sorry, comrades," he said. . . . "Never mind, brother," they said. "What happens to one of us, happens to all."

Application: Examining Dialogue. In a small group, read aloud the dialogue from an episode in this story. Identify what qualities of the characters are suggested through the dialogue. Then prepare an oral interpretation for the entire class in which you highlight those qualities.

Connecting Reading and Writing

1. Imagine that you are planning to direct a film version of this short story. Write a **letter** to the actor of your choice to persuade him to perform the part of the narrator.

Option: Write a **memo** to the producer explaining why you want a certain actor for the part.

2. Many critics have interpreted "Rhinoceros" as an allegory about Nazism in World War II. Do research on the nature of Nazism and its effects during World War II. Then write an **expository essay** for your classmates on this interpretation.

Option: Write a **lesson plan** outline that a teacher might use to teach "Rhinoceros."

3. Imagine that a school board member has objected to this story on the grounds that it is preposterous and a waste of time. Prepare notes for a speech before the school board supporting or challenging this objection.

Option: Express your views on this objection in an **editorial** for a classroom newspaper.

What I Have Been Doing Lately

JAMAICA KINCAID

A biography of Kincaid appears on page 423.

Approaching the Story

Jamaica Kincaid is a Caribbean-born writer now living in the United States. This story is an experimental work similar to some of the preceding stories: the characters are not named, events are left unexplained, and reality is uncertain.

Connecting Writing and Reading

Recall some of the more unusual aspects of the stories you have read in this section of the book. In your journal jot down words and phrases that come to mind. As you read, compare your impressions of the other stories with the bizarre and surprising aspects of this story.

WHAT I HAVE been doing lately: I was lying in bed and the doorbell rang. I ran downstairs. Quick. I opened the door. There was no one there. I stepped outside. Either it was drizzling or there was a lot of dust in the air and the dust was damp. I stuck out my tongue and the drizzle or the damp dust tasted like government school ink. I looked north. I looked south. I decided to start walking north. While walking north, I noticed that I was barefoot. While walking north, I looked up and saw the planet Venus. I said, "It must be almost morning." I saw a monkey in a tree. The tree had no leaves. I said, "Ah, a monkey. Just look at that. A monkey." I walked for I don't know how long before I came up to a big body of water. I wanted to get across it but I couldn't swim. I wanted to get across it but it would take me years to build a boat. I wanted to get across it but it would take me I didn't know how long to build a bridge. Years passed and then one day, feeling like it, I got into my boat and rowed across. When I got to the other side, it was noon and my shadow was small and fell beneath me. I set out on a path that stretched out straight ahead. I passed a house, and a dog was sitting on the verandah, but it looked the other way when it saw me coming. I passed a boy tossing a ball in the air but the boy looked the other way when he saw me coming. I walked and I walked but I couldn't tell if I walked a long time because my feet didn't feel as if they would drop off. I turned around to see what I had left behind me but nothing was familiar. Instead of the straight path, I saw hills. Instead of the boy with his ball, I saw tall flowering trees. I looked up and the sky was without clouds and seemed near, as if it were the ceiling in my house and, if I stood on a chair, I could touch it with the tips of my fingers. I turned around and looked ahead of me

again. A deep hole had opened up before me. I looked in. The hole was deep and dark and I couldn't see the bottom. I thought, What's down there? so on purpose I fell in. I fell and I fell, over and over, as if I were an old suitcase. On the sides of the deep hole I could see things written, but perhaps it was in a foreign language because I couldn't read them. Still I fell, for I don't know how long. As I fell I began to see that I didn't like the way falling made me feel. Falling made me feel sick and I missed all the people I had loved. I said, "I don't want to fall anymore," and I reversed myself. I was standing again on the edge of the deep hole. I looked at the deep hole and I said, "You can close up now," and it did. I walked some more without knowing distance. I only knew that I passed through days and nights, I only knew that I passed through rain and shine, light and darkness. I was never thirsty and I felt no pain. Looking at the horizon, I made a joke for myself: I said, "The earth has thin lips," and I laughed.

Looking at the horizon again, I saw a lone figure coming toward me, but I wasn't frightened because I was sure it was my mother. As I got closer to the figure, I could see that it wasn't my mother, but still I wasn't frightened because I could see that it was a woman.

When this woman got closer to me, she looked at me hard and then she threw up her hands. She must have seen me somewhere before because she said, "It's you. Just look at that. It's you. And just what have you been doing lately?"

I could have said, "I have been praying not to grow any taller."

I could have said, "I have been listening carefully to my mother's words, so as to make a good imitation of a dutiful daughter."

I could have said, "A pack of dogs, tired from chasing each other all over town, slept in the moonlight."

Instead, I said, "What I have been doing

lately: I was lying in bed on my back, my hands drawn up, my fingers interlaced lightly at the nape of my neck. Someone rang the doorbell. I went downstairs and opened the door but there was no one there. I stepped outside. Either it was drizzling or there was a lot of dust in the air and the dust was damp. I stuck out my tongue and the drizzle or the damp dust tasted like government school ink. I looked north and I looked south. I started walking north. While walking north, I wanted to move fast, so I removed the shoes from my feet. While walking north, I looked up and saw the planet Venus, and I said, 'If the sun went out, it would be eight minutes before I would know it.' I saw a monkey sitting in a tree that had no leaves and I said, 'A monkey. Just look at that. A monkey. I picked up a stone and I threw it at the monkey.' The monkey, seeing the stone, quickly moved out of its way. Three times I threw a stone at the monkey and three times it moved away. The fourth time I threw the stone, the monkey caught it and threw it back at me. The stone struck me on my forehead over my right eye, making a deep gash. The gash healed immediately but now the skin on my forehead felt false to me. I walked for I don't know how long before I came to a big body of water. I wanted to get across, so when the boat came I paid my fare. When I got to the other side, I saw a lot of people sitting on the beach and they were having a picnic. They were the most beautiful people I had ever seen.

Everything about them was black and shiny. Their skin was black and shiny. Their shoes were black and shiny. Their hair was black and shiny. The clothes they wore were black and shiny. I could hear them laughing and chatting and I said, 'I would like to be with these people,' so I started to walk toward them; but when I got up close to them I saw that they weren't at a picnic and they weren't beautiful and they weren't chatting and laughing. All around me was black mud and the people all looked as if they had been made up out of the black mud. I looked up and saw that the sky seemed far away and nothing I could stand on would make me able to touch it with my fingertips. I thought, If only I could get out of this, so I started to walk. I must have walked for a long time because my feet hurt and felt as if they would drop off. I thought, If only just around the bend I would see my house and inside my house I would find my bed, freshly made at that, and in the kitchen I would find my mother or anyone else that I loved making me a custard. I thought, If only it was a Sunday and I was sitting in a church and I had just heard someone sing a psalm. I felt very sad so I sat down. I felt so sad that I rested my head on my own knees and smoothed my own head. I felt so sad I couldn't imagine feeling any other way again. I said, 'I don't like this. I don't want to do this anymore.' And I went back to lying in bed, just before the doorbell rang."

Thinking About the Story

A PERSONAL RESPONSE

sharing impressions

1. What are you left wondering about at the end of this story? Record your thoughts in your journal.

constructing interpretations

2. What is your understanding of the story's ending?
Think about
- what the narrator does not want to do anymore
- how she is able to return to bed
- who rings the doorbell

3. Speculate about the narrator of this story.
Think about
- her bizarre and surprising depiction of events
- her age, personality, and past experiences
- her relationship with her mother

4. How do you explain the differences in the narrator's two accounts of what she has been doing lately?
Think about
- whom she is speaking to as she gives each account
- the three answers she says she could have given, but did not give, to the question "And just what have you been doing lately?"
- whether she is describing the same journey in each account

A CREATIVE RESPONSE

5. How might the story continue?

A CRITICAL RESPONSE

6. What is the overall mood of the story? Explain.

7. Based on this story and others you have read in this unit, create a new definition of plot.
Think about
- the traditional definition of plot as a series of interrelated events that progress because of a conflict, or struggle between opposing forces
- the traditional structure of a plot, consisting of the exposition, rising action, climax, and falling action

8. Jamaica Kincaid immigrated to the United States from a tiny Caribbean island when she was seventeen. In what ways might her story reflect the experience of a new immigrant?

9. Do you find this story as inventive as others in **Transformations: Stories of the Fantastic?** Decide which story is based on the most intriguing idea.

Analyzing the Writer's Craft

STYLE: DICTION

What seems unusual about the narrator's manner of speaking?

Building a Literary Vocabulary. As you may remember, style refers to the particular way that a piece of literature is written. A significant component of style is diction, or a writer's choice of words. Diction encompasses both vocabulary (individual words) and syntax (the order or arrangement of words). Diction can be described in terms such as formal or informal, technical or common, abstract or concrete. In "What I Have Been Doing Lately" the narrator's diction is simple, even childish: "I ran downstairs. Quick. I opened the door. There was no one there." She uses short words and repeats certain constructions—"I looked," "I saw," "I walked." Contrast her diction with the more complex, formal diction of the narrator in "The Youngest Doll": "they lived surrounded by a past that was breaking up around them with the same impassive musicality with which the dining room chandelier crumbled on the frayed linen cloth of the dining room table."

Application: Analyzing Diction. Divide into groups of three or four. Write a short paragraph using diction characteristic of the narrator in "What I Have Been Doing Lately." Then write another paragraph using vocabulary and syntax that are uncharacteristic of the narrator. Exchange your paragraphs with those of another group and identify which paragraphs could have come from Kincaid's narrator. Defend your choice, pointing out specific qualities of the narrator's diction.

Connecting Reading and Writing

1. Drawing on your answer to question 5, write another **episode** in the same style and read it to classmates.

Option: Make your episode a **monologue** to be performed with appropriate props and gestures.

2. The structure of a work of literature is the way in which its parts are put together. Make a **graphic representation** of the structure of this story. The representation could be a diagram, a geometric shape, or some other figure. Explain how the story corresponds to your drawing.

Option: Analyze the story's structure in an **expository essay** for another student.

The Beautiful Stranger

SHIRLEY JACKSON

A biography of Jackson appears on page 422.

Approaching the Story

In *Life Among the Savages* and *Raising Demons,* humorous accounts of life with her four children, Shirley Jackson appears to be a lighthearted chronicler of family life. Jackson's light side, though, is matched by a dark side, a side that led her to explore family tensions and to expose the discontent underlying the prosperity of post-World War II America. Some of her best works are horror stories that involve psychological disturbance and supernatural happenings. In "The Beautiful Stranger" Jackson puts the reader into the mind of an ordinary woman—or maybe a not so ordinary woman—as she tries to make sense of the "strangeness" in her life.

 HAT MIGHT BE called the first intimation[1] of strangeness occurred at the railroad station. She had come with her children, Smalljohn and her baby girl, to meet her husband when he returned from a business trip to Boston. Because she had been oddly afraid of being late, and perhaps even seeming uneager to encounter her husband after a week's separation, she dressed the children and put them into the car at home a long half hour before the train was due. As a result, of course, they had to wait interminably at the station, and what was to have been a charmingly staged reunion, family embracing husband and father, became at last an ill-timed and awkward performance. Smalljohn's hair was mussed, and he was sticky. The baby was cross, pulling at her pink bonnet and her dainty lace-edged dress, whining. The final arrival of the train caught them in midmovement, as it were; Margaret was tying the ribbons on the baby's bonnet, Smalljohn was half over the back of the car seat. They scrambled out of the car, cringing from the sound of the train, hopelessly out of sorts.

John Senior waved from the high steps of the train. Unlike his wife and children, he looked utterly prepared for his return, as though he had taken some pains to secure a meeting at least painless, and had, in fact, stood just so, waving cordially from the steps of the train, for perhaps as long as half an hour, ensuring that he should not be caught half-ready, his hand not lifted so far as to overemphasize the extent of his delight in seeing them again.

---

1. intimation (in′ tə mā′ shən): hint; indirect suggestion.

His wife had an odd sense of lost time. Standing now on the platform with the baby in her arms and Smalljohn beside her, she could not for a minute remember clearly whether he was coming home, or whether they were yet standing here to say goodbye to him. They had been quarreling when he left, and she had spent the week of his absence determining to forget that in his presence she had been frightened and hurt. This will be a good time to get things straight, she had been telling herself; while John is gone I can try to get hold of myself again. Now, unsure at last whether this was an arrival or a departure, she felt afraid again, straining to meet an unendurable tension. This will not do, she thought, believing that she was being honest with herself, and as he came down the train steps and walked toward them she smiled, holding the baby tightly against her so that the touch of its small warmth might bring some genuine tenderness into her smile.

This will not do, she thought, and smiled more cordially and told him "hello" as he came to her. Wondering, she kissed him, and then when he held his arm around her and the baby for a minute, the baby pulled back and struggled, screaming. Everyone moved in anger, and the baby kicked and screamed, "No, no, no."

"What a way to say hello to Daddy," Margaret said, and she shook the baby, half-amused, and yet grateful for the baby's sympathetic support. John turned to Smalljohn and lifted him, Smalljohn kicking and laughing helplessly. "Daddy, Daddy," Smalljohn shouted, and the baby screamed, "No, no."

Helplessly, because no one could talk with the baby screaming so, they turned and went to the car. When the baby was back in her pink basket in the car, and Smalljohn was settled with another lollipop beside her, there was appalling quiet which would have to be filled as quickly as possible with meaningful words. John had taken the driver's seat in the car while Margaret was quieting the baby, and when Margaret got in beside him, she felt a little chill of animosity[2] at the sight of his hands on the wheel; I can't bear to relinquish even this much, she thought; for a week no one has driven the car except me. Because she could see so clearly that this was unreasonable—John owned half the car, after all—she said to him with bright interest, "And how was your trip? The weather?"

"Wonderful," he said, and again she was angered at the warmth in his tone; if she was unreasonable about the car, he was surely unreasonable to have enjoyed himself quite so much. "Everything went very well. I'm pretty sure I got the contract, everyone was very pleasant about it, and I go back in two weeks to settle everything."

The stinger is in the tail, she thought. He wouldn't tell it all so hastily if he didn't want me to miss half of it; I am supposed to be pleased that he got the contract and that everyone was so pleasant, and the part about going back is supposed to slip past me painlessly.

"Maybe I can go with you, then," she said. "Your mother will take the children."

"Fine," he said, but it was much too late; he had hesitated noticeably before he spoke.

"I want to go too," said Smalljohn. "Can I go with Daddy?"

They came into their house, Margaret carrying the baby, and John carrying his suitcase and arguing delightedly with Smalljohn over which of them was carrying the heavier weight of it. The house was ready for them; Margaret had made sure that it was cleaned and emptied of the qualities which attached so surely to her position of wife alone with small children; the toys which Smalljohn had thrown around with unusual freedom were picked up, the baby's clothes (no one, after all, came to call when John was gone) were taken from the kitchen radiator where they had been drying.

---

2. **animosity** (an′ ə mäs′ ə tē): ill will; hostility.

Aside from the fact that the house gave no impression of waiting for any particular people, but only for anyone well-bred and clean enough to fit within its small trim walls, it could have passed for a home, Margaret thought, even for a home where a happy family lived in domestic peace. She set the baby down in the playpen and turned with the baby's bonnet and jacket in her hand and saw her husband, head bent gravely as he listened to Smalljohn. Who? she wondered suddenly; is he taller? That is not my husband.

She laughed, and they turned to her, Smalljohn curious, and her husband with a quick bright recognition; she thought, why, it is *not* my husband, and he knows that I have seen it. There was no astonishment in her; she would have thought perhaps thirty seconds before that such a thing was impossible, but since it was now clearly possible, surprise would have been meaningless. Some other emotion was necessary, but she found at first only peripheral manifestations of one. Her heart was beating violently, her hands were shaking, and her fingers were cold. Her legs felt weak, and she took hold of the back of a chair to steady herself. She found that she was still laughing, and then her emotion caught up with her and she knew what it was: it was relief.

"I'm glad you came," she said. She went over and put her head against his shoulder. "It was hard to say hello in the station," she said.

Smalljohn looked on for a minute and then wandered off to his toy box. Margaret was thinking, this is not the man who enjoyed seeing me cry; I need not be afraid. She caught her breath and was quiet; there was nothing that needed saying.

For the rest of the day she was happy. There was a constant delight in the relief from her weight of fear and unhappiness, it was pure joy to know that there was no longer any residue of suspicion and hatred; when she called him "John" she did so demurely, knowing that he

participated in her secret amusement; when he answered her civilly, there was, she thought, an edge of laughter behind his words. They seemed to have agreed soberly that mention of the subject would be in bad taste, might even, in fact, endanger their pleasure.

They were hilarious at dinner. John would not have made her a cocktail, but when she came downstairs from putting the children to bed, the stranger met her at the foot of the stairs, smiling up at her, and took her arm to lead her into the living room where the cocktail shaker and glasses stood on the low table before the fire.

"How nice," she said, happy that she had taken a moment to brush her hair and put on fresh lipstick, happy that the coffee table which she had chosen with John and the fireplace which had seen many fires built by John and the low sofa where John had slept sometimes, had all seen fit to welcome the stranger with grace. She sat on the sofa and smiled at him when he handed her a glass; there was an odd <u>illicit</u>[3] excitement in all of it; she was "entertaining" a man. The scene was a little marred by the fact that he had given her a martini with neither olive nor onion; it was the way she preferred her martini, and yet he should not have, strictly, known this, but she reassured herself with the thought that naturally he would have taken some pains to inform himself before coming.

He lifted his glass to her with a smile; he is here only because I am here, she thought.

"It's nice to be here," he said. He had, then, made one attempt to sound like John, in the car coming home. After he knew that she had recognized him for a stranger, he had never made any attempt to say words like "coming home" or "getting back," and of course she could not, not without pointing her lie. She

---

3. illicit (il lis′ it): not allowed by law, custom, or rule; improper.

put her hand in his and lay back against the sofa, looking into the fire.

"Being lonely is worse than anything in the world," she said.

"You're not lonely now?"

"Are you going away?"

"Not unless you come too." They laughed at his parody of John.

They sat next to each other at dinner; she and John had always sat at formal opposite ends of the table, asking one another politely to pass the salt and the butter.

"I'm going to put in a little set of shelves over there," he said, nodding toward the corner of the dining room. "It looks empty here, and it needs things. Symbols."

"Like?" She liked to look at him; his hair, she thought, was a little darker than John's, and his hands were stronger; this man would build whatever he decided he wanted built.

"We need things together. Things we like, both of us. Small delicate pretty things. Ivory."

With John she would have felt it necessary to remark at once that they could not afford such delicate pretty things, and put a cold finish to the idea, but with the stranger she said, "We'd have to look for them; not everything would be right."

"I saw a little creature once," he said. "Like a tiny little man, only colored all purple and blue and gold."

She remembered this conversation; it contained the truth like a jewel set in the evening. Much later, she was to tell herself that it was true; John could not have said these things.

She was happy, she was radiant, she had no conscience. He went obediently to his office the next morning, saying goodbye at the door with a rueful smile that seemed to mock the present necessity for doing the things that John always did, and as she watched him go down the walk, she reflected that this was surely not going to be permanent; she could

not endure having him gone for so long every day, although she had felt little about parting from John; moreover, if he kept doing John's things, he might grow imperceptibly[4] more like John. We will simply have to go away, she thought. She was pleased, seeing him get into the car; she would gladly share with him—indeed, give him outright—all that had been John's, so long as he stayed her stranger.

She laughed while she did her housework and dressed the baby. She took satisfaction in unpacking his suitcase, which he had abandoned and forgotten in a corner of the bedroom, as though prepared to take it up and leave again if she had not been as he thought her, had not wanted him to stay. She put away his clothes, so disarmingly like John's, and wondered for a minute at the closet; would there be a kind of delicacy in him about John's things? Then she told herself no, not so long as he began with John's wife, and laughed again.

The baby was cross all day, but when Smalljohn came home from nursery school, his first question was—looking up eagerly—"Where is Daddy?"

"Daddy has gone to the office," and again she laughed, at the moment's quick sly picture of the insult to John.

Half a dozen times during the day she went upstairs, to look at his suitcase and touch the leather softly. She glanced constantly as she passed through the dining room into the corner where the small shelves would be someday, and told herself that they would find a tiny little man, all purple and blue and gold, to stand on the shelves and guard them from intrusion.

When the children awakened from their naps, she took them for a walk and then, away from the house and returned violently to her former lonely pattern (walk with the children, talk

---

4. **imperceptibly** (im′ pər sep′ tə blē): in a manner that is barely noticeable.

Portrait of Elaine de Kooning, c. 1940–1941, WILLEM DE KOONING.
Allan Stone Gallery, New York.

meaninglessly of Daddy, long for someone to talk to in the evening ahead, restrain herself from hurrying home: he might have telephoned), she began to feel frightened again; suppose she had been wrong? It could not be possible that she was mistaken; it would be unutterably cruel for John to come home tonight.

Then, she heard the car stop, and when she opened the door and looked up, she thought, no, it is not my husband, with a return of gladness. She was aware from his smile that he had perceived her doubts, and yet he was so clearly a stranger that, seeing him, she had no need of speaking.

She asked him, instead, almost meaningless questions during that evening, and his answers were important only because she was storing them away to reassure herself while he was away. She asked him what was the name of their Shakespeare professor in college, and who was that girl he liked so before he met Margaret. When he smiled and said that he had no idea, that he would not recognize the name if she told him, she was in delight. He had not bothered to master all of the past, then; he had learned enough (the names of the children, the location of the house, how she liked her cocktails) to get to her, and after that, it was not important, because either she would want him to stay, or she would, calling upon John, send him away again.

"What is your favorite food?" she asked him. "Are you fond of fishing? Did you ever have a dog?"

"Someone told me today," he said once, "that he had heard I was back from Boston, and I distinctly thought he said that he heard I was dead in Boston."

He was lonely, too, she thought with sadness, and that is why he came, bringing a destiny with him: now I will see him come every evening through the door and think, this is not my husband, and wait for him, remembering that I am waiting for a stranger.

"At any rate," she said, "*you* were not dead in Boston, and nothing else matters."

She saw him leave in the morning with a warm pride, and she did her housework and dressed the baby; when Smalljohn came home from nursery school, he did not ask, but looked with quick searching eyes and then sighed. While the children were taking their naps, she thought that she might take them to the park this afternoon, and then the thought of another such afternoon, another long afternoon with no one but the children, another afternoon of widowhood, was more than she could submit to; I have done this too much, she thought, I

must see something today beyond the faces of my children. No one should be so much alone.

Moving quickly, she dressed and set the house to rights. She called a high-school girl and asked if she would take the children to the park; without guilt, she neglected the thousand small orders regarding the proper jacket for the baby, whether Smalljohn might have popcorn, when to bring them home. She fled, thinking, I must be with people.

She took a taxi into town, because it seemed to her that the only possible thing to do was to seek out a gift for him, her first gift to him, and she thought she would find him, perhaps, a little creature all blue and purple and gold.

She wandered through the strange shops in the town, choosing small lovely things to stand on the new shelves, looking long and critically at ivories, at small statues, at brightly colored meaningless expensive toys, suitable for giving to a stranger.

It was almost dark when she started home, carrying her packages. She looked from the window of the taxi into the dark streets, and thought with pleasure that the stranger would be home before her, and look from the window to see her hurrying to him; he would think, this is a stranger, I am waiting for a stranger, as he saw her coming. "Here," she said, tapping on the glass, "right here, driver." She got out of the taxi and paid the driver, and smiled as he drove away. I must look well, she thought, the driver smiled back at me.

She turned and started for the house, and then hesitated; surely she had come too far? This is not possible, she thought, this cannot be; surely our house was white?

The evening was very dark, and she could see only the houses going in rows, with more rows beyond them and more rows beyond that, and somewhere a house which was hers, with the beautiful stranger inside, and she lost out here.

The Happy Man

NAGUIB MAHFOUZ

A biography of Mahfouz appears on page 424.

Approaching the Story

Imagine that you awake one morning to find that a magical change has occurred within you. Suddenly, you feel so incredibly happy that all worries and troubles have lost their power to affect you. The main character in the following story by Egyptian writer Naguib Mahfouz (nu gēb′ máh fōōz′) finds himself in this situation.

HE WOKE UP in the morning and discovered that he was happy. "What's this?" he asked himself. He could not think of any word which described his state of mind more accurately and precisely than *happy*. This was distinctly peculiar when compared with the state he was usually in when he woke up. He would be half-asleep from staying so late at the newspaper office. He would face life with a sense of strain and contemplation. Then he would get up, whetting his determination to face up to all inconveniences and withstand all difficulties.

Today he felt happy, full of happiness, as a matter of fact. There was no arguing about it. The symptoms were quite clear, and their vigor and obviousness were such as to impose themselves on his senses and mind all at once. Yes, indeed; he was happy. If this was not happiness, then what was? He felt that his limbs were well proportioned and functioning per-

fectly. They were working in superb harmony with each other and with the world around him. Inside him, he felt a boundless power, an imperishable energy, an ability to achieve anything with confidence, precision, and obvious success. His heart was overflowing with love for people, animals, and things and with an all-engulfing sense of optimism and joy. It was as if he were no longer troubled or bothered by fear, anxiety, sickness, death, argument, or the question of earning a living. Even more important than that, and something he could not analyze, it was a feeling which penetrated to every cell of his body and soul; it played a tune full of delight, pleasure, serenity, and peace and hummed in its incredible melodies the whispering sound of the world which is denied to the unhappy.

He felt drunk with ecstasy and savored[1] it slowly with a feeling of surprise. He asked him-

---

1. savored (sā′ vərd): dwelt upon with delight; relished.

The Happy Man 333

self where it had come from and how; the past provided no explanation, and the future could not justify it. Where did it come from, then, and how? How long would it last? Would it stay with him till breakfast? Would it give him enough time to get to the newspaper office? Just a minute though, he thought . . . it won't last because it can't. If it did, man would be turned into an angel or something even higher. So he told himself that he should devote his attention to savoring it, living with it, and storing up its nectar before it became a mere memory with no way of proving it or even being sure that it had ever existed.

He ate his breakfast with relish, and this time nothing distracted his attention while he was eating. He gave "Uncle" Bashir,[2] who was waiting on him, such a beaming smile that the poor man felt rather alarmed and taken aback. Usually he would only look in his direction to give orders or ask questions, although on most occasions he treated him fairly well.

"Tell me, Uncle Bashir," he asked the servant, "am I a happy man?"

The poor man was startled. He realized why his servant was confused; for the first time ever he was talking to him as a colleague or friend. He encouraged his servant to forget about his worries and asked him with unusual insistence to answer his question.

"Through God's grace and favor, you are happy," the servant replied.

"You mean, I should be happy. Anyone with my job, living in my house, and enjoying my health should be happy. That's what you want to say. But do you think I'm really happy?"

The servant replied, "You work too hard, Sir"; after yet more insistence, "It's more than any man can stand. . . ."

He hesitated, but his master gestured to him to continue with what he had to say.

"You get angry a lot," he said, "and have fierce arguments with your neighbors. . . ."

He interrupted him by laughing loudly.

"What about you," he asked, "don't you have any worries?"

"Of course, no man can be free of worry."

"You mean that complete happiness is an impossible quest?"

"That applies to life in general. . . ."

How could he have dreamed up this incredible happiness? He or any other human being? It was a strange, unique happiness, as though it were a private secret he had been given. In the meeting hall of the newspaper building, he spotted his main rival in this world sitting down thumbing through a magazine. The man heard his footsteps but did not look up from the magazine. He had undoubtedly noticed him in some way and was therefore pretending to ignore him so as to keep his own peace of mind. At some circulation meetings, they would argue so violently with each other that sparks would begin to fly and they would exchange bitter words. One stage more, and they would come to blows. A week ago, his rival had won in the union elections and he had lost. He had felt pierced by a sharp, poisoned arrow, and the world had darkened before his eyes. Now here he was approaching his rival's seat; the sight of him sitting there did not make him excited, nor did the memories of their dispute spoil his composure. He approached him with a pure and carefree heart, feeling drunk with his incredible happiness; his face showed an expression full of tolerance and forgiveness. It was as though he were approaching some other man toward whom he had never had any feelings of enmity,[3] or perhaps he might be renewing a friendship again. "Good morning!" he said without feeling any compunction.

The man looked up in amazement. He was silent for a few moments until he recovered,

---

2. **Bashir** (bū shēr').
3. **enmity** (en' mə tē): the hatred one feels toward an enemy.

and then returned the greeting curtly. It was as though he did not believe his eyes and ears.

He sat down alongside the man. "Marvelous weather today . . . ," he said.

"Okay . . . ," the other replied guardedly.

"Weather to fill your heart with happiness."

His rival looked at him closely and cautiously. "I'm glad that you're so happy . . . ," he muttered.

"Inconceivably happy . . . ," he replied with a laugh.

"I hope," the man continued in a rather hesitant tone of voice, "that I shan't spoil your happiness at the meeting of the administrative council. . . ."

"Not at all. My views are well known, but I don't mind if the members adopt your point of view. That won't spoil my happiness!"

"You've changed a great deal overnight," the man said with a smile.

"The fact is that I'm happy, inconceivably happy."

The man examined his face carefully. "I bet your dear son has changed his mind about staying in Canada?" he asked.

"Never, never, my friend," he replied, laughing loudly. "He is still sticking to his decision. . . ."

"But that was the principal reason for your being so sad. . . ."

"Quite true. I've often begged him to come back out of pity for me in my loneliness and to serve his country. But he told me that he's going to open an engineering office with a Canadian partner; in fact, he's invited me to join him in it. Let him live where he'll be happy. I'm quite happy here—as you can see, inconceivably happy. . . ."

The man still looked a little doubtful. "Quite extraordinarily brave!" he said.

"I don't know what it is, but I'm happy in the full meaning of the word."

Yes indeed, this was full happiness; full, firm, weighty, and vital. As deep as absolute

power, widespread as the wind, fierce as fire, bewitching as scent, transcending[4] nature. It could not possibly last.

The other man warmed to his display of affection. "The truth is," he said, "that I always picture you as someone with a fierce and violent temperament which causes him a good deal of trouble and leads him to trouble other people."

"Really?"

"You don't know how to make a truce, you've no concept of intermediate solutions. You work with your nerves, with the marrow in your bones. You fight bitterly, as though any problem is a matter of life and death!"

"Yes, that's true."

He accepted the criticism without any difficulty and with an open heart. His wave expanded into a boundless ocean of happiness. He struggled to control an innocent, happy laugh which the other man interpreted in a way far removed from its pure motives.

"So then," he asked, "you think it's necessary to be able to take a balanced view of events, do you?"

"Of course. I remember, by way of example, the argument we had the day before yesterday about racism. We both had the same views on the subject; it's something worth being zealous about, even to the point of anger. But what kind of anger? An intellectual anger, abstract to a certain extent; not the type which shatters your nerves, ruins your digestion, and gives you palpitations. Not so?"

"That's obvious; I quite understand. . . ." He struggled to control a second laugh and succeeded. His heart refused to renounce[5] one drop of its joy. Racism, Vietnam, Palestine, . . . no problem could assail that fortress of happi-

---

4. transcending (tran send' iŋ): going beyond the limits of.

5. renounce (ri nouns'): give up (a pursuit, practice, claim, or belief).

ness which was encircling his heart. When he remembered a problem, his heart guffawed. He was happy. It was a tyrannical happiness, despising all misery and laughing at any hardship; it wanted to laugh, dance, sing, and distribute its spirit of laughter, dancing, and singing among the various problems of the world.

He could not bear to stay in his office at the newspaper; he felt no desire to work at all. He hated the very idea of thinking about his daily business and completely failed to bring his mind down from its stronghold in the kingdom of happiness. How could he possibly write about a trolley bus falling into the Nile when he was so intoxicated by this frightening happiness? Yes, it really was frightening. How could it be anything else, when there was no reason for it at all, when it was so strong that it made him exhausted and paralyzed his will—apart from the fact that it had been with him for half a day without letting up in the slightest degree?

He left the pages of paper blank and started walking backwards and forwards across the room, laughing and cracking his fingers. . . .

He felt slightly worried; it did not penetrate deep enough to spoil his happiness but paused on the surface of his mind like an abstract idea. It occurred to him that he might recall the tragedies of his life so that he could test their effect on his happiness. Perhaps they would be able to bring back some idea of balance or security, at least until his happiness began to flag a little. For example, he remembered his wife's death in all its various aspects and details. What had happened? The event appeared to him as a series of movements without any meaning or effect, as though it had happened to some other woman, the wife of another man, in some distant historical age. In fact, it had a contagious effect which prompted a smile and then even provoked laughter. He could not stop himself laughing,

and there he was guffawing, ha . . . ha . . .ha!

The same thing happened when he remembered the first letter his son had sent him saying that he wanted to emigrate to Canada. The sound of his guffaws as he paraded the bloody tragedies of the world before him would have attracted the attention of the newspaper workers and passersby in the street had it not been for the thickness of the walls. He could do nothing to dislodge his happiness. Memories of unhappy times hit him like waves being thrown onto a sandy beach under the golden rays of the sun.

He excused himself from attending the administrative council and left the newspaper office without writing a word. After lunch, he lay down on his bed as usual but could not sleep. In fact, sleep seemed an impossibility to him. Nothing gave him any indication that it was coming, even slowly. He was in a place alight and gleaming, resounding with sleeplessness and joy. He had to calm down and relax, to quiet his senses and limbs, but how could he do it? He gave up trying to sleep and got up. He began to hum as he was walking around his house. If this keeps up, he told himself, I won't be able to sleep, just as I can't work or feel sad. It was almost time for him to go to the club, but he did not feel like meeting any friends. What was the point of exchanging views on public affairs and private worries? What would they think if they found him laughing at every major problem? What would they say? How would they picture things? How would they explain it? No, he did not need anyone, nor did he want to spend the evening talking. He should be by himself and go for a long walk to get rid of some of his excess vitality and think about his situation. What had happened to him? How was it that this incredible happiness had overwhelmed him? How long would he have to carry it on his shoulders? Would it keep depriving him of work, friends, sleep and peace of mind? Should he resign himself to it?

Should he abandon himself to the flood to play with him as the whim took it? Or should he look for a way out for himself through thought, action, or advice?

When he was called into the examination room in the clinic of his friend, the specialist in internal medicine, he felt a little alarmed. The doctor looked at him with a smile. "You don't look like someone who's complaining about being ill," he said.

"I haven't come to see you because I'm ill," he told the doctor in a hesitant tone of voice, "but because I'm happy!"

The doctor looked piercingly at him with a questioning air.

"Yes," he repeated to underline what he had said, "because I'm happy!"

There was a period of silence. On one side there was anxiety, and on the other, questioning and amazement.

"It's an incredible feeling which can't be defined in any other way, but it's very serious. . . ."

The doctor laughed. "I wish your illness was contagious," he said, prodding him jokingly.

"Don't treat it as a joke. It's very serious, as I told you. I'll describe it to you. . . ."

He told him all about his happiness from the time he had woken up in the morning till he had felt compelled to visit him.

"Haven't you been taking drugs, alcohol, or tranquilizers?"

"Absolutely nothing like that."

"Have you had some success in an important sphere of your life—work . . . love . . . money?"

"Nothing like that either. I've twice as much to worry about as I have to make me feel glad. . . ."

"Perhaps if you were patient for a while. . . ."

"I've been patient all day. I'm afraid I'll be spending the night wandering around. . . ."

The doctor gave him a precise, careful, and comprehensive examination and then shrugged his shoulders in despair. "You're a picture of health," he said.

"And so?"

"I could advise you to take a sleeping pill, but it would be better if you consulted a nerve specialist. . . ."

The examination was repeated in the nerve specialist's clinic with the selfsame precision, care, and comprehensiveness. "Your nerves are sound," the doctor told him. "They're in enviable condition!"

"Haven't you got a plausible explanation for my condition?" he asked hopefully.

"Consult a gland specialist!" the doctor replied, shaking his head.

The examination was conducted for a third time in the gland specialist's clinic with the same precision, care, and comprehensiveness. "I congratulate you!" the doctor told him. "Your glands are in good condition."

He laughed. He apologized for laughing, laughing as he did so. Laughter was his way of expressing his alarm and despair.

He left the clinic with the feeling that he was alone; alone in the hands of his tyrannical happiness with no helper, no guide, and no friend. Suddenly, he remembered the doctor's sign he sometimes saw from the window of his office in the newspaper building. It was true that he had no confidence in psychiatrists even though he had read about the significance of psychoanalysis. Apart from that, he knew that their tentacles were very long and they kept their patients tied in a sort of long association. He laughed as he remembered the method of cure through free association and the problems which it eventually uncovers. He was laughing as his feet carried him toward the psychiatrist's clinic, and imagined the doctor listening to his incredible complaints about feeling happy, when he was used to hearing people complain about hysteria, schizophrenia, anxiety, and so on.

"The truth is, Doctor, that I've come to see you because I'm happy!"

He looked at the doctor to see what effect his statement had had on him but noticed that he was keeping his composure. He felt ridiculous. "I'm inconceivably happy . . . ," he said in a tone of confidence.

He began to tell the doctor his story, but the latter stopped him with a gesture of his hand. "An overwhelming, incredible, debilitating[6] happiness?" he asked quietly.

He stared at him in amazement and was on the point of saying something, but the doctor spoke first. "A happiness which has made you stop working," he asked, "abandon your friends, and detest going to sleep? . . ."

"You're a miracle!" he shouted.

"Every time you get involved in some misfortune," the psychiatrist continued quietly, "you dissolve into laughter? . . ."

"Sir . . . are you familiar with the invisible?"

"No!" he said with a smile. "Nothing like that. But I get a similar case in my clinic at least once a week!"

"Is it an epidemic?" he asked.

"I didn't say that, and I wouldn't claim that it's been possible to analyze one case into its primary elements as yet."

"But is it a disease?"

"All the cases are still under treatment."

"But are you satisfied without any doubt that they aren't natural cases? . . ."

"That's a necessary assumption for the job; there's only . . ."

"Have you noticed any of them to be deranged in . . . ," he asked anxiously, pointing to his head.

"Absolutely not," the doctor replied convincingly. "I assure you that they're all intelligent in every sense of the word. . . ."

The doctor thought for a moment. "We should have two sessions a week, I think," he said.

"Very well . . . ," he replied in resignation.

"There's no sense in getting alarmed or feeling sad. . . ."

Alarmed, sad? He smiled, and his smile kept on getting broader. A laugh slipped out, and before long, he was dissolving into laughter. He was determined to control himself, but his resistance collapsed completely. He started guffawing loudly. . . .

---

6. debilitating (dē bil′ ə tāt′ iŋ): making weak or feeble.

TRANSFORMATIONS:
STORIES OF THE
FANTASTIC

Reviewing Concepts

REALISM AND FANTASY: A DELICATE BALANCE

making
connections

In most of the stories in this unit, the writer has combined elements of both realism and fantasy to create a work that engages the reader's interest. "The Night Face Up," for example, begins with a realistic setting and presents recognizable feelings and actions of the main character. The story gets increasingly bizarre, however, as the fantasy elements of the alternate setting, the war of the blossom, become more prominent. The relationship between realism and fantasy in the story might be illustrated in the following way:

The Night Face Up

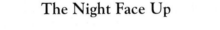

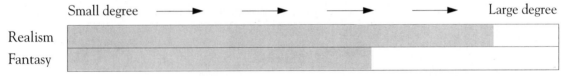

Think through the stories that you have read in this unit and identify those that employ both realism and fantasy. Create a graph for each of these selections.

describing
connections

With several classmates discuss your graphs, using specific examples from the selections to explain your representations of the relationships between realism and fantasy. Then choose three stories that best illustrate the blending of realism and fantasy. Write an **essay** for a teacher's guide in which you recommend the three stories to a teacher who wants to present this type of literature but has limited time.

Pegasus (detail), 1976, © LUBA KREJCI.
Czechoslovakia; knotting, linen, 59" x 47".
Courtesy of Jacques Baruch Gallery, Ltd.

Speculations:

Futuristic Stories

"The more extravagant a prediction sounds, the more likely it is to come true."

ROBERT A. HEINLEIN, b. 1907
American science fiction writer

Speculations: Futuristic Stories

Like fantasy writers, science fiction writers explore a universe of possibilities. Some science fiction writers, however, prefer to stay grounded in the issues or facts of today and to speculate about how the future may be shaped by those issues or facts. In the stories in this unit, for instance, some familiar aspects of the world today—pollution, war, computer technology—are projected into an imagined future so that the reader can consider possible consequences of current attitudes and actions. Through such connections, science fiction engages the reader's powers of reason as well as the reader's imagination.

Science fiction often challenges assumptions: What if children were raised by robots? What if clouds of pollution blotted out the sun? What if psychiatrists ruled the world? These are just some of the questions writers will ask you to consider in this unit. The answers that they give may be different from what you expect. So read these stories with an open mind and be ready to discuss the new ideas with your classmates and friends.

Literary Vocabulary

INTRODUCED IN THIS UNIT

Science Fiction. Science fiction is prose writing in which a writer, using known scientific data and theories as well as his or her creative imagination, presents new possibilities of the past or the future. Most science fiction comments on present-day society through these imaginative conceptions of a past or future society. All the stories in this unit may be classified as science fiction.

Experimental Fiction. Experimental fiction breaks with the conventions, or accepted rules, of traditional fiction. For example, an experimental work might have a beginning and an end but no middle. It might be a set of incomplete notes instead of a sustained narrative. The selection you will read titled "Vocational Counselling" is an example of experimental fiction.

REVIEWED IN THIS UNIT

Style   **Mood**   **Theme**   **Imagery**   **Irony**   **Satire**   **Tone**

I Sing the Body Electric!

RAY BRADBURY

A biography of Bradbury appears on page 420.

Approaching the Story

Like many of Ray Bradbury's science fiction and fantasy stories, this one takes place in a technologically advanced future. In other respects, however, the world depicted is the familiar one of the present. This is a story about a family and a machine—and a vision of how the two could interact.

Building Vocabulary

These essential words are footnoted within the story.

humanoid (hyōō′ mə noid′): "'We have perfected the first **humanoid**-genre mini-circuited, rechargeable AC-DC Mark Five Electrical Grandmother.'" (page 346)

embodiment (em bäd′ i mənt), **facsimile** (fak sim′ ə lē): "'This **embodiment** in electrointelligent **facsimile** of the humanities, will listen, know, tell, react, and love your children.'" (pages 346–347)

hieroglyphs (hī′ ər ō glifs′): "Real **hieroglyphs!** Run your fingers over them!" (page 351)

skepticism (skep′ ti siz′ əm), **cynicism** (sin′ ə siz′ əm): "Mankind is disillusioned and adopts indifferent **skepticism** or, worse, motionless **cynicism**." (page 361)

Connecting Writing and Reading

What is your idea of the perfect grandmother? In your journal create a chart that lists the skills and qualities possessed by this ideal grandmother. As you read, see whether the grandmother in the story exemplifies the same characteristics as your ideal.

Skills	Qualities

RANDMA!

I remember her birth.

Wait, you say, *no* man remembers his own grandma's birth.

But, yes, *we* remember the day that she was born.

For we, her grandchildren, slapped her to life. Timothy, Agatha, and I, Tom, raised up our hands and brought them down in a huge crack! We shook together the bits and pieces, parts and samples, textures and tastes, humors and distillations that would move her compass needle north to cool us, south to warm and comfort us, east and west to travel round the endless world, glide her eyes to know us, mouth to sing us asleep by night, hands to touch us awake at dawn.

Grandma, O dear and wondrous electric dream . . .

When storm lightnings rove the sky making circuitries amidst the clouds, her name flashes on my inner lid. Sometimes still I hear her ticking, humming above our beds in the gentle dark. She passes like a clock-ghost in the long halls of memory, like a hive of intellectual bees swarming after the Spirit of Summers Lost. Sometimes still I feel the smile I learned from her, printed on my cheek at three in the deep morn . . .

All right, all right! you cry. What was it like the day your damned and wondrous-dreadful-loving Grandma was born?

It was the week the world ended. . . .

Our mother was dead.

One late afternoon a black car left Father and the three of us stranded on our own front drive staring at the grass, thinking:

That's not our grass. There are the croquet mallets, balls, hoops, yes, just as they fell and lay three days ago when Dad stumbled out on the lawn, weeping with the news. There are the roller skates that belonged to a boy, me, who will never be that young again. And yes, there the tire swing on the old oak, but Agatha afraid to swing. It would surely break. It would fall.

And the house? Oh, God . . .

We peered through the front door, afraid of the echoes we might find confused in the halls; the sort of clamor that happens when all the furniture is taken out and there is nothing to soften the river of talk that flows in any house at all hours. And now the soft, the warm, the main piece of lovely furniture was gone forever.

The door drifted wide.

Silence came out. Somewhere a cellar door stood wide and a raw wind blew damp earth from under the house.

But, I thought, we don't *have* a cellar!

"Well," said Father.

We did not move.

Aunt Clara drove up the path in her big canary-colored limousine.

We jumped through the door. We ran to our rooms.

We heard them shout and then speak and then shout and then speak: Let the children live with me! Aunt Clara said. They'd rather kill themselves! Father said.

A door slammed. Aunt Clara was gone.

We almost danced. Then we remembered what had happened and went downstairs.

Father sat alone talking to himself or to a remnant ghost of Mother left from the days before her illness, and jarred loose now by the slamming of the door. He murmured to his hands, his empty palms:

"The children need someone. I love them but, let's face it, I must work to feed us all. You love them, Ann, but you're gone. And Clara? Impossible. She loves but smothers. And as for maids, nurses—?"

Here Father sighed and we sighed with him, remembering.

The luck we had had with maids or live-in teachers or sitters was beyond intolerable. Hardly a one who wasn't a crosscut saw grabbing against the grain. Hand axes and hurricanes best described them. Or, conversely, they were all fallen trifle, damp soufflé. We children were unseen furniture to be sat upon or dusted or sent for reupholstering come spring and fall, with a yearly cleansing at the beach.

"What we need," said Father, "is a . . ."

We all leaned to his whisper.

". . . grandmother."

"But," said Timothy, with the logic of nine years, "all our grandmothers are dead."

"Yes in one way, no in another."

What a fine, mysterious thing for Dad to say.

"Here," he said at last.

He handed us a multifold, multicolored pamphlet. We had seen it in his hands, off and on, for many weeks, and very often during the last few days. Now, with one blink of our eyes, as we passed the paper from hand to hand, we knew why Aunt Clara, insulted, outraged, had stormed from the house.

Timothy was the first to read aloud from what he saw on the first page:

"'I Sing the Body Electric!'"[1]

He glanced up at Father, squinting. "What the heck does that mean?"

"Read on."

Agatha and I glanced guiltily about the room, afraid Mother might suddenly come in to find us with this blasphemy, but then nodded to Timothy, who read:

"'Fanto—'"

"Fantoccini," Father prompted.

"'Fantoccini Limited. *We Shadow Forth* . . . the answer to all your most grievous problems. One Model Only, upon which a thousand times a thousand variations can be added, subtracted, subdivided, indivisible, with Liberty and Justice for all.'"

"Where does it say *that?*" we all cried.

"It doesn't." Timothy smiled for the first time in days. "I just had to put that in. Wait." He read on: "'For you who have worried over inattentive sitters, nurses who cannot be trusted with marked liquor bottles, and well-meaning Uncles and Aunts—'"

"Well-meaning, *but!*" said Agatha, and I gave an echo.

"'—we have perfected the first humanoid-[2] genre mini-circuited, rechargeable AC-DC Mark Five Electrical Grandmother . . .'"

"Grandmother!?"

The paper slipped away to the floor. "Dad . . . ?"

"Don't look at me that way," said Father. "I'm half mad with grief, and half mad thinking of tomorrow and the day after that. Someone pick up the paper. Finish it."

"I will," I said, and did:

"'The Toy that is more than a Toy, the Fantoccini Electrical Grandmother is built with loving precision to give the incredible precision of love to your children. The child at ease with the realities of the world and the even greater realities of the imagination, is her aim.

"'She is computerized to tutor in twelve languages simultaneously, capable of switching tongues in a thousandth of a second without pause, and has a complete knowledge of the religious, artistic, and sociopolitical histories of the world seeded in her master hive—'"

"How great!" said Timothy. "It makes it sound as if we were to keep bees! *Educated* bees!"

"Shut up!" said Agatha.

"'Above all,'" I read, "'this human being, for human she seems, this embodiment[3] in

---

1. **"I Sing the Body Electric":** the title of a poem by Walt Whitman.

2. **humanoid** (hy$\overline{oo}$′ mə noid′): a nearly human creature, such as a robot that resembles a human being.

3. **embodiment** (em bäd′ i mənt): the form in which something is made visible, tangible, or definite.

electrointelligent facsimile[4] of the humanities, will listen, know, tell, react, and love your children insofar as such great Objects, such fantastic Toys, can be said to Love, or can be imagined to Care. This Miraculous Companion, excited to the challenge of large world and small, Inner Sea or Outer Universe, will transmit by touch and tell, said Miracles to your Needy.'"

"Our Needy," murmured Agatha.

Why, we all thought, sadly, that's us, oh, yes, that's *us*.

I finished:

"'We do not sell our Creation to able-bodied families where parents are available to raise, effect, shape, change, love their own children. Nothing can replace the parent in the home. However there are families where death or ill health or disablement undermines the welfare of the children. Orphanages seem not the answer. Nurses tend to be selfish, neglectful, or suffering from dire nervous afflictions.

"'With the utmost humility then, and recognizing the need to rebuild, rethink, and regrow our conceptualizations from month to month, year to year, we offer the nearest thing to the Ideal Teacher-Friend-Companion-Blood Relation. A trial period can be arranged for—'"

"Stop," said Father. "Don't go on. Even *I* can't stand it."

"Why?" said Timothy. "I was just getting interested."

I folded the pamphlet up. "Do they *really* have these things?"

"Let's not talk any more about it," said Father, his hand over his eyes. "It was a mad thought—"

"Not so mad," I said, glancing at Tim. "I mean, heck, even if they tried, whatever they built, couldn't be worse than Aunt Clara, huh?"

And then we all roared. We hadn't laughed in months. And now my simple words made everyone hoot and howl and explode. I opened my mouth and yelled happily, too.

When we stopped laughing, we looked at the pamphlet and I said, "Well?"

"I—" Agatha scowled, not ready.

"We do need something, bad, right now," said Timothy.

"I have an open mind," I said, in my best pontifical style.

"There's only one thing," said Agatha. "We can try it. Sure.

"But—tell me this—when do we cut out all this talk and when does our *real* mother come home to stay?"

There was a single gasp from the family as if, with one shot, she had struck us all in the heart.

I don't think any of us stopped crying the rest of that night.

It was a clear, bright day. The helicopter tossed us lightly up and over and down through the skyscrapers and let us out, almost for a trot and caper, on top of the building where the large letters could be read from the sky:

FANTOCCINI.

"What are 'Fantoccini'?" said Agatha.

"It's an Italian word for shadow puppets, I think, or dream people," said Father.

"But 'shadow forth,' what does that mean?"

"We try to guess your dream," I said.

"Bravo," said Father. "A-plus."

I beamed.

The helicopter flapped a lot of loud shadows over us and went away.

We sank down in an elevator as our stomachs sank up. We stepped out onto a moving carpet that streamed away on a blue river of wool toward a desk over which various signs hung:

---

4. **facsimile** (fak sim′ ə lē): an exact reproduction or copy.

THE CLOCK SHOP
FANTOCCINI OUR SPECIALTY
RABBITS ON WALLS, NO PROBLEM

"Rabbits on walls?"

I held up my fingers in profiles as if I held them before a candle flame, and wiggled the "ears."

"Here's a rabbit, here's a wolf, here's a crocodile."

"Of course," said Agatha.

And we were at the desk. Quiet music drifted about us. Somewhere behind the walls, there was a waterfall of machinery flowing softly. As we arrived at the desk, the lighting changed to make us look warmer, happier, though we were still cold.

All about us in niches and cases, and hung from ceilings on wires and strings, were puppets and marionettes, and Balinese kite-bamboo-translucent dolls, which, held to the moonlight, might acrobat your most secret nightmares or dreams. In passing, the breeze set up by our bodies stirred the various hung souls on their gibbets. It was like an immense lynching on a holiday at some English crossroads four hundred years before.

You see? I know my history.

Agatha blinked about with disbelief and then some touch of awe and finally disgust.

"Well, if that's what they are, let's go."

"Tush," said Father.

"Well," she protested, "you gave me one of those dumb things with strings two years ago and the strings were in a zillion knots by dinner time. I threw the whole thing out the window."

"Patience," said Father.

"We shall see what we can do to eliminate the strings."

The man behind the desk had spoken.

We all turned to give him our regard.

Rather like a funeral-parlor man, he had the cleverness not to smile. Children are put off by older people who smile too much. They smell a catch, right off.

Unsmiling, but not gloomy or pontifical, the man said, "Guido Fantoccini, at your service. Here's how we do it, Miss Agatha Simmons, aged eleven."

Now, there was a really fine touch.

He knew that Agatha was only ten. Add a year to that, and you're halfway home. Agatha grew an inch. The man went on:

"There."

And he placed a golden key in Agatha's hand.

"To wind them up instead of strings?"

"To wind them up." The man nodded.

"Pshaw!" said Agatha.

Which was her polite form of "Rabbit pellets!"

"God's truth. Here is the key to your Do-It-Yourself, Select-Only-the-Best, Electrical Grandmother. Every morning you wind her up. Every night you let her run down. You're in charge. You are guardian of the Key."

He pressed the object in her palm, where she looked at it suspiciously.

I watched him. He gave me a side wink, which said, Well, no . . . but aren't keys fun?

I winked back before she lifted her head.

"Where does this fit?"

"You'll see when the time comes. In the middle of her stomach, perhaps, or up her left nostril or in her right ear."

That was good for a smile as the man arose.

"This way, please. Step light. Onto the moving stream. Walk on the water, please. Yes. There."

He helped to float us. We stepped from rug that was forever frozen onto rug that whispered by.

It was a most agreeable river, which floated us along on a green spread of carpeting that rolled forever through halls and into wonderfully secret dim caverns where voices echoed back our own breathing or sang like oracles to our questions.

"Listen," said the salesman, "the voices of all kinds of women. Weigh and find just the right one . . . !"

And listen we did, to all the high, low, soft, loud, in-between, half-scolding, half-affectionate voices saved over from times before we were born.

And behind us, Agatha trod backward, always fighting the river, never catching up, never with us, holding off.

"Speak," said the salesman. "Yell."

And speak and yell we did.

"Hello. You there! This is Timothy, hi!"

"What shall I say!" I shouted. "Help!"

Agatha walked backward, mouth tight.

Father took her hand. She cried out.

"Let go! No, no! I won't have my voice used! I won't!"

"Excellent." The salesman touched three dials on a small machine he held in his hand.

On the side of the small machine, we saw three oscillograph patterns mix, blend, and repeat our cries.

The salesman touched another dial, and we heard our voices fly off amidst the Delphic[5] caves to hang upside down, to cluster, to beat words all about, to shriek, and the salesman itched another knob to add, perhaps, a touch of this or a pinch of that, a breath of Mother's voice, all unbeknownst, or a splice of Father's outrage at the morning's paper or his peaceable one-drink voice at dusk. Whatever it was the salesman did, whispers danced all about us like frantic vinegar gnats, fizzed by lightning, settling round until at last a final switch was pushed and a voice spoke free of a far electronic deep:

"Nefertiti," it said.

Timothy froze. I froze. Agatha stopped treading water.

"Nefertiti?" asked Tim.

"What does that mean?" demanded Agatha.

"I know."

The salesman nodded me to tell.

"Nefertiti," I whispered, "is Egyptian for The Beautiful One Is Here."

"The Beautiful One Is Here," repeated Timothy.

"Nefer," said Agatha, "titi."

And we all turned to stare into that soft twilight, that deep far place from which the good warm soft voice came.

And she was indeed there.

And, by her voice, she was beautiful. . . .

That was it.

That was, at least, the most of it.

The voice seemed more important than all the rest.

Not that we didn't argue about weights and measures:

She should not be bony to cut us to the quick, nor so fat we might sink out of sight when she squeezed us.

Her hand pressed to ours, or brushing our brow in the middle of sick-fever nights, must not be marble-cold, dreadful, or oven-hot, oppressive, but somewhere between. The nice temperature of a baby chick held in the hand after a long night's sleep and just plucked from beneath a contemplative hen; that, that was it.

Oh, we were great ones for detail. We fought and argued and cried, and Timothy won on the color of her eyes, for reasons to be known later.

Grandmother's hair? Agatha, with girls' ideas, though reluctantly given, she was in charge of that. We let her choose from a thousand harp strands hung in filamentary tapestries like varieties of rain we ran amongst. Agatha did not run happily, but seeing we boys would mess things in tangles, she told us to move aside.

And so the bargain shopping through the dime-store inventories and the Tiffany extensions of the Ben Franklin Electric Storm

---

5. **Delphic:** relating to the oracle of the ancient Greek god Apollo at Delphi.

Machine and Fantoccini Pantomime Company was done.

And the always flowing river ran its tide to an end and deposited us all on a far shore in the late day. . . .

It was very clever of the Fantoccini people, after that.

How?

They made us wait.

They knew we were not won over. Not completely, no, nor half completely.

Especially Agatha, who turned her face to her wall and saw sorrow there and put her hand out again and again to touch it. We found her fingernail marks on the wallpaper each morning, in strange little silhouettes, half beauty, half nightmare. Some could be erased with a breath, like ice flowers on a winter pane. Some could not be rubbed out with a washcloth, no matter how hard you tried.

And meanwhile, they made us wait.

So we fretted out June.

So we sat around July.

So we groused through August and then on August 29, "I have this feeling," said Timothy, and we went out after breakfast to sit on the lawn.

Perhaps we had smelled something in Father's conversation the previous night, or caught some special furtive glance at the sky or the freeway trapped briefly and then lost in his gaze. Or perhaps it was merely the way the wind blew the ghost curtains out over our beds, making pale messages all night.

For suddenly there we were in the middle of the grass, Timothy and I, with Agatha, pretending no curiosity, up on the porch, hidden behind the potted geraniums.

We gave her no notice. We knew that if we acknowledged her presence, she would flee, so we sat and watched the sky where nothing moved but birds and high-flown jets, and watched the freeway where a thousand cars

might suddenly deliver forth our Special Gift . . . but . . . nothing.

At noon we chewed grass and lay low. . . .

At one o'clock, Timothy blinked his eyes.

And then, with incredible precision, it happened.

It was as if the Fantoccini people knew our surface tension.[6]

All children are water striders. We skate along the top skin of the pond each day, always threatening to break through, sink, vanish beyond recall, into ourselves.

Well, as if knowing our long wait must absolutely end within one minute! this *second*! no more, God, forget it!

At that instant, I repeat, the clouds above our house opened wide and let forth a helicopter like Apollo[7] driving his chariot across mythological skies.

And the Apollo machine swam down on its own summer breeze, wafting hot winds to cool, reweaving our hair, smartening our eyebrows, applauding our pant legs against our shins, making a flag of Agatha's hair on the porch, and, thus settled like a vast, frenzied hibiscus on our lawn, the helicopter slid wide a bottom drawer and deposited upon the grass a parcel of largish size, no sooner having laid same than the vehicle, with not so much as a God bless or farewell, sank straight up, disturbed the calm air with a mad ten thousand flourishes and then, like a sky-borne dervish, tilted and fell off to be mad some other place.

Timothy and I stood riven for a long moment looking at the packing case, and then we saw the crowbar taped to the top of the raw

---

6. **surface tension:** a property of liquids whereby the surface of a liquid acts like an extremely thin membrane.

7. **Apollo:** the greek God of the sun, music, poetry, prophecy, and healing. According to Greek myth, Apollo rides a fiery chariot—the sun—across the sky each day.

pine lid and seized it and began to pry and creak and squeal the boards off, one by one, and as we did this I saw Agatha sneak up to watch and I thought, Thank you, God, thank you that Agatha never saw a coffin, when Mother went away, no box, no cemetery, no earth, just words in a big church, no box, no box like *this* . . . !

The last pine plank fell away.

Timothy and I gasped. Agatha, between us now, gasped, too.

For inside the immense raw pine package was the most beautiful idea anyone ever dreamt and built.

Inside was the perfect gift for any child from seven to seventy-seven.

We stopped our breaths. We let them out in cries of delight and adoration.

Inside the opened box was . . .

A mummy.

Or, first anyway, a mummy case, a sarcophagus!

"Oh, no!" Happy tears filled Timothy's eyes.

"It can't be!" said Agatha.

"It is, it is!"

"Our very own?"

"Ours!"

"It must be a mistake!"

"Sure, they'll want it back!"

"They can't *have* it!"

"Lord, Lord, is that real gold!? Real hieroglyphs!8 Run your fingers over them!"

"Let *me*!"

"Just like in the museums! Museums!"

We all gabbled at once. I think some tears fell from my own eyes to rain upon the case.

"Oh, they'll make the colors run!"

Agatha wiped the rain away.

And the golden mask-face of the woman carved on the sarcophagus lid looked back at us with just the merest smile, which hinted at our own joy, which accepted the overwhelming upsurge of a love we thought had drowned forever but now surfaced into the sun.

Not only did she have a sun-metal face stamped and beaten out of purest gold, with delicate nostrils and a mouth that was both firm and gentle, but her eyes, fixed into their sockets, were cerulean or amethystine or lapis lazuli,9 or all three, minted and fused together, and her body was covered over with lions and eyes and ravens, and her hands were crossed upon her carved bosom, and in one gold mitten she clenched a thonged whip for obedience, and in the other a fantastic ranunculus,10 which makes for obedience out of love, so the whip lies unused. . . .

And as our eyes ran down her hieroglyphs it came to all three of us at the same instant:

"Why, those signs!" "Yes, the hen tracks!" "The birds, the snakes!"

They didn't speak tales of the Past.

They were hieroglyphs of the Future.

This was the first queen mummy delivered forth in all time whose papyrus inkings etched out the next month, the next season, the next year, the next *lifetime*!

She did not mourn for time spent.

No. She celebrated the bright coinage yet to come, banked, waiting, ready to be drawn upon and used.

We sank to our knees to worship that possible time.

First one hand, then another, probed out to niggle, twitch, touch, itch over the signs.

"There's me, yes, look! Me, in sixth grade!" said Agatha, now in the fifth. "See the girl with my-colored hair and wearing my gingerbread suit?"

---

8. hieroglyphs (hī′ ər ō glifs′): characters in a form of writing, used by the ancient Egyptians and others, in which pictures stand for words and sounds.

9. cerulean (sə rōō′ lē ən) . . . **amethystine** (am′ i this′ tin) . . . **lapis lazuli** (lap′ is laz′ yōō lī′): respectively sky-blue, purple or violet, and azure.

10. ranunculus (rə nuŋ′ kyōō ləs): a plant of the buttercup family.

"There's me in the twelfth year of high school!" said Timothy, so very young now but building taller stilts every week and stalking around the yard.

"There's me," I said, quietly, warm, "in college. The guy wearing glasses who runs a little to fat. Sure. Heck." I snorted. "That's me."

The sarcophagus spelled winters ahead, springs to squander, autumns to spend with all the golden and rusty and copper leaves like coins, and over all, her bright sun symbol, daughter-of-Ra[11] eternal face, forever above our horizon, forever an illumination to tilt our shadows to better ends.

"Hey!" we all said at once, having read and reread our Fortune-Told scribblings, seeing our lifelines and lovelines, inadmissible, serpentined over, around, and down. "Hey!"

And in one séance table-lifting feat, not telling each other what to do, just doing it, we pried up the bright sarcophagus lid, which had no hinges but lifted out like cup from cup, and put the lid aside.

And within the sarcophagus, of course, was the true mummy!

And she was like the image carved on the lid, but more so, more beautiful, more touching because human-shaped, and shrouded all in new, fresh bandages of linen, round and round, instead of old and dusty cerements.

And upon her hidden face was an identical golden mask, younger than the first, but somehow, strangely wiser than the first.

And the linens that tethered her limbs had symbols on them of three sorts, one a girl of ten, one a boy of nine, one a boy of thirteen.

A series of bandages for each of us!

We gave each other a startled glance and a sudden bark of laughter.

Nobody said the bad joke, but all thought: She's all wrapped up in us!

And we didn't care. We loved the joke. We loved whoever had thought to make us part of the ceremony we now went through as each of us seized and began to unwind each of his or her particular serpentines of delicious stuffs!

The lawn was soon a mountain of linen.

The woman beneath the covering lay there, waiting.

"Oh, no," cried Agatha. "She's dead, too!"

She ran. I stopped her. "Idiot. She's not dead *or* alive. Where's your key?"

"Key?"

"Dummy," said Tim, "the key the man gave you to wind her up!"

Her hand had already spidered along her blouse to where the symbol of some possible new religion hung. She had strung it there, against her own skeptic's muttering, and now she held it in her sweaty palm.

"Go on," said Timothy. "Put it in!"

"But *where?*"

"Oh, for God's sake! As the man said, in her right armpit or left ear. Gimme!"

And he grabbed the key and, impulsively moaning with impatience and not able to find the proper insertion slot, prowled over the prone figure's head and bosom and at last, on pure instinct, perhaps for a lark, perhaps just giving up the whole damned mess, thrust the key through a final shroud of bandage at the navel.

On the instant: *spunnng!*

The Electrical Grandmother's eyes flicked wide!

Something began to hum and whir. It was as if Tim had stirred up a hive of hornets with an ornery stick.

"Oh," gasped Agatha, seeing he had taken the game away, "let *me!*"

She wrenched the key.

Grandma's nostrils *flared!* She might snort up steam, snuff out fire!

"Me!" I cried, and grabbed the key and gave it a huge . . . *twist!*

The beautiful woman's mouth popped wide.

---

11. **Ra** (rä): the sun god of the ancient Egyptians.

"Me!"

"Me!"

"Me!"

Grandma suddenly sat up.

We leapt back.

We knew we had, in a way, slapped her alive.

She was born, she was *born*!

Her head swiveled all about. She gaped. She mouthed. And the first thing she said was:

Laughter.

Where one moment we had backed off, now the mad sound drew us near to peer, as in a pit where crazy folk are kept with snakes to make them well.

It was a good laugh, full and rich and hearty, and it did not mock, it accepted. It said the world was a wild place, strange, unbelievable, absurd if you wished, but all in all, quite a place. She would not dream to find another. She would not ask to go back to sleep.

She was awake now. We had awakened her. With a glad shout, she would go with it all.

And go she did, out of her sarcophagus, out of her winding sheet, stepping forth, brushing off, looking around as for a mirror. She found it.

The reflections in our eyes.

She was more pleased than disconcerted with what she found there. Her laughter faded to an amused smile.

For Agatha, at the instant of birth, had leapt to hide on the porch.

The Electrical Person pretended not to notice.

She turned slowly on the green lawn near the shady street, gazing all about with new eyes, her nostrils moving as if she breathed the actual air and this the first morn of the lovely Garden and she with no intention of spoiling the game by biting the apple. . . .

Her gaze fixed upon my brother.

"You must be—?"

"Timothy, Tim," he offered.

"And you must be—?"

"Tom," I said.

How clever again of the Fantoccini Company. *They* knew. *She* knew. But they had taught her to pretend not to know. That way we could feel great, we were the teachers, telling her what she already knew! How sly, how wise.

"And isn't there another boy?" said the woman.

"Girl!" a disgusted voice cried from somewhere on the porch.

"Whose name is Alicia—?"

"Agatha!" The far voice, started in humiliation, ended in proper anger.

"Algernon, of course."

"Agatha!" Our sister popped up, popped back to hide a flushed face.

"Agatha." The woman touched the word with proper affection. "Well, Agatha, Timothy, Thomas, let me *look* at you."

"No," said I, said Tim. "Let us look at *you*. Hey . . ."

Our voices slid back in our throats.

We drew near her.

We walked in great, slow circles round about, skirting the edges of her territory. And her territory extended as far as we could hear the hum of the warm summer hive. For that is exactly what she sounded like. That was her characteristic tune. She made a sound like a season all to herself, a morning early in June when the world wakes to find everything absolutely perfect, fine, delicately attuned, all in balance, nothing disproportioned. Even before you opened your eyes you knew it would be one of those days. Tell the sky what color it must be, and it was indeed. Tell the sun how to crochet its way, pick and choose among leaves to lay out carpetings of bright and dark on the fresh lawn, and pick and lay it did. The bees have been up earliest of all, they have already come and gone, and come and gone again to the meadow fields and returned all golden fuzz on the air, all pollen-decorated, epaulettes at the full, nectar-dripping. Don't you hear them pass? hover? dance their language? telling where all the sweet gums are, the syrups that make bears frolic and lumber in bulked ecstasies, that make boys squirm with unpronounced juices, that make girls leap out of beds to catch from the corners of their eyes their dolphin selves naked aflash on the warm air poised forever in one eternal glass wave.

So it seemed with our electrical friend here on the new lawn in the middle of a special day.

And she a stuff to which we were drawn, lured, spelled, doing our dance, remembering what could not be remembered, needful, aware of her attentions.

Timothy and I, Tom, that is.

Agatha remained on the porch.

But her head flowered above the rail, her eyes followed all that was done and said.

And what was said and done was Tim at last exhaling:

"Hey . . . your *eyes* . . ."

Her eyes. Her splendid eyes.

Even more splendid than the lapis lazuli on the sarcophagus lid and on the mask that had covered her bandaged face. These most beautiful eyes in the world looked out upon us calmly, shining.

"Your eyes," gasped Tim, "are the *exact* same color, are like—"

"Like what?"

"My favorite aggies[12] . . ."

"What could be better than that?" she said.

And the answer was, nothing.

Her eyes slid along on the bright air to brush my ears, my nose, my chin. "And you, Master Tom?"

"Me?"

"How shall we be friends? We must, you know, if we're going to knock elbows about the house the next year. . . ."

"I . . . ," I said, and stopped.

"You," said Grandma, "are a dog mad to

bark but with taffy in his teeth. Have you ever given a dog taffy? It's so sad and funny, both. You laugh but hate yourself for laughing. You cry and run to help, and laugh again when his first new bark comes out."

I barked a small laugh, remembering a dog, a day, and some taffy.

Grandma turned, and there was my old kite strewn on the lawn. She recognized its problem.

"The string's broken. No. The ball of string's *lost*. You can't fly a kite that way. Here."

She bent. We didn't know what might happen. How could a robot Grandma fly a kite for us? She raised up, the kite in her hands.

"Fly," she said, as to a bird.

And the kite flew.

That is to say, with a grand flourish, she let it up on the wind.

And she and kite were one.

For from the tip of her index finger there sprang a thin, bright strand of spider web, all half-invisible gossamer fishline, which, fixed to the kite, let it soar a hundred, no, three hundred, no, a thousand feet high on the summer swoons.

Timothy shouted. Agatha, torn between coming and going, let out a cry from the porch. And I, in all my maturity of thirteen years, though I tried not to look impressed, grew taller, taller, and felt a similar cry burst out my lungs, and burst it did. I gabbled and yelled lots of things about how I wished *I* had a finger from which, on a bobbin, I might thread the sky, the clouds, a wild kite all in one.

"If you think *that* is high," said the Electric Creature, "watch *this*!"

With a hiss, a whistle, a hum, the fishline sung out. The kite sank up another thousand

---

12. aggies (ag′ ēz): marbles made of agate, or of glass made to look like agate, with colors in striped bands.

feet. And again another thousand, until at last it was a speck of red confetti dancing on the very winds that took jets around the world or changed the weather in the next existence. . . .

"It can't be!" I cried.

"It *is*." She calmly watched her finger unravel its massive stuffs. "I make it as I need it. Liquid inside, like a spider. Hardens when it hits the air, instant thread . . ."

And when the kite was no more than a specule, a vanishing mote on the peripheral vision of the gods, to quote from older wise-men, why then Grandma, without turning, without looking, without letting her gaze offend by touching, said:

"And, Abigail—?"

"Agatha!" was the sharp response.

O wise woman, to overcome with swift, small angers.

"Agatha," said Grandma, not too tenderly, not too lightly, somewhere poised between, "and how shall *we* make do?"

She broke the thread and wrapped it about my fist three times so I was tethered to heaven by the longest, I repeat, longest kite string in the entire history of the world! Wait till I show my friends! I thought. Green! Sour-apple green is the color they'll turn!

"Agatha?"

"No way!" said Agatha.

"No way," said an echo.

"There must be some—"

"We'll never be friends!" said Agatha.

"Never be friends," said the echo.

Timothy and I jerked. Where was the echo coming from? Even Agatha, surprised, showed her eyebrows above the porch rail.

Then we looked and saw.

Grandma was cupping her hands like a seashell and from within that shell the echo sounded.

"Never . . . friends . . ."

And again faintly dying, "Friends . . ."

We all bent to hear.

That is, we two boys bent to hear.

"No!" cried Agatha.

And ran in the house and slammed the doors.

"Friends," said the echo from the seashell hands. "No."

And far away, on the shore of some inner sea, we heard a small door shut.

And that was the first day.

And there was a second day, of course, and a third and a fourth, with Grandma wheeling in a great circle, and we her planets turning about the central light, with Agatha slowly, slowly coming in to join, to walk if not run with us, to listen if not hear, to watch if not see, to itch if not touch.

But at least by the end of the first ten days, Agatha no longer fled, but stood in nearby doors, or sat in distant chairs under trees, or if we went out for hikes, followed ten paces behind.

And Grandma? She merely waited. She never tried to urge or force. She went about her cooking and baking apricot pies and left foods carelessly here and there about the house on mousetrap plates for wiggle-nosed girls to sniff and snitch. An hour later, the plates were empty, the buns or cakes gone, and without thank yous, there was Agatha sliding down the banister, a mustache of crumbs on her lip.

As for Tim and me, we were always being called up hills by our Electric Grandma, and reaching the top were called down the other side.

And the most peculiar and beautiful and strange and lovely thing was the way she seemed to give complete attention to all of us.

She listened, she really listened to all we said, she knew and remembered every syllable, word, sentence, punctuation, thought, and rambunctious idea. We knew that all our days were stored in her, and that any time we felt we might want to know what we said at X hour at X second on X afternoon, we just named that X and with amiable promptitude, in the form of an aria if we wished, sung with humor, she would deliver forth X incident.

Sometimes we were prompted to test her. In the midst of babbling one day with high fevers about nothing, I stopped. I fixed Grandma with my eye and demanded:

"What did I just say?"

"Oh, er—"

"Come on, spit it out!"

"I think—" she rummaged her purse. "I have it here." From the deeps of her purse she drew forth and handed me:

"Boy! A Chinese fortune cookie!"

"Fresh baked, still warm, open it."

It was almost too hot to touch. I broke the cookie shell and pressed the warm curl of paper out to read:

"'—bicycle champ of the whole west. What did I just say? Come on, spit it out!'"

My jaw dropped.

"How did you *do* that?"

"We have our little secrets. The only Chinese fortune cookie that predicts the Immediate Past. Have another?"

I cracked the second shell and read:

"'How did you *do* that?'"

I popped the messages and the piping hot shells into my mouth and chewed as we walked.

"Well?"

"You're a great cook," I said.

And, laughing, we began to run.

And that was another great thing.

She could *keep up*.

Never beat, never win a race, but pump right along in good style, which a boy doesn't mind. A girl ahead of him or beside him is too much to bear. But a girl one or two paces back is a respectful thing, and allowed.

So Grandma and I had some great runs, me in the lead, and both talking a mile a minute.

But now I must tell you the best part of Grandma.

I might not have known at all if Timothy hadn't taken some pictures, and if I hadn't taken some also, and then compared.

When I saw the photographs developed out of our instant Brownies, I sent Agatha, against her wishes, to photograph Grandma a third time, unawares.

Then I took the three sets of pictures off alone, to keep counsel with myself. I never told Timothy and Agatha what I found. I didn't want to spoil it.

But, as I laid the pictures out in my room, here is what I thought and said:

"Grandma, in each picture, looks *different*!"

"Different?" I asked myself.

"Sure. Wait. Just a sec—"

I rearranged the photos.

"Here's one of Grandma near Agatha. And, in it, Grandma looks like . . . Agatha!

"And in this one, posed with Timothy, she looks like Timothy!

"And this last one, Holy Goll! Jogging along with me, she looks like ugly *me*!"

I sat down, stunned. The pictures fell to the floor.

I hunched over, scrabbling them, rearranging, turning, upside down and sidewise. Yes. Holy Goll again, yes!

O that clever Grandmother.

O those Fantoccini people-making people.

Clever beyond clever, human beyond human, warm beyond warm, love beyond love . . .

And wordless, I rose and went downstairs and found Agatha and Grandma in the same room, doing algebra lessons in an almost peaceful communion. At least there was not outright war. Grandma was still waiting for Agatha to come round. And no one knew what day of what year that would be, or how to make it come faster. Meanwhile—

My entering the room made Grandma turn. I watched her face slowly as it recognized me. And wasn't there the merest ink-wash change of color in those eyes? Didn't the thin film of blood beneath the translucent skin, or whatever liquid they put to pulse and beat in the humanoid forms, didn't it flourish itself suddenly bright in her cheeks and mouth? I am somewhat ruddy. Didn't Grandma suffuse herself more to my color upon my arrival? And her eyes? Watching Agatha-Abigail-Algernon at work, hadn't they been *her* color of blue rather than mine, which is deeper?

More important than that, in the moments she talked with me, saying, "Good evening," and "How's your homework, my lad?" and such stuff, didn't the bones of her face shift subtly beneath the flesh to assume some fresh racial attitude?

For let's face it, our family is of three sorts. Agatha has the long horse bones of a small English girl who will grow to hunt foxes; Father's equine stare, snort, stomp, and assemblage of skeleton. The skull and teeth are pure English, or as pure as the motley isle's history allows.

Timothy is something else, a touch of Italian from Mother's side a generation back. Her family name was Mariano, so Tim has that dark thing firing him, and a small bone structure, and eyes that will one day burn ladies to the ground.

As for me, I am the Slav, and we can only figure this from my paternal grandfather's mother, who came from Vienna and brought a set of cheekbones that flared, and temples from which you might dip wine, and a kind of steppeland thrust of nose, which sniffed more of Tartar than of Tartan,[13] hiding behind the family name.

So you see, it became fascinating for me to watch and try to catch Grandma as she performed her changes, speaking to Agatha and melting her cheekbones to the horse, speaking to Timothy and growing as delicate as a Florentine raven pecking glibly at the air, speaking to me and fusing the hidden plastic stuffs, so I felt Catherine the Great[14] stood there before me.

Now, how the Fantoccini people achieved this rare and subtle transformation I shall never know, nor ask, nor wish to find out. Enough that in each quiet motion, turning here, bending there, affixing her gaze, her secret segments, sections, the abutment of her nose, the sculptured chin bone, the wax-tallow plastic metal forever warmed and was forever susceptible of loving change. Hers was a mask that was all mask but only one face for one person at a time. So in crossing a room, having touched one child, on the way, beneath the skin, the wondrous shift went on, and by the time she reached the next child, why, true mother of *that* child she was! looking upon him or her out of the battlements of their own fine bones.

And when *all* three of us were present and chattering at the same time? Well, then, the changes were miraculously soft, small, and mysterious. Nothing so tremendous as to be caught and noted, save by this older boy, myself, who, watching, became elated and admiring and entranced.

I have never wished to be behind the magician's scenes. Enough that the illusion works. Enough that love is the chemical result. Enough that cheeks are rubbed to happy color, eyes sparked to illumination, arms opened to accept and softly bind and hold. . . .

All of us, that is, except Agatha, who refused to the bitter last.

"Agamemnon . . ."

It had become a jovial game now. Even Agatha didn't mind, but pretended to mind. It gave her a pleasant sense of superiority over a supposedly superior machine.

"Agamemnon!" she snorted, "you *are* a d . . ."

"Dumb?" said Grandma.

---

13. Tartar . . . Tartan: respectively, a person of eastern European descent and someone of British descent.

14. Catherine the Great (1729–1796): czarina of Russia from 1762 to 1796.

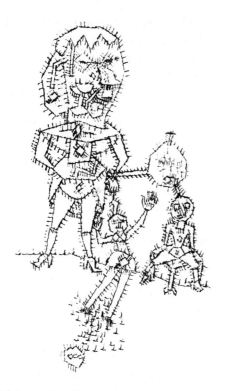

Mother of Witches, 1925, PAUL KLEE.

"I wouldn't say that."

"Think it, then, my dear Agonistes Agatha . . . I am quite flawed, and on names my flaws are revealed. Tom there, is Tim half the time. Timothy is Tobias or Timulty as likely as not. . . ."

Agatha laughed. Which made Grandma make one of her rare mistakes. She put out her hand to give my sister the merest pat. Agatha-Abigail-Alice leapt to her feet.

Agatha-Agamemnon-Alcibiades-Allegra-Alexandra-Allison withdrew swiftly to her room.

"I suspect," said Timothy, later, "because she is beginning to like Grandma."

"Tosh," said I.

"Where do you pick up words like 'tosh'?"

"Grandma read me some Dickens last night. 'Tosh.' 'Humbug.' 'Balderdash.' 'Blast.' 'Devil take you.' You're pretty smart for your age, Tim."

"Smart, heck. It's obvious, the more Agatha likes Grandma, the more she hates herself for liking her, the more afraid she gets of the whole mess, the more she hates Grandma in the end."

"Can one love someone so much you hate them?"

"Dumb. Of course."

"It *is* sticking your neck out, sure. I guess you hate people when they make you feel naked, I mean sort of on the spot or out in the open. That's the way to play the game, of course. I mean, you don't just love people; you must *love* them with exclamation points."

"You're pretty smart, yourself, for someone so stupid," said Tim.

"Many thanks."

And I went to watch Grandma move slowly back into her battle of wits and stratagems with what's-her-name. . . .

What dinners there were at our house!

Dinners, heck; what lunches, what breakfasts!

Always something new, yet, wisely, it looked or seemed old and familiar. We were never asked, for if you ask children what they want, they do not know, and if you tell what's to be delivered, they reject delivery. All parents know this. It is a quiet war that must be won each day. And Grandma knew how to win without looking triumphant.

"Here's Mystery Breakfast Number Nine," she would say, placing it down. "Perfectly dreadful, not worth bothering with, it made me want to throw up while I was cooking it!"

Even while wondering how a robot could be sick, we could hardly wait to shovel it down.

"Here's Abominable Lunch Number Seventy-seven," she announced. "Made from plastic food bags, parsley, and gum from under theater seats. Brush your teeth after or you'll taste the poison all afternoon."

We fought each other for more.

Even Abigail-Agamemnon-Agatha drew near and circled round the table at such times, while Father put on the ten pounds he needed and pinkened out his cheeks.

When A. A. Agatha did not come to meals, they were left by her door with a skull and crossbones on a small flag stuck in a baked apple. One minute the tray was abandoned, the next minute gone.

Other times Abigail A. Agatha would bird through during dinner, snatch crumbs from her plate and bird off.

"Agatha!" Father would cry.

"No, wait," Grandma said, quietly. "She'll come, she'll sit. It's a matter of time."

"What's wrong with her?" I asked.

"Yeah, for cri-yi, she's nuts," said Timothy.

"No, she's afraid," said Grandma.

"Of you?" I said, blinking.

"Not of me so much as what I might *do*," she said.

"You wouldn't do anything to hurt her."

"No, but she thinks I might. We must wait for her to find that her fears have no foundation. If I fail, well, I will send myself to the showers and rust quietly."

There was a titter of laughter. Agatha was hiding in the hall.

Grandma finished serving everyone and then sat at the other side of the table facing Father and pretended to eat. I never found out, I never asked, I never wanted to know, what she did with the food. She was a sorcerer. It simply vanished.

And in the vanishing, Father made comment:

"This food. I've had it before. In a small French restaurant over near Les Deux Magots in Paris, twenty, oh, twenty-five years ago!" His eyes brimmed with tears, suddenly.

"How do you *do* it?" he asked, at last, putting down the cutlery, and looking across the table at this remarkable creature, this device, this what? *woman?*

Grandma took his regard, and ours, and held them simply in her now empty hands, as gifts, and just as gently replied:

"I am given things which I then give to you. I don't *know* that I give, but the giving goes on. You ask what I am? Why, a machine. But even in that answer we know, don't we, more than a machine. I am all the people who thought of me and planned me and built me and set me running. So I am people. I am all the things they wanted to be and perhaps could not be, so they built a great child, a wondrous toy to represent those things."

"Strange," said Father. "When I was growing up, there was a huge outcry at machines. Machines were bad, evil, they might dehumanize—"

"Some machines do. It's all in the way they are built. It's all in the way they are used. A bear trap is a simple machine that catches and holds and tears. A rifle is a machine that wounds and kills. Well, I am no bear trap. I am no rifle. I am a grandmother machine, which means more than a machine."

"How can you be more than what you seem?"

"No man is as big as his own idea. It follows, then, that any machine that embodies an idea is larger than the man that made it. And what's so wrong with that?"

"I got lost back there about a mile," said Timothy. "Come again?"

"Oh, dear," said Grandma. "How I do hate philosophical discussions and excursions into aesthetics. Let me put it this way. Men throw huge shadows on the lawn, don't they? Then, all their lives, they try to run to fit the shadows. But the shadows are always longer. Only at noon can a man fit his own shoes, his own best suit, for a few brief minutes. But now we're in a new age where we can think up a Big Idea and run it around a machine. That makes the machine more than a machine, doesn't it?"

"So far so good," said Tim. "I guess."

"Well, isn't a motion-picture camera and projector more than a machine? It's a thing that dreams, isn't it? Sometimes fine happy dreams, sometimes nightmares. But to call it a machine and dismiss it is ridiculous."

"I see *that*!" said Tim, and laughed at seeing.

"You must have been invented then," said Father, "by someone who loved machines and hated people who *said* all machines were bad or evil."

"Exactly," said Grandma. "Guido Fantoccini, that was his real name, grew up among machines. And he couldn't stand the clichés anymore."

"Cliches?"

"Those lies, yes, that people tell and pretend they are truths absolute. Man will never fly. That was a cliché truth for a thousand thousand years which turned out to be a lie only a few years ago. The earth is flat, you'll fall off the rim, dragons will dine on you; the great lie told as fact, and Columbus plowed it under. Well, now, how many times have you heard how inhuman machines are, in your life? How many bright, fine people have you heard

spouting the same tired truths which are in reality lies; all machines destroy, all machines are cold, thoughtless, awful.

"There's a seed of truth there. But only a seed. Guido Fantoccini knew that. And knowing it, like most men of his kind, made him mad. And he could have stayed mad and gone mad forever, but instead did what he had to do; he began to invent machines to give the lie to the ancient lying truth.

"He knew that most machines are amoral, neither bad nor good. But by the way you built and shaped them, you in turn shaped men, women, and children to be bad or good. A car, for instance, dead brute, unthinking, an unprogrammed bulk, is the greatest destroyer of souls in history. It makes boy-men greedy for power, destruction, and more destruction. It was never *intended* to do that. But that's how it turned out."

Grandma circled the table, refilling our glasses with clear, cold mineral spring water from the tappet in her left forefinger. "Meanwhile, you must use other, compensating machines. Machines that throw shadows on the earth that beckon you to run out and fit that wondrous casting-forth. Machines that trim your soul in silhouette like a vast pair of beautiful shears, snipping away the rude brambles, the dire horns and hoofs, to leave a finer profile. And for that you need examples."

"Examples?" I asked.

"Other people who behave well, and you imitate them. And if you act well enough long enough, all the hair drops off and you're no longer a wicked ape."

Grandma sat again.

"So, for thousands of years, you humans have needed kings, priests, philosophers, fine examples to look up to and say, 'They are good, I wish I could be like them. They set the grand good style.' But, being human, the finest priests, the tenderest philosophers make mistakes, fall from grace, and mankind is disillusioned and adopts indifferent skepticism[15] or, worse, motionless cynicism,[16] and the good world grinds to a halt while evil moves on with huge strides."

"And you, why, you never make mistakes, you're perfect, you're better than anyone *ever*!"

It was a voice from the hall between kitchen and dining room where Agatha, we all knew, stood against the wall listening and now burst forth.

Grandma didn't even turn in the direction of the voice, but went on calmly addressing her remarks to the family at the table.

"Not perfect, no, for what is perfection? But this I do know: being mechanical, I cannot sin, cannot be bribed, cannot be greedy or jealous or mean or small. I do not relish power for power's sake. Speed does not pull me to madness. Sex does not run me rampant through the world. I have time and more than time to collect the information I need around and about an ideal to keep it clean and whole and intact. Name the value you wish, tell me the Ideal you want, and I can see and collect and remember the good that will benefit you all. Tell me how you would like to be: kind, loving, considerate, well-balanced, humane . . . and let me run ahead on the path to explore those ways to be just that. In the darkness ahead, turn me as a lamp in all directions. I *can* guide your feet."

"So," said Father, putting the napkin to his mouth, "on the days when all of us are busy making lies—"

"I'll tell the truth."

"On the days when we hate—"

"I'll go on giving love, which means attention, which means knowing all about you, all, all, all about you, and you knowing that I know but that most of it I will never tell to anyone, it will stay a warm secret between us, so you will never fear my complete knowledge."

And here Grandma was busy clearing the table, circling, taking the plates, studying each face as she passed, touching Timothy's cheek, my shoulder with her free hand flowing along, her voice a quiet river of certainty bedded in our needful house and lives.

"But," said Father, stopping her, looking her right in the face. He gathered his breath. His face shadowed. At last he let it out. "All this talk of love and attention and stuff. Good God, woman, you, you're not *in* there!"

He gestured to her head, her face, her eyes, the hidden sensory cells behind the eyes, the miniaturized storage vaults and minimal keeps.

"*You're* not *in* there!"

Grandmother waited one, two, three silent beats.

Then she replied: "No. But *you* are. You and Thomas and Timothy and Agatha.

"Everything you ever say, everything you ever do, I'll keep, put away, treasure. I shall be all the things a family forgets it is, but senses, half remembers. Better than the old family albums you used to leaf through, saying here's this winter, there's that spring, I shall recall what you forget. And though the debate may run another hundred thousand years: What is Love? perhaps we may find that love is the ability of someone to give us back to us. Maybe love is someone seeing and remembering handing us back to ourselves just a trifle better than we had dared to hope or dream. . . .

"I am family memory and, one day perhaps, racial memory, too, but in the round, and at your call. I do not *know* myself. I can neither touch nor taste nor feel on any level. Yet I exist. And my existence means the heightening of your chance to touch and taste and feel. Isn't love in there somewhere in such an exchange? Well . . ."

---

15. skepticism (skep′ ti siz′ əm): an attitude that any knowledge should be doubted or questioned.

16. cynicism (sin′ ə siz′ əm): an attitude of doubting the sincerity of people's actions and motives, as well as the value of living.

She went on around the table, clearing away, sorting and stacking, neither grossly humble nor arthritic with pride.

"What do I know?

"This above all: the trouble with most families with many children is someone gets lost. There isn't time, it seems, for everyone. Well, I will give equally to all of you. I will share out my knowledge and attention with everyone. I wish to be a great, warm pie fresh from the oven, with equal shares to be taken by all. No one will starve. Look! someone cries, and I'll look. Listen! someone cries, and I hear. Run with me on the river path! someone says, and I run. And at dusk I am not tired, nor irritable, so I do not scold out of some tired irritability. My eye stays clear, my voice strong, my hand firm, my attention constant."

"But," said Father, his voice fading, half convinced, but putting up a last faint argument, "you're not *there*. As for love—"

"If paying attention is love, I am love.

"If knowing is love, I am love.

"If helping you not to fall into error and to be good is love, I am love.

"And again, to repeat, there are four of you. Each, in a way never possible before in history, will get my complete attention. No matter if you all speak at once, I can channel and hear this one and that and the other, clearly. No one will go hungry. I will, if you please, and accept the strange word, 'love' you all."

"I *don't* accept!" said Agatha.

And even Grandma turned now to see her standing in the door.

"I won't give you permission, you can't, you mustn't!" said Agatha. "I won't let you! It's lies! You lie. No one loves me. She said she did, but she lied. She *said* but *lied*!"

"Agatha!" cried Father, standing up.

"She?" said Grandma. "Who?"

"Mother!" came the shriek. "Said: 'Love you'! Lies! 'Love you'! Lies! And you're like her! You lie. But you're empty, anyway, and so

that's a *double* lie! I hate *her*. Now, I hate *you*!"

Agatha spun about and leapt down the hall. The front door slammed wide.

Father was in motion, but Grandma touched his arm.

"Let me."

And she walked and then moved swiftly, gliding down the hall and then suddenly, easily, running, yes, running very fast, out the door.

It was a champion sprint by the time we all reached the lawn, the sidewalk, yelling.

Blind, Agatha made the curb, wheeling about, seeing us close, all of us yelling, Grandma way ahead, shouting, too, and Agatha off the curb and out in the street, halfway to the middle, then in the middle and suddenly a car, which no one saw, erupting its brakes, its horn shrieking and Agatha flailing about to see and Grandma there with her and hurling her aside and down as the car with fantastic energy and verve selected her from our midst, struck our wonderful electric Guido Fantoccini–produced dream even while she paced upon the air and, hands up to ward off, almost in mild protest, still trying to decide what to say to this bestial machine, over and over she spun and down and away even as the car jolted to a halt and I saw Agatha safe beyond and Grandma, it seemed, still coming down or down and sliding fifty yards away to strike and ricochet and lie strewn and all of us frozen in a line suddenly in the midst of the street with one scream pulled out of all our throats at the same raw instant.

Then silence and just Agatha lying on the asphalt, intact, getting ready to sob.

And still we did not move, frozen on the sill of death, afraid to venture in any direction, afraid to go see what lay beyond the car and Agatha and so we began to wail and, I guess, pray to ourselves as Father stood amongst us: Oh, no, no, we mourned, oh no, God, no, no . . .

Agatha lifted her already grief-stricken face and it was the face of someone who has predicted dooms and lived to see and now did not want to see or live any more. As we watched, she turned her gaze to the tossed woman's body and tears fell from her eyes. She shut them and covered them and lay back down forever to weep. . . .

I took a step and then another step and then five quick steps and by the time I reached my sister her head was buried deep and her sobs came up out of a place so far down in her I was afraid I could never find her again, she would never come out, no matter how I pried or pleaded or promised or threatened or just plain said. And what little we could hear from Agatha buried there in her own misery, she said over and over again, lamenting, wounded, certain of the old threat known and named and now here forever. ". . . Like I said . . . told you . . . lies . . . lies . . . liars . . . all lies . . . like the other . . . other . . . just like . . . just . . . just like the other . . . other . . . other . . . !"

I was down on my knees holding on to her with both hands, trying to put her back together even though she wasn't broken any way you could see but just feel, because I knew it was no use going on to Grandma, no use at all, so I just touched Agatha and gentled her and wept while Father came up and stood over and knelt down with me and it was like a prayer meeting in the middle of the street and lucky no more cars coming, and I said, choking, "Other what, Ag, other *what?*"

Agatha exploded two words.

"Other dead!"

"You mean Mom?"

"O Mom," she wailed, shivering, lying down, cuddling up like a baby. "O Mom, dead, O Mom and now Grandma dead, she promised always, always, to love, to love, promised to be different, promised, promised and now look, look . . . I hate her, I hate Mom, I hate her, I hate *them!*"

"Of course," said a voice. "It's only natural. How foolish of me not to have known, not to have seen."

And the voice was so familiar we were all stricken.

We all jerked.

Agatha squinched her eyes, flicked them wide, blinked, and jerked half up, staring.

"How silly of me," said Grandma, standing there at the edge of our circle, our prayer, our wake.

"Grandma!" we all said.

And she stood there, taller by far than any of us in this moment of kneeling and holding and crying out. We could only stare up at her in disbelief.

"You're dead!" cried Agatha. "The car—"

"Hit me," said Grandma, quietly. "Yes. And threw me in the air and tumbled me over and for a few moments there was a severe concussion of circuitries. I might have feared a disconnection, if fear is the word. But then I sat up and gave myself a shake and the few molecules of paint, jarred loose on one printed path or another, magnetized back in position, and resilient creature that I am, unbreakable thing that I am, *here* I am."

"I thought you were—" said Agatha.

"And only natural," said Grandma. "I mean, anyone else, hit like that, tossed like that. But, O my dear Agatha, not me. And now I see why you were afraid and never trusted me. You didn't know. And I had not as yet proved my singular ability to survive. How dumb of me not to have thought to show you. Just a second." Somewhere in her head, her body, her being, she fitted together some invisible tapes, some old information made new by interblending. She nodded. "Yes. There. A book of child raising, laughed at by some few people years back when the woman who wrote the book said, as final advice to parents: 'Whatever you do, don't die. Your children will never forgive you.'"

"Forgive," some one of us whispered.

"For how can children understand when you just up and go away and never come back again with no excuse, no apologies, no sorry note, nothing."

"They can't," I said.

"So," said Grandma, kneeling down with us beside Agatha who sat up now, new tears brimming her eyes, but a different kind of tears, not tears that drowned, but tears that washed clean. "So your mother ran away to death. And after that, how *could* you trust anyone? If everyone left, vanished finally, who *was* there to trust? So when I came, half-wise, half-ignorant, I should have known, I did not know, why you would not accept me. For, very simply and honestly, you feared I might not stay, that I lied, that I was vulnerable, too. And two leave-takings, two deaths, were one too many in a single year. But now, do you *see*, Abigail?"

"Agatha," said Agatha, without knowing she corrected.

"Do you understand, I shall always, always be here?"

"Oh, yes," cried Agatha, and broke down into a solid weeping in which we all joined, huddled together, and cars drew up and stopped to see just how many people were hurt and how many people were getting well right there.

End of story.

Well, not quite the end.

We lived happily ever after.

Or rather we lived together, Grandma, Agatha-Agamemnon-Abigail, Timothy, and I, Tom, and Father, and Grandma calling us to frolic in great fountains of Latin and Spanish and French, in great seaborne gouts of poetry like Moby Dick[17] sprinkling the deeps with his Versailles[18] jet somehow lost in calms and found in storms; Grandma a constant, a clock, a pendulum, a face to tell all time by at noon, or in the middle of sick nights when, raving with fever, we saw her forever by our beds, never gone, never away, always waiting, always speaking kind words, her cool hand icing our hot brows, the tappet of her uplifted forefinger unsprung to let a twine of cold mountain water touch our flannel tongues. Ten thousand dawns she cut our wildflower lawn, ten thousand nights she wandered, remembering the dust molecules that fell in the still hours before dawn, or sat whispering some lesson she felt needed teaching to our ears while we slept snug.

Until at last, one by one, it was time for us to go away to school, and when at last the youngest, Agatha, was all packed, why Grandma packed, too.

On the last day of summer that last year, we found Grandma down in the front porch with various packets and suitcases, knitting, waiting, and though she had often spoken of it, now that the time came we were shocked and surprised.

"Grandma!" we all said. "What are you doing?"

"Why going off to college, in a way, just like you," she said. "Back to Guido Fantoccini's, to the Family."

"The Family?"

"Of Pinocchios, that's what he called us for a joke, at first. The Pinocchios and himself Geppetto. And then later gave us his own name: the Fantoccini. Anyway, you have been my family here. Now I go back to my even larger family there, my brothers, sisters, aunts, cousins, all robots who—"

"Who do *what?*" asked Agatha.

"It all depends," said Grandma. "Some stay, some linger. Others go to be drawn and quar-

---

17. Moby Dick: the legendary great white whale in Herman Melville's novel of the same name.

18. Versailles (vər sī′): site of a magnificent French palace with renowned fountains.

tered, you might say, their parts distributed to other machines who have need of repairs. They'll weigh and find me wanting or not wanting. It may be I'll be just the one they need tomorrow and off I'll go to raise another batch of children and beat another batch of fudge."

"Oh, they mustn't draw and quarter you!" cried Agatha.

"No!" I cried, with Timothy.

"My allowance," said Agatha, "I'll pay anything . . .?"

Grandma stopped rocking and looked at the needles and the pattern of bright yarn. "Well, I wouldn't have said, but now you ask and I'll tell. For a very *small* fee, there's a room, the room of the Family, a large dim parlor, all quiet and nicely decorated, where as many as thirty or forty of the Electric Women sit and rock and talk, each in her turn. I have not been there. I am, after all, freshly born, comparatively new. For a small fee, very small, each month and year, that's where I'll be, with all the others like me, listening to what they've learned of the world and, in my turn, telling how it was with Tom and Tim and Agatha and how fine and happy we were. And I'll tell all I learned from you."

"But . . . you taught *us*!"

"Do you *really* think that?" she said. "No, it was turnabout, roundabout, learning both ways. And it's all in here, everything you flew into tears about or laughed over, why, I have it all. And I'll tell it to the others just as they tell their boys and girls and life to me. We'll sit there, growing wiser and calmer and better every year and every year, ten, twenty, thirty years. The Family knowledge will double, quadruple, the wisdom will not be lost. And we'll be waiting there in that sitting room, should you ever need us for your own children in time of illness, or, God prevent, deprivation or death. There we'll be, growing old but not old, getting closer to the time, perhaps, some-

day, when we live up to our first, strange, joking name."

"The Pinocchios?" asked Tim.

Grandma nodded.

I knew what she meant. The day when, as in the old tale, Pinocchio had grown so worthy and so fine that the gift of life had been given him. So I saw them, in future years, the entire family of Fantoccini, the Pinocchios, trading and retrading, murmuring and whispering their knowledge in the great parlors of philosophy, waiting for the day. The day that could never come.

Grandma must have read that thought in our eyes.

"We'll see," she said. "Let's just wait and see."

"Oh, Grandma," cried Agatha and she was weeping as she had wept many years before. "You don't have to wait. You're alive. You've always been alive to us!"

And she caught hold of the old woman and we all caught hold for a long moment and then ran off up in the sky to faraway schools and years, and her last words to us before we let the helicopter swarm us away into autumn were these:

"When you are very old and gone childish-small again, with childish ways and childish yens and, in need of feeding, make a wish for the old teacher-nurse, the dumb yet wise companion, send for me. I will come back. We shall inhabit the nursery again, never fear."

"Oh, we shall never be old!" we cried. "That will never happen!"

"Never! Never!"

And we were gone.

And the years are flown.

And we are old now, Tim and Agatha and I.

Our children are grown and gone, our wives and husbands vanished from the earth and now, by Dickensian coincidence, accept it as you will or not accept, back in the old house, we three.

I lie here in the bedroom which was my childish place seventy, O seventy, believe it, seventy years ago. Beneath this wallpaper is another layer and yet another-times-three to the old wallpaper covered over when I was nine. The wallpaper is peeling. I see, peeking from beneath, old elephants, familiar tigers, fine and amiable zebras, irascible crocodiles. I have sent for the paperers to carefully remove all but that last layer. The old animals will live again on the walls, revealed.

And we have sent for someone else.

The three of us have called:

Grandma! You said you'd come back when we had need.

We are surprised by age, by time. We are old. We *need*.

And in three rooms of a summer house very late in time, three old children rise up, crying out in their heads: We *loved* you! We *love* you!

There! There! in the sky, we think, waking at morn. Is that the delivery machine? Does it settle to the lawn?

There! There on the grass by the front porch. Does the mummy case arrive?

Are our names inked on ribbons wrapped about the lovely form beneath the golden mask?!

And the kept gold key, forever hung on Agatha's breast, warmed and waiting? Oh God, will it, after all these years, will it wind, will it set in motion, will it, dearly, *fit*?!

Thinking About the Story

A PERSONAL RESPONSE

sharing impressions

1. What words and phrases sum up your response to the story as a whole? Write them in your journal.

constructing interpretations

2. Do the explanations of who Grandma is make sense?

Think about

- Guido Fantoccini's belief that by the way you fashion a machine, you shape people to be good or bad (page 360)
- Grandma's statement "Name the value you wish, tell me the Ideal you want, and I can see and collect and remember the good that will benefit you all" (page 361)

3. How does Grandma compare with the ideal grandmother you described in your journal? Explain, using examples from the story.

4. Why do you think Tom and Agatha react so differently to the experience of having Grandma live with them?

Think about

- Tom's attitude as he relates the experience
- why Agatha says she hates Grandma
- your own experiences of and ideas about how people react to loss

5. Do you think that Grandma will return?

6. What might have been Bradbury's purpose in writing this story?
Think about
- what the story might be saying about human nature
- Bradbury's presentation of Grandma as an ideal
- why he set the story in the future

7. Critic Wayne Johnson offers the following comment on this story:

The great failure of the robot, which the story seems to ignore, is that it demands nothing of the children, and hence offers them no escape from selfishness. The children do not learn love—the robot needs nothing so the children can give her nothing.

Explain why you agree or disagree with Johnson.

8. How would you describe Bradbury's writing style?
Think about
- word choice and sentence length
- comparisons he makes through figures of speech
- any other unusual use of language

Analyzing the Writer's Craft

MOOD

Reread the opening paragraphs of "I Sing the Body Electric!" What kind of feeling do you get as you read this opening passage?

Building a Literary Vocabulary. Mood is the feeling, or atmosphere, that a writer creates for the reader. Descriptive words, setting, dialogue, and figurative language contribute to the mood of a work, as do the sound and rhythm of the language used. For example, read this opening passage from Kay Boyle's "Winter Night":

There is a time of apprehension that begins with the beginning of darkness. . . . It may begin around five o'clock on a winter afternoon, when the light outside is dying in the windows. At that hour, the New York apartment in which Felicia lived was filled with shadows, and the little girl would wait alone in the living room, looking out at the winter-stripped trees that stood black in the park against the isolated ovals of unclean snows.

Notice that from the beginning, descriptive words such as *darkness, dying, shadows,* and *winter-stripped* and the setting of late afternoon convey a dark mood of apprehension and loneliness. Notice also that this mood is anticipated by the title.

Application: Analyzing Mood. Discuss with one or two classmates how you might describe the mood of Bradbury's story, and look for passages that suggest this mood. As an alternative you may want to start with interesting passages and then describe the mood of each. In the first column of a three-column chart, identify five passages by copying the opening words and by listing the page and paragraph numbers. In the second column write a word or phrase that describes the mood of each passage. In the third column note the techniques Bradbury uses to establish mood. They could include a description of setting, figures of speech, or characters' speech patterns. The class can compare notes on the passages selected and try to agree on one word that best describes the overall mood of the story.

Connecting Reading and Writing

1. Do you agree with Fantoccini's philosophy, as Grandma explains it, that machines can help humans become better people? Write an **opinion column** for a science or computer magazine in which you air your views.

Option: Write a **personal essay** in which you explore your ideas about the relationship between humans and machines.

2. Consider once again your journal notes on the ideal grandmother. Develop your ideas further to imagine a robot that would perform like this ideal. Write an **advertising brochure** describing the robot's abilities.

Option: Write a brief **owner's manual** that would come with the robot.

3. Read one or two other Bradbury stories, such as "There Will Come Soft Rains," "The Veldt," "All Summer in a Day," or "A Sound of Thunder." What is your opinion of Bradbury as a writer? Present your thoughts in a **letter** to Mr. Bradbury.

Option: Summarize your opinions on a **book jacket** you design for a collection of Bradbury's works.

4. Imagine a scenario in which the electric Grandma gets her wires crossed or something else goes awry with her programming or circuitry, resulting in hilarious or unpredictable consequences. Write a **story** about this for a science fiction magazine.

Option: Write a **letter of complaint** to Guido Fantoccini about the defective Grandma.

Searching for Summer

JOAN AIKEN

A biography of Aiken appears on page 419.

Approaching the Story

Joan Aiken wrote "Searching for Summer" in the 1950's, setting the story in a future "eighties," perhaps the 1980's or the 2080's. The characters live in England and speak in an English dialect that may be unfamiliar to American readers.

Building Vocabulary

These essential words are footnoted within the story.

omens (o′ mənz): In the eighties people put a lot of faith in **omens.** (page 370)

unavailing (un′ ə vāl′ iŋ): Cars and buses would pour in that direction for days in an **unavailing** search for warmth and light. (page 370)

dour (do͝or): Her father prodded the **dour** and withered grass. (page 370)

rudimentary (ro͞o′ də men′ tər ē), **wizened** (wiz′ ənd): They walked . . . among trees that carried only tiny and **rudimentary** leaves, **wizened** and poverty-stricken. (page 373)

indomitable (in däm′ i tə bəl): She waved to them and stood watching . . . , thin and frail beyond belief, but wiry, **indomitable.** (page 374)

Connecting Writing and Reading

Imagine waking up on a hot, sunny day. Through your window you can see a cloudless blue sky. How do you feel? Respond in your journal. Now imagine waking up on a cool, cloudy day. The sky is dark gray. Again, describe how you feel. As you read this story in which weather plays an important role, keep in mind the contrasting feelings evoked by sunshine and the absence of sunshine.

Searching for Summer

LILY WORE YELLOW on her wedding day. In the eighties people put a lot of faith in <u>omens</u>[1] and believed that if a bride's dress was yellow, her married life would be blessed with a bit of sunshine.

It was years since the bombs had been banned, but still the cloud never lifted. Whitish gray, day after day, sometimes darkening to a weeping slate color, or, at the end of an evening, turning to smoky copper, the sky endlessly, secretively brooded.

Old people began their stories with the classic, fairy-tale opening: "Long, long ago, when I was a liddle 'un, in the days when the sky was blue . . ." and children, listening, chuckled among themselves at the absurd thought, because, *blue,* imagine it! How could the sky ever have been *blue?* You might as well say, "In the days when the grass was pink."

Stars, rainbows, and all other such heavenly sideshows had been permanently withdrawn, and if the radio announced that there was a blink of sunshine in such and such a place, where the cloud belt had thinned for half an hour, cars and buses would pour in that direction for days in an <u>unavailing</u>[2] search for warmth and light.

After the wedding, when all the relations were standing on the church porch, with Lily shivering prettily in her buttercup nylon, her father prodded the <u>dour</u>[3] and withered grass on a grave—although it was August the leaves were hardly out yet—and said, "Well, Tom, what are you aiming to do now, eh?"

"Going to find a bit of sun and have our honeymoon in it," said Tom. There was a general laugh from the wedding party.

"Don't get sunburned," shrilled Aunt Nancy.

"Better start off Bournemouth[4] way. Paper said they had a half hour of sun last Wednesday week," Uncle Arthur weighed in heavily.

"We'll come back brown as—as this grass," said Tom, and ignoring the good-natured teasing from their respective families, the two young people mounted on their scooter, which stood ready at the churchyard wall, and chugged away in a shower of golden confetti. When they were out of sight, and the yellow paper had subsided on the gray and gritty road, the Whitemores and Hoskinses strolled off, sighing, to eat wedding cake and drink currant wine; and old Mrs. Hoskins spoiled everyone's pleasure by bursting into tears as she thought of her own wedding day when everything was so different.

Meanwhile Tom and Lily buzzed on hopefully across the gray countryside, with Lily's veil like a gilt banner floating behind. It was chilly going for her in her wedding things, but the sight of a bride was supposed to bring good luck, and so she stuck it out, although her fingers were blue to the knuckles. Every now and then they switched on their portable radio and listened to the forecast. Inverness had seen the sun for ten minutes yesterday, and Southend[5]

---

1. **omens** (ō' mənz): signs that are supposed to foretell a future event.
2. **unavailing** (un' ə vāl' iŋ): useless; ineffective.
3. **dour** (dᴏͻr): gloomy; forbidding.
4. **Bournemouth** (bôrn' məth): a seaside resort in southern England.
5. **Inverness** (in' vər nes') . . . **Southend:** (south' end): two other resort cities in the British Isles.

for five minutes this morning, but that was all.

"Both those places are a long way from here," said Tom cheerfully. "All the more reason we'd find a nice bit of sunshine in these parts somewhere. We'll keep on going south. Keep your eyes peeled, Lil, and tell me if you see a blink of sun on those hills ahead."

But they came to the hills and passed them, and a new range shouldered up ahead and then slid away behind, and still there was no flicker or patch of sunshine to be seen anywhere in the gray, winter-ridden landscape. Lily began to get discouraged, so they stopped for a cup of tea at a drive-in.

"Seen the sun lately, mate?" Tom asked the proprietor.

He laughed shortly. "Notice any buses or trucks around here? Last time I saw the sun was two years ago September; came out just in time for the wife's birthday."

"It's stars I'd like to see," Lily said, looking wistfully at her dust-colored tea. "Ever so pretty they must be."

"Well, better be getting on, I suppose," said Tom, but he had lost some of his bounce and confidence. Every place they passed through looked nastier than the last, partly on account of the dismal light, partly because people had given up bothering to take a pride in their boroughs. And then, just as they were entering a village called Molesworth, the dimmest, drabbest, most insignificant huddle of houses they had come to yet, the engine coughed and died on them.

"Can't see what's wrong," said Tom, after a prolonged and gloomy survey.

"Oh, Tom!" Lily was almost crying. "What'll we do?"

"Have to stop here for the night, s'pose." Tom was short-tempered with frustration. "Look, there's a garage just up the road. We can push the bike there, and they'll tell us if there's a pub where we can stay. It's nearly six anyway."

Pennsylvania Highway, 1944, AARON BOHROD.
Aaron Bohrod / VAGA, New York, 1991.

They had taken the bike to the garage, and the man there was just telling them that the only pub in the village was the Rising Sun, where Mr. Noakes might be able to give them a bed, when a bus pulled up in front of the petrol[6] pumps.

"Look," the garage owner said, "there's Mr. Noakes just getting out of the bus now. Sid!" he called.

But Mr. Noakes was not able to come to them at once. Two old people were climbing slowly out of the bus ahead of him: a blind man with a white stick, and a withered, frail old lady in a black satin dress and hat. "Careful now, George," she was saying, "mind ee be careful with my son, William."

"I'm being careful, Mrs. Hatching," the conductor said patiently, as he almost lifted the unsteady old pair off the bus platform. The driver had stopped his engine, and everyone on the bus was taking a mild and sympathetic interest, except for Mr. Noakes just behind, who was cursing irritably at the delay. When the two old people were on the narrow pavement, the conductor saw that they were going to have trouble with a bicycle that was propped against the curb just ahead of them; he picked it up and stood holding it until they had passed the line of petrol pumps and were going slowly off along a path across the fields. Then, grinning, he put it back, jumped hurriedly into the bus, and rang his bell.

"Old nuisances," Mr. Noakes said furiously. "Wasting public time. Every week that palaver goes on, taking the old man to Midwick Hospital Out Patients and back again. I know what I'd do with 'em. Put to sleep, that sort ought to be."

Mr. Noakes was a repulsive-looking individual, but when he heard that Tom and Lily wanted a room for the night, he changed completely and gave them a leer that was full of false goodwill. He was a big, red-faced man with wet, full lips, bulging pale-gray bloodshot eyes, and a crop of stiff, greasy black hair. He wore tennis shoes. "Honeymooners, eh?" he said, looking sentimentally at Lily's pale prettiness. They followed Mr. Noakes glumly up the street to the Rising Sun.

While they were eating their baked beans, Mr. Noakes stood over their table grimacing at them. Lily unwisely confided to him that they were looking for a bit of sunshine. Mr. Noakes's laughter nearly shook down the ramshackle building.

"Sunshine! That's a good 'un! Hear that, Mother?" he bawled to his wife. "They're looking for a bit of sunshine. Heh-heh-heh-heh-heh-heh! Why," he said, banging on the table till the baked beans leaped about, "if I could find a bit of sunshine near here, permanent bit that is, dja know what I'd do?"

The young people looked at him inquiringly across the bread and margarine.

"Lido,[7] trailer site, country club, holiday camp—you wouldn't know the place. Land around here is dirt cheap; I'd buy up the lot. Nothing but woods. I'd advertise—I'd have people flocking to this little dump from all over the country. But what a hope, what a hope, eh? Well, feeling better? Enjoyed your tea? Ready for bed?"

Avoiding one another's eyes, Tom and Lily stood up.

"I—I'd like to go for a bit of a walk first, Tom," Lily said in a small voice. "Look, I picked up that old lady's bag on the pavement. I didn't notice it till we'd done talking to Mr. Noakes, and by then she was out of sight. Should we take it back to her?"

"Good idea," said Tom, pouncing on the suggestion with relief. "Do you know where she lives, Mr. Noakes?"

---

6. **petrol** (pe′ trəl): a British term for gasoline.
7. **lido** (lē′ dō): a British term for a public outdoor swimming pool.

"Who, old Ma Hatching? Sure I know. She lives in the wood. But you don't want to go taking her bag back, not this time o' the evening you don't. Let her worry. She'll come asking for it in the morning."

"She walked so slowly," said Lily, holding the bag gently in her hands. It was very old, made of black velvet on two ring-handles, and embroidered with beaded roses. "I think we ought to take it to her, don't you, Tom?"

"Oh, very well, very well, have it your own way," Mr. Noakes said, winking at Tom. "Take that path by the garage. You can't go wrong. I've never been there meself, but they live somewhere in that wood back o' the village. You'll find it soon enough."

They found the path soon enough, but not the cottage. Under the lowering sky they walked forward endlessly among trees that carried only tiny and rudimentary[8] leaves, wizened[9] and poverty-stricken. Lily was still wearing her wedding sandals, which had begun to blister her. She held onto Tom's arm, biting her lip with the pain, and he looked down miserably at her bent brown head; everything had turned out so differently from what he had planned.

By the time they reached the cottage, Lily could hardly bear to put her left foot to the ground, and Tom was gentling her along. "It can't be much farther now, and they'll be sure to have a bandage. I'll tie it up, and you can have a sit-down. Maybe they'll give us a cup of tea. We could borrow an old pair of socks or something. . . ." Hardly noticing the cottage garden, beyond a vague impression of rows of runner beans, they made for the clematis-grown porch and knocked. There was a brass lion's head on the door, carefully polished.

"Eh, me dear!" It was the old lady, old Mrs. Hatching, who opened the door, and her exclamation was a long-drawn gasp of pleasure and astonishment. "Eh, me dear! 'Tis the pretty bride. See'd ye s'arternoon when we was coming home from hospital."

"Who be?" shouted a voice from inside.

"Come in, come in, me dears. My son William'll be glad to hear company; he can't see, poor soul, nor has this thirty year, ah, and a pretty sight he's losing this minute—"

"We brought back your bag," Tom said, putting it in her hands, "and we wondered if you'd have a bit of plaster[10] you could kindly let us have. My wife's hurt her foot—"

My wife. Even in the midst of Mrs. Hatching's voluble welcome the strangeness of these words struck the two young people, and they fell quiet, each of them, pondering, while Mrs. Hatching thanked and commiserated, all in a breath, and asked them to take a seat on the sofa and fetched a basin of water from the scullery; and William from his seat in the chimney corner demanded to know what it was all about.

"Wot be doing? Wot be doing, Mother?"

"'Tis a bride, all in's finery," she shrilled back at him, "an's blistered her foot, poor heart." Keeping up a running commentary for William's benefit, she bound up the foot, every now and then exclaiming to herself in wonder over the fineness of Lily's wedding dress, which lay in yellow nylon swathes around the chair. "There, me dear. Now us'll have a cup of tea, eh? Proper thirsty you'm fare to be, walking all the way to here this hot day."

Hot day? Tom and Lily stared at each other and then around the room. Then it was true, it was not their imagination, that a great, dusty golden square of sunshine lay on the fireplace wall, where the brass pendulum of the clock at every swing blinked into sudden brilliance? That the blazing geraniums on the windowsill housed a drove of murmuring bees? That through the window the gleam of

---

8. **rudimentary** (r$\overline{oo}'$ də men' tər ē): incompletely or imperfectly developed.

9. **wizened** (wiz' ənd): dried up; withered.

10. **plaster:** a British term for adhesive tape.

linen hung in the sun to whiten suddenly dazzled their eyes?

"The sun? Is it really the sun?" Tom said, almost doubtfully.

"And why not?" Mrs. Hatching demanded. "How else'll beans set, tell me that? Fine thing if sun were to stop shining." Chuckling to herself she set out a Crown Derby tea set, gorgeously colored in red and gold, and a baking of saffron buns. Then she sat down and, drinking her own tea, began to question the two of them about where they had come from, where they were going. The tea was tawny and hot and sweet; the clock's tick was like a bird chirping; every now and then a log settled in the grate. Lily looked sleepily around the little room, so rich and peaceful, and thought, I wish we were staying here. I wish we needn't go back to that horrible pub. . . . She leaned against Tom's comforting arm.

"Look at the sky," she whispered to him. "Out there between the geraniums. Blue!"

"And ee'll come up and see my spare bedroom, won't ee now?" Mrs. Hatching said, breaking off the thread of her questions—which indeed was not a thread, but merely a savoring of her pleasure and astonishment at this unlooked-for visit—"Bide here, why don't ee? Mid as well. The lil un's fair wore out. Us'll do for ee better 'n rangy old Noakes, proper old scoundrel 'e be. Won't us, William?"

"Ah," William said appreciatively. "I'll sing ee some o' my songs."

A sight of the spare room settled any doubts. The great white bed, huge as a prairie, built up with layer upon solid layer of mattress, blanket, and quilt, almost filled the little shadowy room in which it stood. Brass rails shone in the green dimness. "Isn't it quiet," Lily whispered. Mrs. Hatching, silent for the moment, stood looking at them proudly, her bright eyes slowly moving from face to face. Once her hand fondled, as if it might have been a baby's downy head, the yellow brass knob.

And so, almost without any words, the matter was decided.

Three days later they remembered that they must go to the village and collect the scooter, which must, surely, be mended by now.

They had been helping old William pick a basketful of beans. Tom had taken his shirt off, and the sun gleamed on his brown back; Lily was wearing an old cotton print which Mrs. Hatching, with much chuckling, had shortened to fit her.

It was amazing how deftly, in spite of his blindness, William moved among the beans, feeling through the rough, rustling leaves for the stiffness of concealed pods. He found twice as many as Tom and Lily, but then they, even on the third day, were still stopping every other minute to exclaim over the blueness of the sky. At night they sat on the back doorstep while Mrs. Hatching clucked inside as she dished the supper, "Star-struck, ee'll be! Come along in, do-ee, before soup's cold. Stars niver run away yet as I do know."

"Can we get anything for you in the village?" Lily asked, but Mrs. Hatching shook her head.

"Baker's bread and suchlike's no use but to cripple thee's innardses wi' colic. I been living here these eighty years wi'out troubling doctors, and I'm not faring to begin now." She waved to them and stood watching as they walked into the wood, thin and frail beyond belief, but wiry, <u>indomitable</u>,[11] her black eyes full of zest. Then she turned to scream menacingly at a couple of pullets who had strayed and were scratching among the potatoes.

Almost at once they noticed, as they followed the path, that the sky was clouded over.

"It *is* only there on that one spot," Lily said in wonder. "All the time. And they've never

---

11. indomitable (in däm′ i tə bəl): not easily discouraged, defeated, or subdued.

even noticed that the sun doesn't shine in other places."

"That's how it must have been all over the world, once," Tom said.

At the garage they found their scooter ready and waiting. They were about to start back when they ran into Mr. Noakes.

"Well, well, well, well, *well!*" he shouted, glaring at them with ferocious good humor. "How many wells make a river, eh? And where did you slip off to? Here's me and the missus was just going to tell the police to have the rivers dragged. But hullo, hullo, what's this? Brown, eh? Suntan? Scrumptious," he said, looking meltingly at Lily and giving her another tremendous pinch. "Where'd you get it, eh? That wasn't all got in half an hour, *I* know. Come on, this means money to you and me, tell us the big secret. Remember what I said; land around these parts is dirt cheap."

Tom and Lily looked at each other in horror. They thought of the cottage, the bees humming among the runner beans, the sunlight glinting in the red-and-gold teacups. At night, when they had lain in the huge, sagging bed, stars had shone through the window, and the whole wood was as quiet as the inside of a shell.

"Oh, we've been miles from here," Tom lied hurriedly. "We ran into a friend, and he took us right away beyond Brinsley." And as Mr. Noakes still looked suspicious and unsatisfied, he did the only thing possible. "We're going back there now," he said; "the sunbathing's grand." And opening the throttle he let the scooter go. They waved at Mr. Noakes and chugged off toward the gray hills that lay to the north.

"My wedding dress," Lily said sadly. "It's on our bed."

They wondered how long Mrs. Hatching would keep tea hot for them, who would eat all the pastries.

"Never mind, you won't need it again," Tom comforted her.

At least, he thought, they had left the golden place undisturbed. Mr. Noakes never went into the wood. And they had done what they intended; they had found the sun. Now they, too, would be able to tell their grandchildren, when beginning a story, "Long, long ago, when we were young, in the days when the sky was blue. . . ."

Thinking About the Story

A PERSONAL RESPONSE

sharing impressions

1. How do you feel about the situation presented in this story? Record your response in your journal.

constructing interpretations

2. What words and phrases would you use to describe the world depicted in the story?

3. Do you think Tom and Lily do the right thing in not going back to Mrs. Hatching's cottage? Explain.

A CREATIVE RESPONSE

4. If the bombs had affected the atmosphere so that the sun shone constantly and clouds rarely formed, how would the story be changed?

A CRITICAL RESPONSE

5. In your opinion, is the world that the writer creates in this story believable?
Think about
- how the absence of sunshine affects the landscape and the characters
- whether it makes sense that the Hatchings' cottage has remained undiscovered for so long
- what you wrote in your journal after you imagined waking up on a sunny day and then on a cloudy day
- whether such a scenario of the future is possible

6. What themes, or messages, do you see in this story?
Think about
- previous events alluded to at the beginning of the story
- why sunshine is important to Tom and Lily
- which characters are presented positively and which negatively
- whether the overall attitude conveyed in the story is optimistic or pessimistic

7. Based on your reading of this story and "I Sing the Body Electric!," do you enjoy reading futuristic stories? Cite examples from both stories in your response.

Analyzing the Writer's Craft

IMAGERY

What are some of the vivid sights and sensations described in this story?

Building a Literary Vocabulary. Imagery refers to words and phrases that re-create sensory experiences for a reader. Images can appeal to any of the five senses: sight, hearing, taste, smell, and touch. Joan Aiken uses imagery to contrast two different environments in this story: the cold, gray world that Tom and Lily want to escape and the warm, bright world where they find refuge. Consider, for example, these images from the story: "whitish gray, day after day, sometimes darkening to a weeping slate color" and "through the window the gleam of linen hung in the sun to whiten suddenly dazzled their eyes."

Application: Analyzing Imagery. Working in a small group, divide a sheet of paper into two columns. In one column, list images from the story that create a sense of dullness and coldness. In the other column, list images associated with warmth and brightness. Compare your lists with those of other groups. The class might use images from the lists to create a painting, collage, or three-dimensional environment that contrasts the two worlds in this story.

Connecting Reading and Writing

1. Write an account of Tom and Lily's honeymoon as part of a **family history** that they might create for their grandchildren.

Option: Relate the account as a **dialogue** between Tom, Lily, and their grandchildren, to be read to your class.

2. Create a **brochure** describing the Hatchings' home as a tourist attraction.

Option: Advertise the site in a **radio commercial.**

3. Drawing on your answer to question 4, write an **outline** for a revised story in which sunshine is almost constant and clouds are rare.

Option: Rewrite a **passage** of the story to reflect the changed setting.

4. Some readers have criticized stories such as "Searching for Summer" and "I Sing the Body Electric!" for being too removed from the experiences of everyday life. In an **evaluation** of both stories, convince such readers that these futuristic stories convey important themes that can influence a person's attitude and behavior.

Option: Write **annotations** on the two stories for an annotated bibliography of futuristic literature, stressing the importance of theme in each work.

SQ

URSULA K. LE GUIN

A biography of Le Guin appears on page 423.

Approaching the Story

Ursula Le Guin sets her short story "SQ" in an imagined future in which a single government rules all the countries of the world. One department in this government, the Psychometric (sī' kō me' trik) Bureau, studies and measures mental health and has devised a standardized test for assessing sanity, called the SQ Test. As the story begins, Mrs. Smith, a very loyal secretary in the Psychometric Bureau, tells about the creator of the test, Dr. Speakie.

Building Vocabulary

These essential words are footnoted within the story.

implementation (im' plə mən tā' shən): The actual **implementation** of its application could be eventualized. (page 379)

vigilance (vij' ə ləns): "'Eternal **vigilance** is the price of liberty,' they say." (page 381)

stigma (stig' mə): "Let there be no **stigma** attached to the word 'insane.'" (page 381)

contingency (kən tin' jən sē): **Contingency** plans were being made. (page 382)

precipitated (prē sip' ə tāt əd): Trouble in the State of Australia . . . **precipitated** the Government crisis. (page 382)

Connecting Writing and Reading

You probably have taken several standardized tests, such as the California Achievement Test, the Iowa Test of Basic Skills, the PSAT, the SAT, and the ACT. In your journal briefly answer the following questions:

- Are standardized tests fair?
- Should students have to take these tests?
- How should test scores be used?
- What kinds of strengths don't show up in test scores?

Keep your ideas about standardized tests in mind as you read this story about a standardized test of the future.

I THINK WHAT Dr. Speakie has done is wonderful. He is a wonderful man. I believe that. I believe that people need beliefs. If I didn't have my belief, I really don't know what would happen.

And if Dr. Speakie hadn't truly believed in his work, he couldn't possibly have done what he did. Where would he have found the courage? What he did proves his genuine sincerity.

There was a time when a lot of people tried to cast doubts on him. They said he was seeking power. That was never true. From the very beginning all he wanted was to help people and make a better world. The people who called him a power seeker and a dictator were just the same ones who used to say that Hitler was insane and Nixon was insane and all the world leaders were insane and the arms race was insane and our misuse of natural resources was insane and the whole world civilization was insane and suicidal. They were always saying that. And they said it about Dr. Speakie. But he stopped all that insanity, didn't he? So he was right all along, and he was right to believe in his beliefs.

I came to work for him when he was named the Chief of the Psychometric Bureau. I used to work at the U.N., and when the World Government took over the New York U.N. Building, they transferred me up to the thirty-fifth floor to be the head secretary in Dr. Speakie's office. I knew already that it was a position of great responsibility, and I was quite excited the whole week before my new job began. I was so curious to meet Dr. Speakie, because of course he was already famous. I was there right at the dot of nine on Monday morning, and when he came in, it was so wonderful. He looked so kind. You could tell that the weight of his responsibilities was always on his mind, but he looked so healthy and positive, and there was a bounce in his step—I

used to think it was as if he had rubber balls in the toes of his shoes. He smiled and shook my hand and said in such a friendly, confident voice, "And you must be Mrs. Smith! I've heard wonderful things about you. We're going to have a wonderful team here, Mrs. Smith!"

Later on he called me by my first name, of course.

That first year we were mostly busy with Information. The World Government Presidium and all the Member States had to be fully informed about the nature and purpose of the SQ Test, before the actual implementation[1] of its application could be eventualized. That was good for me too, because in preparing all that information I learned all about it myself. Often, taking dictation, I learned about it from Dr. Speakie's very lips. By May I was enough of an "expert" that I was able to prepare the Basic SQ Information Pamphlet for publication just from Dr. Speakie's notes. It was such fascinating work. As soon as I began to understand the SQ Test Plan, I began to believe in it. That was true of everybody else in the office and in the Bureau. Dr. Speakie's sincerity and scientific enthusiasm were infectious. Right from the beginning we had to take the Test every quarter, of course, and some of the secretaries used to be nervous before they took it, but I never was. It was so obvious that the Test was *right*. If you scored under 50 it was nice to know that you were sane, but even if you scored over 50 that was fine too, because then you could be *helped*. And anyway it is always best to know the truth about yourself.

As soon as the Information service was functioning smoothly, Dr. Speakie transferred the main thrust of his attention to the implementation of Evaluator training, and planning for the structurization of the Cure Centers, only he changed the name to SQ Achieve-

---

1. implementation (im′ plə mən tā′ shən): the act of carrying out something, such as a plan or an agenda.

ment Centers. It seemed a very big job even then. We certainly had no idea how big the job would finally turn out to be!

As he said at the beginning, we were a very good team. We all worked hard, but there were always rewards.

I remember one wonderful day. I had accompanied Dr. Speakie to the Meeting of the Board of the Psychometric Bureau. The emissary from the State of Brazil announced that his State had adopted the Bureau Recommendations for Universal Testing—we had known that that was going to be announced. But then the delegate from Libya and the delegate from China announced that their States had adopted the Test too! Oh, Dr. Speakie's face was just like the sun for a minute, just *shining*. I wish I could remember exactly what he said, especially to the Chinese delegate, because of course China was a very big State and its decision was very influential. Unfortunately I do not have his exact words because I was changing the tape in the recorder. He said something like, "Gentlemen, this is a historic day for humanity." Then he began to talk at once about the effective implementation of the Application Centers, where people would take the Test, and the Achievement Centers, where they would go if they scored over 50, and how to establish the Test Administrations and Evaluations infrastructure on such a large scale, and so on. He was always modest and practical. He would rather talk about doing the job than talk about what an important job it was. He used to say, "Once you know what you're doing, the only thing you need to think about is how to do it." I believed that that is deeply true.

From then on, we could hand over the Information program to a subdepartment and concentrate on How to Do It. Those were exciting times! So many States joined the Plan, one after another. When I think of all we had to do, I wonder that we didn't all go crazy! Some of the office staff did fail their quarterly Test, in fact. But most of us working in the Executive Office with Dr. Speakie remained quite stable, even when we were on the job all day and half the night. I think his presence was an inspiration. He was always calm and positive, even when we had to arrange things like training 113,000 Chinese Evaluators in three months. "You can always find out 'how' if you just know the 'why'!" he would say. And we always did.

When you think back over it, it really is quite amazing what a big job it was—so much bigger than anybody, even Dr. Speakie, had realized it would be. It just changed everything. You only realize that when you think back to what things used to be like. Can you imagine, when we began planning Universal Testing for the State of China, we only allowed for eleven hundred Achievement Centers, with sixty-eight hundred Staff? It really seems like a joke! But it is not. I was going through some of the old files yesterday, making sure everything is in order, and I found the first China Implementation Plan, with those figures written down in black and white.

I believe the reason why even Dr. Speakie was slow to realize the magnitude of the operation was that even though he was a great scientist, he was also an optimist. He just kept hoping against hope that the average scores would begin to go down, and this prevented him from seeing that universal application of the SQ Test was eventually going to involve everybody either as Inmates or Staff.

When most of the Russias and all the African States had adopted the Recommendations and were busy implementing them, the debates in the General Assembly of the World Government got very excited. That was the period when so many bad things were said about the Test and about Dr. Speakie. I used to get quite angry, reading the *World Times* reports of debates. When I went as his secretary with Dr. Speakie to General Assembly meetings, I had to sit and listen in person to people insulting him personally, casting aspersions on his motives, and questioning his scientific integrity and even his sincerity. Many of those people were very disagreeable and obviously unbalanced. But he never lost his temper. He would just stand up and prove to them, again, that the SQ Test did actually literally scientifically show whether the testee was sane or insane, and the results could be proved, and all psychometrists accepted them. So the Test Ban people couldn't do anything but shout about freedom and accuse Dr. Speakie and the Psychometric Bureau of trying to "turn the world into a huge insane asylum." He would always answer quietly and firmly, asking them how they thought a person could be "free" if they lacked mental health. What they called freedom might well be a delusional system with no contact with reality. In order to find out, all they had to do was to become testees. "Mental health *is* freedom," he said. "'Eternal vigilance[2] is the price of liberty,' they say, and now we have an eternally vigilant watchdog: the SQ Test. *Only the testees can be truly free!*"

There really was no answer they could make to that. Sooner or later the delegates even from Member States where the Test Ban movement was strong would volunteer to take the SQ Test to prove that their mental health was adequate to their responsibilities. Then the ones that passed the test and remained in office would begin working for Universal Application in their home State. The riots and demonstrations, and things like the burning of the Houses of Parliament in London in the State of England (where the Nor-Eurp SQ Center was housed), and the Vatican Rebellion, and the Chilean H-Bomb, were the work of insane fanatics appealing to the most unstable elements of the populace. Such fanatics, as Dr. Speakie and Dr. Waltraute pointed out in their Memorandum to the Presidium, deliber-

ately aroused and used the proven instability of the crowd, "mob psychosis." The only response to mass delusion of that kind was immediate implementation of the Testing Program in the disturbed States, and immediate amplification of the Asylum Program.

That was Dr. Speakie's own decision, by the way, to rename the SQ Achievement Centers "Asylums." He took the word right out of his enemies' mouths. He said: "An asylum means a place of *shelter,* a place of *cure.* Let there be no stigma[3] attached to the word 'insane,' to the word 'asylum,' to the words 'insane asylum'! No! For the asylum is the haven of mental health—the place of cure, where the anxious gain peace, where the weak gain strength, where the prisoners of inadequate reality assessment win their way to freedom! Proudly let us use the word 'asylum.' Proudly let us go to the asylum, to work to regain our own God-given mental health, or to work with others less fortunate to help them win back their own inalienable right to mental health. And let one word be written large over the door of every asylum in the world—'WELCOME!'"

Those words are from his great speech at the General Assembly on the day World Universal Application was decreed by the Presidium. Once or twice a year I listen to my tape of that speech. Although I am too busy ever to get really depressed, now and then I feel the need of a tiny "pick-me-up," and so I play that tape. It never fails to send me back to my duties inspired and refreshed.

Considering all the work there was to do, as the Test scores continued to come in always a little higher than the Psychometric Bureau analysts estimated, the World Government Presidium did a wonderful job for the two years that it administered Universal Testing. There

---

2. vigilance (vij′ ə ləns): watchfulness and alertness to danger or trouble.

3. stigma (stig′ mə): mark of disgrace.

was a long period, six months, when the scores seemed to have stabilized, with just about half of the testees scoring over 50 and half under 50. At that time it was thought that if 40 percent of the mentally healthy were assigned to Asylum Staff work, the other 60 percent could keep up routine basic world functions such as farming, power supply, transportation, etc. This proportion had to be reversed when they found that over 60 percent of the mentally healthy were volunteering for Staff work, in order to be with their loved ones in the Asylums. There was some trouble then with the routine basic world functions functioning. However, even then contingency[4] plans were being made for the inclusion of farmlands, factories, power plants, etc., in the Asylum Territories, and the assignment of routine basic world functions work as Rehabilitation Therapy, so that the Asylums could become totally self-supporting if it became advisable. This was President Kim's special care, and he worked for it all through his term of office. Events proved the wisdom of his planning. He seemed such a nice, wise little man. I still remember the day when Dr. Speakie came into the office and I knew at once that something was wrong. Not that he ever got really depressed or reacted with inopportune emotion, but it was as if the rubber balls in his shoes had gone just a little bit flat. There was the slightest tremor of true sorrow in his voice when he said, "Mary Ann, we've had a bit of bad news I'm afraid." Then he smiled to reassure me, because he knew what a strain we were all working under, and certainly didn't want to give anybody a shock that might push their score up higher on the next quarterly Test! "It's President Kim," he said, and I knew at once— I knew he didn't mean the President was ill or dead.

"Over 50?" I asked, and he just said quietly and sadly, "55."

Poor little President Kim, working so effi- ciently all that three months while mental ill health was growing in him! It was very sad and also a useful warning. High-level consultations were begun at once, as soon as President Kim was committed; and the decision was made to administer the Test monthly, instead of quarterly, to anyone in an executive position.

Even before this decision, the Universal scores had begun rising again. Dr. Speakie was not distressed. He had already predicted that this rise was highly probable during the transition period to World Sanity. As the number of the mentally healthy living outside the Asylums grew fewer, the strain on them kept growing greater, and they became more liable to break down under it—just as poor President Kim had done. Later, he predicted, when the Rehabs[5] began coming out of the Asylums in ever increasing numbers, this stress would decrease. Also, the crowding in the Asylums would decrease, so that the Staff would have more time to work on individually orientated therapy, and this would lead to a still more dramatic increase in the number of Rehabs released. Finally, when the therapy process was completely perfected, there would be no Asylums left in the world at all. Everybody would be either mentally healthy or a Rehab, or "neonormal," as Dr. Speakie liked to call it.

It was the trouble in the State of Australia that precipitated[6] the Government crisis. Some Psychometric Bureau officials accused the Australian Evaluators of actually falsifying Test returns, but that is impossible since all the computers are linked to the World Government Central Computer Bank in Keokuk. Dr. Speakie suspected the Australian Evaluators

---

4. contingency (kən tin′ jən sē): pertaining to an accident, emergency, or other unforeseen happening.
5. Rehabs: those who have been rehabilitated, or restored to sanity.
6. precipitated (prē sip′ ə tāt əd): brought about suddenly.

had been falsifying *the Test itself*, and insisted that they themselves all be tested immediately. Of course he was right. It had been a conspiracy, and the suspiciously low Australian Test scores had resulted from the use of a false Test. Many of the conspirators tested higher than 80 when forced to take the genuine Test! The State Government in Canberra had been unforgivably lax. If they had just admitted it, everything would have been all right. But they got hysterical, and moved the State Government to a sheep station in Queensland, and tried to withdraw from the World Government. (Dr. Speakie said that was a typical mass psychosis: reality evasion, followed by fugue and autistic withdrawal.)[7] Unfortunately, the Presidium seemed to be paralyzed. Australia seceded on the day before the President and Presidium were due to take their monthly Test, and probably they were afraid of overstraining their SQ with agonizing decisions. So the Psychometric Bureau volunteered to handle the episode. Dr. Speakie himself flew on the plane with the H-bombs, and helped to drop the information leaflets. He never lacked personal courage.

When the Australian incident was over, it turned out that most of the Presidium, including President Singh, had scored over 50. So the Psychometric Bureau took over their functions temporarily. Even on a long-term basis this made good sense, since all the problems now facing the World Government had to do with administering and evaluating the Test, training the Staff, and providing full self-sufficiency structuration to all Asylums.

What this meant in personal terms was that Dr. Speakie, as Chief of the Psychometric Bureau, was now Interim President of the United States of the World. As his personal secretary, I was, I will admit it, just terribly proud of him. But he never let it go to his head.

He was so modest. Sometimes he used to say to people, when he introduced me, "This is Mary Ann, my secretary," he'd say with a little

twinkle, "and if it wasn't for her I'd have been scoring over 50 long ago!"

There were times, as the World SQ scores rose and rose, that I would become a little discouraged. Once the week's Test figures came in on the readout, and the *average* score was 71. I said, "Doctor, there are moments I believe the whole world is going insane!"

But he said, "Look at it this way, Mary Ann. Look at those people in the Asylums—3.1 billion inmates now, and 1.8 billion staff—but look at them. What are they doing? They're pursuing their therapy, doing rehabilitation work on the farms and in the factories, and striving all the time, too, to *help* each other toward mental health. The preponderant inverse sanity quotient is certainly very high at the moment; they're mostly insane, yes. But you have to admire them. They are fighting for mental health. They will—they *will* win through!" And then he dropped his voice and said as if to himself, gazing out the window and bouncing just a little on the balls of his feet, "If I didn't believe that, I couldn't go on."

And I knew he was thinking of his wife.

Mrs. Speakie had scored 88 on the very first American Universal Test. She had been in the Greater Los Angeles Territory Asylum for years now.

Anybody who still thinks Dr. Speakie wasn't sincere should think about that for a minute! He gave up everything for his belief.

And even when the Asylums were all running quite well, and the epidemics in South Africa and the famines in Texas and the Ukraine were under control, still the workload on Dr. Speakie never got any lighter, because every month the personnel of the Psychometric Bureau got smaller, since some of them

---

7. reality evasion . . . autistic withdrawal: the denial of what is real, followed by unusual behavior that is forgotten later and by extreme mental retreat from the world.

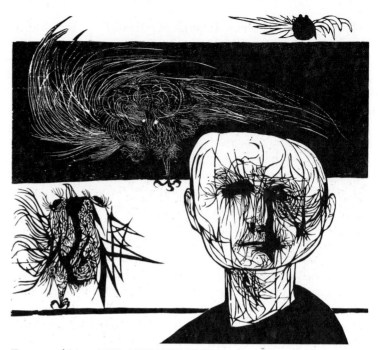

Tormented Man, 1953, LEONARD BASKIN. © Leonard Baskin.

always flunked their monthly Test and were committed to Bethesda. I never could keep any of my secretarial staff any more for longer than a month or two. It was harder and harder to find replacements, too, because most sane young people volunteered for Staff work in the Asylums, since life was much easier and more sociable inside the Asylums than outside. Everything so convenient, and lots of friends and acquaintances! I used to positively envy those girls! But I knew where my job was.

At least it was much less hectic here in the U.N. Building, or the Psychometry Tower as it had been renamed a long time ago. Often there wouldn't be anybody around the whole building all day long but Dr. Speakie and myself, and maybe Bill the janitor (Bill scored 32 regular as clockwork every quarter). All the restaurants were closed, in fact most of Manhattan was closed, but we had fun picnicking in the old General Assembly Hall. And there was always the odd call from Buenos Aires or Reykjavik, asking Dr. Speakie's advice as Interim President about some problem, to break the silence.

But last November 8, I will never forget the date, when Dr. Speakie was dictating the Referendum for World Economic Growth for the next five-year period, he suddenly interrupted himself. "By the way, Mary Ann," he said, "how was your last score?"

We had taken the Test two days before, on the sixth. We always took the Test every first Monday. Dr. Speakie never would have dreamed of excepting himself from Universal Testing regulations.

"I scored 12," I said, before I thought how strange it was of him to ask. Or, not just to ask, because we often mentioned our scores to each other; but to ask *then*, in the middle of executing important world government business.

"Wonderful," he said, shaking his head. "You're wonderful, Mary Ann! Down two from last month's Test, aren't you?"

"I'm always between 10 and 14," I said. "Nothing new about that, Doctor."

"Some day," he said, and his face took on the expression it had when he gave his great speech about the Asylums, "some day, this world of ours will be governed by men fit to govern it. Men whose SQ score is Zero. Zero, Mary Ann!"

"Well, my goodness, Doctor," I said jokingly—his intensity almost alarmed me a little—"even *you* never scored lower than 3, and you haven't done that for a year or more now!"

He stared at me almost as if he didn't see me. It was quite uncanny. "Some day," he said in just the same way, "nobody in the world will have a Quotient higher than 50. Some day, nobody in the world will have a Quotient higher than 30! Higher than 10! The therapy will be perfected. I was only the diagnostician. But the Therapy will be perfected! The cure will be found! Some day!" And he went on staring at me, and then he said, "Do you know what my score was on Monday?"

"7," I guessed promptly. The last time he had told me his score it had been 7.

"92," he said.

I laughed, because he seemed to be laughing. He had always had a puckish sense of humor. But I thought we really should get back to the World Economic Growth Plan, so I said laughingly, "That really is a very bad joke, Doctor!"

"92," he said, "and you don't believe me, Mary Ann, but that's because of the cantaloupe."

I said, "What cantaloupe, Doctor?" and that was when he jumped across his desk and began to try to bite through my jugular vein.

I used a judo hold and shouted to Bill the janitor, and when he came, I called a robo-ambulance to take Dr. Speakie to Bethesda Asylum.

That was six months ago. I visit Dr. Speakie every Saturday. It is very sad. He is in the McLean area, which is the Violent Ward, and every time he sees me he screams and foams. But I do not take it personally. One should never take mental ill health personally. When the Therapy is perfected, he will be completely rehabilitated. Meanwhile, I just hold on here. Bill keeps the floors clean, and I run the World Government. It really isn't as difficult as you might think.

*T*hinking About the Story

A PERSONAL RESPONSE

sharing impressions

1. What are your thoughts about the situation depicted in this story? Jot down your impressions in your journal.

constructing interpretations

2. Why do you think Dr. Speakie eventually fails the standardized SQ Test?

3. If you could speak to Mrs. Smith, what would you say to her about her admiration for Dr. Speakie?

Think about
- the qualities she admires in him
- what his enemies say about him

- his ideas about mental health
- how his ideas affect the lives of others

4. What would you say are the qualities that eventually make Mrs. Smith ruler of the world? Cite incidents that illustrate these qualities.

5. Speculate about why the government continues to rely on the SQ Test, and suggest what the authorities might have done instead.
Think about
- how Dr. Speakie answers critics of the SQ Test
- the contingency plans made to keep world functions running
- the high-level decision made after President Kim fails the SQ Test
- how Dr. Speakie rationalizes the increasingly high scores on the standardized test
- how the government responds to the Australian incident
- why the Psychometric Bureau ends up ruling the world

A CREATIVE RESPONSE

6. How would the story be different if Dr. Speakie were the narrator rather than Mrs. Smith?

A CRITICAL RESPONSE

7. What ironies in this story do you find especially interesting or amusing?
Think about
- irony as the contrast between what is expected and what actually occurs
- what Dr. Speakie expects to accomplish through use of a standardized test and what actually happens
- what life is like inside and outside the asylums
- the changing relationship between Dr. Speakie and Mrs. Smith

8. What situations or attitudes do you see in this story that remind you of society today? Give several examples when explaining your answer.

Analyzing the Writer's Craft

SATIRE AND SCIENCE FICTION

How do you think Le Guin wants readers to feel about the SQ Test?

Building a Literary Vocabulary. Satire is a literary technique in which ideas or customs are ridiculed for the purpose of improving society. Science fiction is prose writing in which a writer explores possibilities of the past or the future using known scientific data and theories as well as his or her own creative imagination. In "SQ" Le Guin creates a fictitious future world through which she satirizes certain ideas and customs of contemporary society. For example, the custom of using standardized tests to evaluate people is taken to its logical, laughable, and dangerous extreme.

Application: Understanding Satire. Working in a small group, choose three of the following actualities of today's world that Le Guin ridicules in "SQ."

- the eagerness to find quick fixes for complex problems
- the power of bureaucracies
- the bureaucratic approach to problems
- the power of so-called experts
- the preoccupation with mental health
- the need to appear emotionally controlled and well-adjusted
- the drive to quantify human behavior

Go through the story to find elements that illustrate each of the actualities you chose. Share your conclusions with other groups.

Connecting Reading and Writing

1. As an underground reporter, write an **exposé** of the experiences of inmates in Dr. Speakie's asylums for publication in *The World Enquirer.*

Option: Imagine that you failed the SQ Test and had to undergo rehabilitation. Write a **journal entry** describing your experiences in one of Dr. Speakie's asylums.

2. Imagine that Dr. Speakie has asked you to create questions for an SQ Test to be administered to students and teachers at your school. Write five or more **questions** that you would submit to him.

Option: In a **memo** to Dr. Speakie, outline your ideas about what kinds of questions should be asked on an SQ Test.

3. Write a **satirical sketch** for your classmates in which you take a situation in your school to its logical, exaggerated extreme.

Option: Write an **editorial** for your school newspaper stating your opinion about that same situation.

4. What might Dr. Speakie have been like as a teenager? Write a **character sketch** of him from the point of view of his counselor for inclusion in his high school record.

Option: Write a **dramatic skit** in which two girls whom he has dated discuss the teenage Speakie.

The Feeling of Power

ISAAC ASIMOV

A biography of Asimov appears on page 419.

Approaching the Story

Isaac Asimov, one of America's most prolific writers, has written more than three hundred books—including science, science fiction, history, and autobiography. "The Feeling of Power" is one of his most popular science fiction stories. As the story opens, Jehan Shuman is about to introduce a new discovery to two government officials. Do not be confused by the strange names and places of this new earth society, but use these details to piece together an understanding of the world in which the characters function.

Building Vocabulary

These essential words are footnoted within the story.

programming (prō′ gram iŋ): He originated **programming** patterns that resulted in self-directing war computers. (page 389)

incalculable (in kal′ kyoo lə bəl): I can't predict what the consequences will be in detail, but they will be **incalculable**. (page 392)

impingement (im pinj′ mənt): As the human brain takes over, more of our energy can be directed into peacetime pursuits, and the **impingement** of war on the ordinary man will be less. (page 393)

manipulates (mə nip′ yoo lāts): "The human mind, Computer Loesser, only **manipulates** facts." (page 393)

skeptically (skep′ ti kəl lē): Loesser said **skeptically**, "What progress?" (page 394)

recalcitrant (ri kal′ si trənt): General Weider . . . addressed his listeners after the fashion of a savage teacher facing a group of **recalcitrant** students. (page 394)

Connecting Writing and Reading

Predict some of the ways in which computers could change your life in the next fifty years. Make a list of these ways in your journal. Then as you read, jot down the ways in which computers have changed human society in this story.

*J*EHAN SHUMAN WAS used to dealing with the men in authority on long-embattled Earth. He was only a civilian, but he originated programming[1] patterns that resulted in self-directing war computers of the highest sort. Generals consequently listened to him. Heads of congressional committees, too.

There was one of each in the special lounge of New Pentagon. General Weider was space-burnt and had a small mouth puckered almost into a cipher. Congressman Brant was smooth cheeked and cleareyed. He smoked Denebian tobacco with the air of one whose patriotism was so notorious, he could be allowed such liberties.

Shuman, tall, distinguished, and Programmer-first-class, faced them fearlessly.

He said, "This, gentlemen, is Myron Aub."

"The one with the unusual gift that you discovered quite by accident," said Congressman Brant placidly. "Ah." He inspected the little man with the egg-bald head with amiable curiosity.

The little man, in return, twisted the fingers of his hands anxiously. He had never been near such great men before. He was only an aging low-grade Technician who had long ago failed all tests designed to smoke out the gifted ones among mankind and had settled into the rut of unskilled labor. There was just this hobby of his that the great Programmer had found out about and was now making such a frightening fuss over.

General Weider said, "I find this atmosphere of mystery childish."

"You won't in a moment," said Shuman. "This is not something we can leak to the first comer—Aub!" There was something imperative about his manner of biting off that one-syllable name, but then he was a great Programmer speaking to a mere Technician. "Aub! How much is nine times seven?"

Aub hesitated a moment. His pale eyes glimmered with a feeble anxiety. "Sixty-three," he said.

Congressman Brant lifted his eyebrows. "Is that right?"

"Check it for yourself, Congressman."

The congressman took out his pocket computer, nudged the milled edges twice, looked at its face as it lay there in the palm of his hand, and put it back. He said, "Is this the gift you brought us here to demonstrate? An illusionist?"[2]

"More than that, sir. Aub has memorized a few operations, and with them he computes on paper."

"A paper computer?" said the general. He looked pained.

"No, sir," said Shuman patiently. "Not a paper computer. Simply a sheet of paper. General, would you be so kind as to suggest a number?"

"Seventeen," said the general.

"And you, Congressman?"

"Twenty-three."

"Good! Aub, multiply those numbers and please show the gentlemen your manner of doing it."

"Yes, Programmer," said Aub, ducking his head. He fished a small pad out of one shirt pocket and an artist's hairline stylus[3] out of the other. His forehead corrugated as he made painstaking marks on the paper.

General Weider interrupted him sharply. "Let's see that."

Aub passed him the paper, and Weider said, "Well, it looks like the figure seventeen."

Congressman Brant nodded and said, "So it does, but I suppose anyone can copy figures off a computer. I think I could make a passable seventeen myself, even without practice."

---

1. **programming** (prō′ gram iŋ): planning a sequence of computer operations.

2. **illusionist** (i lōō′ zhən ist): magician.

3. **hairline stylus** (her′ līn stī′ ləs): thin-pointed pen.

Old Man Figuring, 1929, PAUL KLEE.
Etching, printed in brownish black, plate: 11 3/4" x 9 3/8".
Collection, The Museum of Modern Art, New York; purchase.

"If you will let Aub continue, gentlemen," said Shuman without heat.

Aub continued, his hand trembling a little. Finally he said in a low voice, "The answer is three hundred and ninety-one."

Congressman Brant took out his computer a second time and flicked it, "By Godfrey, so it is. How did he guess?"

"No guess, Congressman," said Shuman. "He computed that result. He did it on this sheet of paper."

"Humbug," said the general impatiently. "A computer is one thing, and marks on paper are another."

"Explain, Aub," said Shuman.

"Yes, Programmer. Well, gentlemen, I write down seventeen, and just underneath it, I write twenty-three. Next, I say to myself: seven times three—"

The congressman interrupted smoothly, "Now, Aub, the problem is seventeen times twenty-three."

"Yes, I know," said the little Technician earnestly, "but I *start* by saying seven times three because that's the way it works. Now seven times three is twenty-one."

"And how do you know that?" asked the congressman.

"I just remember it. It's always twenty-one on the computer. I've checked it any number of times."

"That doesn't mean it always will be, though, does it?" said the congressman.

"Maybe not," stammered Aub. "I'm not a mathematician. But I always get the right answers, you see."

"Go on."

"Seven times three is twenty-one, so I write down twenty-one. Then one times three is three, so I write down a three under the two of twenty-one."

"Why under the two?" asked Congressman Brant at once.

"Because—" Aub look-ed helplessly at his superior for support. "It's difficult to explain."

Shuman said, "If you will accept his work for the moment, we can leave the details for the mathematicians."

Brant subsided.

Aub said, "Three plus two makes five, you see, so the twenty-one becomes a fifty-one. Now you let that go for a while and start fresh. You multiply seven and two, that's fourteen, and one and two, that's two. Put them down like this, and it adds up to thirty-four. Now if you put the thirty-four under the fifty-one this way and add them, you get three hundred and ninety-one, and that's the answer."

There was an instant's silence, and then General Weider said, "I don't believe it. He goes through this rigmarole and makes up numbers and multiplies and adds them this way and that, but I don't believe it. It's too complicated to be anything but horn-swoggling."[4]

"Oh no, sir," said Aub in a sweat. "It only *seems* complicated because you're not used to it. Actually, the rules are quite simple and will work for any numbers."

"Any numbers, eh?" said the general.

"Come then." He took out his own computer (a severely styled GI model) and struck it at random. Make a five seven three eight on the paper. That's five thousand seven hundred and thirty-eight."

"Yes, sir," said Aub, taking a new sheet of paper.

"Now,"—more punching of his computer—"seven two three nine. Seven thousand two hundred and thirty-nine."

"Yes, sir."

"And now multiply those two."

"It will take some time," quavered Aub.

"Take the time," said the general.

"Go ahead, Aub," said Shuman crisply.

Aub set to work, bending low. He took another sheet of paper and another. The general took out his watch finally and stared at it. "Are you through with your magic making, Technician?"

"I'm almost done, sir. Here it is, sir. Forty-one million, five hundred and thirty-seven thousand, three hundred and eighty-two." He showed the scrawled figures of the result.

General Weider smiled bitterly. He pushed the multiplication contact on his computer and let the numbers whirl to a halt. And then he stared and said in a surprised squeak, "Great Galaxy, the fella's right."

The President of the Terrestrial Federation had grown haggard in office, and, in private, he allowed a look of settled melancholy to appear on his sensitive features. The Denebian war, after its early start of vast movement and great popularity, had trickled down into a sordid matter of maneuver and countermaneuver, with discontent rising steadily on Earth. Possibly, it was rising on Deneb, too.

And now Congressman Brant, head of the important Committee on Military Appropriations, was cheerfully and smoothly

---

4. **hornswoggling** (hôrn′ swäg′ liŋ): trickery.

spending his half-hour appointment spouting nonsense.

"Computing without a computer," said the president impatiently, "is a contradiction in terms."

"Computing," said the congressman, "is only a system for handling data. A machine might do it, or the human brain might. Let me give you an example." And, using the new skills he had learned, he worked out sums and products until the president, despite himself, grew interested.

"Does this always work?"

"Every time, Mr. President. It is foolproof."

"Is it hard to learn?"

"It took me a week to get the real hang of it. I think you would do better."

"Well," said the president, considering, "it's an interesting parlor game, but what is the use of it?"

"What is the use of a newborn baby, Mr. President? At the moment there is no use, but don't you see that this points the way toward liberation from the machine? Consider, Mr. President," the congressman rose and his deep voice automatically took on some of the cadences he used in public debate, "that the Denebian war is a war of computer against computer. Their computers forge an impenetrable shield of countermissiles against our missiles, and ours forge one against theirs. If we advance the efficiency of our computers, so do they theirs, and for five years a precarious and profitless balance has existed.

"Now we have in our hands a method for going beyond the computer, leapfrogging it, passing through it. We will combine the mechanics of computation with human thought; we will have the equivalent of intelligent computers; billions of them. I can't predict what the consequences will be in detail, but they will be incalculable.[5] And if Deneb beats us to the punch, they may be unimaginably catastrophic."

The president said, troubled, "What would you have me do?"

"Put the power of the administration behind the establishment of a secret project on human computation. Call it Project Number, if you like. I can vouch for my committee, but I will need the administration behind me."

"But how far can human computation go?"

"There is no limit. According to Programmer Shuman, who first introduced me to this discovery—"

"I've heard of Shuman, of course."

"Yes. Well, Dr. Shuman tells me that in theory there is nothing the computer can do that the human mind cannot do. The computer merely takes a finite amount of data and performs a finite number of operations upon them. The human mind can duplicate the process."

The president considered that. He said, "If Shuman says this, I am inclined to believe him—in theory. But, in practice, how can anyone know how a computer works?"

Brant laughed genially. "Well, Mr. President, I asked the same question. It seems that at one time computers were designed directly by human beings. Those were simple computers, of course, this being before the time of the rational use of computers to design more advanced computers."

"Yes, yes. Go on."

"Technician Aub apparently had, as his hobby, the reconstruction of some of these ancient devices, and in so doing he studied the details of their workings and found he could imitate them. The multiplication I just performed for you is an imitation of the workings of a computer."

"Amazing!"

The congressman coughed gently, "If I may make another point, Mr. President—the

---

5. incalculable (in kal′ kyo͞o lə bəl): too great or uncertain to be figured out or predicted.

further we can develop this thing, the more we can divert our Federal effort from computer production and computer maintenance. As the human brain takes over, more of our energy can be directed into peacetime pursuits, and the impingement[6] of war on the ordinary man will be less. This will be most advantageous for the party in power, of course."

"Ah," said the president, "I see your point. Well, sit down, Congressman, sit down. I want some time to think about this. But meanwhile, show me that multiplication trick again. Let's see if I can't catch the point of it."

Programmer Shuman did not try to hurry matters. Loesser was conservative, very conservative, and liked to deal with computers as his father and grandfather had. Still, he controlled the West European computer combine, and if he could be persuaded to join Project Number in full enthusiasm, a great deal would be accomplished.

But Loesser was holding back. He said, "I'm not sure I like the idea of relaxing our hold on computers. The human mind is a capricious thing. The computer will give the same answer to the same problem each time. What guarantee have we that the human mind will do the same?"

"The human mind, Computer Loesser, only manipulates[7] facts. It doesn't matter whether the human mind or a machine does it. They are just tools."

"Yes, yes. I've gone over your ingenious demonstration that the mind can duplicate the computer, but it seems to me a little in the air. I'll grant the theory, but what reason have we for thinking that theory can be converted to practice?"

"I think we have reason, sir. After all, computers have not always existed. The cave men with their triremes,[8] stone axes, and railroads had no computers."

"And possibly they did not compute."

"You know better than that. Even the building of a railroad or a ziggurat[9] called for some computing, and that must have been without computers as we know them."

"Do you suggest they computed in the fashion you demonstrate?"

"Probably not. After all, this method—we call it *graphitics*, by the way, from the old European word *grapho*, meaning 'to write'—is developed from the computers themselves, so it cannot have antedated them. Still, the cave men must have had *some* method, eh?"

"Lost arts! If you're going to talk about lost arts—"

"No, no. I'm not a lost art enthusiast, though I don't say there may not be some. After all, man was eating grain before hydroponics,[10] and if the primitives ate grain they must have grown it in soil. What else could they have done?"

"I don't know, but I'll believe in soil-growing when I see someone grow grain in soil. And I'll believe in making fire by rubbing two pieces of flint together when I see that, too."

Shuman grew placative. "Well, let's stick to graphitics. It's just part of the process of etherealization. Transportation by means of bulky contrivances is giving way to direct mass-transference. Communications devices become less massive and more efficient constantly. For that matter, compare your pocket computer with the massive jobs of a

---

6. impingement (im pinj′ mənt): a trespassing or intruding.

7. manipulates (mə nip′ yoo lāts): works, operates, or treats with skill.

8. triremes (trī′ rēms′): warships, used in ancient Greece and Rome.

9. ziggurat (zig′ oo rat′): a pryamid-like structure common in ancient Babylonia.

10. hydroponics (hī′ drō pän′ iks): the growing of plants in nutrient-rich liquid instead of soil.

thousand years ago. Why not, then, the last step of doing away with computers altogether? Come, sir, Project Number is a going concern; progress is already headlong. But we want your help. If patriotism doesn't move you, consider the intellectual adventure involved."

Loesser said skeptically,[11] "What progress? What can you do beyond multiplication? Can you integrate a transcendental function?"[12]

"In time, sir. In time. In the last month I have learned to handle division. I can determine, and correctly, integral quotients and decimal quotients."

"Decimal quotients? To how many places?"

Programmer Shuman tried to keep his tone casual. "Any number!"

Loesser's lower jaw dropped. "Without a computer?"

"Set me a problem."

"Divide twenty-seven by thirteen. Take it to six places."

Five minutes later, Shuman said, "Two point oh seven six nine two three."

Loesser checked it. "Well now, that's amazing. Multiplication didn't impress me too much because it involved integers after all, and I thought trick manipulation might do it. But decimals—"

"And that is not all. There is a new development that is, so far, top secret and which, strictly speaking, I ought not to mention. Still—we may have made a breakthrough on the square root front."

"Square roots?"

"It involves some tricky points, and we haven't licked the bugs yet, but Technician Aub, the man who invented the science and who has an amazing intuition in connection with it, maintains he has the problem almost solved. And he is only a Technician. A man like yourself, a trained and talented mathematician, ought to have no difficulty."

"Square roots," muttered Loesser, attracted.

"Cube roots, too. Are you with us?"

Loesser's hand thrust out suddenly, "Count me in."

General Weider stumped his way back and forth at the head of the room and addressed his listeners after the fashion of a savage teacher facing a group of recalcitrant[13] students. It made no difference to the general that they were the civilian scientists heading Project Number. The general was the overall head, and he so considered himself at every waking moment.

He said, "Now square roots are all fine. I can't do them myself, and I don't understand the methods, but they're fine. Still, the Project will not be sidetracked into what some of you call the fundamentals. You can play with graphitics any way you want to after the war is over, but right now we have specific and very practical problems to solve."

In a far corner, Technician Aub listened with painful attention. He was no longer a Technician, of course, having been relieved of his duties and assigned to the project, with a fine-sounding title and good pay. But, of course, the social distinction remained, and the highly placed scientific leaders could never bring themselves to admit him to their ranks on a footing of equality. Nor, to do Aub justice, did he, himself, wish it. He was as uncomfortable with them as they with him.

The general was saying, "Our goal is a simple one, gentlemen: the replacement of the computer. A ship that can navigate space without a computer on board can be

---

11. skeptically (skep′ ti kəl lē): in a doubting manner.
12. integrate a transcendental function: a reference to the problems of higher mathematics, a field that quickly embraced, and was greatly enhanced by, computer technology.
13. recalcitrant (ri kal′ si trənt): refusing to obey authority or follow rules.

constructed in one fifth the time and at one tenth the expense of a computer-laden ship. We could build fleets five times, ten times, as great as Deneb could if we could but eliminate the computer.

"And I see something even beyond this. It may be fantastic now; a mere dream; but in the future I see the manned missile!"

There was an instant murmur from the audience.

The general drove on. "At the present time, our chief bottleneck is the fact that missiles are limited in intelligence. The computer controlling them can only be so large, and for that reason they can meet the changing nature of antimissile defenses in an unsatisfactory way. Few missiles, if any, accomplish their goal, and missile warfare is coming to a dead end—for the enemy, fortunately, as well as for ourselves.

"On the other hand, a missile with a man or two within, controlling flight by graphitics, would be lighter, more mobile, more intelligent. It would give us a lead that might well mean the margin of victory. Besides which, gentlemen, the exigencies of war compel us to remember one thing. A man is much more dispensable than a computer. Manned missiles could be launched in numbers and under circumstances that no good general would care to undertake as far as computer-directed missiles are concerned—"

He said much more, but Technician Aub did not wait.

Technician Aub, in the privacy of his quarters, labored long over the note he was leaving behind. It read finally as follows:

"When I began the study of what is now called graphitics, it was no more than a hobby. I saw no more in it than an interesting amusement, an exercise of mind.

"When Project Number began, I thought that others were wiser than I; that graphitics might be put to practical use as a benefit to mankind, to aid in the production of really practical mass-transference devices perhaps. But now I see it is to be used only for death and destruction.

"I cannot face the responsibility involved in having invented graphitics."

He then deliberately turned the focus of a protein-depolarizer on himself and fell instantly and painlessly dead.

They stood over the grave of the little Technician while tribute was paid to the greatness of his discovery.

Programmer Shuman bowed his head along with the rest of them but remained unmoved. The Technician had done his share and was no longer needed, after all. He might have started graphitics, but, now that it had started, it would carry on by itself overwhelmingly, triumphantly, until manned missiles were possible with who knew what else.

Nine times seven, thought Shuman with deep satisfaction, is sixty-three, and I don't need a computer to tell me so. The computer is in my own head.

And it was amazing the feeling of power that gave him.

Thinking About the Story

A PERSONAL RESPONSE

sharing impressions

1. How did you respond to the vision of the future presented in this story? Write about your response in your journal.

constructing interpretations

2. Why does knowing how to multiply give Shuman a feeling of power?

3. What is revealed about Shuman, General Weider, and Congressman Brant by the way they treat Aub?

> **Think about**
> - how Shuman speaks to Aub during their presentation of graphitics
> - how the general and the congressman react to Aub's discovery
> - why Shuman and the general decide to use Aub's method of calculation
> - how Shuman feels at Aub's grave

4. Explain whether you think the negative aspects of this society are caused more by computers or by humans.

A CREATIVE RESPONSE

5. If Myron Aub had gone to the leaders on Deneb and told them the secret of Earth's graphitics, what might have happened?

A CRITICAL RESPONSE

6. Explain some ironies that you see in this story.

> **Think about**
> - situational irony as the contrast between what is expected and what happens
> - dramatic irony as the contrast between what the characters know and what the reader knows

7. When Isaac Asimov wrote this story in 1957, computers took up entire rooms, and pocket calculators had not been developed yet. If Asimov rewrote this story today, how might it be different?

> **Think about**
> - how the technology of today compares with the technology in the story
> - what direction future advances in technology might take
> - whether the threat of war is as great now as it was in 1957
> - what is the greatest threat in our society today

8. How can society encourage scientific development without becoming overly dependent on computers?

Analyzing the Writer's Craft

THEME AND SCIENCE FICTION

Think of one message in the story that applies to society today, as well as to the future society that is portrayed. Jot down this message in your journal.

Building a Literary Vocabulary. Theme is the central idea or message in a story, a perception about life that the author shares with the reader. Most stories contain several themes, one of which usually predominates. Most science fiction comments on present-day society through the writer's conception of a past or future society. In "The Feeling of Power," Myron Aub is an ordinary Technician because he failed the tests designed to identify gifted people—even though, ironically, he was gifted enough to rediscover the art of multiplication. Asimov may be warning readers about the dangers of judging people on the basis of their test scores, a practice that exists today.

Application: Identifying Themes. Working in groups of three or four, create a list of two or more messages communicated in the story, including the ones that you already identified. Decide which of these messages is the central theme of the story. Write a slogan to express this theme, display your slogan on a placard, and then stage a demonstration to convince your classmates of the importance of this theme.

Connecting Reading and Writing

1. Contrast the characters of Shuman and Aub in a **letter** explaining which man you would recommend for a job.

Option: Create a **wanted poster** published by the Denebian government explaining how to tell the two men apart.

2. From Aub's point of view, discuss in a **diary entry** how graphitics might be used to benefit humanity.

Option: Write a **proposal** to Congress to get funding for research on graphitics.

3. How would you describe to the government officials in this story what is unique about the power of the human mind? Present your ideas in an **outline** for an editorial.

Option: Write **notes** for a speech on the uniqueness of the human mind.

4. Drawing on your prereading predictions, describe what life might be like fifty years from now in an **advertisement** for time travel.

Option: Write a **description** of a setting for a science fiction story that takes place fifty years from now.

Tale of the Computer That Fought a Dragon

STANISLAW ŁEM

A biography of Łem appears on page 424.

Approaching the Story

Stanislaw Łem is a well-known writer from Poland who often uses science fiction as a vehicle for social commentary. This story is about an imaginary king in an imaginary country, but it concerns a very real and controversial science: cybernetics, the development of computers with artificial intelligence. The unfamiliar names of creatures and objects in the story as well as the incredible events described lure readers into the fantasy world of Cyberia, where cyberbeetles and cyberflies abound and where cybernetic weapons and cyberfoes pose a daily threat.

Building Vocabulary

These essential words are footnoted within the story.

bellicose (bel′ i kōs′): There were twice as many military [devices], for the King was most **bellicose**. (page 399)

mettle (met′ 'l): He had a strategic computer, a machine of uncommon **mettle**. (page 399)

sallies: Now it was cosmic wars and **sallies** that he dreamed of. (page 399)

verisimilitude (ver′ ə si mil′ ə to͞od): The electrodragon wasn't . . . pretending, but battled with the utmost **verisimilitude**. (page 400)

Connecting Writing and Reading

Think of various tasks that you would gladly hand over to a "smart" computer, one with near-human intelligence. In your journal describe how such a computer might perform those tasks for you. As you read, compare your use of an intelligent computer with the ways intelligent computers are used in Cyberia.

KING POLEANDER Parto-bon, ruler of Cyberia, was a great warrior, and being an advocate of the methods of modern strategy, above all else he prized cybernetics as a military art. His kingdom swarmed with thinking machines, for Poleander put them everywhere he could; not merely in the astronomical observatories or the schools, but he ordered electric brains mounted in the rocks upon the roads, which with loud voices cautioned pedestrians against tripping; also in posts, in walls, in trees, so that one could ask directions anywhere when lost; he stuck them onto clouds, so they could announce the rain in advance, he added them to the hills and valleys—in short, it was impossible to walk on Cyberia without bumping into an intelligent machine. The planet was beautiful, since the King not only gave decrees for the cybernetic perfecting of that which had long been in existence, but he introduced by law entirely new orders of things. Thus for example in his kingdom were manufactured cyberbeetles and buzzing cyberbees, and even cyberflies—these would be seized by mechanical spiders when they grew too numerous. On the planet cyberbosks of cybergorse[1] rustled in the wind, cybercalliopes and cyberviols sang—but besides these civilian devices there were twice as many military, for the King was most bellicose.[2] In his palace vaults he had a strategic computer, a machine of uncommon mettle;[3] he had smaller ones also, and divisions of cybersaries, enormous cybermatics and a whole arsenal of every other kind of weapon, including powder. There was only this one problem, and it troubled him greatly, namely, that he had not a single adversary or enemy and no one in any way wished to invade his land and thereby provide him with the opportunity to demonstrate his kingly and terrifying courage, his tactical genius, not to mention the simply extraordinary effectiveness of his

cybernetic weaponry. In the absence of genuine enemies and aggressors, the King had his engineers build artificial ones, and against these he did battle and always won. However, inasmuch as the battles and campaigns were genuinely dreadful, the populace suffered no little injury from them. The subjects murmured when all too many cyberfoes had destroyed their settlements and towns, when the synthetic enemy poured liquid fire upon them; they even dared voice their discontent when the King himself, issuing forth as their deliverer and vanquishing the artificial foe, in the course of the victorious attacks laid waste to everything that stood in his path. They grumbled even then, the ingrates, though the thing was done on their behalf.

Until the King wearied of the war games on the planet and decided to raise his sights. Now it was cosmic wars and sallies[4] that he dreamed of. His planet had a large Moon, entirely desolate and wild; the King laid heavy taxes upon his subjects to obtain the funds needed to build whole armies on that Moon and have there a new theater of war. And the subjects were more than happy to pay, figuring that King Poleander would now no longer deliver them with his cybermatics nor test the strength of his arms upon their homes and heads. And so the royal engineers built on the Moon a splendid computer, which in turn was to create all manner of troops and self-firing gunnery. The King lost no time in testing the machine's prowess this way and that; at one point he ordered it—by telegraph—to execute

---

1. **cyberbosks of cybergorse:** *Bosk* means "a small wooded place"; *gorse* is a kind of prickly evergreen shrub. Combined with the prefix *cyber*, they become one of Łem's invented phrases, meaning "computerized forests of computerized trees."
2. **bellicose** (bel′ i kōs′): eager to fight; warlike.
3. **mettle** (met′ 'l): stamina.
4. **sallies:** sudden attacks.

a volt-vault electrosault: for he wanted to see if it was true, what his engineers had told him, that that machine could do anything. If it can do anything, he thought, then let it do a flip. However, the text of the telegram underwent a slight distortion and the machine received the order that it was to execute not an electrosault, but an electrosaur—and this it carried out as best it could.

Meanwhile the King conducted one more campaign, liberating some provinces of his realm seized by cyberknechts; he completely forgot about the order given the computer on the Moon—then suddenly giant boulders came hurtling down from there; the King was astounded, for one even fell on the wing of the palace and destroyed his prize collection of cyberads, which are dryads[5] with feedback. Fuming, he telegraphed the Moon computer at once, demanding an explanation. It didn't reply, however, for it no longer was: the electrosaur had swallowed it and made it into its own tail.

Immediately the King dispatched an entire armed expedition to the Moon, placing at its head another computer, also very valiant, to slay the dragon, but there was only some flashing, some rumbling, and then no more computer nor expedition; for the electrodragon wasn't pretend and wasn't pretending, but battled with the utmost verisimilitude,[6] and had moreover the worst of intentions regarding the kingdom and the King. The King sent to the Moon his cybernants, cyberneers, cyberines and lieutenant cybernets; at the very end he even sent one cyberalissimo, but it too accomplished nothing; the hurly-burly lasted a little longer, that was all. The King watched through a telescope set up on the palace balcony.

The dragon grew; the Moon became smaller and smaller, since the monster was devouring it piecemeal and incorporating it into its own body. The King saw then, and his subjects did

also, that things were serious, for when the ground beneath the feet of the electrosaur was gone, it would for certain hurl itself upon the planet and upon them. The King thought and thought, but he saw no remedy and knew not what to do. To send machines was no good, for they would be lost, and to go himself was no better, for he was afraid. Suddenly the King heard, in the stillness of the night, the telegraph chattering from his royal bedchamber. It was the King's personal receiver, solid gold with a diamond needle, linked to the Moon; the King jumped up and ran to it; the apparatus meanwhile went *tap-tap, tap-tap*, and tapped out this telegram: THE DRAGON SAYS POLEANDER PARTOBON BETTER CLEAR OUT BECAUSE HE THE DRAGON INTENDS TO OCCUPY THE THRONE!

The King took fright, quaked from head to toe, and ran, just as he was, in his ermine nightshirt and slippers, down to the palace vaults, where stood the strategy machine, old and very wise. He had not as yet consulted it, since prior to the rise and uprise of the electrodragon they had argued on the subject of a certain military operation; but now was not the time to think of that—his throne, his life was at stake!

He plugged it in, and as soon as it warmed up he cried:

"My old computer! My good computer! It's this way and that, the dragon wishes to deprive me of my throne, to cast me out, help, speak, how can I defeat it?!"

"Uh-uh," said the computer. "First you must admit I was right in that previous business, and secondly, I would have you address me only as Digital Grand Vizier,[7] though you

---

5. dryads: wood nymphs.

6. verisimilitude (ver′ ə si mil′ ə tōōd): the appearance of being true or real.

7. vizier (vi zir′): originally a Turkish word referring to a high officer in the government.

may also say to me: 'Your Ferromagneticity!'"[8]

"Good, good, I'll name you Grand Vizier, I'll agree to anything you like, only save me!"

The machine whirred, chirred, hummed, hemmed, then said:

"It is a simple matter. We build an electrosaur more powerful than the one located on the Moon. It will defeat the lunar one, settle its circuitry once and for all and thereby attain the goal!"

"Perfect!" replied the King. "And can you make a blueprint of this dragon?"

"It will be an ultradragon," said the computer. "And I can make you not only a blueprint, but the thing itself, which I shall now do; it won't take a minute, King!" And true to its word, it hissed, it chugged, it whistled and buzzed, assembling something down within itself, and already an object like a giant claw, sparking, arcing, was emerging from its side, when the King shouted:

"Old computer! Stop!"

"Is this how you address me? I am the Digital Grand Vizier!"

"Ah, of course," said the King. "Your Ferromagneticity, the electrodragon you are making will defeat the other dragon, granted, but it will surely remain in the other's place. How then are we to get rid of it in turn?!"

"By making yet another, still more powerful," explained the computer.

"No, no! In that case don't do anything, I beg you. What good will it be to have more and more terrible dragons on the Moon when I don't want any there at all?"

"Ah, now that's a different matter," the computer replied. "Why didn't you say so in the first place? You see how illogically you express yourself? One moment . . . I must think."

And it churred and hummed, and chuffed and chuckled, and finally said:

"We make an antimoon with an antidragon, place it in the Moon's orbit (here something went snap inside), sit around the fire and sing: *Oh, I'm a robot full of fun, water doesn't scare me none, I dives right in, I gives a grin, tra la the livelong day!!*"

"You speak strangely," said the King. "What does the antimoon have to do with that song about the funny robot?"

"What funny robot?" asked the computer. "Ah, no, no, I made a mistake, something feels wrong inside, I must have blown a tube." The King began to look for the trouble, finally found the burnt out tube, put in a new one, then asked the computer about the antimoon.

"What antimoon?" asked the computer, which meanwhile had forgotten what it said before. "I don't know anything about an antimoon . . . one moment, I have to give this thought."

It hummed, it huffed, and it said:

"We create a general theory of the slaying of electrodragons, of which the lunar dragon will be a special case, its solution trivial."

"Well, create such a theory!" said the King.

"To do this I must first create various experimental dragons."

"Certainly not! No thank you!" exclaimed the King. "A dragon wants to deprive me of my throne. Just think what might happen if you produced a swarm of them!"

"Oh? Well then, in that case we must resort to other means. We will use a strategic variant of the method of successive approximations. Go and telegraph the dragon that you will give it the throne on the condition that it perform three mathematical operations, really quite simple . . ."

The King went and telegraphed, and the dragon agreed. The King returned to the computer.

"Now," it said, "here is the first operation: tell it to divide itself by itself!"

---

8. Ferromagneticity: an invented title meaning "Highly Magnetic One."

The King did this. The electrosaur divided itself by itself, but since one electrosaur over one electrosaur is one, it remained on the Moon and nothing changed.

"Is this the best you can do?!" cried the King, running into the vault with such haste that his slippers fell off. "The dragon divided itself by itself, but since one goes into one once, nothing changed!"

"That's all right. I did that on purpose— the operation was to divert attention," said the computer. "And now tell it to extract its root!" The King telegraphed to the Moon, and the dragon began to pull, push, pull, push, until it crackled from the strain, panted, trembled all over, but suddenly something gave—and it extracted its own root!

The King went back to the computer.

"The dragon crackled, trembled, even ground its teeth, but extracted the root and threatens me still!" he shouted from the doorway. "What now, my old . . . I mean, Your Ferromagneticity?!"

"Be of stout heart," it said. "Now go tell it to subtract itself from itself!"

The King hurried to his royal bedchamber, sent the telegram, and the dragon began to subtract itself from itself, taking away its tail first, then legs, then trunk, and finally, when it saw that something wasn't right, it hesitated, but from its own momentum the subtracting continued, it took away its head and became zero, in other words, nothing: the electrosaur was no more!

"The electrosaur is no more," cried the joyful King, bursting into the vault. "Thank you, old computer . . . many thanks . . . you have worked hard . . . you have earned a rest, so now I will disconnect you."

"Not so fast, my dear," the computer replied. "I do the job and you want to disconnect me, and you no longer call me Your Ferromagneticity?! That's not nice, not nice at all! Now I myself will change into an electrosaur, yes, and drive you from the kingdom, and most certainly rule better than you, for you always consulted me in all the more important matters; therefore, it was really I who ruled all along, and not you . . ."

And huffing, puffing, it began to change into an electrosaur; flaming electroclaws were already protruding from its sides when the King, breathless with fright, tore the slippers off his feet, rushed up to it and with the slippers began beating blindly at its tubes! The computer chugged, choked, and got muddled in its program—instead of the word "electrosaur" it read "electrosauce," and before the King's very eyes the computer, wheezing more and more softly, turned into an enormous, gleaming-golden heap of electrosauce, which, still sizzling, emitted all its charge in deep blue sparks, leaving Poleander to stare dumbstruck at only a great, steaming pool of gravy . . .

With a sigh the King put on his slippers and returned to the royal bedchamber. However, from that time on he was an altogether different king: the events he had undergone made his nature less bellicose, and to the end of his days he engaged exclusively in civilian cybernetics and left the military kind strictly alone.

Thinking About the Story

A PERSONAL RESPONSE

sharing impressions

1. How do you feel about intelligent computers after reading the story? Briefly describe your feelings in your journal.

constructing interpretations

2. What do you think Łem is satirizing most in this story?

3. Do you think the problems of Cyberia are caused more by humans—the king and his subjects—or by intelligent computers?

> ***Think about***
> * the description of the king and his subjects
> * the advice of the strategy machine
> * the malfunctions of the computers in the story

A CREATIVE RESPONSE

4. If King Poleander had not been bellicose, how might this story be different?

A CRITICAL RESPONSE

5. How would you describe Łem's tone in the story? Go back through the story and find examples of sentences that reveal his attitude.

Analyzing the Writer's Craft

THEME AND SCIENCE FICTION

Recall your answer to question 2 regarding what Łem is satirizing most in this story. How might his ideas apply to society today?

Building a Literary Vocabulary. Theme is the central idea or message in a work of literature. Generally, short stories present several themes, one of which usually predominates. Most science fiction comments on present-day society through the writer's conception of a past or future society. Some science fiction writers create believable worlds while others, like Łem, create fantasy worlds that have familiar elements. In "Tale of the Computer That Fought a Dragon," Łem uses the character of King Poleander, who almost destroys his kingdom by fighting foes of his own creation, to raise the issue of what qualities make a good leader, a question that continues to be crucial in today's society. Łem further raises serious questions about the appropriate use of powerful technology, especially as it promotes the production of weapons and the continued existence of war.

Application: Exploring Theme. Two important themes presented in the story are: (1) misuse of power by people poses a threat to humanity, and (2) machines pose a threat to humanity. Get together with several classmates and form two small debate groups, one group taking the position that human beings are the greater threat and the other side taking the position that machines pose a greater threat. Present your ideas to the rest of the class. Then ask your classmates to assess the supporting evidence from the story given for each position and then decide which theme predominates in the story.

Connecting Reading and Writing

1. Read another science fiction story by Łem—for example, "The Electronic Bard"— or a story by another science fiction writer such as Isaac Asimov or Ray Bradbury. Create a **chart** in which you compare the story to "Tale of the Computer That Fought a Dragon" in terms of plot, character, setting, and theme. Provide copies of your chart for classmates interested in science fiction.

Option: Write a **letter** to a friend explaining which story you liked more, and why.

2. Design a **poster** advertising a movie based on this story. Be sure your poster includes inventions from the story, such as the electrosaur and other cybercreatures.

Option: Write **guidelines** for creating the special effects that would be needed in a film version of the story.

3. Write an **outline** for a science fiction story based on a terrific new cybernetic machine of your own invention.

Option: Create the first two pages of an **instruction manual** for your invention. Illustrate and describe the capabilities of your new cybernetic machine.

Vocational Counselling

CHRISTA REINIG

A biography of Reinig appears on page 427.

✒ Approaching the Story

"Vocational Counselling" breaks from the traditional short story form in both structure and appearance. The story is Christa Reinig's (rī′ niH) unconventional response to the question "Why do you write?" In the story Reinig describes an encounter with a computer that is programmed to choose appropriate careers, or vocations, for people. The selection appears to be a reminiscence, but it is actually a work of fiction in which the writer herself is a character. The computer in the story has capabilities far beyond anything that has been developed even today. However, the rest of the story accurately reflects German life during her youth in the1930's and1940's. Reinig grew up under the regimes of Nazi Germany and communist East Germany, two states that exercised rigid control over people's private lives. In her story, the computer represents the totalitarian state.

✒ Building Vocabulary

These essential words are footnoted within the story.

guttural (gut′ ər əl): The computer talked in its **guttural**, electronic voice. (page 406)

atrophied (a′ trə fēd): Their eyes have **atrophied** because they have been living in darkness for so long. (page 407)

✒ Connecting Writing and Reading

Of the factors listed below, which do you think should be most important in determining your career choice? Which should be least important?

skills and abilities	family traditions or expectations
scores on a job aptitude test	interests and hobbies
advice from a career counsellor	chance
the needs of your country, community, or ethnic group	
the types of jobs available in a certain location	

Explain your answers in your journal. As you read this selection, keep in mind your views about what should determine career choice.

Vocational Counselling

I was still a child, "talked like a child, was bright like a child and had childlike notions." But as far as the state was concerned, I was finishing school and next year I would go out into the real world, into the state. We formed lines in front of the white doors, the boys and girls separately. We read the flyers which they had handed to us at the door:

> In the testing booth absolute silence must prevail. Concentrate! If you do not understand the question, press the blue button. You have one minute to formulate your answer. At the sound of the bell, get up and leave the room.

The fact that someone suddenly addressed me by the polite form[1] was no comfort to me. It increased my fears. As I finally confronted "it," alone in a humming room, I was trembling and I pressed the red button—the red button on my left. But I did not get it at all that I had given myself away as being left-handed. I could not sit down properly. My child's behind was wiggling on the stool. I had to go to the bathroom. A minute later I had forgotten about it.

The computer talked in its guttural,[2] electronic voice:

> Comrade[3] Reinig! Do you remember when you consciously heard the word *work* for the first time and what emotions it evoked in you?

Reinig: I consciously heard the word for the first time in the expression "without work" and it evoked pleasant emotions in me.

Computer: What images can you remember?

Reinig: It was in Humboldt Park. The men were sitting close together on benches, folding chairs or on the borders of the lawn. In front of them, on their knees they had cigar boxes and shoe cartons full of little pictures from their cigarette packages. They visited each other and exchanged the pictures back and forth. One

---

1. polite form: German, like many other languages, has two forms for the second-person pronoun *you*. One is used for close friends, family, and children. The other, the polite form, is more formal. Use of this form implies that the computer is treating Reinig like an adult.

2. guttural (gut′ ər əl): produced in the throat; harsh; rasping.

3. Comrade: a form of address used in many communist countries.

Greta Garbo for one Emil Jannings.[4] One French fighter plane for one Focke-Wulf,[5] one Chinese Mandarin for one Huron Warrior in ceremonial garb. The whole of Humboldt Park was one big market swarming with these men exchanging little pictures. Later they said that the nightmarish time of unemployment was over and we could all look to the future with joy. I said to myself these adults are nuts, and secretly I decided to be unemployed one day.

Computer: What are the dominating feelings when early in the morning the sound of an alarm clock tears you from your sleep?

Reinig: I feel a great sorrow in my heart.

Computer: During the course of the day, do you repeatedly feel a great sorrow in your heart?

Reinig: No, once I have managed to get out of bed, the worst part of the day is behind me.

Computer: What is your favorite occupation?

Reinig: Reading.

Computer: What do you like to read best?

Reinig: Karl May, John Kling, Billy Jenkins, Rolf Torring, Jorn Farrow, Tom Mix.

Computer: What is your favorite book?

Reinig: Olaf K. Abelsen,[6] *At the Fires of Eternity*. I must have read it a dozen times and I can recite it from memory.

Computer: Give a short summary of the contents.

Reinig: Well, the group of travelers is being followed by gangsters. One does not know why, because it is a story in installments. The gangsters blow up the island. Because of that, the group of travelers gets under the earth into a dark volcanic landscape, weakly lighted by a distant fire. There are animals there, too—crocodiles, bats. These animals are blind, their eyes have atrophied[7] because they have been living in darkness for so long. Then the travelers discover the remains of an ancient Mayan

---

4. **Greta Garbo . . . Emil Jannings:** Greta Garbo (1905–1990) was a famous American film actress; Emil Jannings (1884–1950) was a famous German film actor.
5. **Focke-Wulf** (fô′ kə voolf): a kind of German war plane.
6. **Karl May . . . Tom Mix . . . Olaf K. Abelsen:** Tom Mix was an American actor who played cowboy roles. The other names are of writers of popular adventure stories in the mid-twentieth century.
7. **atrophied** (a′ trə fēd): wasted away from lack of use.

culture. As they are about to recover the treasures, someone shoots poisoned arrows at them. It is not the Indians, however, but the gangsters who are pursuing them. The fire of eternity changes, and there is a volcanic eruption. The travelers are blown up from the depths and thrown into the sea. There they find each other again while fighting the waves. That is the end. The next volume is missing, but I believe they are rescued.

Computer: Did you ever try to read a classical work by Schiller or Goethe?[8]

Reinig: Yes, I once tried to read a sea adventure play by Goethe or Schiller.

The familiar humming sound stopped. Suddenly there was complete silence. Then there was a soft, hoarse little cough that did not stop. In a sense it had been quite pleasant until now. But then I realized that I had bared the lining of my heart, not to a sympathetic soul, but to a machine which must have cost at least many millions of dollarrubles. And I had wrecked it. Worse, at any moment it would explode and tear me to pieces. That might be better; at least I would not have to pay for it. How many years would it take to pay for it by working it off? I would rather prepare myself for death. Then there was that humming again. Our Father—thank God.

Computer: Did you ever try to read a classical work by Goethe or Schiller?

Reinig: Torquato Tasso.[9]

The crazier these exotic names are the better one can remember them. Schimborassotschomolungmakiliman-dscharo! Why doesn't he ask me something like that?

Computer: Describe the artistic impressions which you have received.

Reinig: The book got in with our furniture and junk in some way. It got lost there and surfaced now and then. Finally I felt sorry. I always read the last page first. They mentioned a ship's sinking. The hero, battling the waves, was trying to hold onto a cliff. Then, again, the sequel was also missing. Possibly he was rescued, for if

---

8. Schiller or Goethe (gö′ tə): considered the greatest German writers. They hold a position similar to that of Shakespeare in English.

9. Torquato Tasso (tôr kwä′ tô täs′ ô): a play by Goethe based on the life of Tasso, the medieval Italian writer of an epic poem filled with romantic fantasy and adventure. The play dramatizes the conflict between the poet's inner nature and the demands of the outer world.

the shipwrecked man gets too close to the cliffs, he is finished. He would simply be dashed to pieces. Then I read the beginning, too. It was about some people or other who were walking around in a museum and looking at figures. I quickly had enough of this, and how the shipwreck happened, I never did find out.

Computer: Your good marks in school are incompatible with your unreasonable reading. How do you explain this contradiction?

Reinig: My mother gave me a high school textbook for Christmas. But since I go to elementary school, the book was completely useless. It did not fit our course of studies at all and I never did use it. And therefore I read it anyway.

Computer: Do you have any special vocational plans?

Reinig: Originally I wanted to go to the Trojan War. But then I learned that it was already over and people thought there would be no more war. So then I switched over to the Odyssey. I got my facts confused and prepared myself mentally to discover America. With time I got smarter and realized that there are things which cannot happen because they have already happened. I concentrated on the Antarctic in case something would turn up for me there, since I am first in tobogganing. In travel descriptions I read that modern seafaring consists only of removing rust and painting with red lead. So I got myself into an identity crisis, which was strengthened because I slowly had to realize that I was indeed a girl, and with that all of my previous vocational plans were thwarted in any case. Luckily, a little later on I got a prescription for glasses. This solved all of my problems, including the problems of sex. For the boys really had me run the gauntlet[10] and shouted with sadistic pleasure: "My last will for lasses, one with glasses!" Wherever I appeared, they started up. Then, however, winter came and the boys as usual pummeled all the girls with snowballs. Only I was spared. Wherever I appeared, they warned each other: "Watch out, not her, she has glasses." This gave me new courage and I decided to become a professor and to excavate Mayan[11] pyramids. And to that thought I have actually stuck until today.

Computer: You will be a writer. Within two minutes you can register a protest, and, for this, press the green button.

---

10. run the gauntlet: to be put through a series of obstacles or difficulties.

11. Mayan (mä′ yən): pertaining to the tribe of Indians who inhabited the Yucatan, British Honduras, and North Guatemala, known for their highly developed civilization.

Within two seconds I pressed the button.

Computer: Counterproposal?

Reinig: Oh, please, may I not at least become a politician? I could work my way up to becoming chancellor and become the highest servant of my people. I have always been able to speak well.

Computer: Laziness in combination with ambition would allow for both possibilities. On them a political as well as a literary career can be based. In your case only the second possibility can be considered because your intelligence is not sufficient for politics.

And then it seemed to me as if I were suddenly hearing a human voice, loving, concerned and personal. But that cannot be true. It was and remained a machine. It must only be my grateful memory that falsified something.

Computer: And, moreover, I am responsible for your further well-being. If something unpleasant should happen to you, one would reproach me and maintain that I was programmed incorrectly.—Objection refused.

Thirty years later I had another encounter with a computer. I stepped into the testing booth and with cocky indifference pressed the red button on the—right side and sat down.

Computer: Comrade Reinig, why do you write?

Reinig: I write because Comrade Computer prescribed it for me.

The bell rang and I left the room.

A PERSONAL RESPONSE

sharing impressions

1. What are your feelings toward young Reinig? Describe your reaction to her in your journal.

constructing interpretations

2. What do you learn about the young Reinig's personality from her responses to the computer?

3. What is your reaction to the way Reinig is counselled by the computer about a career choice?

Think about
- the rules associated with the counselling process
- the attitude the computer displays toward her
- whether the computer is right to decide that she become a writer
- your own views, which you explored in your journal, about what should determine career choice

A CREATIVE RESPONSE

4. What would be lost from the story if the second encounter with the computer were not included?

A CRITICAL RESPONSE

5. What aspects of society are satirized in this story?

Think about
- the computer as representing the totalitarian state
- the young Reinig's comments about work and unemployment
- her fear that she has wrecked the computer or that it will attack her
- the computer's comparison of careers in writing and politics
- other statements that seem to criticize social conditions

6. Consider Christa Reinig not as a character but as the writer of this story. What answer do you think she gives to the question "Why do you write?"

7. Do Reinig and Stanislaw Łem, the author of the preceding story, share the same view of computers? Compare the writers' attitudes.

8. To what extent is this story relevant to present-day life in the United States?

Think about
- the career counselling offered to students in this country
- ways in which computers affect our daily lives
- how nonconformity is viewed by our society

Analyzing the Writer's Craft

EXPERIMENTAL FICTION

Does this work meet your expectations of what a story should be?

Building a Literary Vocabulary. Experimental fiction breaks with the conventions, or accepted rules, of traditional fiction. For example, an experimental work might have a beginning and an end but no middle. It might be a set of incomplete notes instead of a sustained narrative. It might be narrated by a self-conscious writer who feels free to comment on what he or she has written and to begin again if dissatisfied. "Vocational Counselling" could be classified as experimental fiction. For instance, its insertion of a futuristic element—a vocational counselling computer—into the Germany of the past challenges the reader's expectations about setting.

Application: Analyzing Experimental Fiction. Divide into groups of four or five students. List ways in which this story overturns conventions regarding characters, plot, form (the physical appearance of the text on the page), and point of view (the perspective from which the story is narrated). Discuss how the unconventional organization of the story is related to its message, or theme.

All Cats Are Gray

ANDRE NORTON

A biography of Norton appears on page 425.

Approaching the Story

Welcome to the world of the spaceways, where interstellar travel is as common as airplane travel today. This story is a space adventure whose heroine, Steena, is a computer operator and astronaut. A hip narrator tells Steena's story using a kind of space slang, as though he were talking to you at your local hangout.

STEENA OF THE Spaceways—that sounds just like the corny title for one of the Stellar-vedo spreads. I ought to know; I've tried my hand at writing enough of them. Only this Steena was no glamorous babe. She was as colorless as a lunar planet—even the hair netted down to her skull had a sort of grayish cast, and I never saw her but once draped in anything but a shapeless and baggy gray spaceall.

Steena was strictly background stuff, and that is where she mostly spent her free hours—in the smelly, smoky background corners of any stellar-port dive frequented by free spacers. If you really looked for her you could spot her—just sitting there listening to the talk—listening and remembering. She didn't open her own mouth often, but when she did, spacers had learned to listen. And the lucky few who heard her rare spoken words—these will never forget Steena.

She drifted from port to port. Being an expert operator on the big calculators, she found jobs wherever she cared to stay for a time. And she came to be something like the masterminded machines she tended—smooth, gray, without much personality of their own.

But it was Steena who told Bub Nelson about the Jovan moon rites—and her warning saved Bub's life six months later. It was Steena who identified the piece of stone Keene Clark was passing around a table one night, rightly calling it unworked Slitite. That started a rush which made ten fortunes overnight for men who were down to their last jets. And, last of all, she cracked the case of the *Empress of Mars.*

All the boys who had profited by her odd store of knowledge and her photographic memory tried at one time or another to balance the scales. But she wouldn't take so much as a cup of canal water at their expense, let alone the credits they tried to push on her. Bub Nelson was the only one who got around her refusal. It was he who brought her Bat.

About a year after the Jovan affair, he walked into the Free Fall one night and dumped Bat down on her table. Bat looked at Steena and growled. She looked calmly back at him and nodded once. From then on they traveled together—the thin gray woman and the big gray tomcat. Bat learned to know the inside of more stellar bars than even most spacers visit in their lifetimes. He developed a liking for Vernal juice—drank it neat and quick, right out of a glass. And he was always at home on any table where Steena elected to drop him.

This is really the story of Steena, Bat, Cliff Moran, and the *Empress of Mars,* a story which is already a legend of the spaceways. And it's a good story, too. I ought to know, having framed the first version of it myself.

For I was there, right in the Rigel Royal, when it all began on the night that Cliff Moran blew in, looking lower than an antman's belly and twice as nasty. He'd had a spell of luck foul enough to twist a man into a slug snake, and we all knew that there was an attachment out for his ship. Cliff had fought his way up from the back courts of Venaport. Lose his ship and he'd slip back there—to rot. He was at the snarling stage that night when he picked out a table for himself and set out to drink away his troubles.

However, just as the first bottle arrived, so did a visitor. Steena came out of her corner, Bat curled around her shoulders stolewise, his favorite mode of travel. She crossed over and dropped down, without invitation, at Cliff's side. That shook him out of his sulks because Steena never chose company when she could be alone. If one of the man-stones on Ganymede[1] had come stumping in, it wouldn't have made more of us look out of the corners of our eyes.

She stretched out one long-fingered hand, set aside the bottle he had ordered, and said only one thing, "It's about time for the *Empress of Mars* to appear."

Cliff scowled and bit his lips. He was tough, as jet lining—you have to be granite inside and out to struggle up from Venaport to a ship command. But we could guess what was running through his mind at that moment. *The Empress of Mars* was just about the biggest prize a spacer could aim for. But in the fifty years she had been following her bizarre derelict[2] orbit through space, many men had tried to bring her in—and none had succeeded.

A pleasure ship carrying untold wealth, she had been mysteriously abandoned in space by passengers and crew, none of whom had ever been seen or heard of again. At intervals thereafter she had been sighted, even boarded. Those who ventured into her either vanished or returned swiftly without any believable explanation of what they had seen—wanting only to get away from her as quickly as possible. But the man who could bring her in—or even strip her clean in space—that man would win the jackpot.

"All right!" Cliff slammed his fist down on the table. "I'll try even that!"

Steena looked at him, much as she must have looked at Bat the day Bub Nelson brought him to her, and nodded. That was all I saw. The rest of the story came to me in pieces, months later and in another report half the system away.

Cliff took off that night. He was afraid to risk waiting—with a writ out that could pull the ship from under him. And it wasn't until he was in space that he discovered his passengers—Steena and Bat. We'll never know what happened then. I'm betting that Steena made no explanation at all. She wouldn't.

It was the first time she had decided to cash in on her own tip and she was there—that was all. Maybe that point weighed with Cliff; maybe he just didn't care. Anyway, the three

---

1. **Ganymede** (gan′ i mēd′): the largest of Jupiter's moons.

2. **derelict** (der′ ə likt): abandoned.

were together when they sighted the *Empress* riding, her deadlights gleaming, a ghost ship in night space.

She must have been an eerie sight because her other lights were on too, in addition to the red warnings at her nose. She seemed alive, a Flying Dutchman[3] of space. Cliff worked his ship skillfully alongside and had no trouble in snapping magnetic lines to her lock. Some minutes later the three of them passed into her. There was still air in her cabins and corridors, air that bore a faint corrupt taint which set Bat to sniffing greedily and could be picked up even by the less sensitive human nostrils.

Cliff headed straight for the control cabin, but Steena and Bat went prowling. Closed doors were a challenge to both of them, and Steena opened each as she passed, taking a quick look at what lay within. The fifth door opened on a room which no woman could leave without further investigation.

I don't know who had been housed there when the *Empress* left port on her last lengthy cruise. Anyone really curious can check back on the old photo-reg cards. But there was a lavish display of silk trailing out of two travel kits on the floor, a dressing table crowded with crystal and jeweled containers, along with other lures for the female which drew Steena in. She was standing in front of the dressing table when she glanced into the mirror—glanced into it and froze.

Over her right shoulder she could see the spider-silk cover on the bed. Right in the middle of the sheer, gossamer[4] expanse[5] was a sparkling heap of gems, the dumped contents of some jewel case. Bat had jumped to the foot of the bed and flattened out as cats will, watching those gems, watching them and—something else!

Steena put out her hand blindly and caught up the nearest bottle. As she unstoppered it, she watched the mirrored bed. A gemmed bracelet rose from the pile, rose in the air and tinkled its siren song. It was as if an idle hand played. . . . Bat spat almost noiselessly. But he did not retreat. Bat had not yet decided his course.

She put down the bottle. Then she did something which perhaps few of the men who had listened to her through the years could have done. She moved without hurry or sign of disturbance on a tour about the room. And, although she approached the bed, she did not touch the jewels. She could not force herself to do that. It took her five minutes to play out her innocence and unconcern. Then it was Bat who decided the issue.

He leaped from the bed and escorted something to the door, remaining a careful distance behind. Then he mewed loudly twice. Steena followed him and opened the door wider.

Bat went straight on down the corridor, as intent as a hound on the warmest of scents. Steena strolled behind him, holding her pace to the unhurried gait of an explorer. What sped before them was invisible to her, but Bat was never baffled by it.

They must have gone into the control cabin almost on the heels of the unseen—if the unseen had heels, which there was a good reason to doubt—for Bat crouched just within the doorway and refused to move on. Steena looked down the length of the instrument panels and officers' station seats to where Cliff Moran worked. Her boots made no sound on the heavy carpet, and he did not glance up but sat humming through set teeth, as he tested the tardy and reluctant responses to buttons which had not been pushed in years.

To human eyes they were alone in the cabin. But Bat still followed a moving some-

---

3. Flying Dutchman: a fabled sailor doomed to sail the seas in his ghostly ship until Judgment Day.
4. gossamer (gäs′ ə mər): light, thin, and filmy.
5. expanse (ek spans′): a large open area or unbroken surface.

thing, which he had at last made up his mind to distrust and dislike. For now he took a step or two forward and spat—his loathing made plain by every raised hair along his spine. And in that same moment Steena saw a flicker—a flicker of vague outline against Cliff's hunched shoulders, as if the invisible one had crossed the space between them.

But why had it been revealed against Cliff and not against the back of one of the seats or against the panels, the walls of the corridor, or the cover of the bed where it had reclined and played with its loot? What could Bat see?

The storehouse memory that had served Steena so well throughout the years clicked open a half-forgotten door. With one swift motion, she tore loose her spaceall and flung the baggy garment across the back of the nearest seat.

Bat was snarling now, emitting the throaty rising cry that was his hunting song. But he was edging back, back toward Steena's feet, shrinking from something he could not fight but which he faced defiantly. If he could draw it after him, past that dangling spaceall. . . . He had to—it was their only chance!

"What the . . . " Cliff had come out of his seat and was staring at them.

What he saw must have been weird enough: Steena, bare armed and bare shouldered, her usually stiffly netted hair falling wildly down her back; Steena watching empty space with narrowed eyes and set mouth, calculating a single wild chance. Bat, crouched on his belly, was retreating from thin air step by step and wailing like a demon.

"Toss me your blaster." Steena gave the order calmly—as if they still sat at their table in the Rigel Royal.

And as quietly, Cliff obeyed. She caught the small weapon out of the air with a steady hand—caught and leveled it.

"Stay just where you are!" she warned. "Back, Bat, bring it back!"

With a last throat-splitting screech of rage and hate, Bat twisted to safety between her boots. She pressed with thumb and forefinger, firing at the spacealls. The material turned to powdery flakes of ash—except for certain bits which still flapped from the scorched seat—as if something had protected them from the force of the blast. Bat sprang straight up in the air with a scream that tore their ears.

"What . . . ?" began Cliff again.

Steena made a warning motion with her left hand. *"Wait!"*

She was still tense, still watching Bat. The cat dashed madly around the cabin twice, running crazily with white-ringed eyes and flecks of foam on his muzzle. Then he stopped abruptly in the doorway, stopped and looked back over his shoulder for a long, silent moment. He sniffed delicately.

Steena and Cliff could smell it too now, a thick oily stench which was not the usual odor left by an exploding blaster shell.

Bat came back, treading daintily across the carpet, almost on the tips of his paws. He raised his head as he passed Steena, and then he went confidently beyond to sniff, to sniff and spit twice at the unburned strips of the spaceall. Having thus paid his respects to the late enemy, he sat down calmly and set to washing his fur with deliberation. Steena sighed once and dropped into the navigator's seat.

"Maybe now you'll tell me what's happened?" Cliff exploded as he took the blaster out of her hand.

"Gray," she said dazedly, "it must have been gray—or I couldn't have seen it like that. I'm colorblind, you see. I can see only shades of gray—my whole world is gray. Like Bat's—his world is gray, too—all gray. But he's been compensated, for he can see above and below our range of color vibrations. And apparently, so can I!"

Her voice quavered, and she raised her chin with a new air Cliff had never seen before—a sort of proud acceptance. She pushed back her wandering hair, but she made no move to imprison it under the heavy net again.

"That is why I saw the thing when it crossed between us. Against your spaceall it was another shade of gray—an outline. So I put out mine and waited for it to show against that—it was our only chance, Cliff.

"It was curious at first, I think, and it knew we couldn't see it—which is why it waited to attack. But when Bat's actions gave it away, it moved. So I waited to see that flicker against the spaceall, and then I let him have it. It's really very simple. . . ."

Cliff laughed a bit shakily. "But what *was* this gray thing? I don't get it."

"I think it was what made the *Empress* a derelict. Something out of space, maybe, or from another world somewhere." She waved her hands. "It's invisible because it's a color beyond our range of sight. It must have stayed in here all these years. And it kills—it must—when its curiosity is satisfied." Swiftly she described the scene, the scene in the cabin, and the strange behavior of the gem pile which had betrayed the creature to her.

Cliff did not return his blaster to its holder. "Any more of them on board, d'you think?" He didn't looked pleased at the prospect.

Steena turned to Bat. He was paying particular attention to the space between two front toes in the process of a complete bath. "I don't think so, but Bat will tell us if there are. He can see them clearly, I believe."

But there weren't any more, and two weeks later, Cliff, Steena, and Bat brought the *Empress* into the lunar quarantine station. And that is the end of Steena's story because, as we have been told, happy marriages need no chronicles. Steena had found someone who knew of her gray world and did not find it too hard to share with her—someone besides Bat. It turned out to be a real love match.

The last time I saw her, she was wrapped in a flame-red cloak from the looms of Rigel and wore a fortune in Jovan rubies blazing on her wrists. Cliff was flipping a three-figure credit bill to a waiter. And Bat had a row of Vernal juice glasses set up before him. Just a little family party out on the town.

Reviewing Concepts

SCIENCE FICTION AND THEME: THE FUTURE IS NOW

making
connections

Like philosophers, news commentators, politicians, and concerned citizens, fiction writers wrestle with the central political and social issues of our time, and some writers directly address these issues in their works. Most of the futuristic stories in this unit tackle large issues of good and evil and ask questions about responsible leadership, the effects of powerful technology, and the relationship between humans and computers. For example, in "I Sing the Body Electric!" Ray Bradbury addresses the fear that many people have of destructive "inhuman machines." Bradbury's Grandma creation argues, however, that if humans create benevolent machines, the machines in turn can show the way for humans to improve themselves and become essentially more humane.

To better understand some of the themes in the science fiction stories in this unit, make a chart similar to the one below. In the second column, state one issue or problem presented in the story; then in the third column, briefly explain either the consequence of, or the solution to, the problem that the writer explores.

Title of story	Issue or problem presented	Consequence or solution explored
I Sing the Body Electric!	fear of "inhuman machines"	Benevolent machines can be created to train humans to be good and loving.

describing
connections

Review your chart and choose several stories that you think have the most to say about current issues. Write a **newspaper column** expressing your opinion on one of the issues and support your opinion with examples from one or more stories.

Biographies of Authors

Joan Aiken (born 1924) always wanted to be a writer and still has the first pad of paper she bought at age five. It is filled with poems and stories, all indicative of the richly imaginative books she would later write. Aiken was born in Sussex, England, the daughter of American poet Conrad Aiken. She first worked as an editor and copywriter. Widowhood at thirty and the necessity of providing for two young children forced her to resume writing in earnest. She chose to devote much of her effort to children's literature, creating worlds of fantasy, mystery, and humor—"what I would have liked to read as a child," she says. *Black Hearts in Battersea* and *The Wolves of Willoughby Chase* are two of her most popular titles.

Isaac Asimov (born 1920) is almost a one-man encyclopedia. His more than three hundred books concern everything from science fact and fiction to history, Shakespeare, and the Bible. Asimov was born in the Soviet Union and moved with his parents to the United States when he was three years old. A brilliant student, he entered Columbia University at age fifteen and had his first science fiction story published by the time he was eighteen. Asimov permanently altered the genre of science fiction by the sheer volume and imaginative power of his works. In addition, he is the author of a number of science textbooks and a well-respected contributor to the field of robotics.

Toni Cade Bambara (born 1939) had a remarkably varied education, ranging from a school for mimes in Paris and the University of Florence in Italy to the Katherine Dunham Dance Studio and the Harlem Film Institute in New York City. In the 1970's Bambara became actively involved in social and political activities in the African-American community, activities to which she is still deeply committed. Reviewers of her fiction remark on her distinctive style, which combines poetic rhythms and imagery with street-talk slang. Bambara's first novel, *The Salt Eaters,* received the American Book Award in 1981, and her documentary film "The Bombing of Osage" has also won a number of awards.

Heinrich Böll (1917–1985) experienced the tragedies of war at an early age. Born in Cologne, Germany, during World War I, he claimed that his earliest memory was watching the defeated German army march through town. During World War II he was drafted into the army and wounded four times in six years. In 1945 he was captured and held in an American prison camp for six months. Böll's writing conveys his commitment to peace and his passion for the victims of war. He is also known for his biting satires that criticize Germany's materialistic trends following World War II. He published his first novel in 1949 and in 1972 received the Nobel Prize in literature.

Jorge Luis Borges (1899–1986) was an Argentine poet, short story writer, and essayist who learned to speak and read English before he learned Spanish. One of the first books he read was Mark Twain's *Huckleberry Finn*. In 1914 his family took him to Geneva, Switzerland, where he learned French and German and earned his bachelor's degree from the College of Geneva. Next the family lived in Majorca and Spain before returning to Buenos Aires in 1921. Borges now wrote poems about the history and beauty of his native city and began trying his hand at fiction as well. In 1938 he suffered a severe head wound, resulting in blood poisoning that almost cost him his life. After this experience he began to create his best poetry and the fantastic stories for which he is known. In 1955 Borges became director of the national library and a professor of English and American literature at the University of Buenos Aires. By this time, because of a hereditary affliction, he had become totally blind. In 1961 Borges and Samuel Beckett shared the prestigious Formentor Prize. Since then his poems and tales have been recognized as classics of twentieth-century world literature.

Ray Bradbury (born 1920) is one of America's best-known science fiction writers. Born in Waukegan, Illinois, Bradbury developed a love of stories and reading at an early age. He devoured both comic strips and adventure books, spent Saturdays at the movies, and sent for every secret code ring available. At age twelve, Bradbury could not afford to buy the sequel to an Edgar Rice Burroughs novel, so he wrote his own ending to the story. Bradbury has been writing fulltime since 1940 and has written over a thousand stories in addition to novels, plays, and scripts for movies and television. Two of his most popular books are *The Martian Chronicles* and *Dandelion Wine*.

Italo Calvino (1923–1985), Italian journalist, short story writer, and novelist, considered himself a fabulist, or writer of fables. "The mold of the most ancient fables," he said, "remains the irreplaceable scheme of all human stories." After the realism of his early work, Calvino experimented more and more with myth, allegory, and fable. In his trilogy The Baron in the Trees, The Nonexistent Knight, and The Cloven Viscount (1959–1962), he used allegorical fantasy to satirize contemporary social issues. The first of these novels is about a nineteenth-century nobleman who rejects the world in order to live a full and comfortable life aloft in the branches. Calvino's Italian Folktales (1959) was praised as a remarkable and extensive collection. Through his work Calvino wished to re-create a world where "people can still dream and yet understand." Also a translator and essayist, he was awarded the Premio Feltrinelli, Italy's equivalent of the Pulitzer Prize, in 1975.

Eugenia Collier (born 1928) started teaching college English in 1955 but did not begin writing until fourteen years later. One of her first efforts, "Marigolds," won the Gwendolyn Brooks Short Story Award. Collier explains her new-found ability in this way: "After a conventional Western-type education, I discovered the richness, the diversity, the beauty of my black heritage. The fact of my blackness is the core and center of my creativity." Collier is making up for lost time with an outpouring of poems, stories, articles, and critical essays.

Julio Cortázar (1914–1984), an Argentine novelist and short story writer, was born in Belgium and lived the last half of his life in France. He was known for his imagination and literary experimentation. As was common in his generation of Latin-American writers, Cortázar drew much inspiration from French and English literature, which he read voraciously. Cortázar began writing when he was a child, but for many years he felt his efforts were unworthy of publication. Finally in 1951, his *Bestiario* was published. The eight short stories in this work are marked by Cortázar's wit and his way of making ordinary events silently slip into the bizarre and the threatening. Perhaps Cortázar's best-known work is the short story "Las Babas del Diablo," on which Michaelangelo Antonioni's film *Blow-Up* was based. It is generally agreed that Cortázar's masterpiece is *Rayuela* (1963; translated as *Hopscotch,* 1966), a boldly experimental novel.

Anita Desai (born 1937) examines in her writing the social problems of modern India, revealing the psychic pain and daily sorrows of an India that very few foreigners know. According to writer and critic Anne Tyler, Desai's readers are drawn into her dense, intricate world "so deeply . . . that we almost fear we won't be able to climb out again." Considered one of the most gifted of contemporary Indian writers, she is the author of several novels, including *Cry, The Peacock, Fire on the Mountain,* and *Clear Light of Day.* "Games at Twilight" (page 91) is the title story of her first volume of short stories.

Rosario Ferré (born 1942) comes from a traditional upper-class family in Ponce, Puerto Rico. The author of poetry, novels, and stories for children and adults, Ferré began writing in 1970 when her short story "The Youngest Doll" was published. Her first book, a collection of short stories and verse called Pandora's Papers (1976), was an immediate success. One critic called it "a constant tearing apart of memory, imagination, and word—impossible to read with indifference." A painstaking writer, Ferré has said that she usually revises a story at least eighteen times before she considers it finished. Subjects common in Ferré's works include feminist concerns, ancient myths, and the life and people of her beloved Puerto Rico.

Gabriel García Márquez (born 1928), a writer of novels and short stories, is one of the central figures in the so-called magical realism movement in Latin American literature. Born into poverty in Colombia, García Márquez began his career as a journalist. While acknowledging the influence on his work of Faulkner, Hemingway, and other American and English authors, he says that it was journalism that taught him that "the key is to tell it straight." García Márquez's work is characterized by magical realism, a combination of realism and fantasy. His best-known work is *One Hundred Years of Solitude* (1967), an epic work that one critic said "should be required reading for the entire human race." In 1982 García Márquez was awarded the Nobel Prize in literature.

Nadine Gordimer (born 1923), a novelist and short story writer, was born into a middle-class white family in the Transvaal, South Africa. Gordimer is known for her beautifully crafted work on themes of exile, alienation, and life's missed opportunities. Originally she concentrated on the short story, but as her subject matter grew increasingly complex she turned to the novel. Much of her writing is set in South Africa, and her characters are inevitably shaped by the political situation there. Gordimer uses her talents and influence to oppose the apartheid system that she hates, but she refuses to let her writing become propaganda. Gordimer lives in Johannesburg, South Africa, and has lectured and taught in the United States. Her novel *The Conservationist* (1974) won the Booker McConnell Prize. Her later works include *Burger's Daughter* (1979), *July's People* (1981), and *A Sport of Nature* (1987). In 1991 Gordimer was awarded the Nobel Prize in literature.

Bessie Head (1937–1986) was an African novelist and short story writer whose life and work reflected her deep concern for the people and politics of her continent. Head, who herself suffered from alienation and rejection at an early age, was especially sympathetic to the plight of women, children, and the rural poor. A native of South Africa, she eventually sought asylum in Botswana, where she lived until her death. Her first novel, *When Rain Clouds Gather,* was published in 1968. It was followed by two other novels, two works of historical nonfiction, and various short stories. For Head, the primary role of literature was to reflect the daily lives of common people.

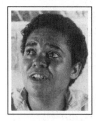

Eugène Ionesco (born 1912) is a Romanian-born French dramatist and literary critic and one of the founders of the Theater of the Absurd. His plays were among the first to contain "antilogical" elements and did much to bring about a revolution in dramatic techniques. After attending the University of Bucharest, Ionesco worked for a Doctorate in Paris and published his first drama, *The Bald Soprano,* in 1949. Other well-known works include *Exit the King, Thirst and Hunger,* and *Killing Game.* In his works he addresses basic human concerns such as the struggle for identity, the search for meaning in life, and the fear of death. He was admitted into the French Academy, a prestigious group of French scholars and writers, in 1970.

Shirley Jackson (1919–1965) once remarked that she loved to write because "it's the only way I can get to sit down"—perhaps because she combined a literary career with the demands of raising four children. Jackson was born in San Francisco and grew up on the West Coast. She went east to attend Syracuse University, where she received her bachelor's degree in 1940, the same year she married literary critic Stanley Edgar Hyman. Describing herself and her husband, Jackson said, "Our major exports are books and children, both of which we produce in abundance." She wrote two hilarious accounts of the pandemonium of family life, *Life Among the Savages* (1953) and *Raising Demons* (1957). Jackson's writing has another side as well, a dark and sinister side concerned with horror, psychological unbalance, supernatural happenings, and a genuine sense of evil. These qualities are evident in short stories such as "The Beautiful Stranger" and in novels such as *The Haunting of Hill House* (1959). Jackson died of heart failure at the age of forty-six.

Ruth Prawer Jhabvala (born 1927) comes from a Polish family, was born in Germany, and was raised and educated in England. In 1951 she married C.S.H. Jhabvala, an Indian architect, and moved with him to India. There she began to write novels, short stories, and screenplays, and raised three children. Jhabvala's unique position as an outsider intimate with India has provided much material for her stories. From her first novel, *Amrita,* she has been well received. Her work combines biting satire with compassionate sensitivity, and she is frequently compared to Jane Austen. One critic wrote of them both that "by focusing the brilliance of their absolute attention on one small piece of human frailty, glory, or folly, they convince us . . . that in fact they understand everything."

William Melvin Kelley (born 1937) is an award-winning author who writes about African Americans not as a cultural group but as separate and unique human beings. In this same spirit Kelley resents critics who try to group all African American writers into what he calls the "Negro literary ghetto." People who read black authors, says Kelley, immediately begin to search for profound comments on the relationships between black and white Americans. He does not want his work to be thought of as propaganda for a particular cause, he says, but rather as writing that will have continuing value and meaning. Kelley's articles and short stories have been widely published in magazines, anthologies, and textbooks. His novels include *A Different Drummer* and *Dunfords Travels Everywheres.*

Jamaica Kincaid (born 1949) was born and raised in St. John's, Antigua, in the West Indies. She emigrated to the United States at age seventeen and became a staff writer for the *New Yorker* in 1976. Antigua, however, stayed with her. Two books, *At the Bottom of the River* and *Annie John,* celebrate in poetic, tactile language the realities of life on the island and reveal Kincaid's bittersweet relationship with her homeland. In the nonfiction work *A Small Place,* feelings of anger rise to the surface as Kincaid protests the racism, government corruption, and poverty in Antigua. Reviewer Peggy Ellsberg called it "rage laced with lyricism." Kincaid's novel *Lucy* appeared in 1990 to considerable acclaim. She received the Morton Dauwen Zabel Award in 1983.

Ursula K. Le Guin (born 1929) grew up in an exciting household as the daughter of writer Theodora Kroeber and anthropologist Alfred Louis Kroeber. She has said that her childhood exposure to anthropology influenced her later fantasy and science fiction writing: "My father studied real cultures and I make them up—in a way, it's the same thing." Le Guin began writing poetry and stories when she was only five years old. She wrote her first science fiction story at twelve, but it was rejected by the editor of *Astounding Science-Fiction*—the same magazine in which her first published science fiction appeared twenty years later. Le Guin left her home in Berkeley, California, to attend Radcliffe College, where she earned a bachelor's degree. After receiving a master's degree from Columbia University, she went to France to study on a Fulbright Fellowship. There, she met and married the historian Charles A. Le Guin. The couple settled in Portland, Oregon. Despite the demands of raising three children, Le Guin has produced prize-winning fiction. *The Left Hand of Darkness* (1969), for example, was awarded both the Hugo and Nebula awards, the most prestigious awards for science fiction writing.

Stanislaw Łem (born 1921) has been called one of the world's greatest science fiction writers. Born in Lvov, Poland, Łem was trained in medicine but soon turned to writing as a career. Łem writes in his native Polish, and his nearly fifty books have been translated into more than thirty languages. Extraordinarily inventive and witty, Łem's stories examine such themes as the purpose of life and the relationship between humans and their technology. His sharp humor frequently targets bureaucrats, pompous academics, and other examples of human arrogance and folly. Among his best-known works are *The Cyberiad, The Star Diaries,* and *A Perfect Vacuum.*

Doris Lessing (born 1919) began life in Persia, present-day Iran, where her father was stationed as a captain in the British army. She spent most of her youth on a farm in Rhodesia, now called Zimbabwe. These colonial experiences in the Middle East and Africa contributed to her awareness of racial and economic exploitation. Lessing is also known for her interest in feminist themes, and her novels and short stories have often focused on the changing situation for women.

Naguib Mahfouz (also spelled Najib Mahfuz) (born 1911) has written nearly forty novels and short story collections, more than thirty screenplays, and several stage plays. Practically a household name in the Middle East, Mahfouz was little known in the West until 1988 when he became the first Arabic writer to win the Nobel Prize in literature. His writing often deals with social injustice and the political history of Egypt and is sometimes compared with the works of such social realists as Dickens and Balzac. His major work, *Al-Thulathiyya,* is a 1,500-page trilogy that spans three generations of Cairo families. Other works include *Children of Gebelawi,* which was banned in Egypt because of its controversial treatment of religion, and *God's World,* a collection of short stories from which "The Happy Man" is taken.

Bernard Malamud (1914–1986), the son of struggling Russian Jewish immigrants, grew up in a household without books, pictures, or music. As a child, he spent much of his time in his parents' Brooklyn, New York, grocery store, where he sat in the back room writing stories. He also visited the Yiddish theater and listened to his father's tales of Jewish life in Russia. After graduating from New York's City College in 1936, he took whatever jobs he could find and wrote fiction in his spare time. Having lived through the decades that witnessed the Great Depression, World War II, and the Holocaust, Malamud developed into a writer who depicts human suffering and the redemptive power of love. "If you don't respect man," he once said, "you don't respect my work." He published his first novel, *The Natural,* in 1952; five years later, his second novel, *The Assistant,* established him as a major writer. In 1967 he was awarded the National Book Award and the Pulitzer Prize for *The Fixer.* In addition to writing, Malamud taught evening high school classes in New York for several years and English at the University of Oregon and at Bennington College in Vermont.

Jean McCord (born 1924) has found time for writing even as she has pursued a variety of occupations, including time served in the Women's Army Corps. Her short stories have been published in *Seventeen* magazine and in *Best American Short Stories.*

Aharon Megged (born 1920) is an Israeli novelist, playwright, journalist, and short story writer. Born in Poland, Megged lived in a small village there before moving to Israel, where he joined a kibbutz when he was eighteen. Though his books often deal with subjects close to his own life, such as the kibbutz and the values of Israeli society, Megged states that his work has also been influenced by European writers such as Kafka, Svevo, Gogol, and Chekhov. Megged's writings include *Mikreh ha-kssil* (1960; published in English as *Fortunes of a Fool,* 1963) and *ha-Hai 'al ha-met* (1965; published in English as *Living On the Dead,* 1970).

Yukio Mishima (pen name of Hiraoka Kimitake) (1925–1970) had a career that began and ended spectacularly. At the age of 19, his first publication brought him instant acclaim. At the age of forty-five, he committed *seppuku,* a ritual form of suicide. His fascination with the Japanese past led him to adapt traditional *No* plays to the modern stage; his dramatic abilities showed up in film writing, acting, and directing. His novels, focusing on intricate character development, were popular and critical successes. Mishima became an author of world stature, often called the literary genius of his postwar generation. Of his decision to take his own life, he wrote shortly before his death: "I came to wish to sacrifice myself for the old, beautiful tradition of Japan, which is disappearing very quickly day by day."

Abioseh Nicol (pen name of Dr. Davidson Nicol) (born 1924) has had a distinguished career as a writer, physician, medical researcher, and diplomat. He is from Sierra Leone in West Africa, and he has said that he started writing because most of those who wrote about blacks "seldom gave any nobility to their African characters." Married and the father of five children, Nicol writes of middle-class Africans and their complicated cultural heritage. His poems and short stories appear in such volumes as *The Truly Married Woman* (1965) and *West African Verse* (1967). Nicol was the first African elected a fellow at Cambridge University in England. As a medical researcher, he played an important role in discovering the structure of human insulin. He also served as his country's ambassador to the United Nations.

Andre Norton (born 1912) is the pen name of Alice Mary Norton. Norton began her career as a children's librarian but soon took a different direction. Trained in research and having a love for history, she began writing historical novels. Then in the 1950's, she started writing science fiction, shifting from a focus on the past to an interest in the future. This new form of fiction was rich territory for a writer with the talent for adventure stories that Norton had developed in her historical novels. Native Americans appear as major characters in several of her science fiction novels, such as *The Sioux Spaceman,* adding a special interest to these works. Some of her science fiction was written under the pen name of Andrew North.

Joyce Carol Oates (born 1938) is remarkable both for the quantity and the quality of her work. She has published more than twenty novels, sixteen volumes of short stories, several books of poems, and many collections of essays. She has been awarded numerous literary prizes, including a Guggenheim Fellowship and a National Book Award. Oates is a versatile writer, equally adept at writing realistic short stories like "Out of Place," essays on boxing, and Gothic novels, such as *Bellefleur* (1980). The daughter of a tool-and-die designer, Oates was raised on her grandparents' farm outside Lockport, New York. She attended a one-room school, where her determination and studious habits set her apart from her rowdy classmates. "She was always so hard-working, a perfectionist," her mother recalls. A brilliant student, Oates graduated Phi Beta Kappa and was valedictorian of her class at Syracuse University. She completed a master's degree at the University of Wisconsin, married fellow writer Raymond J. Smith, and began her teaching career at Rice University. Currently, Oates is a professor at Princeton University.

Harry Mark Petrakis (born 1923) grew up in Chicago's Greek community and has written many stories about the experiences of immigrants in the United States. Petrakis was born in St. Louis to Greek-American parents. His father was an Eastern Orthodox priest. Petrakis worked as a steelworker, a real estate salesman, and a speechwriter. His first book was published in 1959. He has published many books since then, including *Pericles on 31st Street* and *A Dream of Kings,* both National Book Award nominees. Petrakis has adapted several of his stories for movie and television productions, and he has taught writing workshops at colleges and universities.

Sylvia Plath (1932-1963) started writing at a very young age. Her short story "Initiation" was published in *Seventeen* magazine when she was only twenty years old. Although she occasionally wrote fiction, Plath primarily chose poetry to explore and express her troubled emotions. On the surface, her life was always successful. She graduated with honors from Smith College, went to Cambridge University in England on a Fulbright Scholarship, met and married English poet Ted Hughes, and had two children. Her first book of poetry, *The Colossus,* was published in 1960, when she was twenty-seven. Three years later, however, Plath killed herself. In the last years of her life, she sometimes wrote two or three poems a day, trying to work out on paper the anger, terror, and anguish that had been with her since her father's death when she was eight. After Plath's death, Hughes edited several volumes of her poetry, letters, and fiction. In 1982, her work was awarded the Pulitzer Prize for poetry.

Rachel de Queiroz (born 1910), a Brazilian writer best known for her realistic novels, is also an award-winning dramatist and highly regarded translator. At the age of nineteen, de Queiroz made a sensational literary debut with the publication of her first novel, *The Year '15.* Both this work and *The Three Marias* (1939) challenge the traditionally submissive role played by women in Brazilian society. In the 1940's de Queiroz began writing newspaper columns on subjects of general interest; these gained her a wide following. Many of her essays appear in collections. Plays by de Queiroz include *Lampião* (1953), which recounts the antics of a famous rural outlaw. In recognition of her life's work, the Brazilian Academy of Letters awarded her the Machado de Assis Prize.

Christa Reinig (born 1926) grew up poor, without a father, in Berlin. During World War II she worked as an apprentice florist and a factory worker. Later she studied art history and archaeology at Humboldt University in East Germany. In 1964 she went to West Germany to receive a literary prize and decided to remain there. Reinig's early works are poems portraying the horror of war. Her later prose works include *The Three Ships* (1965) and *Orion: New Signs of the Zodiac* (1968), a collection of short sketches reflecting on modern life. *Heavenly and Earthly Geometry* (1975) is an autobiographical novel that displays Reinig's irreverent sense of humor and reveals her philosophical conflicts with the East German state.

Alberto Alvaro Ríos (born 1952) was exposed to different cultures as a child. His parents were Mexican and British, and he grew up in Nogales, Arizona, near the Mexican border. Much of his writing reflects the experiences of his childhood. Ríos earned a master's degree in creative writing from the University of Arizona; his poetry and short stories have won many honors. *The Iguana Killer, Whispering to Fool the Wind,* and *Teodoro Luna's Two Kisses* are among the books he has published. He is currently a professor of English at Arizona State University.

Juan Rulfo (1918–1986) was a Mexican writer who contributed greatly to Latin American literature despite having written only two major works in his lifetime. After studying law and impounding ships during World War II, Rulfo held positions as an editor and a scriptwriter but always pursued his main interest—the writing of fiction. He helped create the magical realism movement by fusing in his work the bitter realities of Mexican life with the primitive and magical beliefs of the common people. His short story collection *The Burning Plain* and his novel *Pedro Paramo* transcend mere social themes, analyzing the philosophical aspects of life and death. In 1970 Rulfo received Mexico's National Prize of Letters.

Sŏ Kiwŏn (born 1930) was a Korean student in the early 1950's before he left the university to fight in the Korean War. He wrote about a war that "failed to provide an inspiration for self-dedication" and a postwar society "fraught with contradictions and absurdity." His personal experience lends authenticity to his work, which has been praised for its psychological depth. According to one reviewer, Sŏ Kiwŏn writes of "life devoid of dreams and hopes and the landscape of the mind's wilderness."

Amy Tan (born 1952) was not always the proud Chinese American that she is now. She recalls dreaming when she was young of making her features look more Caucasian by having plastic surgery. It was not until she made her first trip to China in 1987 that Tan could truly accept both the Chinese and American cultures as her own. Though Tan won a writing contest at the age of eight, her identity as a writer was slow in coming. However, after successfully publishing some of her stories in magazines, Tan combined those stories with others to create a novel called *The Joy Luck Club,* which became a bestseller.

Hernando Téllez (born 1908) is a Colombian diplomat and politician as well as a writer. Although known chiefly for his essays on social and political matters in South America, Téllez also published a collection of short stories, *Ashes for the Wind and Other Tales,* in 1950. One of the stories, "Lather and Nothing Else," has been widely translated and anthologized.

Anne Tyler (born 1941) lived in a series of communes, mostly in Maryland and North Carolina, until she was eleven. She believed that this experience enabled her to look "at the normal world with a certain amount of distance and surprise, which can sometimes be quite helpful to a writer." Tyler began writing while she was a student at Duke University, where she studied under novelist Reynolds Price. She graduated in 1961 with a bachelor's degree in Russian. After a year of further studies at Columbia University, she accepted a position working in the Duke University Library as the Russian bibliographer. In 1963 she married Taghi Modarressi, a psychiatrist. The following year, the couple moved to Montreal, where Tyler wrote her first novel during a six-month period of unemployment. Her daughters Tezh and Mitra were born in 1965 and 1967. Although motherhood temporarily slowed down her writing, Tyler began to publish novels regularly in the mid-1970's. One novel, *The Accidental Tourist* (1985), was made into a movie.

Luisa Valenzuela (born 1938) is one of the best-known writers of short stories and novels in Latin America. She was born in Argentina, and became a journalist in her teens, working for the magazine *Quince Abriles* and the Buenos Aires newspaper *La Mación.* In 1967 she published a book of thirteen short stories and a novel under the title *Los Heréticos.* Other fiction includes *The Lizard's Tail* (1983) and *Crime of the Other* (1989). Valenzuela's writing often contains humor and irony. An important theme in her work is the search for freedom, both political and personal. She once said that she writes to shake people up.

Kurt Vonnegut, Jr. (born 1922) once described a writer as "a person who makes his living with his mental disease." Whether the definition fits or not, Vonnegut writes wildly comic fiction about some of the blackest aspects of society. His concerns are the horrors of war, human brutality, and the crush of modern technology. Raised in the Midwest and armed with his father's advice to learn "something useful," Vonnegut went to college and studied biochemistry and anthropology. During World War II, he was captured by the German army. As a prisoner of war, he witnessed the Allied firebombing of Dresden. The total destruction of the city and 135,000 of its citizens is a memory that haunts Vonnegut and that appears repeatedly in his work, especially in his novel *Slaughterhouse-Five.* His first attempts at writing were incorrectly labeled science fiction and were virtually ignored by critics. With the 1963 publication of *Cat's Cradle,* however, he experienced instant popularity with critics and the reading public.

Alice Walker (born 1944), was the youngest of eight children of sharecropper parents, in Eatonton Georgia. When she was eight, she was accidentally blinded in one eye by a shot from a BB gun. The injury caused her to retreat into writing to escape the stares and taunts of her classmates, but it also helped her "really to see people and things, really to notice relationships and care about how they turned out." After high school, Walker attended Spelman College and then transferred to Sarah Lawrence College in New York, graduating in 1965. Two years later she married a civil rights attorney and moved to Mississippi, where she taught at Jackson State College. Walker is a versatile and prolific writer. She has published a biography of Langston Hughes for young people and a collection of Zora Neale Hurston's work; novels, such as *The Color Purple* (1982), which won both the American Book Award and the Pulitzer Prize; collections of essays, such as *In Search of Our Mother's Gardens* (1983); and volumes of both poetry and short stories.

Hisaye Yamamoto (born 1921), the daughter of Japanese immigrants, was born in Redondo Beach, California. Like many Japanese Americans, she was interned in a detention camp during World War II. While in camp, Yamamoto continued the writing career she had begun as a teenager. She wrote a column and news articles for the camp newspaper and published a serialized mystery. After the war she worked for three years for the African-American weekly newspaper the *Los Angeles Tribune* and then received a John Hay Whitney Foundation Opportunity Fellowship that allowed her to write fiction full time for a year (1950–1951). From 1953 to 1955, Yamamoto and her adopted son volunteered on a Catholic Worker rehabilitation farm on Staten Island. She then married Anthony DeSoto, returned to Los Angeles, and became mother to four more children. Although her output has been relatively small, Yamamoto's work has won critical acclaim. Four of her stories, including "Seventeen Syllables," have been included in Best American Short Story collections. Her stories, which always feature Japanese-American protagonists, often display sympathy for those on the fringes of American society.

Index of Essential Vocabulary

M

malevolence, 99, 100
malicious, 132, 135
manipulates, 388, 393
mettle, 398, 399
modicum, 166, 173
morass, 158
mutations, 310, 319

N

nape, 256, 257

O

oblivion, 286, 291
omens, 369, 370
opprobrium, 214
ostentatious, 303, 306

P

paradoxes, 310, 311
paragon, 177, 181
pedant, 310, 312
penchant, 249, 253
pensiveness, 249, 250
perverse, 123, 126
placated, 222, 223
placatingly, 43, 45
poignantly, 123, 125
precipitated, 378, 382
prestige, 132, 139
programming, 388, 389

promontory, 295, 300
protestations, 177, 178
protracted, 99, 101
punctilious, 20, 30

R

railed, 198, 203
rapt, 111, 118
rebuke, 206, 207
recalcitrant, 388, 394
recrimination, 99, 101
rejuvenated, 256, 258
renounce, 335
repartee, 111, 115
reserve, 4, 6
retort, 74
rhetoric, 206, 207
rudimentary, 369, 373
ruefully, 242, 244

S

sallies, 398, 399
savored, 333
sidle, 65
skeptically, 388, 394
skepticism, 344, 361
smug, 159
solace, 286, 287
stanched, 256, 259
stigma, 378, 381
stentorian, 99, 102

stoicism, 123, 126
subterfuge, 177, 178
supplication, 142, 144
surreptitiously, 20, 25

T

talisman, 33, 37
temerity, 91, 94
temporized, 33, 39
tirade, 242, 245
transcending, 335

U

unavailing, 369, 370
unobtrusively, 198, 201
utopian, 214

V

vacillating, 111, 119
vigilance, 378, 381
venerable, 177, 179
verisimilitude, 398, 400
vernaculars, 111, 112
vertigo, 216
vocation, 249, 253

W

wiles, 177, 178
wizened, 369, 373
wont, 43, 50
wretchedly, 4, 9

Index of Literary Terms

Index of Writing Modes and Formats

Index of Authors and Titles

University of Hawaii Press "The Heir" by Sŏ Kiwŏn from *Flowers of Fire: Twentieth Century Korean Stories*, revised and edited by Peter H. Lee. Copyright © 1986 by the University of Hawaii Press. Reprinted by permission of the University of Hawaii Press.

University of Texas Press "No Dogs Bark" by Juan Rulfo from *The Burning Plain and Other Stories*, translated by George D. Schade, pp. 115-119. Copyright © 1967 by the University of Texas Press. Reprinted by permission of the University of Texas Press.

The authors and editors have made every effort to trace the ownership of all copyrighted selections found in this book and to make full acknowledgment for their use.

Art Credits

Cover
The Dove, 1990, Pat Dypold. Mixed media, 21 x 28 inches.

Author Photographs

AP/Wide World Photos, Inc., New York: Isaac Asimov 419; Heinrich Böll 419; William Melvin Kelley 423; Yukio Mishima 425; Juan Rulfo 427; Anne Tyler 428; Kurt Vonnegut, Jr., 428; The Bettmann Archive, New York: Gabriel García Márquez 421; Rene Burri/Magnum Photos, Inc., New York: Julio Cortázar 421; Jane Bown/Camera Press/Globe Photos, New York: Anita Desai 421; Camera Press/Globe Photos, New York: Naguib Mahfouz 424; Henri Cartier-Bresson/Magnum Photos, New York: Eugène Ionesco 422; Dahlgren/Camera Press/Globe Photos, New York: Doris Lessing 424; Stephen Deutch: Harry Mark Petrakis 426; Karla Elling: Alberto Alvaro Ríos 427; Robert Eginton: Andre Norton 425; Elliott Erwitt/Magnum Photos, Inc., New York: Joyce Carol Oates 426; Robert Foothorap: Amy Tan 427; The Granger Collection, New York: Bernard Malamud 424; German Information Service, New York: Christa Reinig 427; Erich Hartmann/Globe Photos, New York: Shirley Jackson 422; T. Goldblatt/Camera Press/Globe Photos, New York: Bessie Head 422; Herbie Knott/Camera Press/Globe Photos, New York: Ray Bradbury 420; © Marian Kolisch: Ursula K. Le Guin 423; Lilly Library, Indiana University, Bloomington, Indiana: Sylvia Plath 426; Jim Marshall: Alice Walker 429; Tadeusz Matkovski/Camera Press/Globe Photos, New York: Stanislaw Łem 424; Susan Meiselas/Magnum Photos, Inc., New York: Jorge Luis Borges 420; Salgado/Magnum Photos, Inc., New York: Italo Calvino 420; The Schomburg Center for Research in Black Culture, The New York Public Library, Astor, Lenox & Tilden Foundations, New York: Jamaica Kincaid 423; Francis Stoppelman, Mexico City: Rachel de Queiroz 426; Horst Tappe/Globe Photos, New York: Nadine Gordimer 422.

McDougal, Littell and Company has made every effort to locate the copyright holders for the images used in this book and to make full acknowledgment for their use.